Mooncakes

Wendy Xu   Suzanne Walker

Lettered by Joamette Gil

ROAR™

Chapter 1

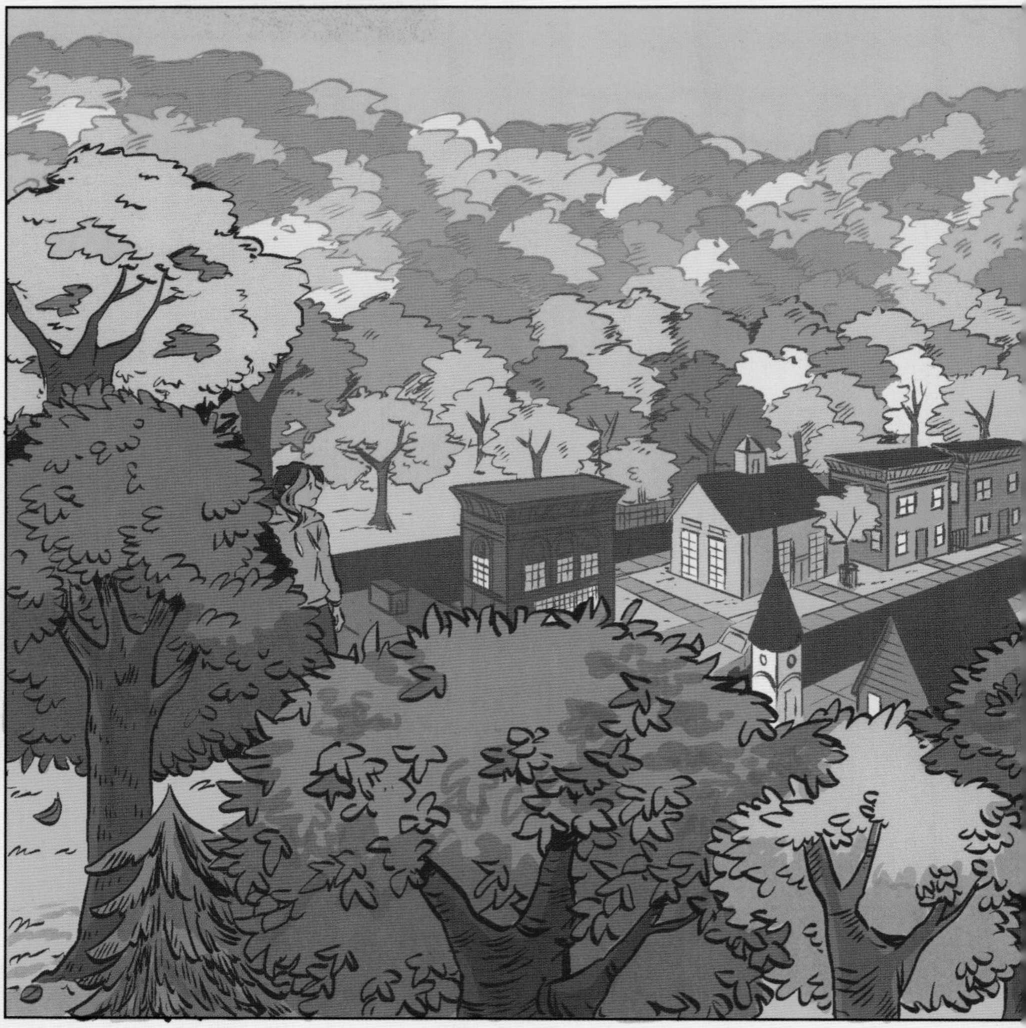

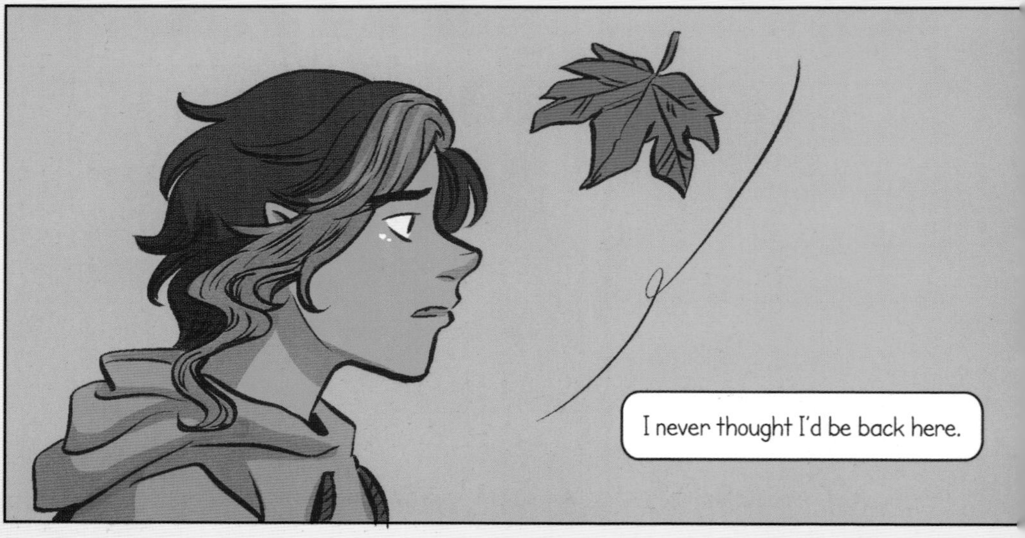
I never thought I'd be back here.

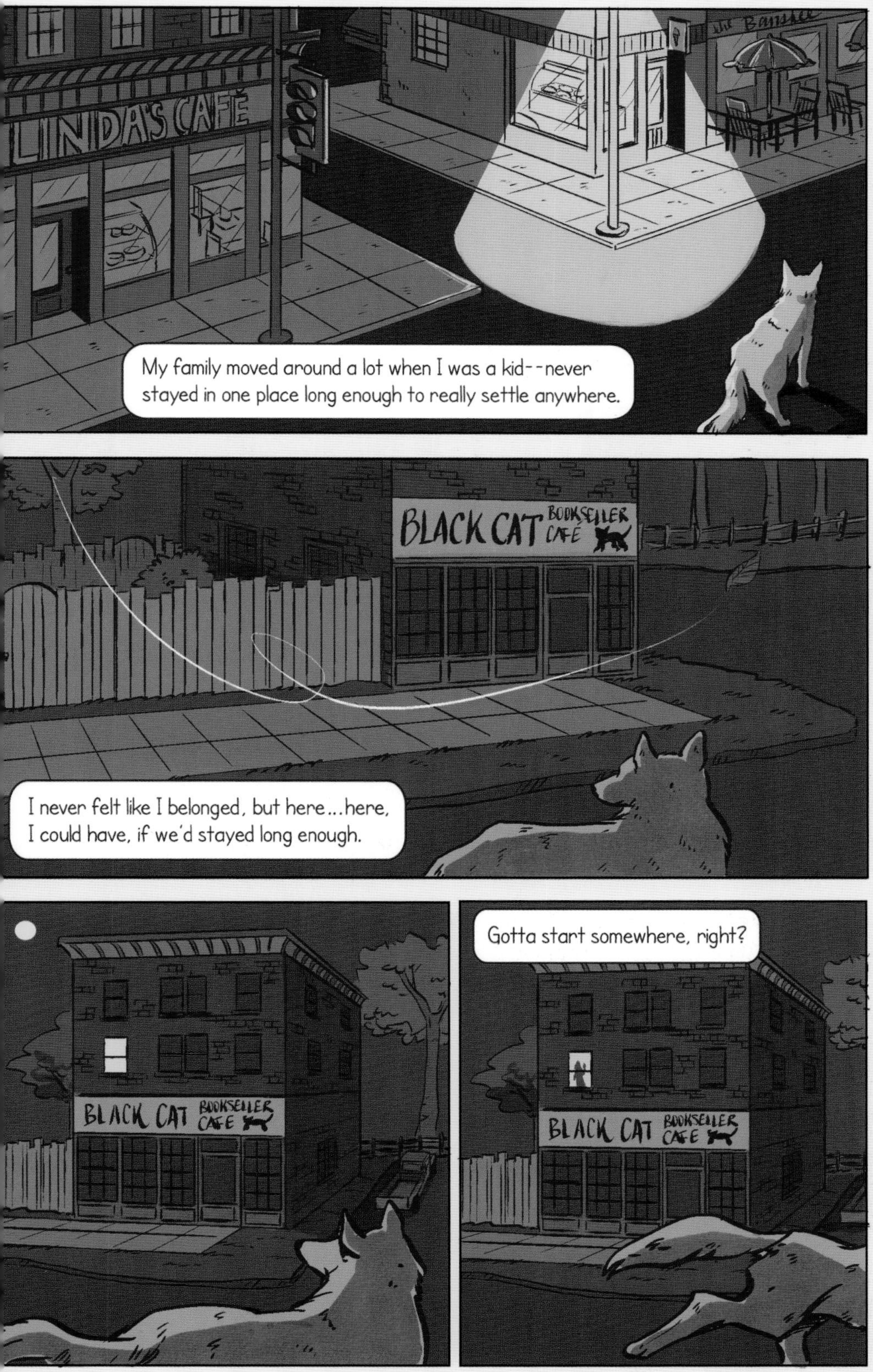
LINDA'S CAFÉ
My family moved around a lot when I was a kid--never stayed in one place long enough to really settle anywhere.
BLACK CAT BOOKSELLER CAFE
I never felt like I belonged, but here...here, I could have, if we'd stayed long enough.
BLACK CAT BOOKSELLER CAFE
Gotta start somewhere, right?
BLACK CAT BOOKSELLER CAFE

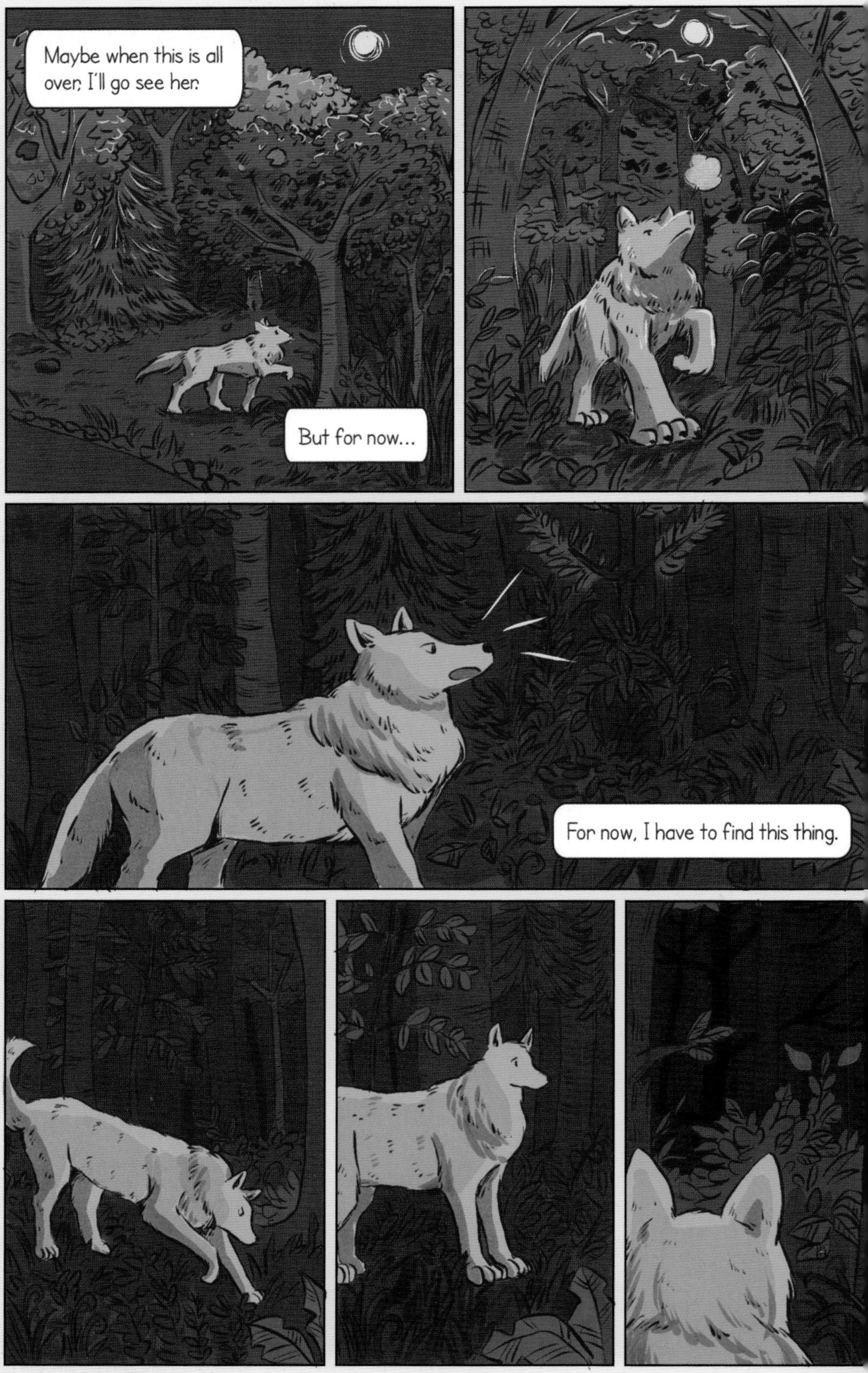
Maybe when this is all over, I'll go see her.
But for now...
For now, I have to find this thing.

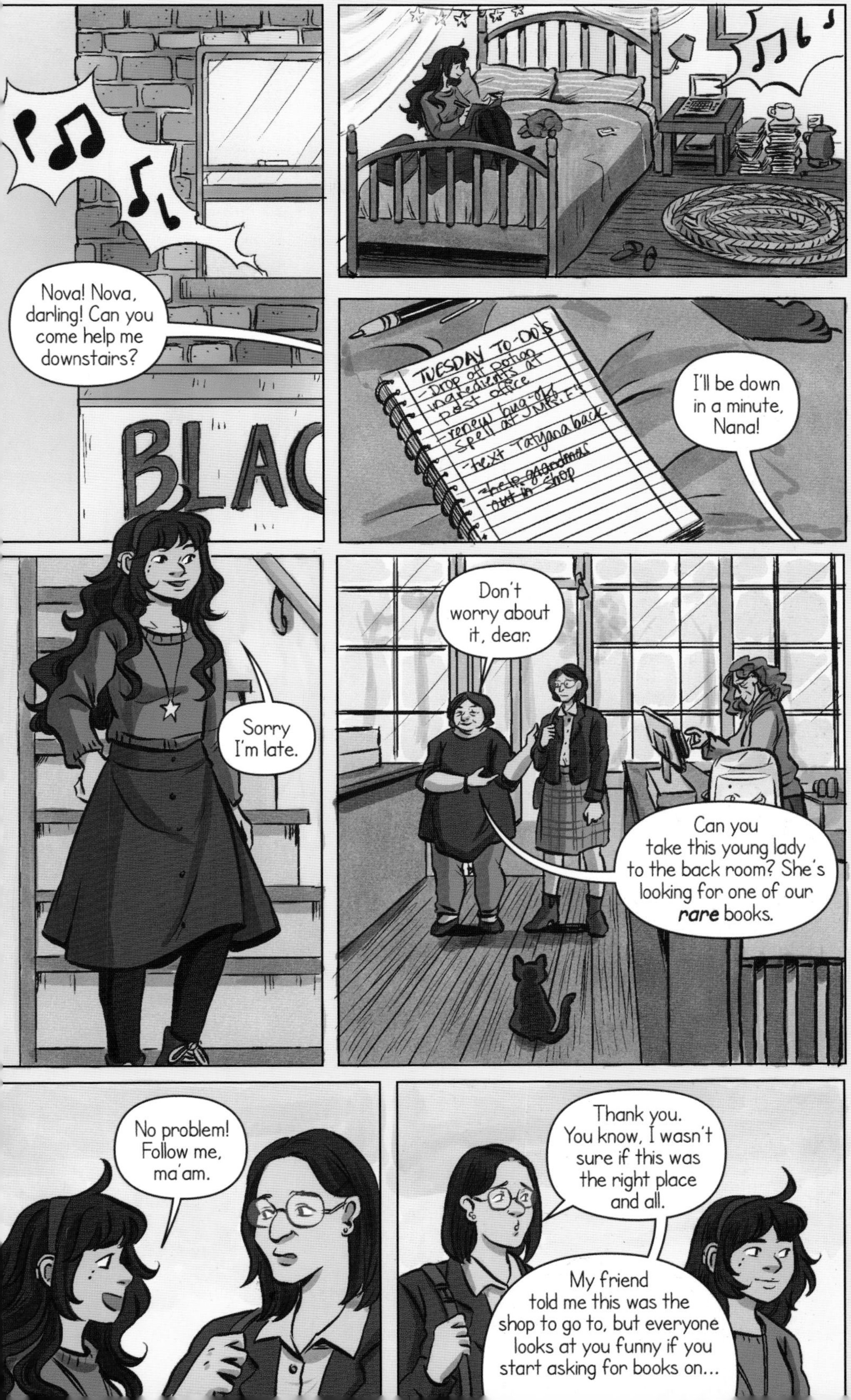

♪♫
Nova! Nova, darling! Can you come help me downstairs?
BLAC
TUESDAY TO-DO'S
-Drop of potion ingredients at post office
-renew bug-off spell at Mrs. F's
-text Tatyana back
-help grandma out in shop
I'll be down in a minute, Nana!
Sorry I'm late.
Don't worry about it, dear.
Can you take this young lady to the back room? She's looking for one of our **rare** books.
No problem! Follow me, ma'am.
Thank you. You know, I wasn't sure if this was the right place and all.
My friend told me this was the shop to go to, but everyone looks at you funny if you start asking for books on...

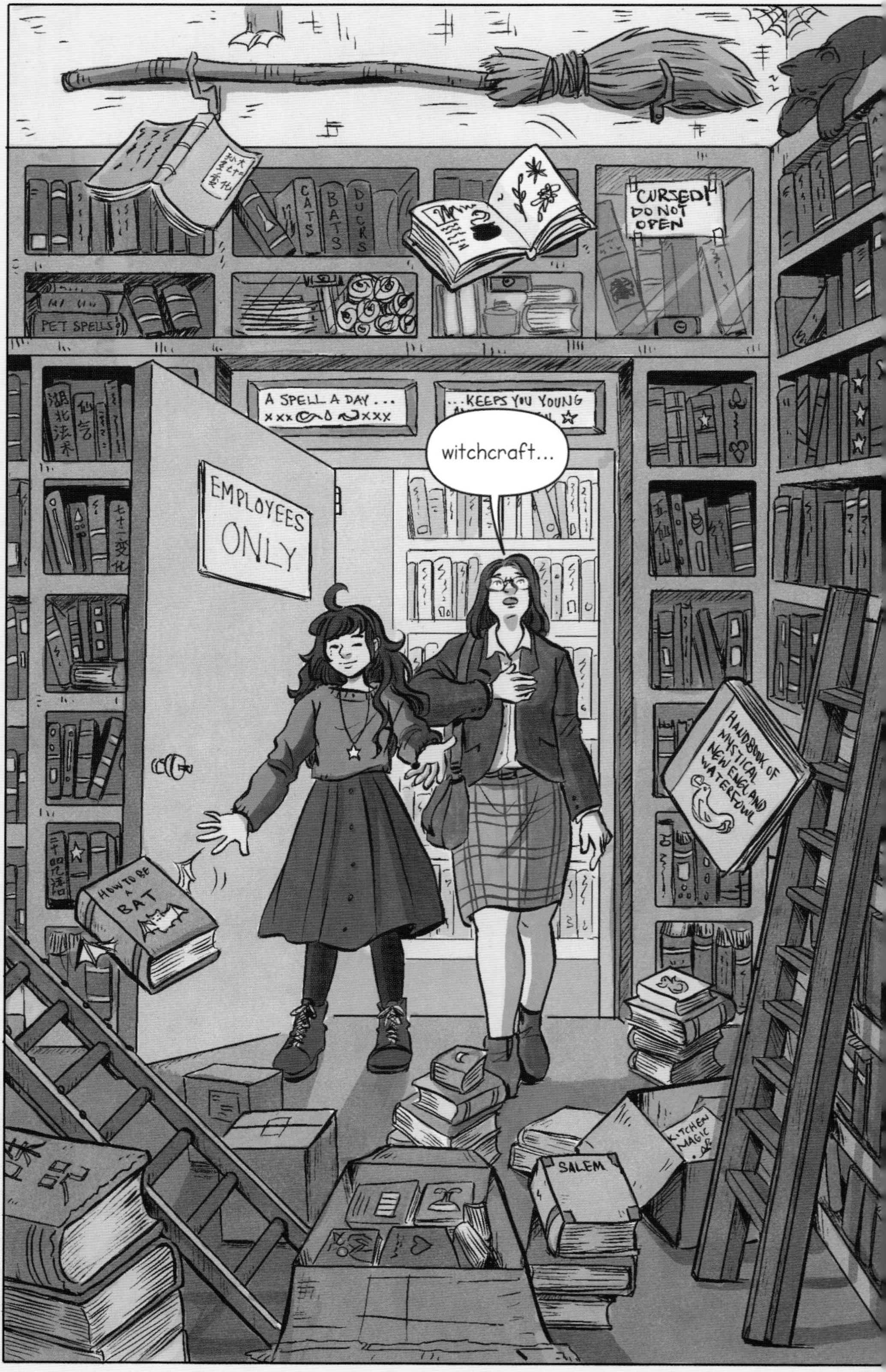
CATS
BATS
DUCKS
CURSED! DO NOT OPEN
PET SPELLS
A SPELL A DAY...
...KEEPS YOU YOUNG
witchcraft...
EMPLOYEES ONLY
HOW TO BE A BAT
HANDBOOK OF MYSTICAL NEW ENGLAND WATERFOWL
SALEM
KITCHEN MAGIC

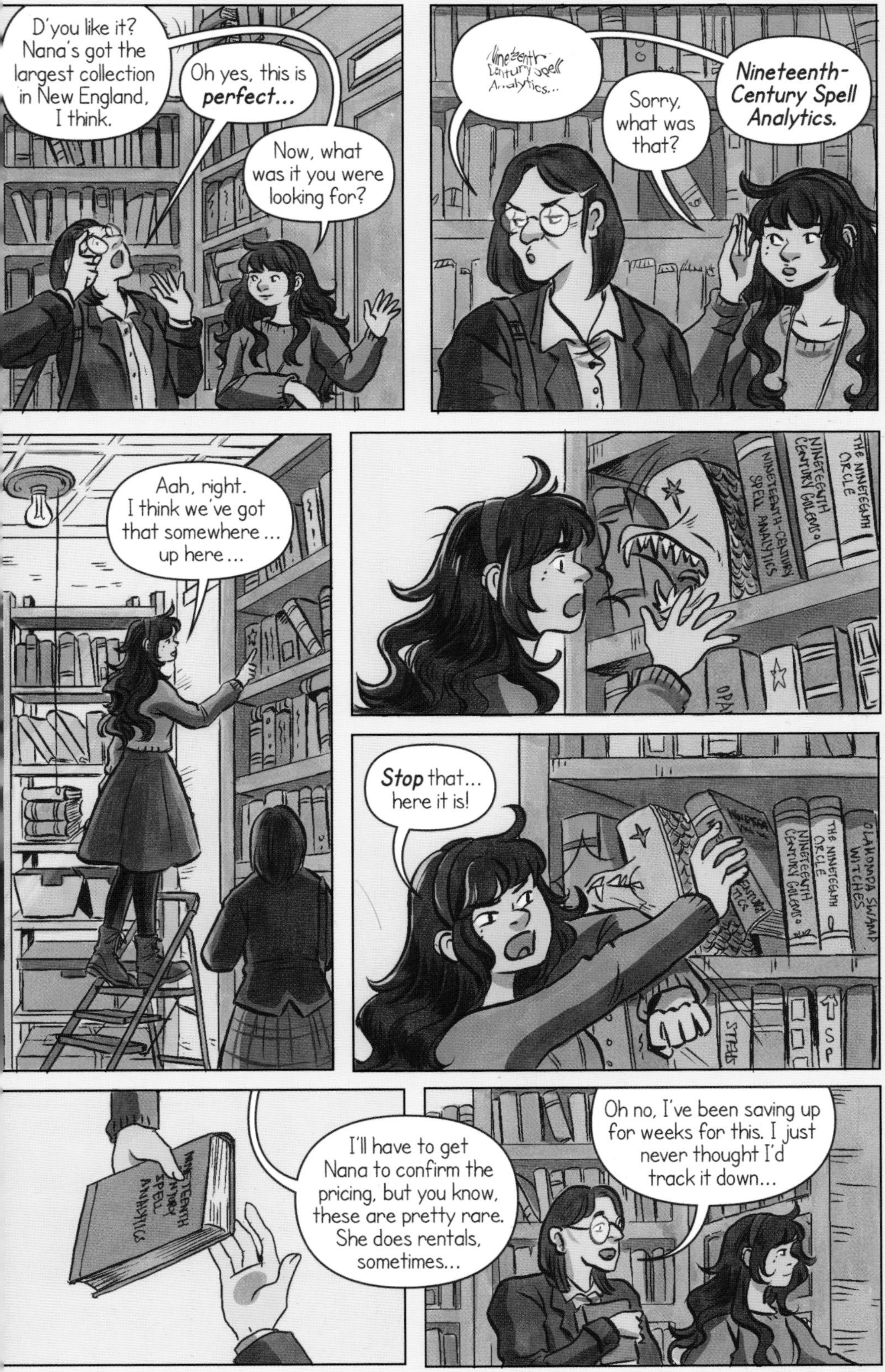

D'you like it? Nana's got the largest collection in New England, I think.
Oh yes, this is *perfect...*
Now, what was it you were looking for?
Nineteenth Century Spell Analytics...
Sorry, what was that?
Nineteenth-Century Spell Analytics.
Aah, right. I think we've got that somewhere ... up here ...
THE NINETEENTH CIRCLE
NINETEENTH CENTURY GOLEMS
NINETEENTH-CENTURY SPELL ANALYTICS
Stop that... here it is!
I'll have to get Nana to confirm the pricing, but you know, these are pretty rare. She does rentals, sometimes...
Oh no, I've been saving up for weeks for this. I just never thought I'd track it down...

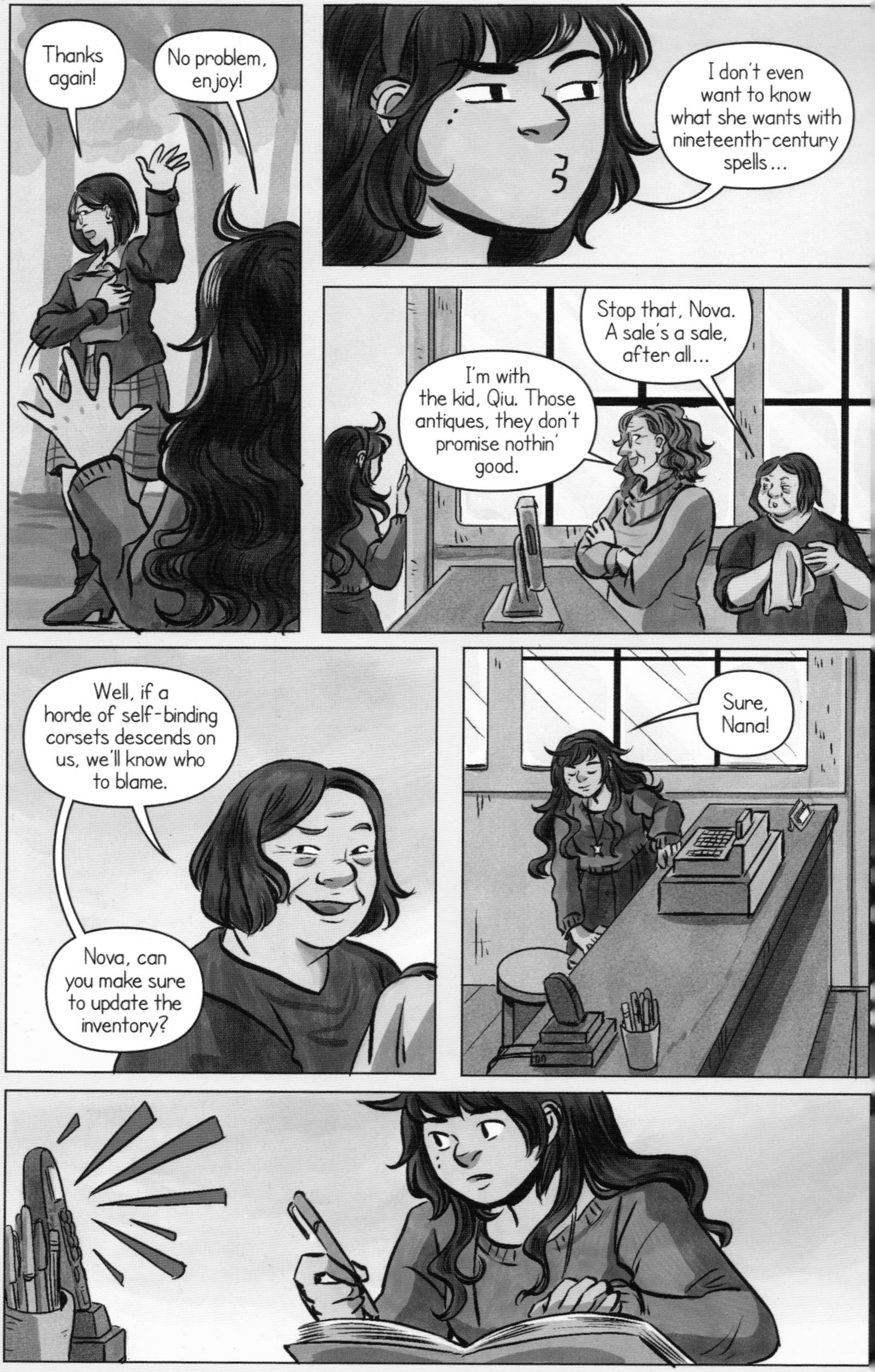
Thanks again!
No problem, enjoy!
I don't even want to know what she wants with nineteenth-century spells...
Stop that, Nova. A sale's a sale, after all...
I'm with the kid, Qiu. Those antiques, they don't promise nothin' good.
Well, if a horde of self-binding corsets descends on us, we'll know who to blame.
Nova, can you make sure to update the inventory?
Sure, Nana!

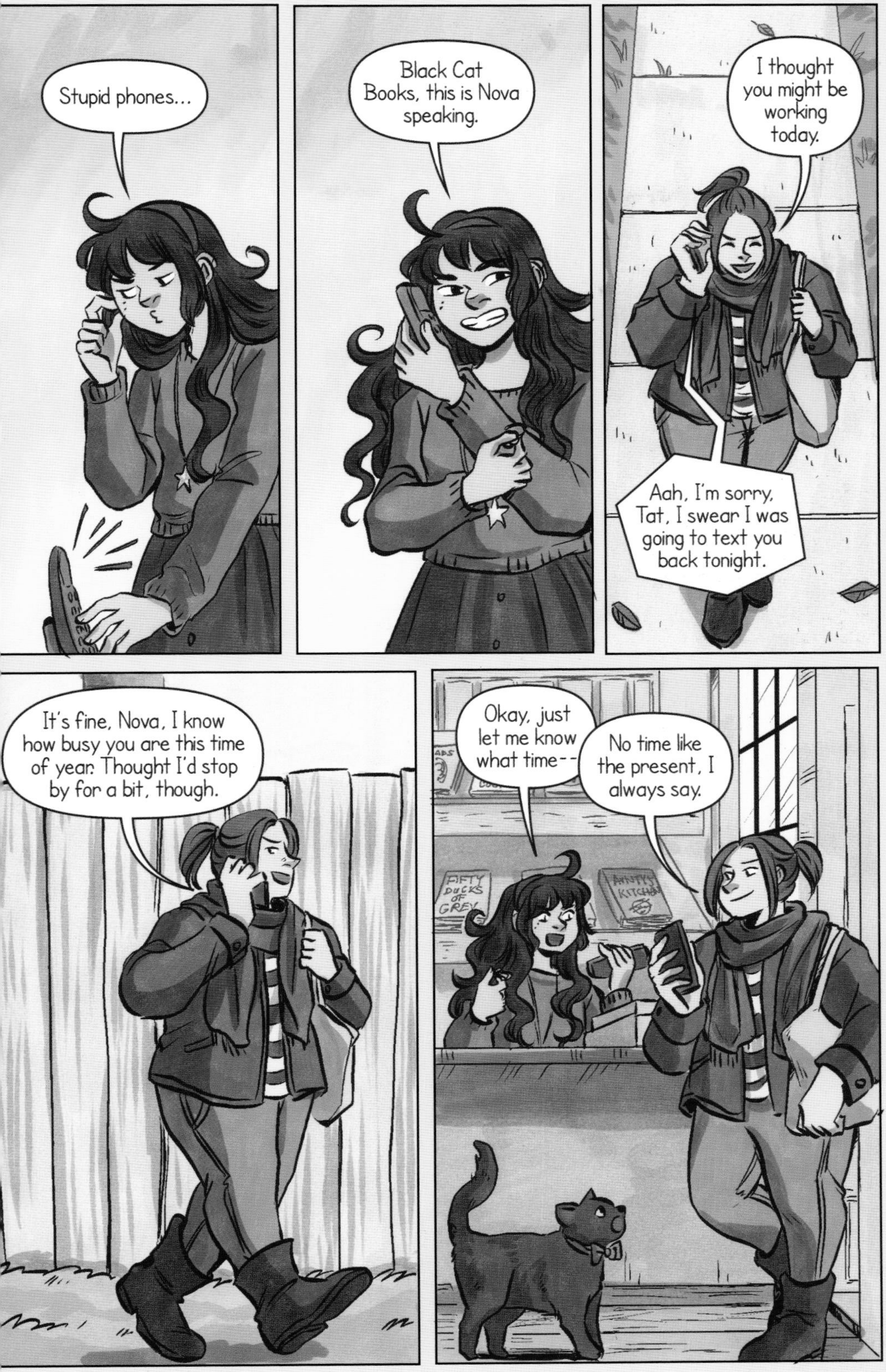

Stupid phones...
Black Cat Books, this is Nova speaking.
I thought you might be working today.
Aah, I'm sorry, Tat, I swear I was going to text you back tonight.
It's fine, Nova, I know how busy you are this time of year. Thought I'd stop by for a bit, though.
Okay, just let me know what time--
No time like the present, I always say.
FIFTY DUCKS OF GREY

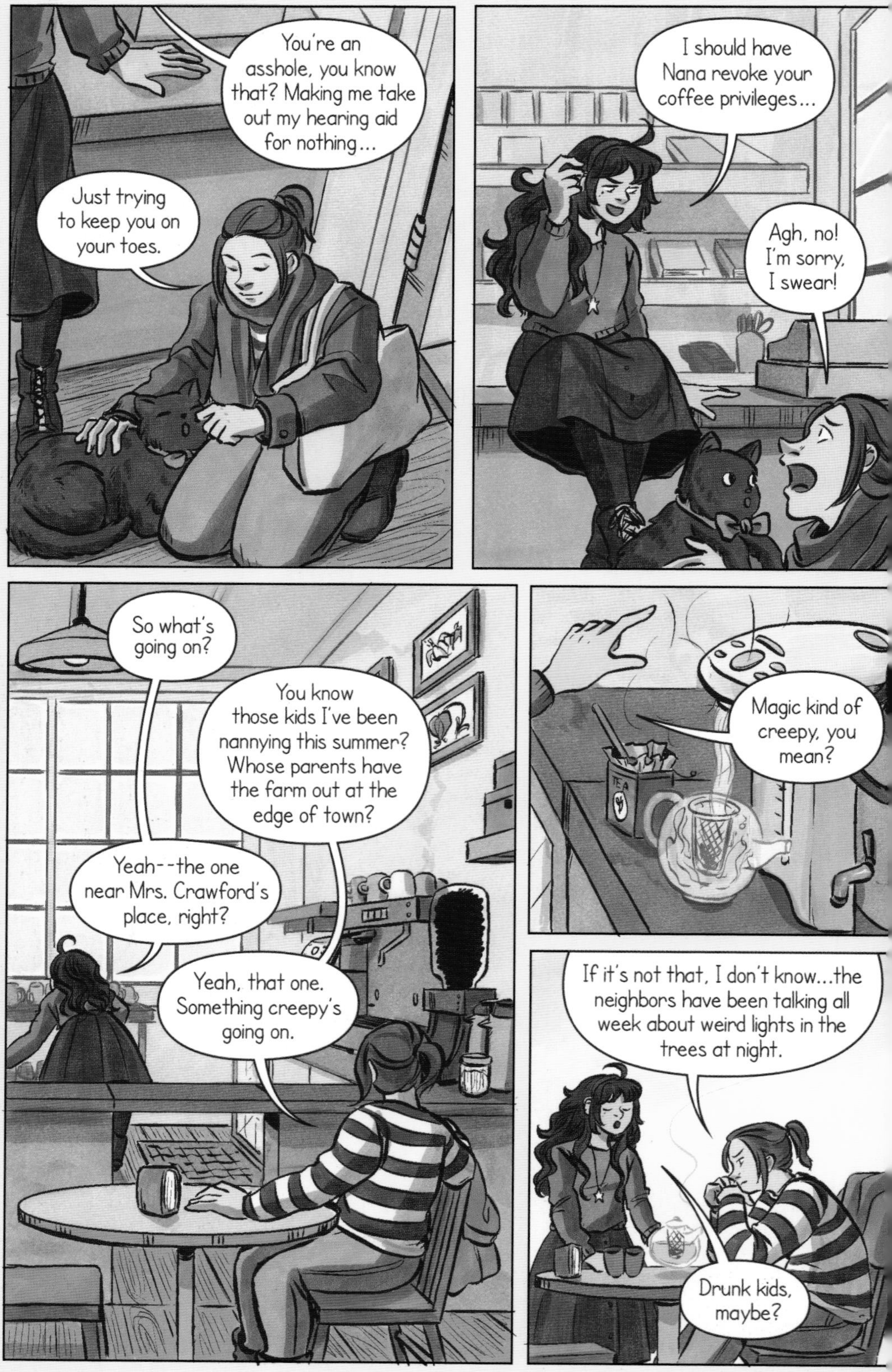
You're an asshole, you know that? Making me take out my hearing aid for nothing...
Just trying to keep you on your toes.
I should have Nana revoke your coffee privileges...
Agh, no! I'm sorry, I swear!
So what's going on?
You know those kids I've been nannying this summer? Whose parents have the farm out at the edge of town?
Yeah--the one near Mrs. Crawford's place, right?
Yeah, that one. Something creepy's going on.
Magic kind of creepy, you mean?
If it's not that, I don't know...the neighbors have been talking all week about weird lights in the trees at night.
Drunk kids, maybe?

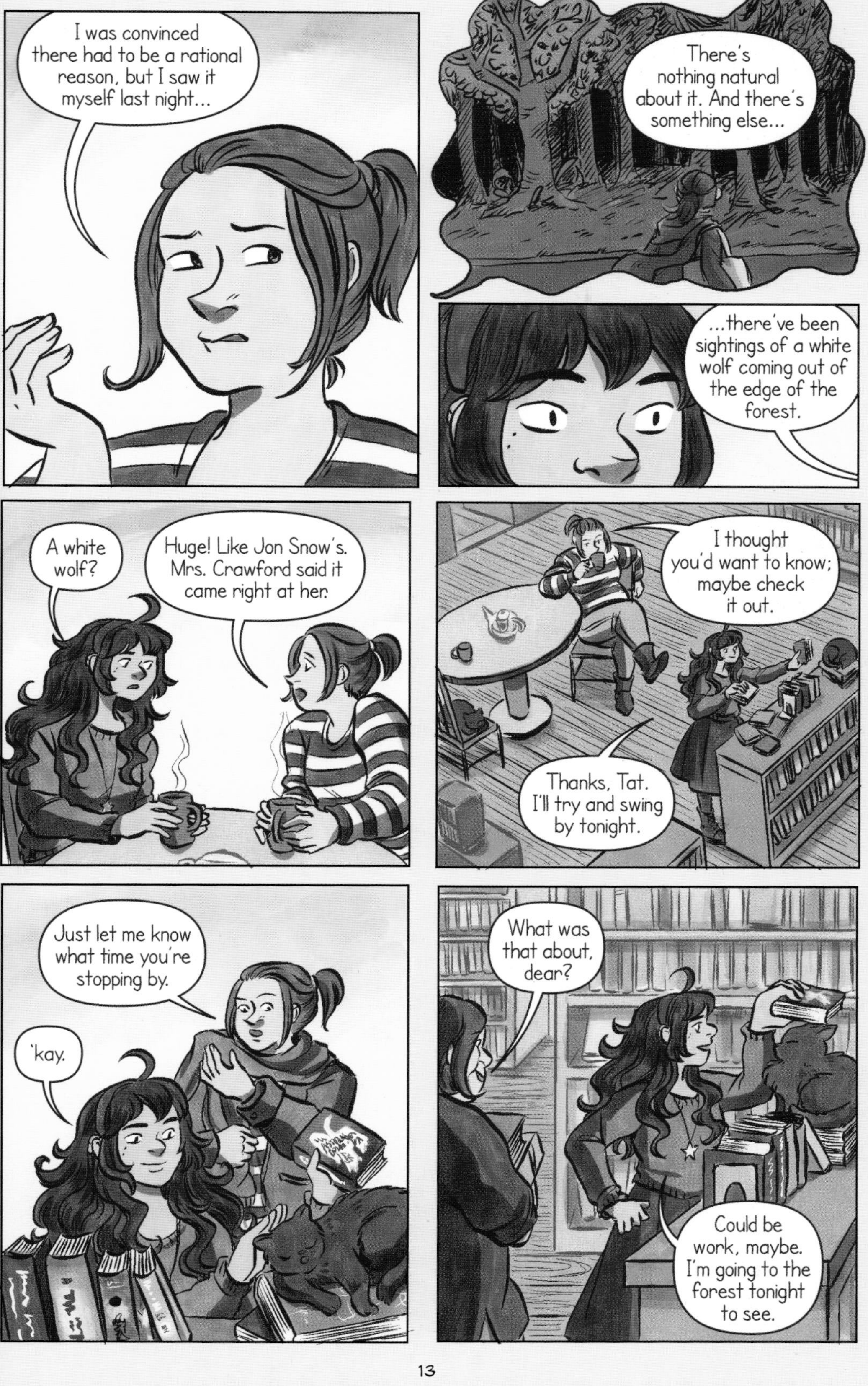
I was convinced there had to be a rational reason, but I saw it myself last night...
There's nothing natural about it. And there's something else...
...there've been sightings of a white wolf coming out of the edge of the forest.
A white wolf?
Huge! Like Jon Snow's. Mrs. Crawford said it came right at her.
I thought you'd want to know; maybe check it out.
Thanks, Tat. I'll try and swing by tonight.
Just let me know what time you're stopping by.
'kay.
What was that about, dear?
Could be work, maybe. I'm going to the forest tonight to see.

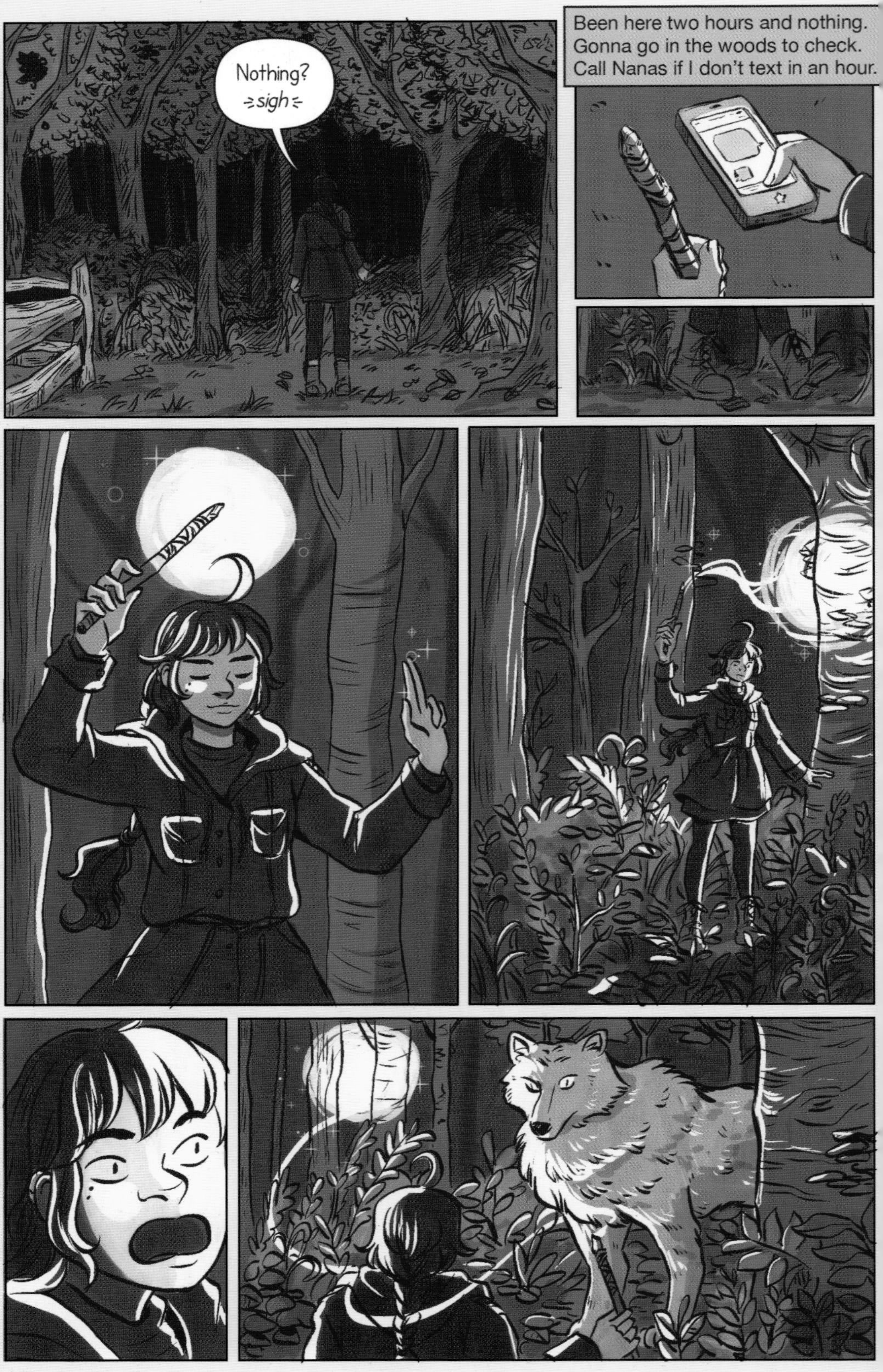
Nothing?
sigh
Been here two hours and nothing.
Gonna go in the woods to check.
Call Nanas if I don't text in an hour.

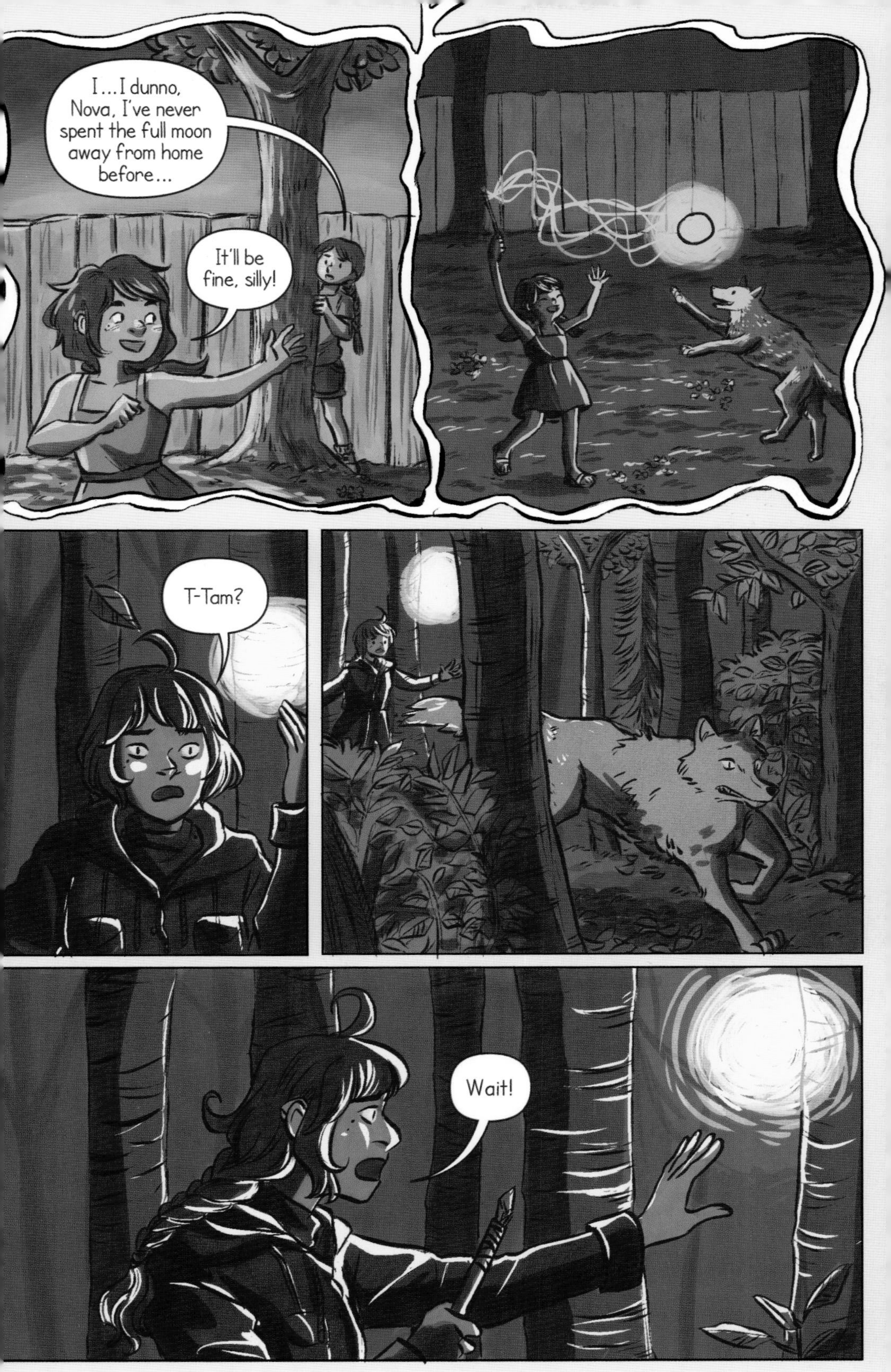
I...I dunno, Nova, I've never spent the full moon away from home before...
It'll be fine, silly!
T-Tam?
Wait!

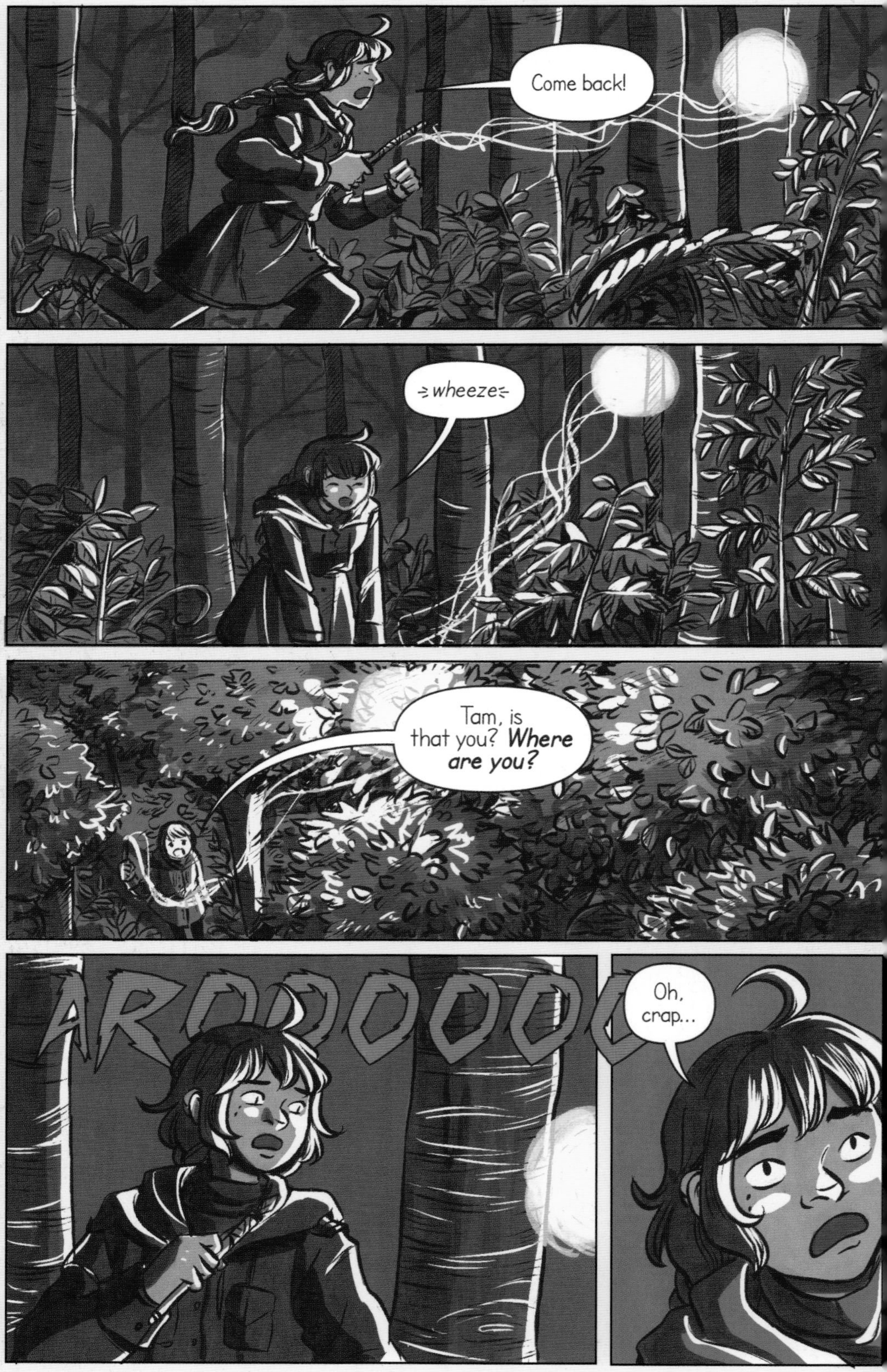
Come back!
wheeze
Tam, is that you? **Where are you?**
AROOOOOO
Oh, crap...

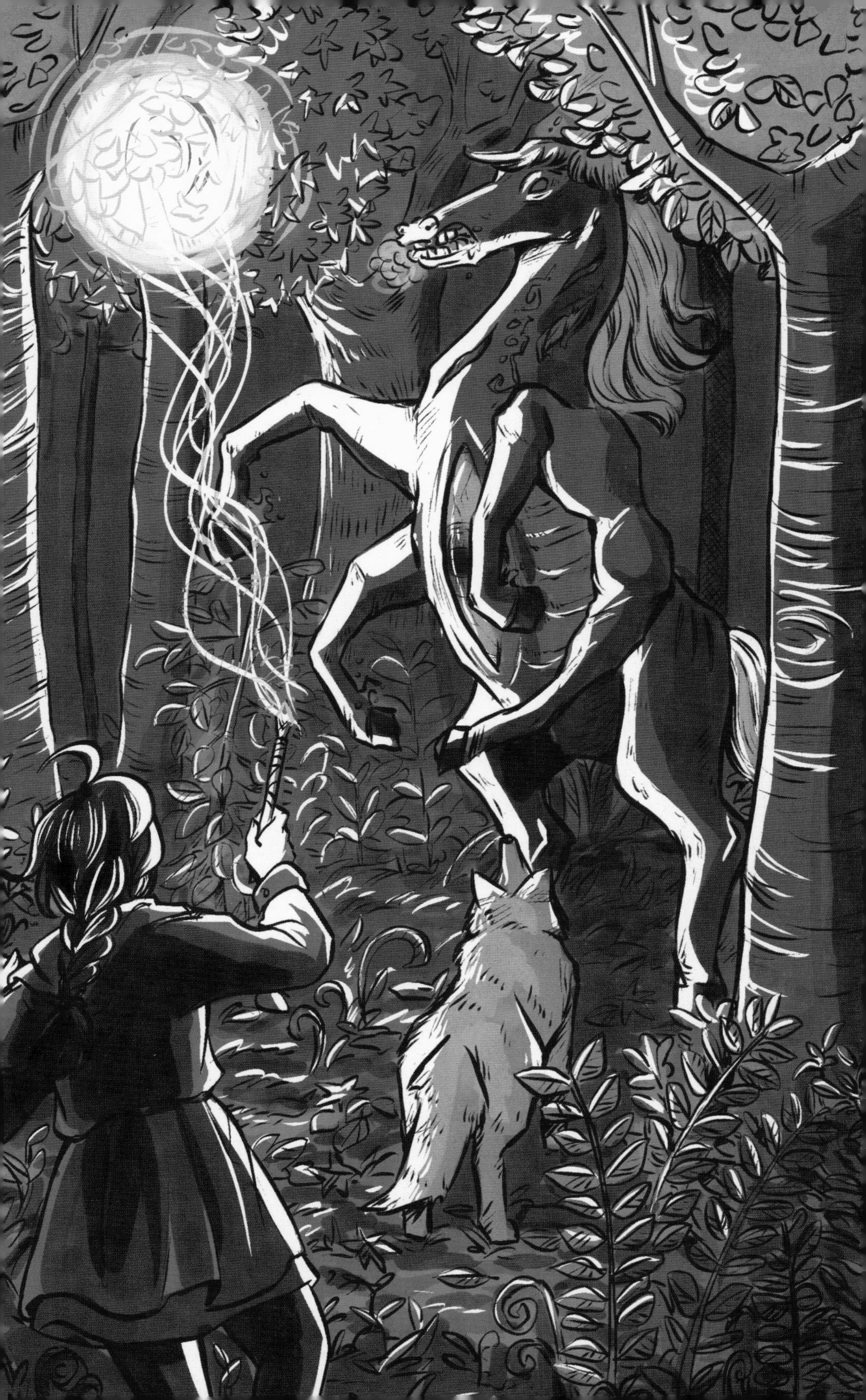

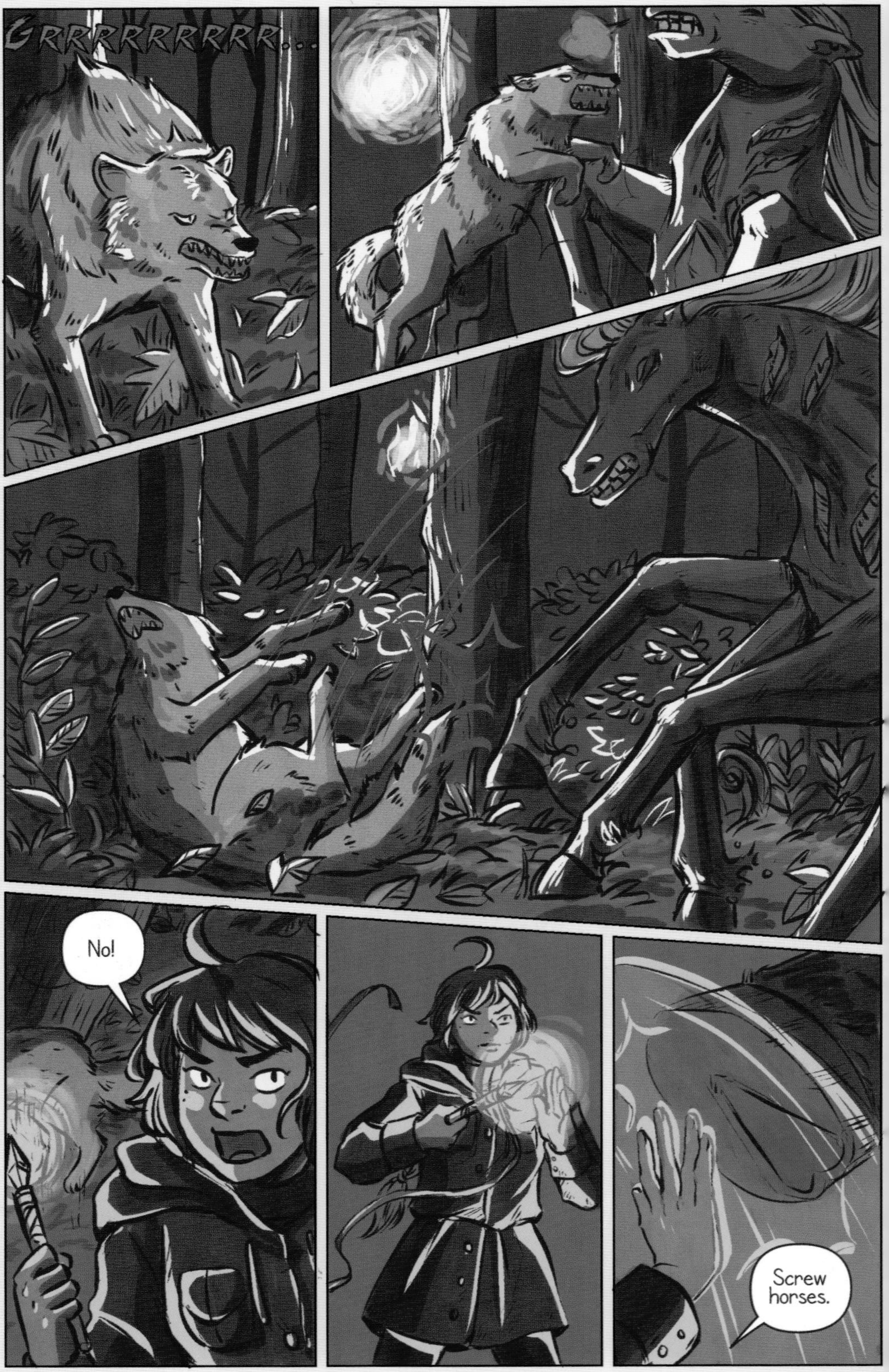
GRRRRRRRRRR...
No!
Screw horses.

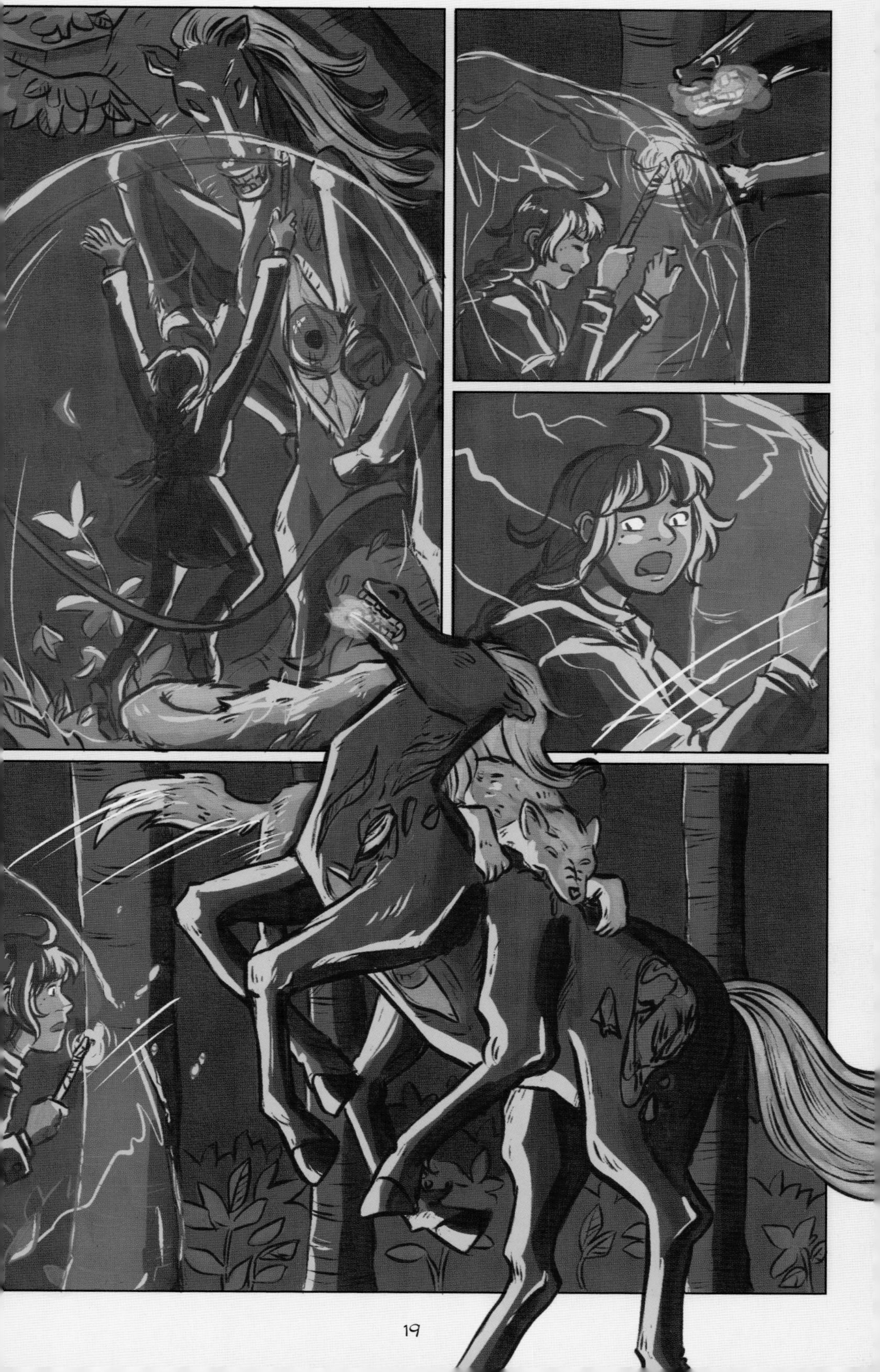

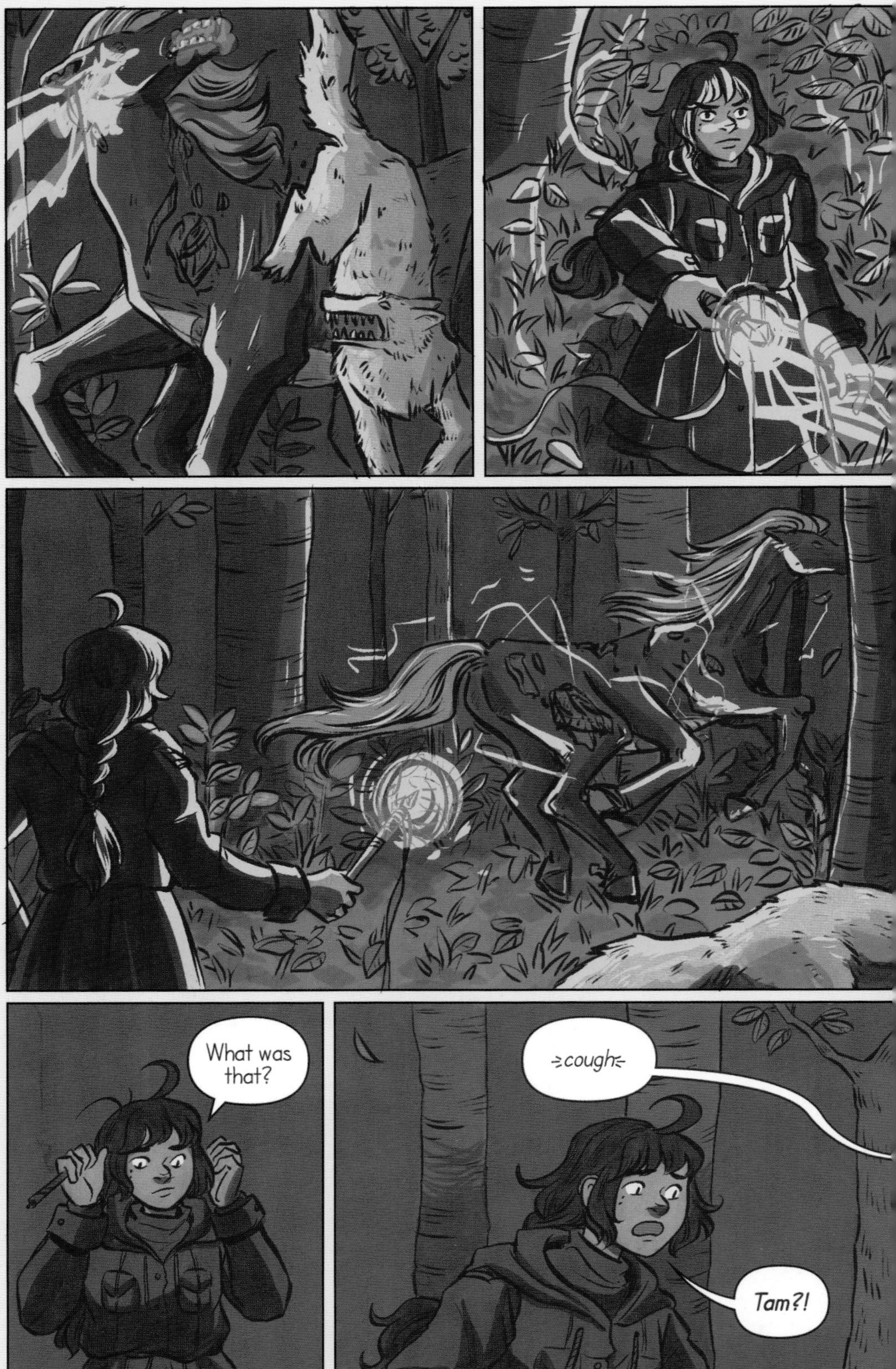
What was that?
cough
Tam?!

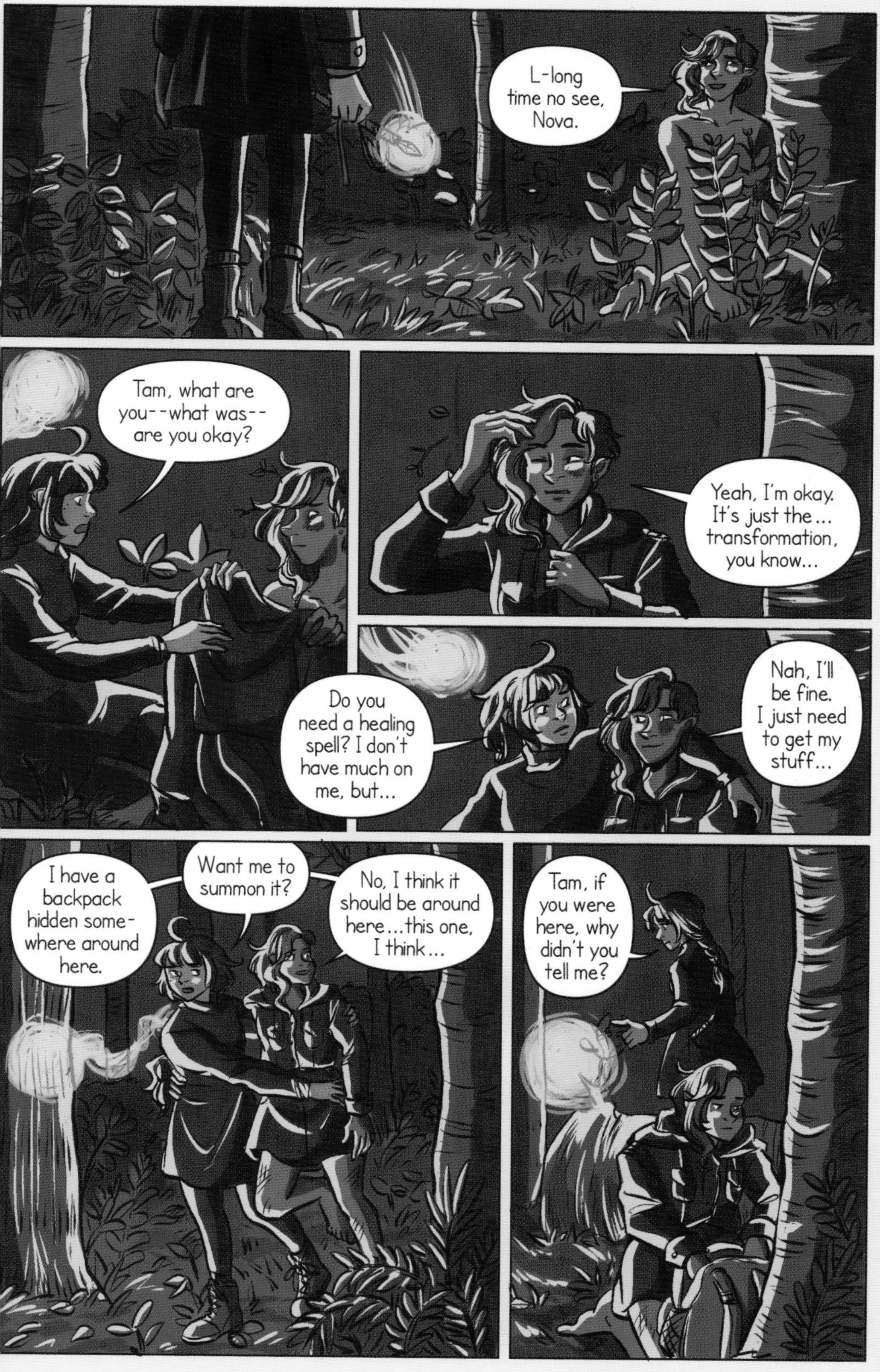
L-long time no see, Nova.
Tam, what are you--what was--are you okay?
Yeah, I'm okay. It's just the... transformation, you know...
Do you need a healing spell? I don't have much on me, but...
Nah, I'll be fine. I just need to get my stuff...
I have a backpack hidden some-where around here.
Want me to summon it?
No, I think it should be around here...this one, I think...
Tam, if you were here, why didn't you tell me?

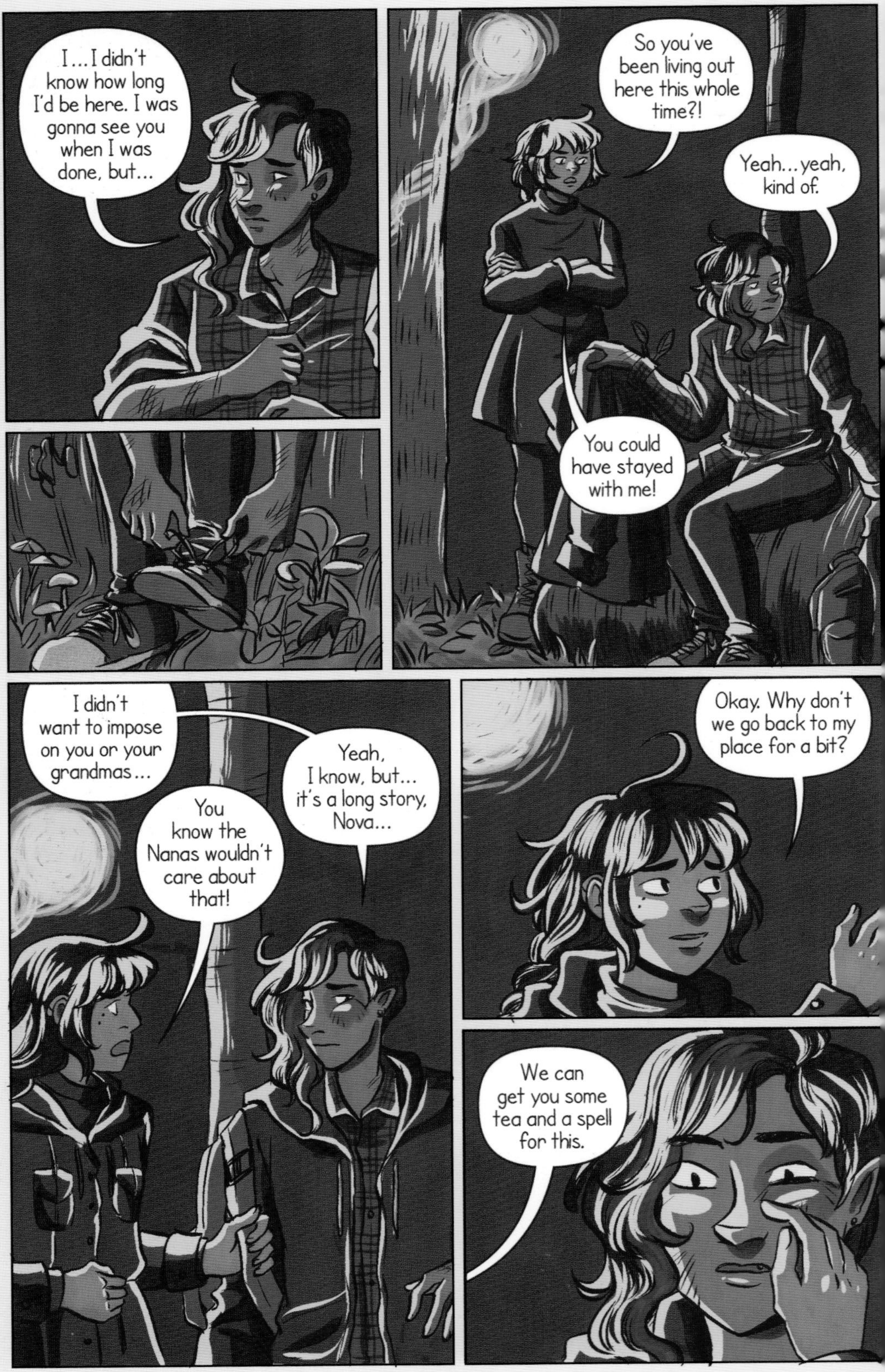

I...I didn't know how long I'd be here. I was gonna see you when I was done, but...
So you've been living out here this whole time?!
Yeah... yeah, kind of.
You could have stayed with me!
I didn't want to impose on you or your grandmas...
You know the Nanas wouldn't care about that!
Yeah, I know, but... it's a long story, Nova...
Okay. Why don't we go back to my place for a bit?
We can get you some tea and a spell for this.

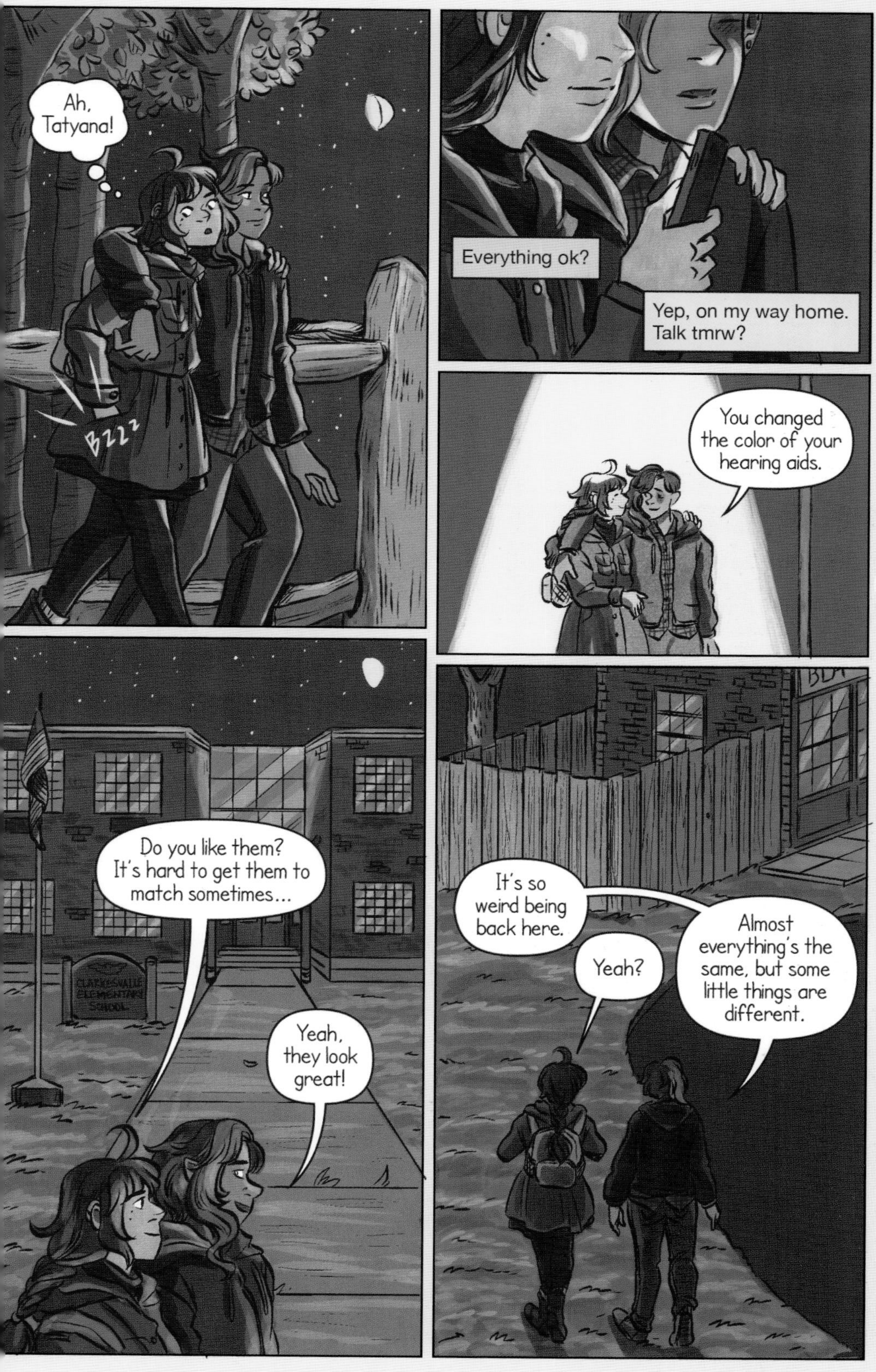
Ah, Tatyana!
BZZZ
Everything ok?
Yep, on my way home. Talk tmrw?
You changed the color of your hearing aids.
Do you like them? It's hard to get them to match sometimes...
Yeah, they look great!
CLARKESVILLE ELEMENTARY SCHOOL
It's so weird being back here.
Yeah?
Almost everything's the same, but some little things are different.

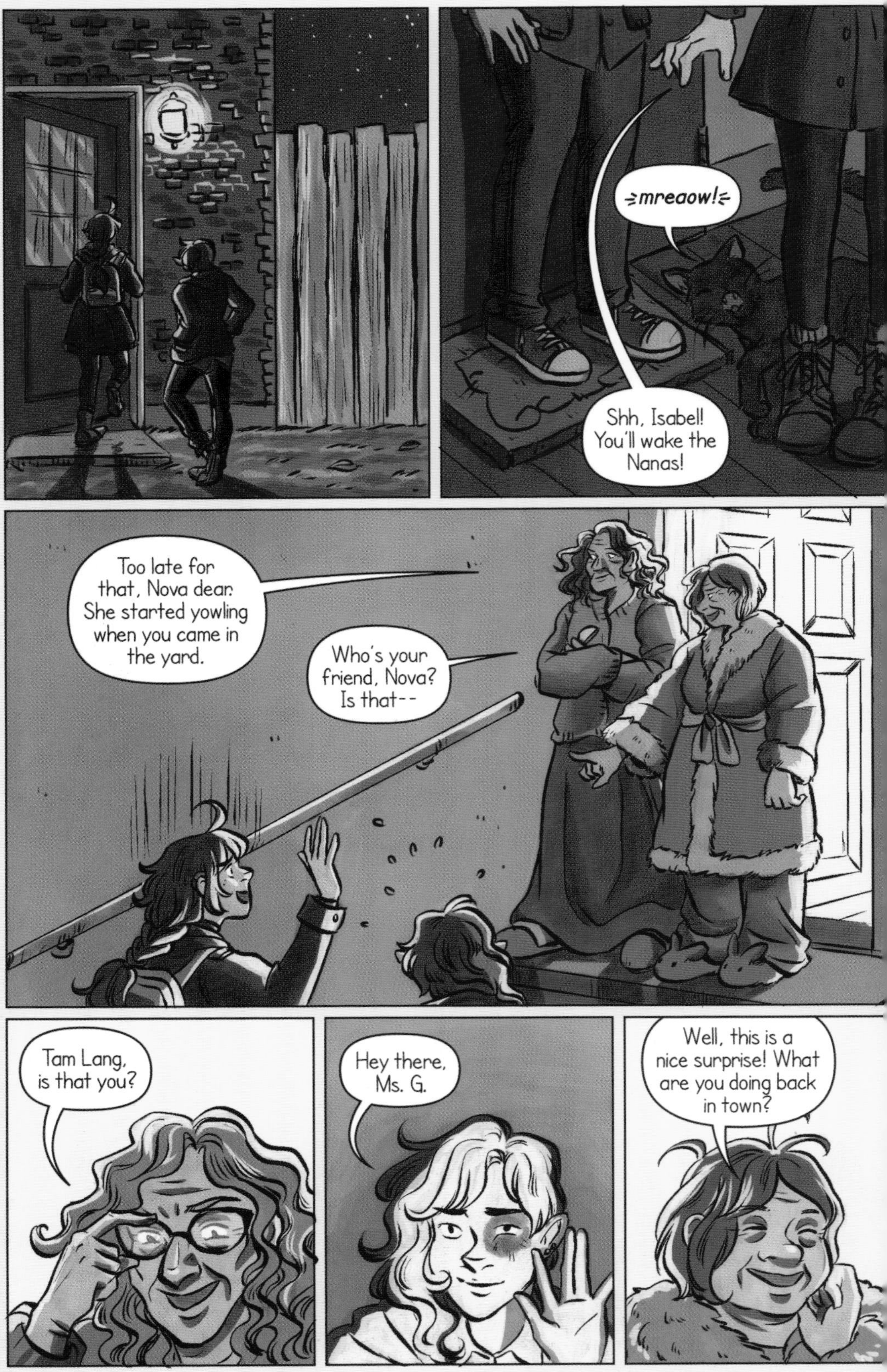
mreaow!
Shh, Isabel! You'll wake the Nanas!
Too late for that, Nova dear. She started yowling when you came in the yard.
Who's your friend, Nova? Is that--
Tam Lang, is that you?
Hey there, Ms. G.
Well, this is a nice surprise! What are you doing back in town?

Is it all right if Tam stays with us for a night or two?

Of course it is.

There are towels in the closet she can use...

They.

Beg pardon?

I use "they" pronouns now.

Of course, I'm sorry, dear! My mistake.

Do either of you need anything? Tea, water...

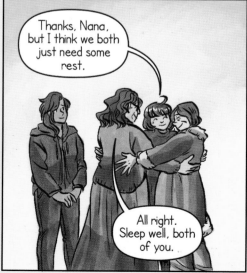

Thanks, Nana, but I think we both just need some rest.

All right. Sleep well, both of you.

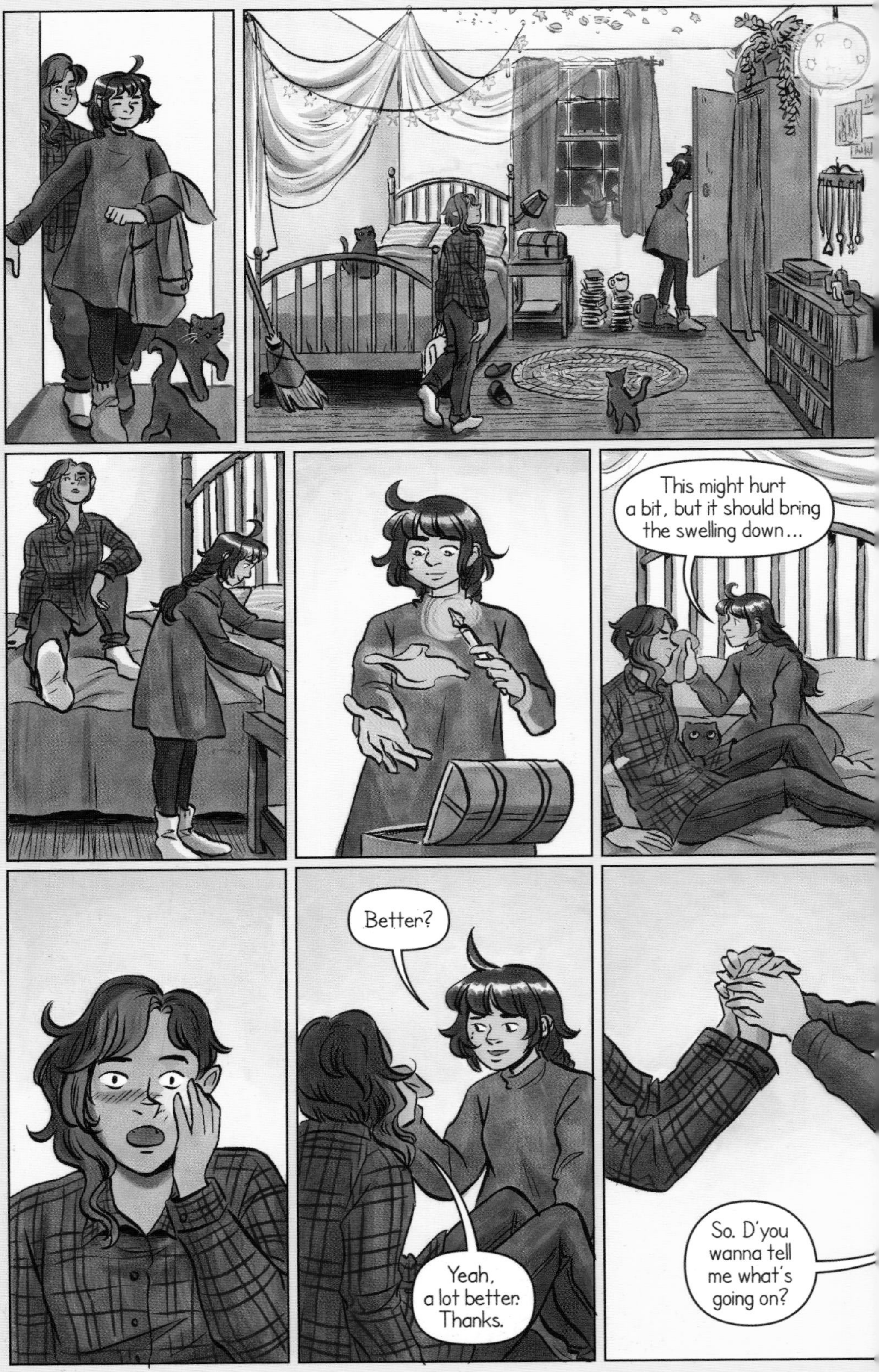
This might hurt a bit, but it should bring the swelling down...
Better?
Yeah, a lot better. Thanks.
So. D'you wanna tell me what's going on?

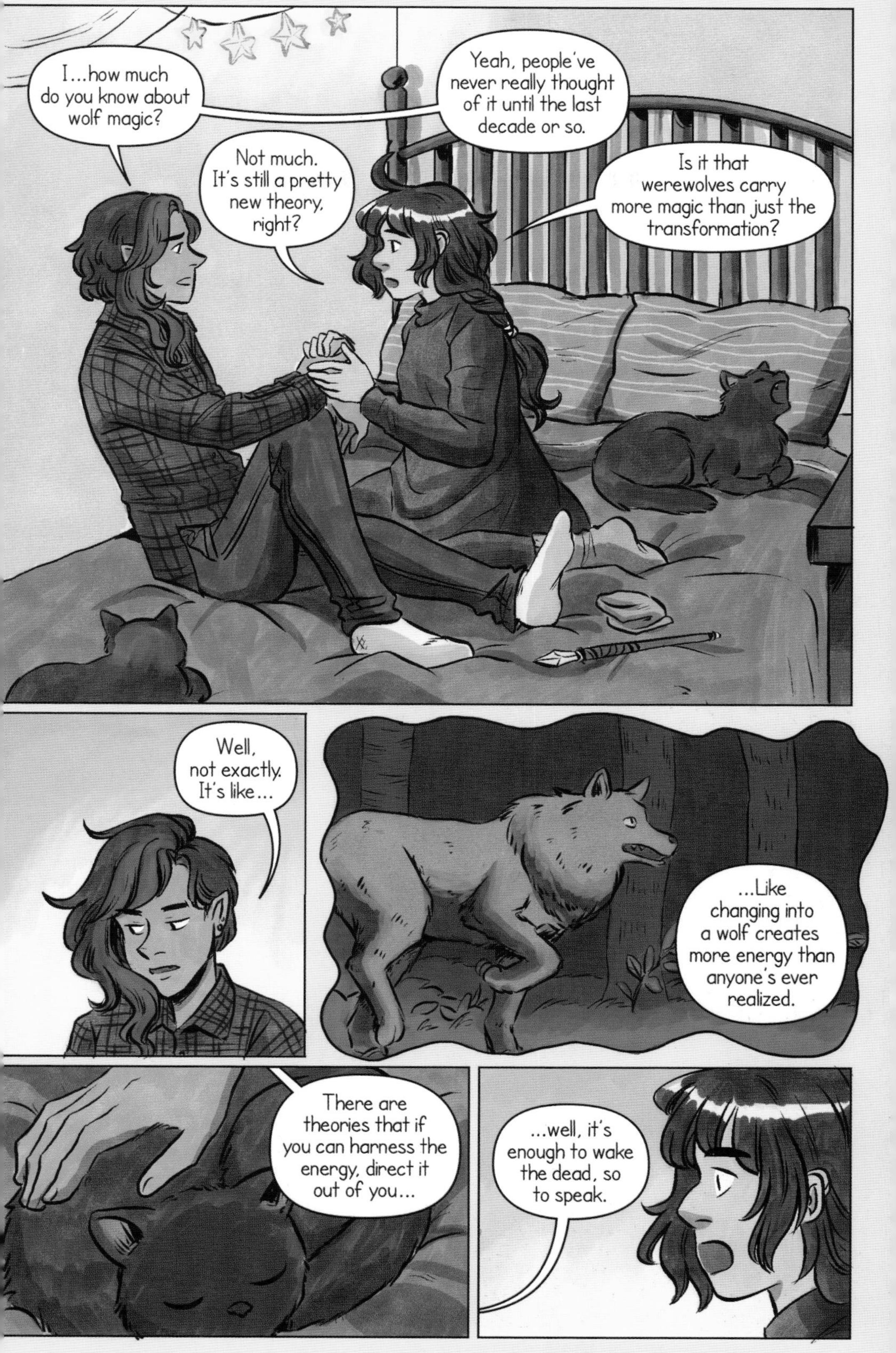
I...how much do you know about wolf magic?
Not much. It's still a pretty new theory, right?
Yeah, people've never really thought of it until the last decade or so.
Is it that werewolves carry more magic than just the transformation?
Well, not exactly. It's like...
...Like changing into a wolf creates more energy than anyone's ever realized.
There are theories that if you can harness the energy, direct it out of you...
...well, it's enough to wake the dead, so to speak.

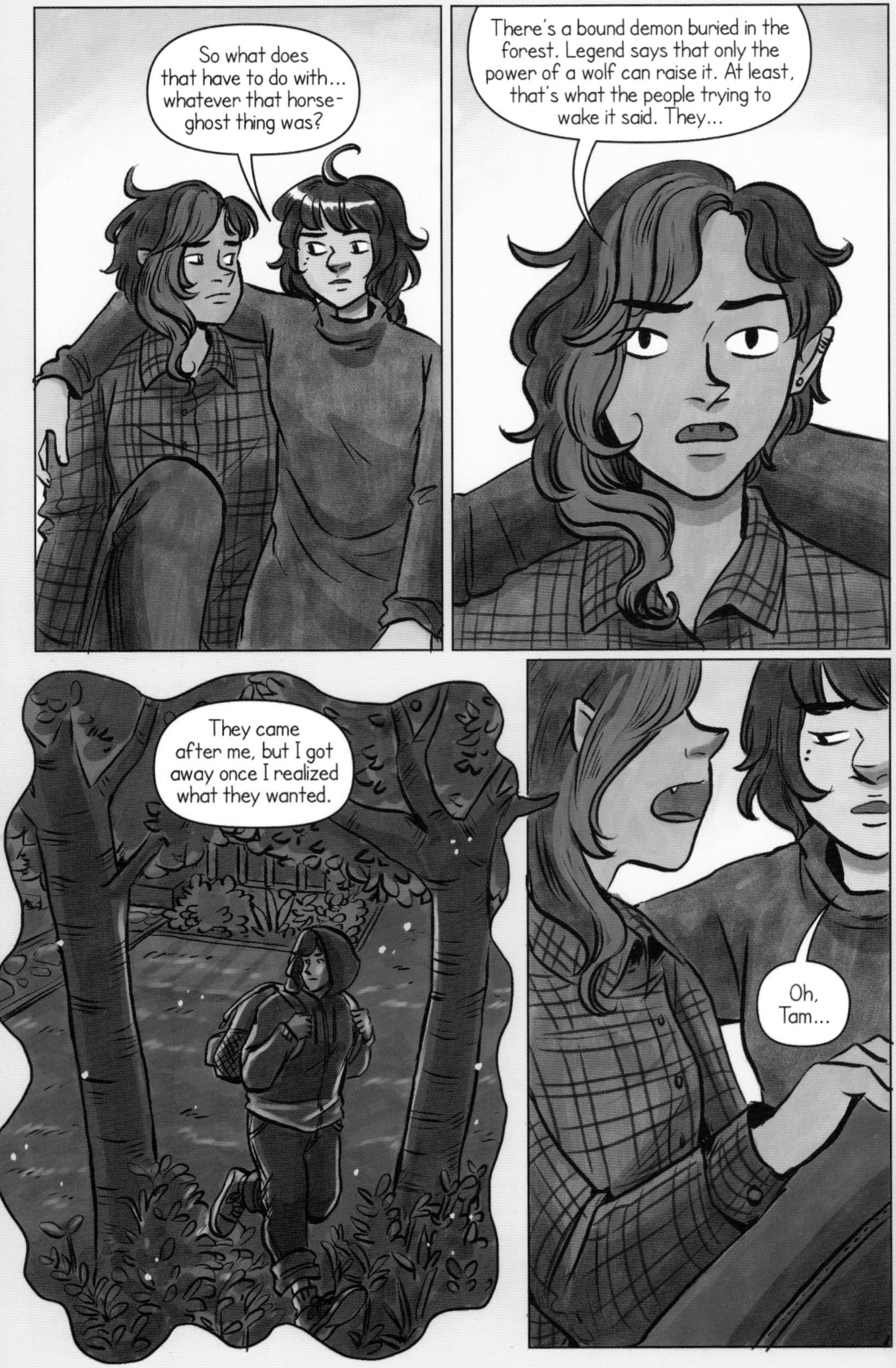
So what does that have to do with... whatever that horse-ghost thing was?
There's a bound demon buried in the forest. Legend says that only the power of a wolf can raise it. At least, that's what the people trying to wake it said. They...
They came after me, but I got away once I realized what they wanted.
Oh, Tam...

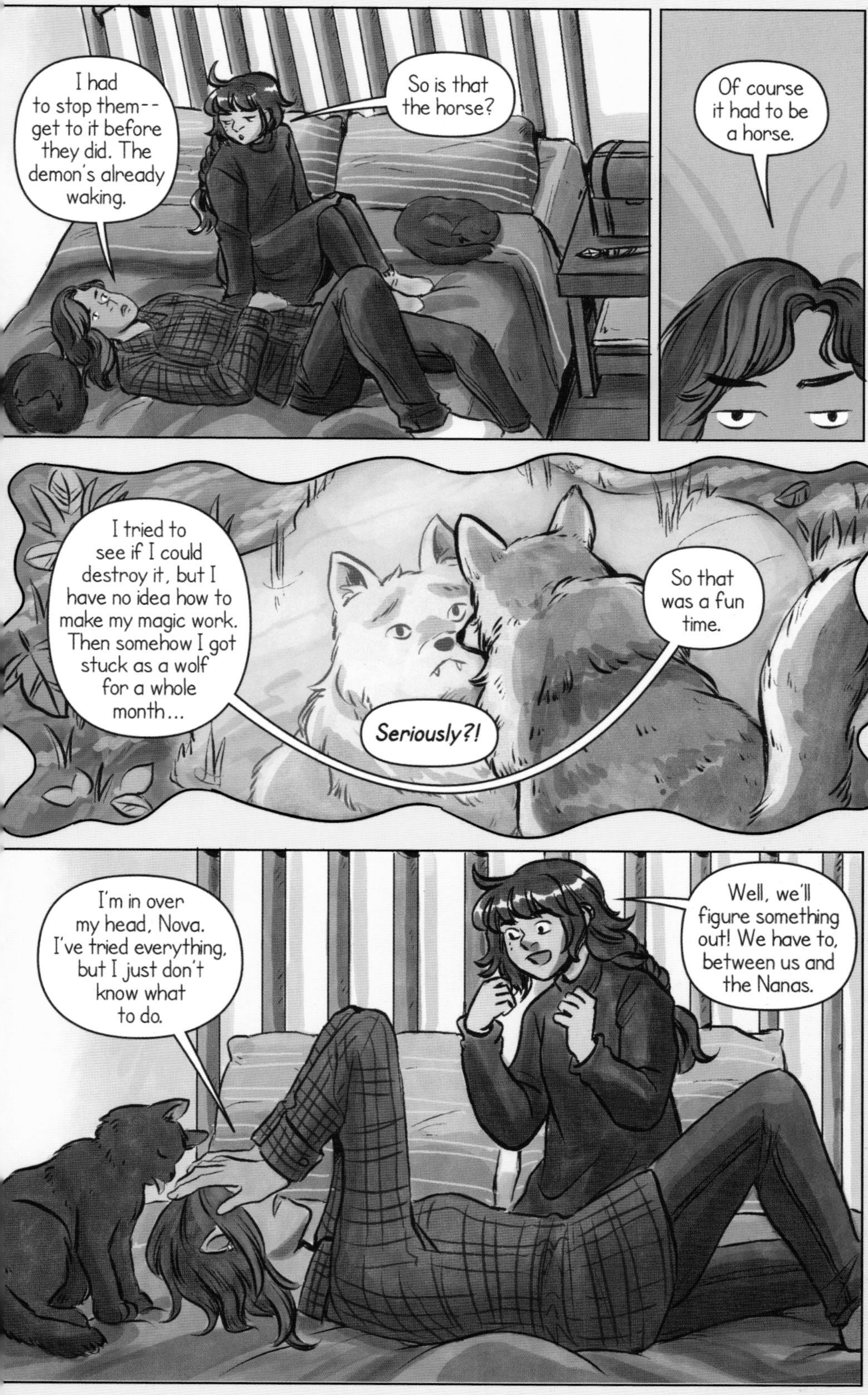
I had to stop them--get to it before they did. The demon's already waking.
So is that the horse?
Of course it had to be a horse.
I tried to see if I could destroy it, but I have no idea how to make my magic work. Then somehow I got stuck as a wolf for a whole month...
Seriously?!
So that was a fun time.
I'm in over my head, Nova. I've tried everything, but I just don't know what to do.
Well, we'll figure something out! We have to, between us and the Nanas.

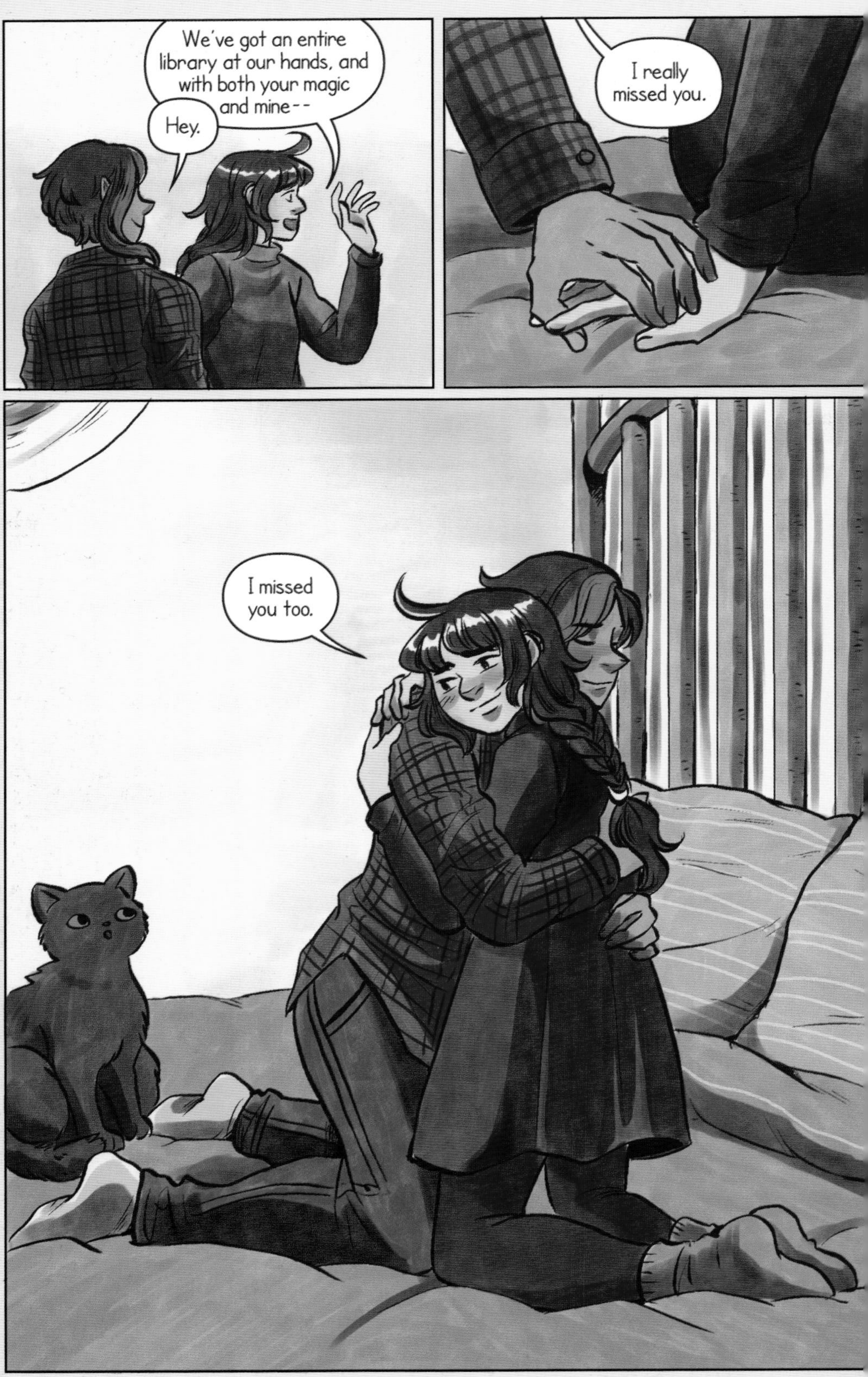
We've got an entire library at our hands, and with both your magic and mine--
Hey.
I really missed you.
I missed you too.

Chapter 2

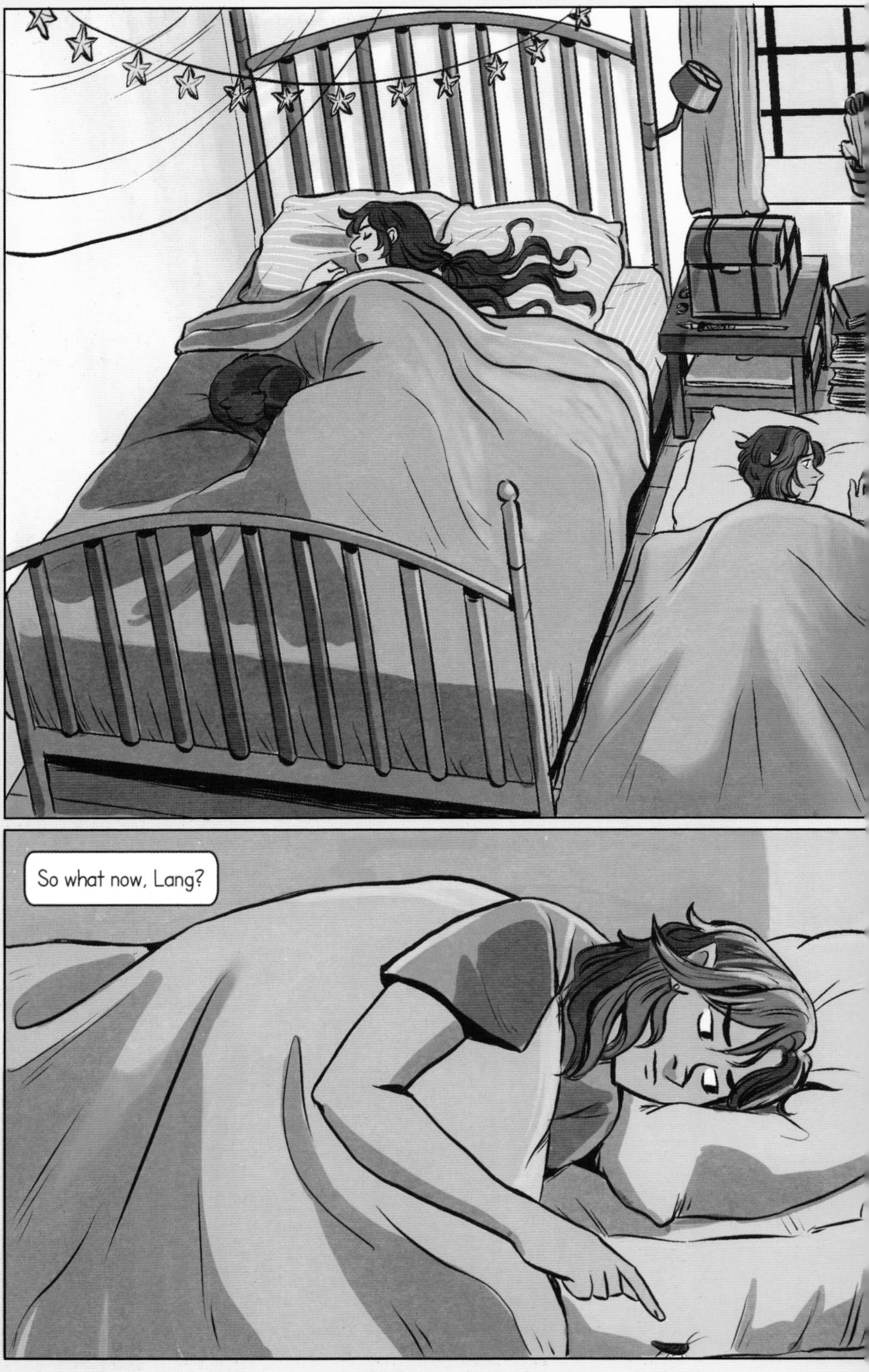
So what now, Lang?

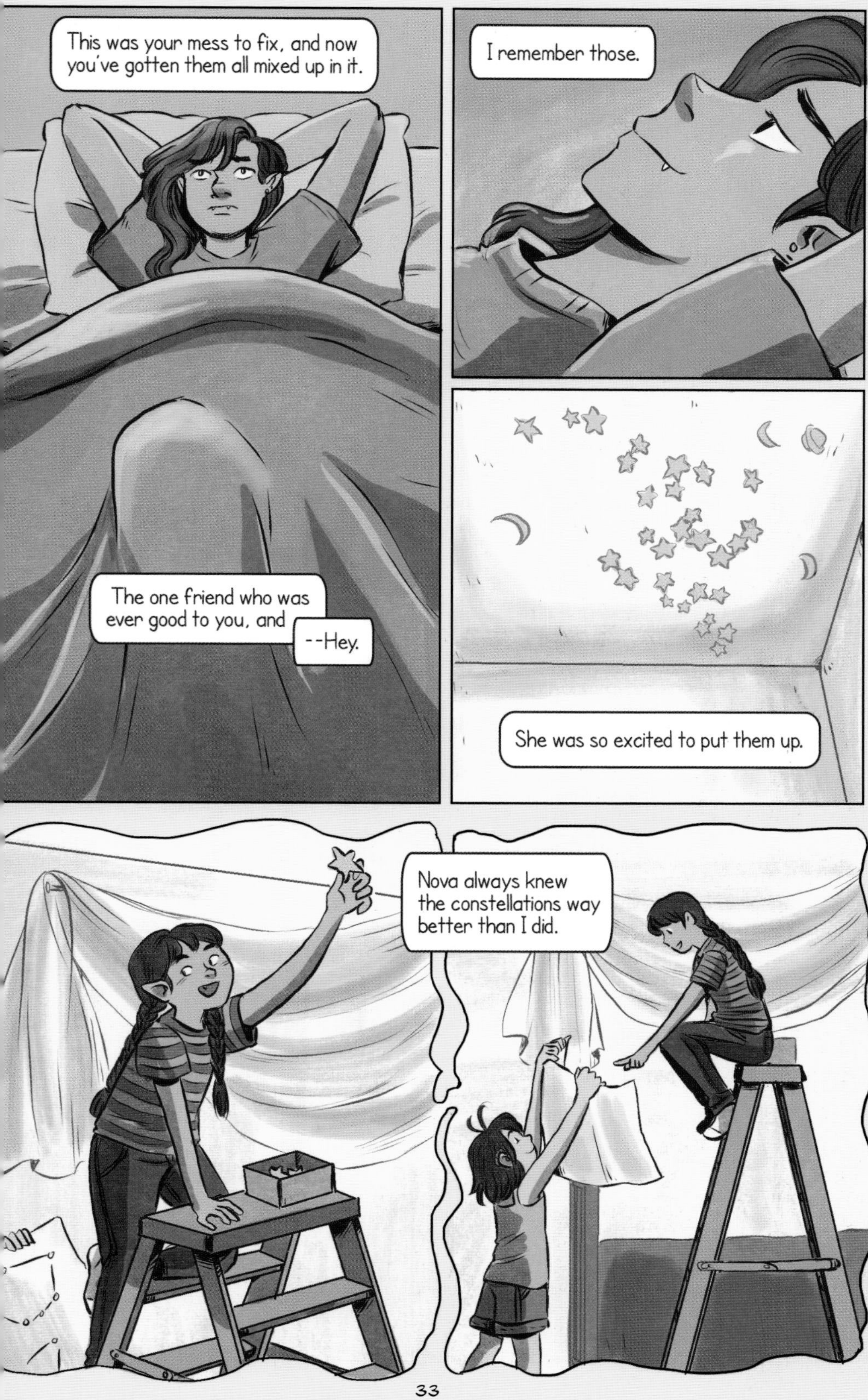
This was your mess to fix, and now you've gotten them all mixed up in it.
I remember those.
The one friend who was ever good to you, and
--Hey.
She was so excited to put them up.
Nova always knew the constellations way better than I did.

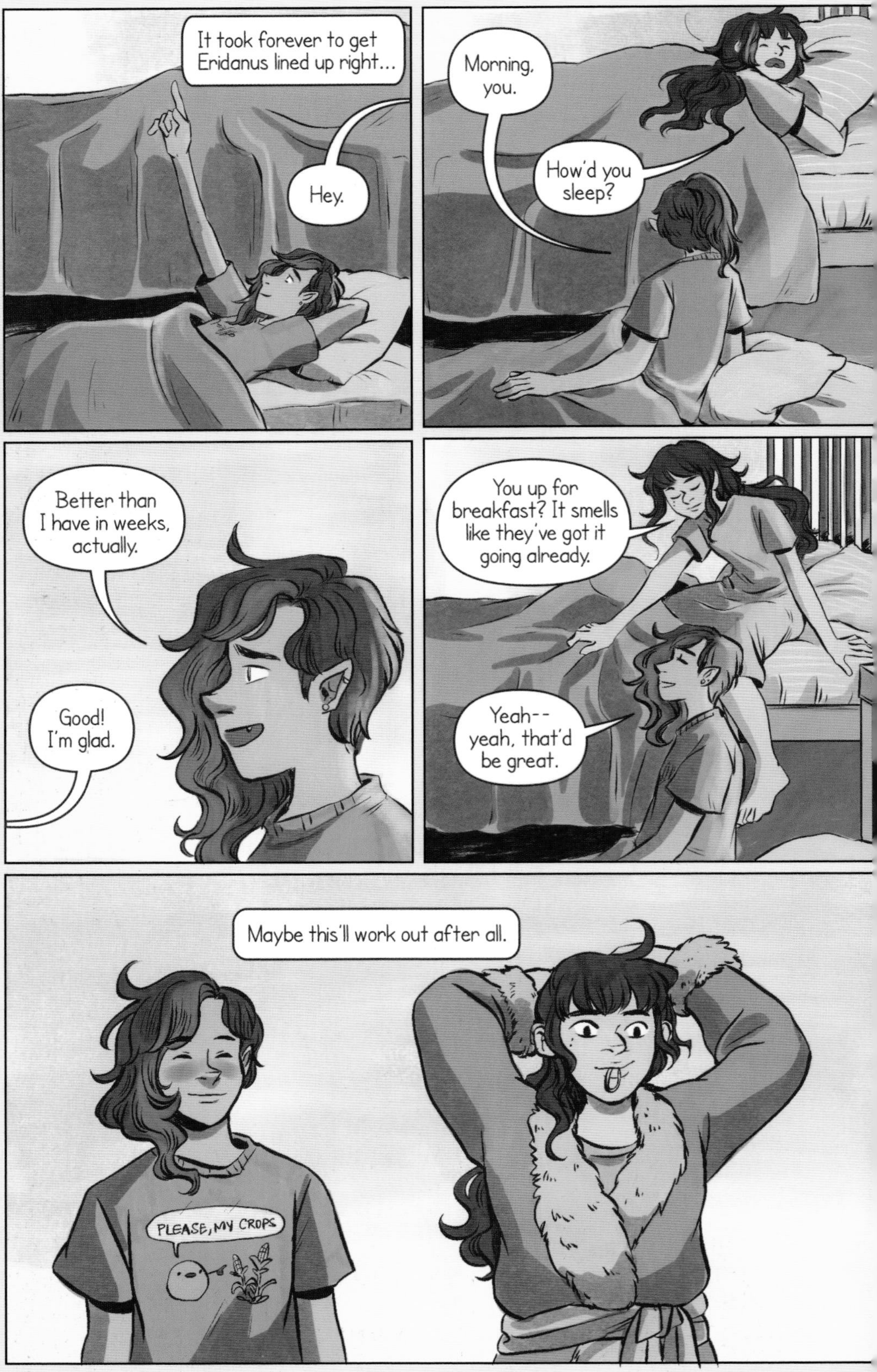
It took forever to get Eridanus lined up right...
Hey.
Morning, you.
How'd you sleep?
Better than I have in weeks, actually.
Good! I'm glad.
You up for breakfast? It smells like they've got it going already.
Yeah-- yeah, that'd be great.
Maybe this'll work out after all.
PLEASE, MY CROPS

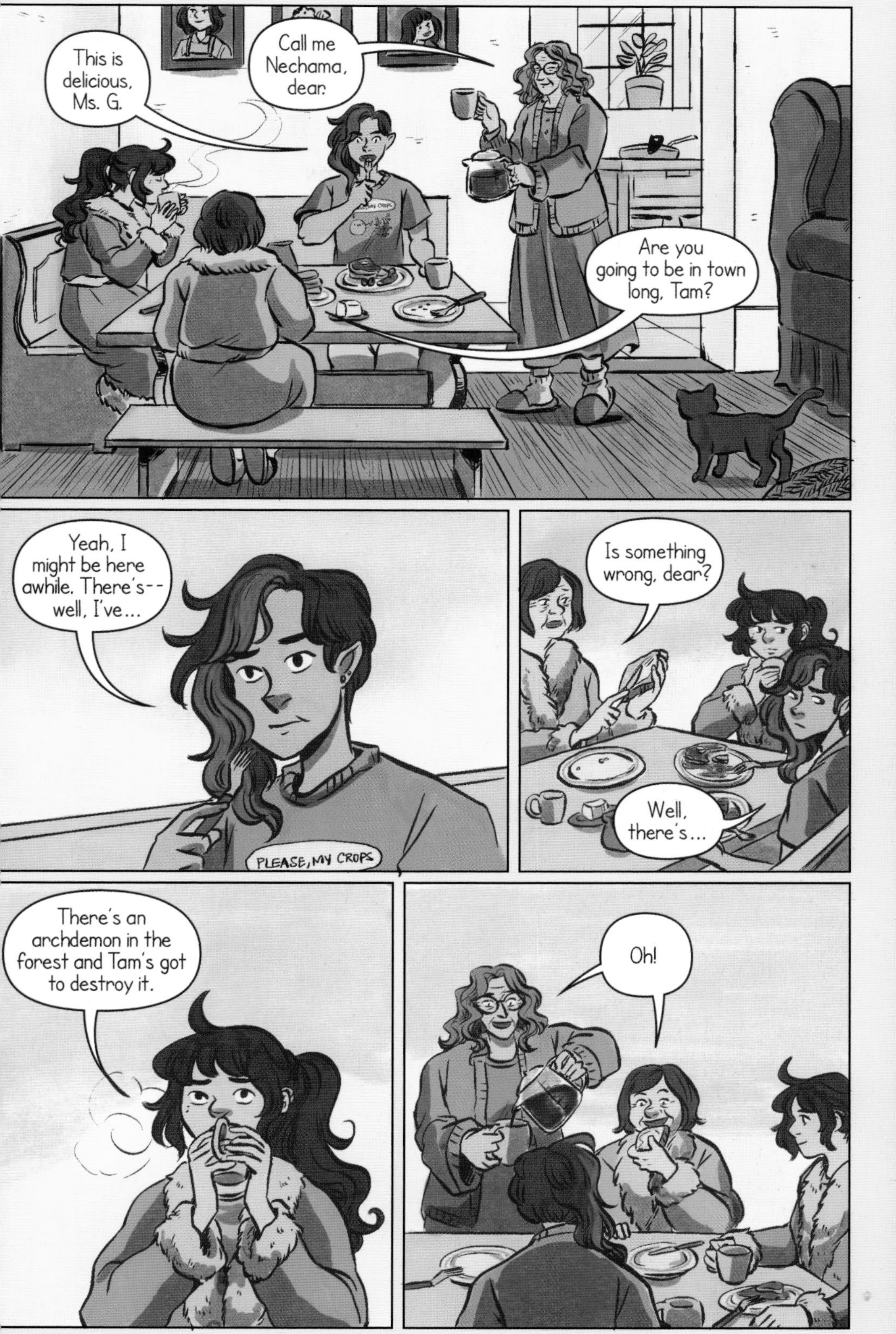
This is delicious, Ms. G.
Call me Nechama, dear.
Are you going to be in town long, Tam?
PLEASE, MY CROPS
Yeah, I might be here awhile. There's--well, I've...
PLEASE, MY CROPS
Is something wrong, dear?
Well, there's...
There's an archdemon in the forest and Tam's got to destroy it.
Oh!

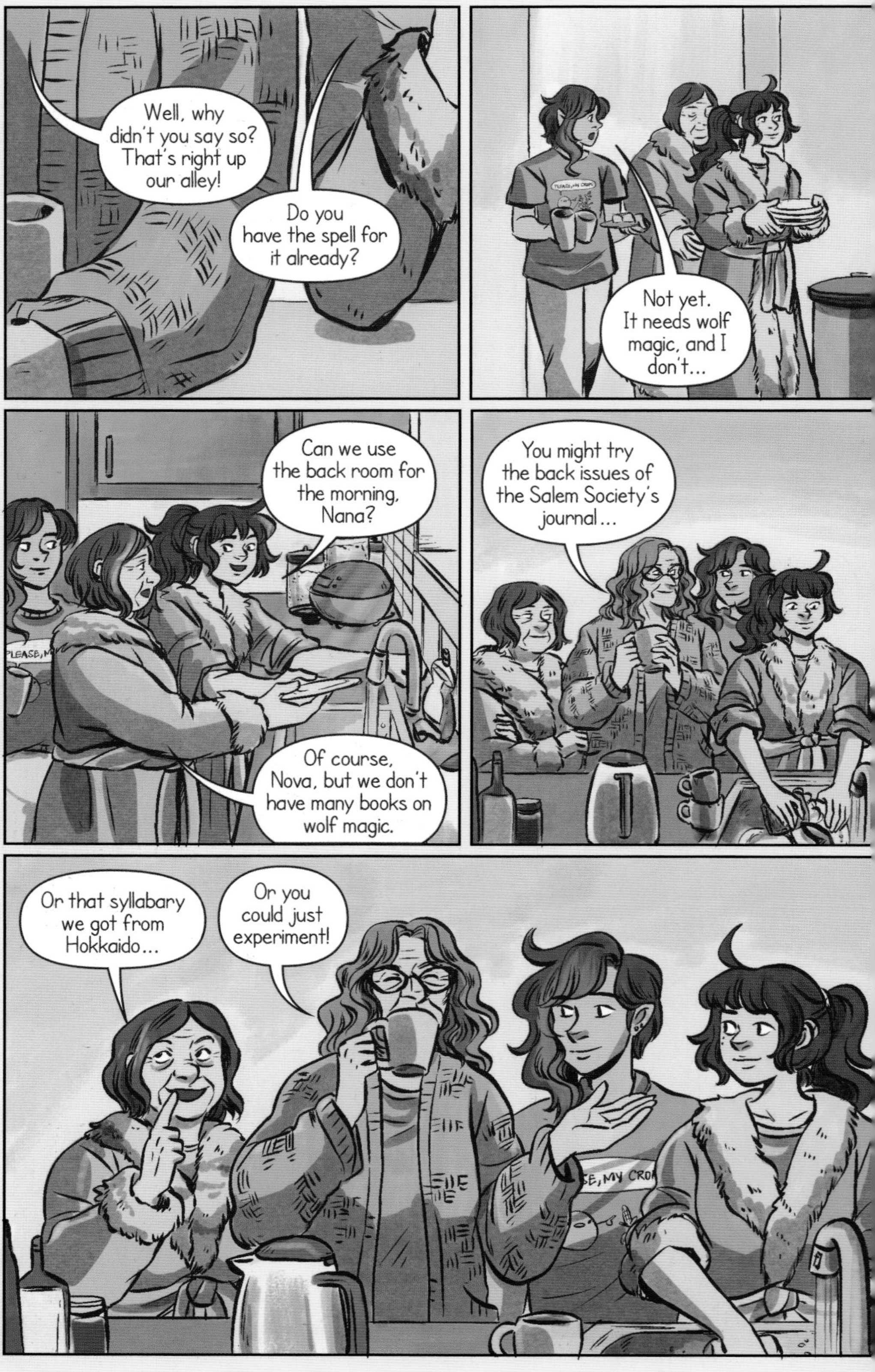

Well, why didn't you say so? That's right up our alley!
Do you have the spell for it already?
Not yet. It needs wolf magic, and I don't...
PLEASE, MY CROPS
Can we use the back room for the morning, Nana?
PLEASE, M
Of course, Nova, but we don't have many books on wolf magic.
You might try the back issues of the Salem Society's journal...
Or that syllabary we got from Hokkaido...
Or you could just experiment!
SE, MY CRO

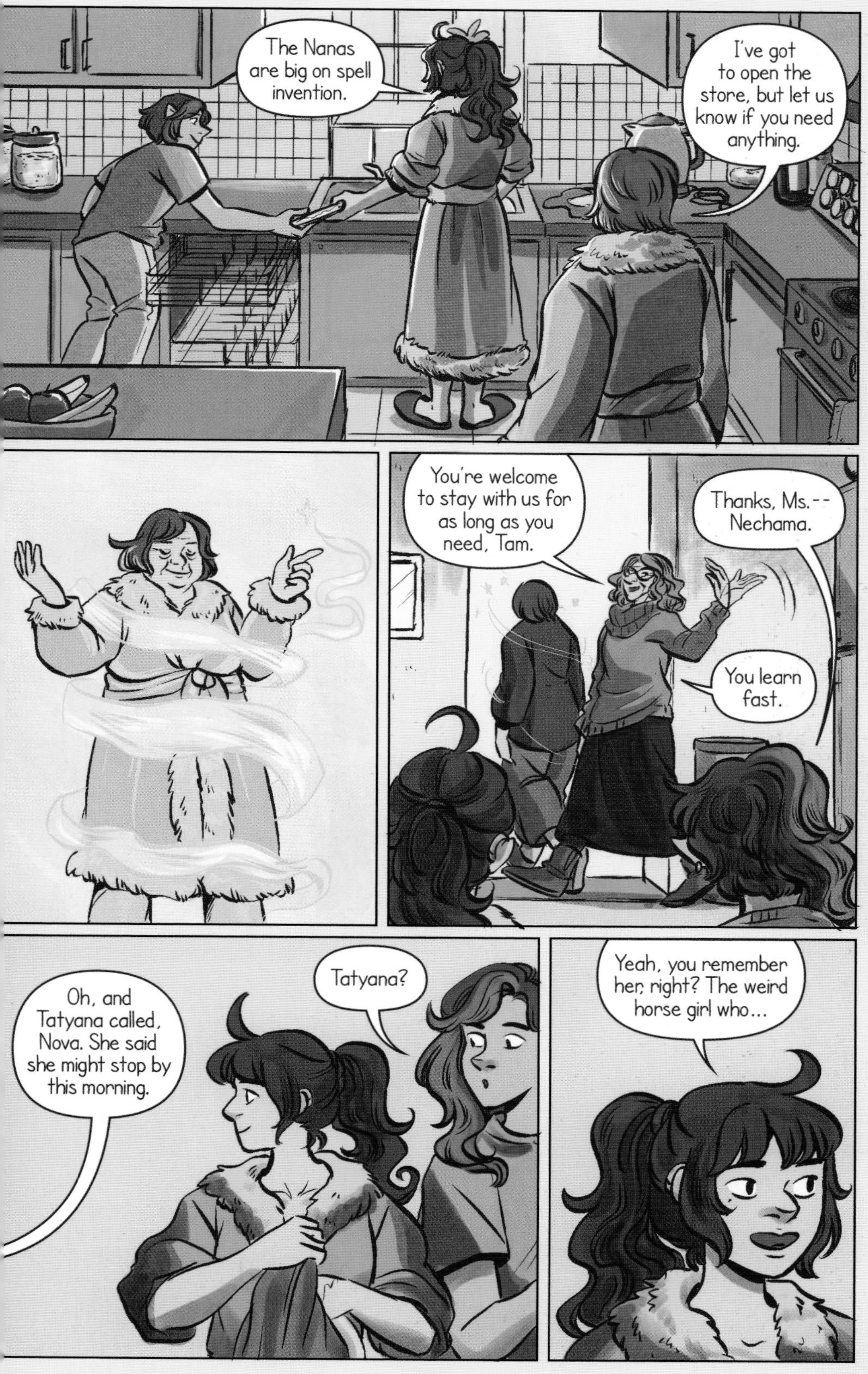
The Nanas are big on spell invention.
I've got to open the store, but let us know if you need anything.
You're welcome to stay with us for as long as you need, Tam.
Thanks, Ms.-- Nechama.
You learn fast.
Oh, and Tatyana called, Nova. She said she might stop by this morning.
Tatyana?
Yeah, you remember her, right? The weird horse girl who...

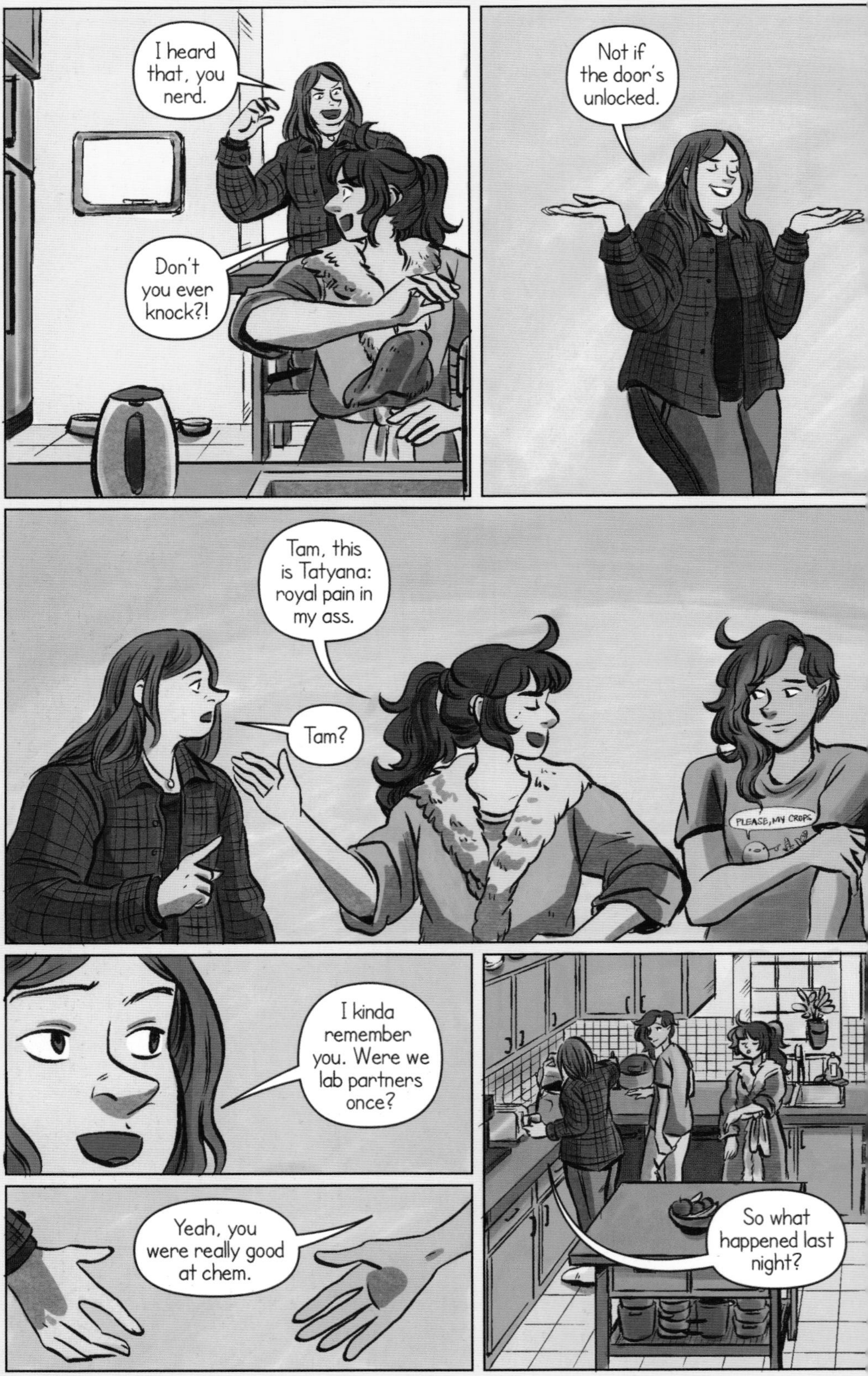
I heard that, you nerd.
Don't you ever knock?!
Not if the door's unlocked.
Tam, this is Tatyana: royal pain in my ass.
Tam?
PLEASE, MY CROPS
I kinda remember you. Were we lab partners once?
Yeah, you were really good at chem.
So what happened last night?

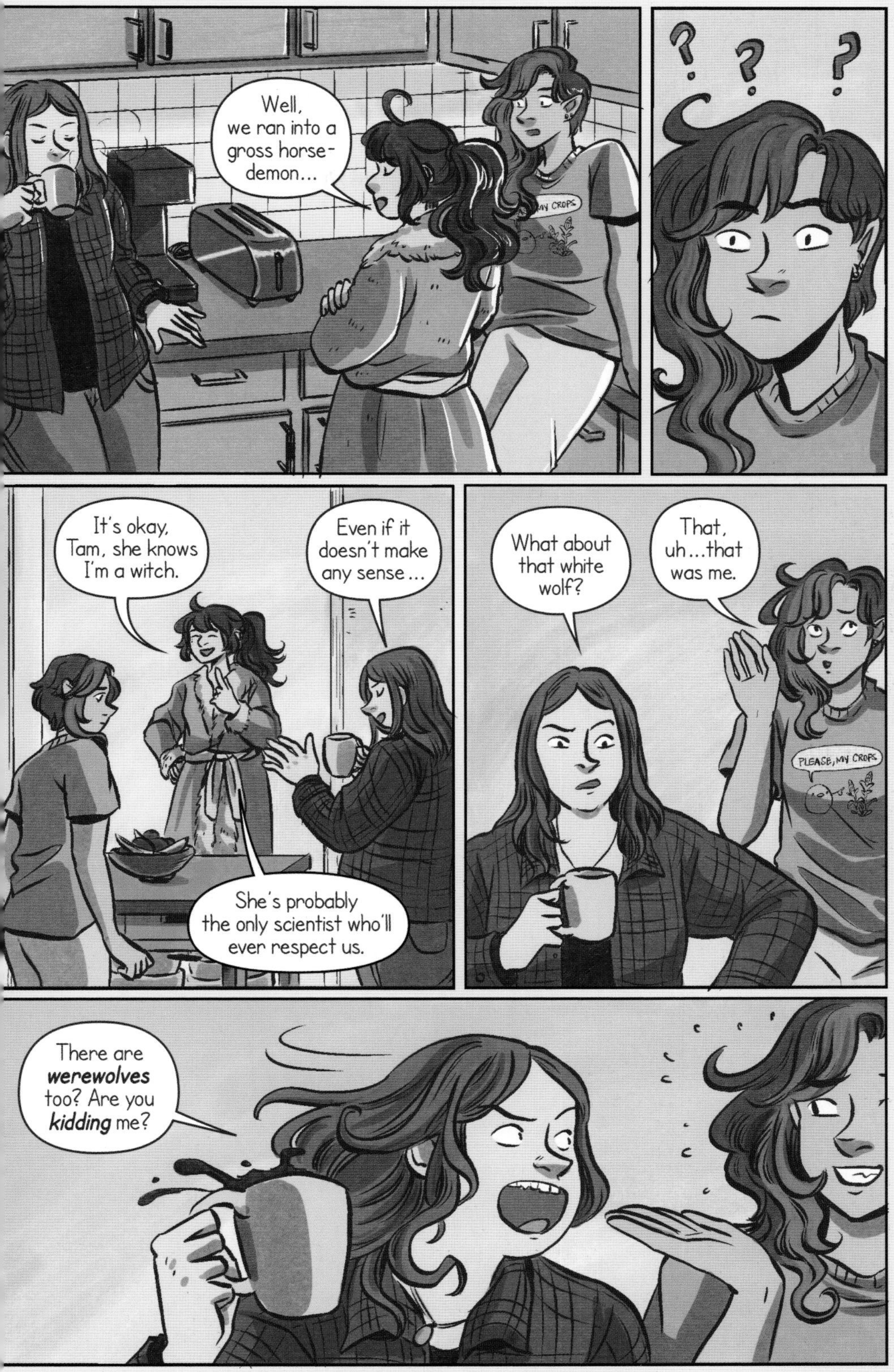
Well, we ran into a gross horse-demon...
MY CROPS
? ? ?
It's okay, Tam, she knows I'm a witch.
Even if it doesn't make any sense...
She's probably the only scientist who'll ever respect us.
What about that white wolf?
That, uh...that was me.
PLEASE, MY CROPS
There are **werewolves** too? Are you **kidding** me?

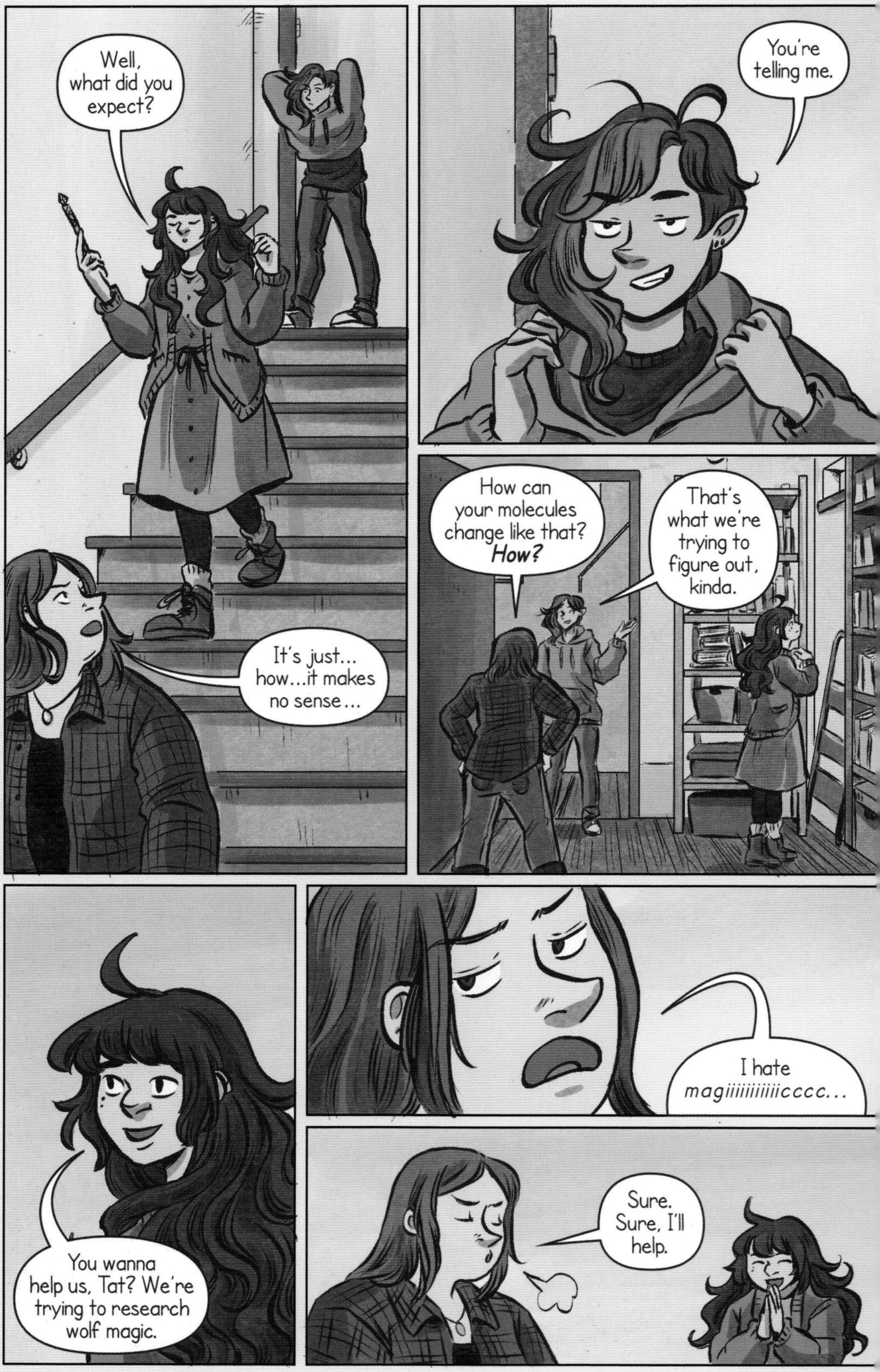
Well, what did you expect?
You're telling me.
It's just... how...it makes no sense...
How can your molecules change like that? **How?**
That's what we're trying to figure out, kinda.
You wanna help us, Tat? We're trying to research wolf magic.
I hate *magiiiiiiiiiiicccc...*
Sure. Sure, I'll help.

FRAGILE

This is useless!

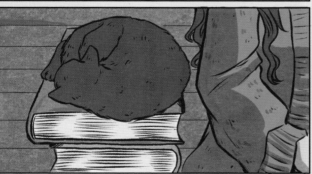

Science and Magic
Are They Really
So Different

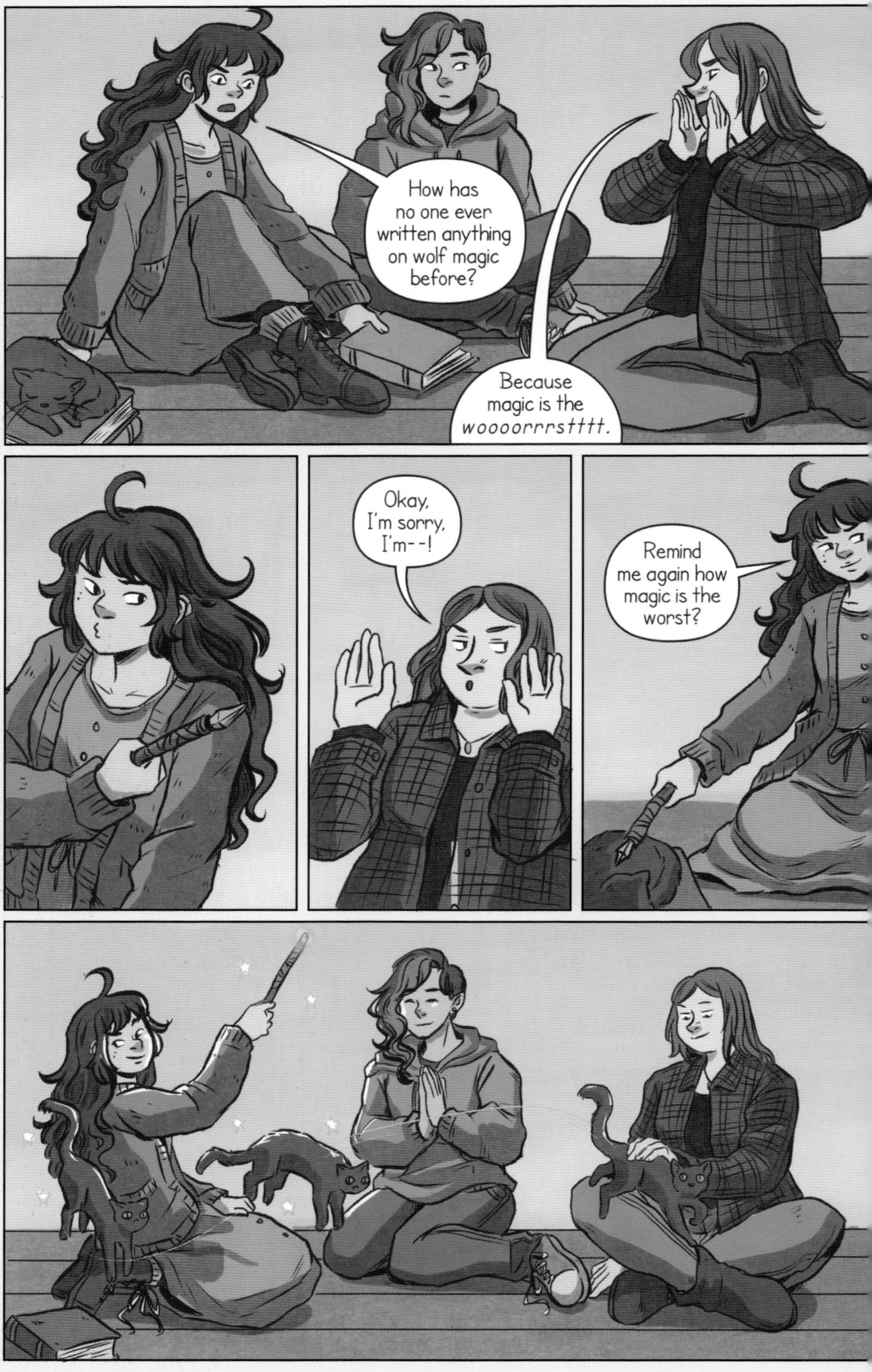
How has no one ever written anything on wolf magic before?
Because magic is the woooorrrsttttt.
Okay, I'm sorry, I'm--!
Remind me again how magic is the worst?

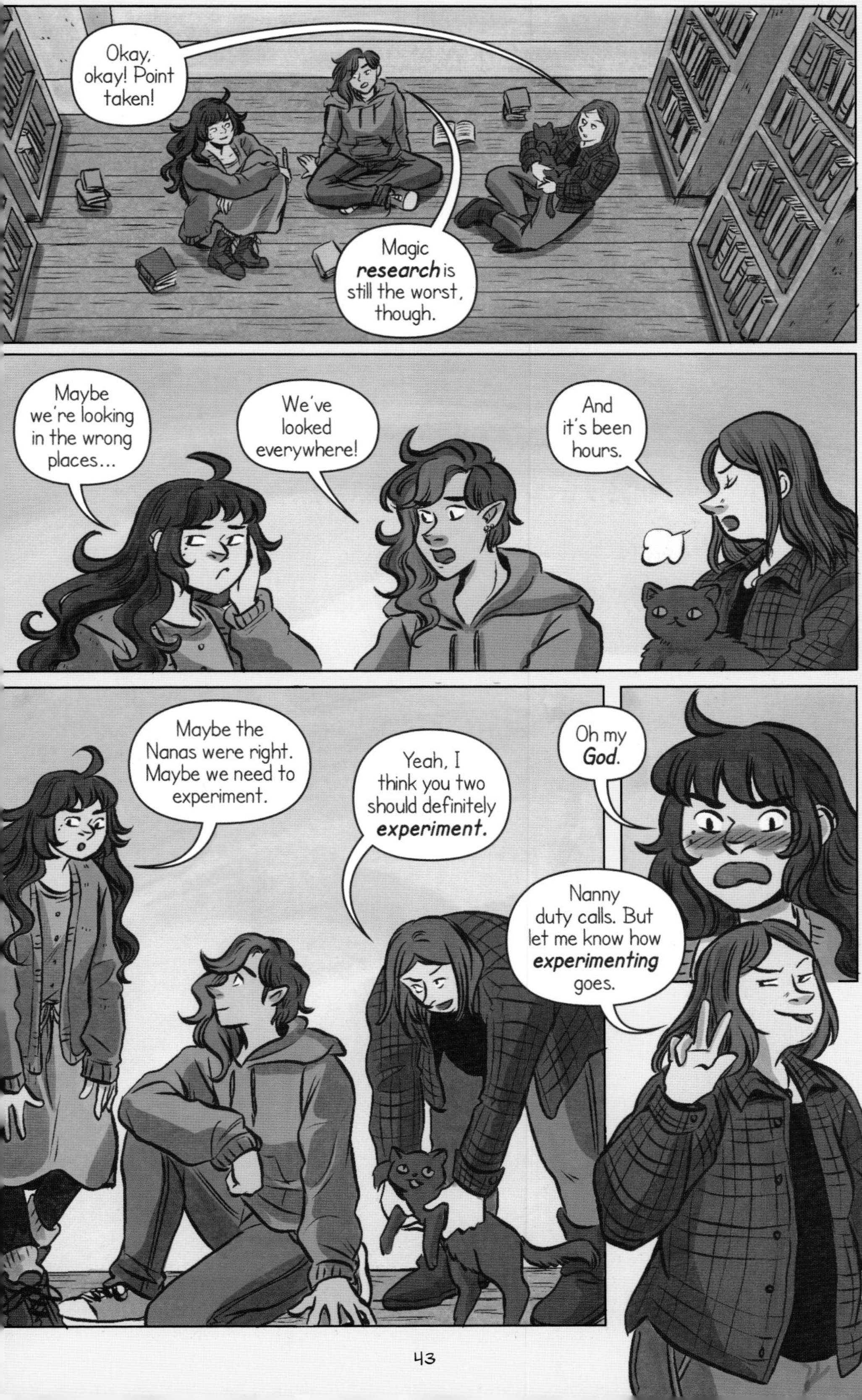
Okay, okay! Point taken!
Magic **research** is still the worst, though.
Maybe we're looking in the wrong places...
We've looked everywhere!
And it's been hours.
Maybe the Nanas were right. Maybe we need to experiment.
Yeah, I think you two should definitely ***experiment.***
Oh my ***God***.
Nanny duty calls. But let me know how ***experimenting*** goes.

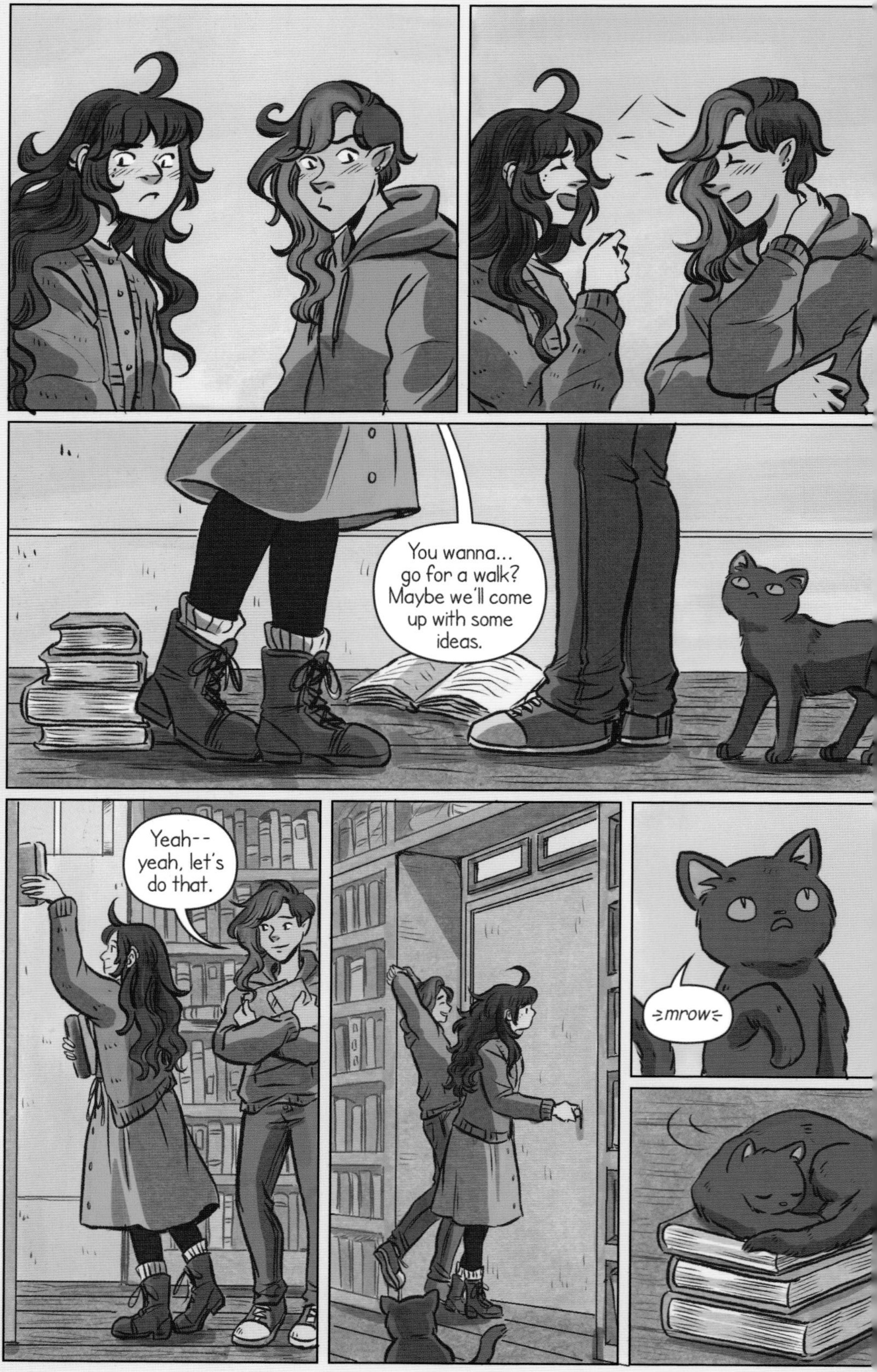
You wanna... go for a walk? Maybe we'll come up with some ideas.
Yeah-- yeah, let's do that.
mrow

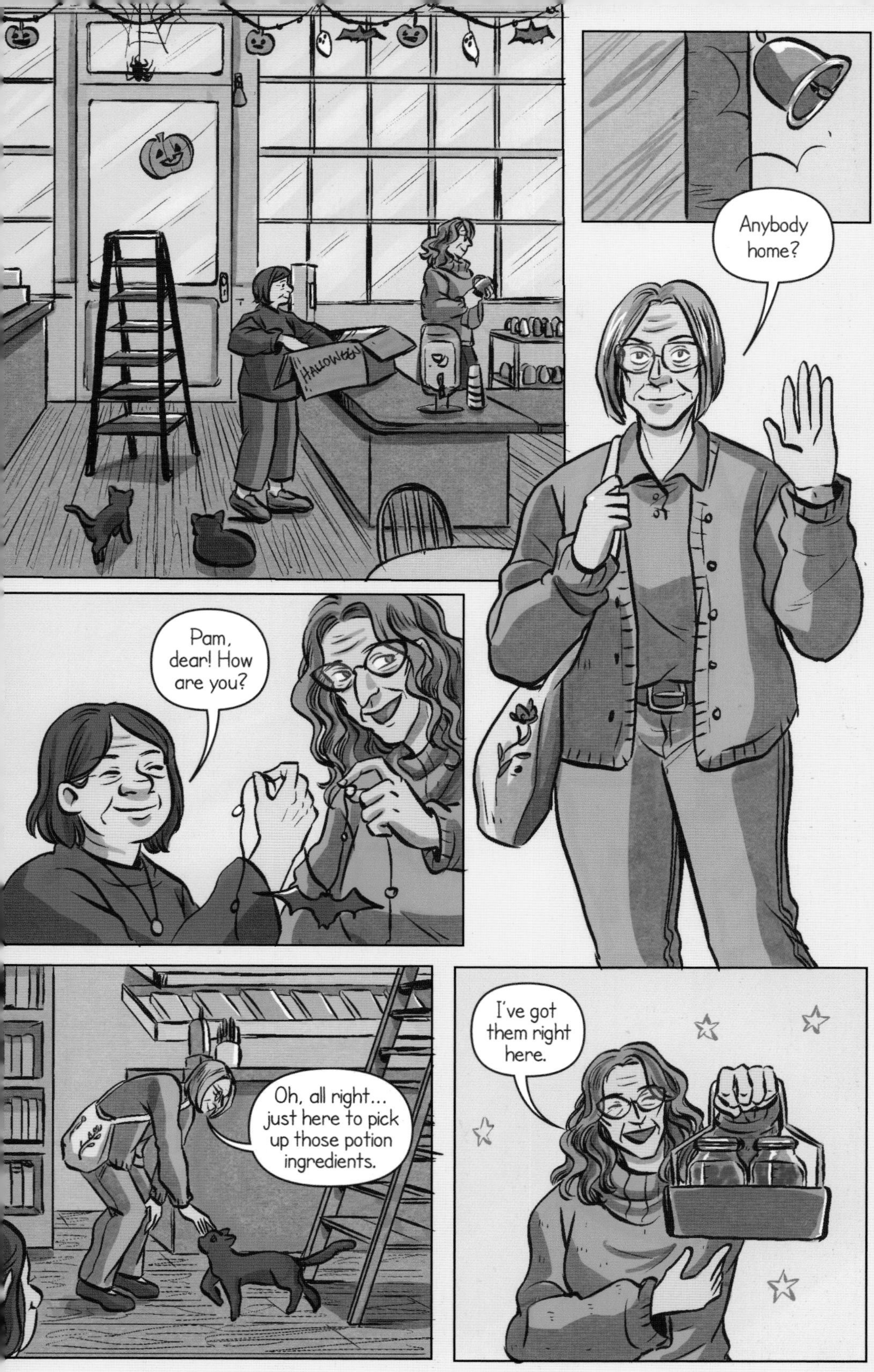
HALLOWEEN
Anybody home?
Pam, dear! How are you?
Oh, all right... just here to pick up those potion ingredients.
I've got them right here.

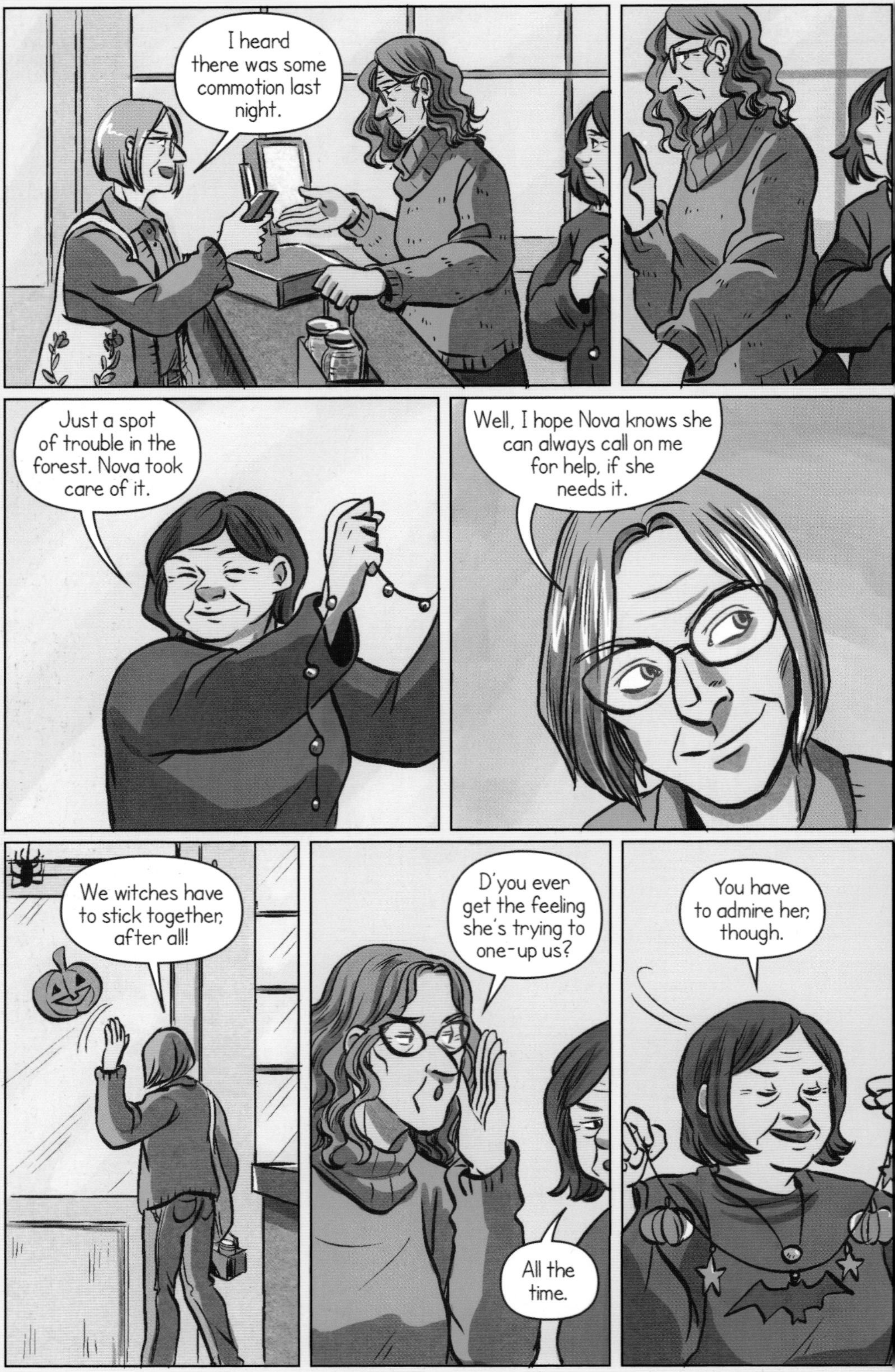
I heard there was some commotion last night.
Just a spot of trouble in the forest. Nova took care of it.
Well, I hope Nova knows she can always call on me for help, if she needs it.
We witches have to stick together, after all!
D'you ever get the feeling she's trying to one-up us?
All the time.
You have to admire her, though.

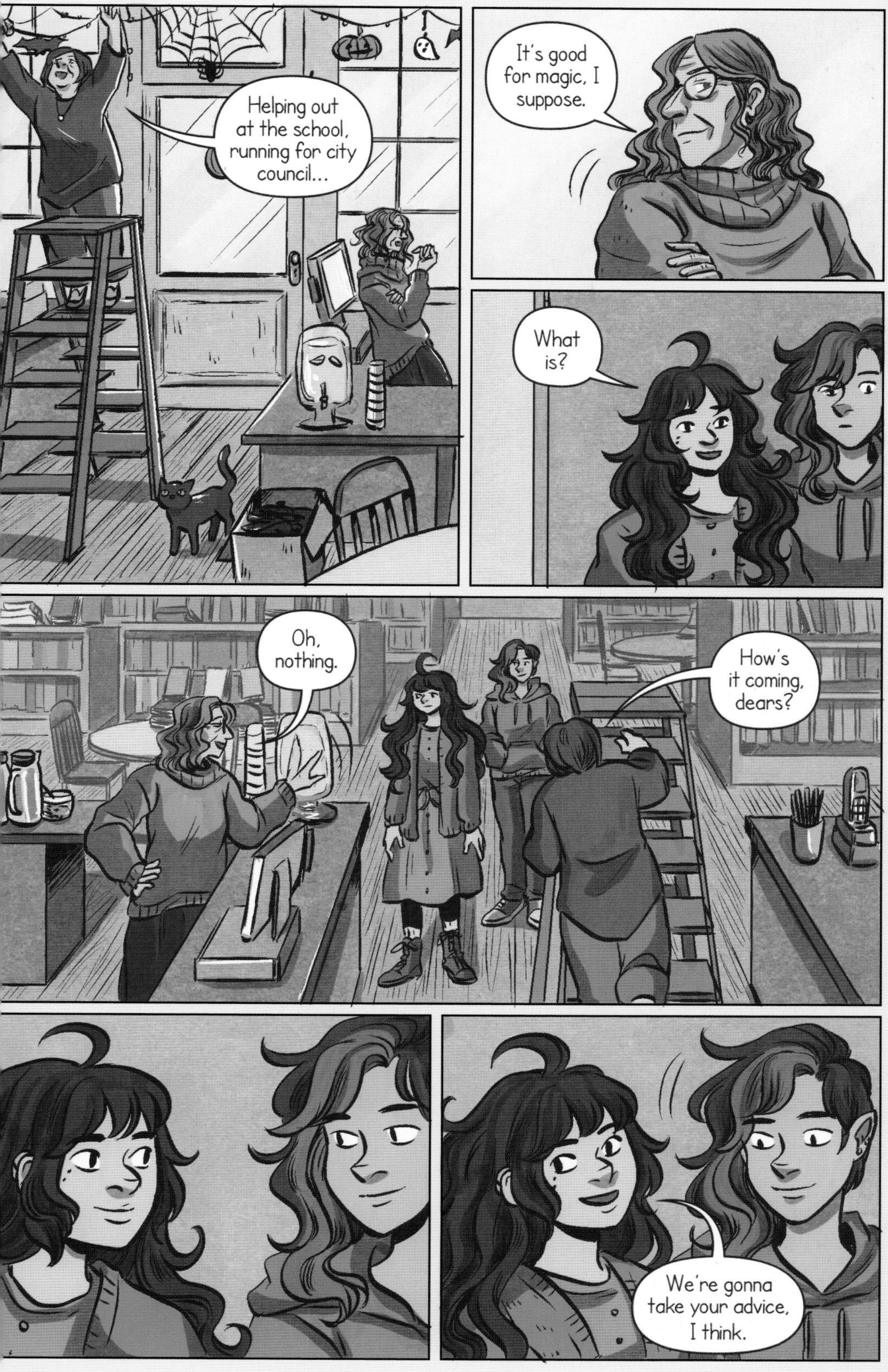
Helping out at the school, running for city council...
It's good for magic, I suppose.
What is?
Oh, nothing.
How's it coming, dears?
We're gonna take your advice, I think.

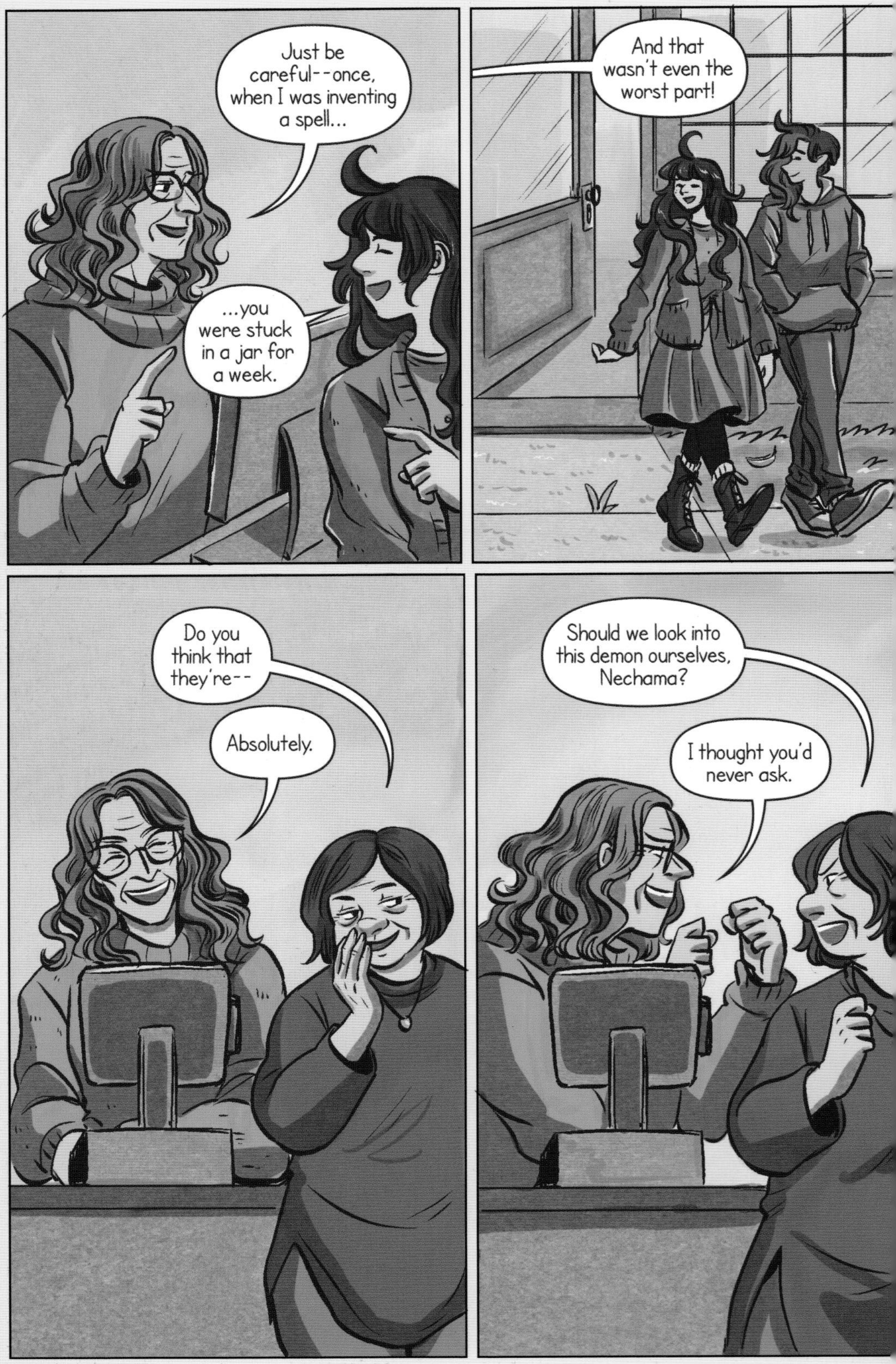
Just be careful--once, when I was inventing a spell...
...you were stuck in a jar for a week.
And that wasn't even the worst part!
Do you think that they're--
Absolutely.
Should we look into this demon ourselves, Nechama?
I thought you'd never ask.

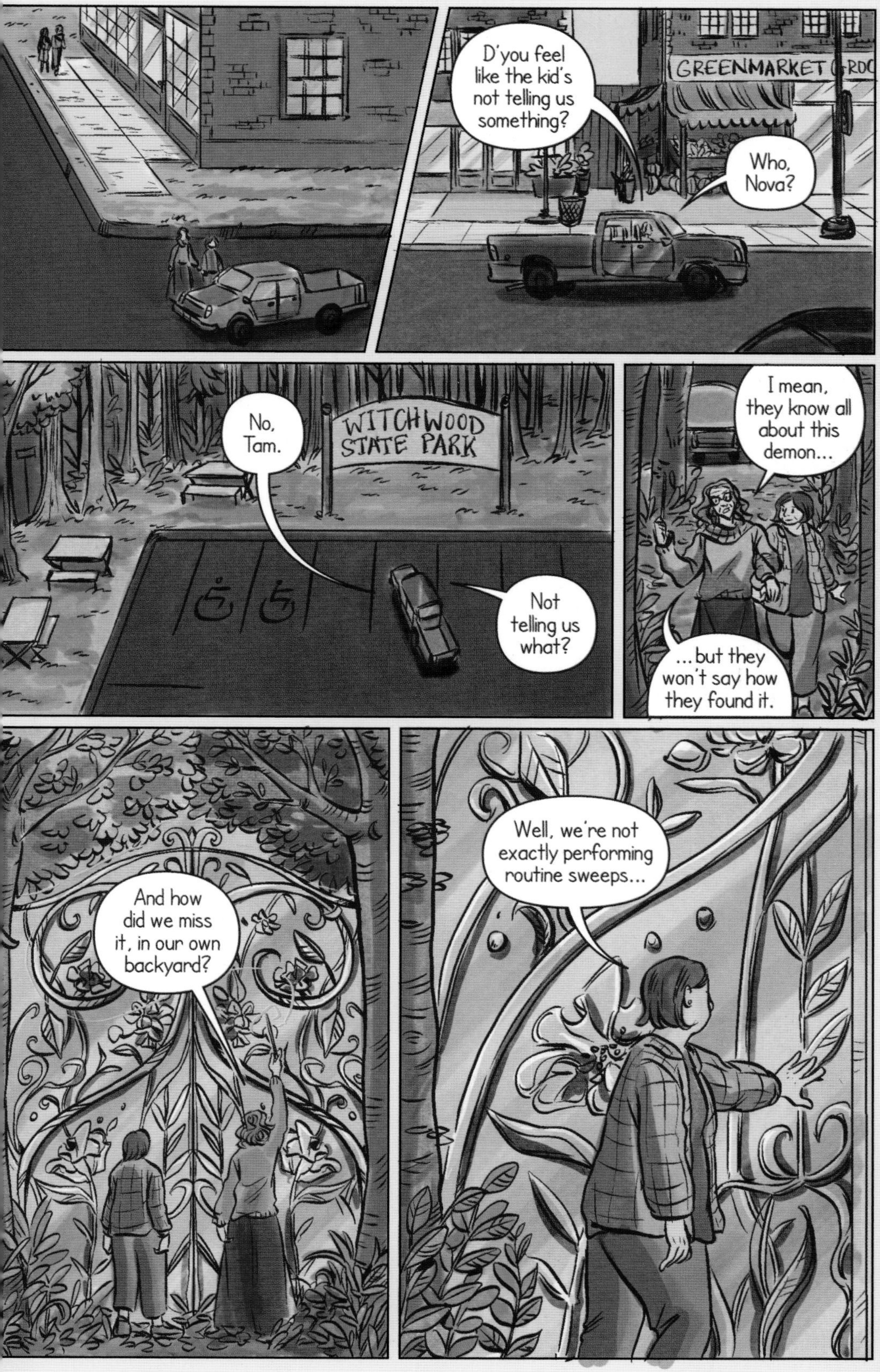
D'you feel like the kid's not telling us something?
GREENMARKET GROC
Who, Nova?
WITCHWOOD STATE PARK
No, Tam.
Not telling us what?
I mean, they know all about this demon...
...but they won't say how they found it.
And how did we miss it, in our own backyard?
Well, we're not exactly performing routine sweeps...

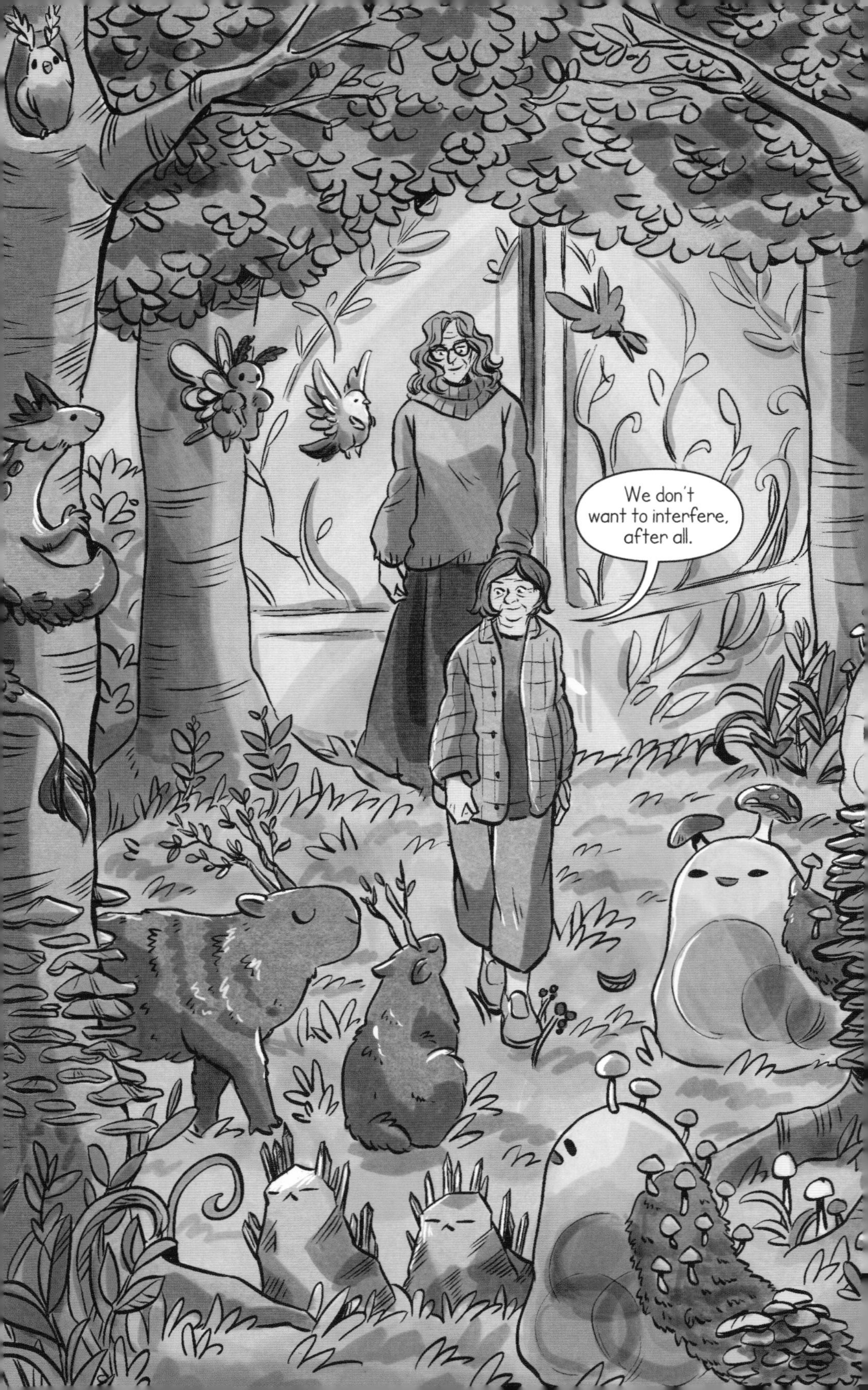
We don't want to interfere, after all.

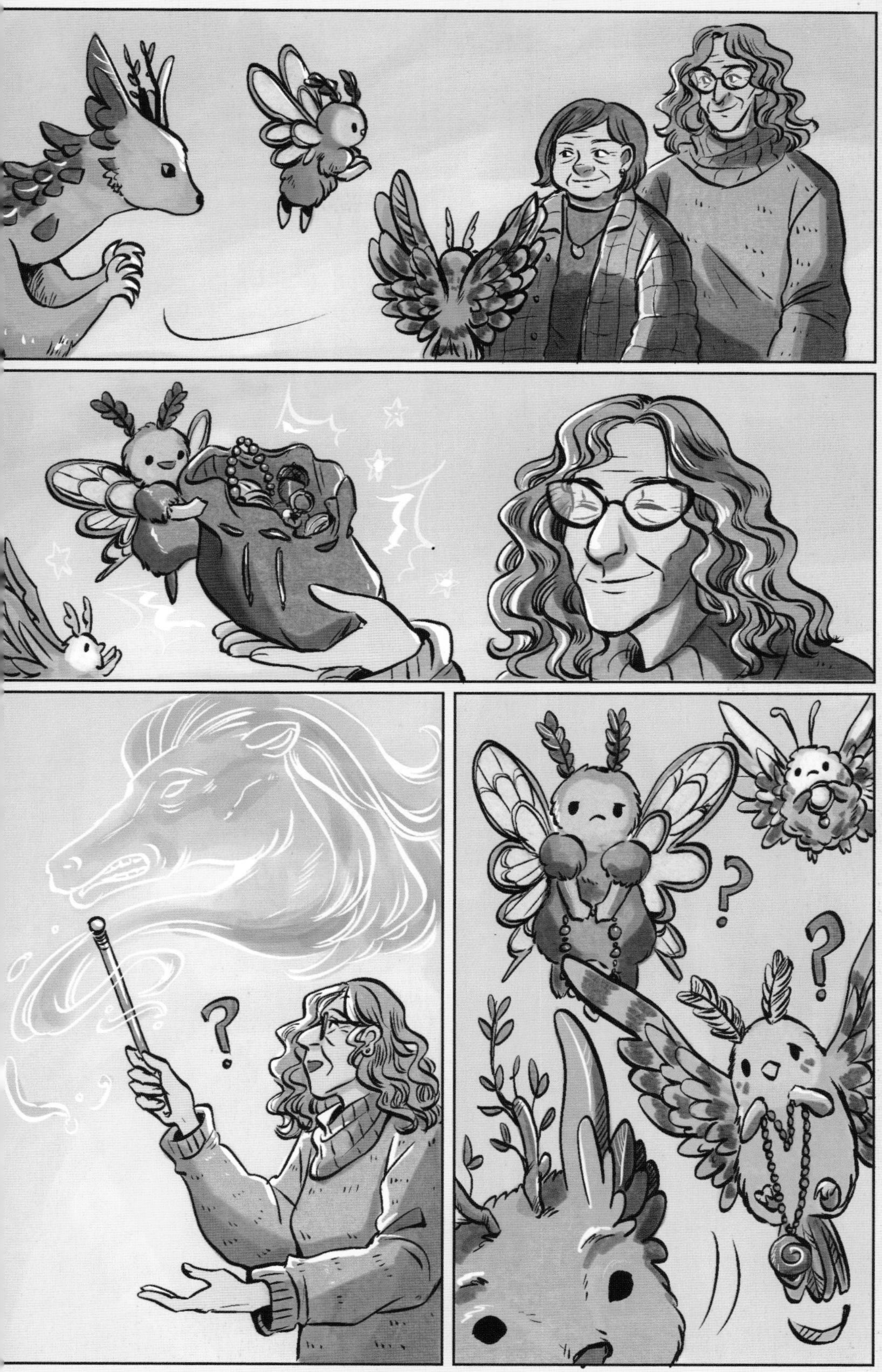

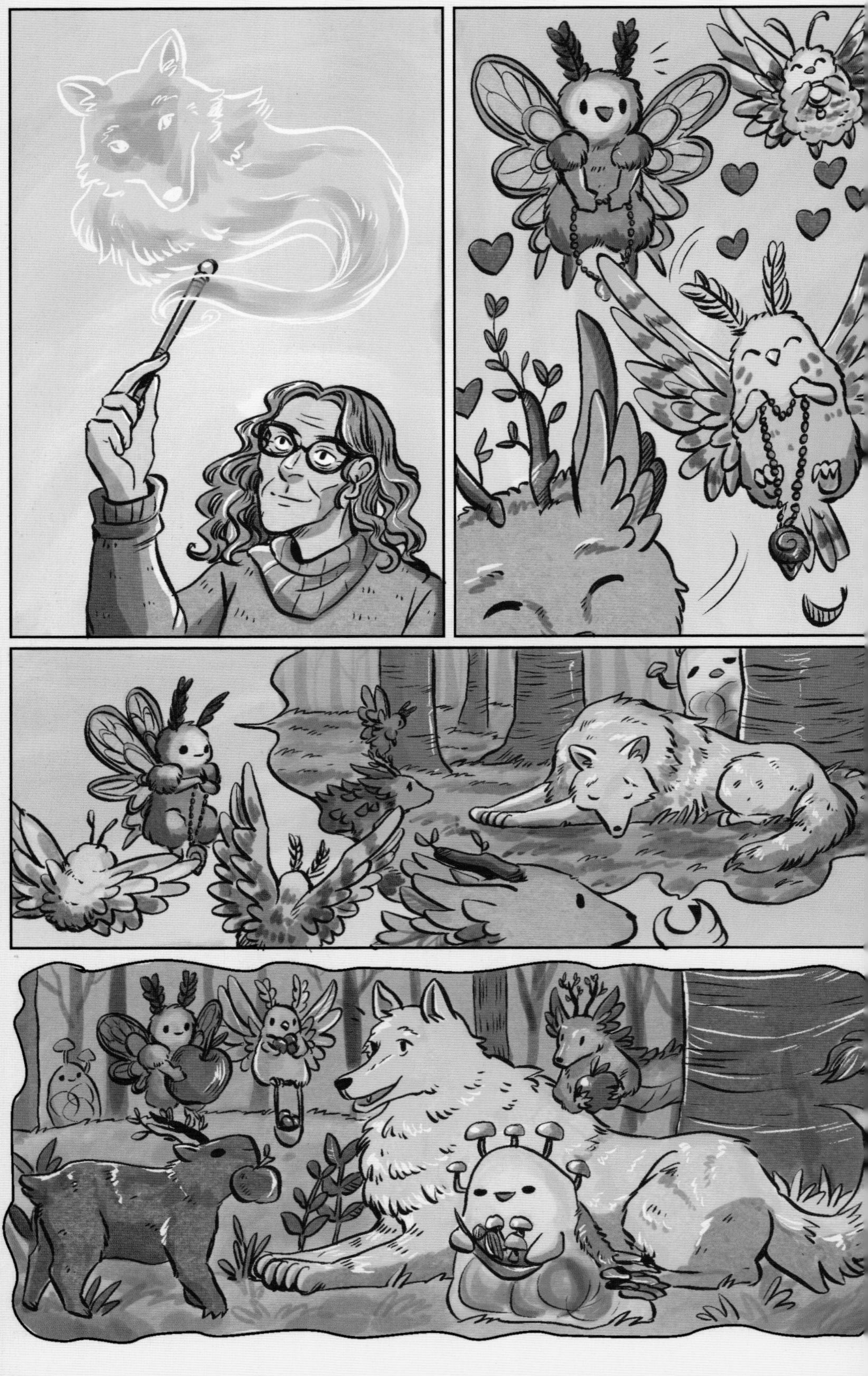

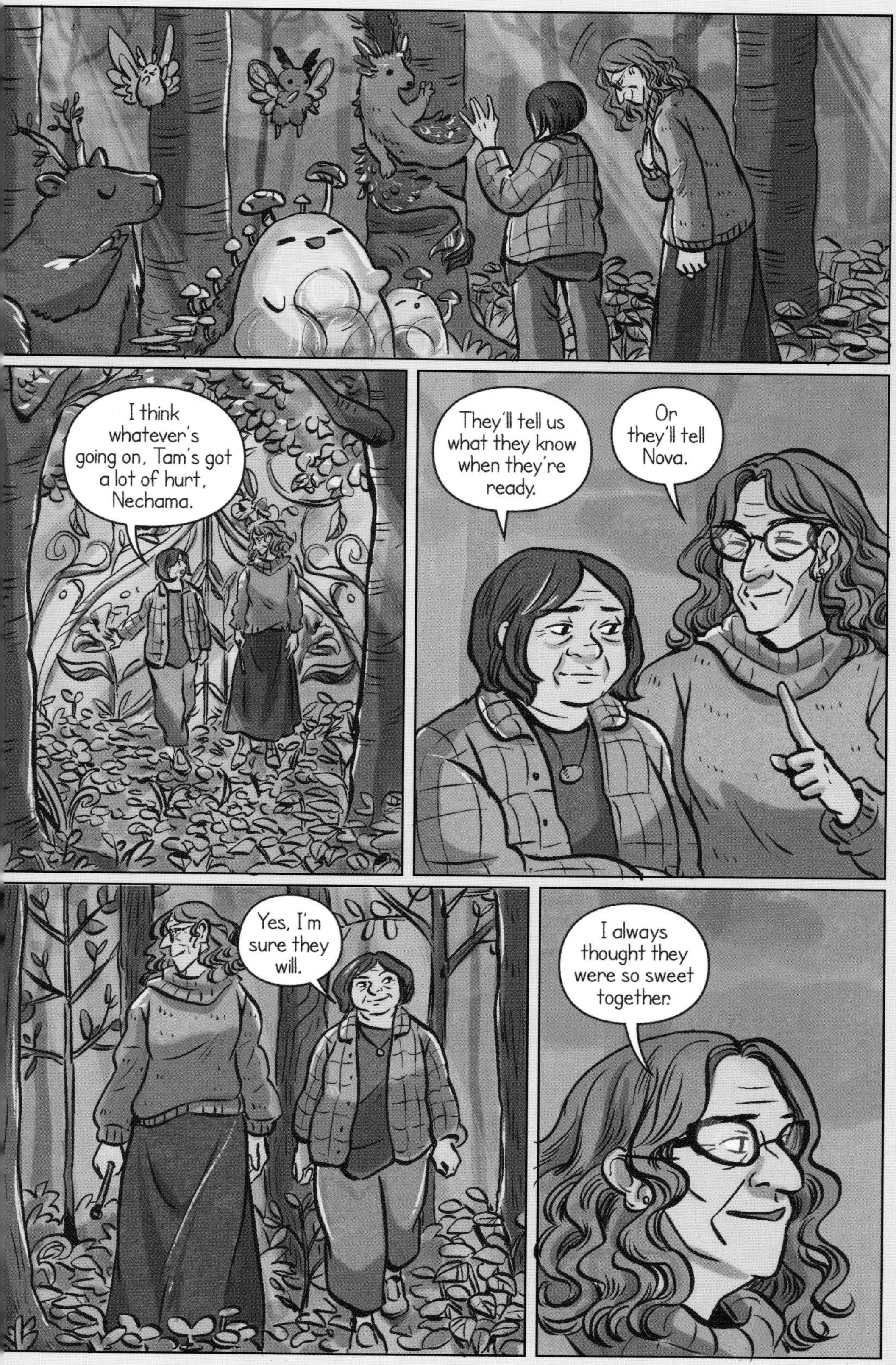
I think whatever's going on, Tam's got a lot of hurt, Nechama.
They'll tell us what they know when they're ready.
Or they'll tell Nova.
Yes, I'm sure they will.
I always thought they were so sweet together.

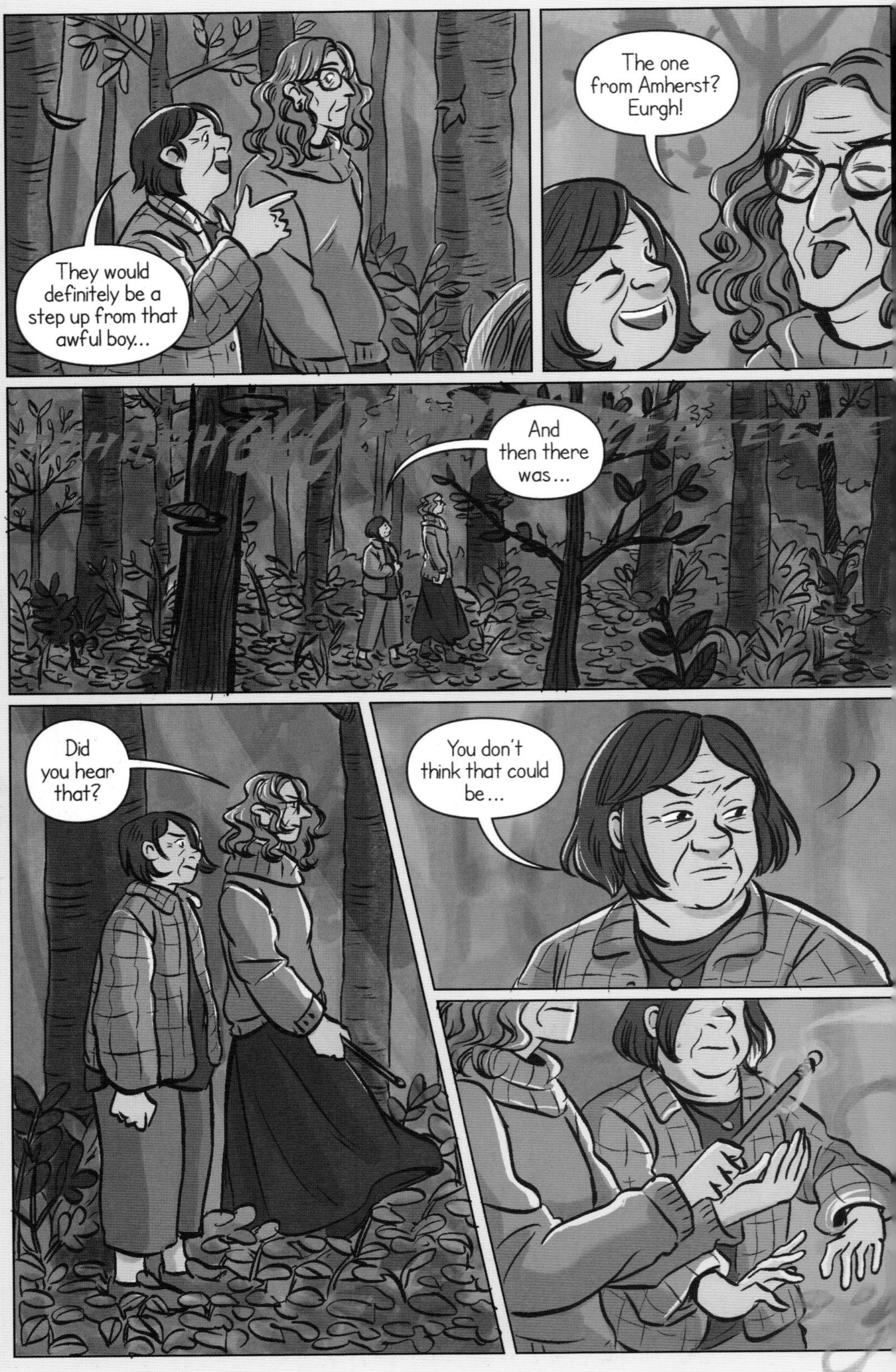
They would definitely be a step up from that awful boy...
The one from Amherst? Eurgh!
And then there was...
Did you hear that?
You don't think that could be...

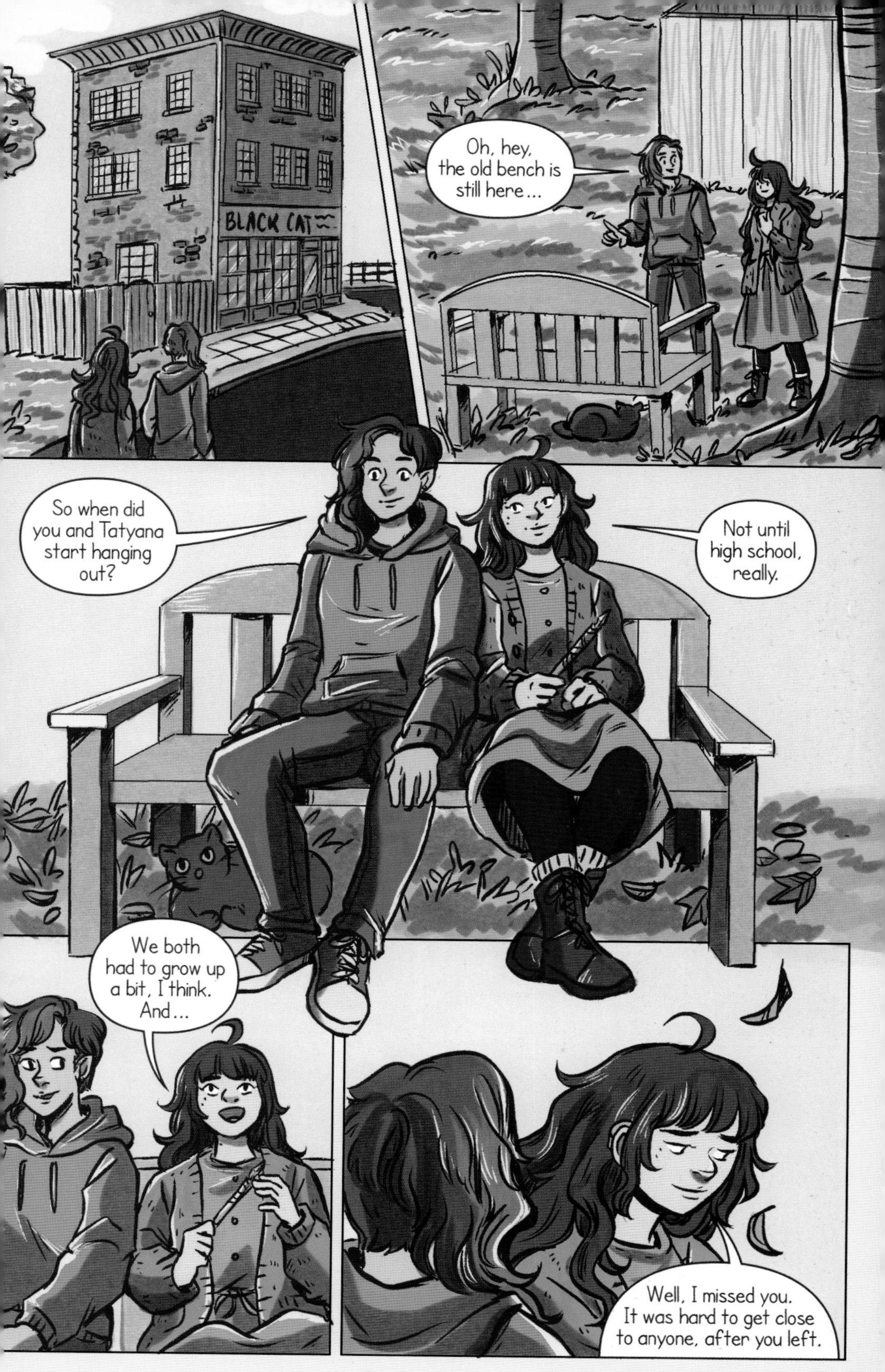
BLACK CAT
Oh, hey, the old bench is still here...
So when did you and Tatyana start hanging out?
Not until high school, really.
We both had to grow up a bit, I think. And...
Well, I missed you. It was hard to get close to anyone, after you left.

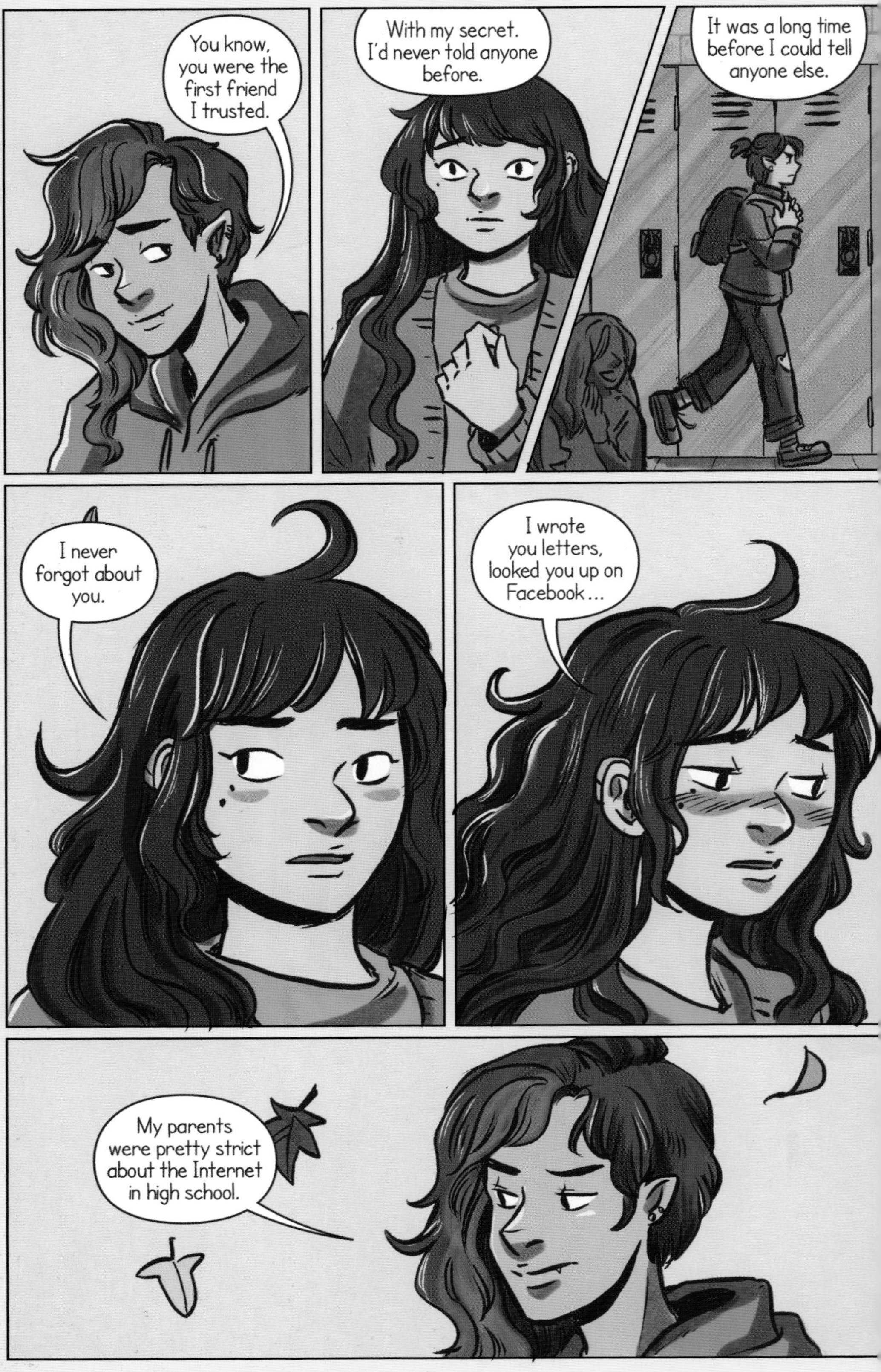
You know, you were the first friend I trusted.
With my secret. I'd never told anyone before.
It was a long time before I could tell anyone else.
I never forgot about you.
I wrote you letters, looked you up on Facebook...
My parents were pretty strict about the Internet in high school.

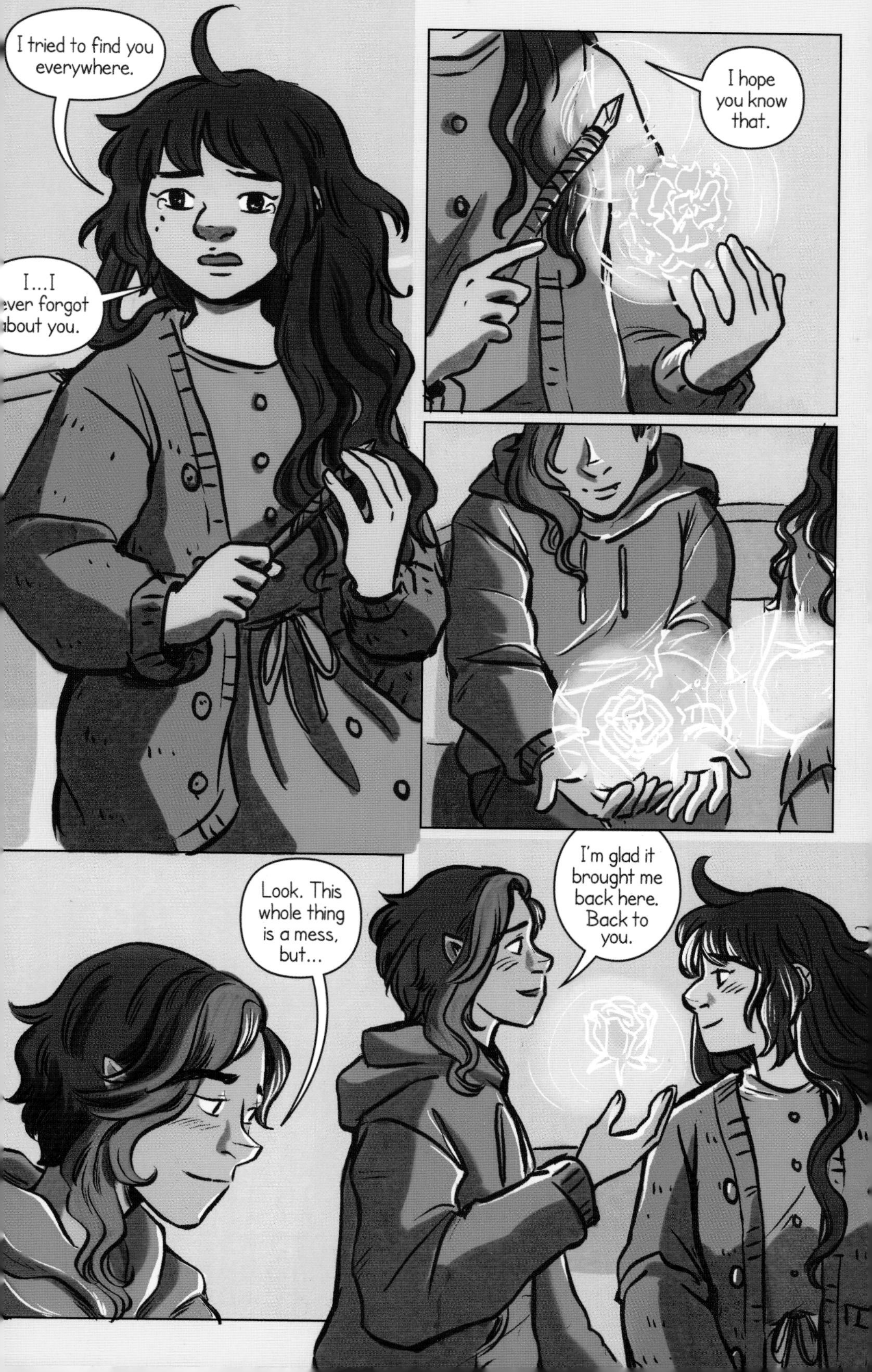

I tried to find you everywhere.
I...I ever forgot about you.
I hope you know that.
Look. This whole thing is a mess, but...
I'm glad it brought me back here. Back to you.

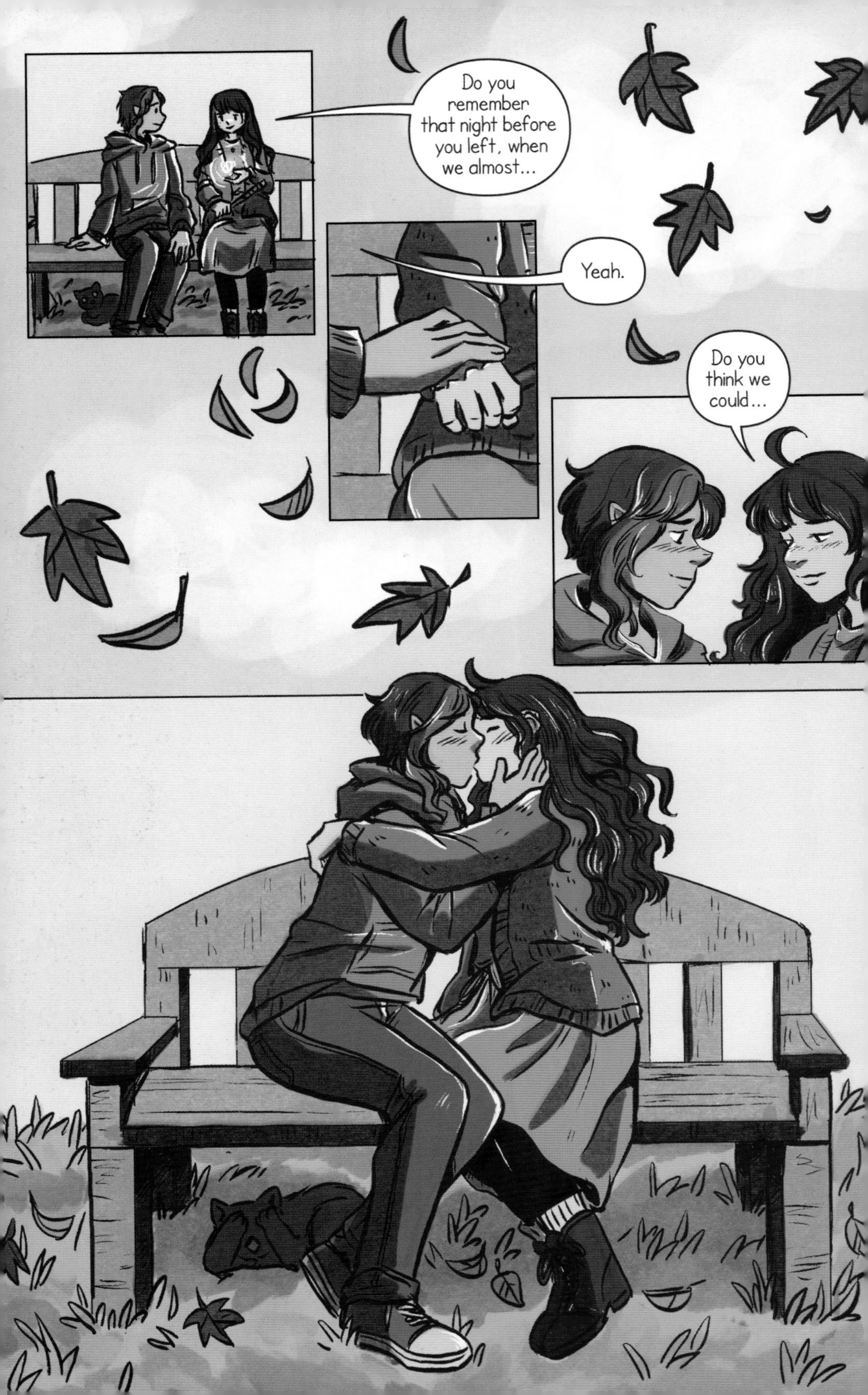
Do you remember that night before you left, when we almost...
Yeah.
Do you think we could...

Chapter 3

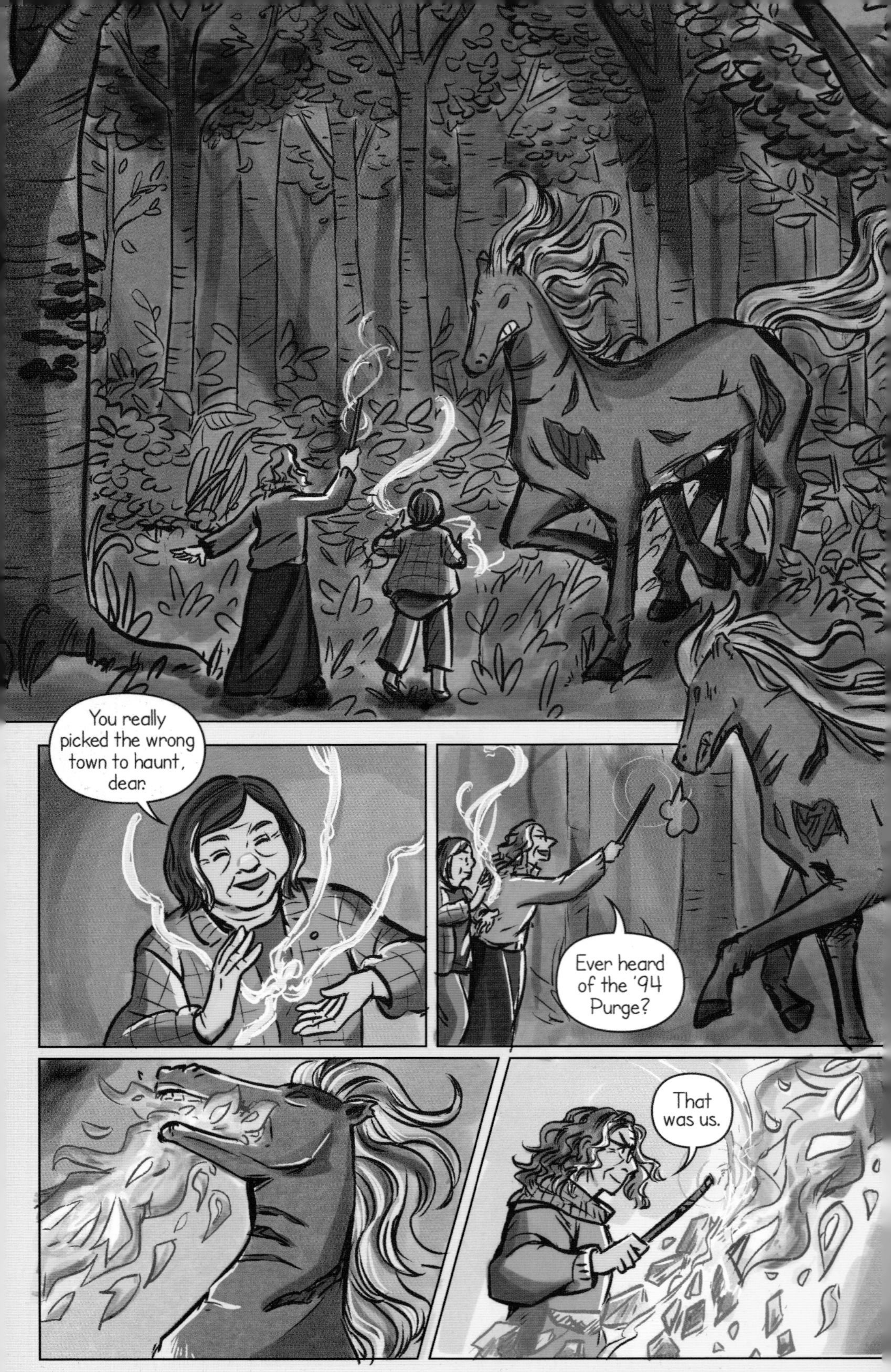
You really picked the wrong town to haunt, dear.
Ever heard of the '94 Purge?
That was us.

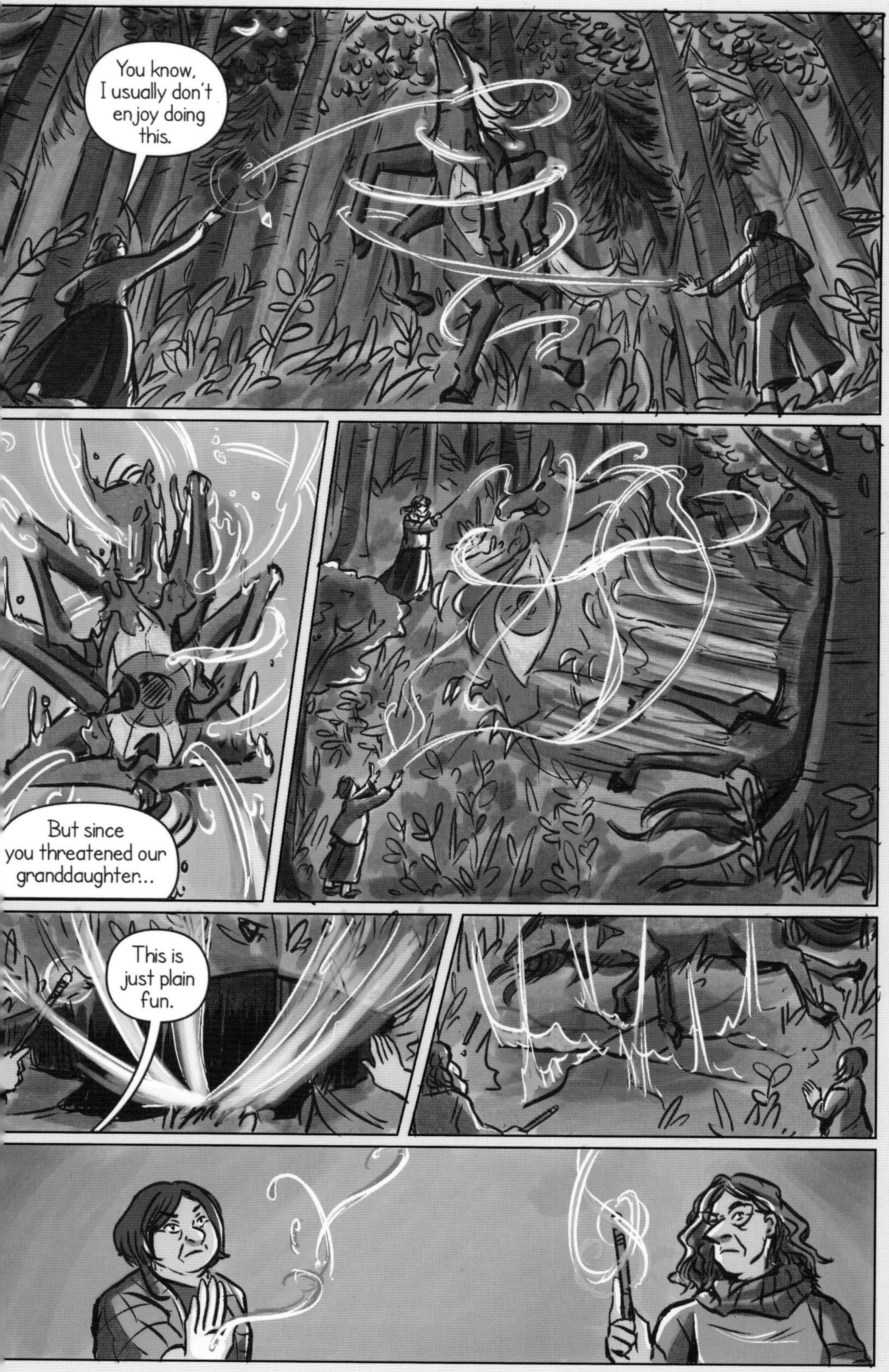

You know, I usually don't enjoy doing this.
But since you threatened our granddaughter...
This is just plain fun.

Oh, for heaven's sake...

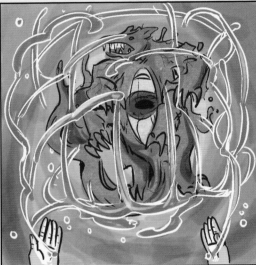

How long d'you think that will hold it?

A couple weeks, at least. Enough time for us to figure out another option.

And to think this looked so simple...

Don't look so glum. When was the last time we had a real challenge?

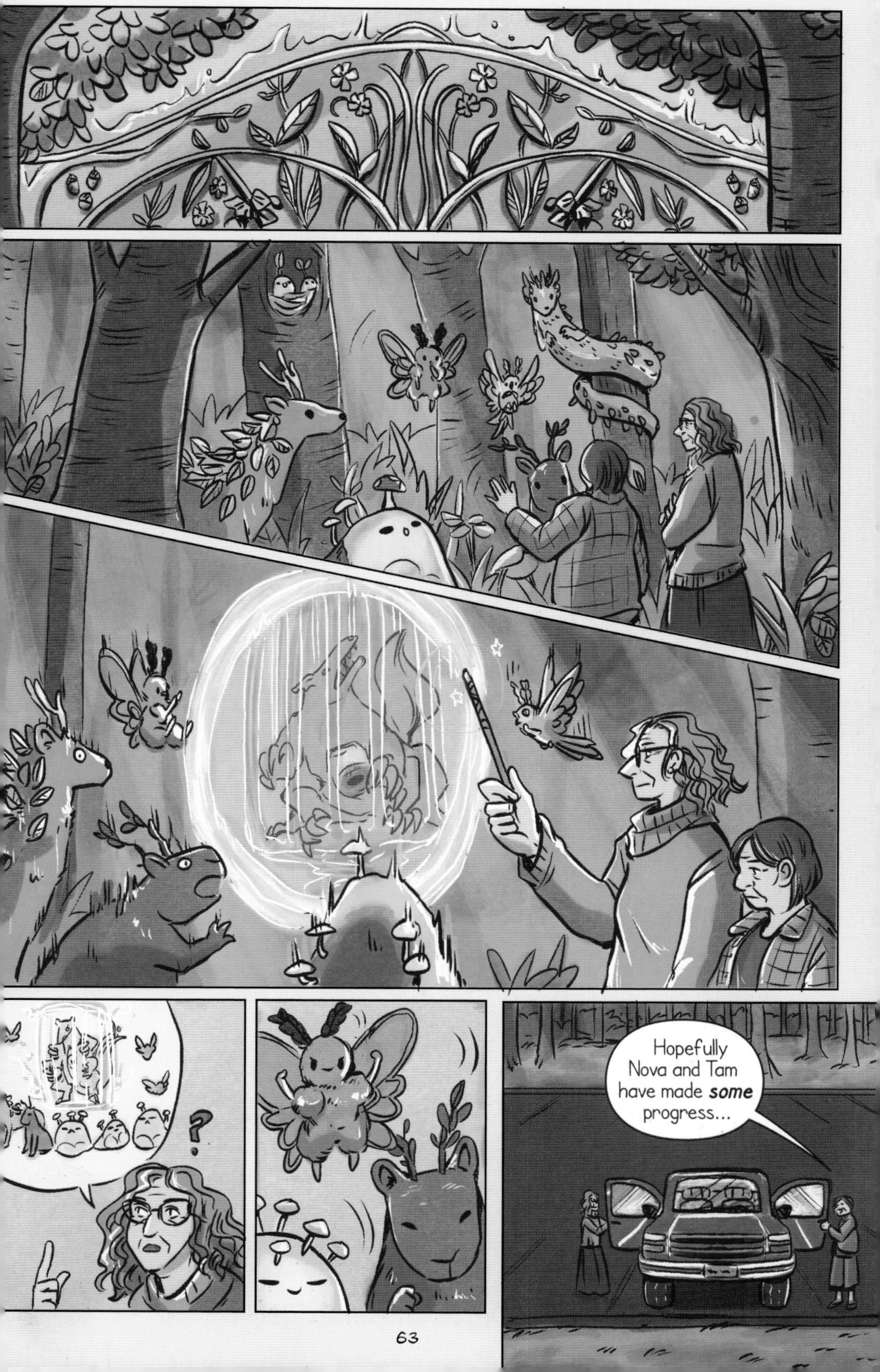
?
Hopefully
Nova and Tam
have made **some**
progress...

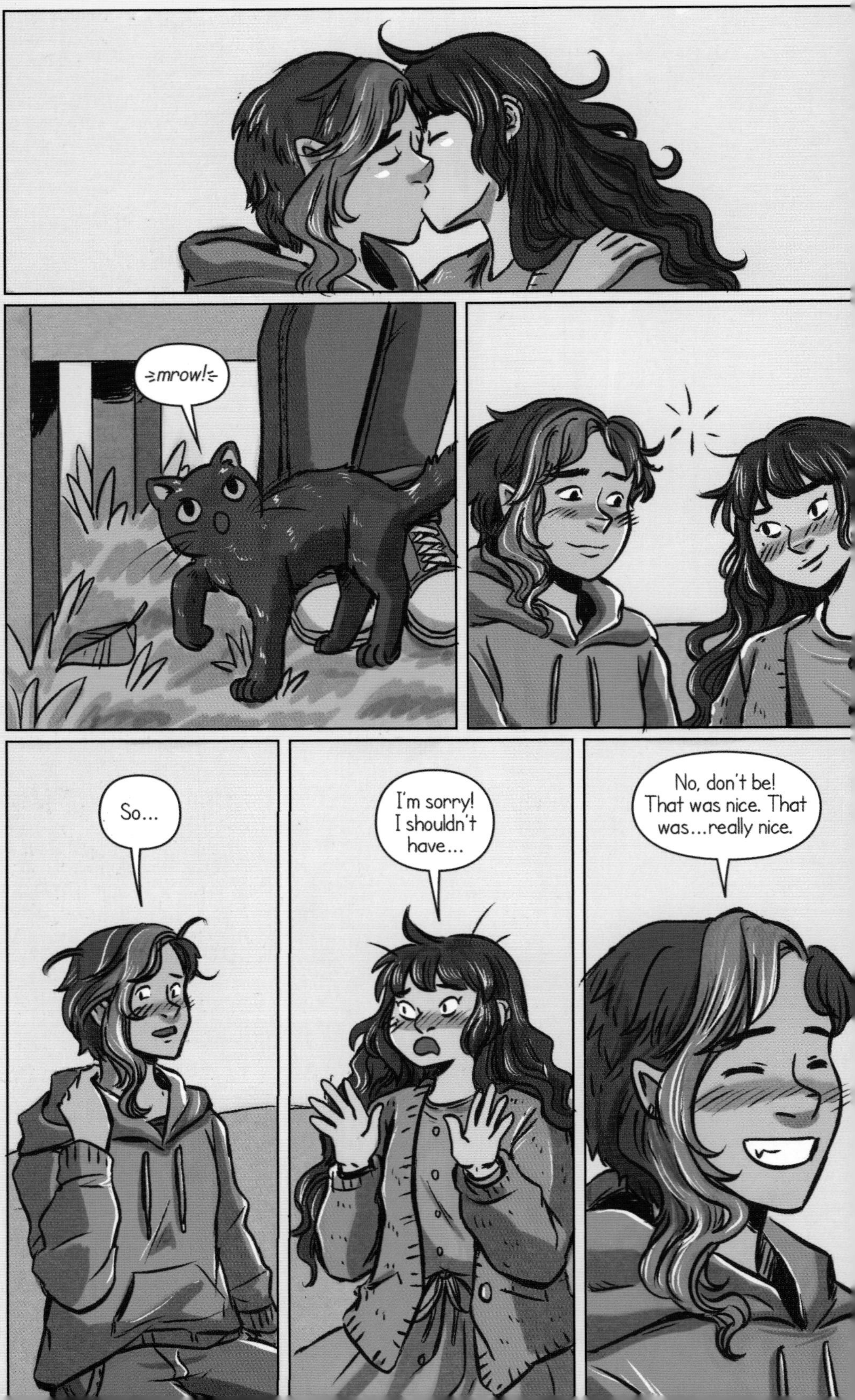
mrow!
So...
I'm sorry! I shouldn't have...
No, don't be! That was nice. That was...really nice.

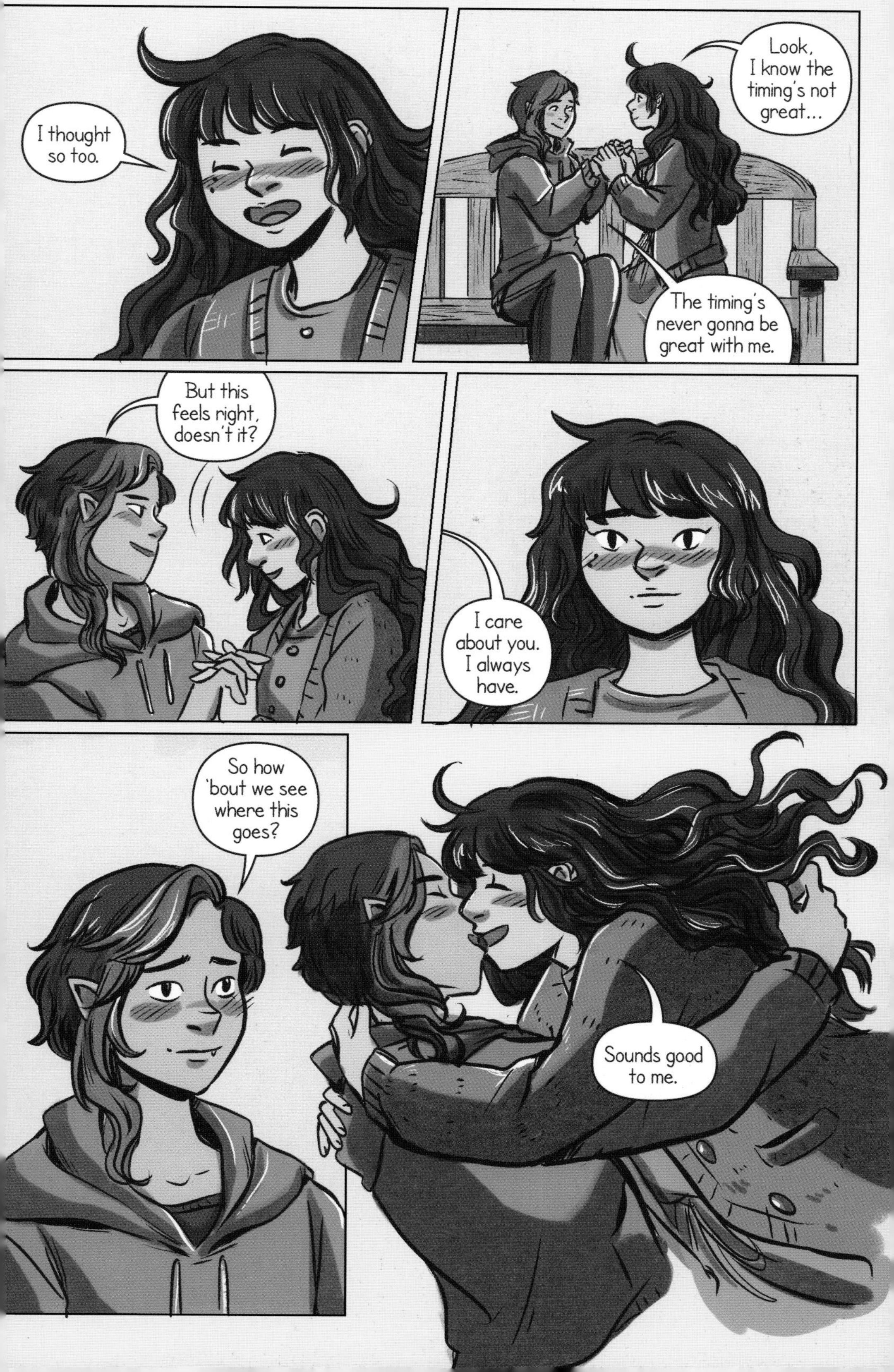
I thought so too.
Look, I know the timing's not great...
The timing's never gonna be great with me.
But this feels right, doesn't it?
I care about you. I always have.
So how 'bout we see where this goes?
Sounds good to me.

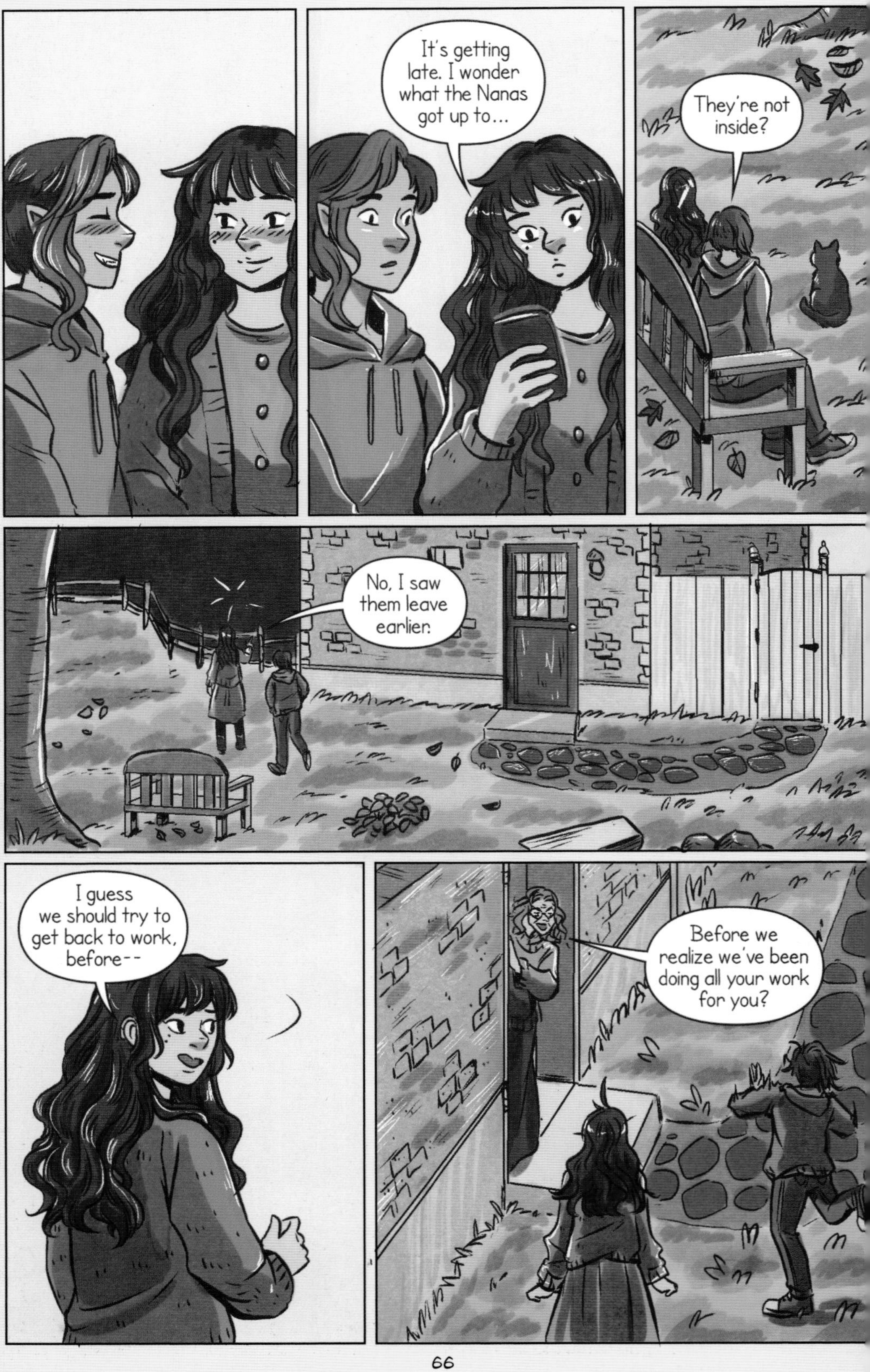
It's getting late. I wonder what the Nanas got up to...
They're not inside?
No, I saw them leave earlier.
I guess we should try to get back to work, before--
Before we realize we've been doing all your work for you?

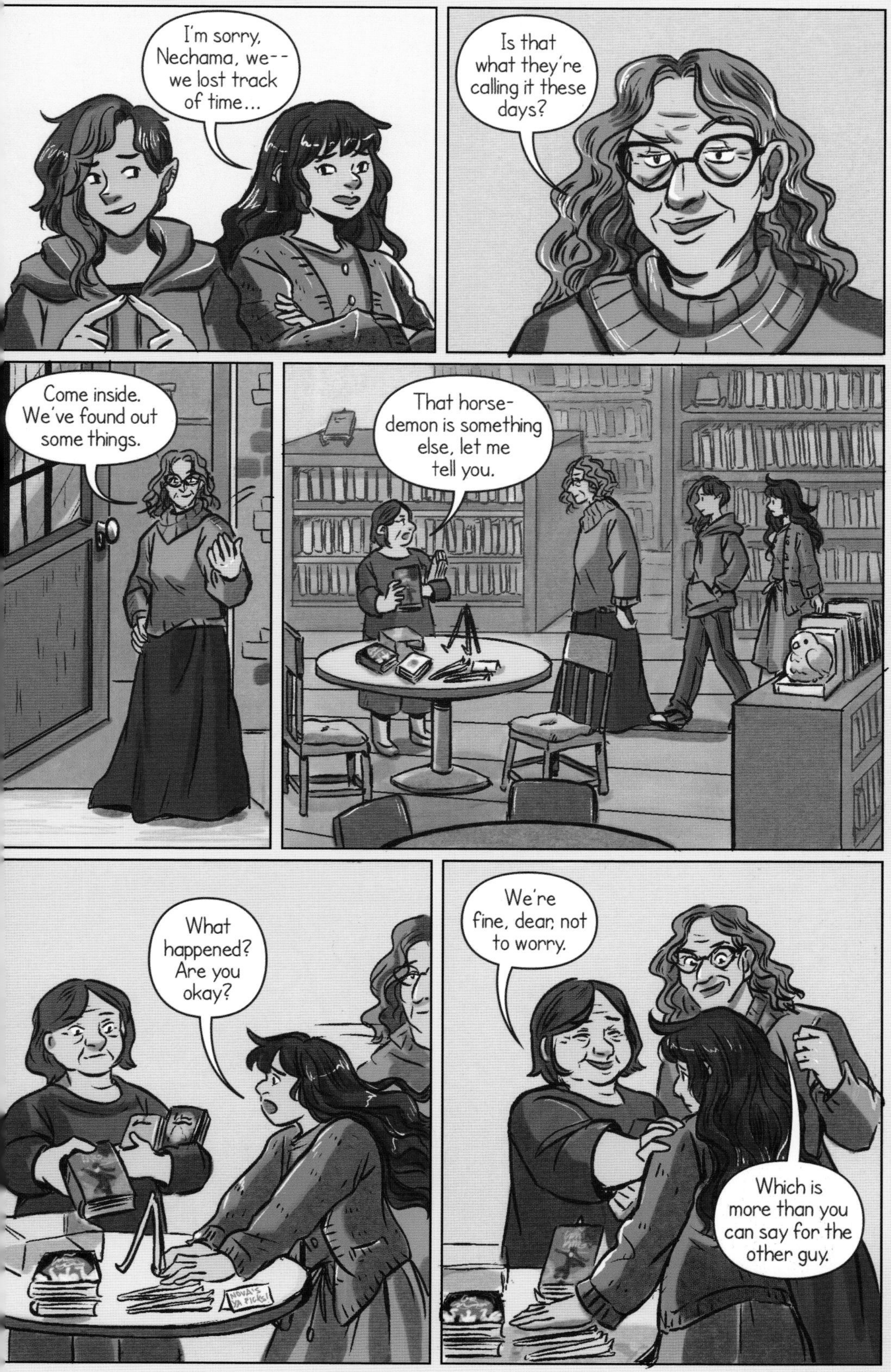
I'm sorry, Nechama, we-- we lost track of time...
Is that what they're calling it these days?
Come inside. We've found out some things.
That horse-demon is something else, let me tell you.
What happened? Are you okay?
NOVA'S YA PICKS!
We're fine, dear, not to worry.
Which is more than you can say for the other guy.

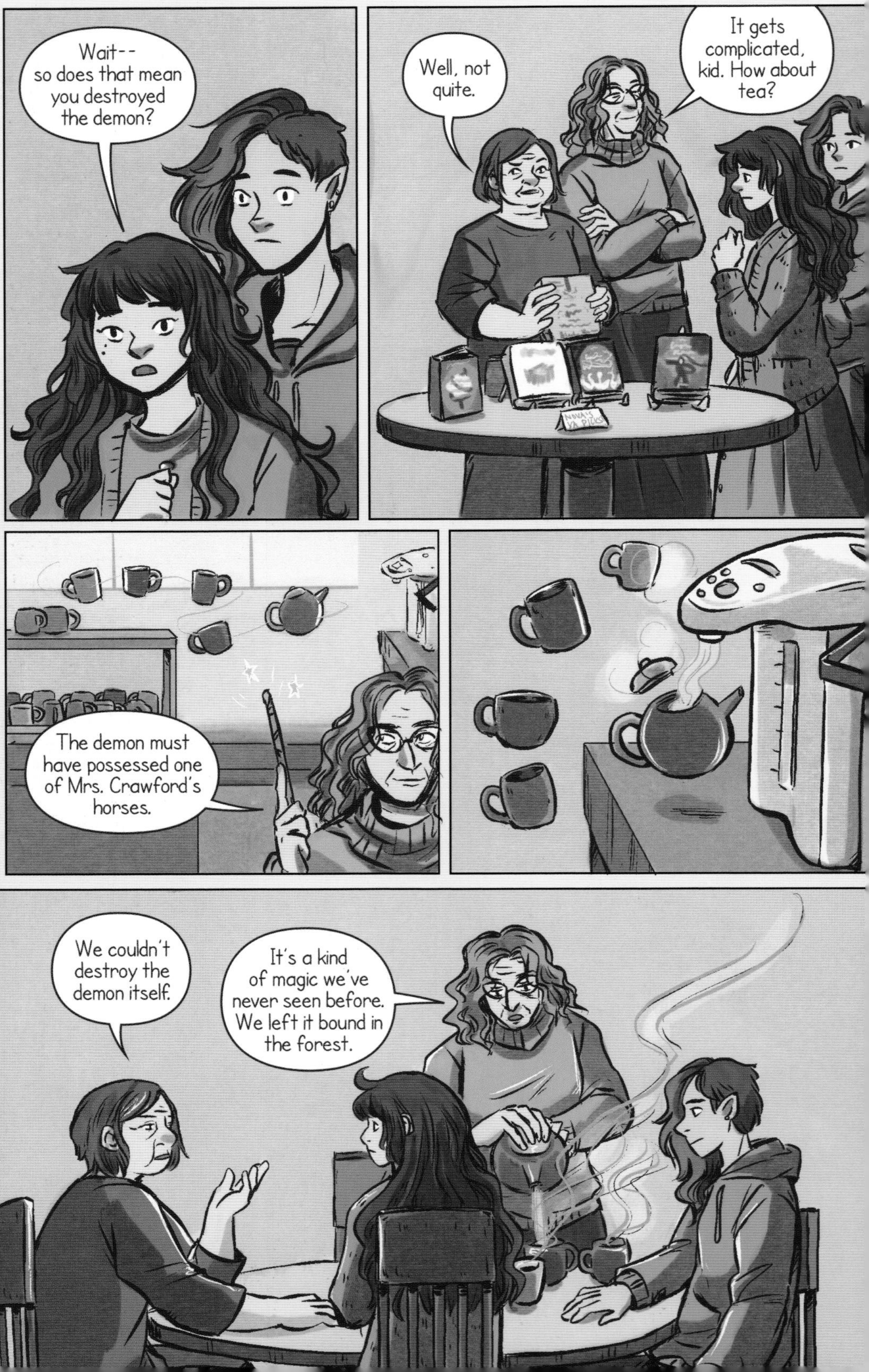
Wait-- so does that mean you destroyed the demon?
Well, not quite.
It gets complicated, kid. How about tea?
NOVA'S YA PICKS
The demon must have possessed one of Mrs. Crawford's horses.
We couldn't destroy the demon itself.
It's a kind of magic we've never seen before. We left it bound in the forest.

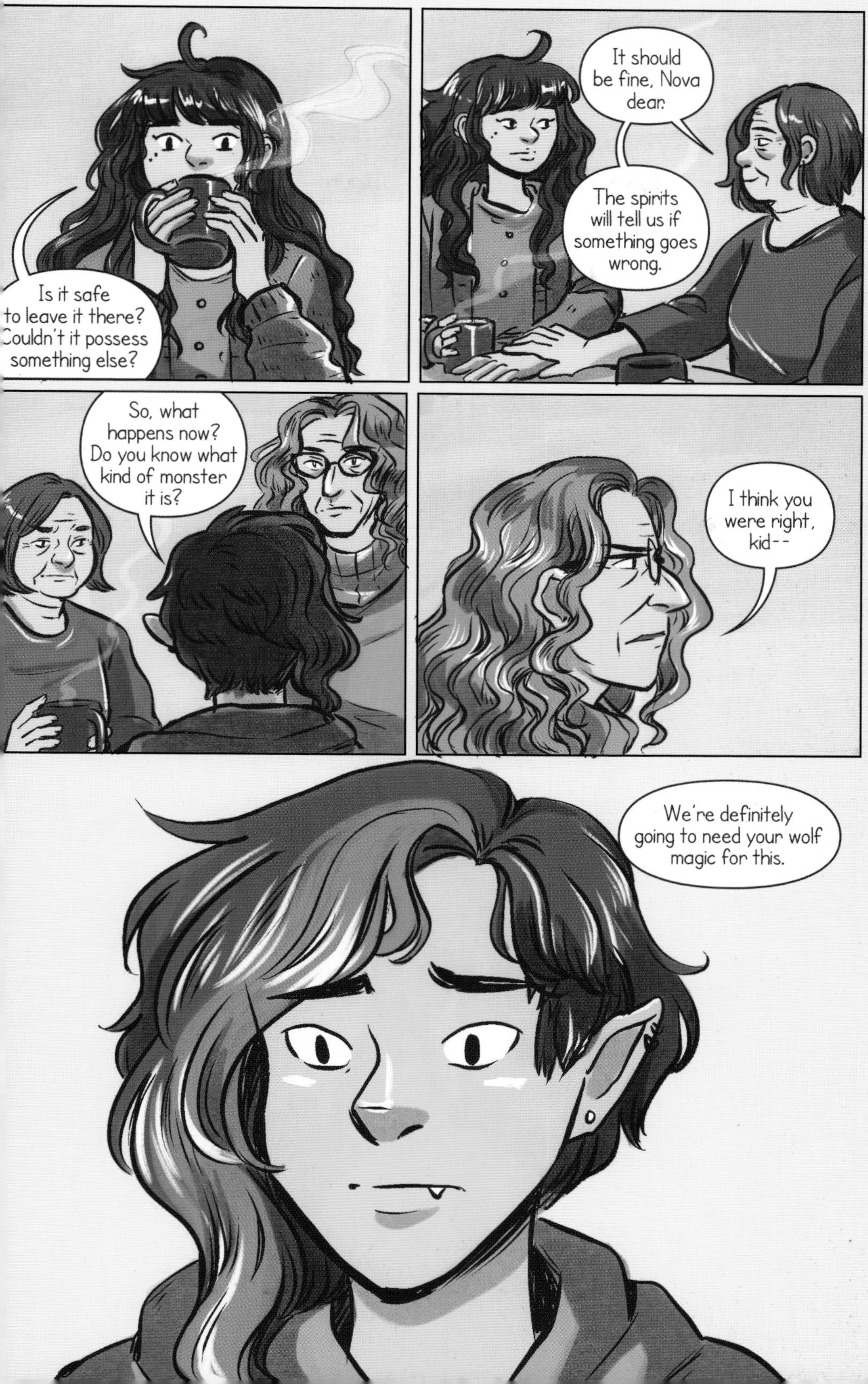
Is it safe to leave it there? Couldn't it possess something else?
It should be fine, Nova dear.
The spirits will tell us if something goes wrong.
So, what happens now? Do you know what kind of monster it is?
I think you were right, kid--
We're definitely going to need your wolf magic for this.

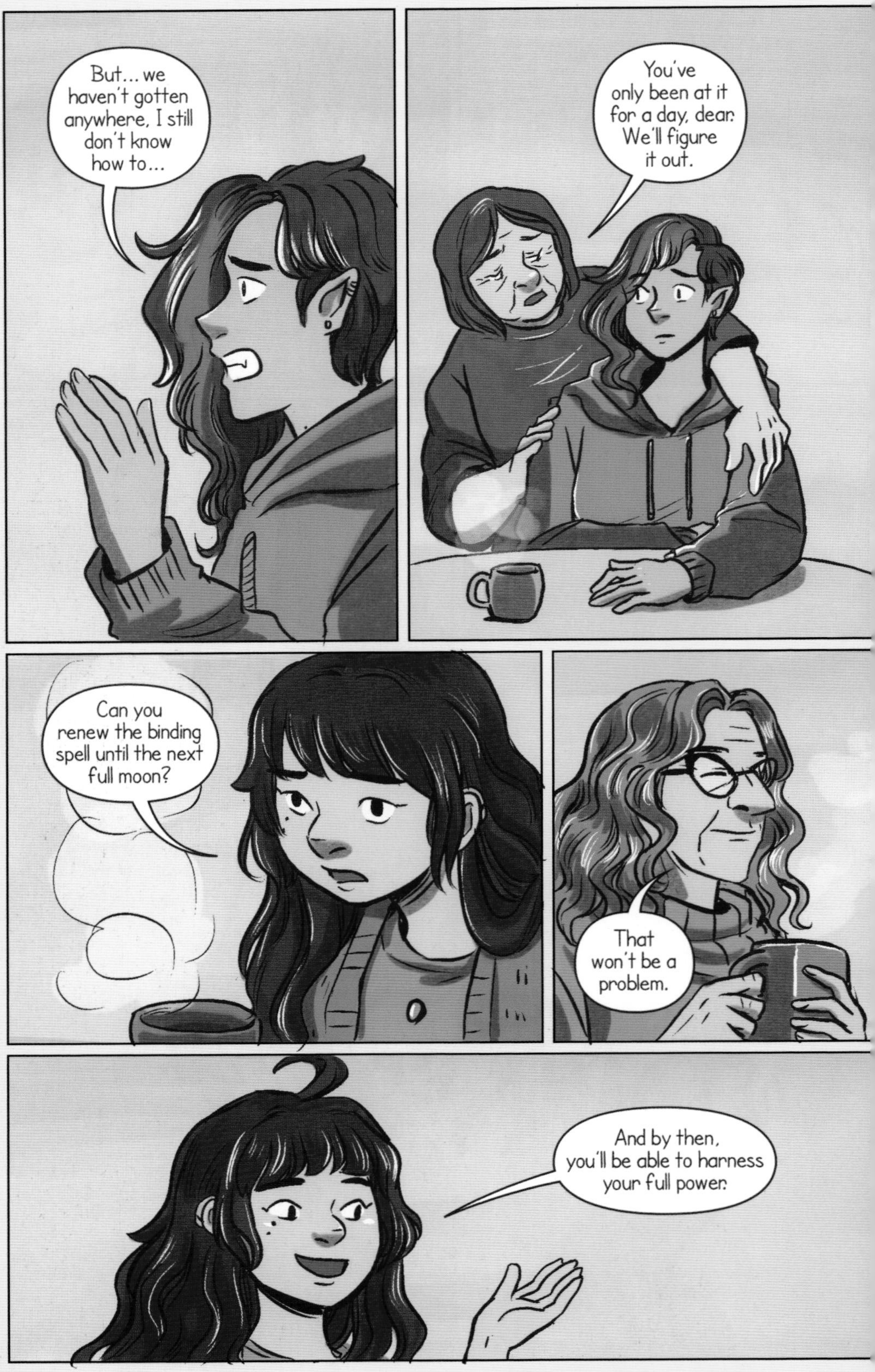
But... we haven't gotten anywhere, I still don't know how to...
You've only been at it for a day, dear. We'll figure it out.
Can you renew the binding spell until the next full moon?
That won't be a problem.
And by then, you'll be able to harness your full power.

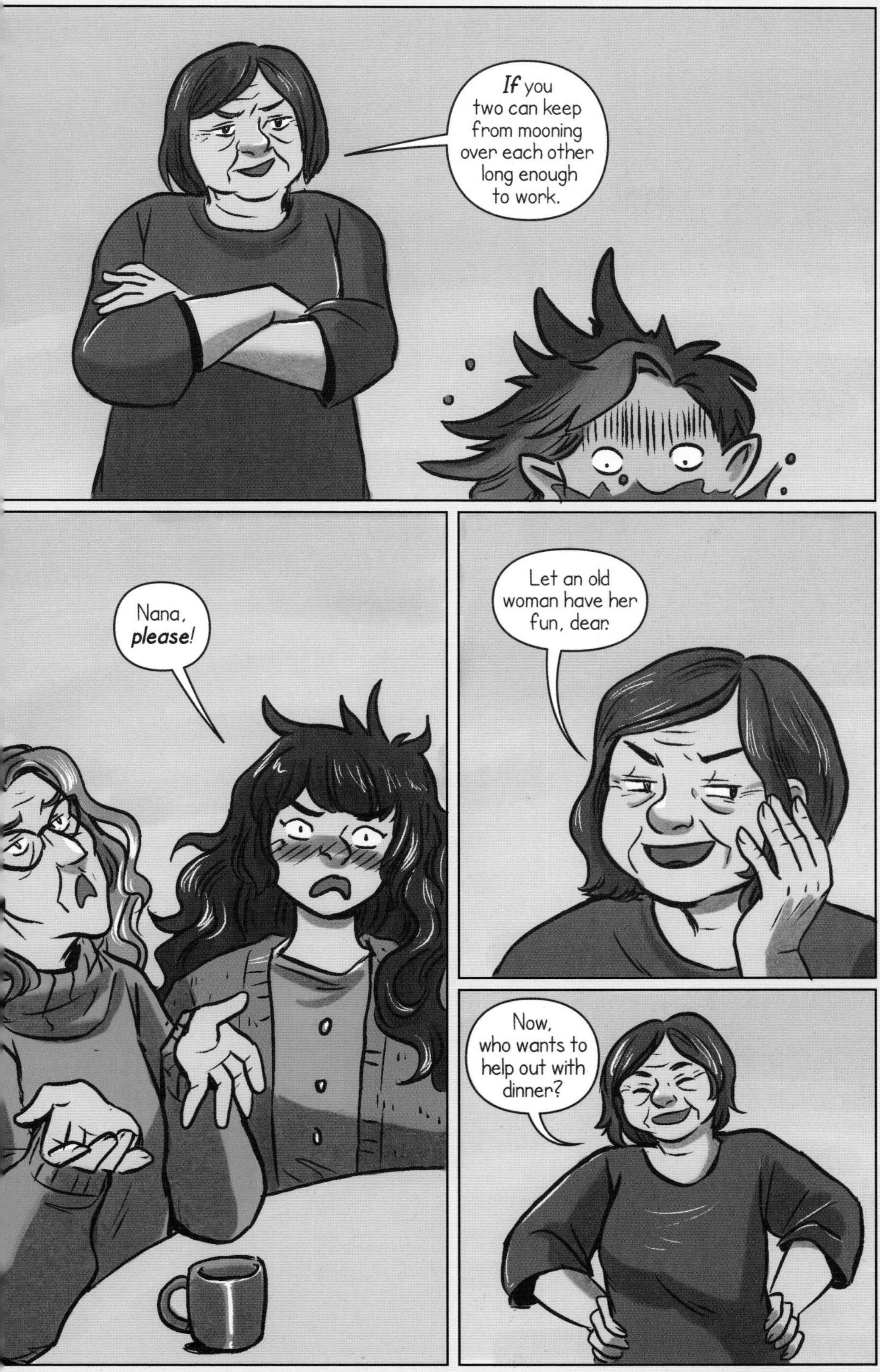

If you two can keep from mooning over each other long enough to work.
Nana, ***please***!
Let an old woman have her fun, dear.
Now, who wants to help out with dinner?

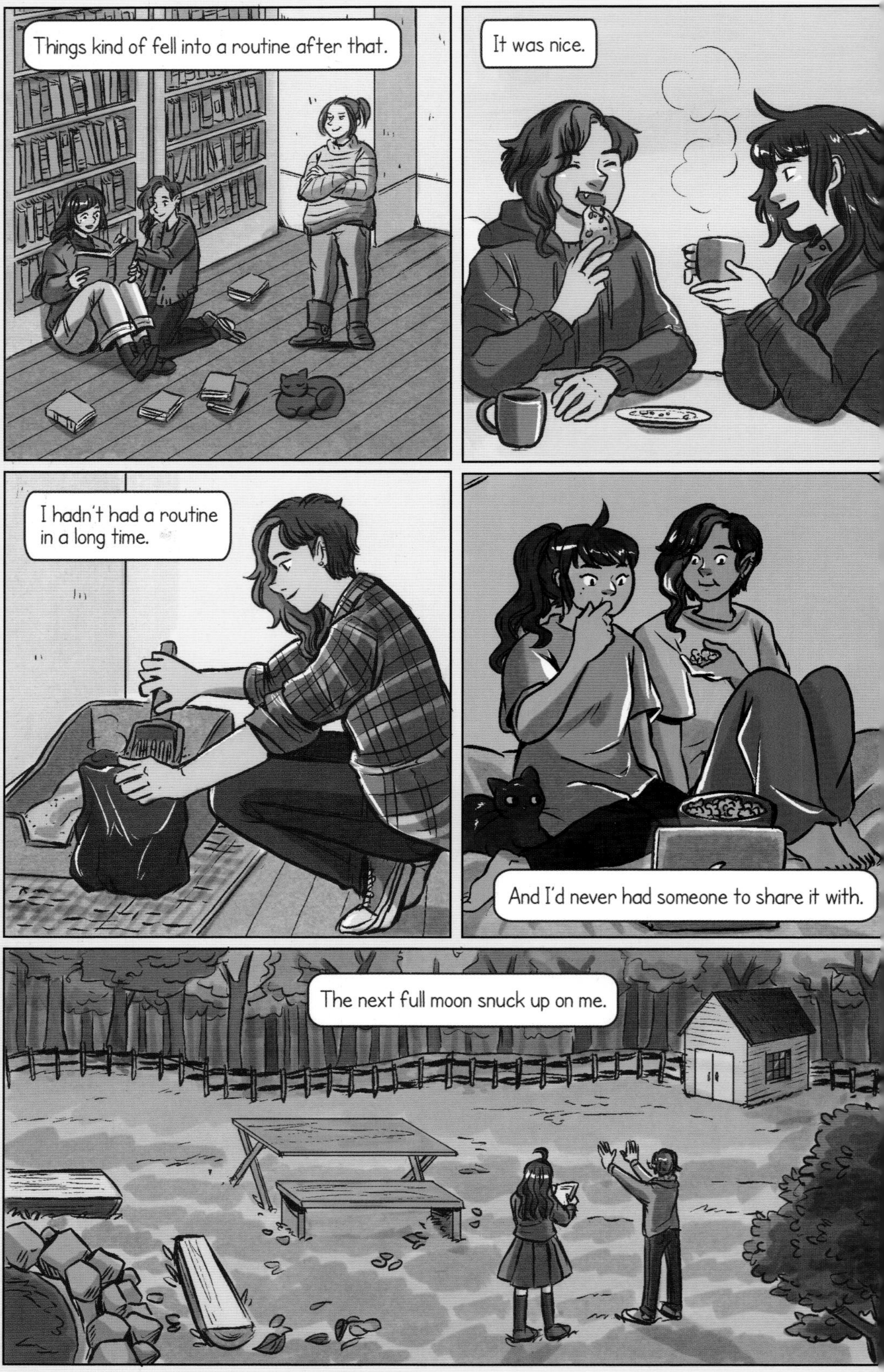
Things kind of fell into a routine after that.
It was nice.
I hadn't had a routine in a long time.
And I'd never had someone to share it with.
The next full moon snuck up on me.

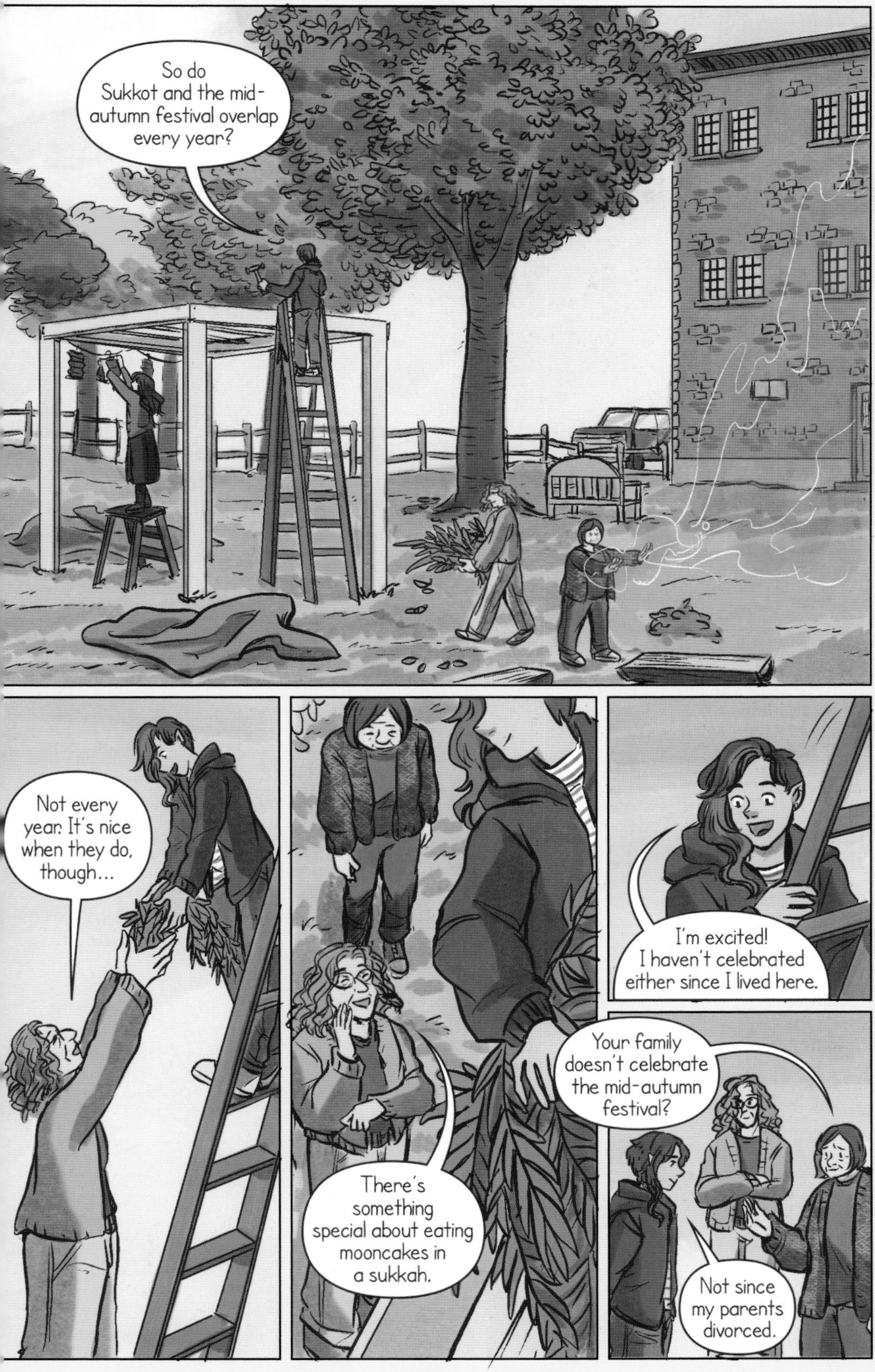
So do Sukkot and the mid-autumn festival overlap every year?
Not every year. It's nice when they do, though...
There's something special about eating mooncakes in a sukkah.
I'm excited! I haven't celebrated either since I lived here.
Your family doesn't celebrate the mid-autumn festival?
Not since my parents divorced.

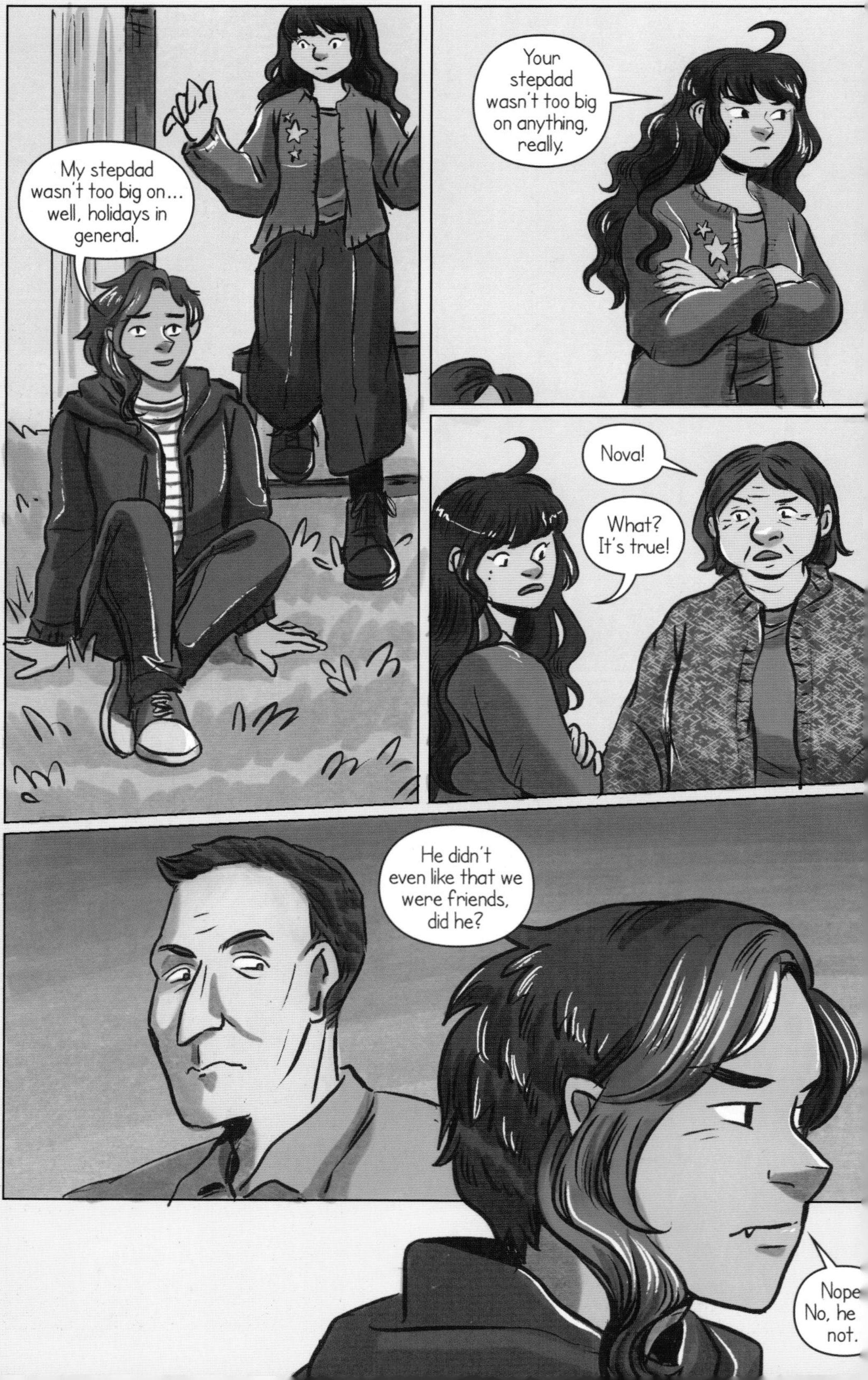
My stepdad wasn't too big on... well, holidays in general.
Your stepdad wasn't too big on anything, really.
Nova!
What? It's true!
He didn't even like that we were friends, did he?
Nope No, he not.

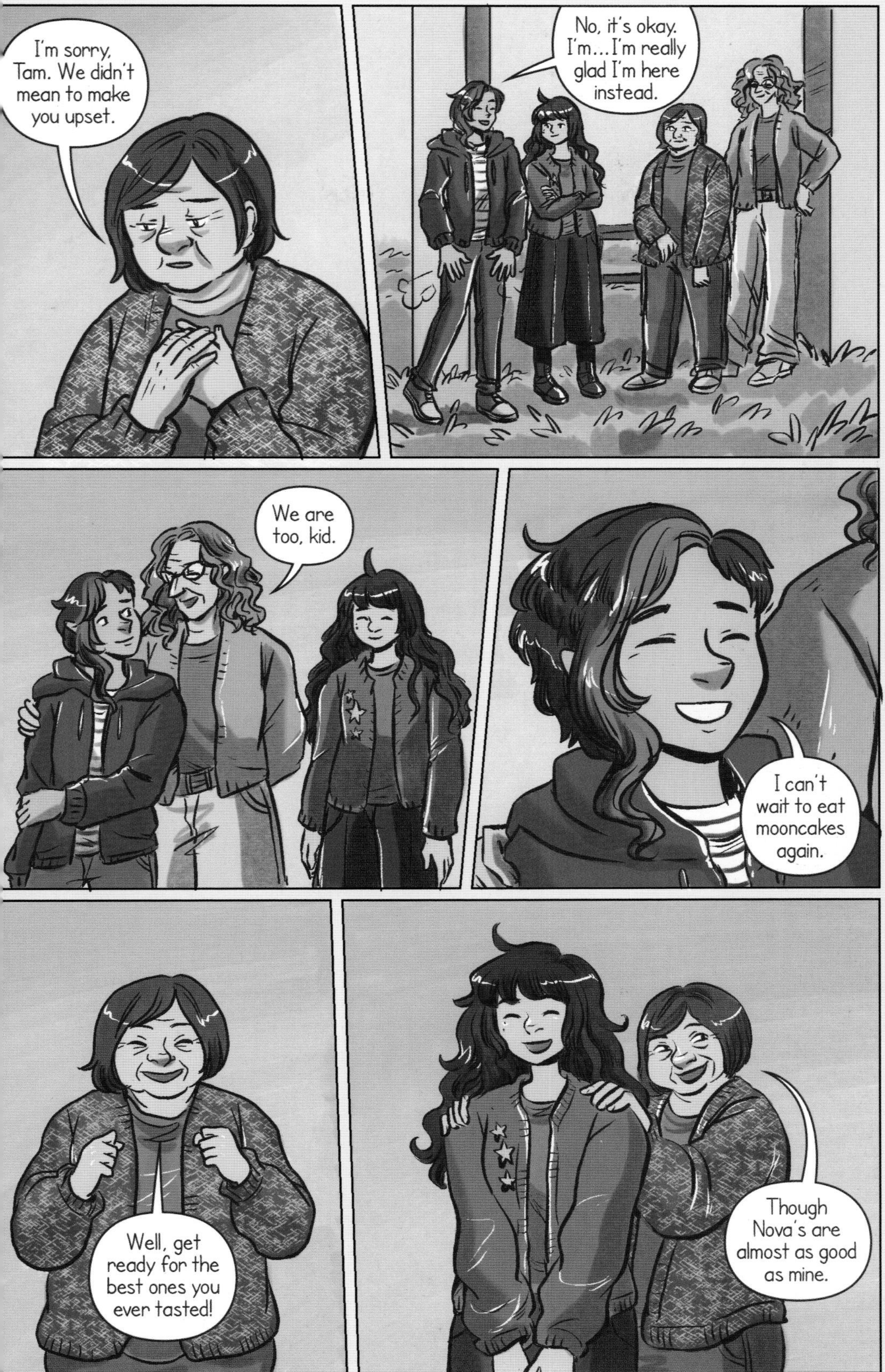
I'm sorry, Tam. We didn't mean to make you upset.
No, it's okay. I'm...I'm really glad I'm here instead.
We are too, kid.
I can't wait to eat mooncakes again.
Well, get ready for the best ones you ever tasted!
Though Nova's are almost as good as mine.

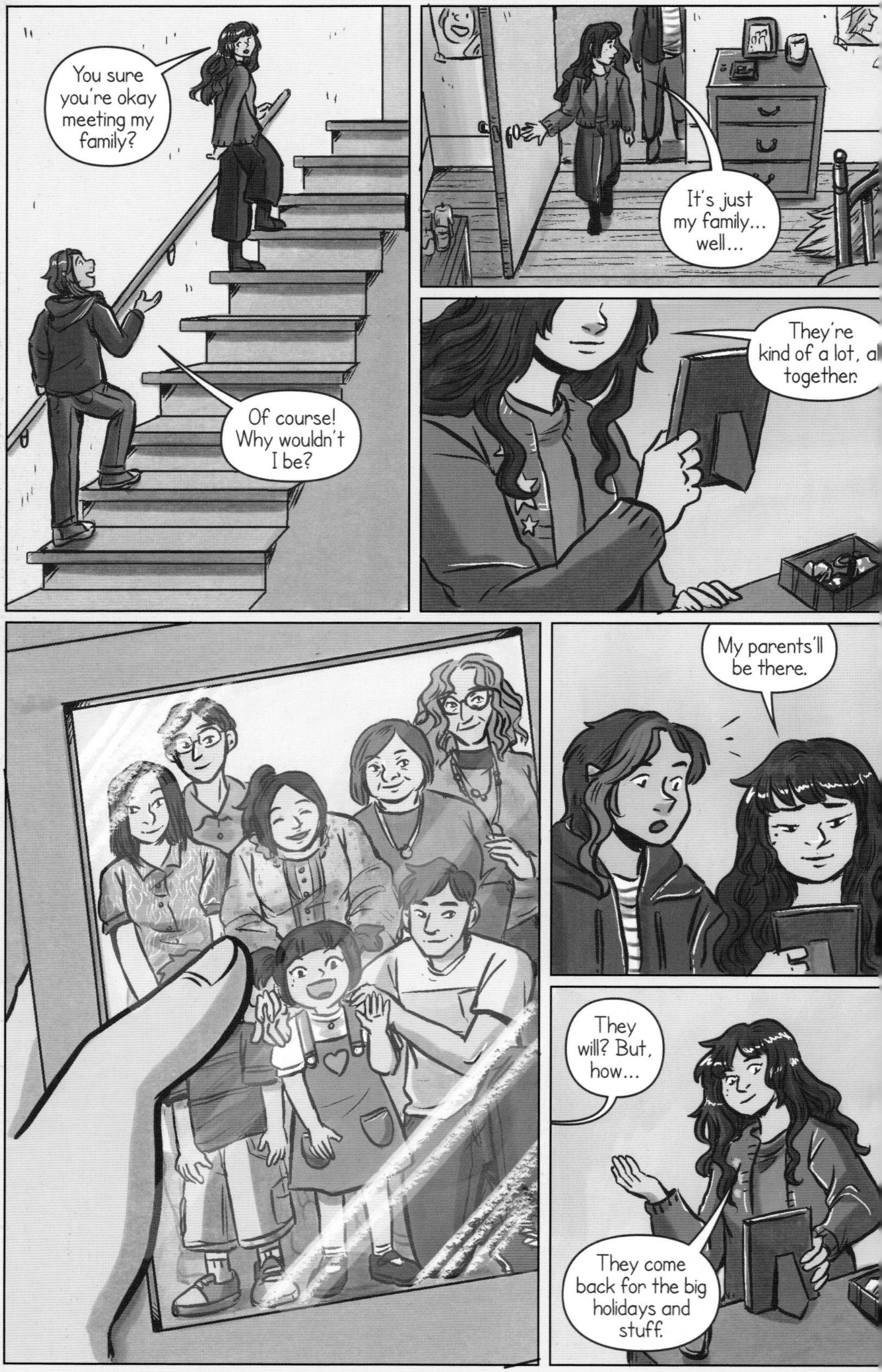

You sure you're okay meeting my family?
Of course! Why wouldn't I be?
It's just my family... well...
They're kind of a lot, al together.
My parents'll be there.
They will? But, how...
They come back for the big holidays and stuff.

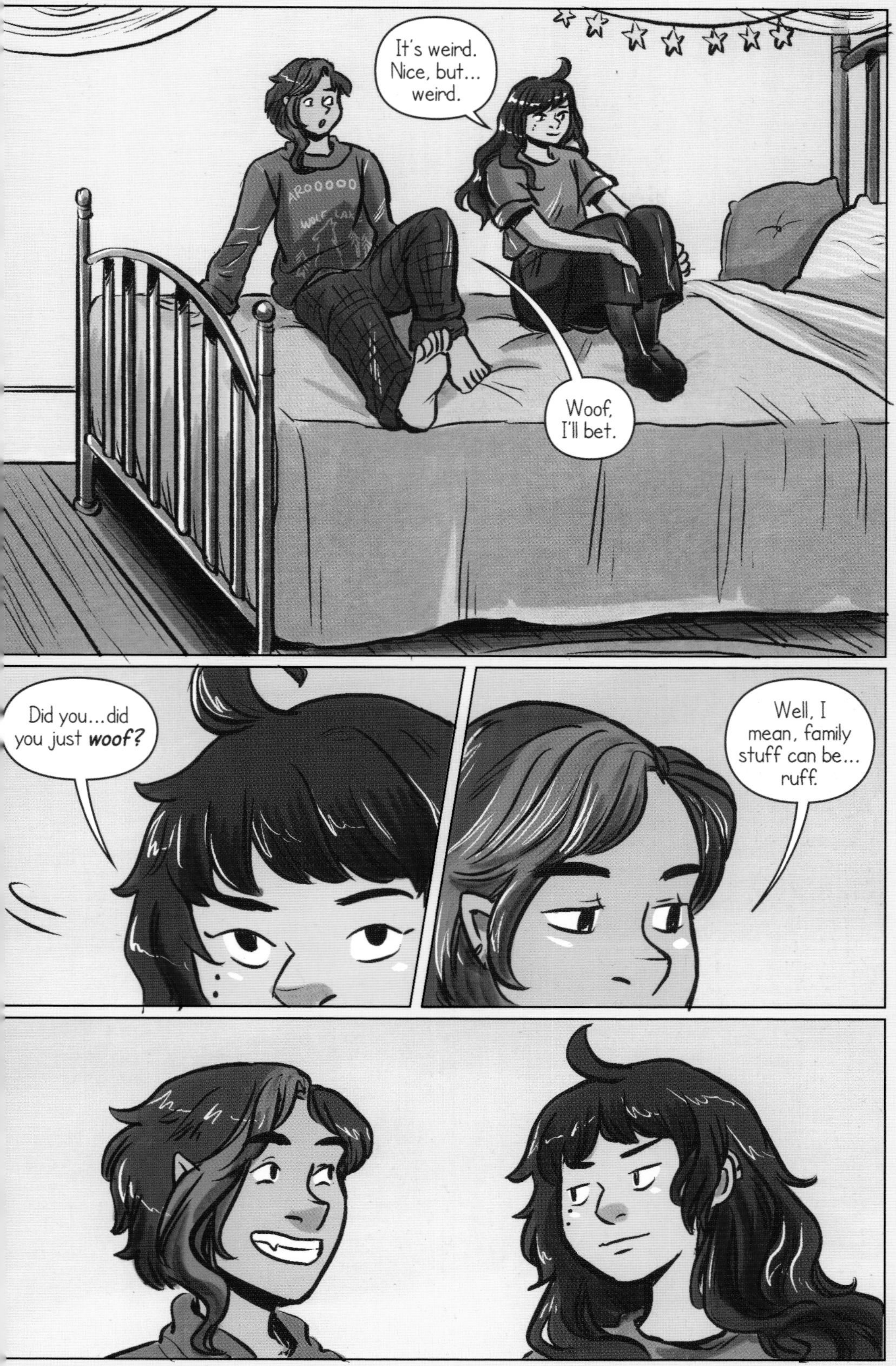
It's weird. Nice, but... weird.
Woof, I'll bet.
Did you...did you just **woof?**
Well, I mean, family stuff can be... ruff.

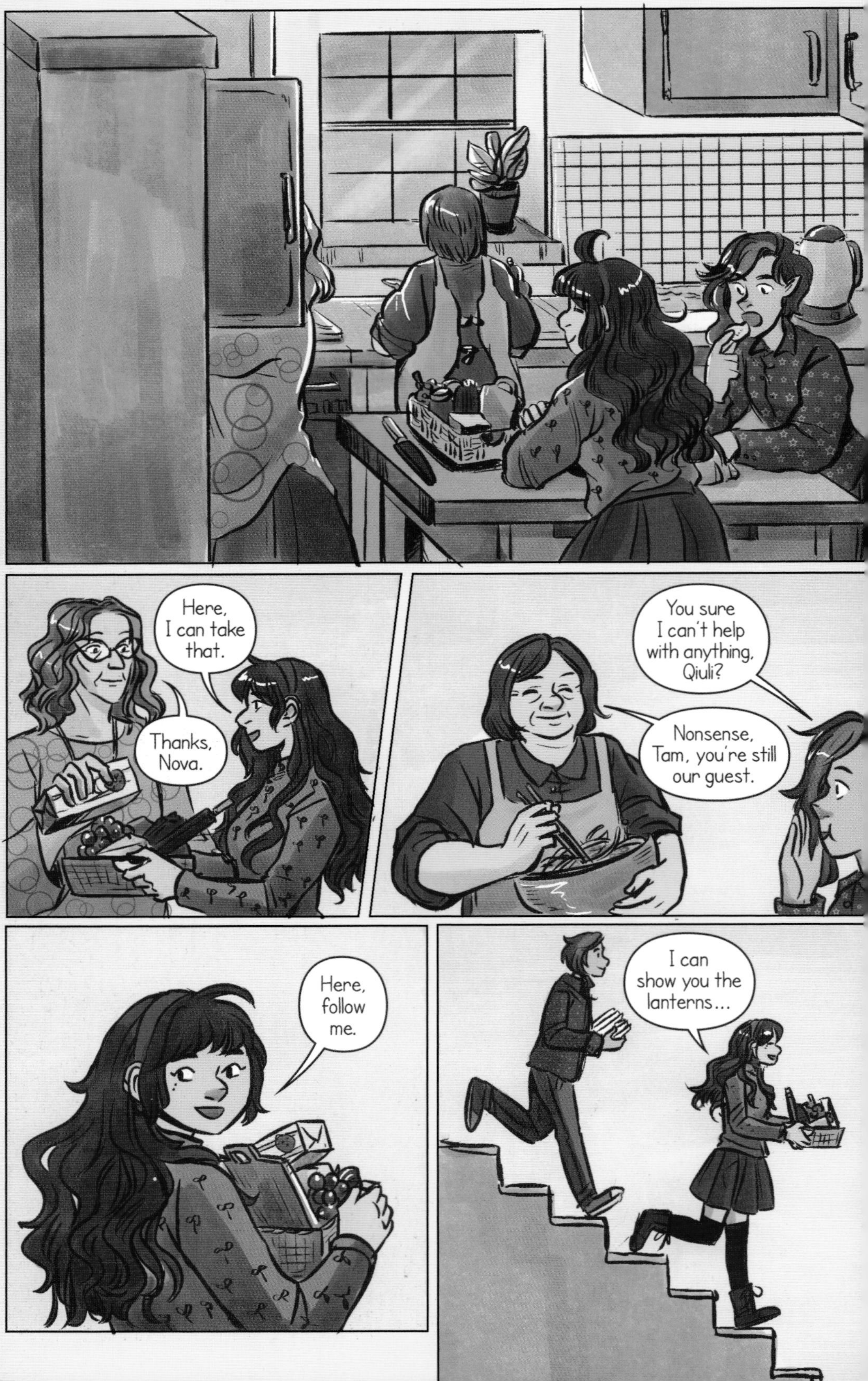
Here, I can take that.
Thanks, Nova.
You sure I can't help with anything, Qiuli?
Nonsense, Tam, you're still our guest.
Here, follow me.
I can show you the lanterns...

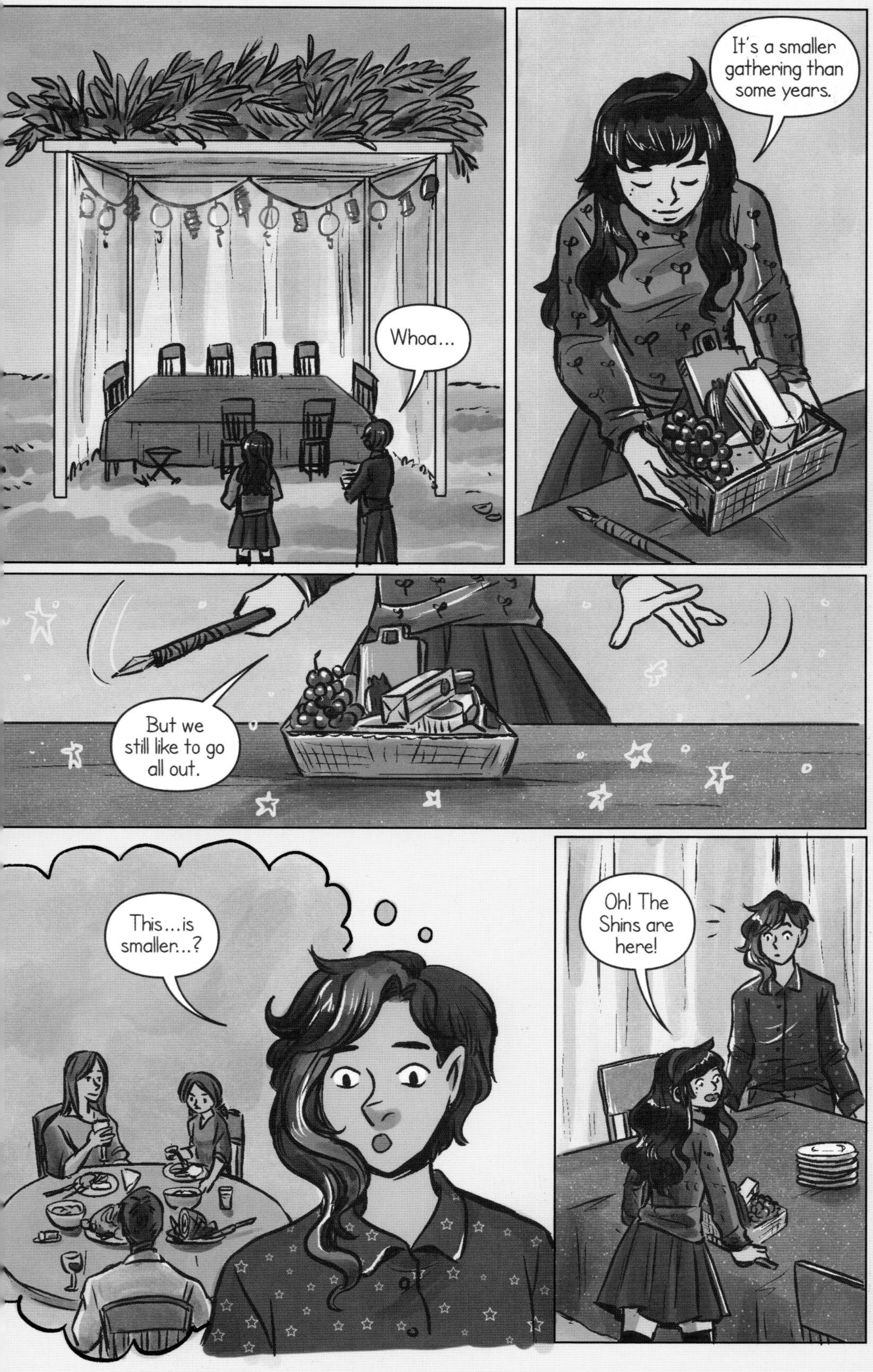
Whoa...
It's a smaller gathering than some years.
But we still like to go all out.
This...is smaller...?
Oh! The Shins are here!

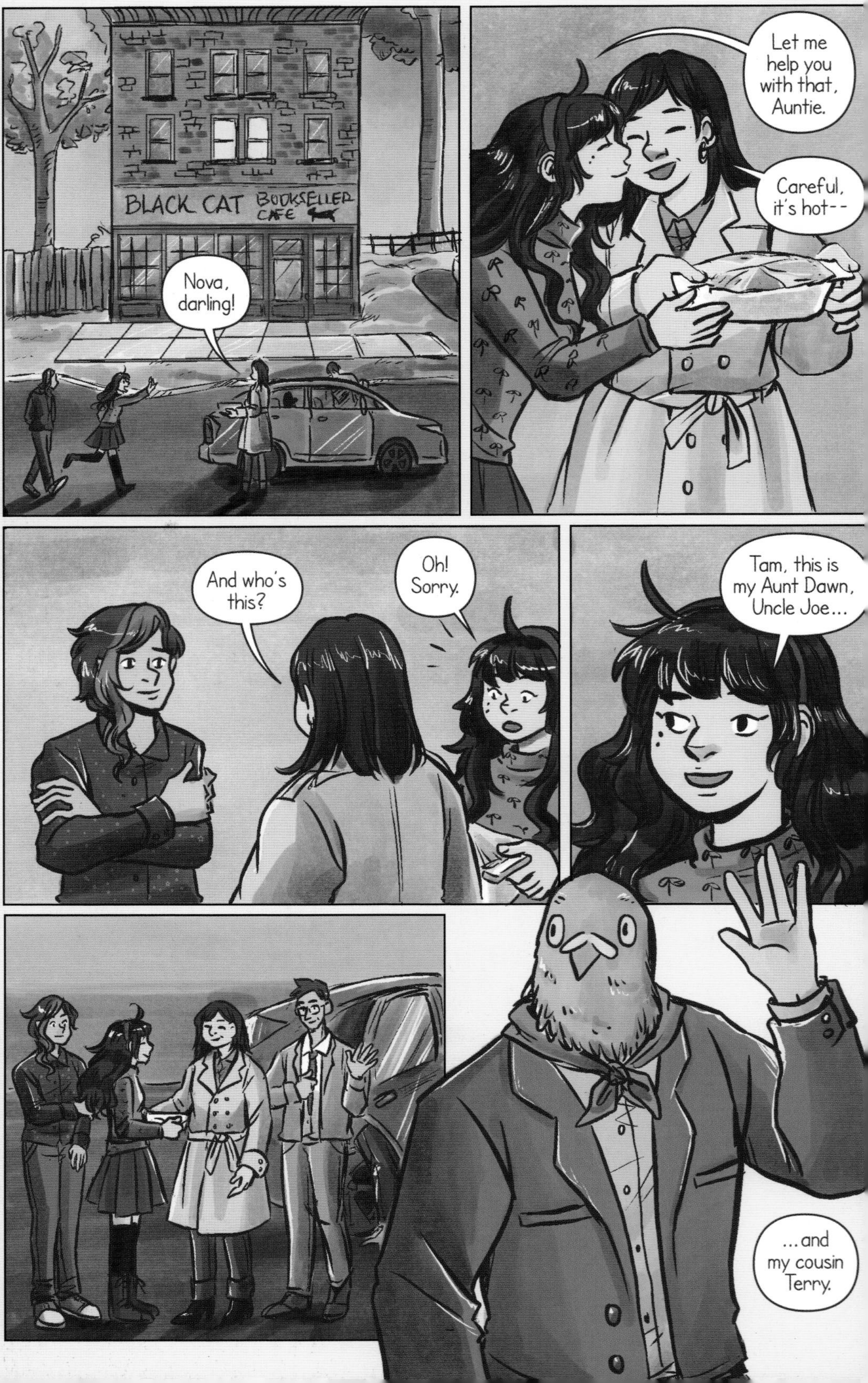
BLACK CAT BOOKSELLER CAFE
Nova, darling!
Let me help you with that, Auntie.
Careful, it's hot--
And who's this?
Oh! Sorry.
Tam, this is my Aunt Dawn, Uncle Joe...
...and my cousin Terry.

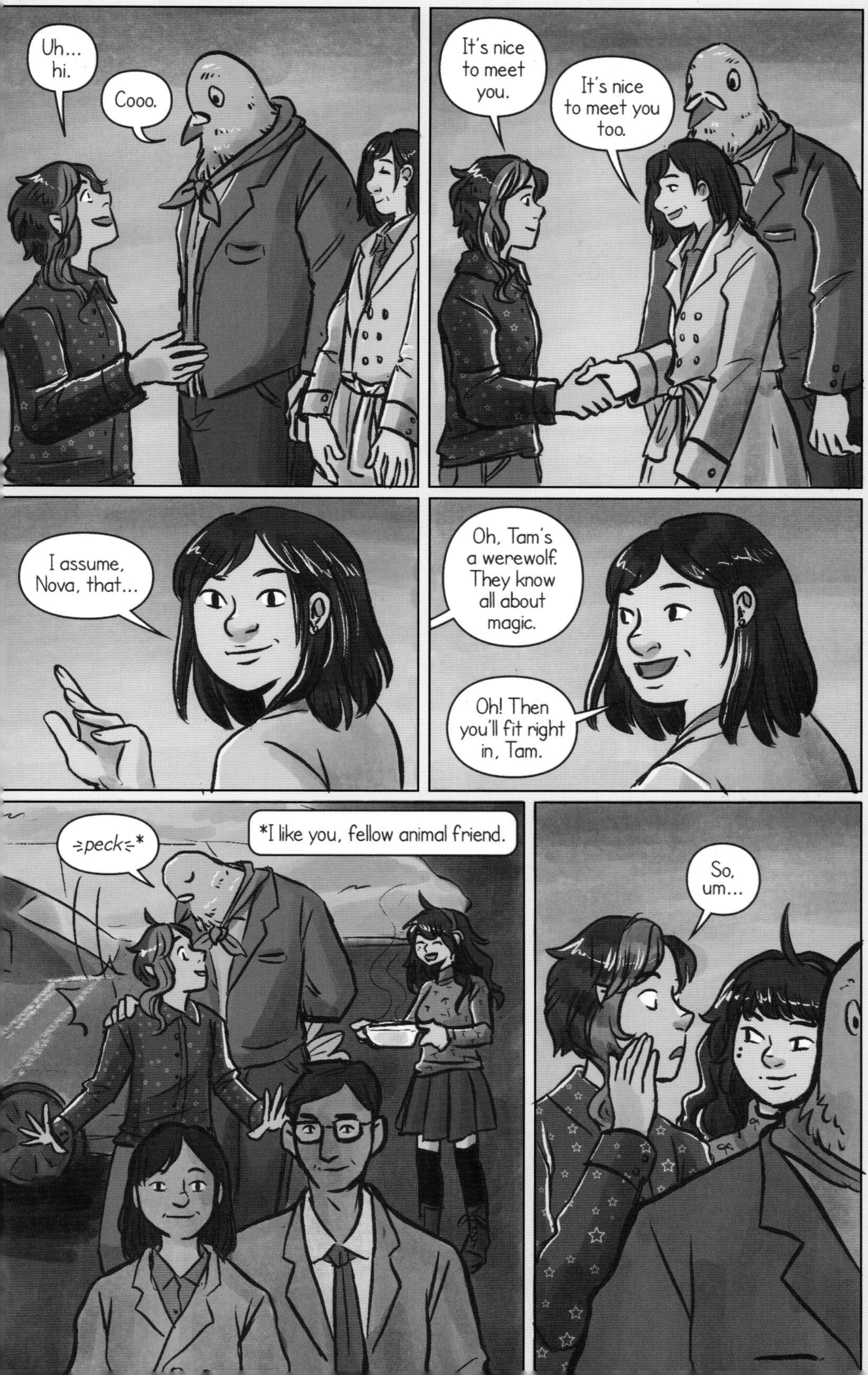
Uh... hi.
Cooo.
It's nice to meet you.
It's nice to meet you too.
I assume, Nova, that...
Oh, Tam's a werewolf. They know all about magic.
Oh! Then you'll fit right in, Tam.
⇉peck⇇*
*I like you, fellow animal friend.
So, um...

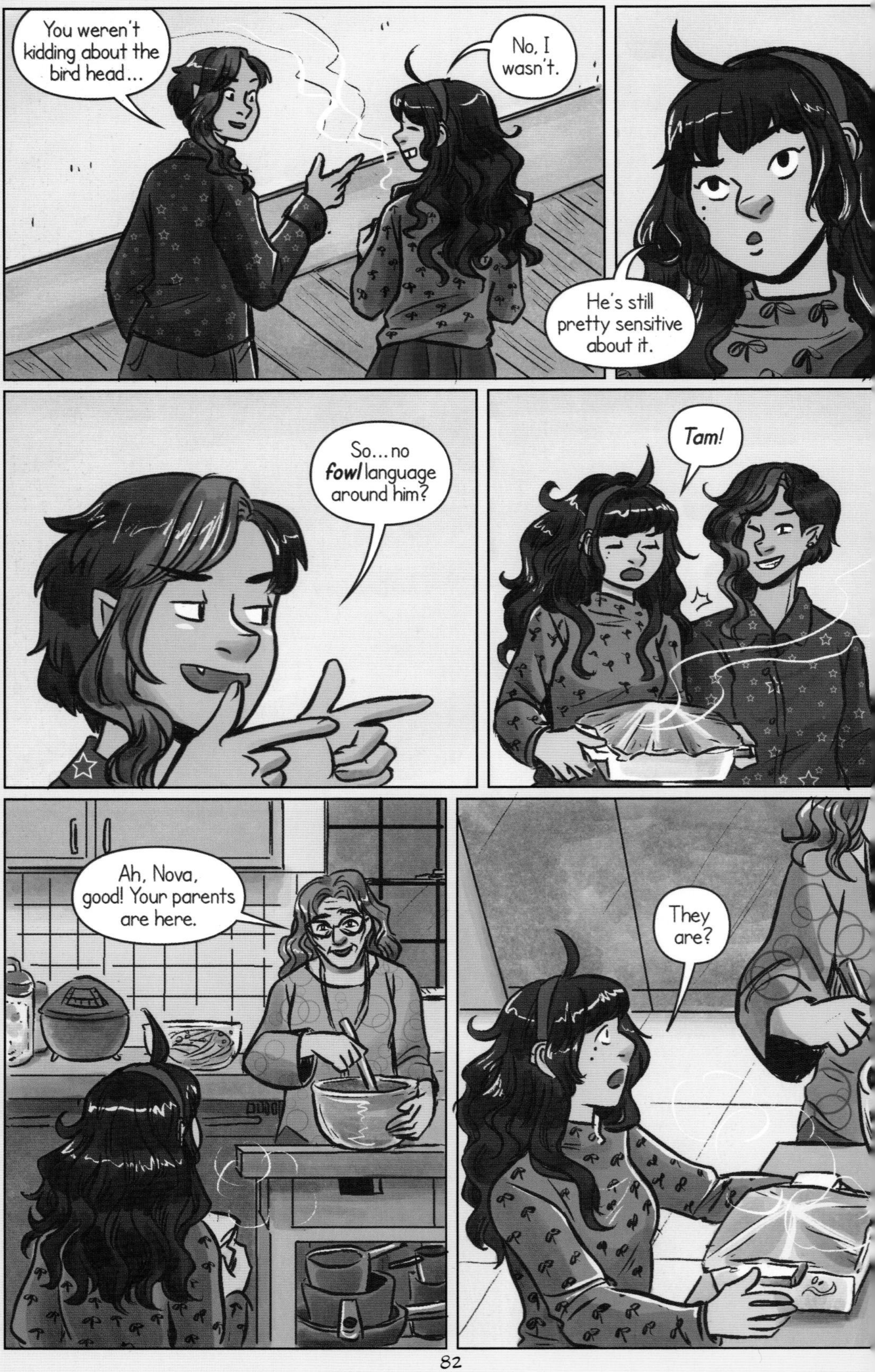
You weren't kidding about the bird head...
No, I wasn't.
He's still pretty sensitive about it.
So... no **fowl** language around him?
Tam!
Ah, Nova, good! Your parents are here.
They are?

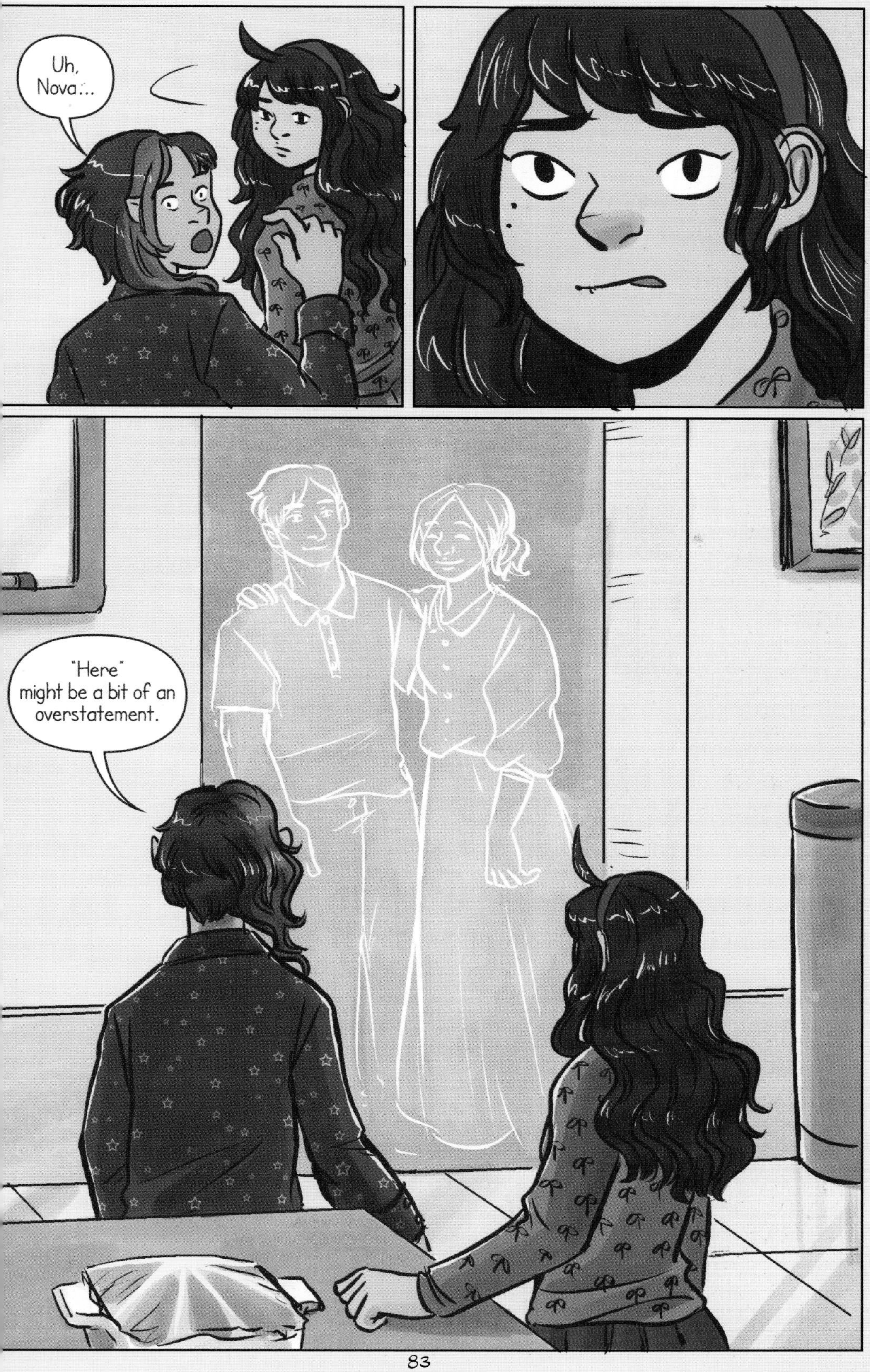
Uh, Nova...
"Here" might be a bit of an overstatement.

Chapter 4

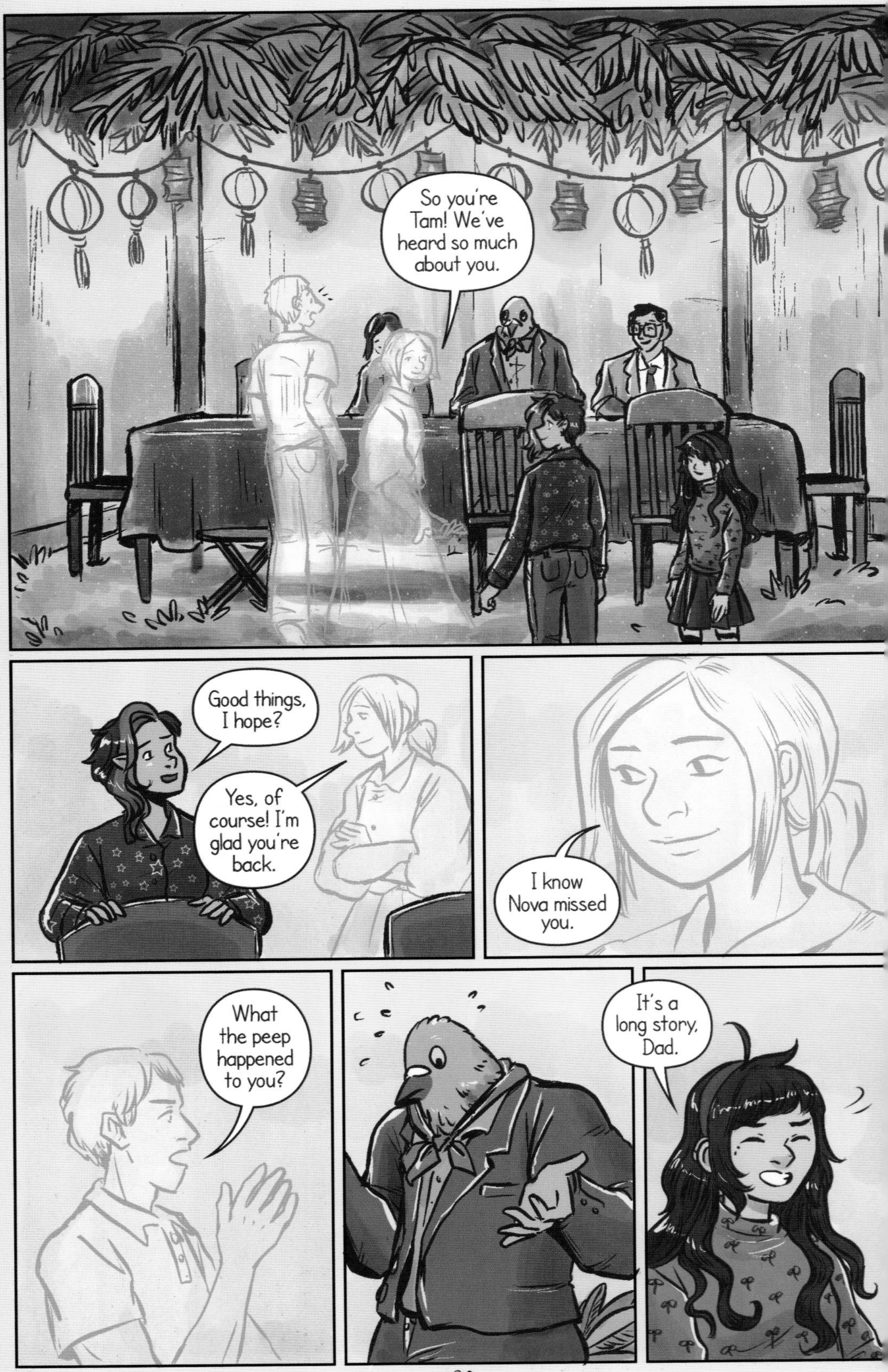

So you're Tam! We've heard so much about you.
Good things, I hope?
Yes, of course! I'm glad you're back.
I know Nova missed you.
What the peep happened to you?
It's a long story, Dad.

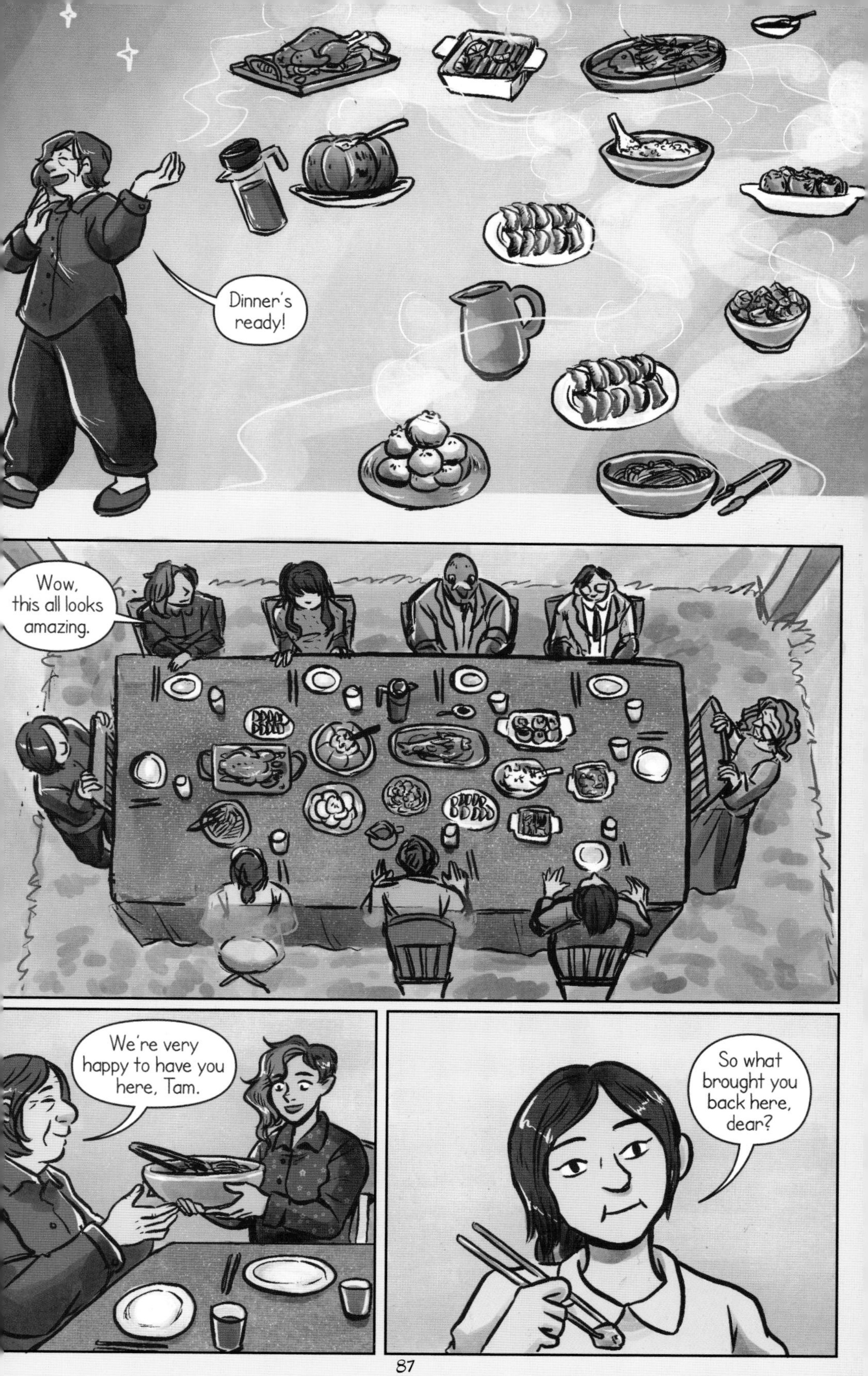
Dinner's ready!
Wow, this all looks amazing.
We're very happy to have you here, Tam.
So what brought you back here, dear?

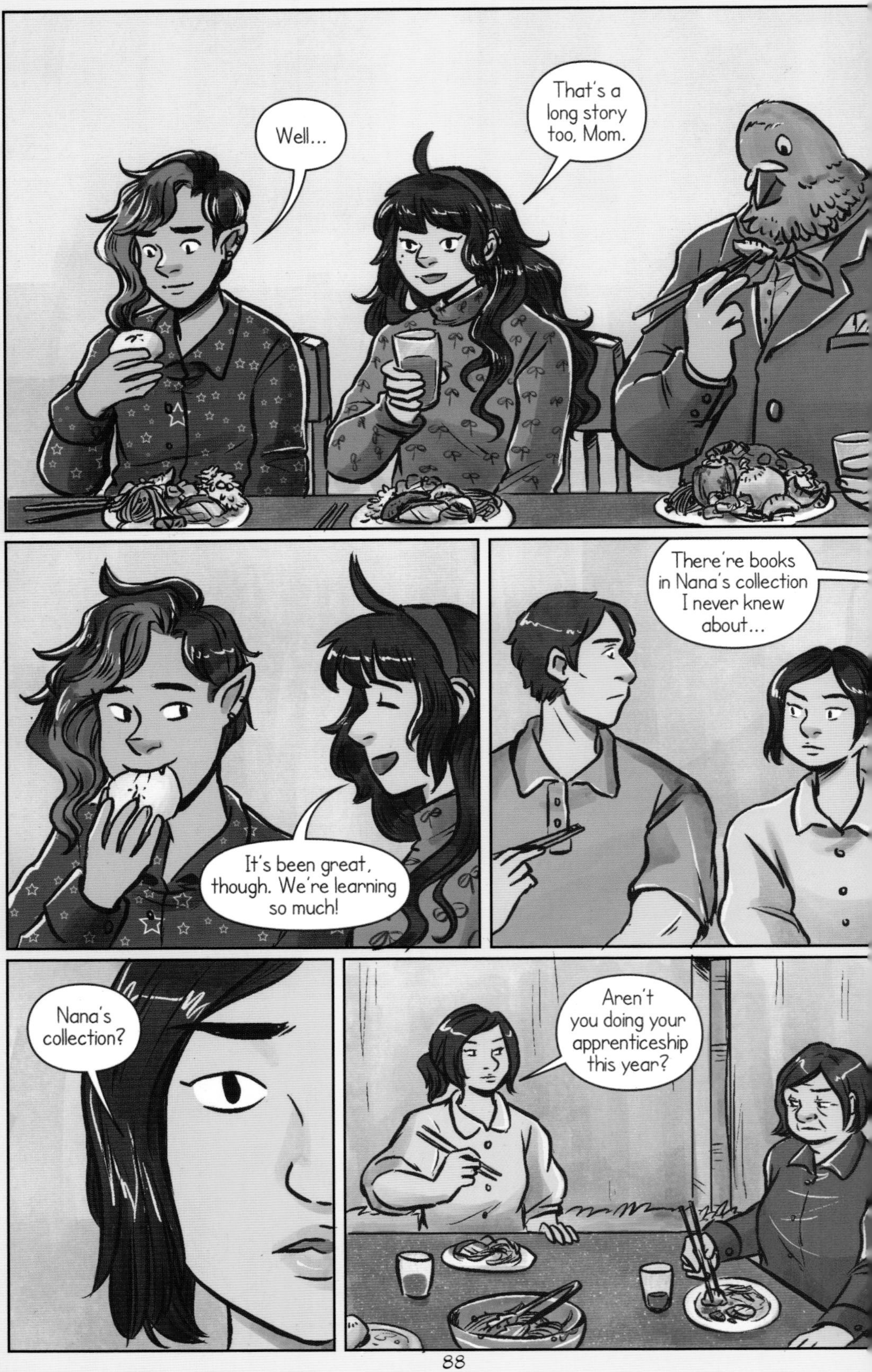
Well...
That's a long story too, Mom.
It's been great, though. We're learning so much!
There're books in Nana's collection I never knew about...
Nana's collection?
Aren't you doing your apprenticeship this year?

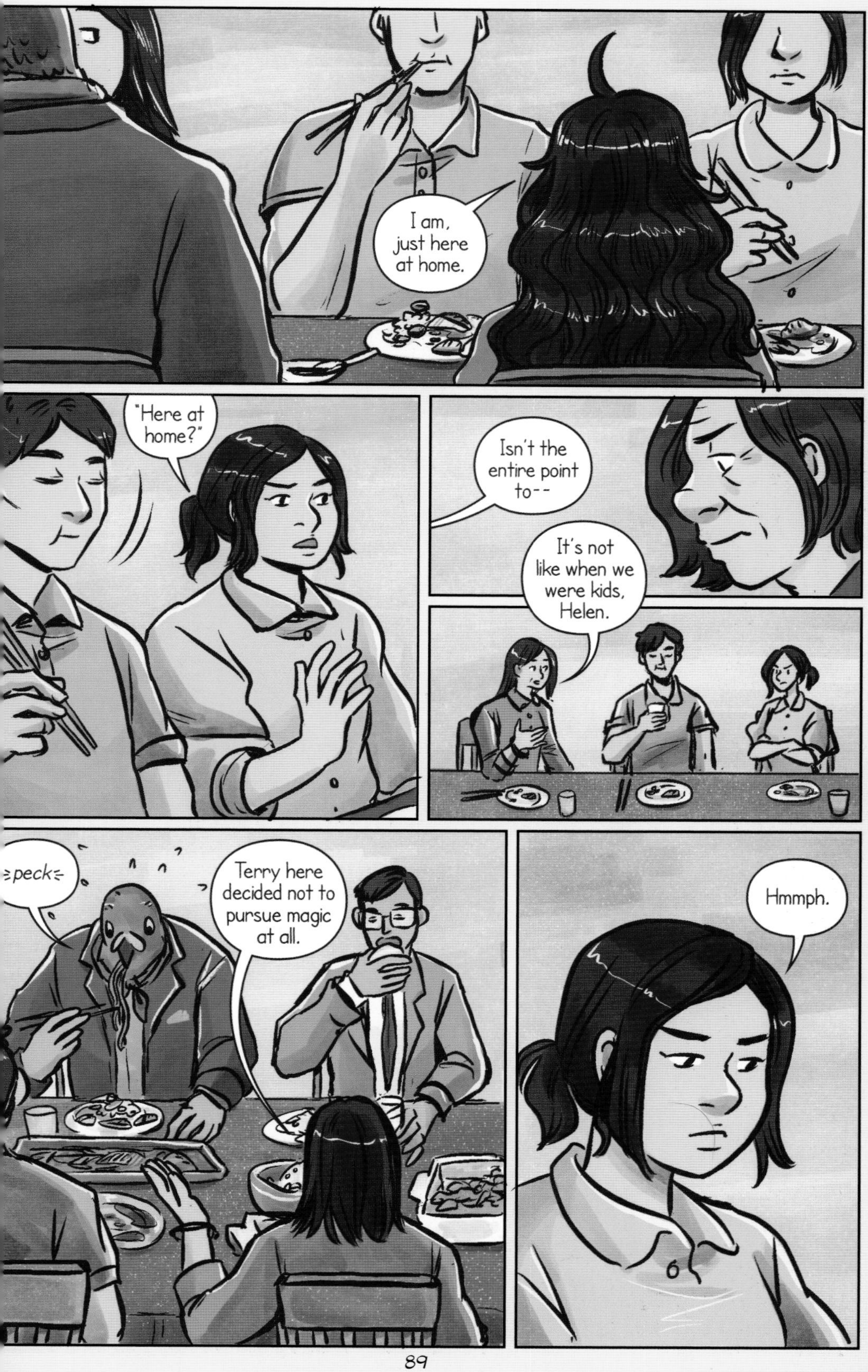
I am, just here at home.
"Here at home?"
Isn't the entire point to--
It's not like when we were kids, Helen.
=peck=
Terry here decided not to pursue magic at all.
Hmmph.

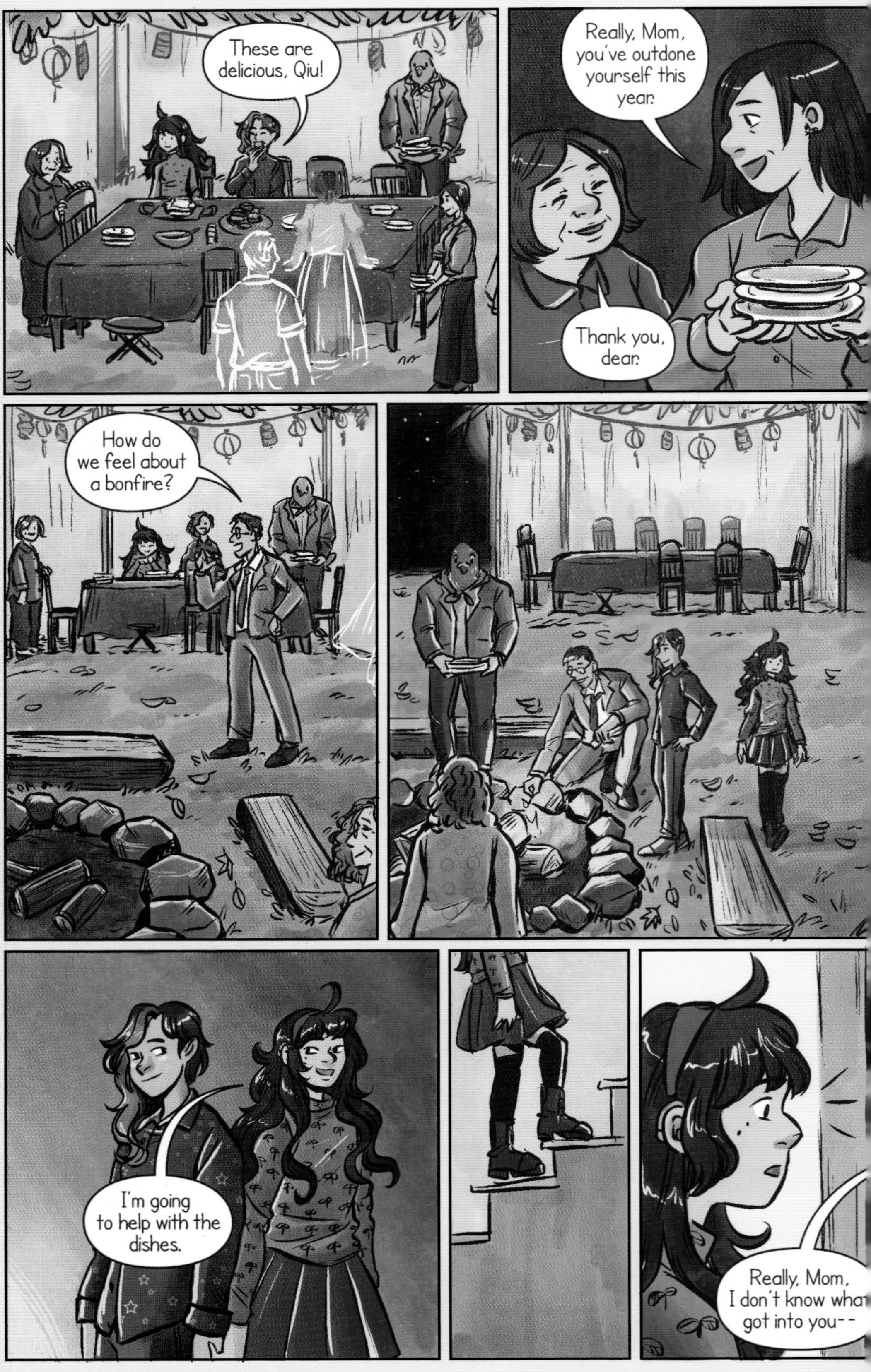
These are delicious, Qiu!
Really, Mom, you've outdone yourself this year.
Thank you, dear.
How do we feel about a bonfire?
I'm going to help with the dishes.
Really, Mom, I don't know what got into you--

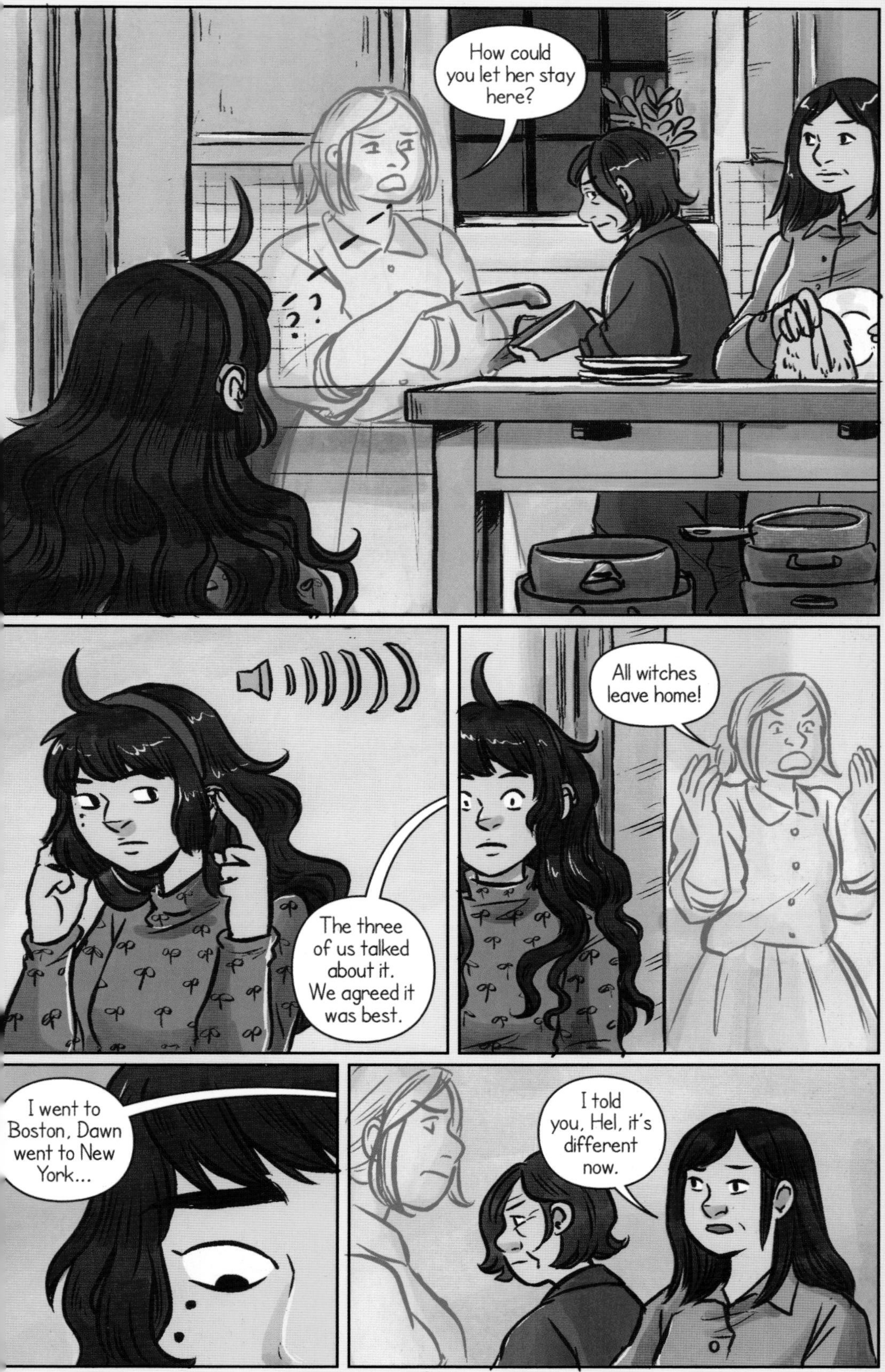
How could you let her stay here?
The three of us talked about it. We agreed it was best.
All witches leave home!
I went to Boston, Dawn went to New York...
I told you, Hel, it's different now.

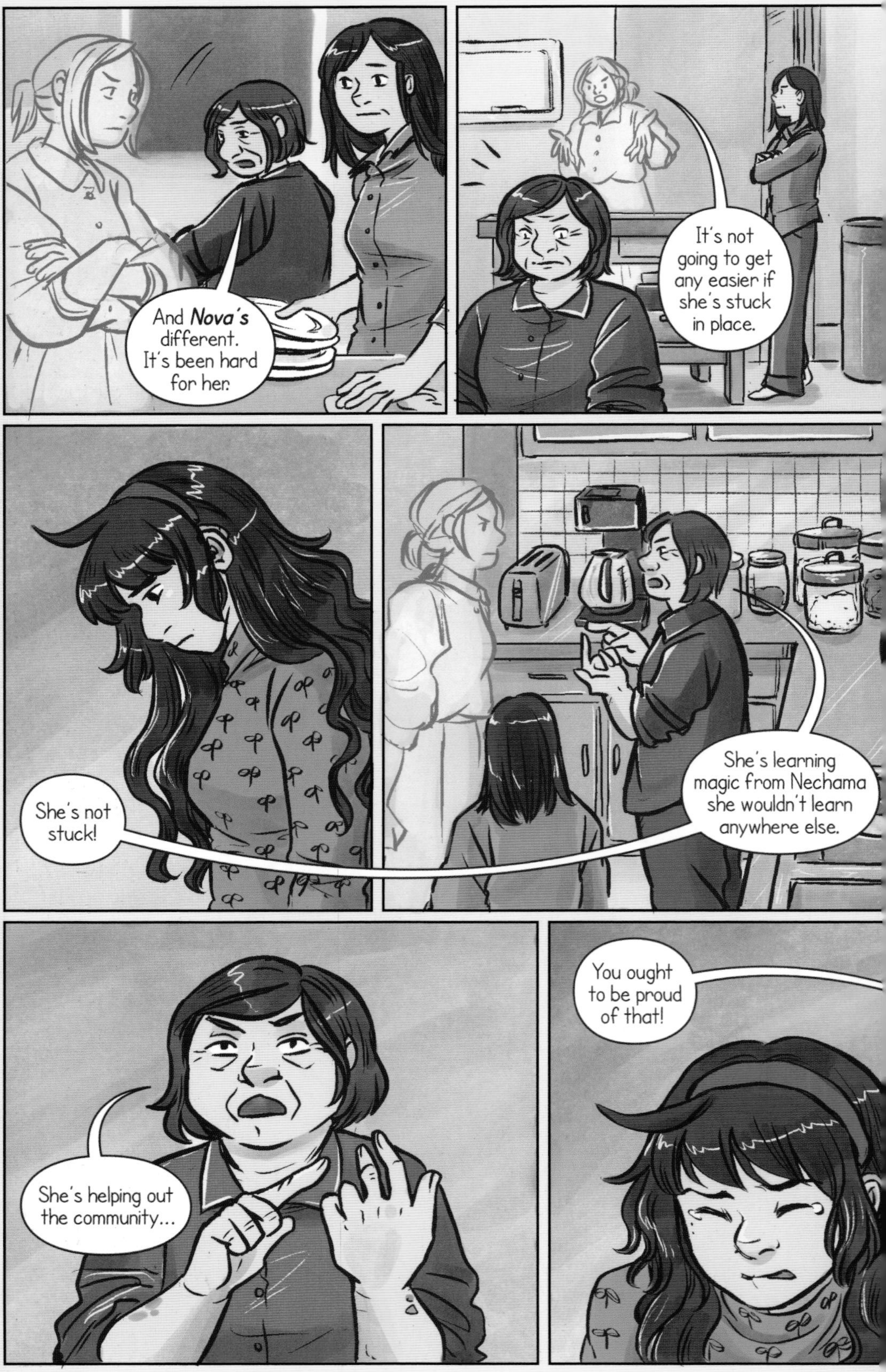

And Nova's different. It's been hard for her.
It's not going to get any easier if she's stuck in place.
She's not stuck!
She's learning magic from Nechama she wouldn't learn anywhere else.
She's helping out the community...
You ought to be proud of that!

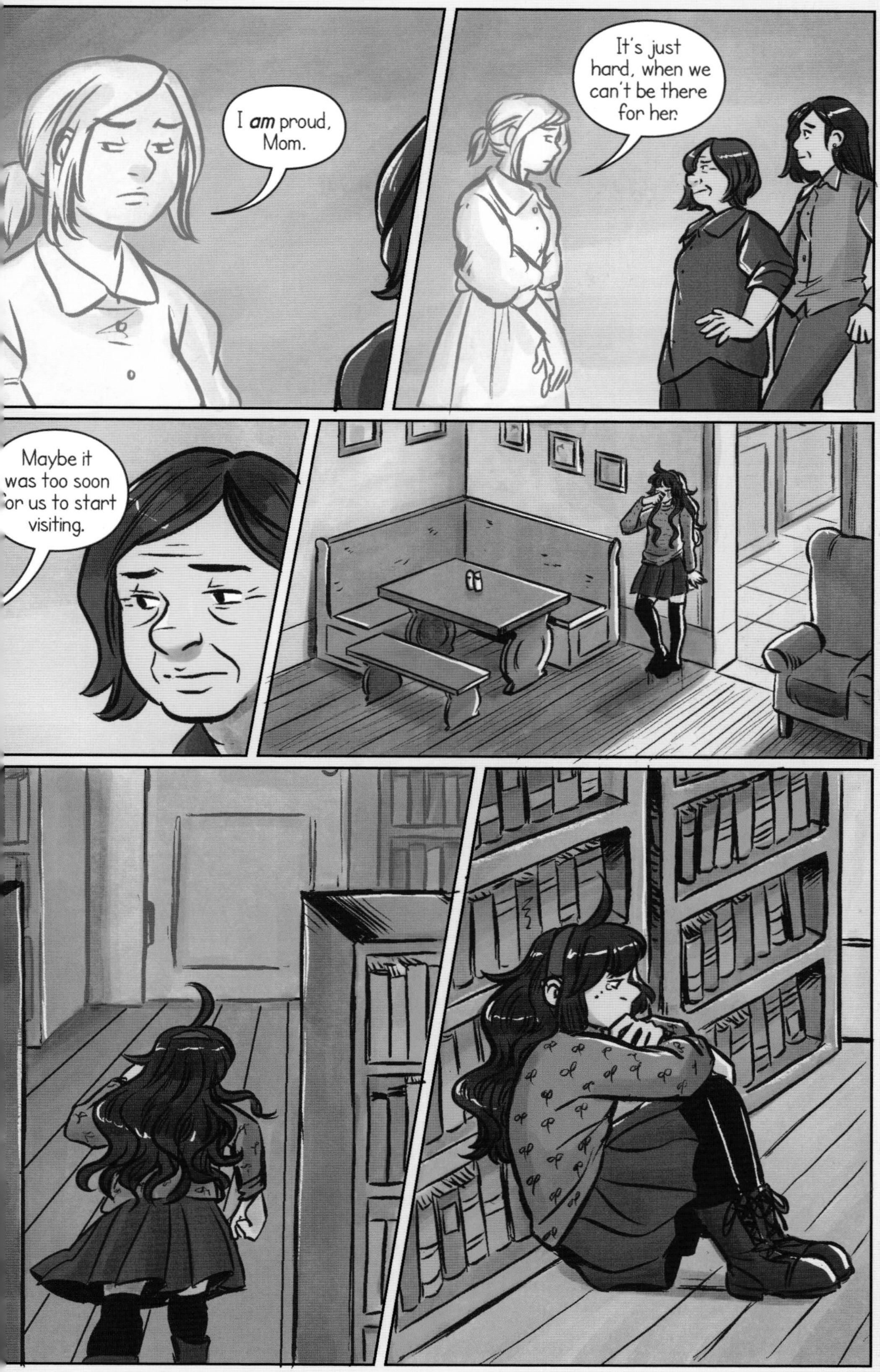
I am proud, Mom.
It's just hard, when we can't be there for her.
Maybe it was too soon for us to start visiting.

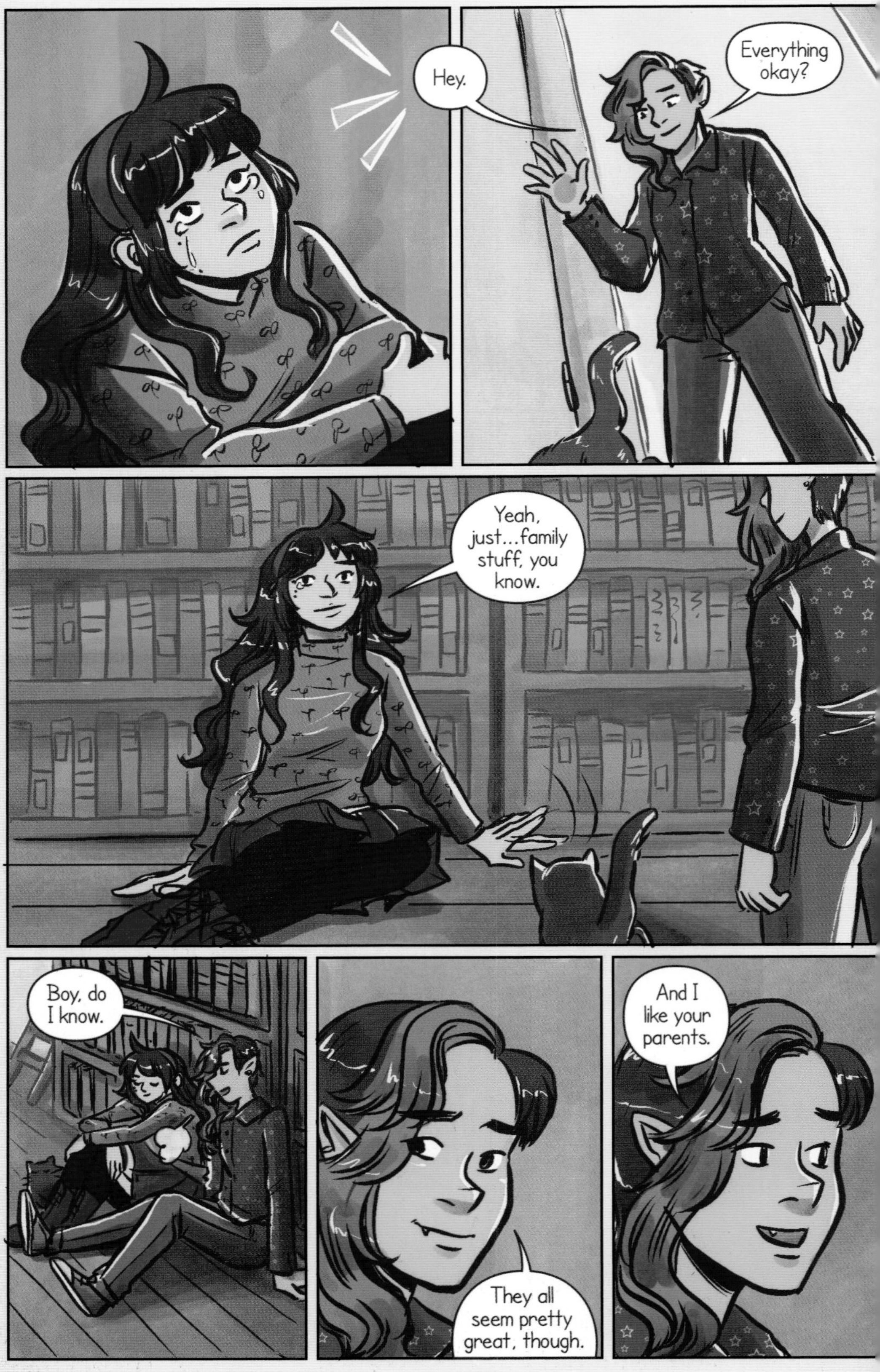

Hey.
Everything okay?
Yeah, just...family stuff, you know.
Boy, do I know.
They all seem pretty great, though.
And I like your parents.

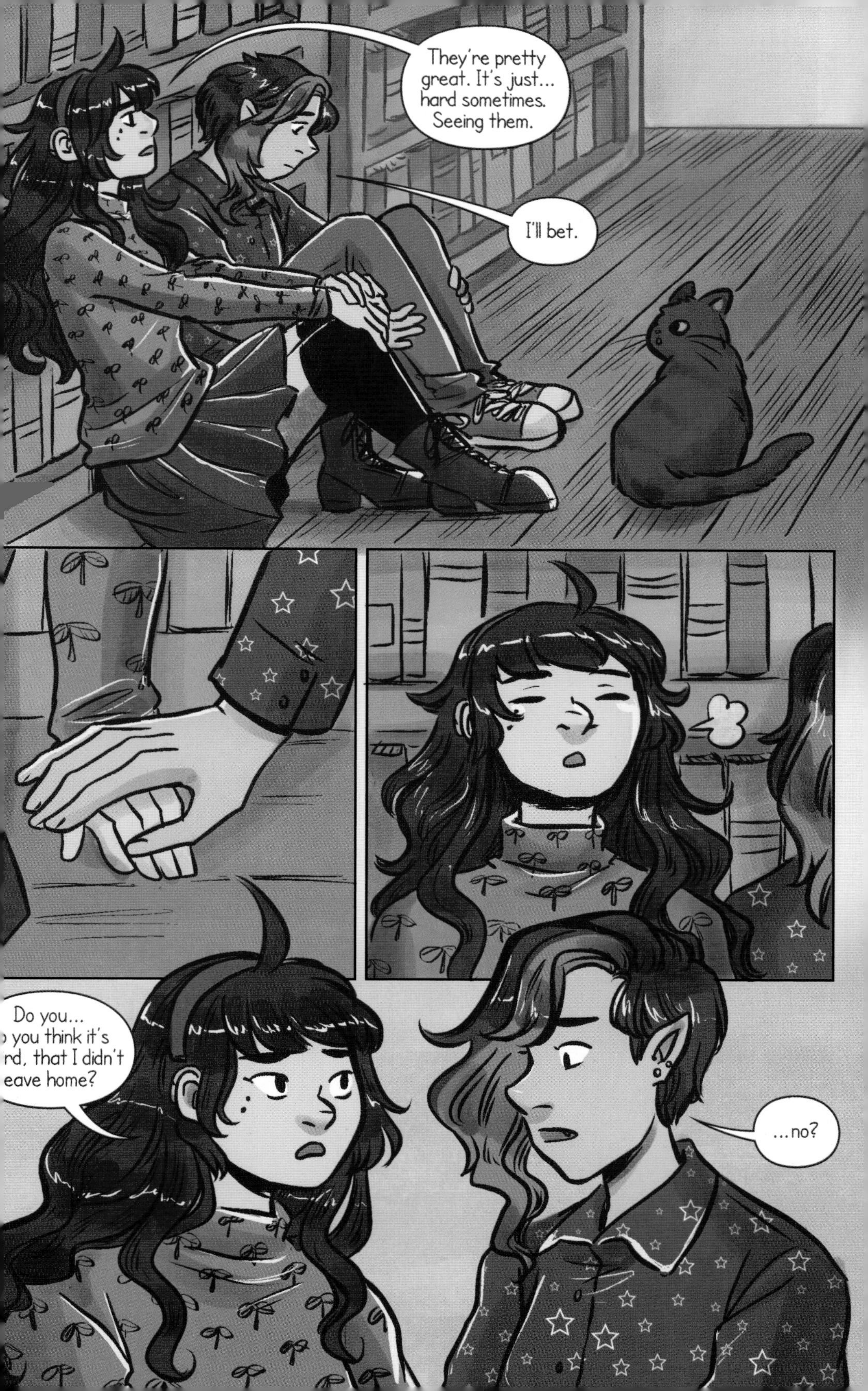
They're pretty great. It's just... hard sometimes. Seeing them.
I'll bet.
Do you... you think it's rd, that I didn't eave home?
...no?

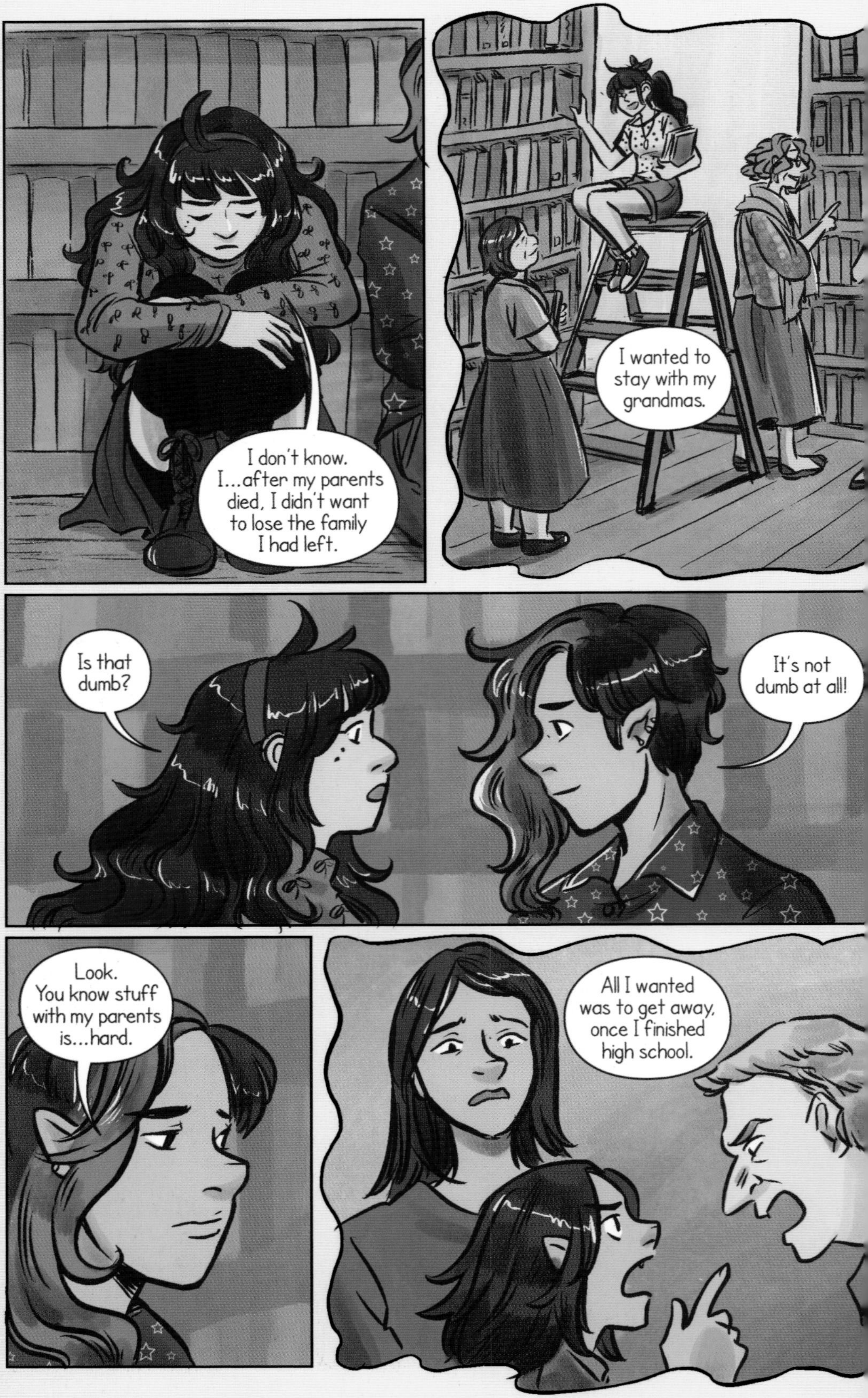
I don't know. I...after my parents died, I didn't want to lose the family I had left.
I wanted to stay with my grandmas.
Is that dumb?
It's not dumb at all!
Look. You know stuff with my parents is...hard.
All I wanted was to get away, once I finished high school.

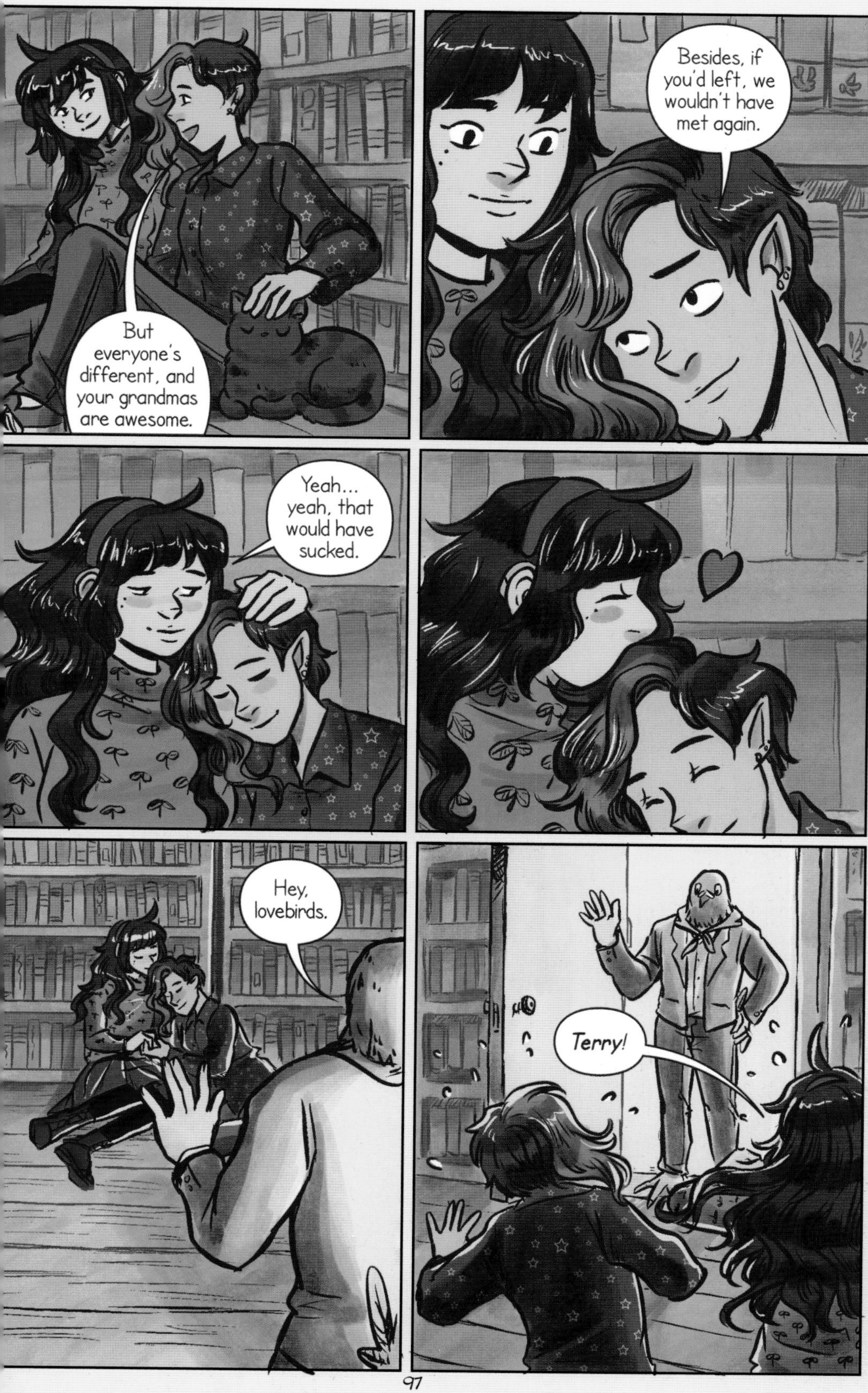
But everyone's different, and your grandmas are awesome.
Besides, if you'd left, we wouldn't have met again.
Yeah... yeah, that would have sucked.
Hey, lovebirds.
Terry!

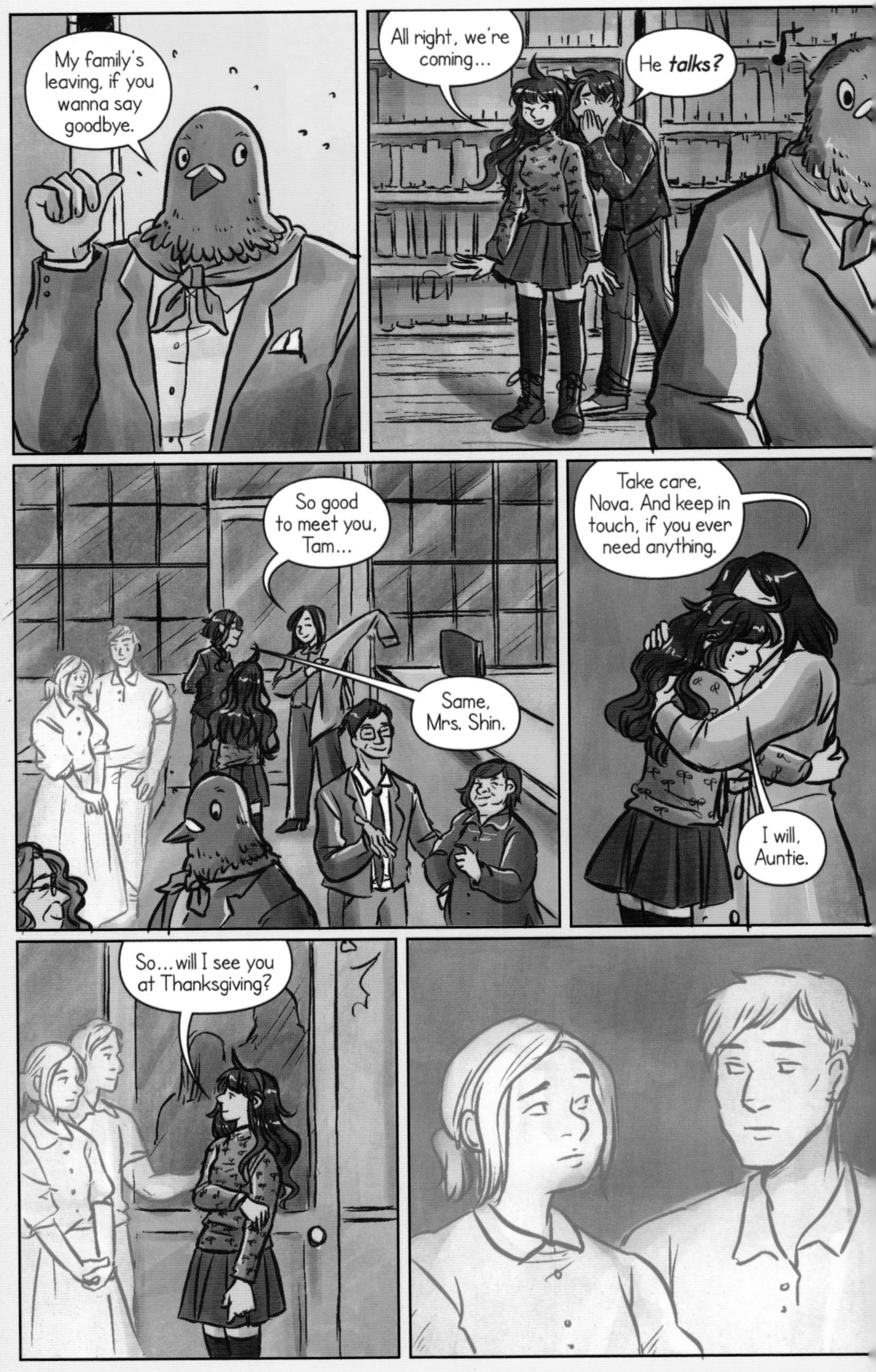
My family's leaving, if you wanna say goodbye.
All right, we're coming...
He *talks?*
So good to meet you, Tam...
Same, Mrs. Shin.
Take care, Nova. And keep in touch, if you ever need anything.
I will, Auntie.
So...will I see you at Thanksgiving?

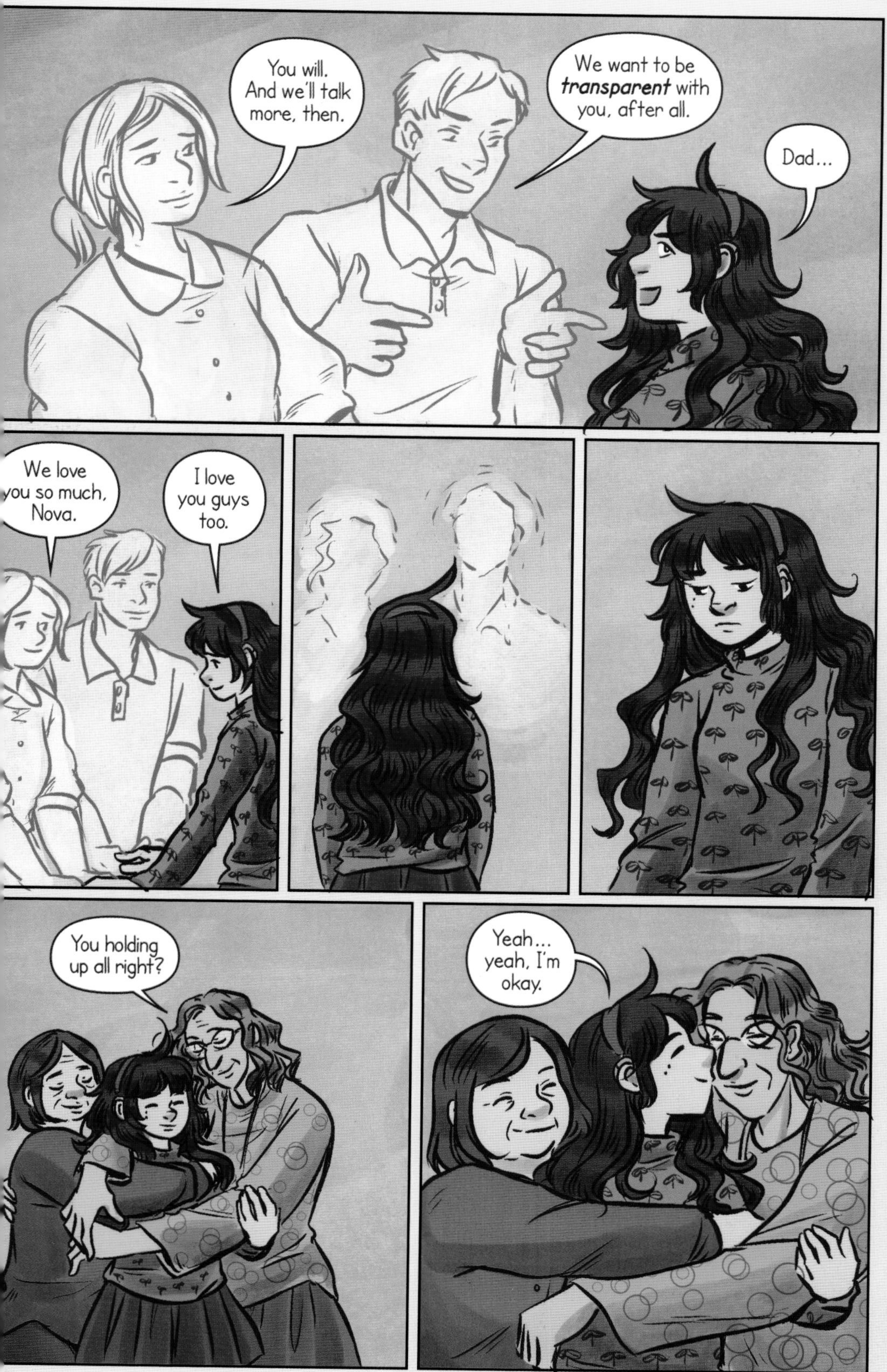
You will. And we'll talk more, then.
We want to be *transparent* with you, after all.
Dad...
We love you so much, Nova.
I love you guys too.
You holding up all right?
Yeah... yeah, I'm okay.

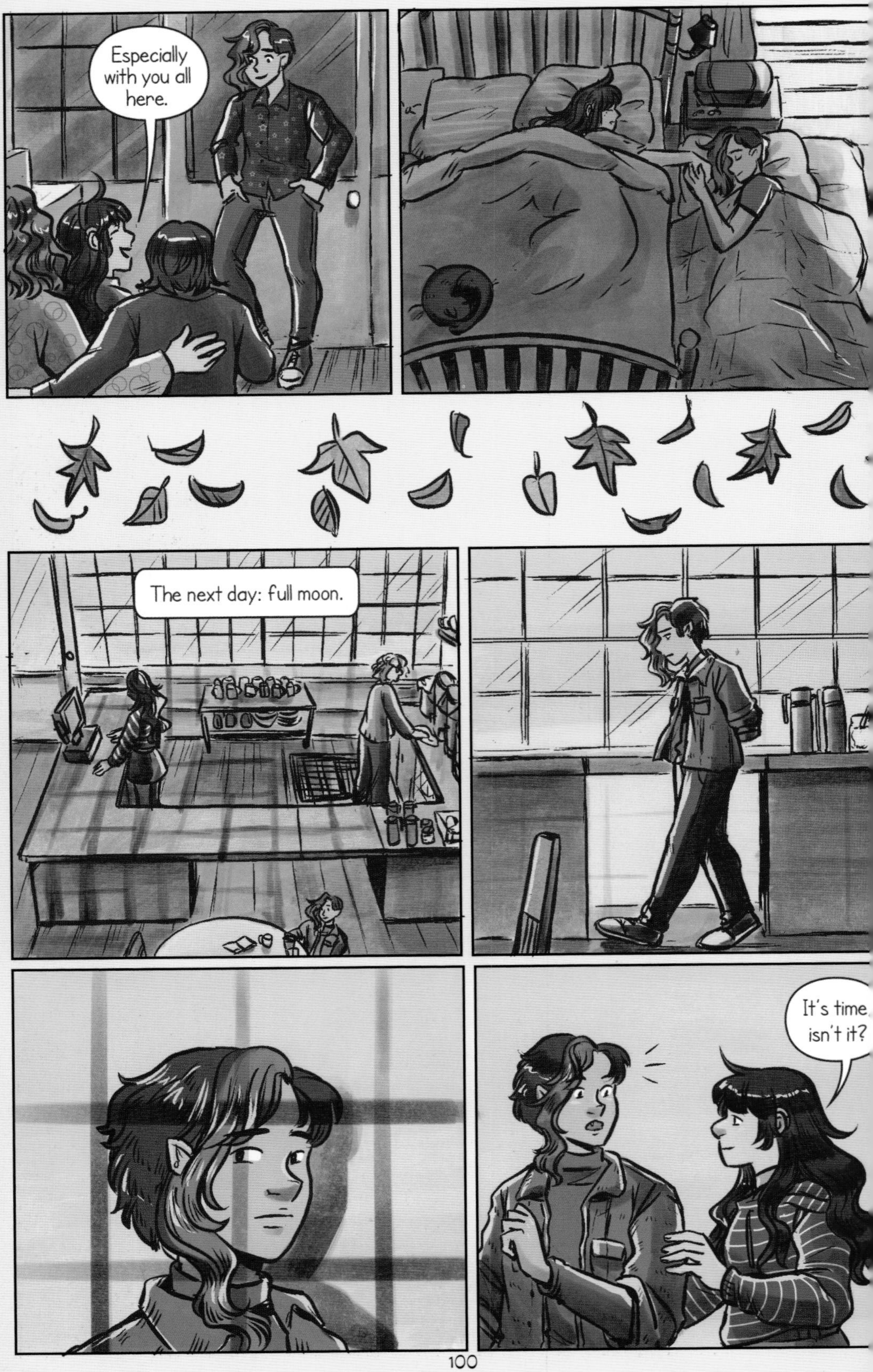
Especially with you all here.
The next day: full moon.
It's time, isn't it?

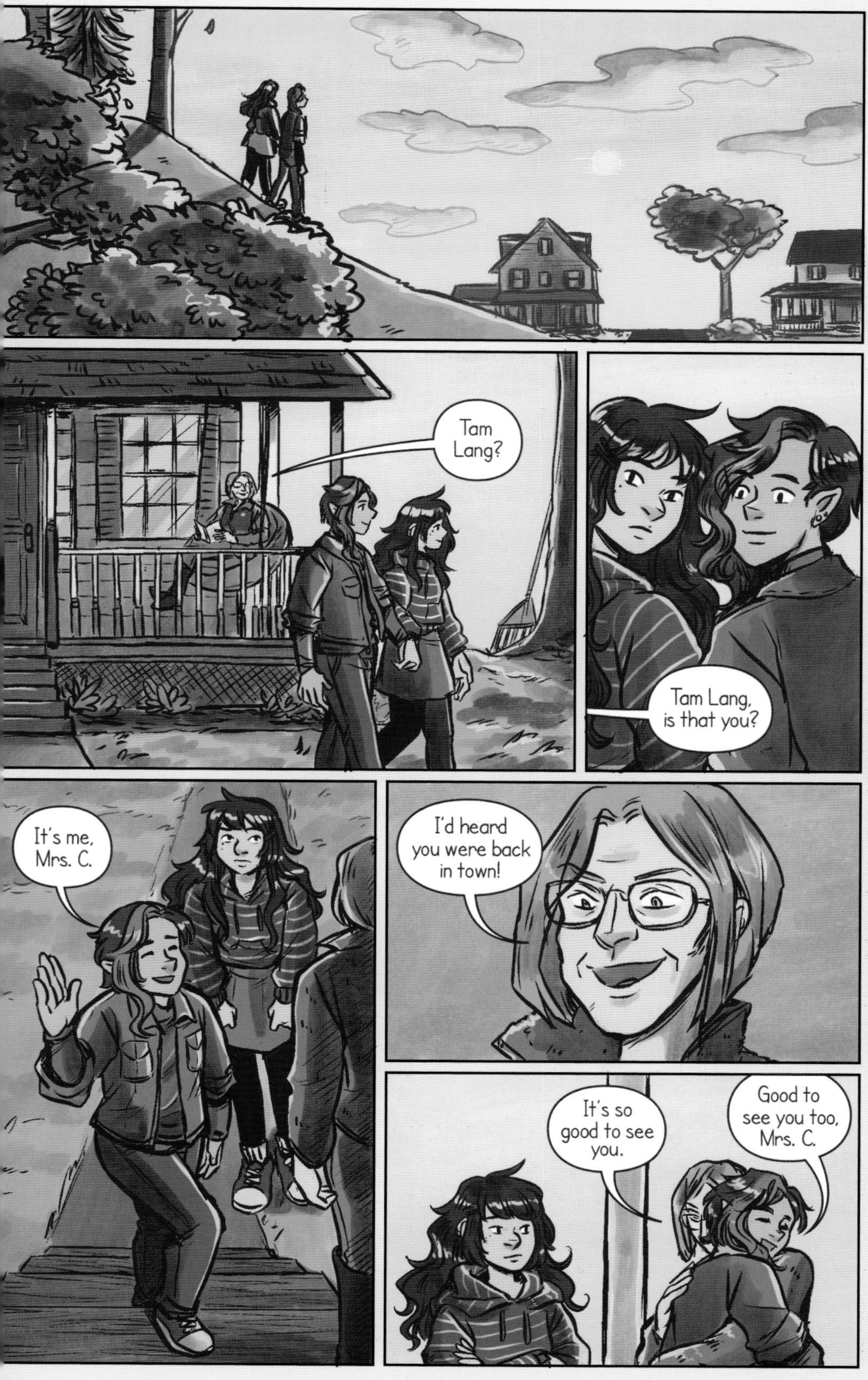
Tam Lang?
Tam Lang, is that you?
It's me, Mrs. C.
I'd heard you were back in town!
It's so good to see you.
Good to see you too, Mrs. C.

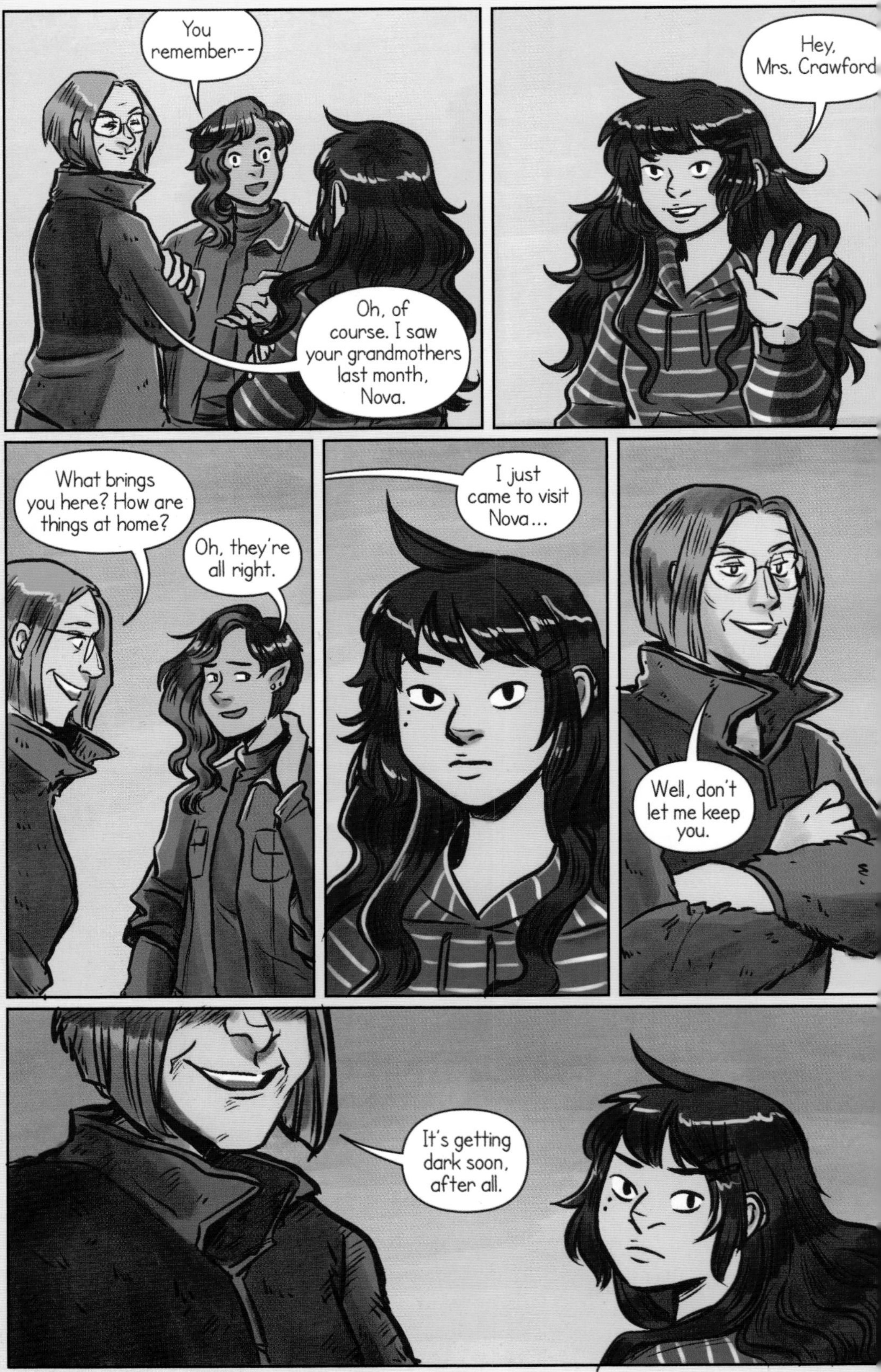
You remember--
Oh, of course. I saw your grandmothers last month, Nova.
Hey, Mrs. Crawford
What brings you here? How are things at home?
Oh, they're all right.
I just came to visit Nova...
Well, don't let me keep you.
It's getting dark soon, after all.

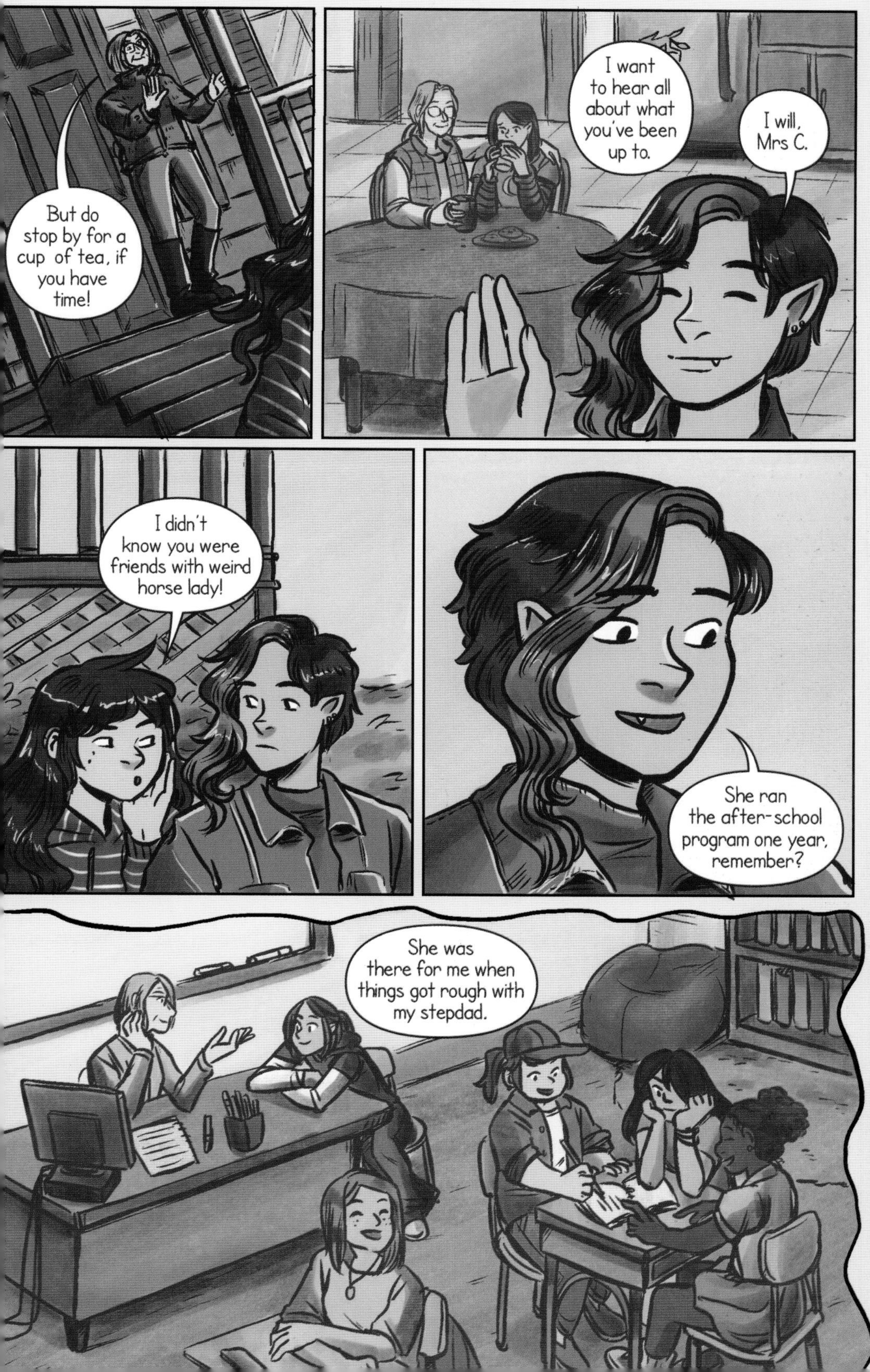
But do stop by for a cup of tea, if you have time!
I want to hear all about what you've been up to.
I will, Mrs C.
I didn't know you were friends with weird horse lady!
She ran the after-school program one year, remember?
She was there for me when things got rough with my stepdad.

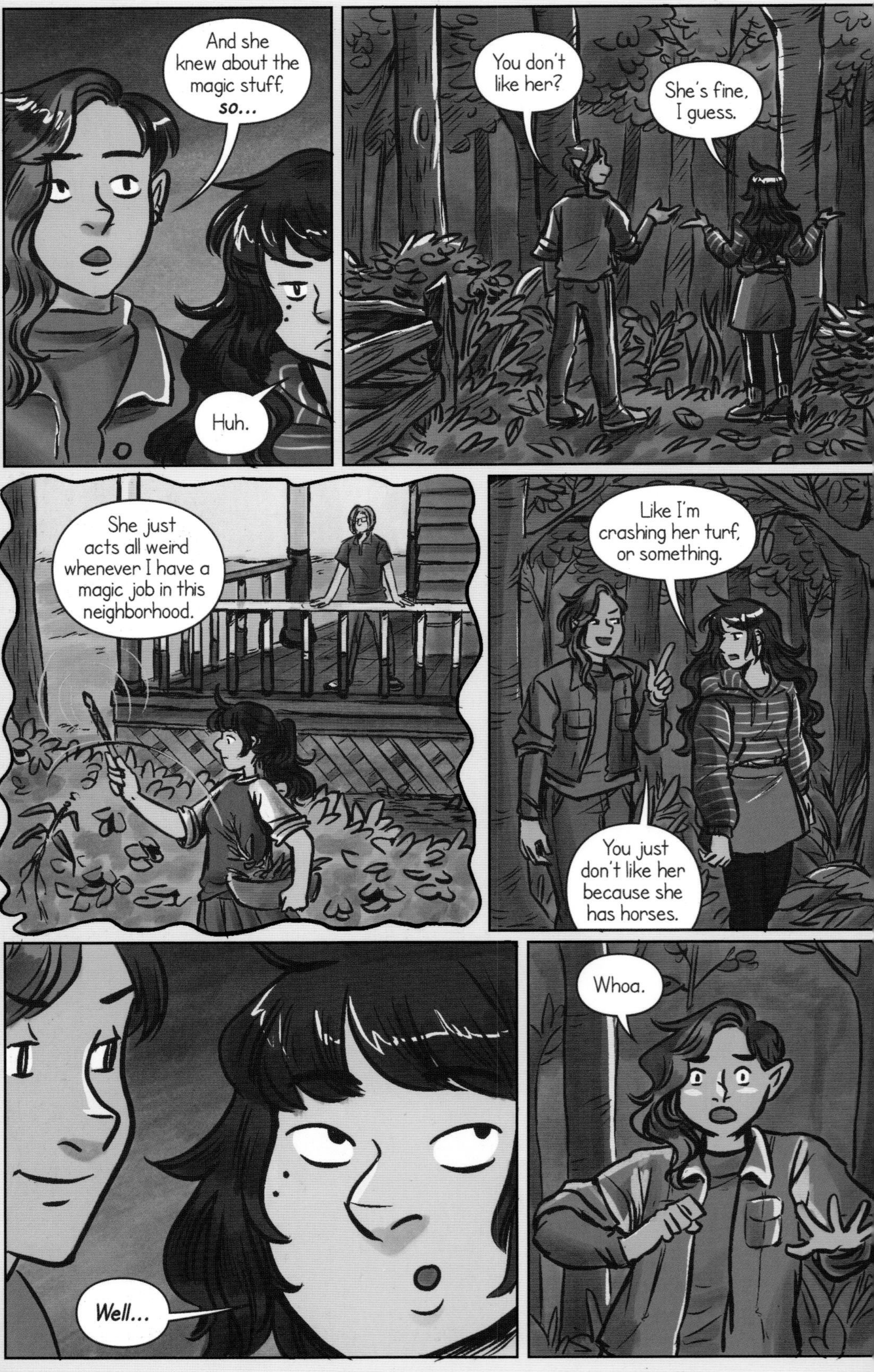
And she knew about the magic stuff, **so...**
Huh.
You don't like her?
She's fine, I guess.
She just acts all weird whenever I have a magic job in this neighborhood.
Like I'm crashing her turf, or something.
You just don't like her because she has horses.
Well...
Whoa.

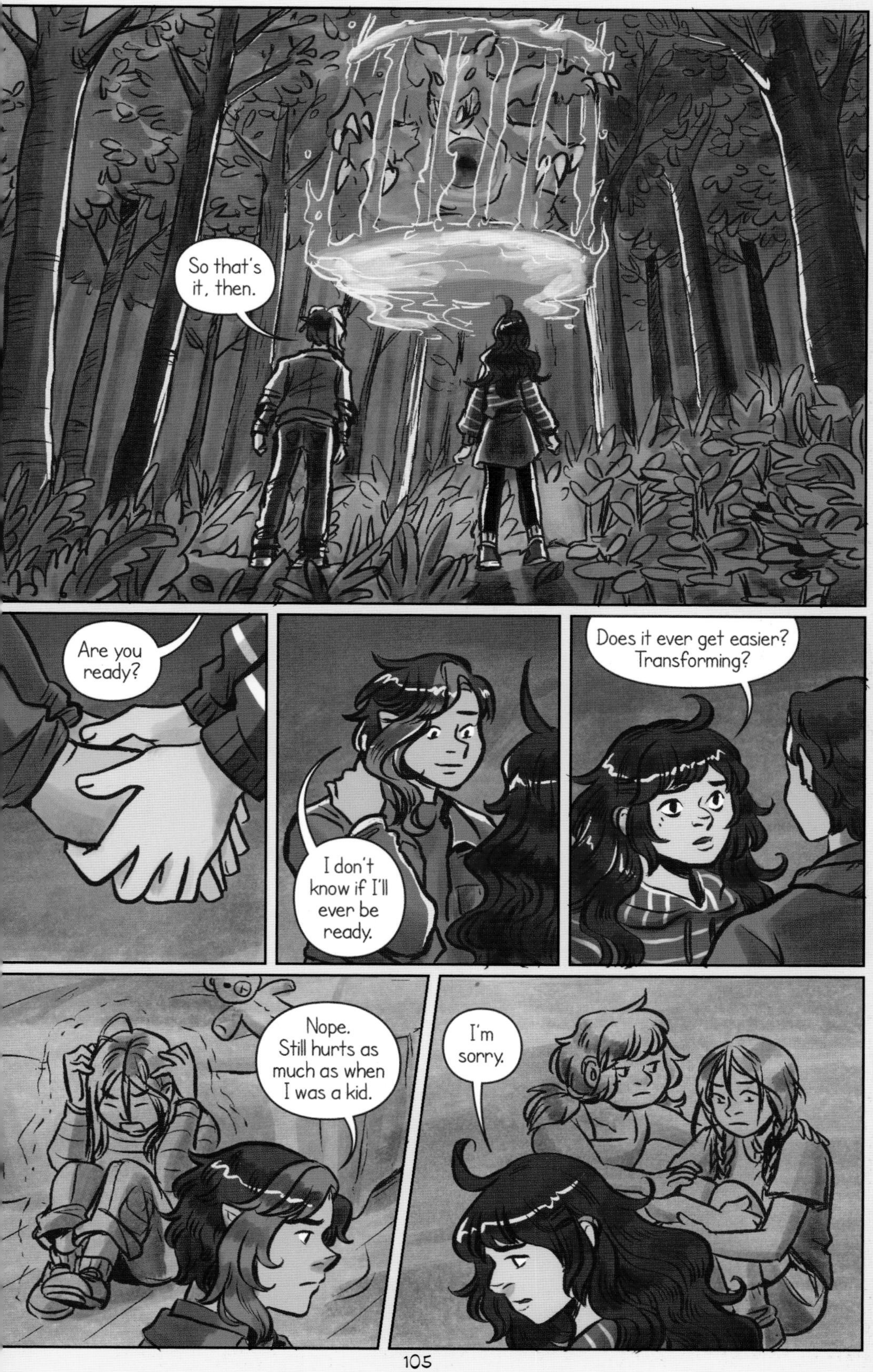
So that's it, then.
Are you ready?
I don't know if I'll ever be ready.
Does it ever get easier? Transforming?
Nope. Still hurts as much as when I was a kid.
I'm sorry.

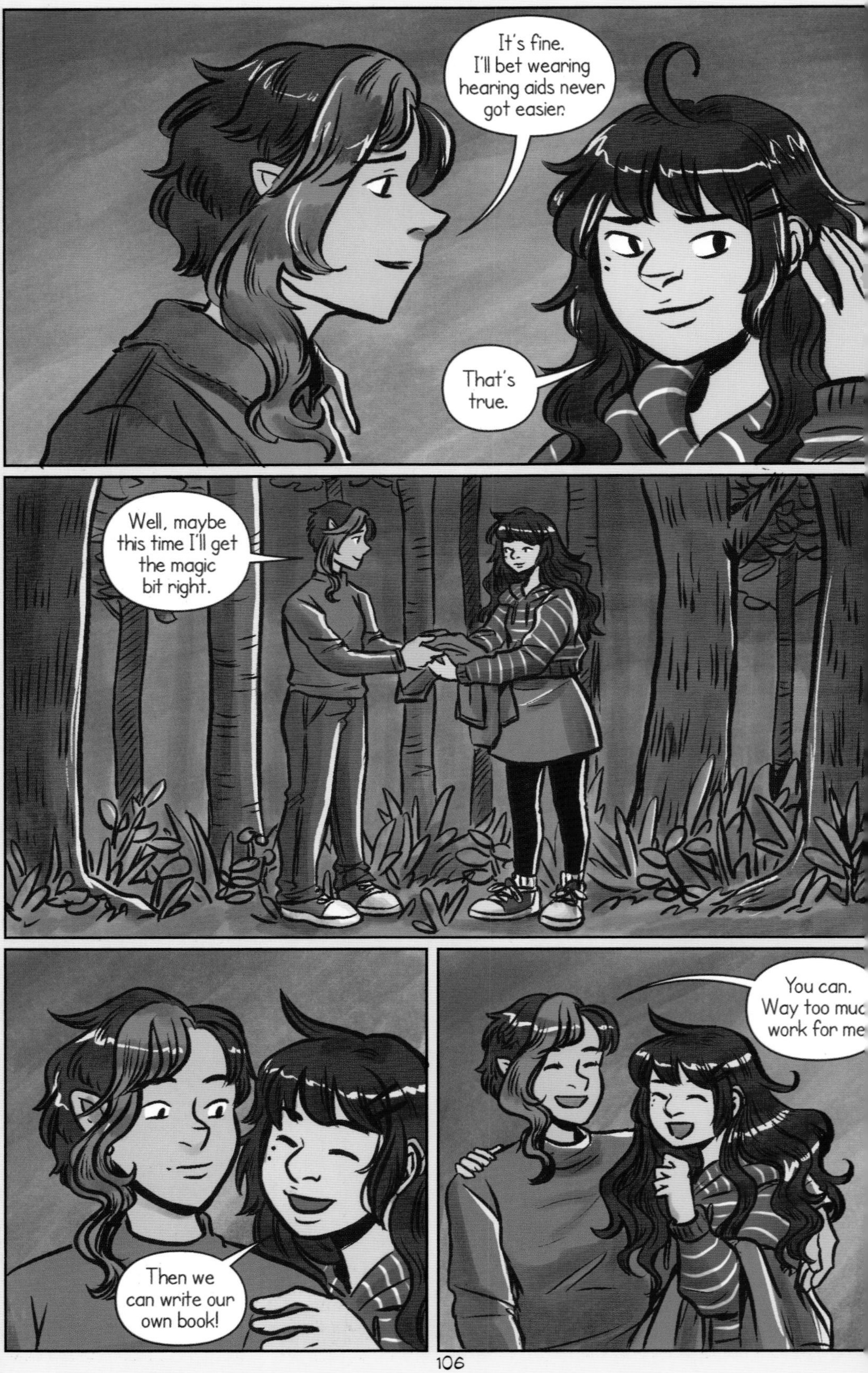

It's fine. I'll bet wearing hearing aids never got easier.
That's true.
Well, maybe this time I'll get the magic bit right.
Then we can write our own book!
You can. Way too muc work for me

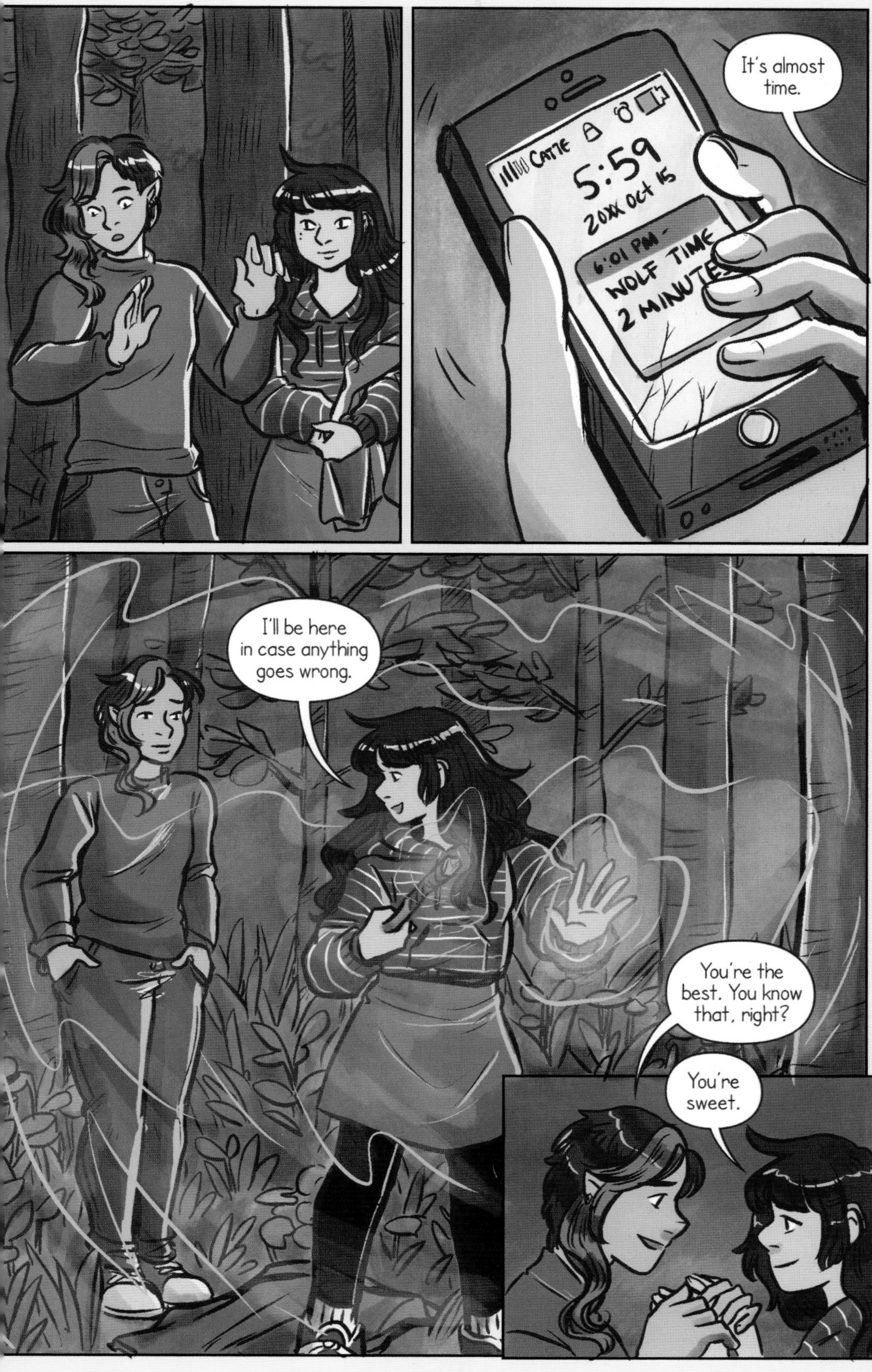

5:59
20XX OCT 15
6:01 PM -
WOLF TIME
2 MINUTE
It's almost time.
I'll be here in case anything goes wrong.
You're the best. You know that, right?
You're sweet.

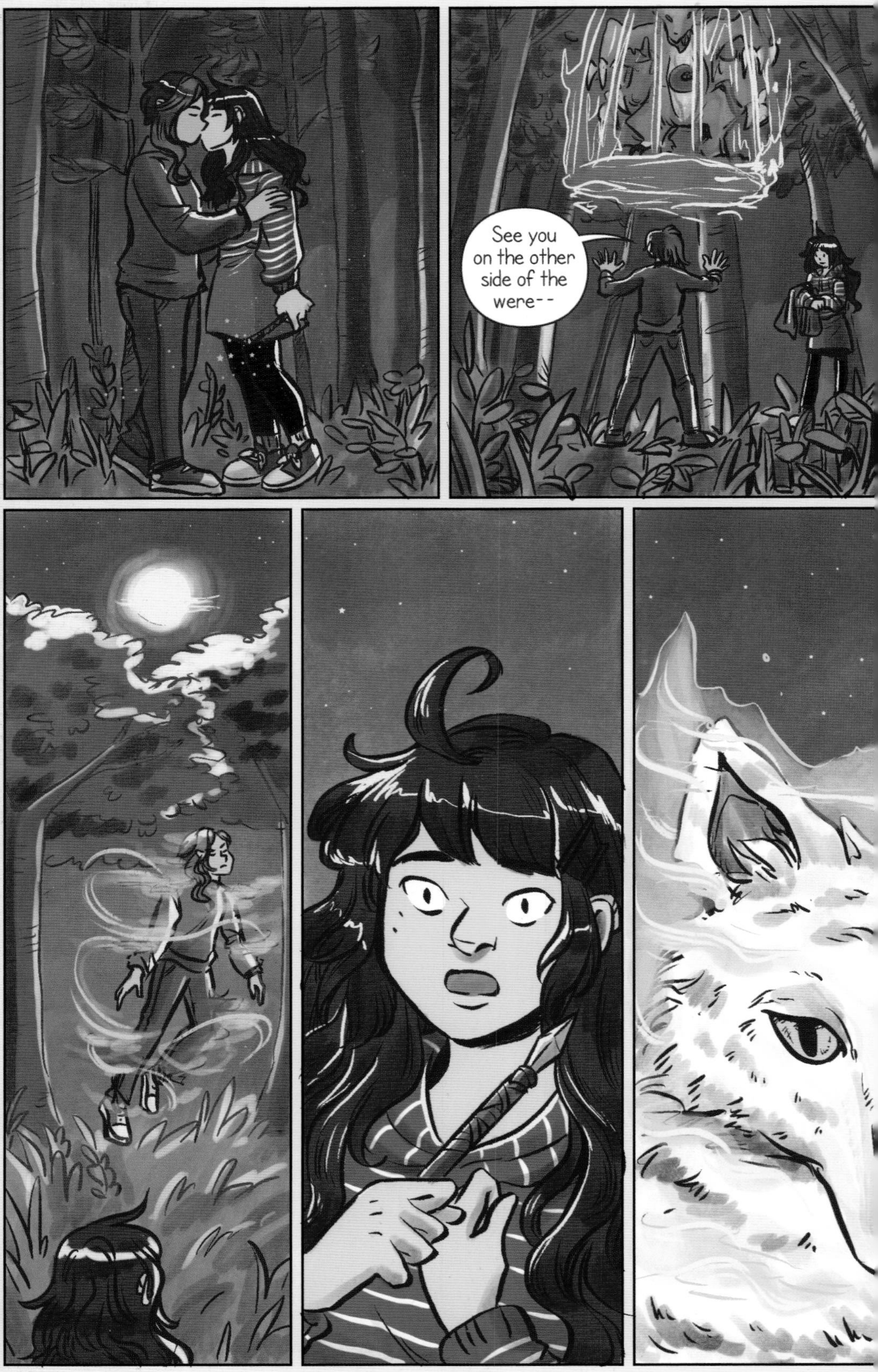
See you on the other side of the were--

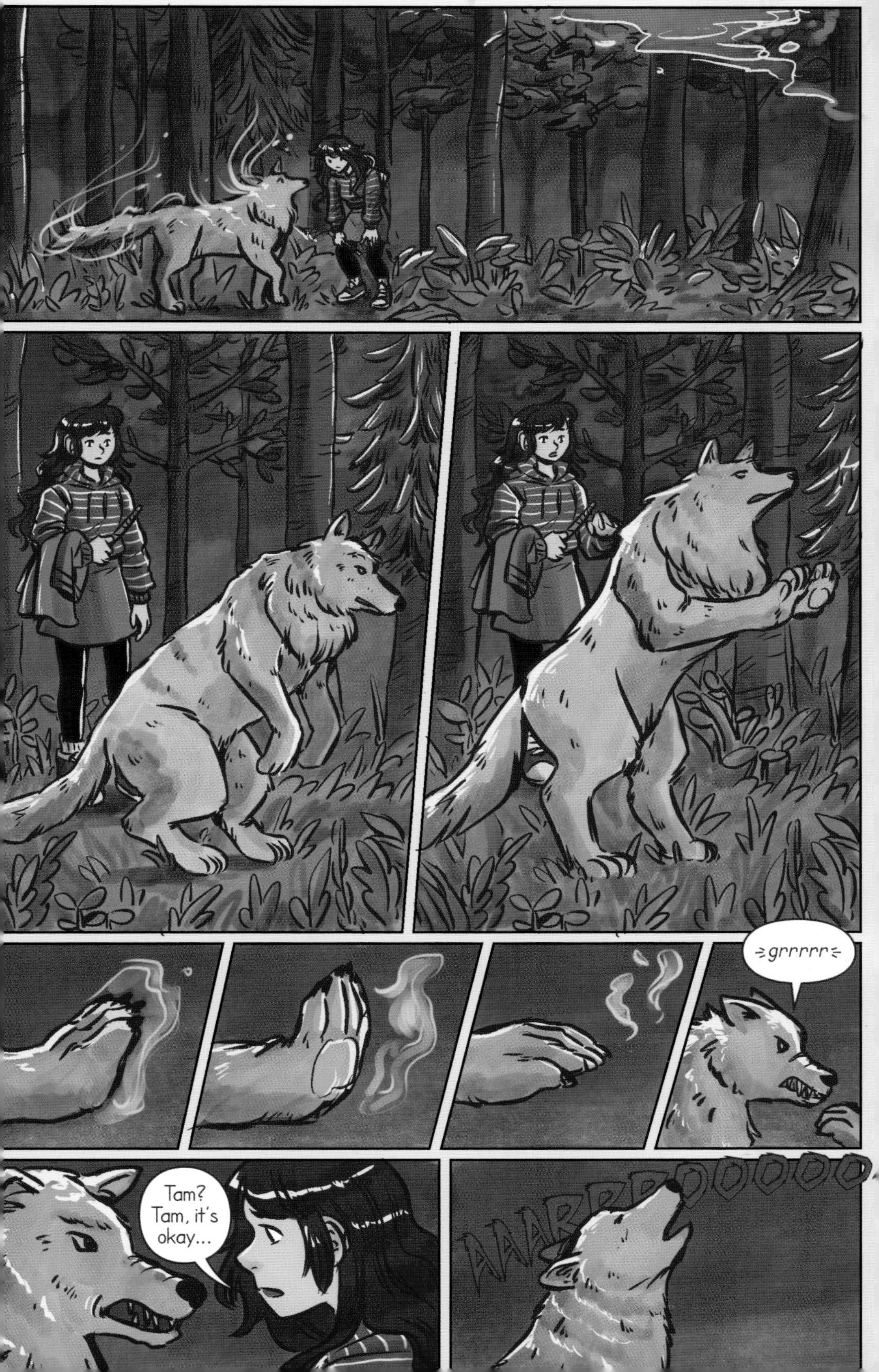
grrrrr
Tam?
Tam, it's
okay...
AAARRROOOOOO

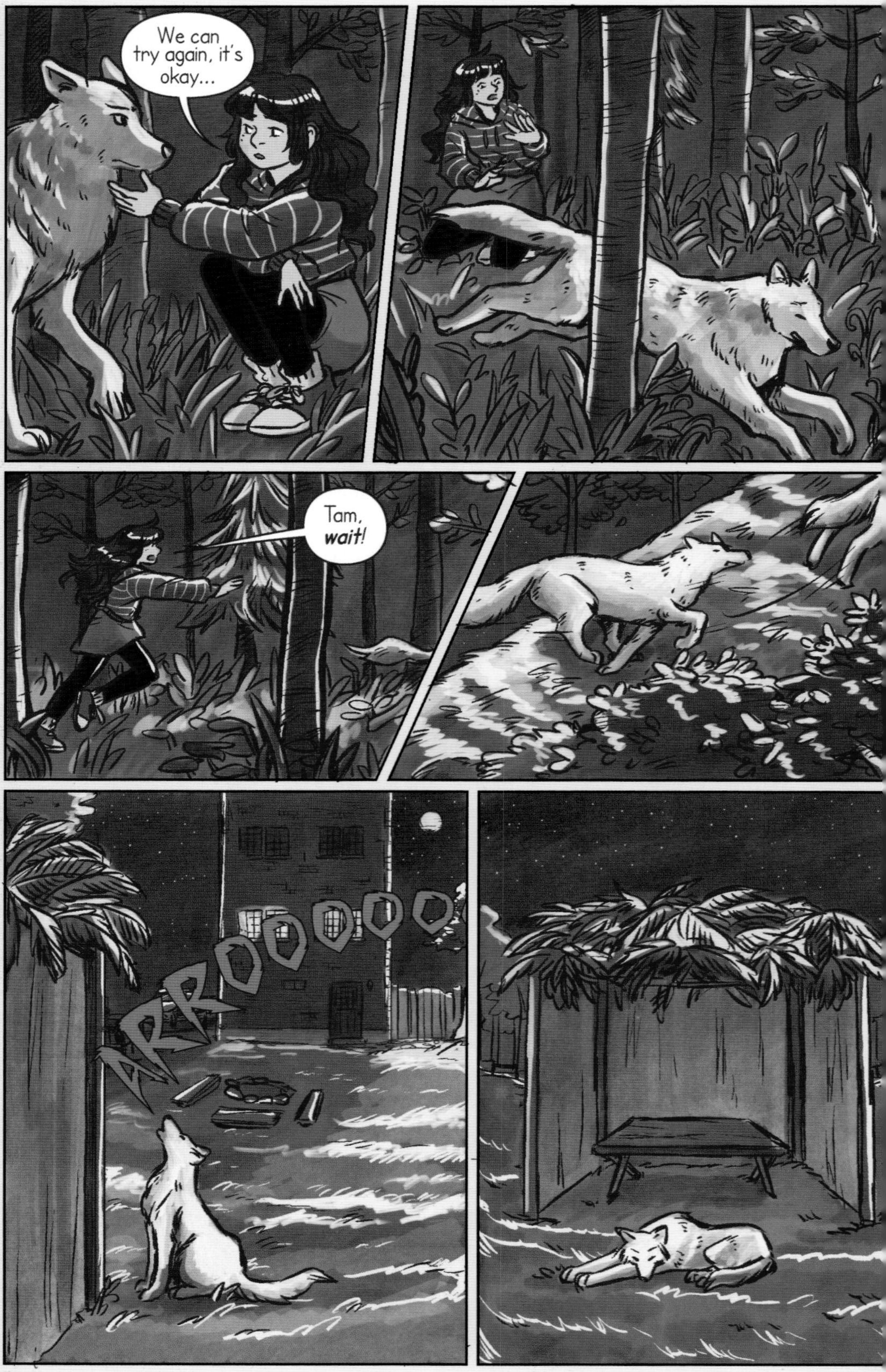
We can try again, it's okay...
Tam, wait!
ARROOOOOO

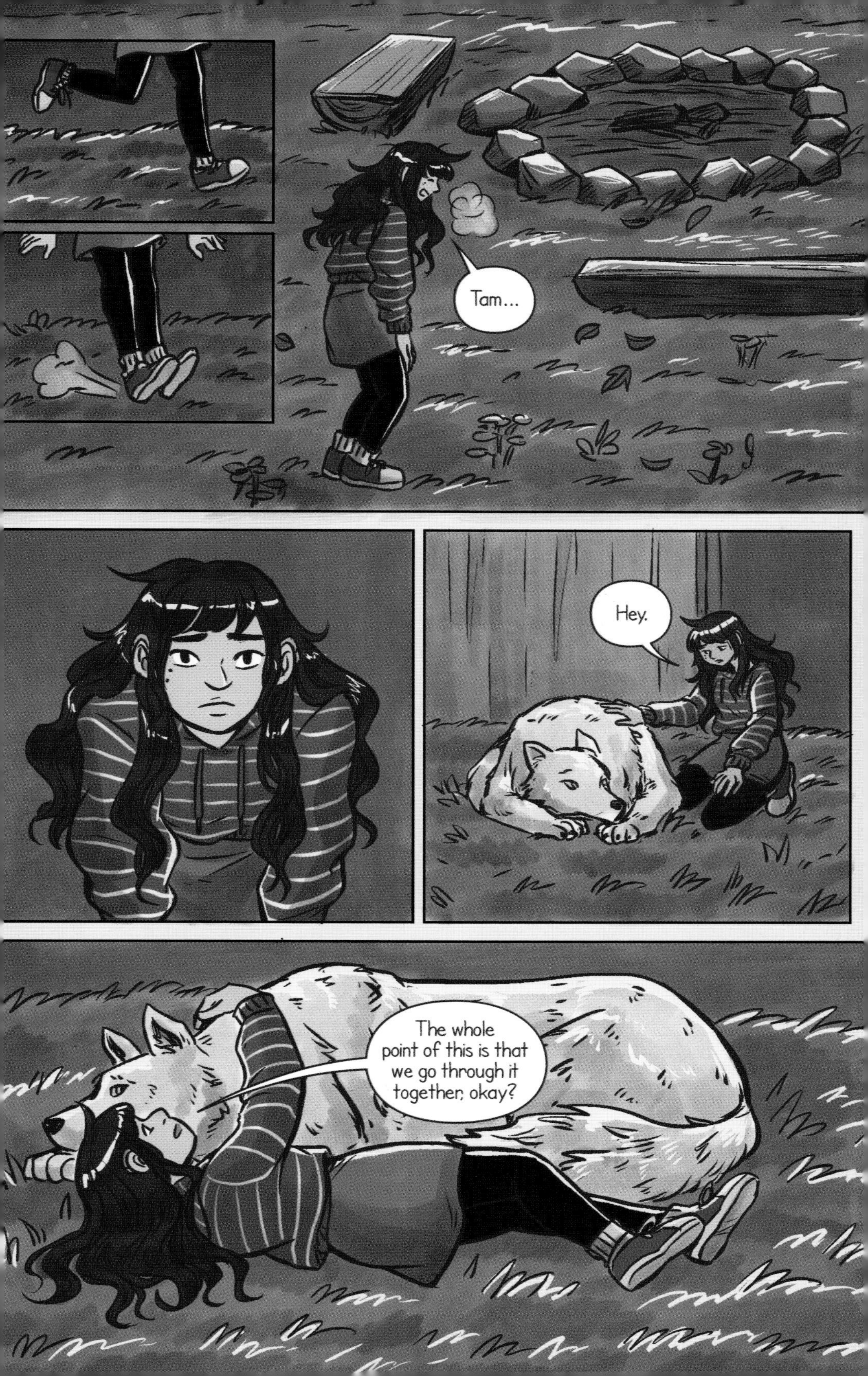
Tam...
Hey.
The whole point of this is that we go through it together, okay?

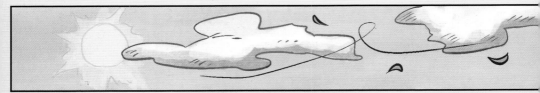

Well, we can certainly renew the binding spell.

Yes, that won't be a problem.

How is Tam doing?

They went straight to bed, but...

I wonder if I should go talk to them...

Give them time, Nova. I'm sure they're exhausted.

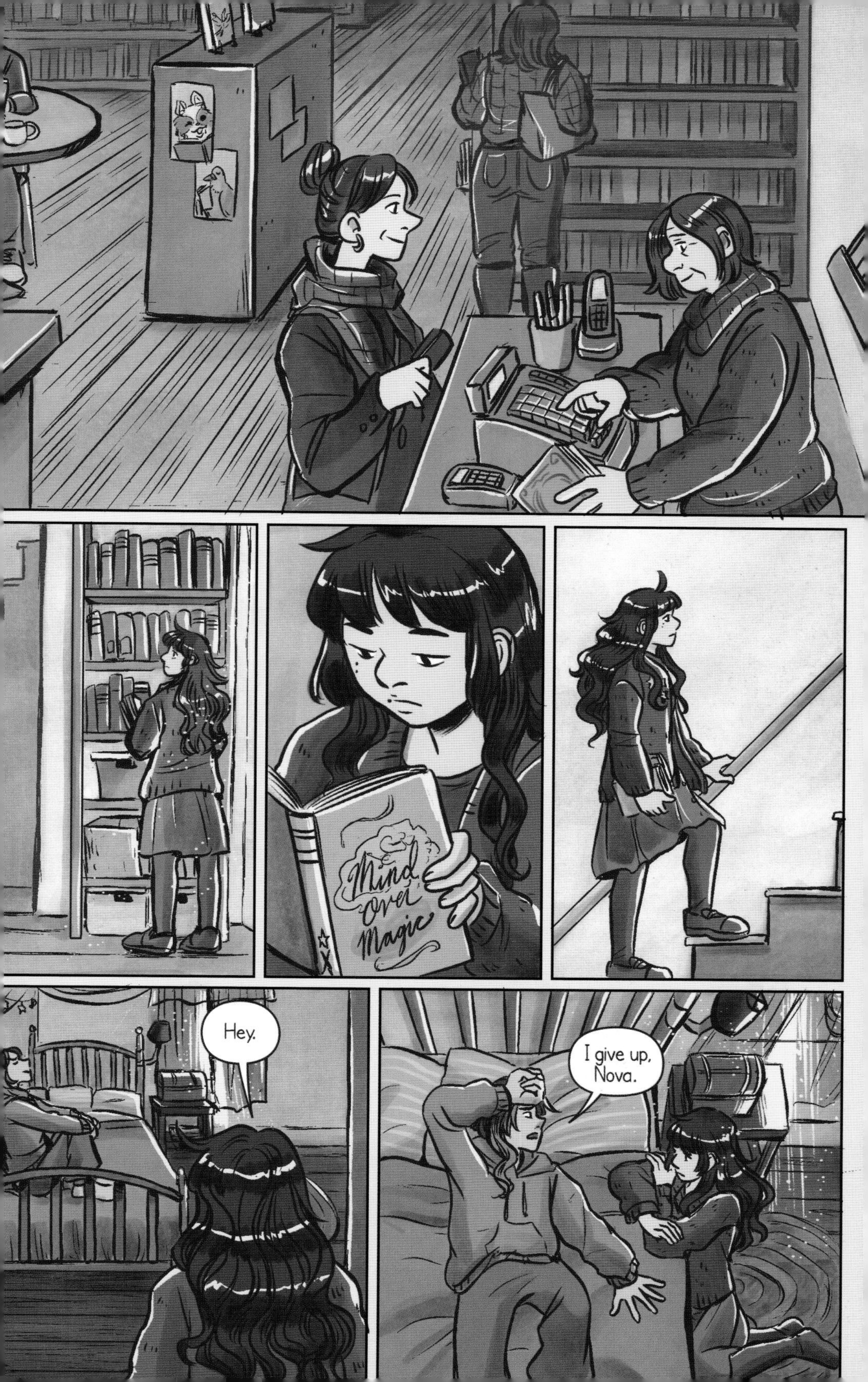
Mind over Magic
Hey.
I give up, Nova.

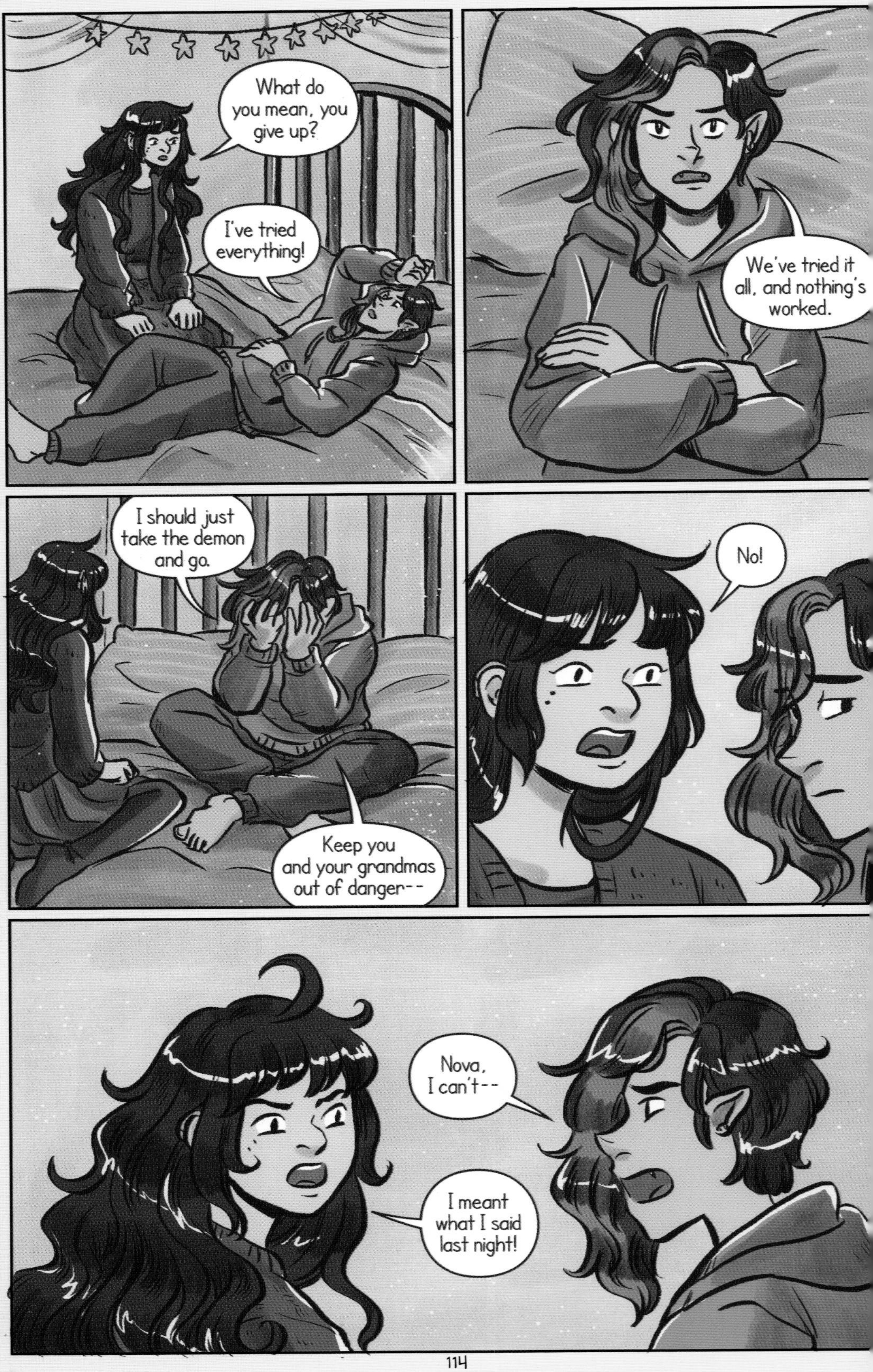
What do you mean, you give up?
I've tried everything!
We've tried it all, and nothing's worked.
I should just take the demon and go.
Keep you and your grandmas out of danger--
No!
Nova, I can't--
I meant what I said last night!

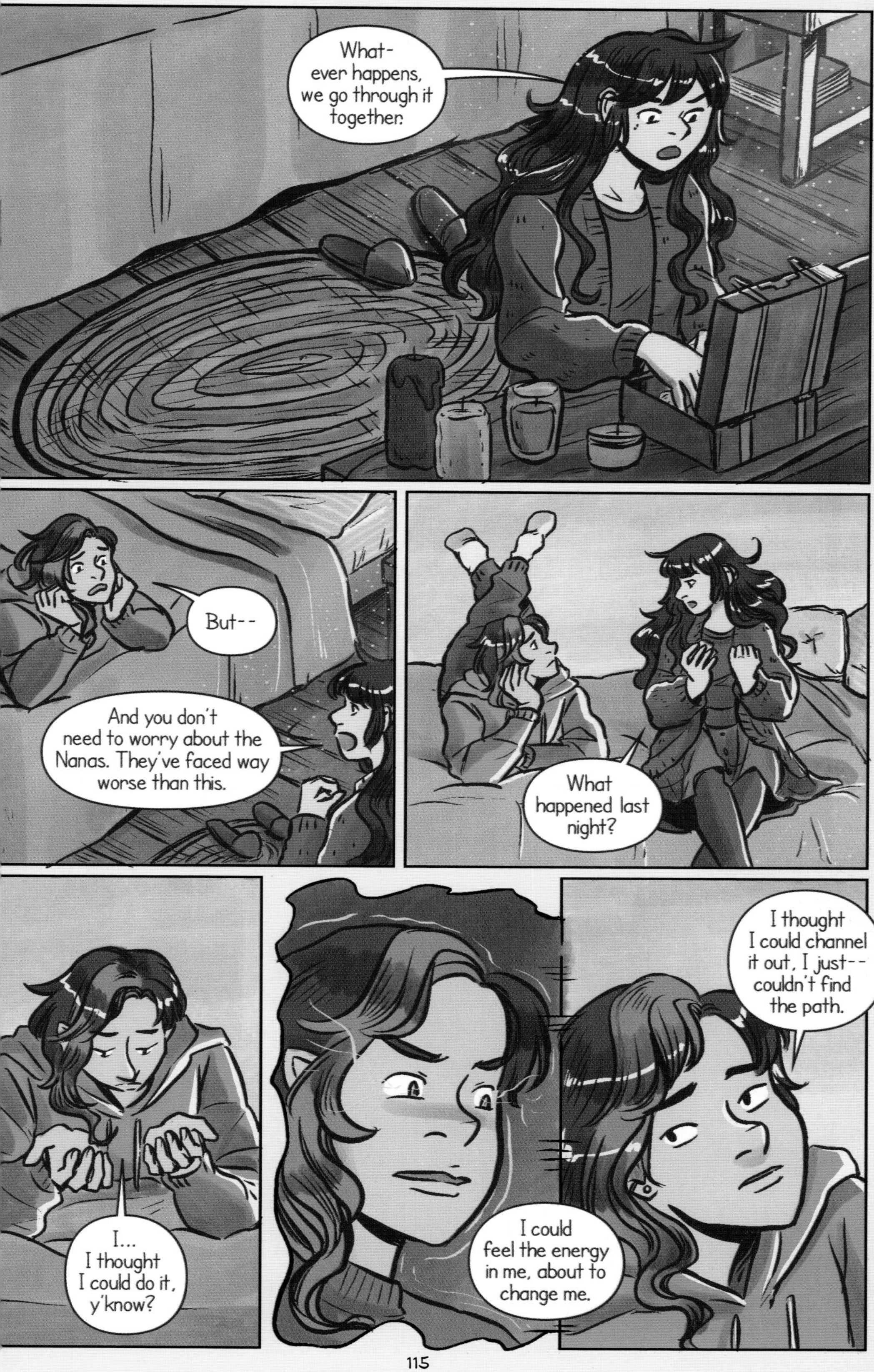
What-
ever happens,
we go through it
together.
But--
And you don't
need to worry about the
Nanas. They've faced way
worse than this.
What
happened last
night?
I...
I thought
I could do it,
y'know?
I could
feel the energy
in me, about to
change me.
I thought
I could channel
it out, I just--
couldn't find
the path.

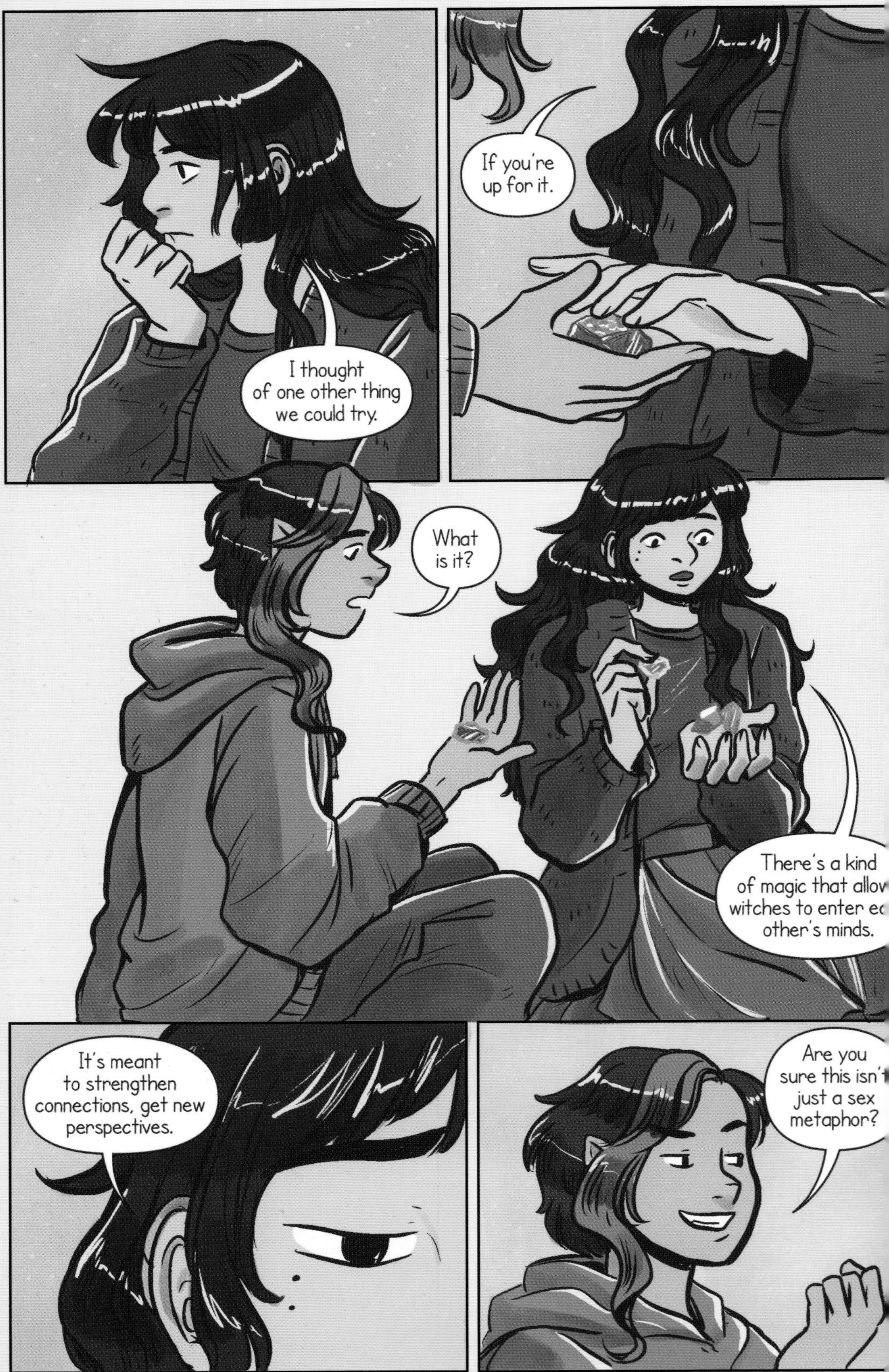
I thought of one other thing we could try.
If you're up for it.
What is it?
There's a kind of magic that allow witches to enter ea other's minds.
It's meant to strengthen connections, get new perspectives.
Are you sure this isn't just a sex metaphor?

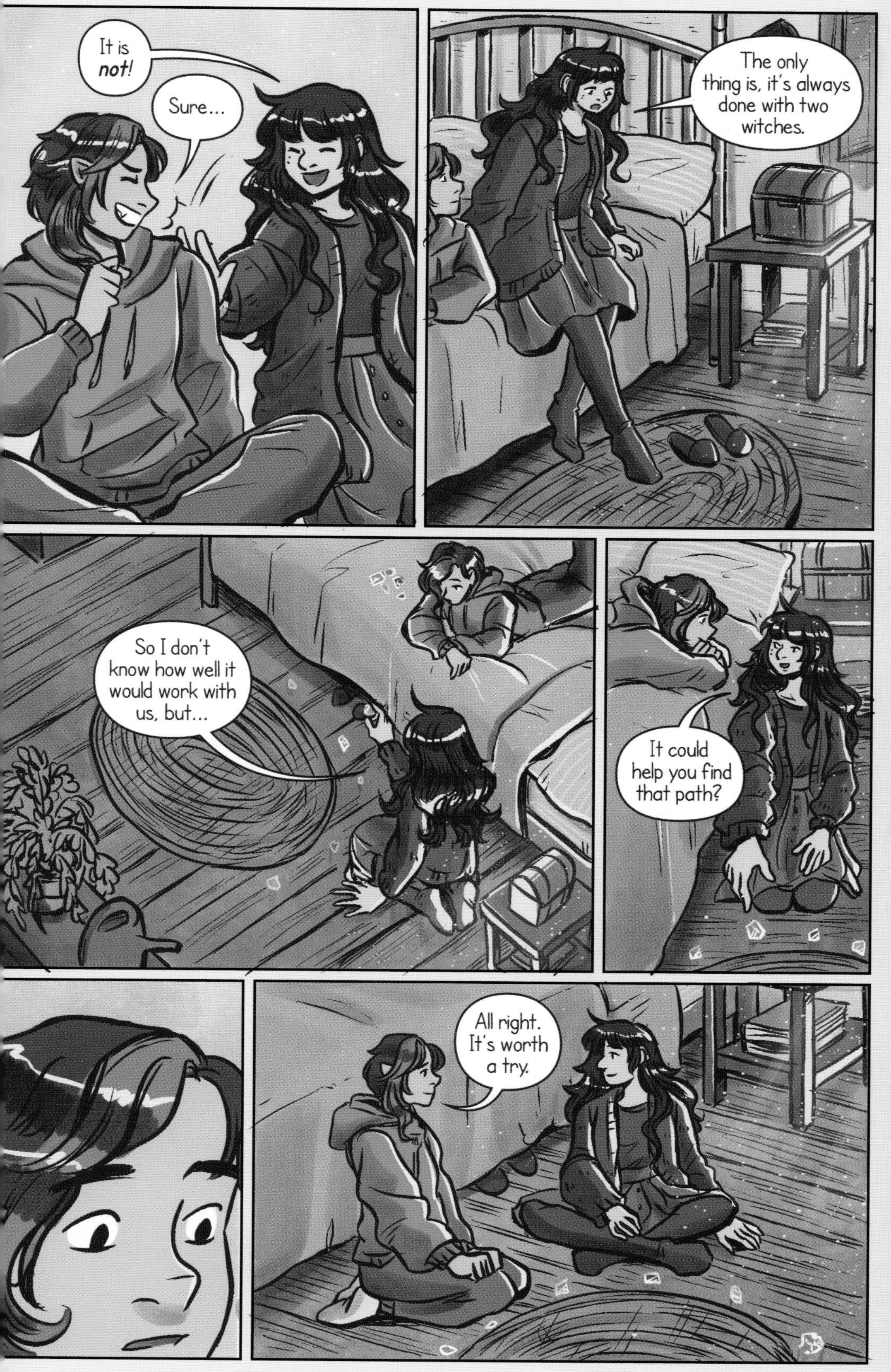
It is *not*!
Sure...
The only thing is, it's always done with two witches.
So I don't know how well it would work with us, but...
It could help you find that path?
All right. It's worth a try.

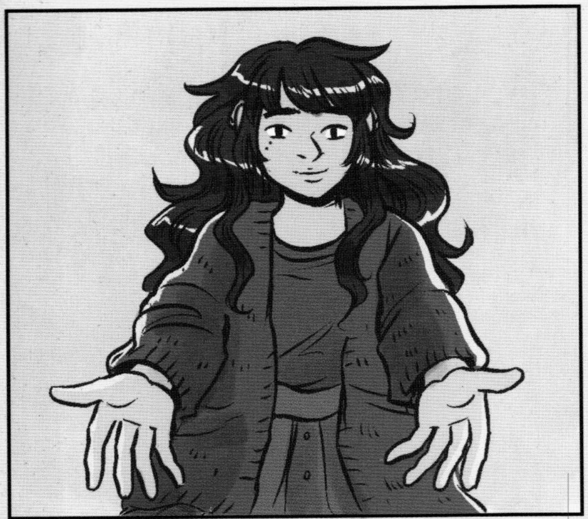

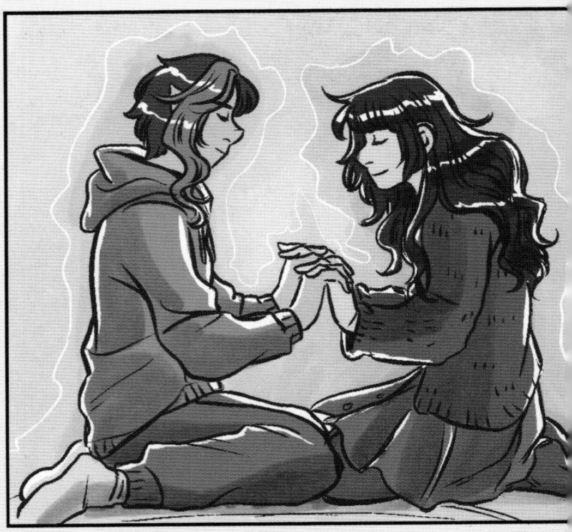

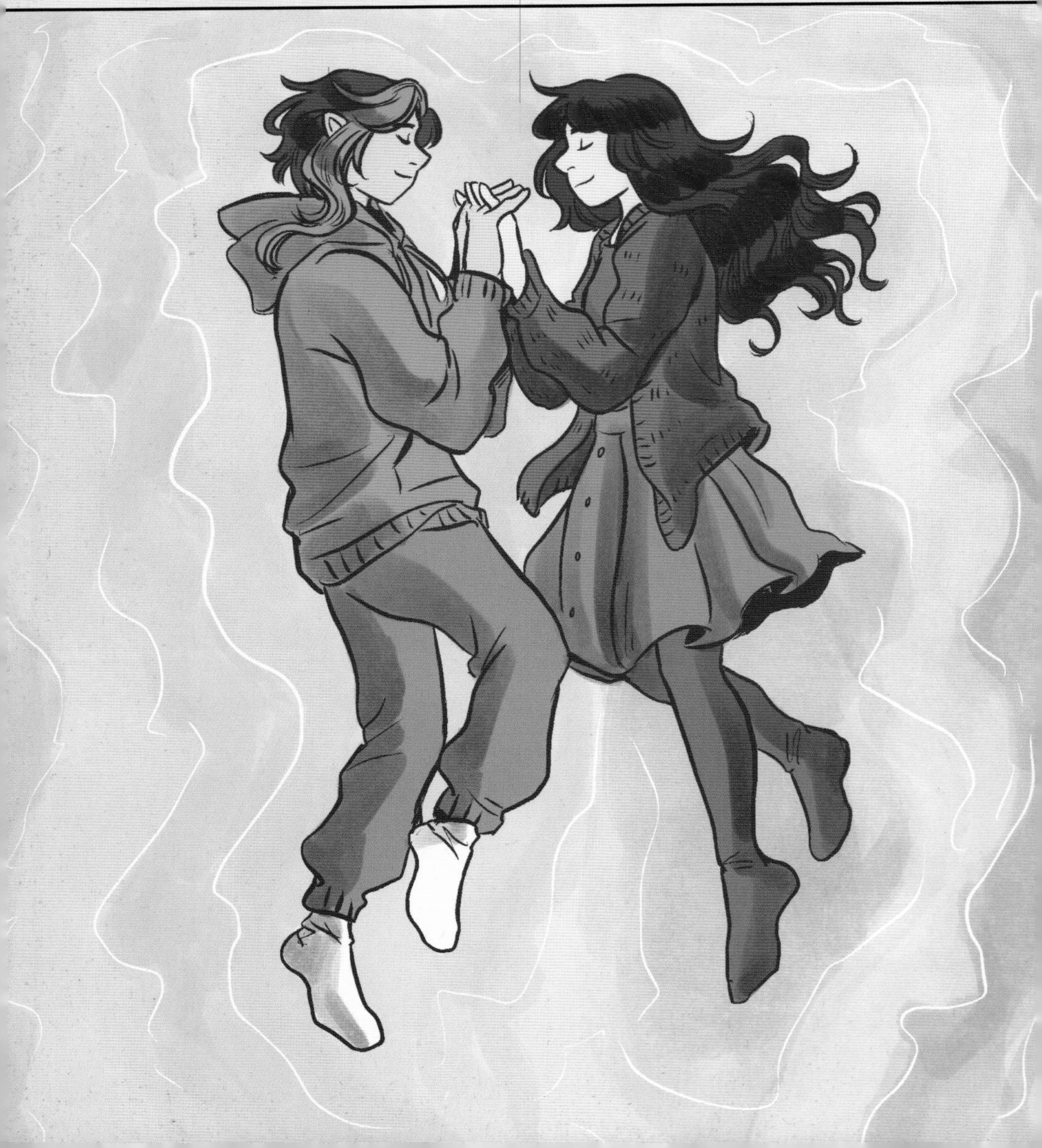

Chapter 5

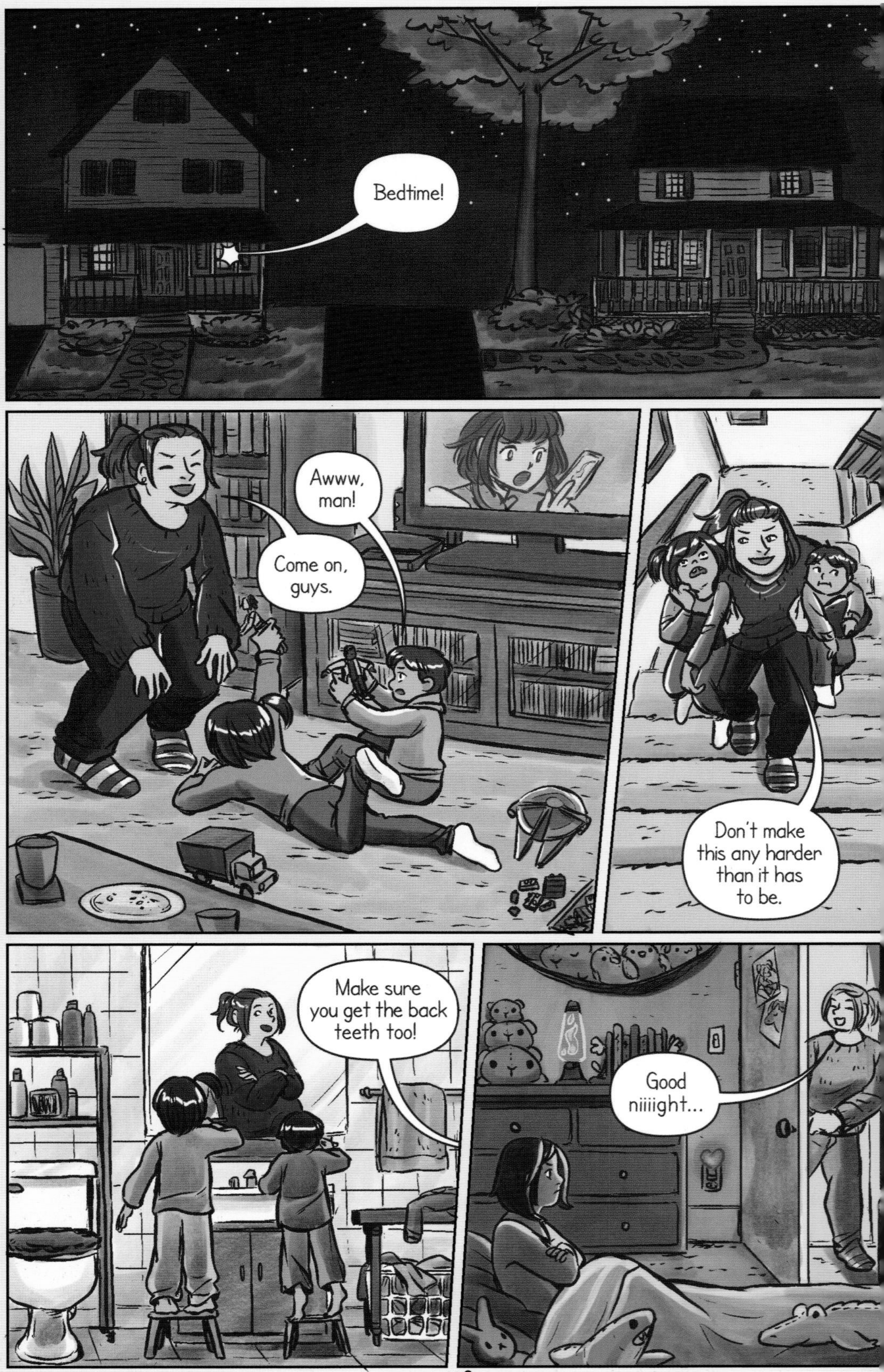
Bedtime!
Come on, guys.
Awww, man!
Don't make this any harder than it has to be.
Make sure you get the back teeth too!
Good niiiight...

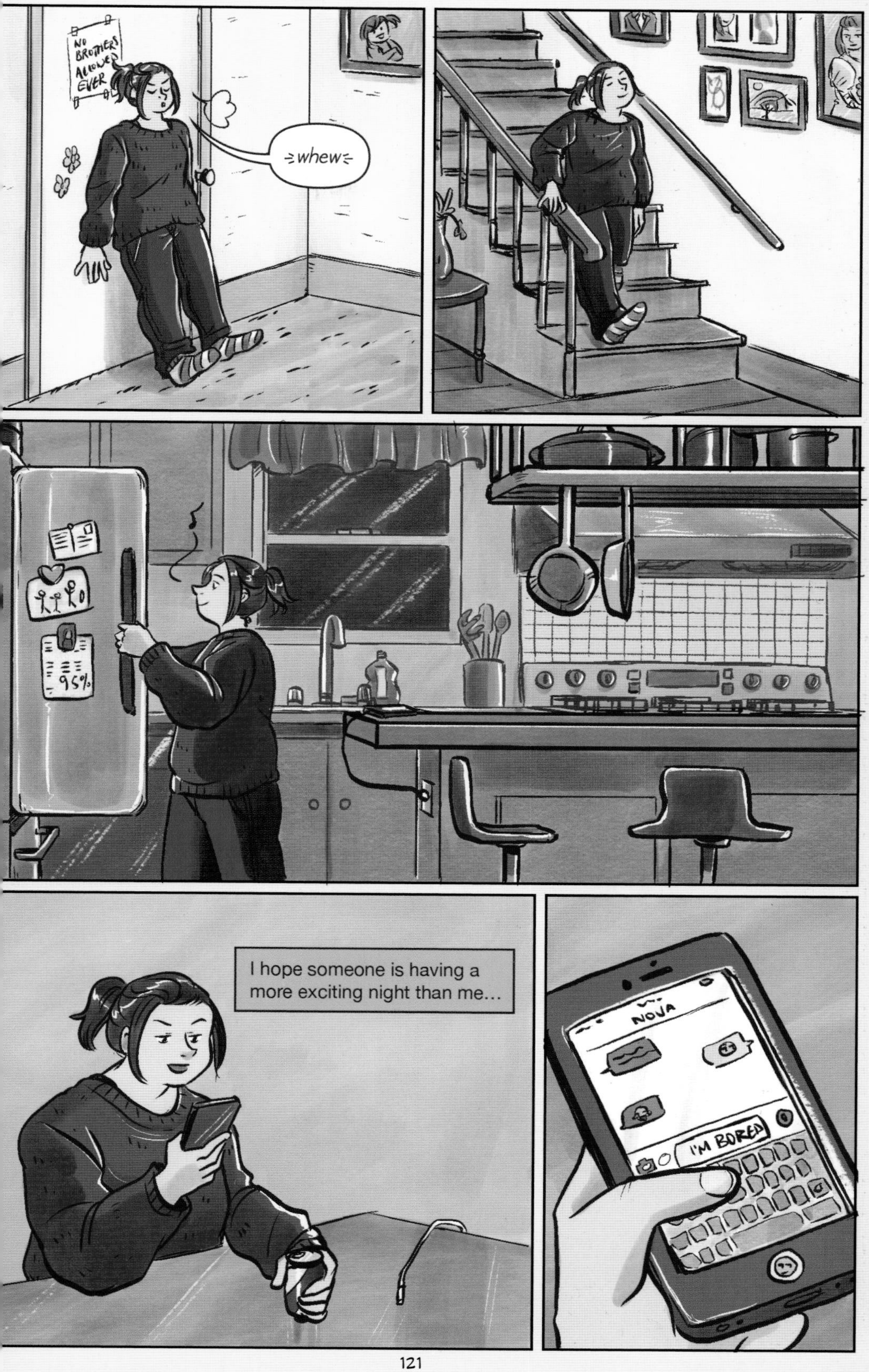
NO BROTHERS ALLOWED EVER
whew
95%
I hope someone is having a more exciting night than me...
NOVA
I'M BORED

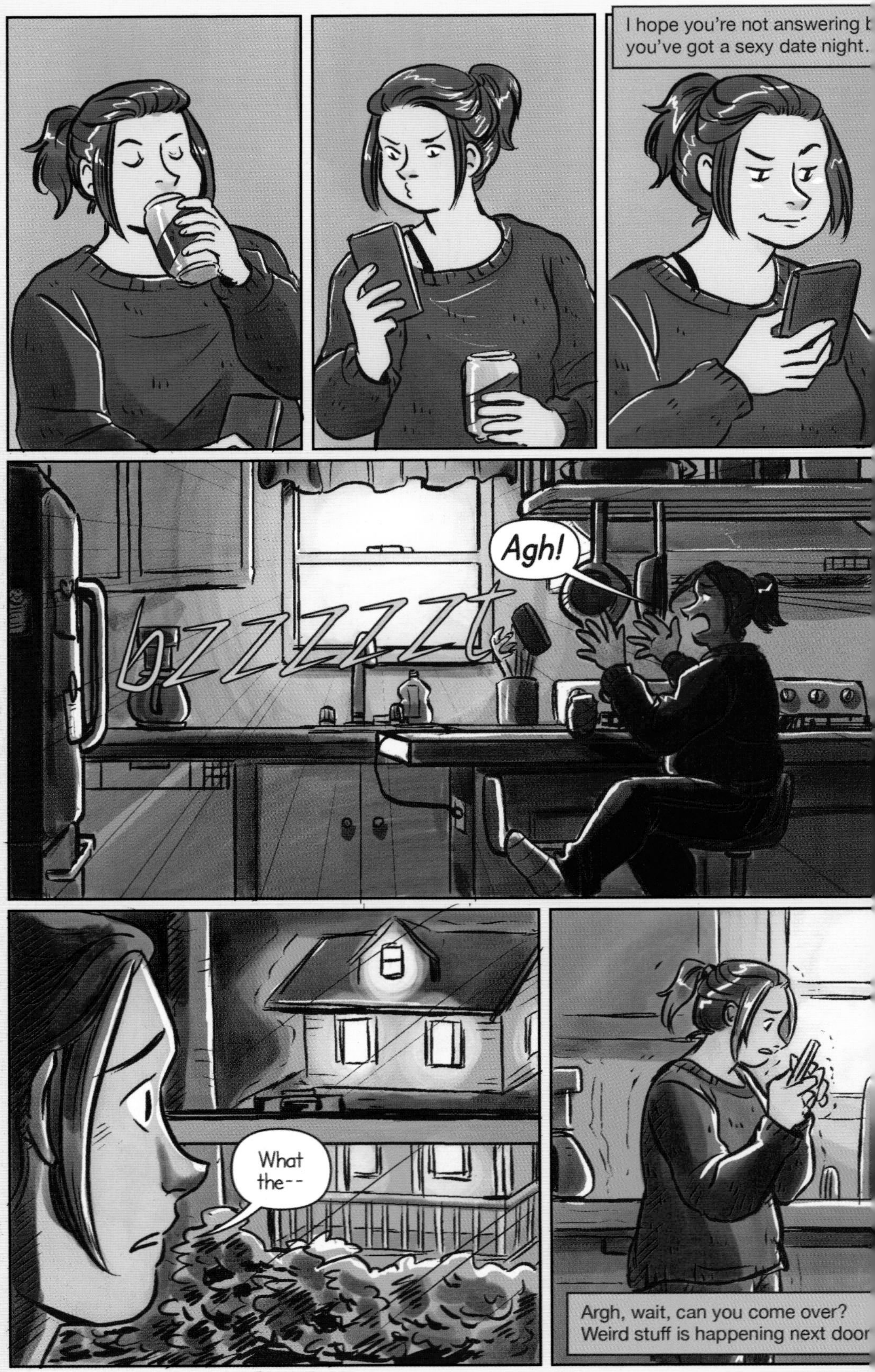
I hope you're not answering b
you've got a sexy date night.
Agh!
bzzzzzzt
What the--
Argh, wait, can you come over?
Weird stuff is happening next door

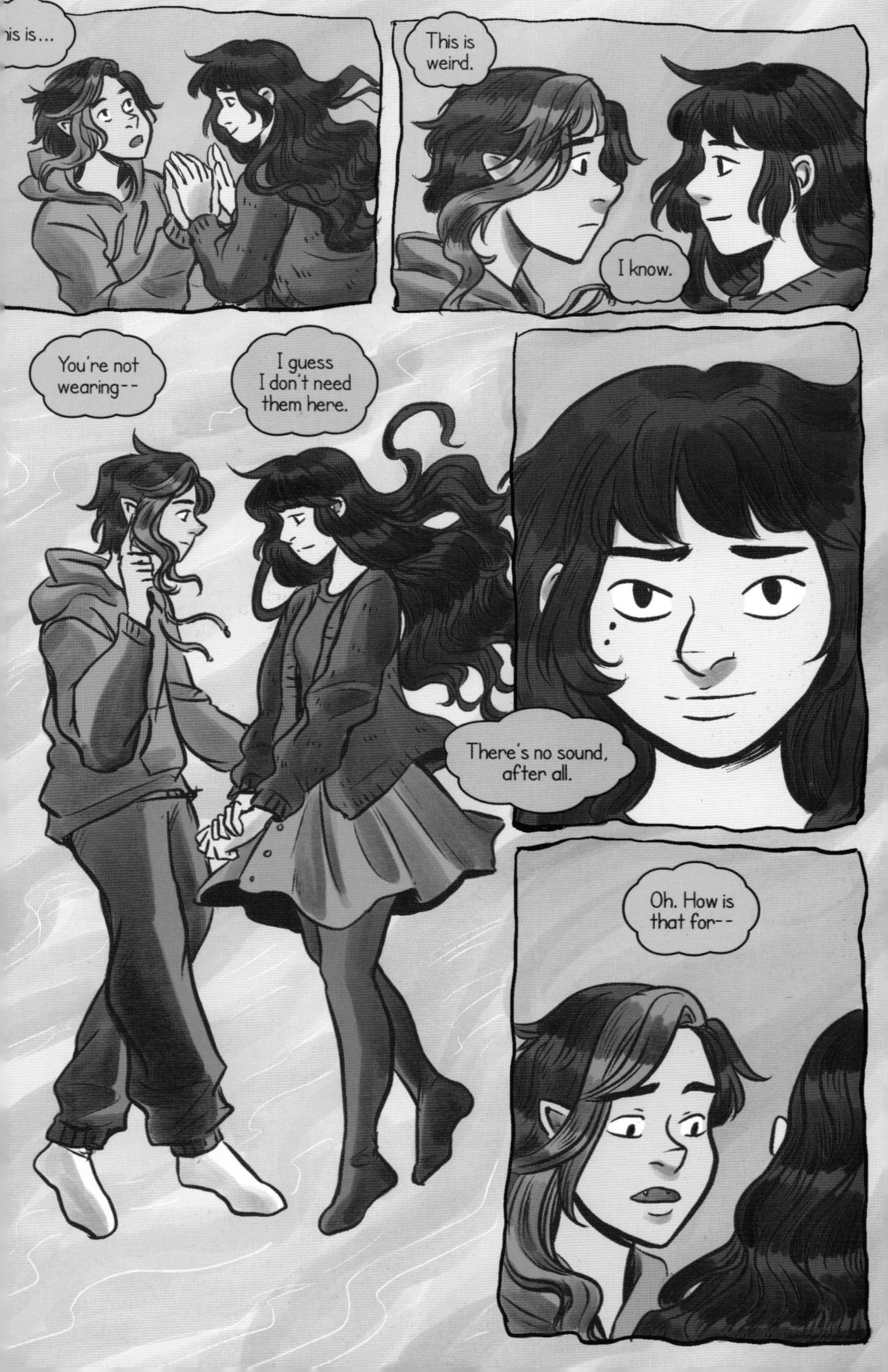

his is...
This is weird.
I know.
You're not wearing--
I guess I don't need them here.
There's no sound, after all.
Oh. How is that for--

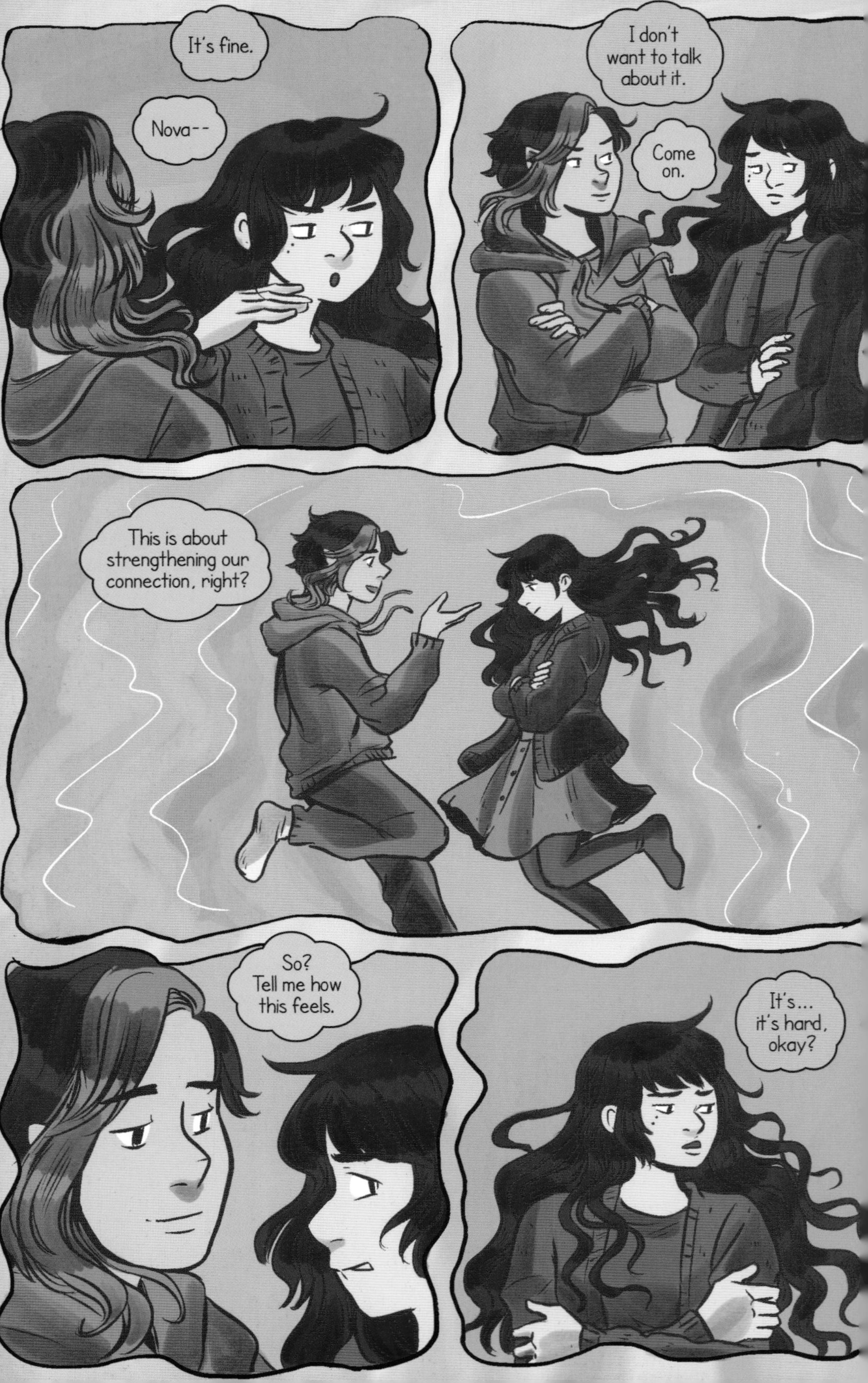
It's fine.
Nova--
I don't want to talk about it.
Come on.
This is about strengthening our connection, right?
So? Tell me how this feels.
It's... it's hard, okay?

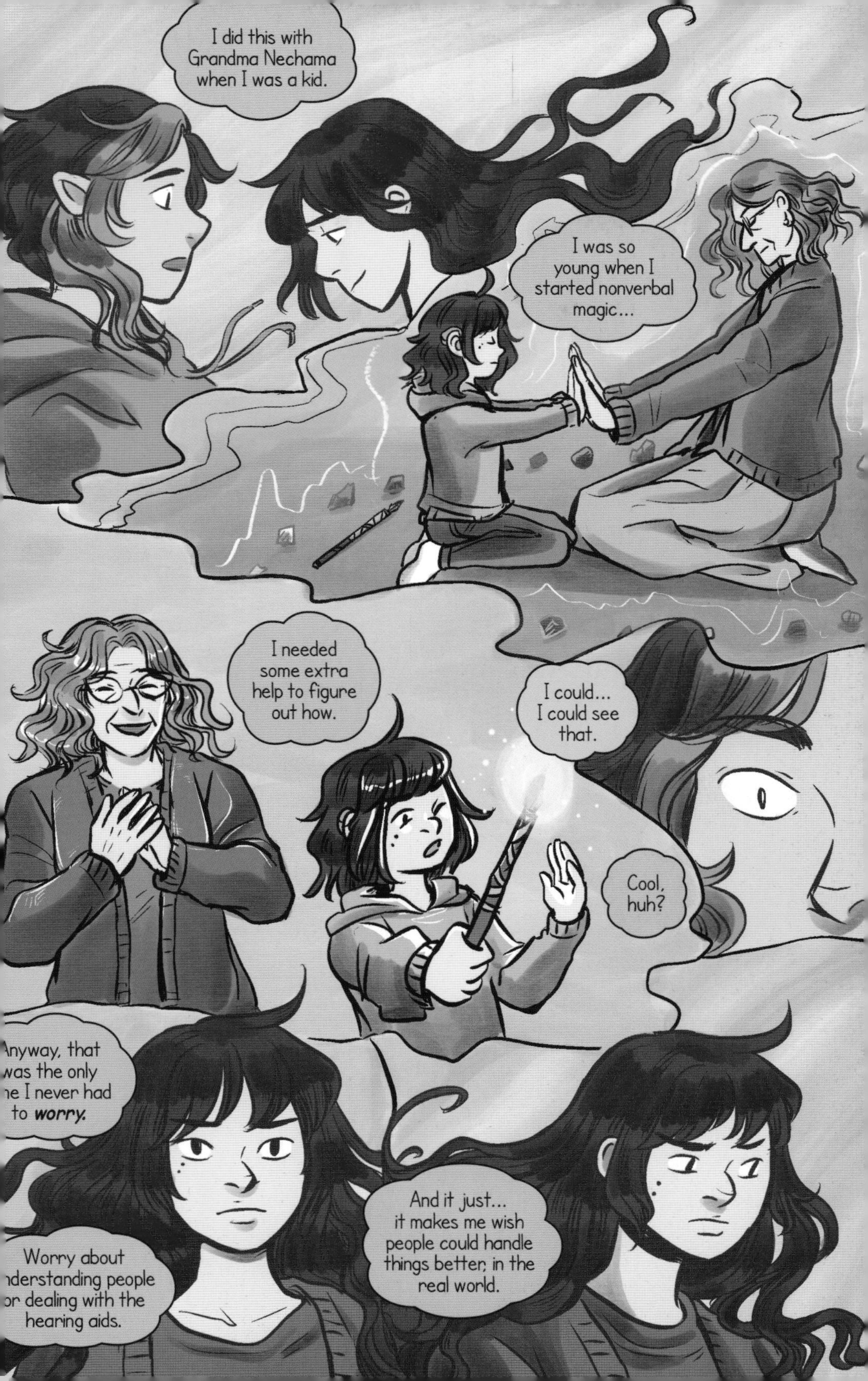
I did this with Grandma Nechama when I was a kid.
I was so young when I started nonverbal magic...
I needed some extra help to figure out how.
I could... I could see that.
Cool, huh?
Anyway, that was the only ne I never had to **worry.**
Worry about nderstanding people or dealing with the hearing aids.
And it just... it makes me wish people could handle things better, in the real world.

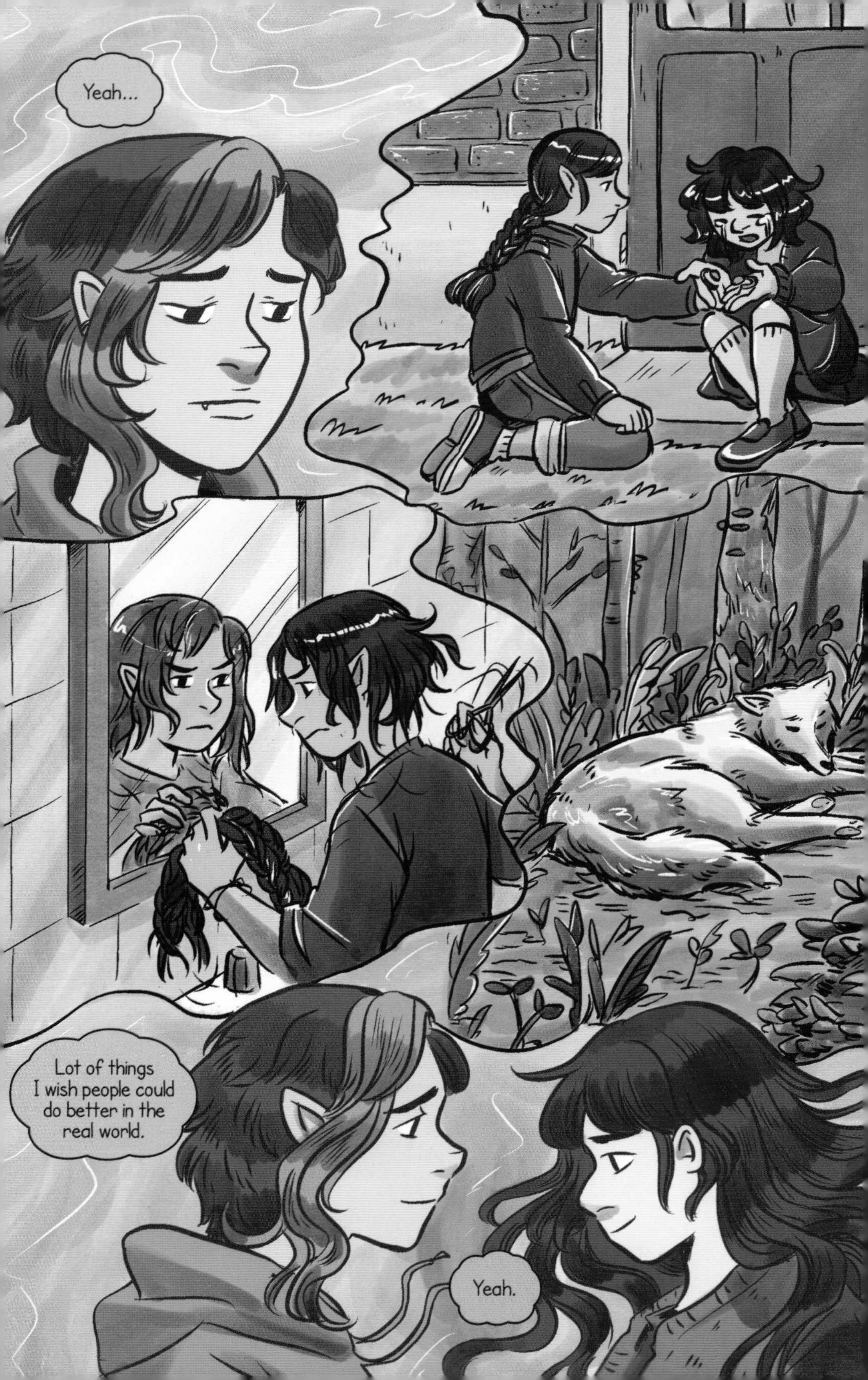
Yeah...
Lot of things I wish people could do better in the real world.
Yeah.

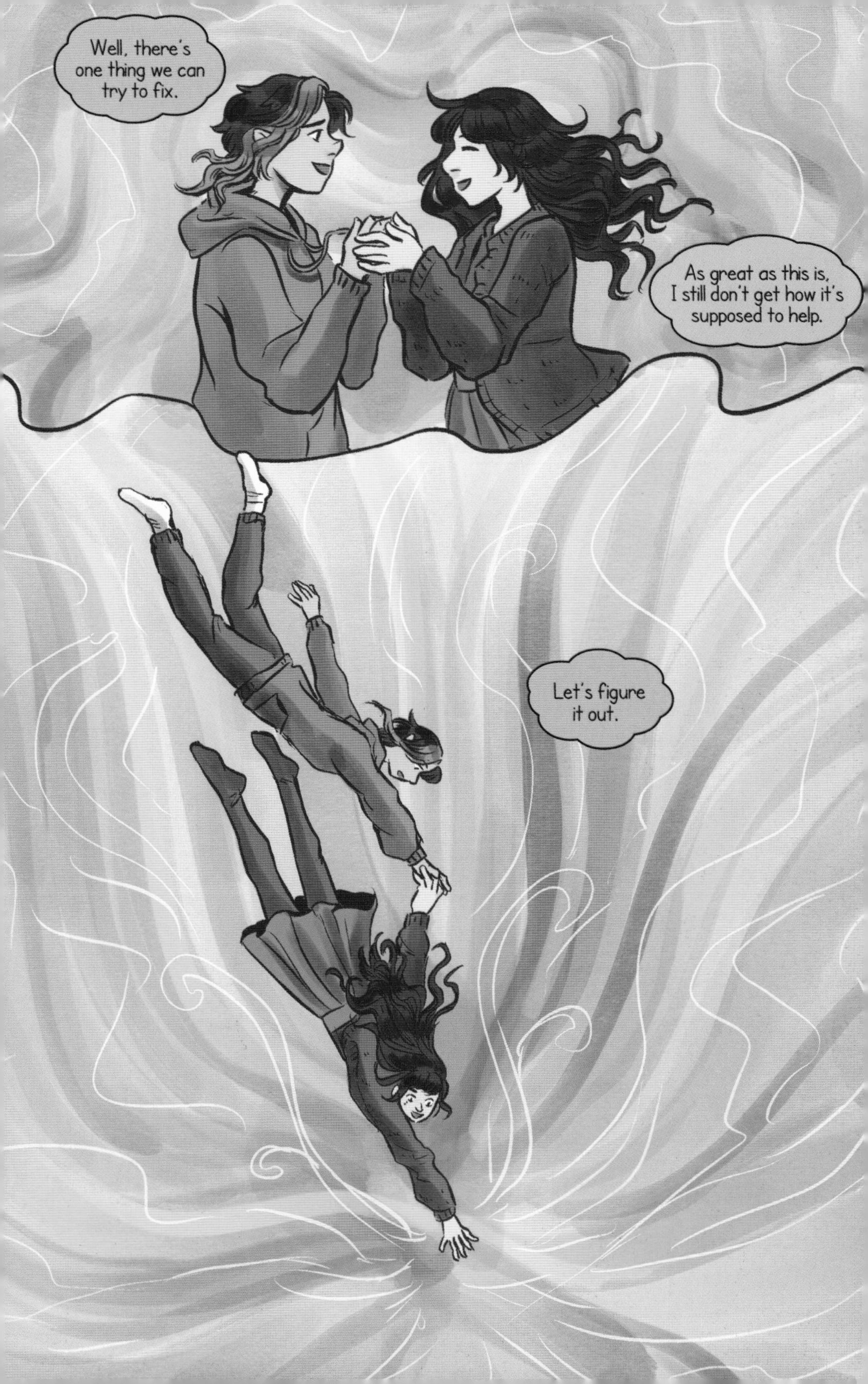
Well, there's one thing we can try to fix.
As great as this is, I still don't get how it's supposed to help.
Let's figure it out.

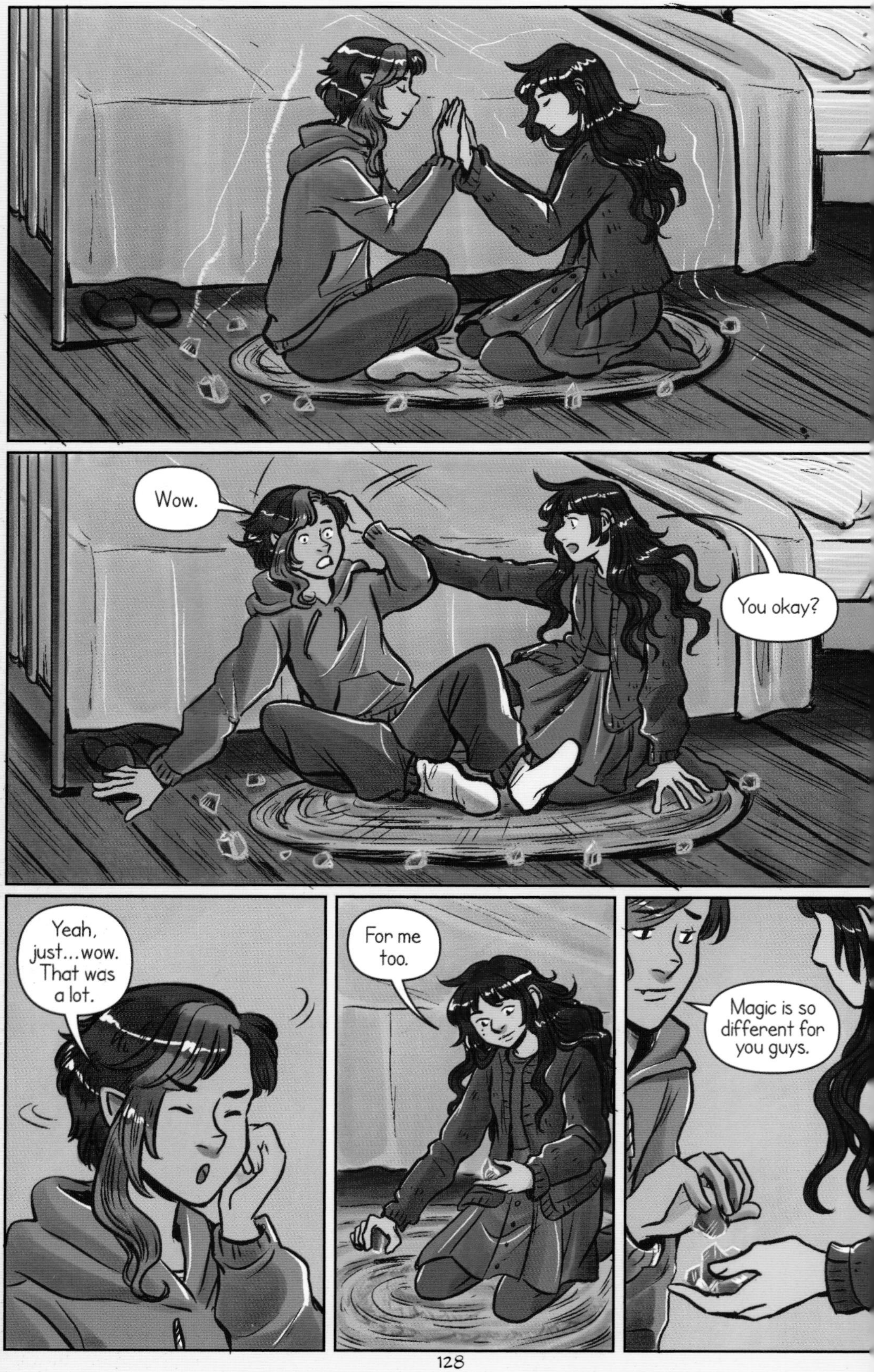
Wow.
You okay?
Yeah, just...wow. That was a lot.
For me too.
Magic is so different for you guys.

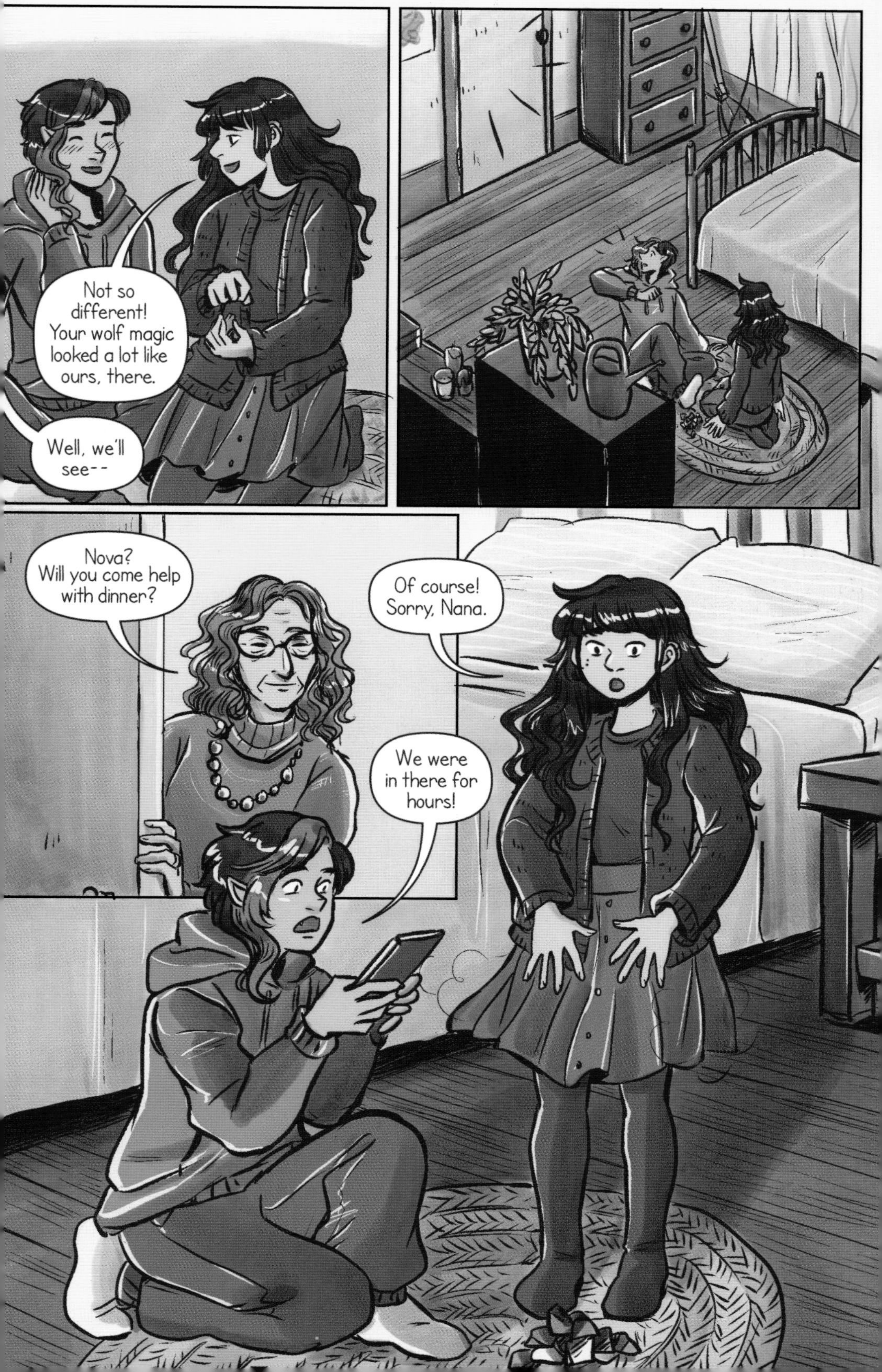

Not so different! Your wolf magic looked a lot like ours, there.
Well, we'll see--
Nova? Will you come help with dinner?
Of course! Sorry, Nana.
We were in there for hours!

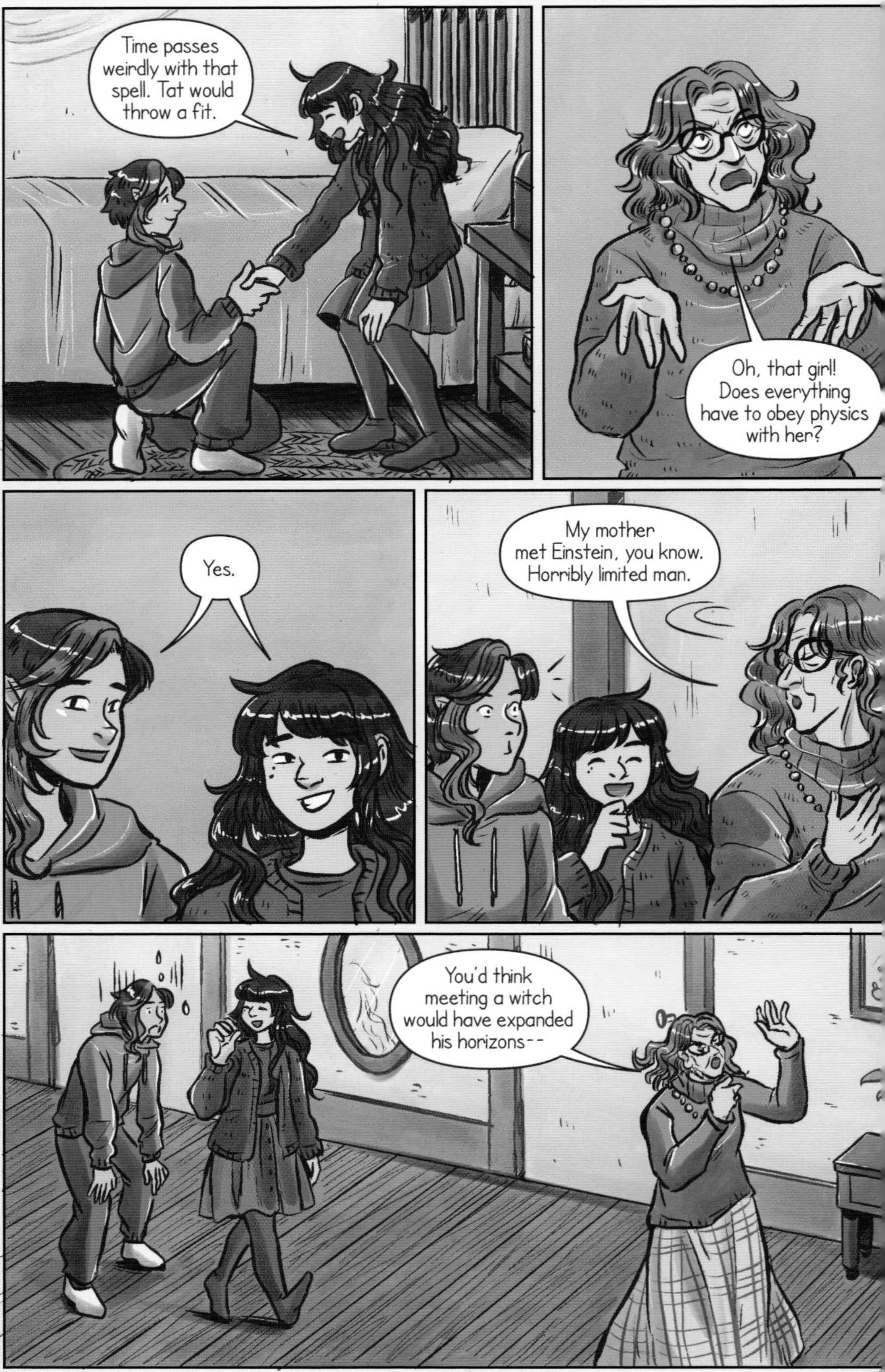
Time passes weirdly with that spell. Tat would throw a fit.
Oh, that girl! Does everything have to obey physics with her?
Yes.
My mother met Einstein, you know. Horribly limited man.
You'd think meeting a witch would have expanded his horizons--

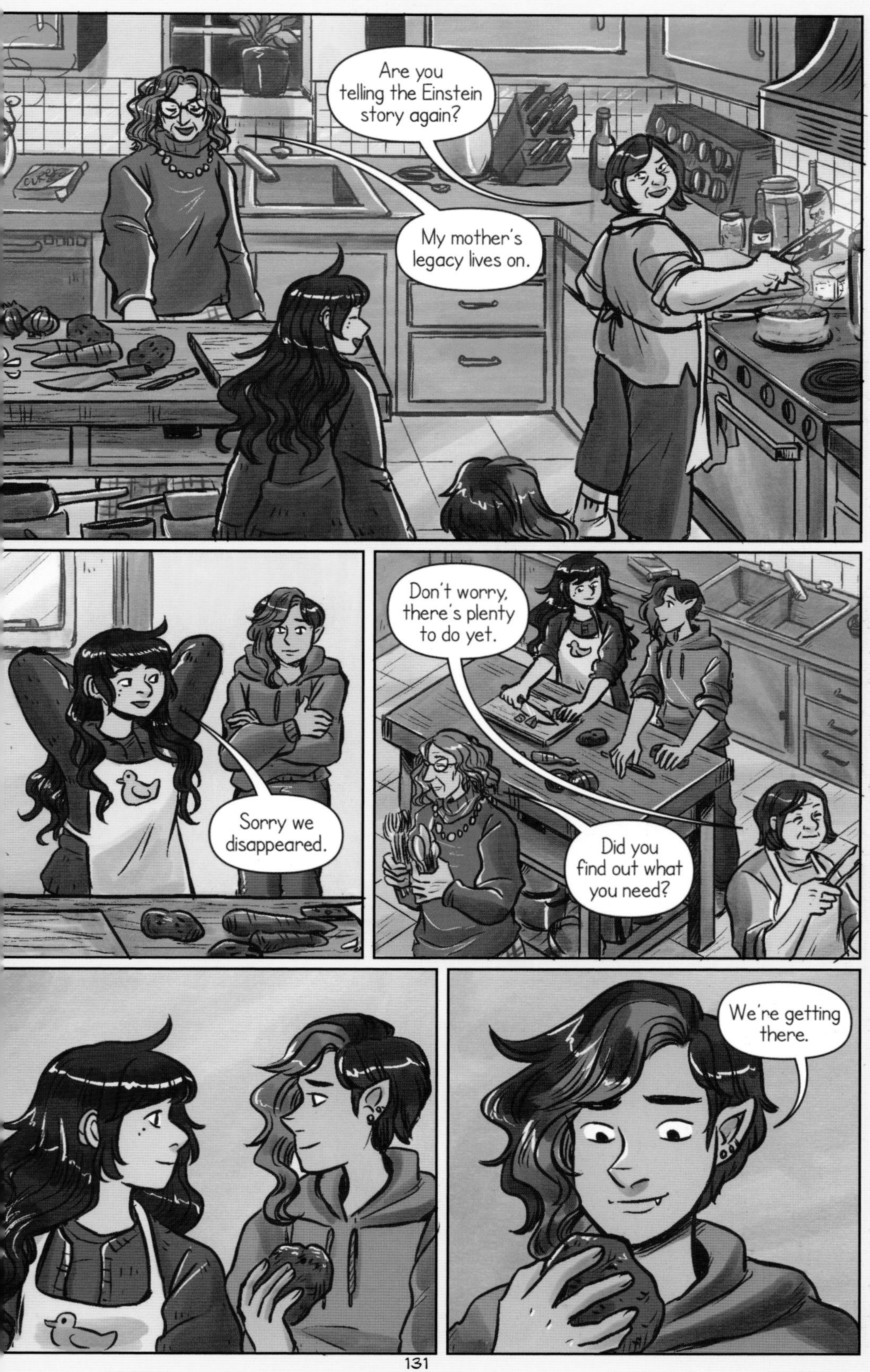
Are you telling the Einstein story again?
My mother's legacy lives on.
Sorry we disappeared.
Don't worry, there's plenty to do yet.
Did you find out what you need?
We're getting there.

Oh! That might be--

Go ahead, dear.

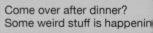

Come over after dinner?
Some weird stuff is happenin

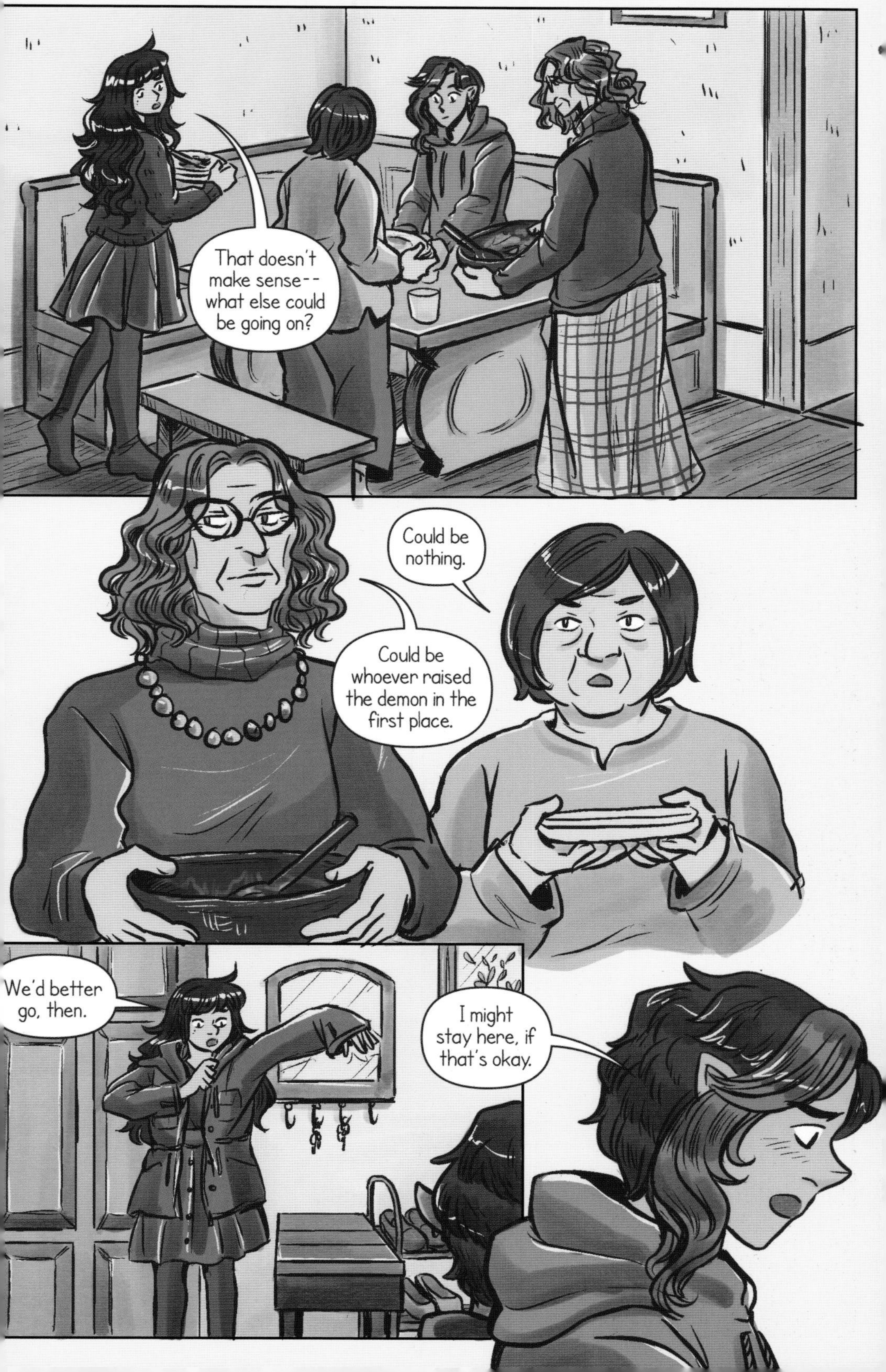
That doesn't make sense--what else could be going on?
Could be nothing.
Could be whoever raised the demon in the first place.
We'd better go, then.
I might stay here, if that's okay.

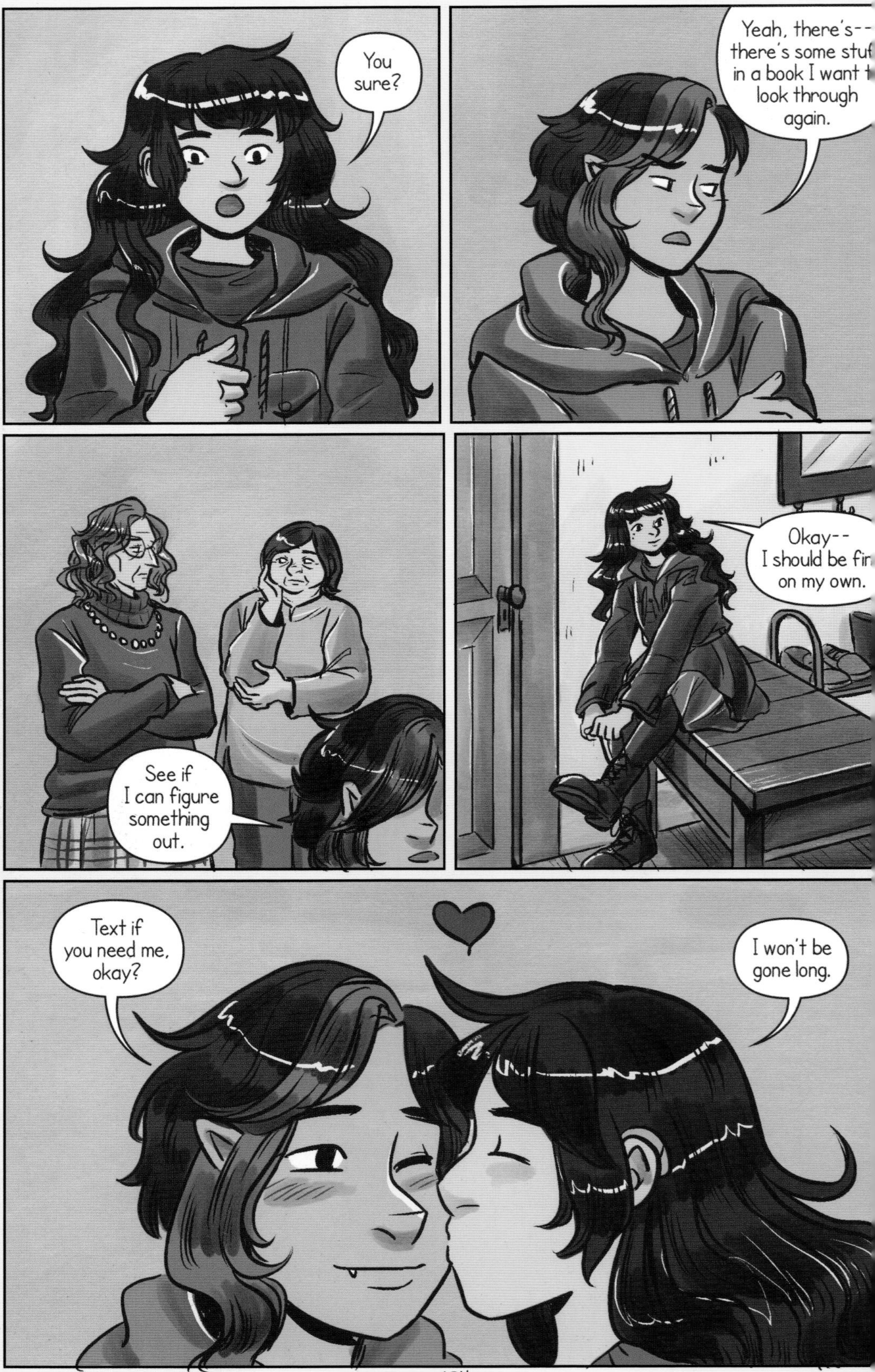
You sure?
Yeah, there's-- there's some stuf in a book I want t look through again.
See if I can figure something out.
Okay-- I should be fin on my own.
Text if you need me, okay?
I won't be gone long.

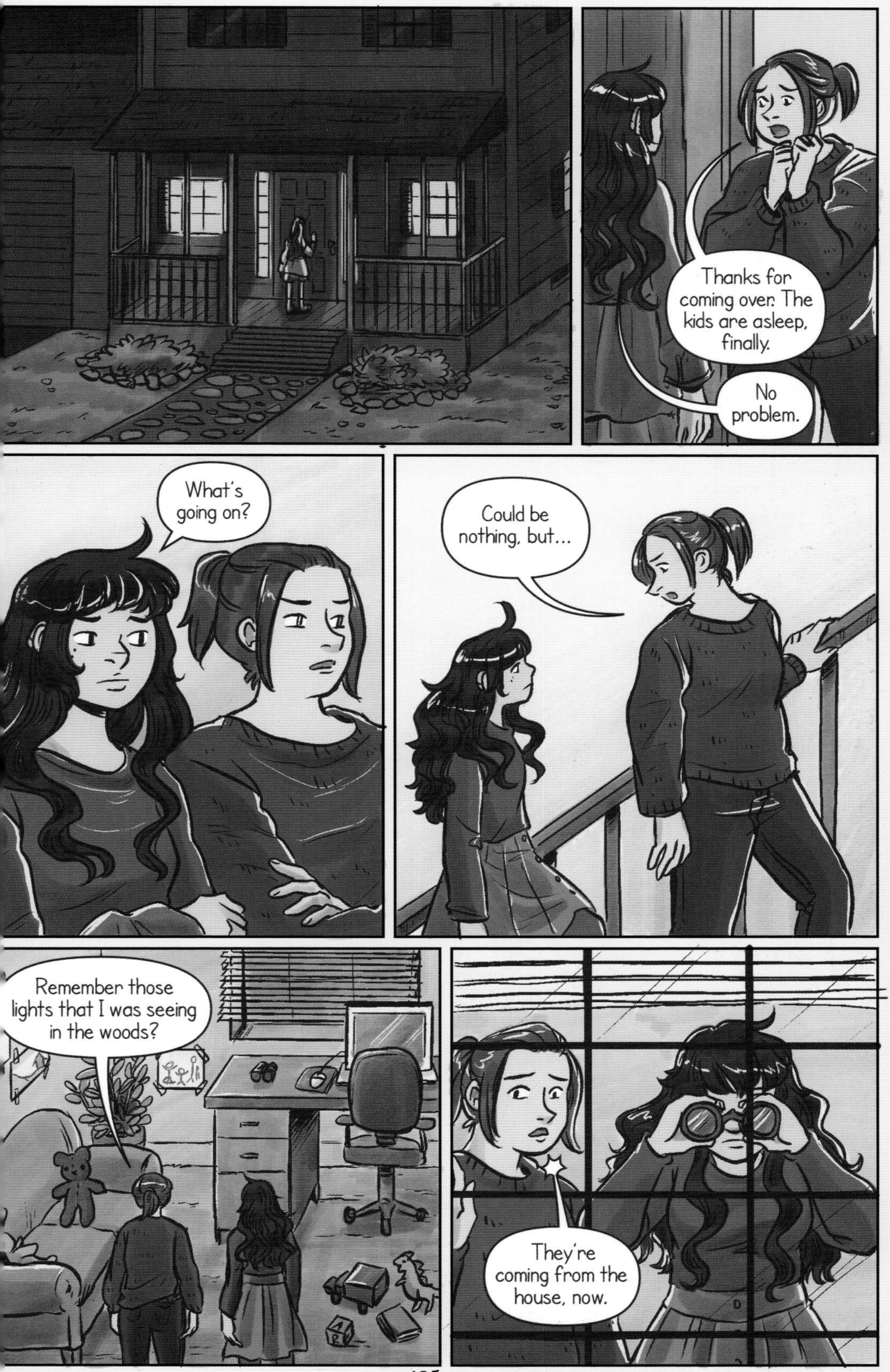
Thanks for coming over. The kids are asleep, finally.
No problem.
What's going on?
Could be nothing, but...
Remember those lights that I was seeing in the woods?
They're coming from the house, now.

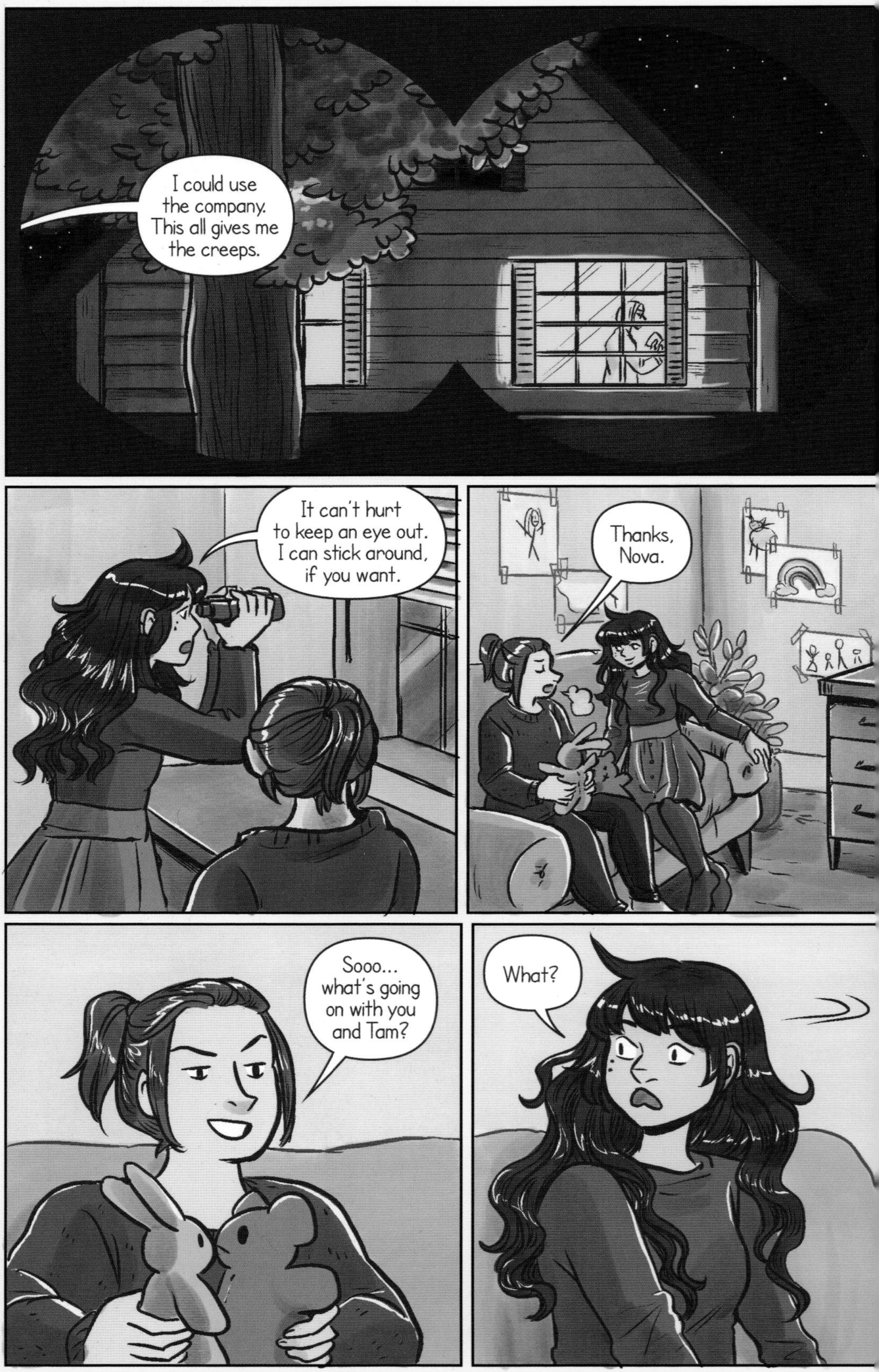
I could use the company. This all gives me the creeps.
It can't hurt to keep an eye out. I can stick around, if you want.
Thanks, Nova.
Sooo... what's going on with you and Tam?
What?

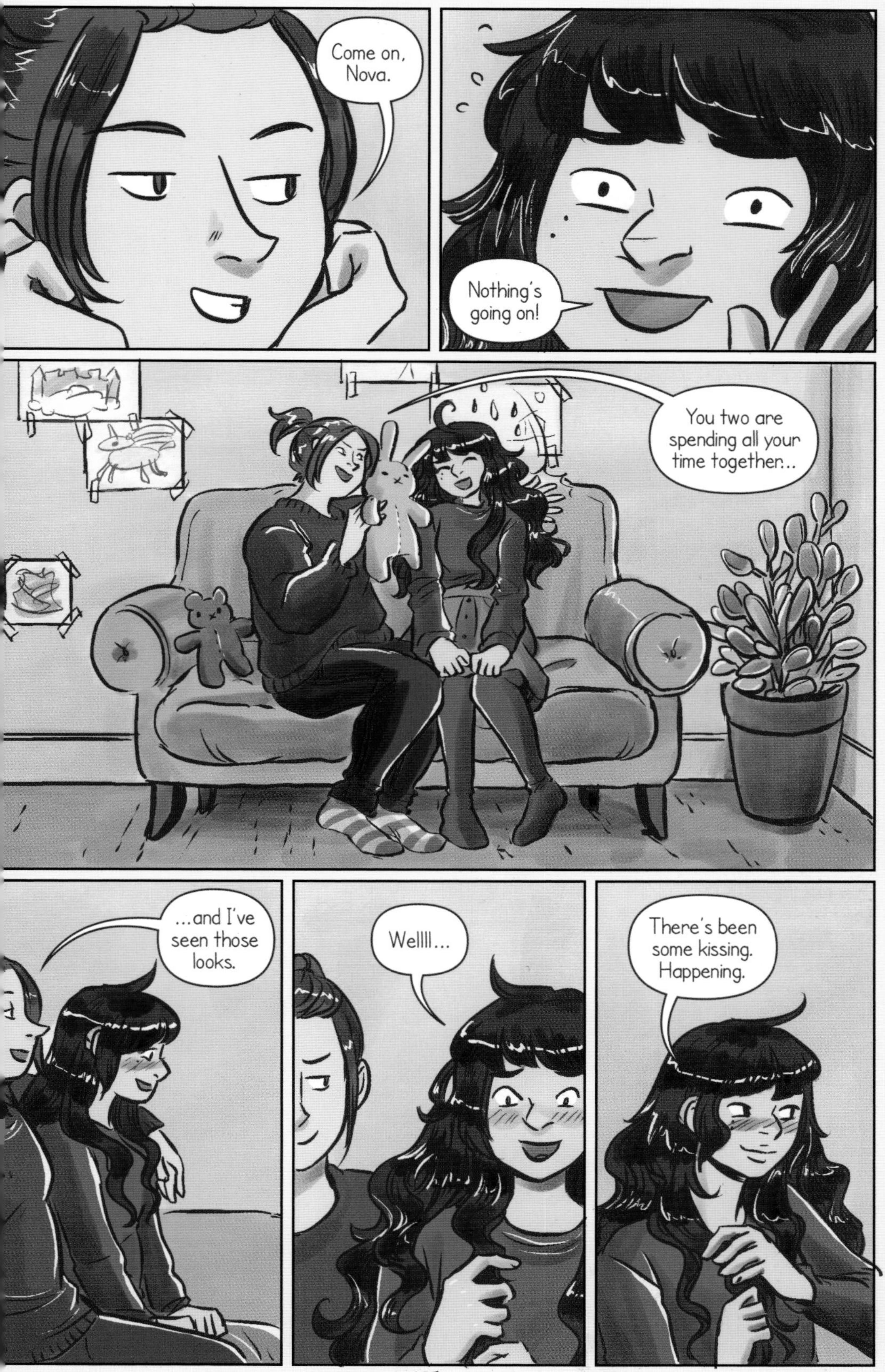
Come on, Nova.
Nothing's going on!
You two are spending all your time together...
...and I've seen those looks.
Wellll...
There's been some kissing. Happening.

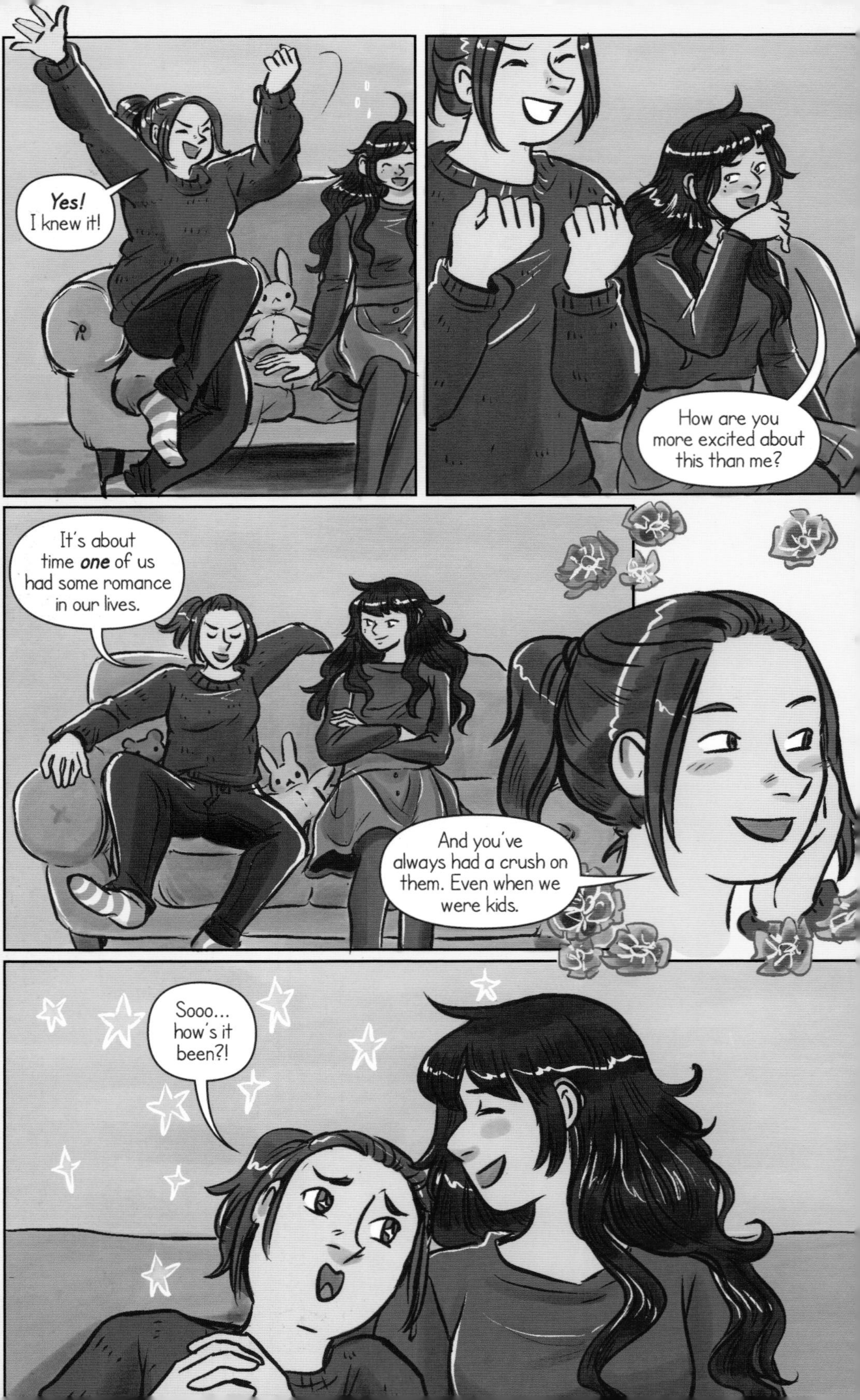

Yes! I knew it!
How are you more excited about this than me?
It's about time ***one*** of us had some romance in our lives.
And you've always had a crush on them. Even when we were kids.
Sooo... how's it been?!

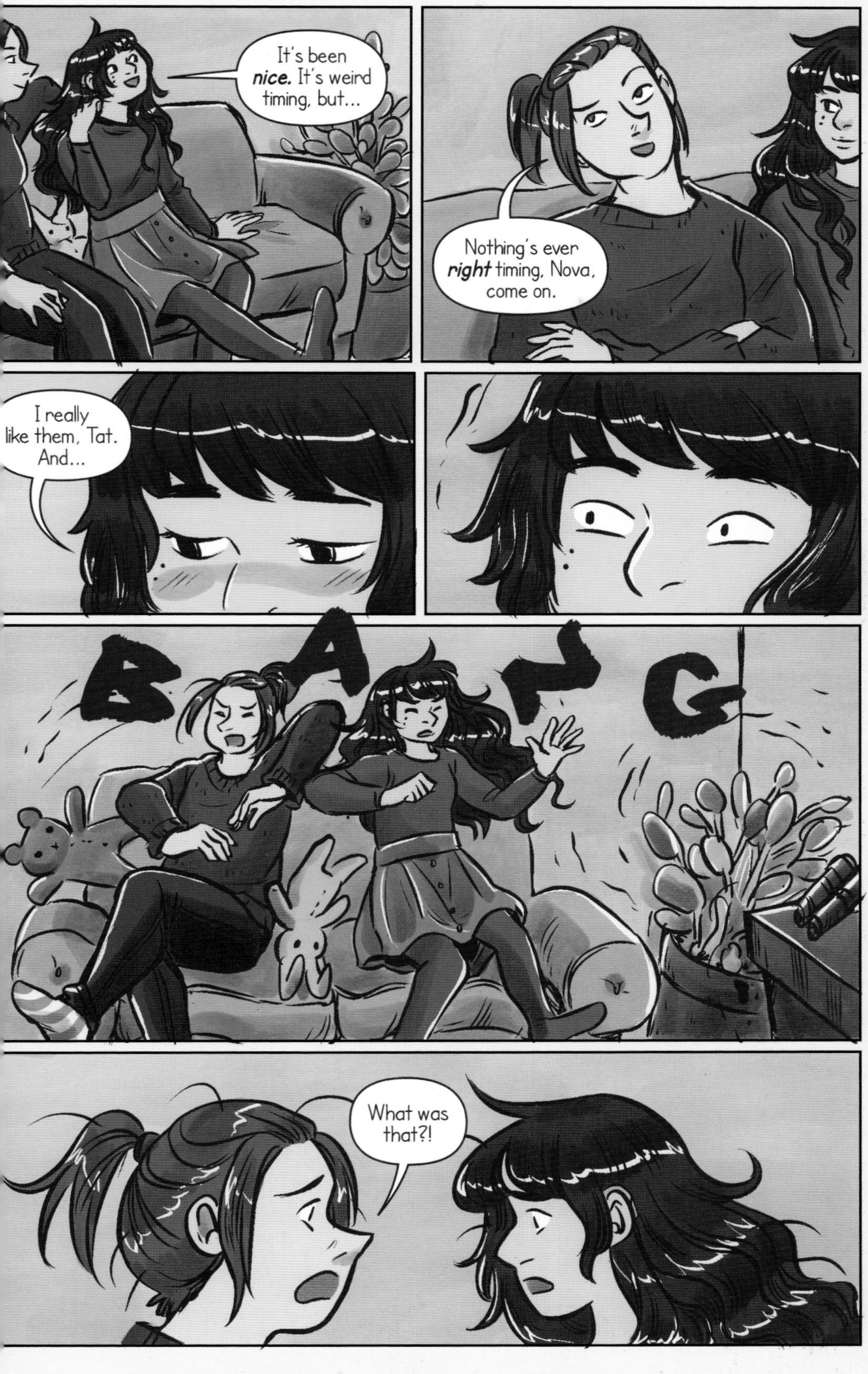
It's been *nice.* It's weird timing, but...
Nothing's ever *right* timing, Nova, come on.
I really like them, Tat. And...
BANG
What was that?!

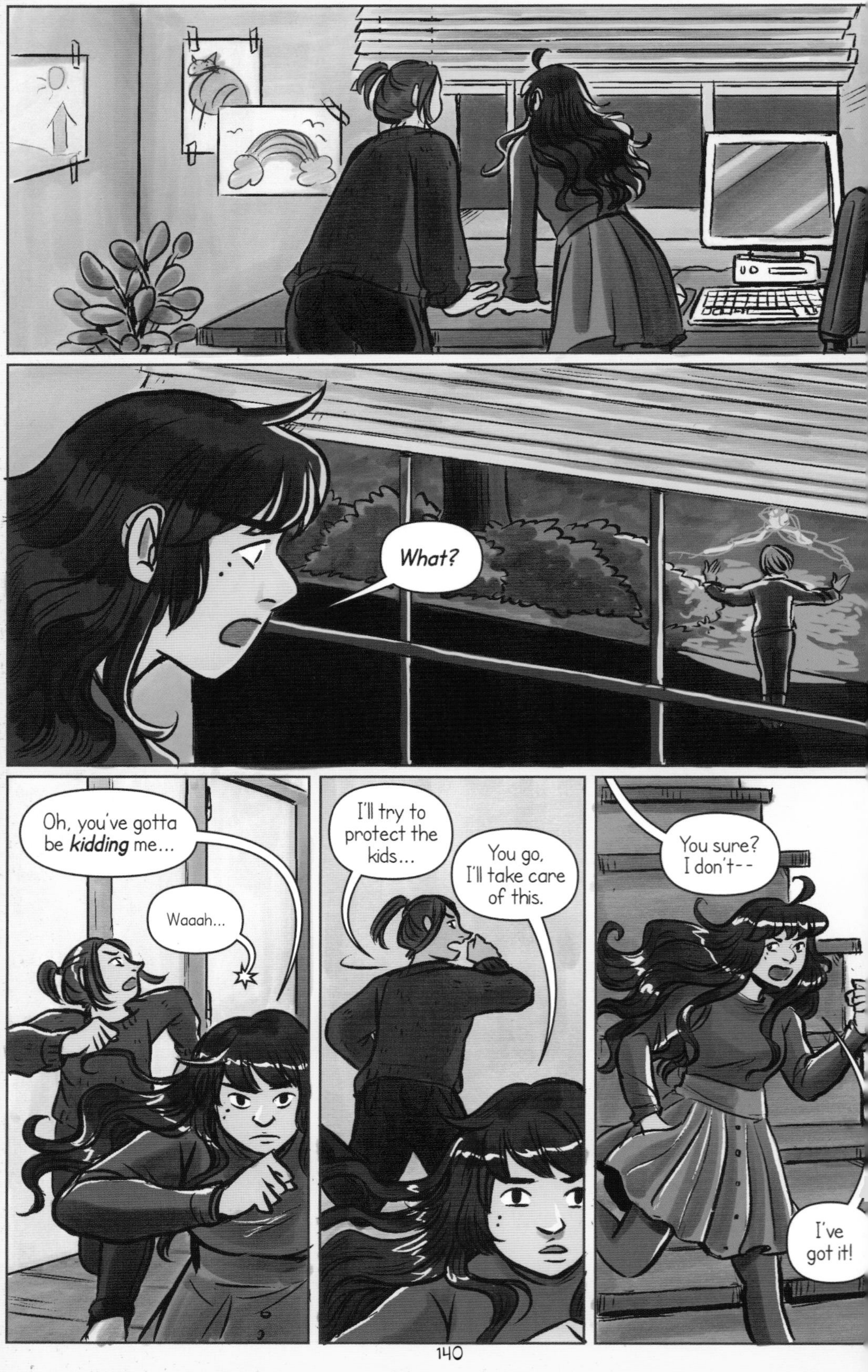
What?
Oh, you've gotta be ***kidding*** me...
Waaah...
I'll try to protect the kids...
You go, I'll take care of this.
You sure? I don't--
I've got it!

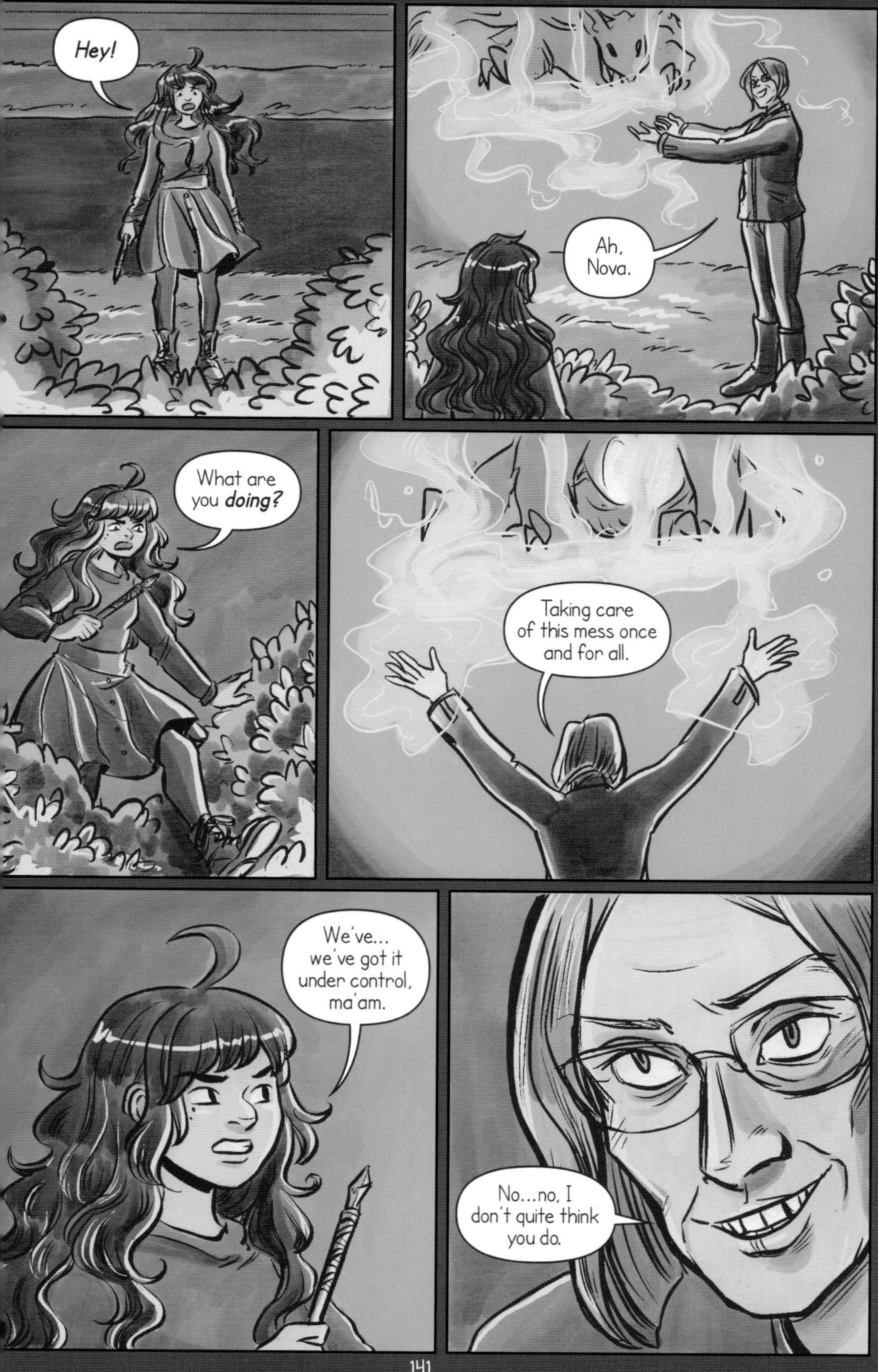
Hey!
Ah, Nova.
What are you *doing?*
Taking care of this mess once and for all.
We've... we've got it under control, ma'am.
No...no, I don't quite think you do.

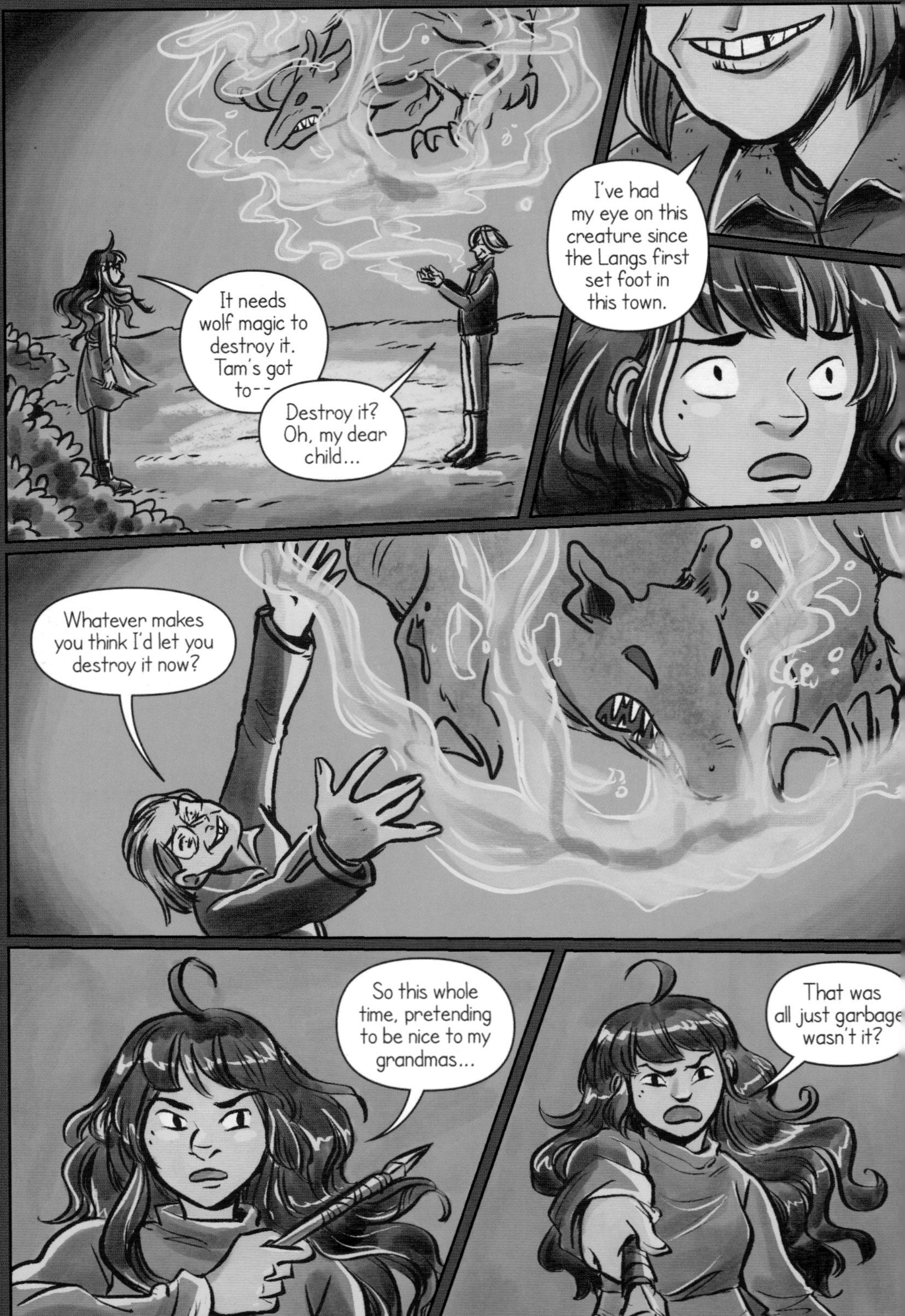
It needs wolf magic to destroy it. Tam's got to--
Destroy it? Oh, my dear child...
I've had my eye on this creature since the Langs first set foot in this town.
Whatever makes you think I'd let you destroy it now?
So this whole time, pretending to be nice to my grandmas...
That was all just garbage wasn't it?

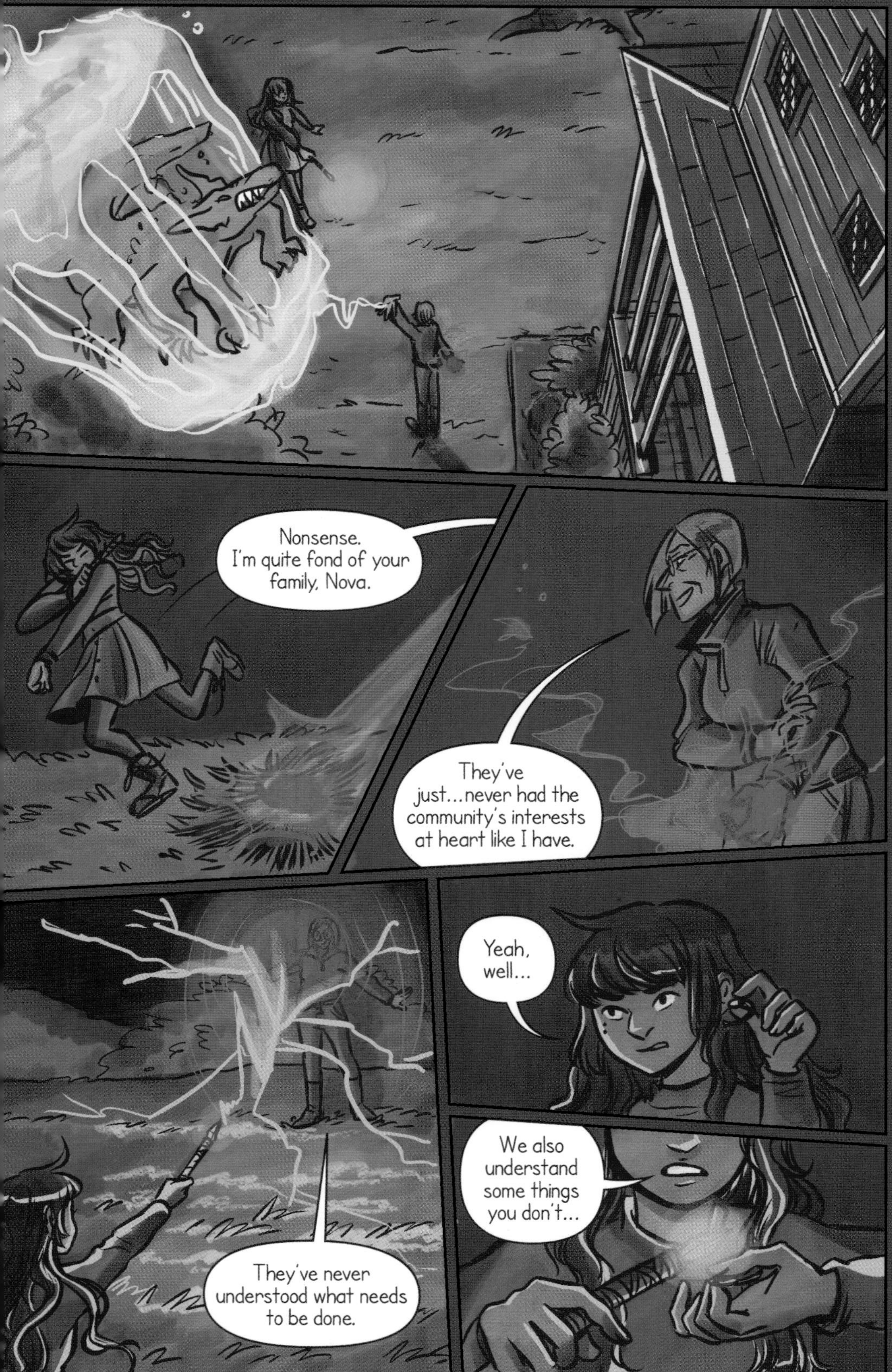
Nonsense. I'm quite fond of your family, Nova.
They've just...never had the community's interests at heart like I have.
They've never understood what needs to be done.
Yeah, well...
We also understand some things you don't...

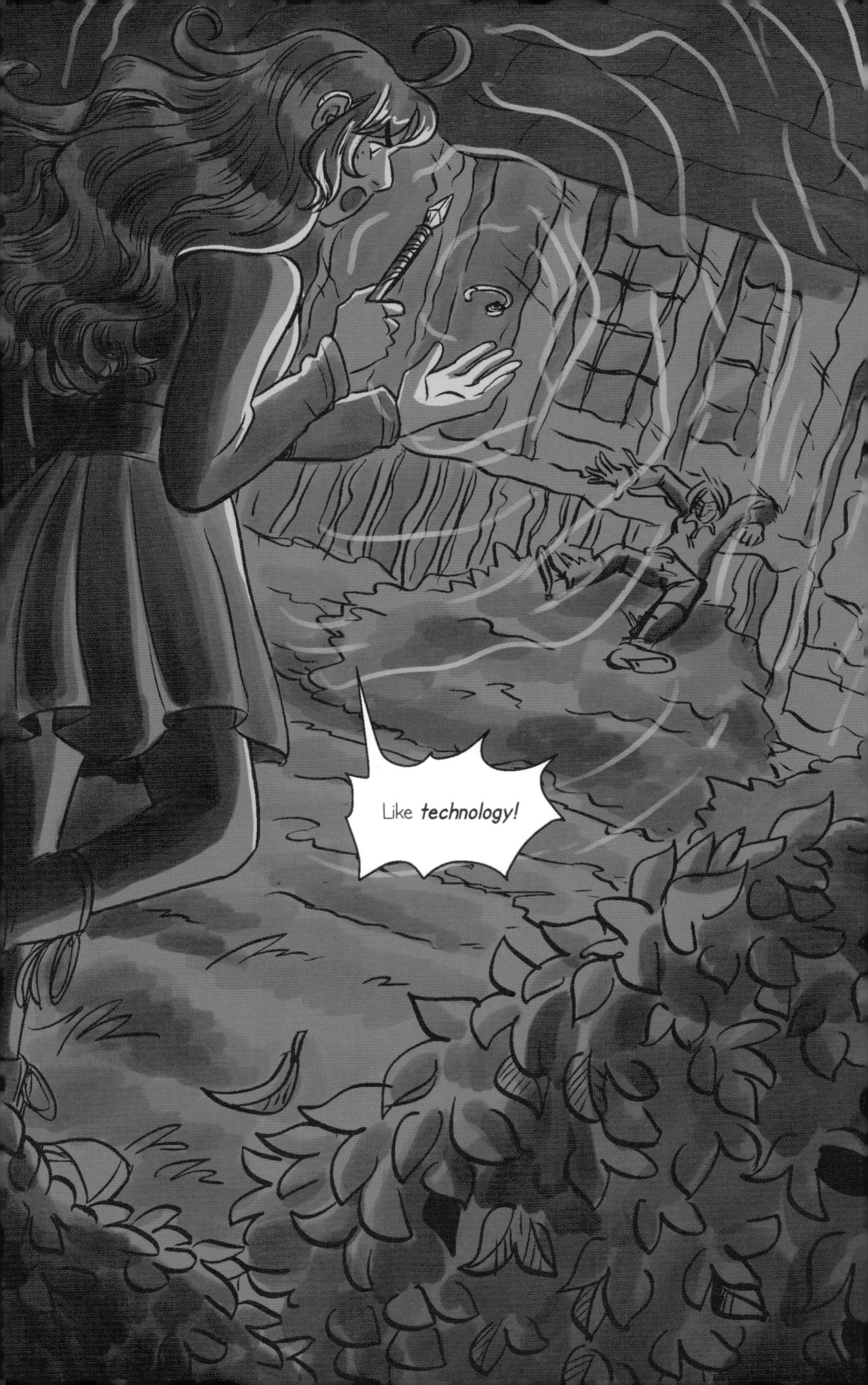
Like technology!

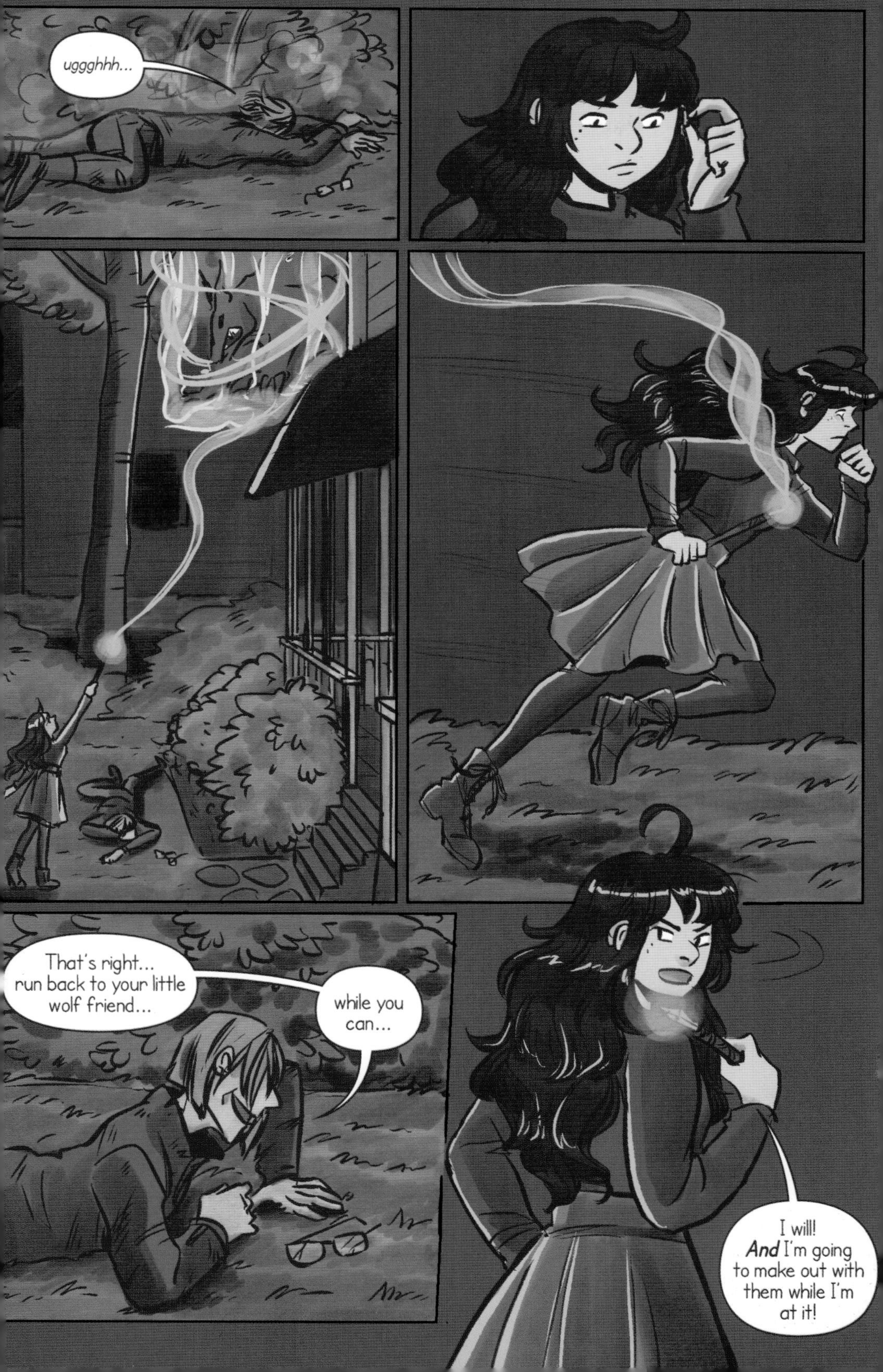
uggghhh...
That's right... run back to your little wolf friend...
while you can...
I will! ***And*** I'm going to make out with them while I'm at it!

Chapter 6

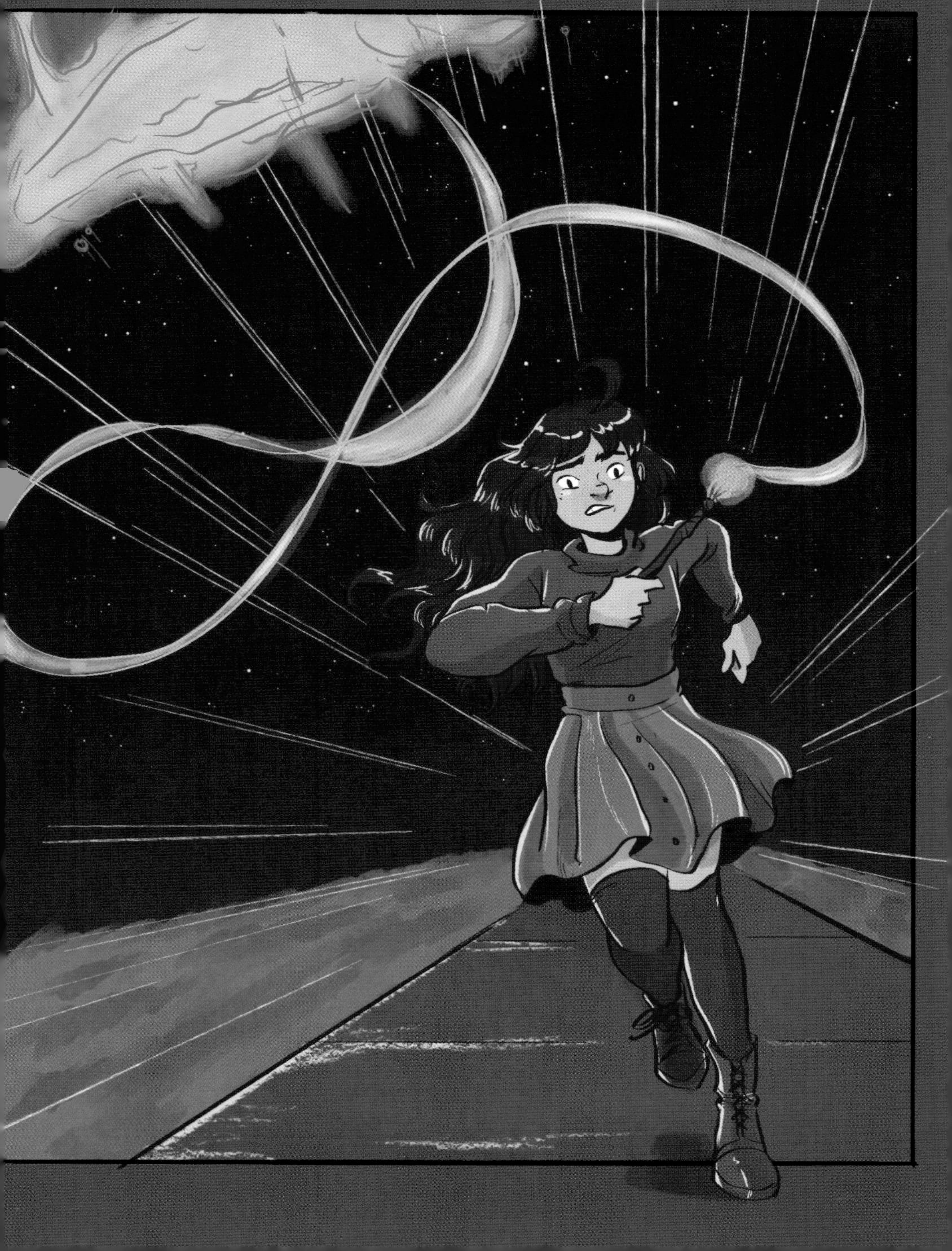

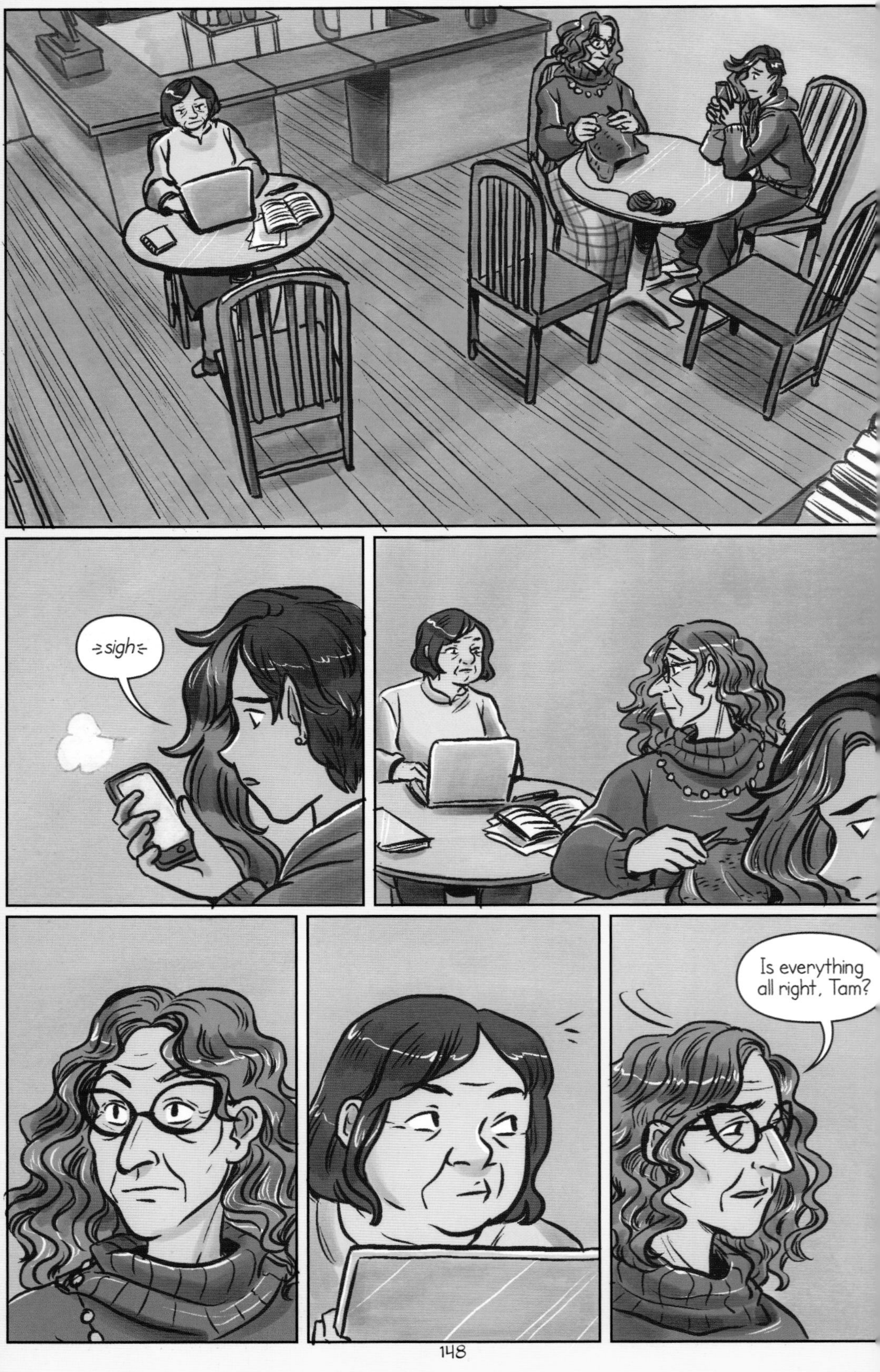
sigh
Is everything all right, Tam?

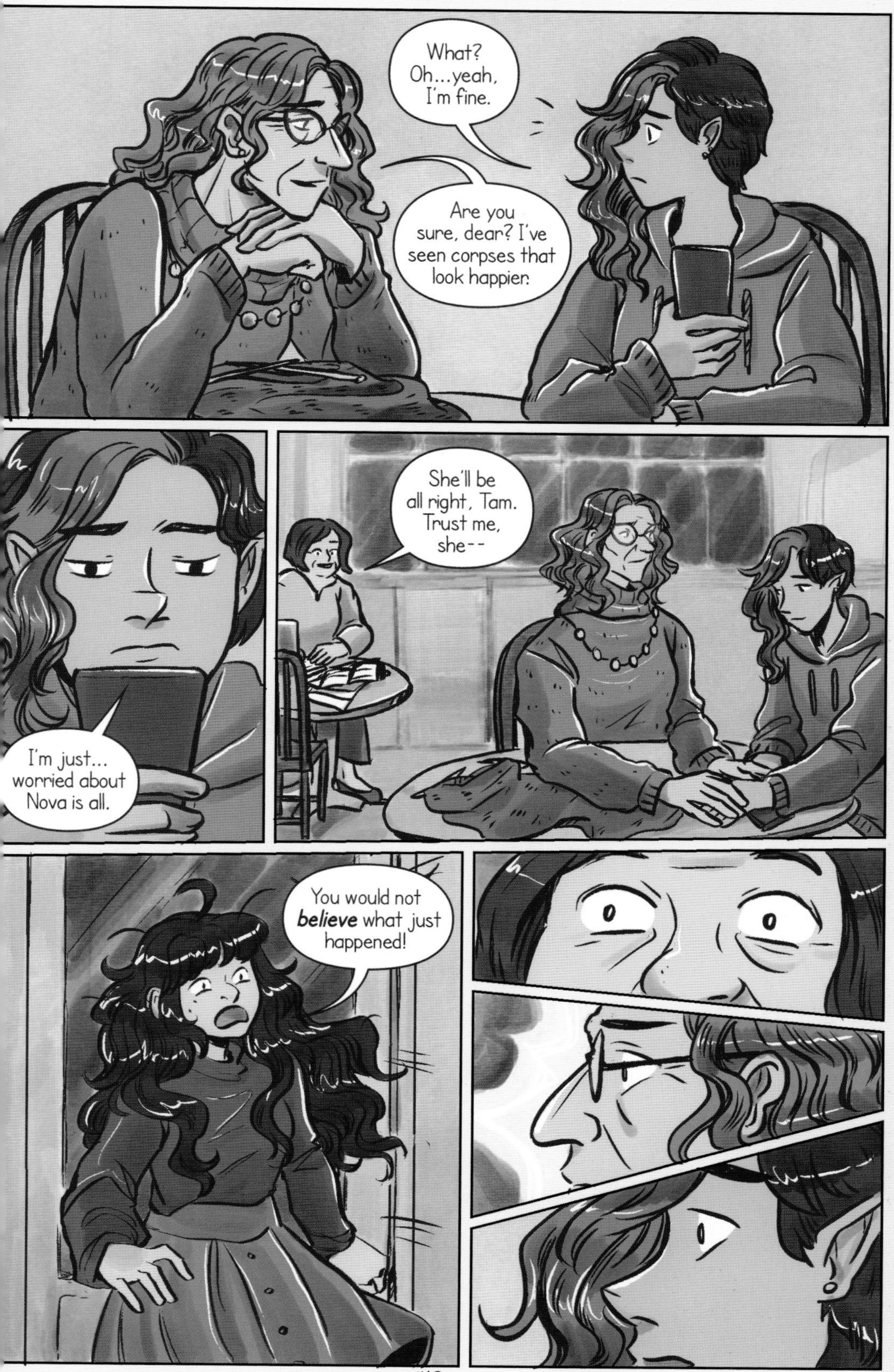
What? Oh...yeah, I'm fine.
Are you sure, dear? I've seen corpses that look happier.
I'm just... worried about Nova is all.
She'll be all right, Tam. Trust me, she--
You would not **believe** what just happened!

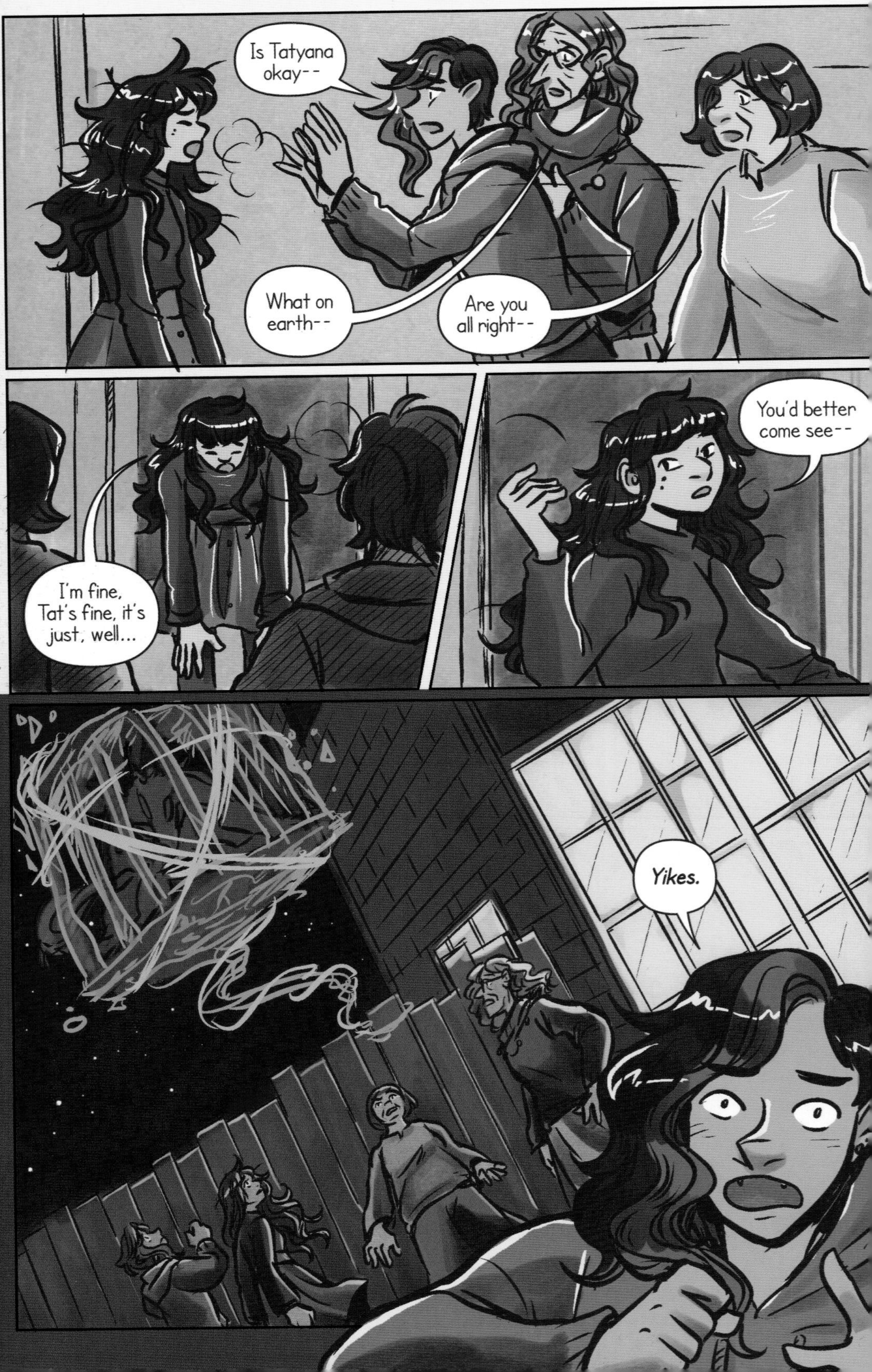
Is Tatyana okay--
What on earth--
Are you all right--
I'm fine, Tat's fine, it's just, well...
You'd better come see--
Yikes.

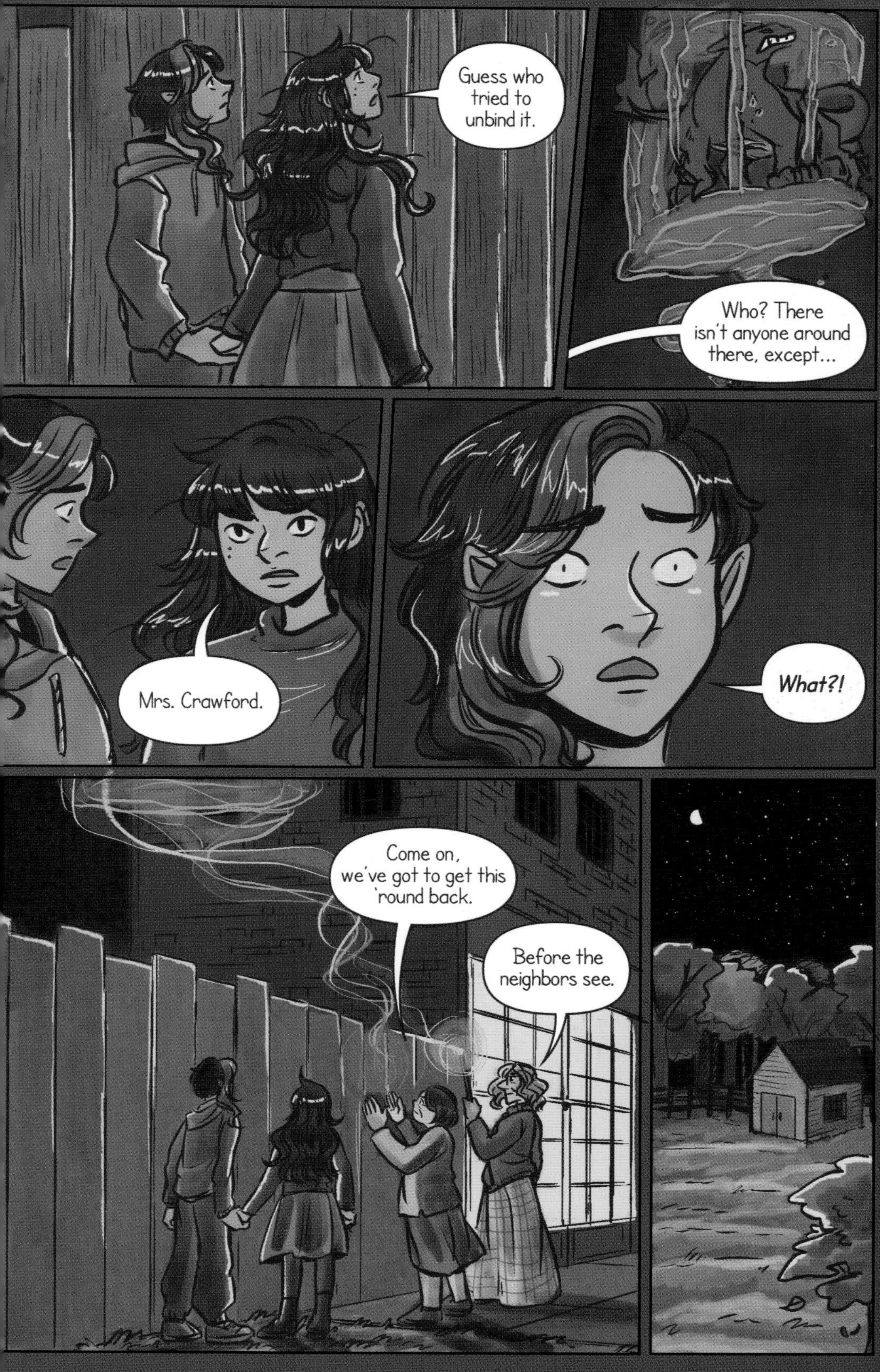
Guess who tried to unbind it.
Who? There isn't anyone around there, except...
Mrs. Crawford.
What?!
Come on, we've got to get this 'round back.
Before the neighbors see.

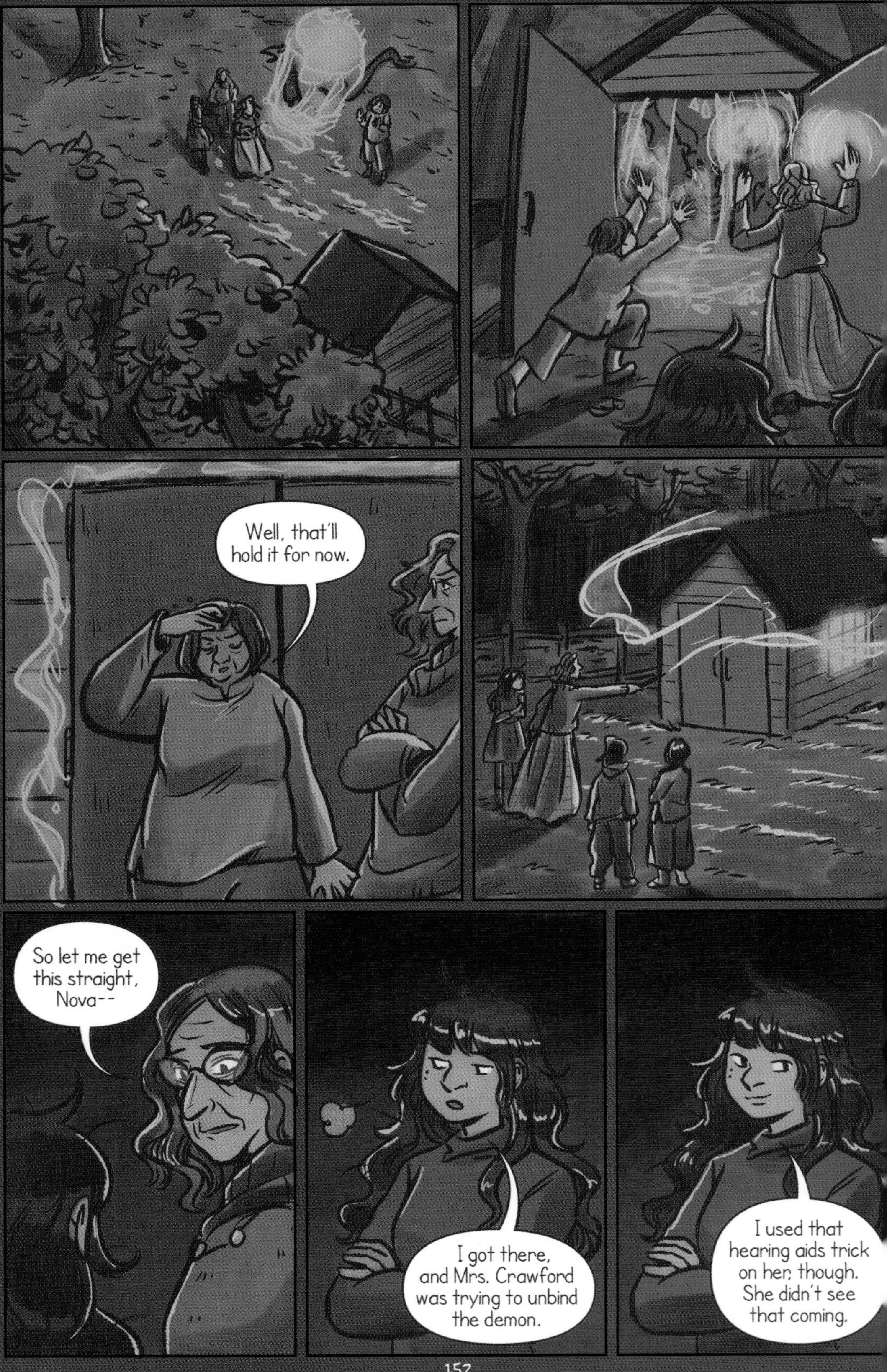
Well, that'll hold it for now.
So let me get this straight, Nova--
I got there, and Mrs. Crawford was trying to unbind the demon.
I used that hearing aids trick on her, though. She didn't see that coming.

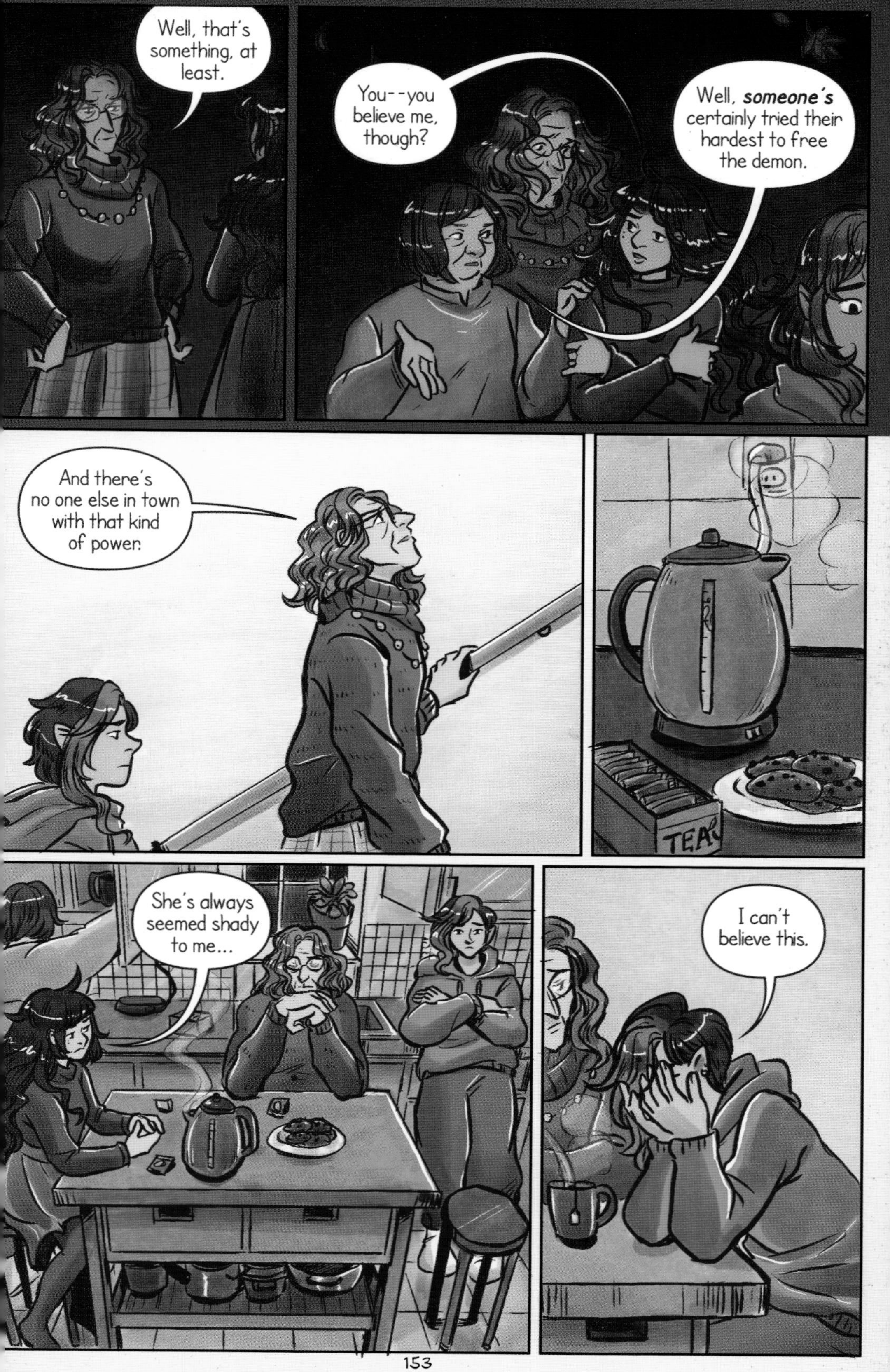

Well, that's something, at least.
You--you believe me, though?
Well, **someone's** certainly tried their hardest to free the demon.
And there's no one else in town with that kind of power.
TEA
She's always seemed shady to me...
I can't believe this.

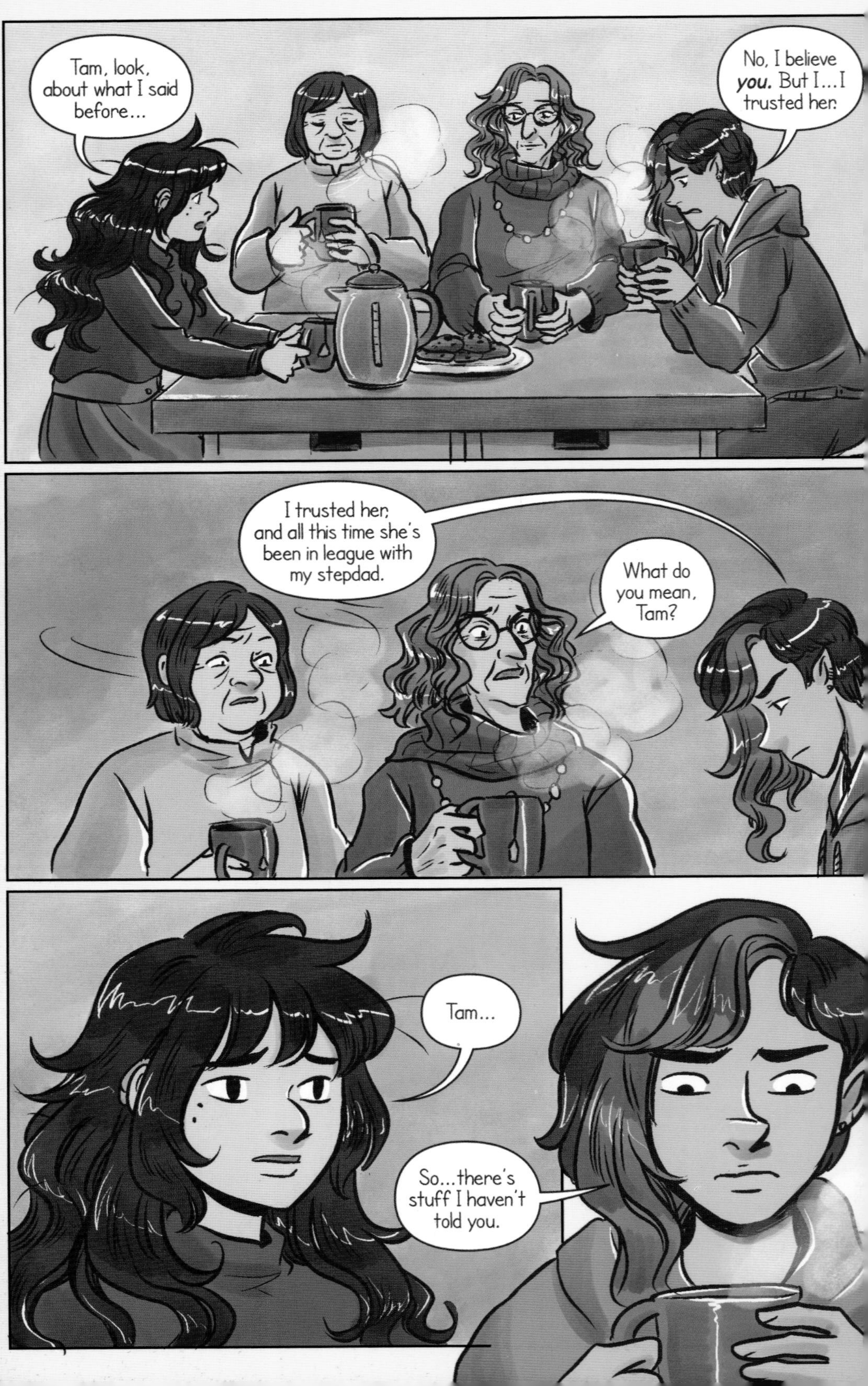
Tam, look, about what I said before...
No, I believe ***you.*** But I...I trusted her.
I trusted her, and all this time she's been in league with my stepdad.
What do you mean, Tam?
Tam...
So...there's stuff I haven't told you.

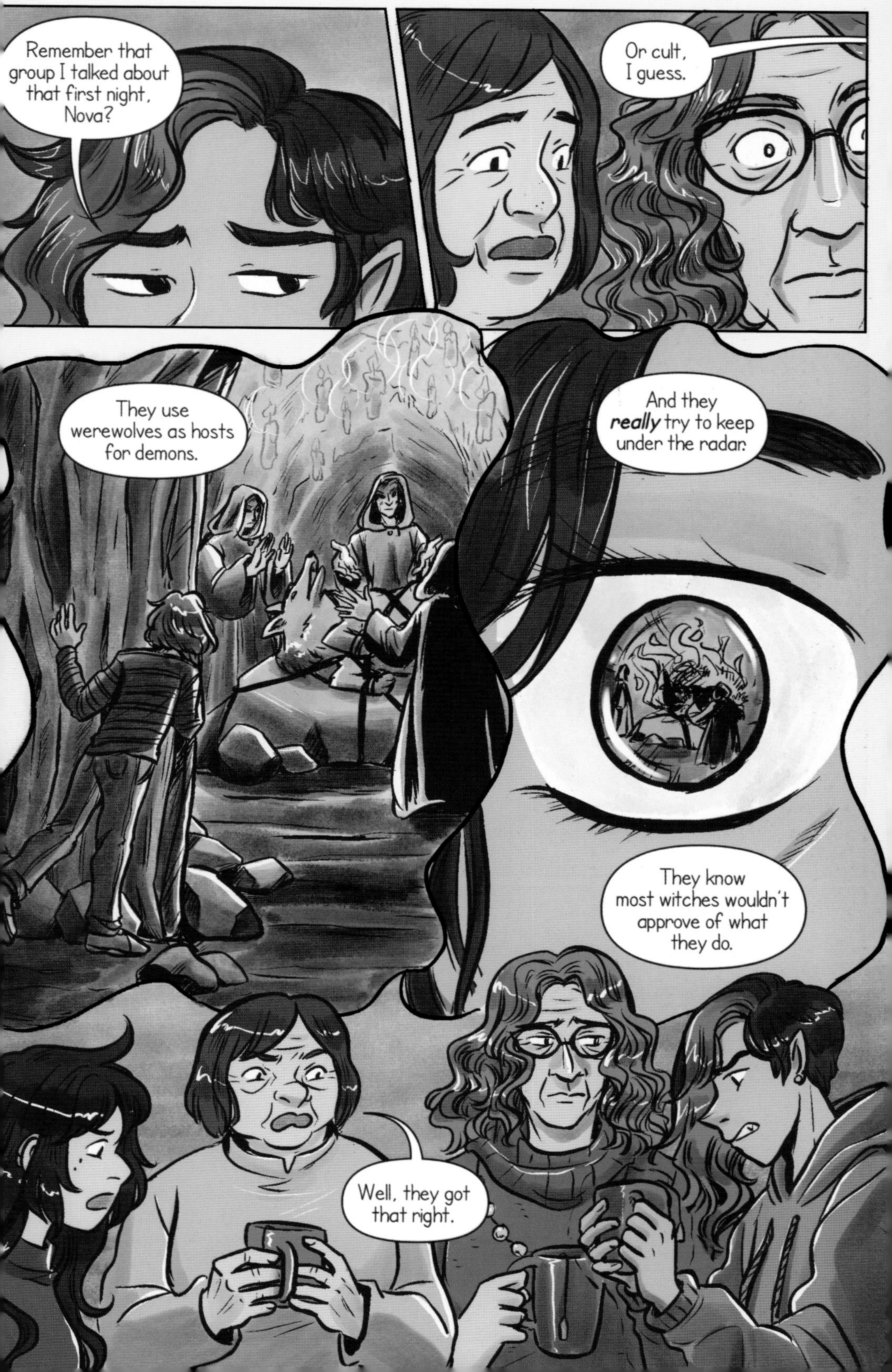
Remember that group I talked about that first night, Nova?
Or cult, I guess.
They use werewolves as hosts for demons.
And they *really* try to keep under the radar.
They know most witches wouldn't approve of what they do.
Well, they got that right.

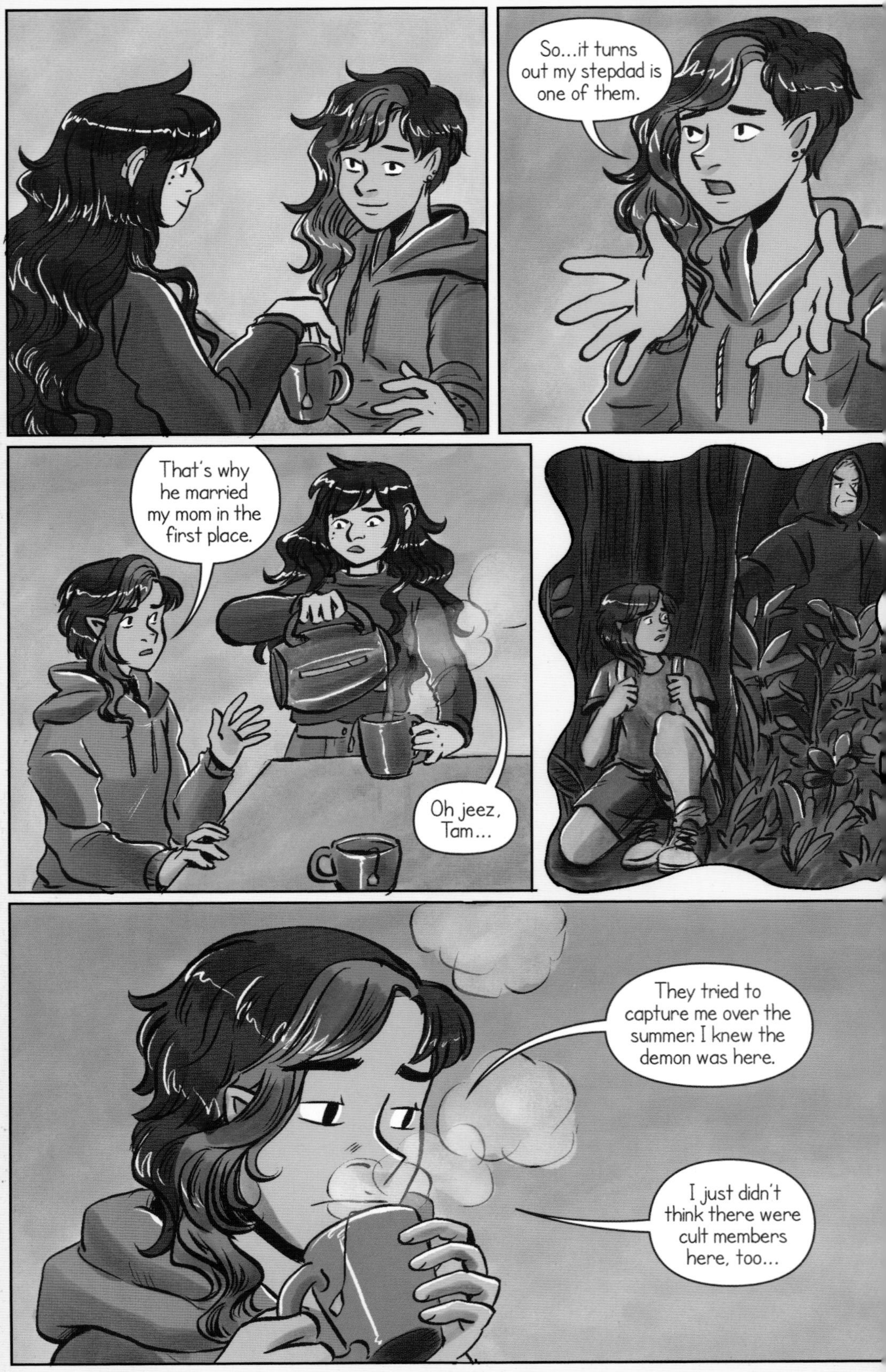
So...it turns out my stepdad is one of them.
That's why he married my mom in the first place.
Oh jeez, Tam...
They tried to capture me over the summer. I knew the demon was here.
I just didn't think there were cult members here, too...

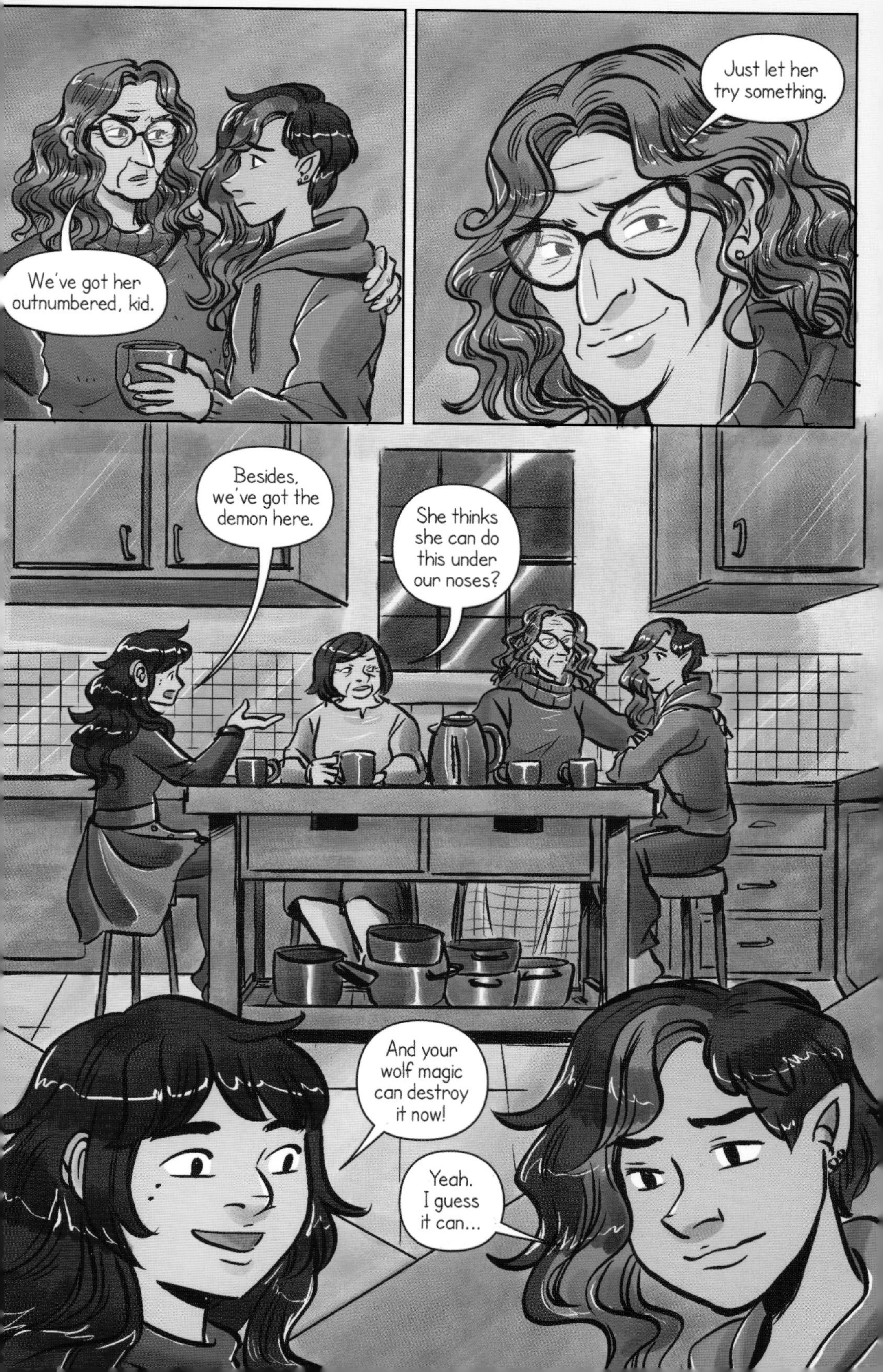
We've got her outnumbered, kid.
Just let her try something.
Besides, we've got the demon here.
She thinks she can do this under our noses?
And your wolf magic can destroy it now!
Yeah. I guess it can...

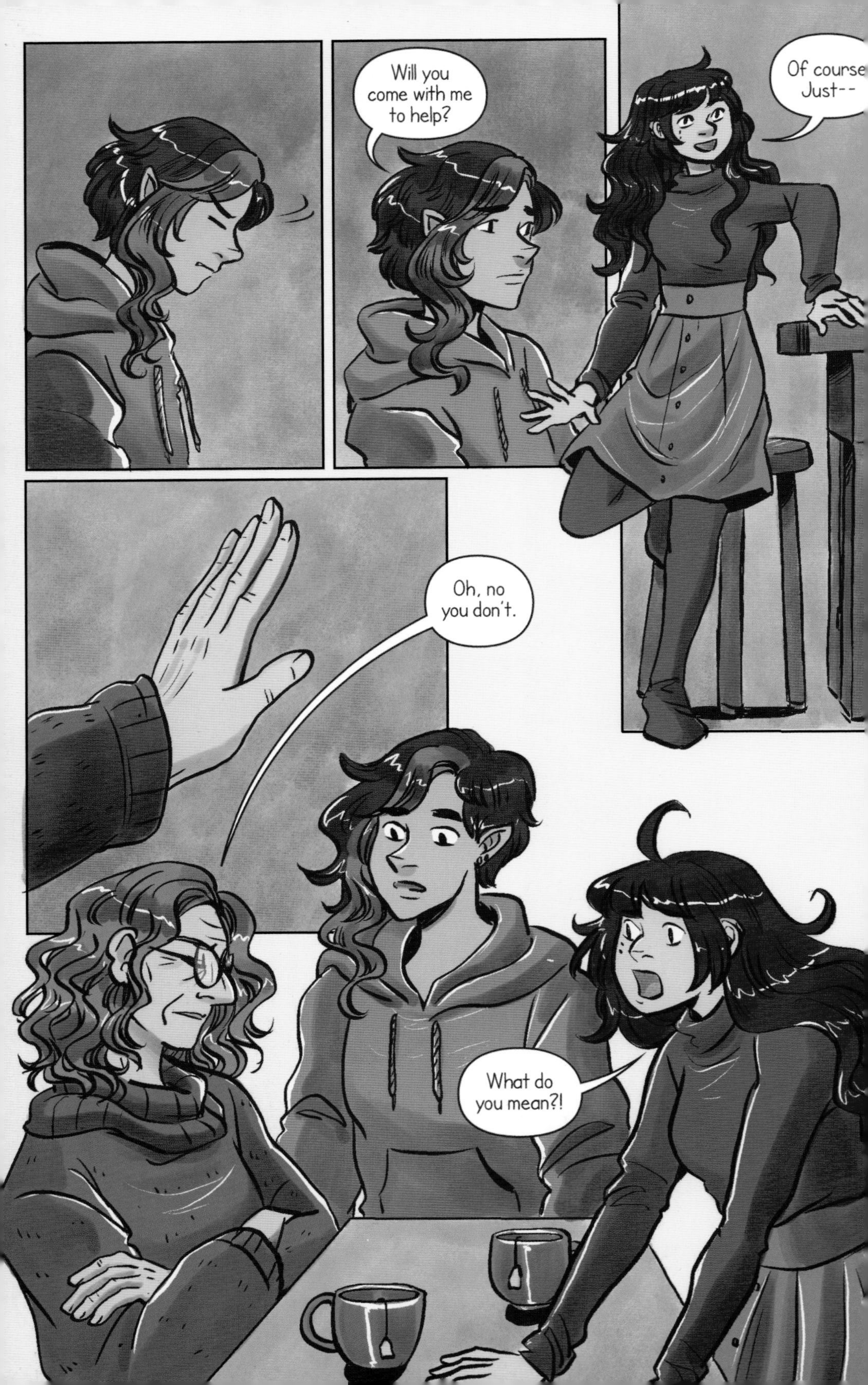
Will you come with me to help?
Of course Just--
Oh, no you don't.
What do you mean?!

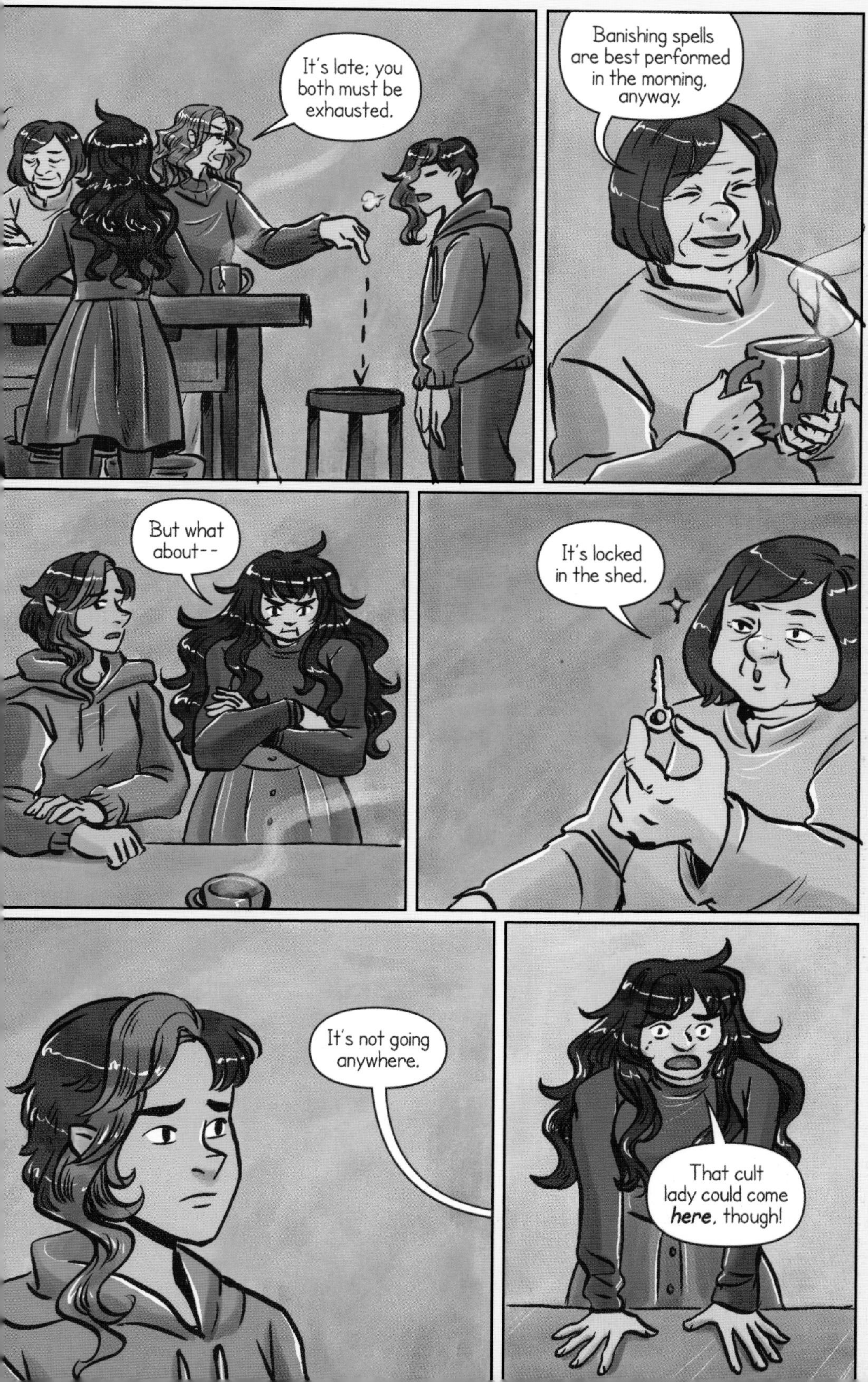
It's late; you both must be exhausted.
Banishing spells are best performed in the morning, anyway.
But what about--
It's locked in the shed.
It's not going anywhere.
That cult lady could come ***here***, though!

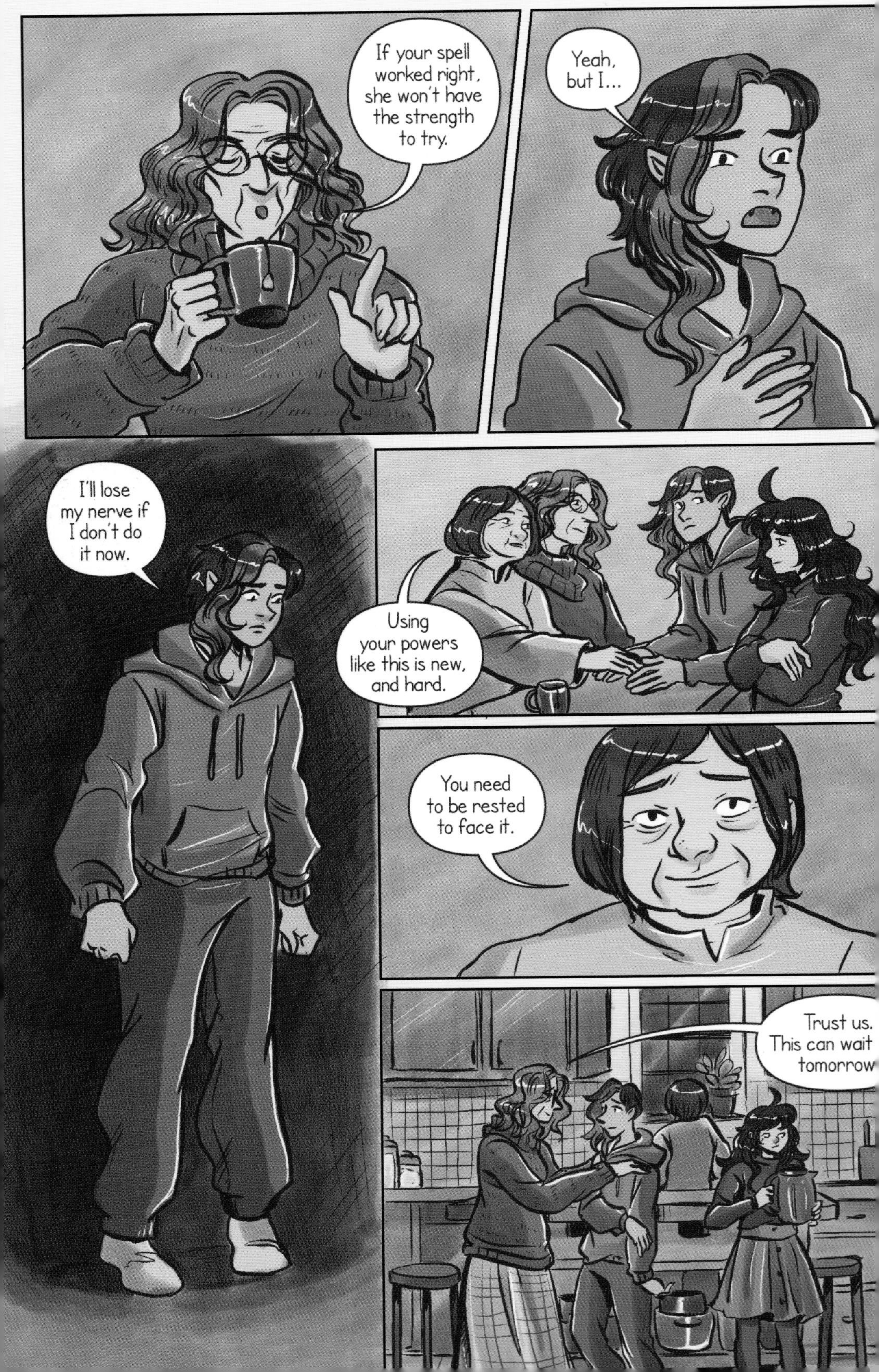
If your spell worked right, she won't have the strength to try.
Yeah, but I...
I'll lose my nerve if I don't do it now.
Using your powers like this is new, and hard.
You need to be rested to face it.
Trust us. This can wait tomorrow

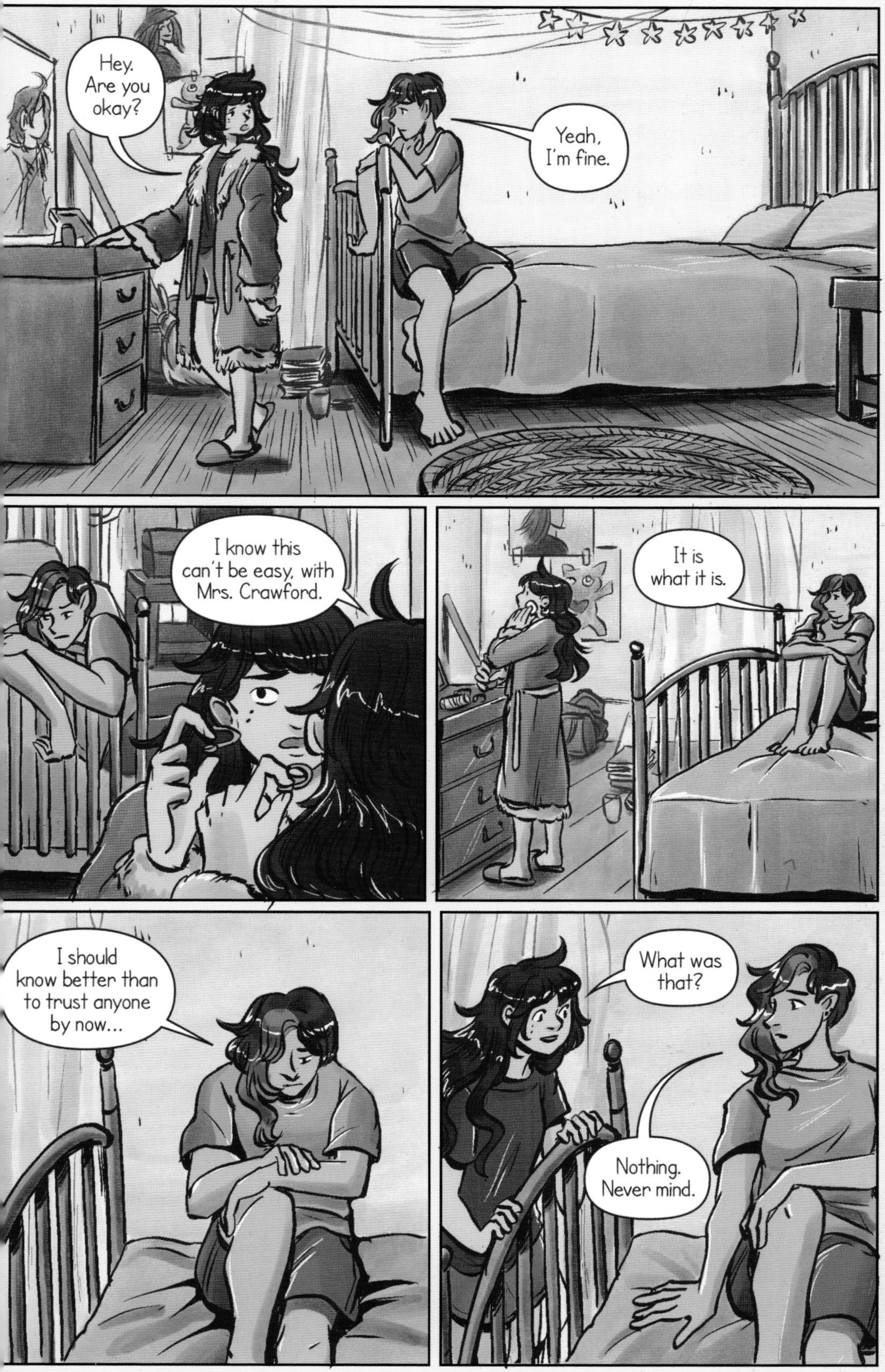
Hey. Are you okay?
Yeah, I'm fine.
I know this can't be easy, with Mrs. Crawford.
It is what it is.
I should know better than to trust anyone by now...
What was that?
Nothing. Never mind.

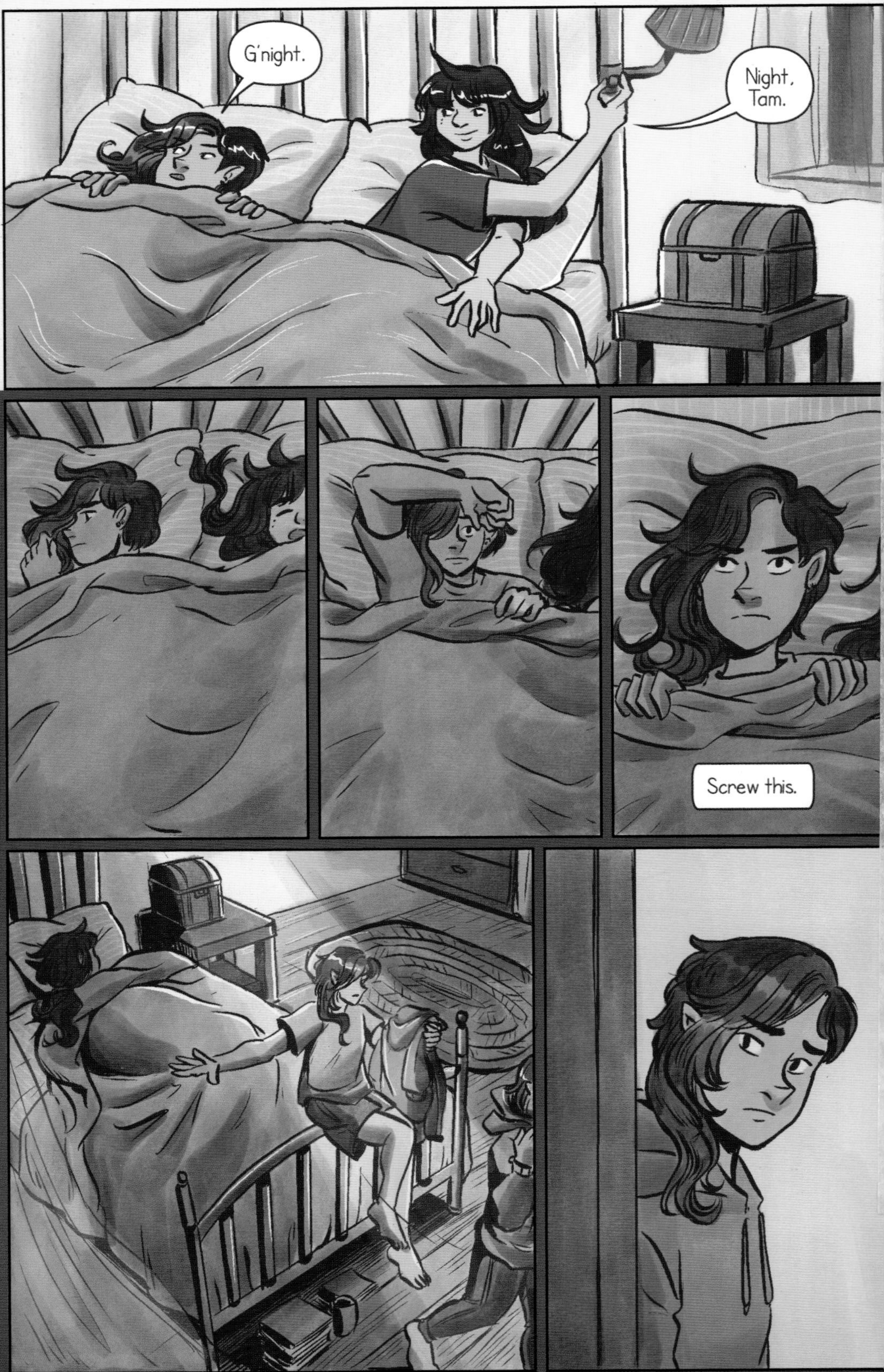
G'night.
Night, Tam.
Screw this.

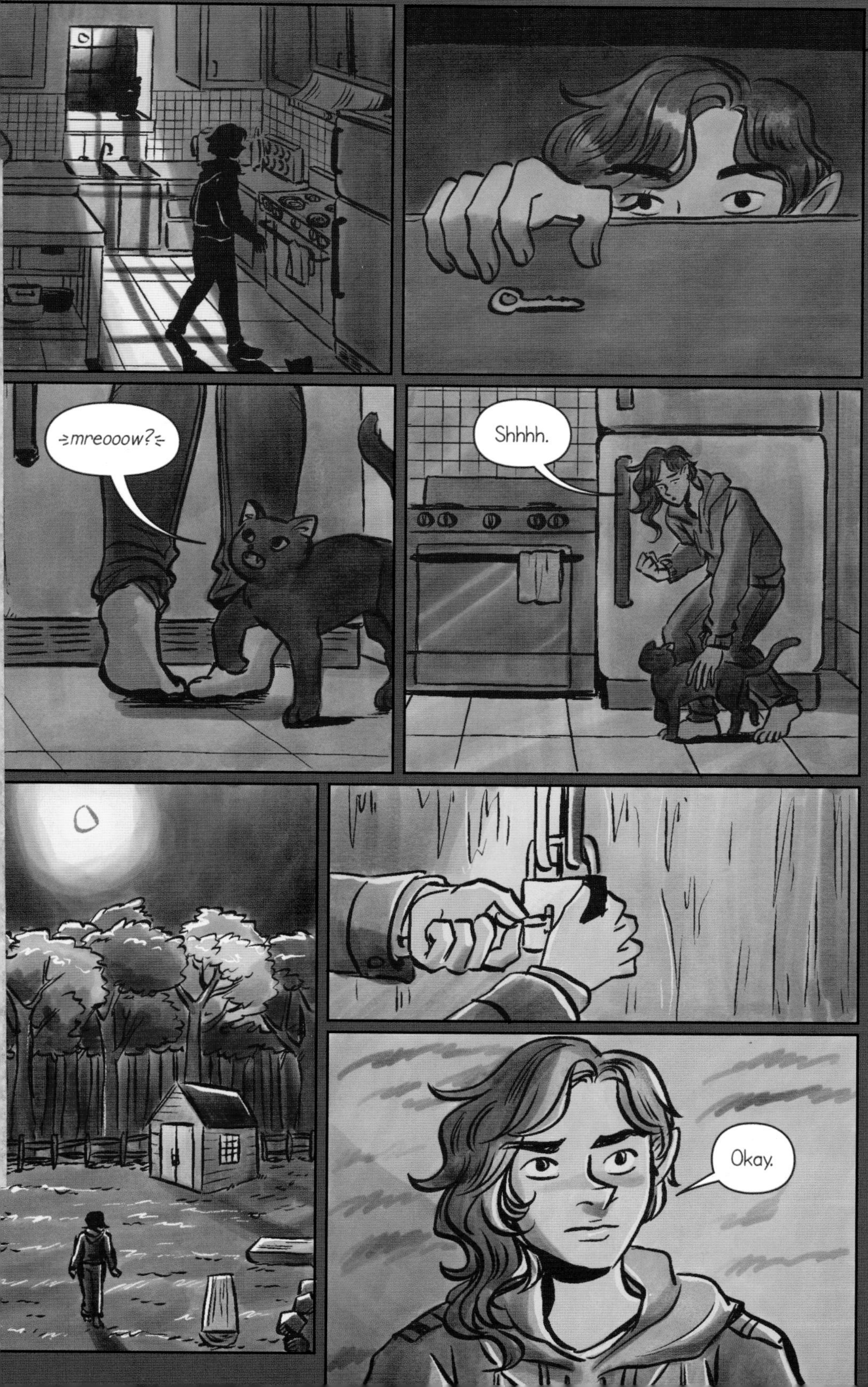
mreooow?
Shhhh.
Okay.

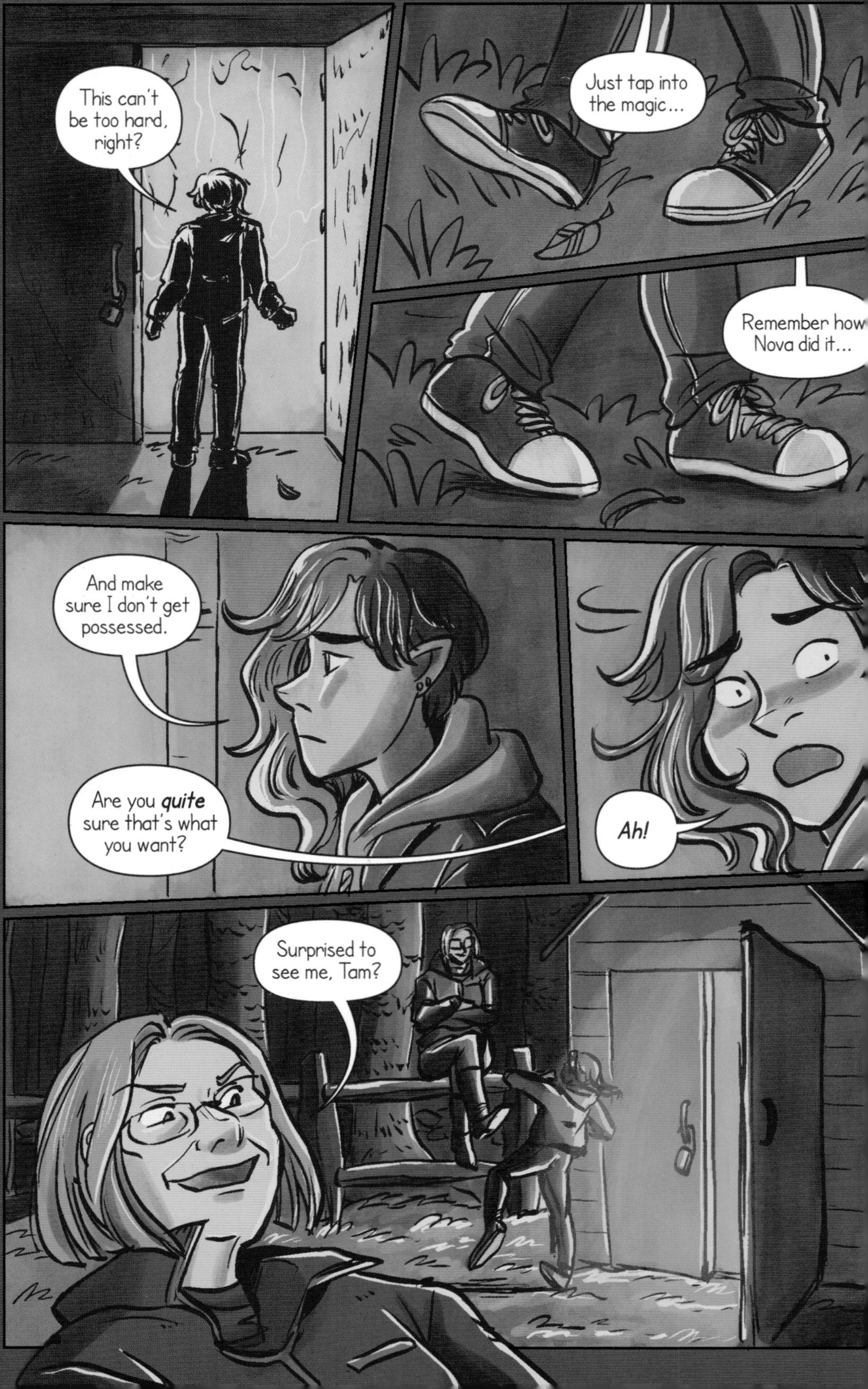
This can't be too hard, right?
Just tap into the magic...
Remember how Nova did it...
And make sure I don't get possessed.
Are you *quite* sure that's what you want?
Ah!
Surprised to see me, Tam?

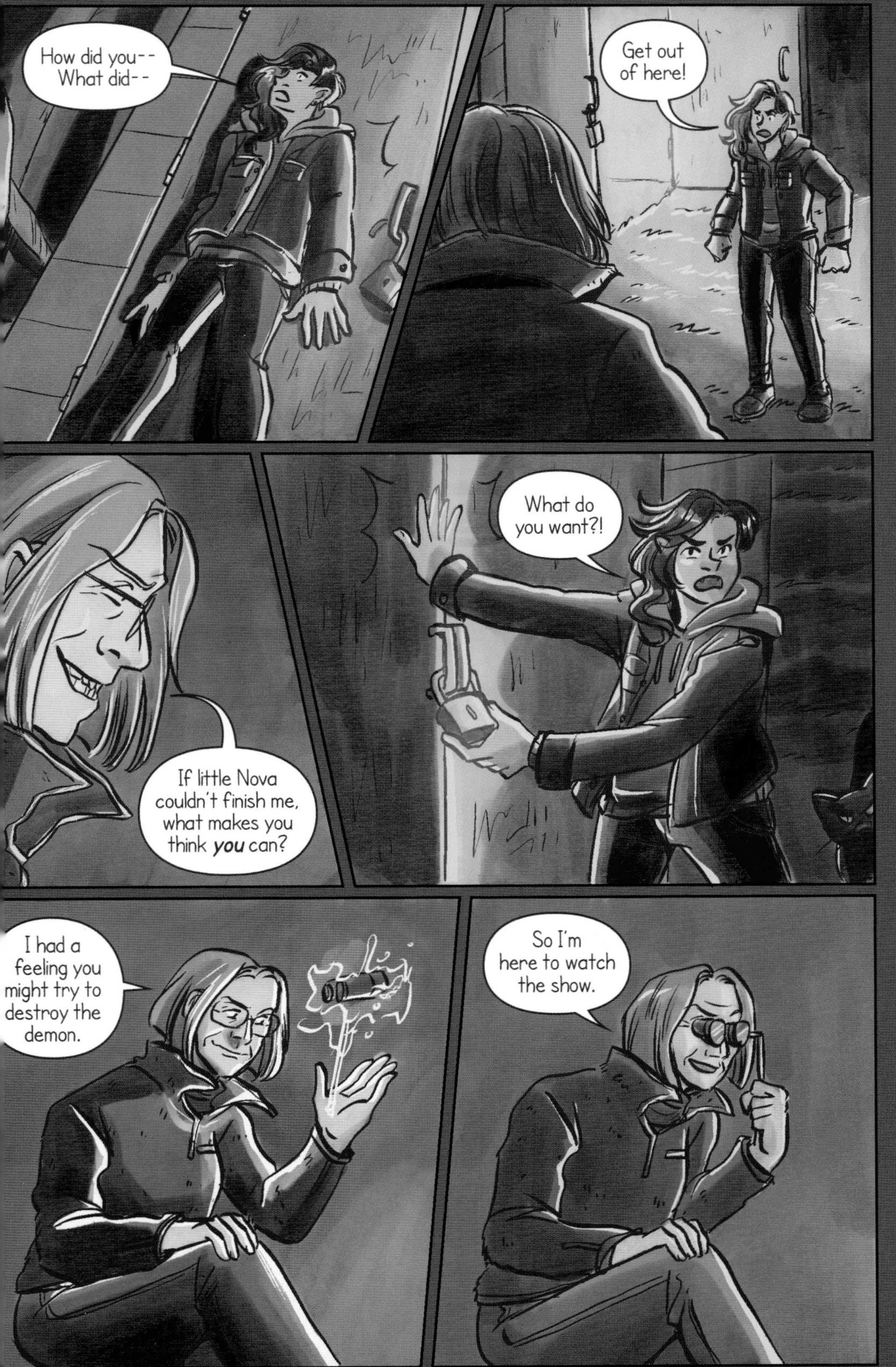
How did you--
What did--
Get out of here!
What do you want?!
If little Nova couldn't finish me, what makes you think ***you*** can?
I had a feeling you might try to destroy the demon.
So I'm here to watch the show.

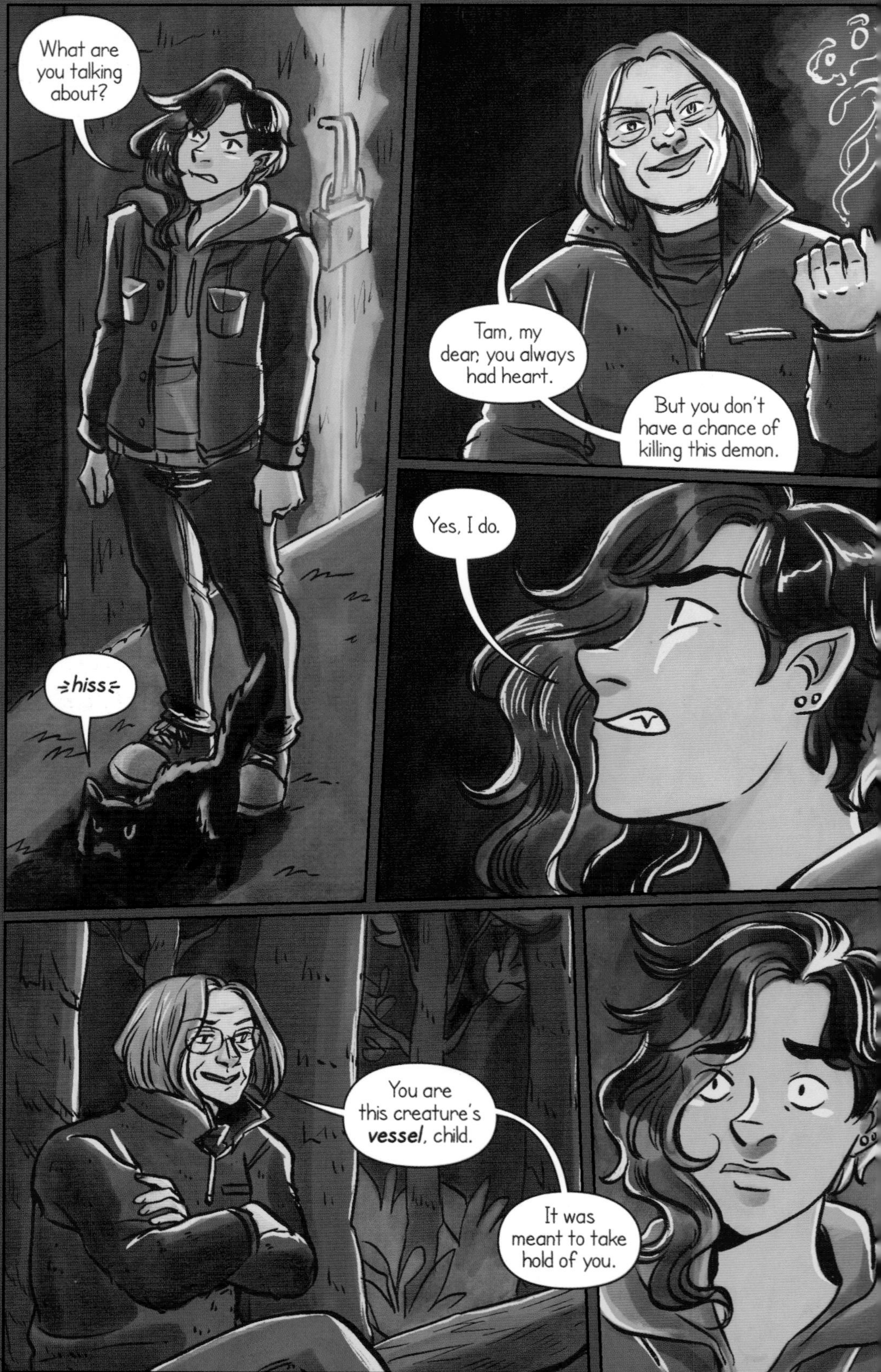
What are you talking about?
hiss
Tam, my dear, you always had heart.
But you don't have a chance of killing this demon.
Yes, I do.
You are this creature's **vessel**, child.
It was meant to take hold of you.

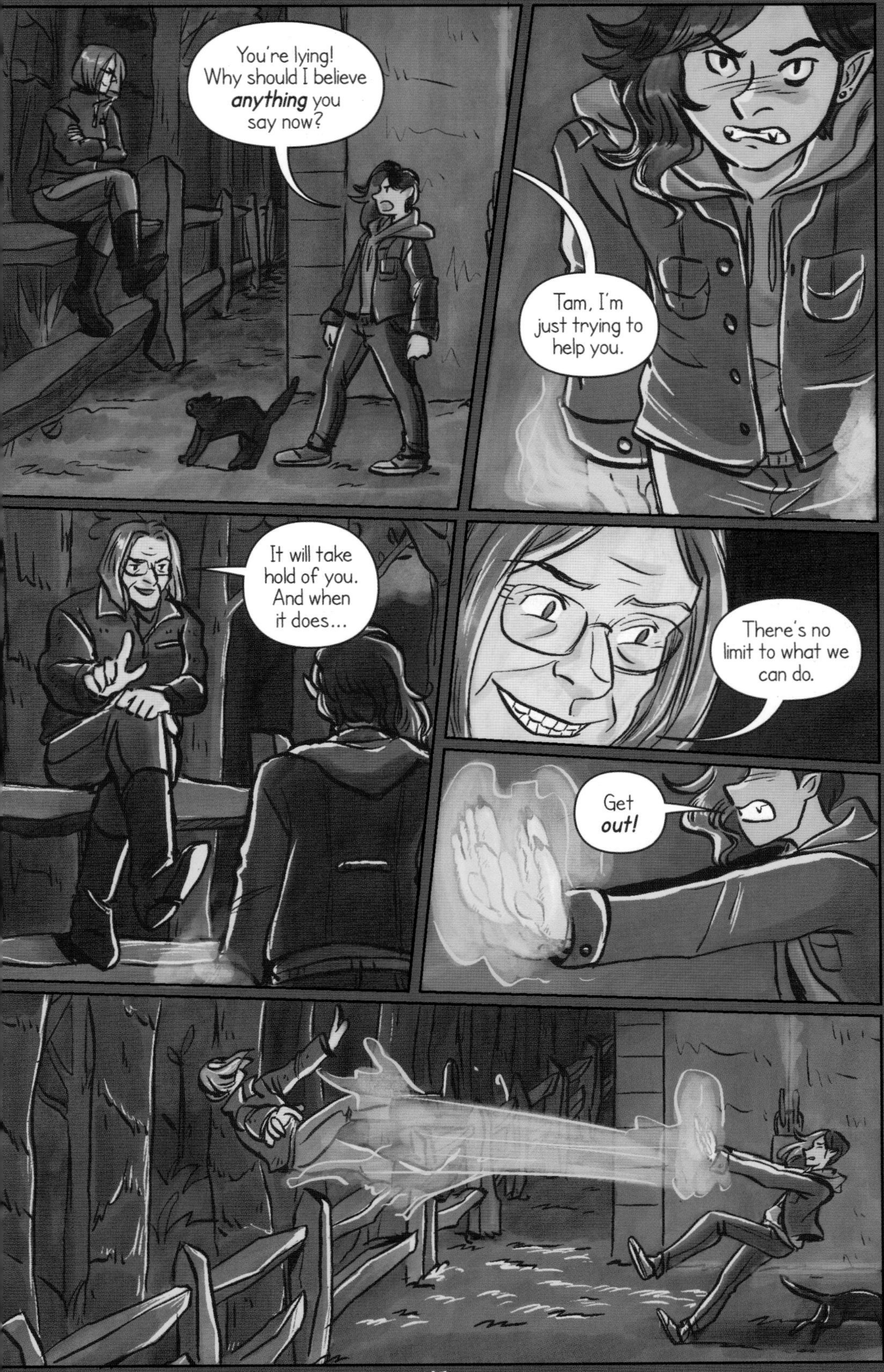
You're lying! Why should I believe *anything* you say now?
Tam, I'm just trying to help you.
It will take hold of you. And when it does...
There's no limit to what we can do.
Get *out!*

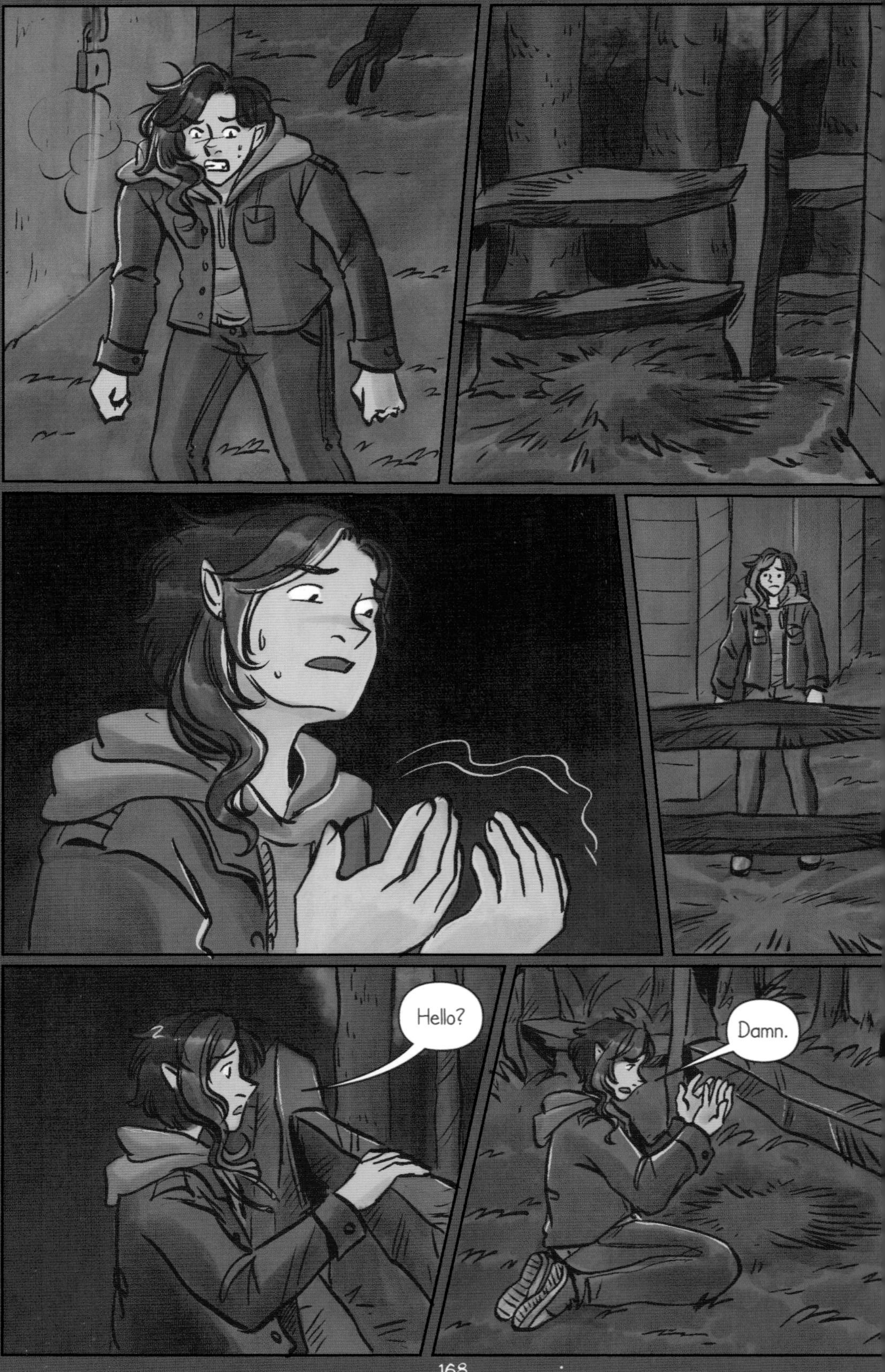
Hello?
Damn.

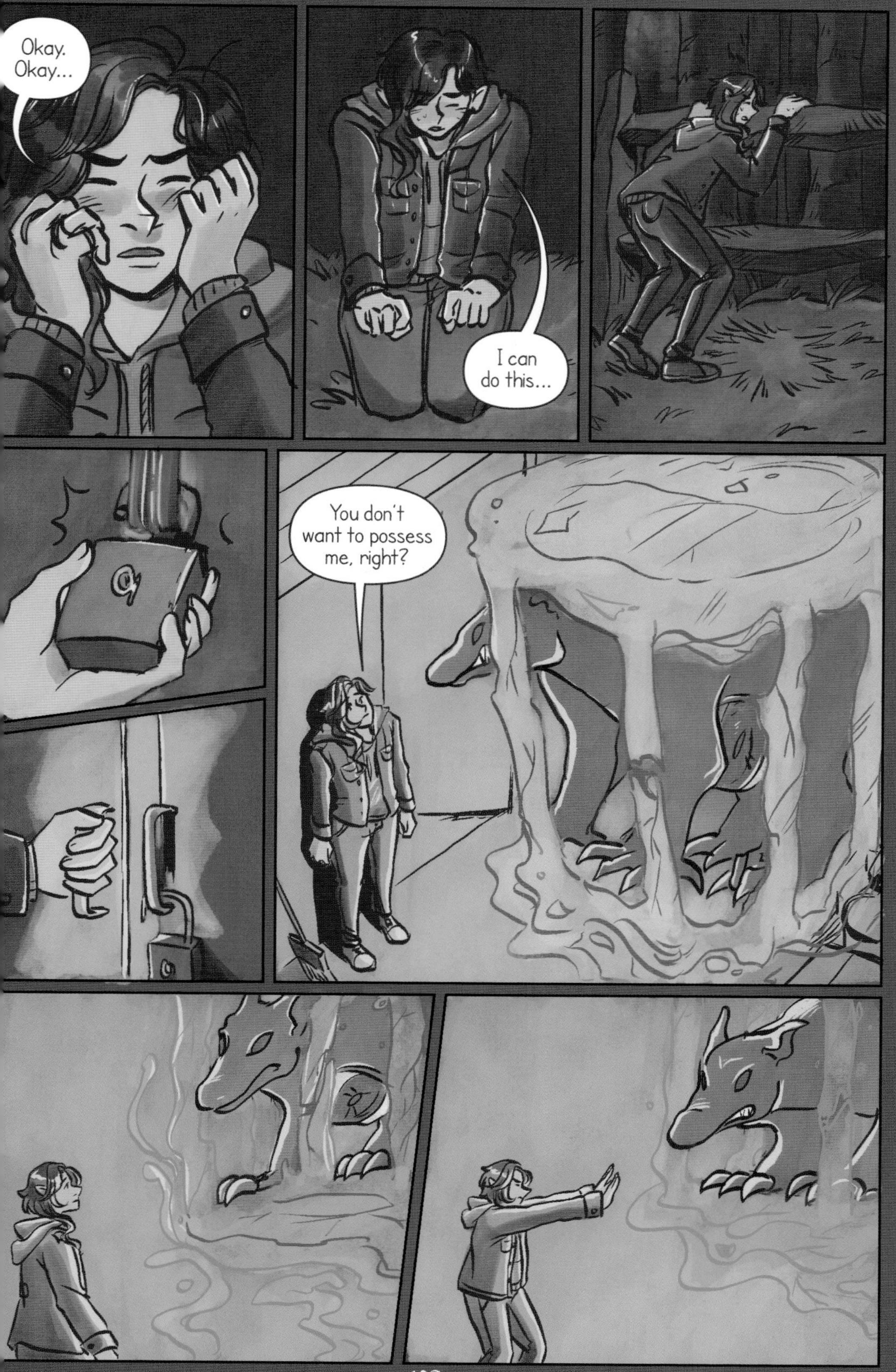
Okay.
Okay...
I can do this...
You don't want to possess me, right?

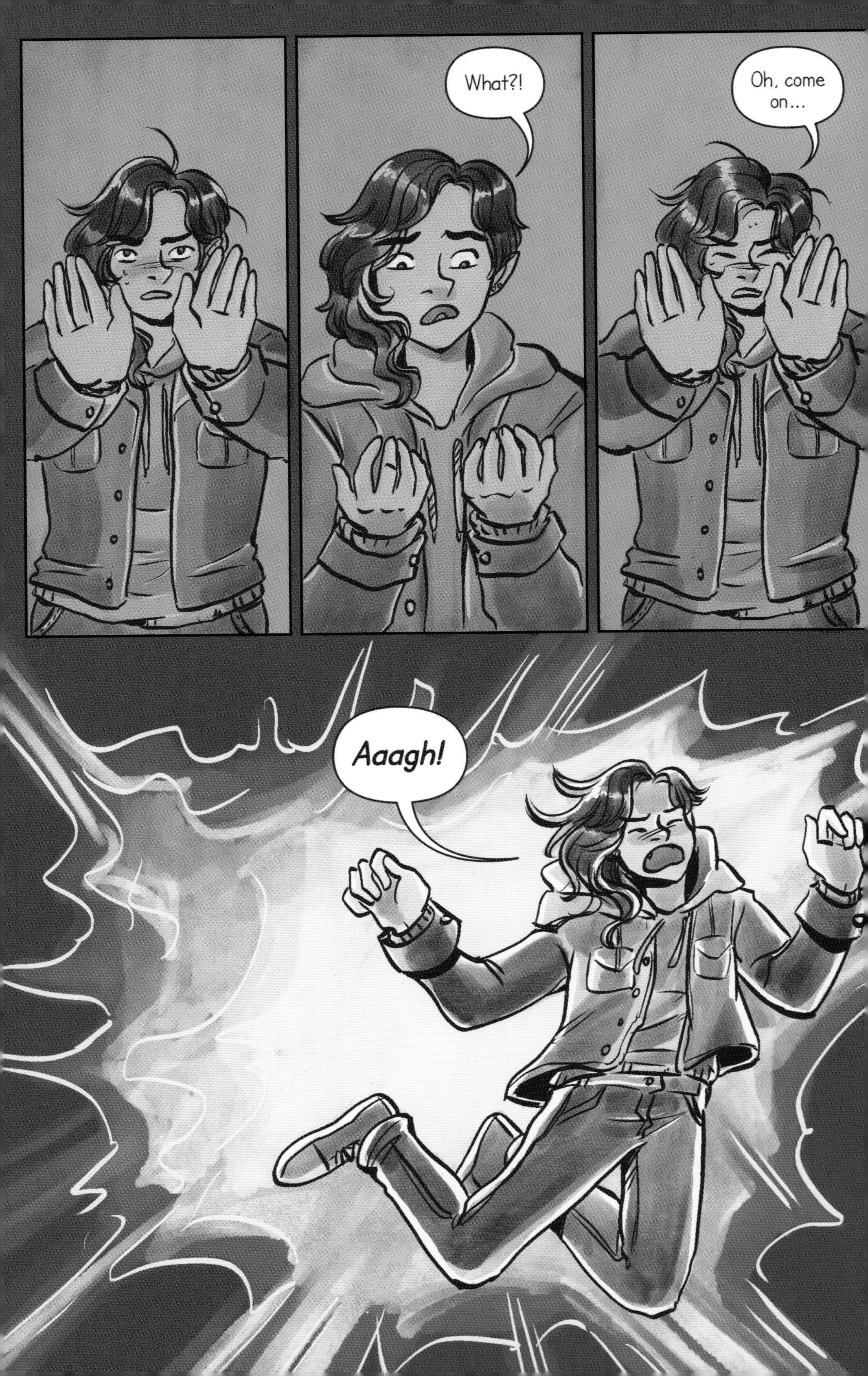
What?!
Oh, come on...
Aaagh!

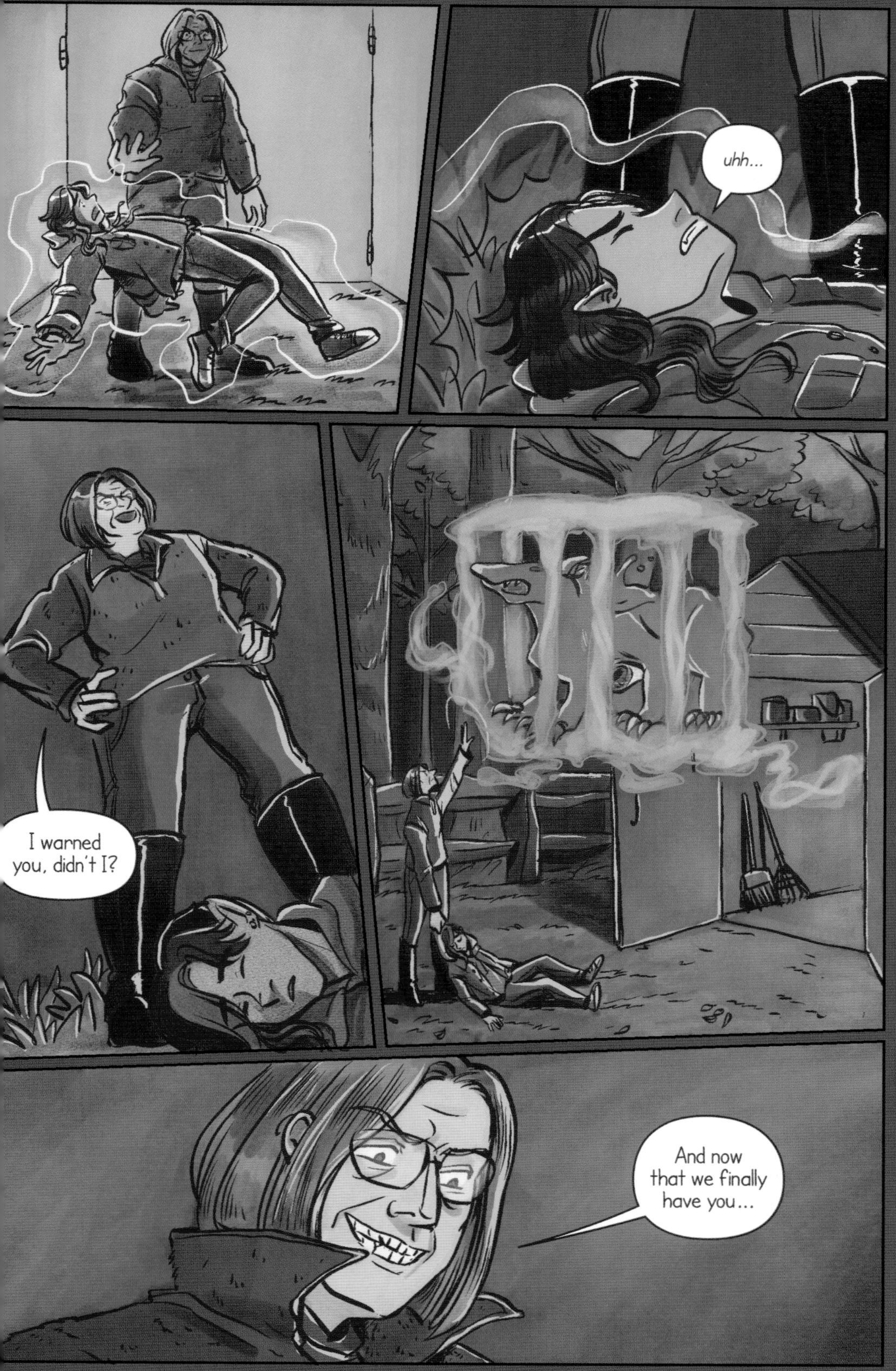
uhh...
I warned you, didn't I?
And now that we finally have you...

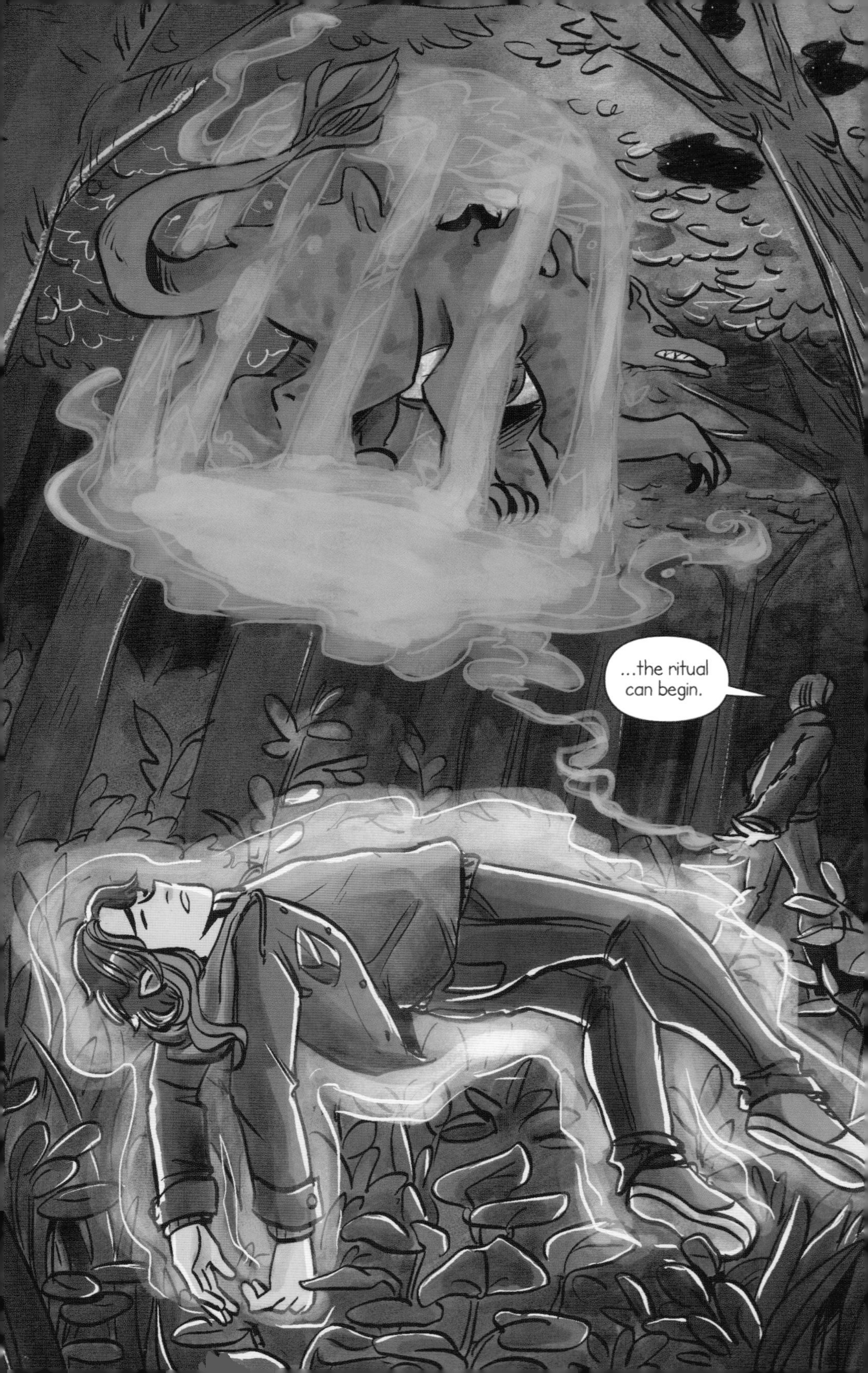
...the ritual can begin.

Chapter 7

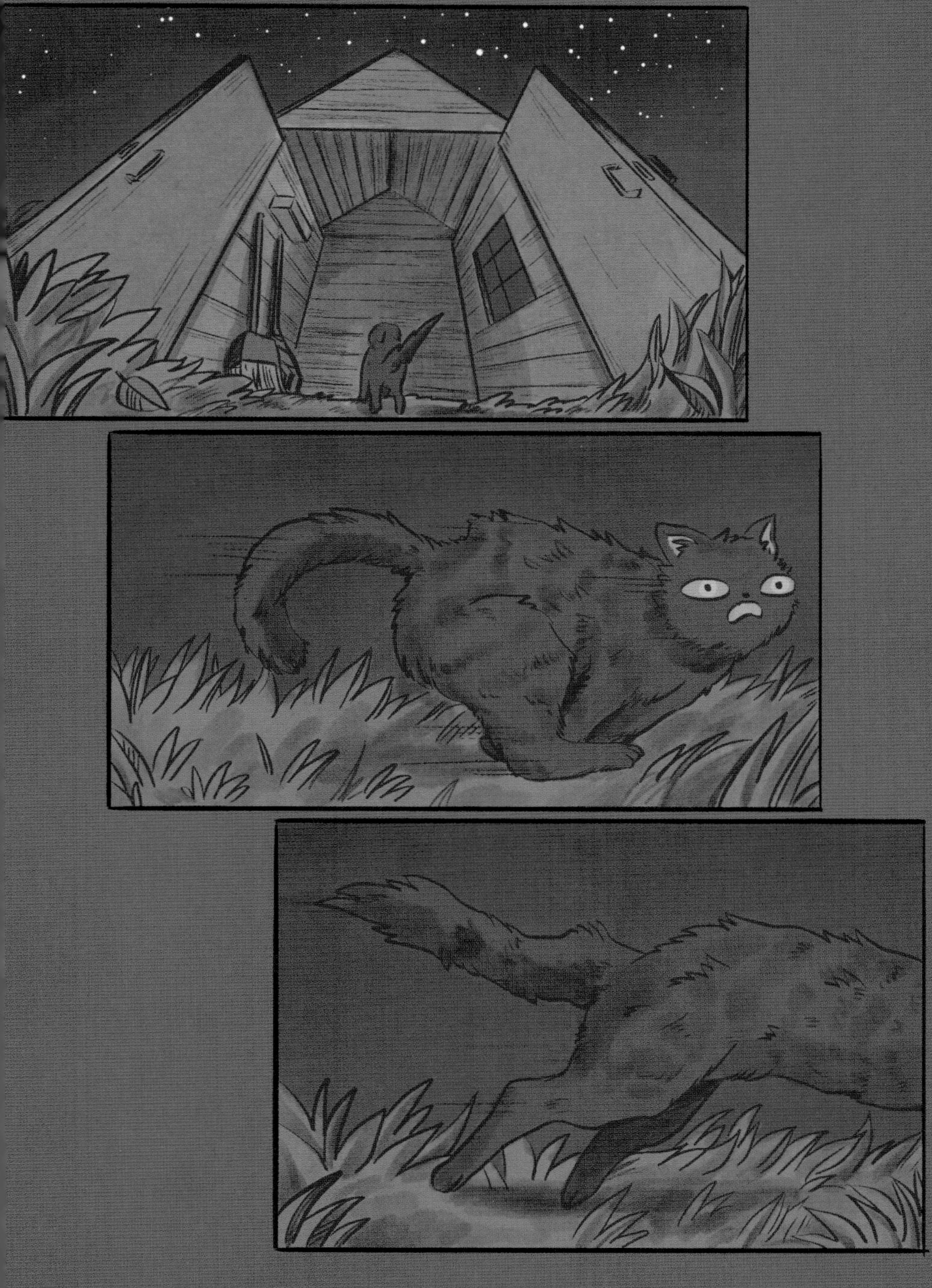

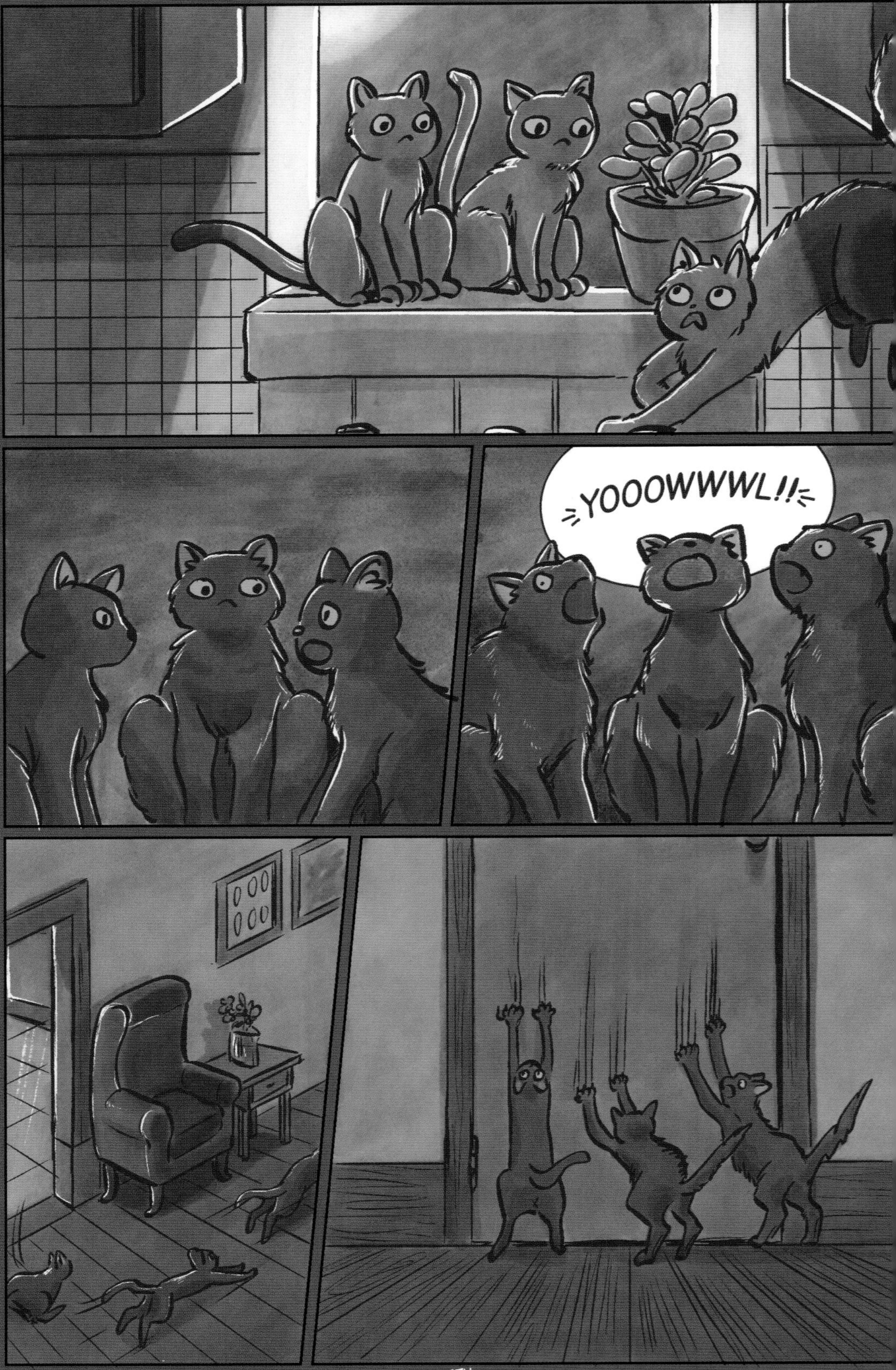
YOOOWWWL!!

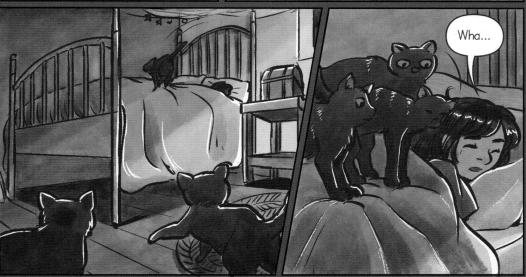

Wha...

...Tam?

Jeez, Isabel, you're gonna wake...

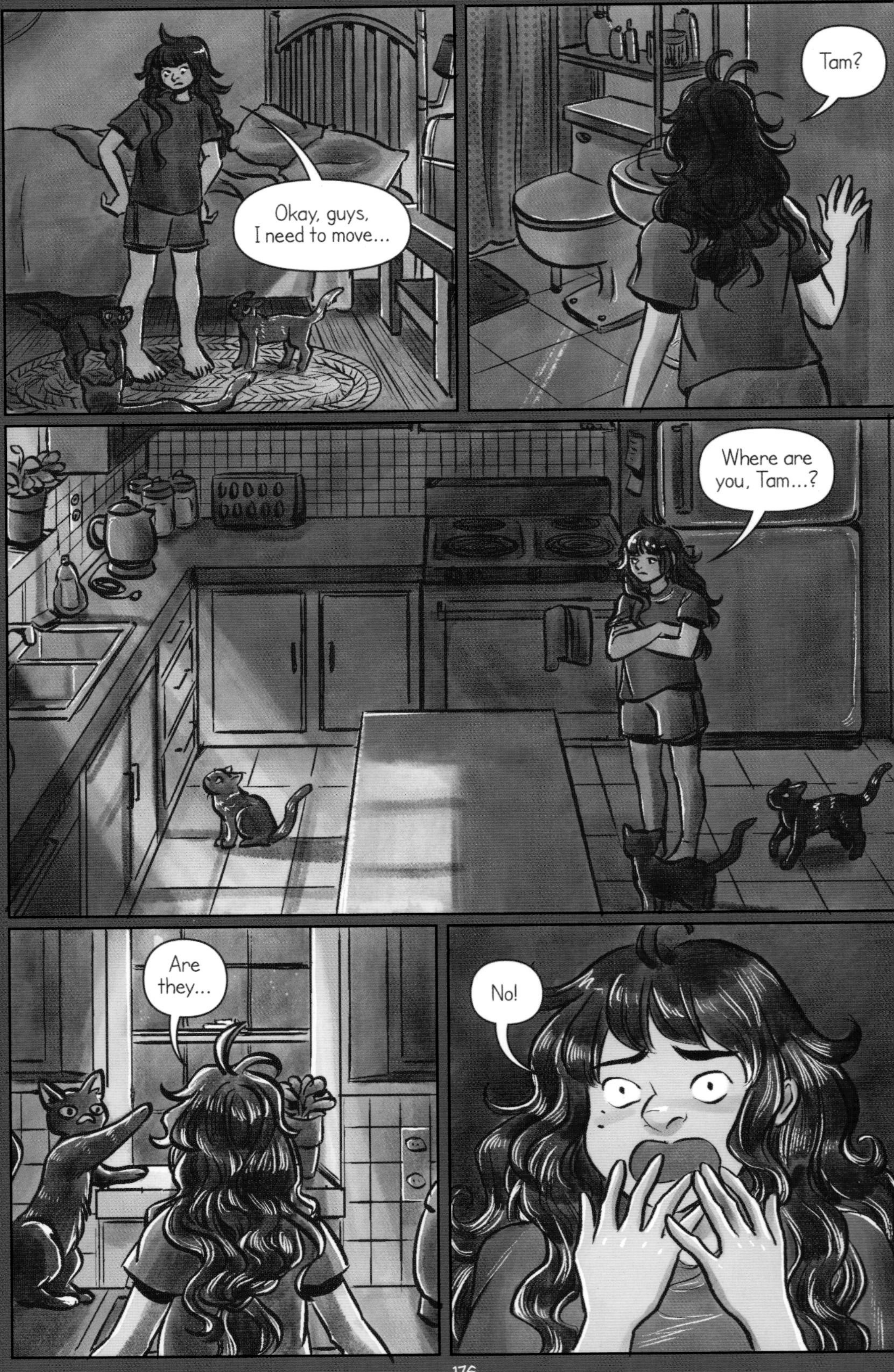
Okay, guys, I need to move...
Tam?
Where are you, Tam...?
Are they...
No!

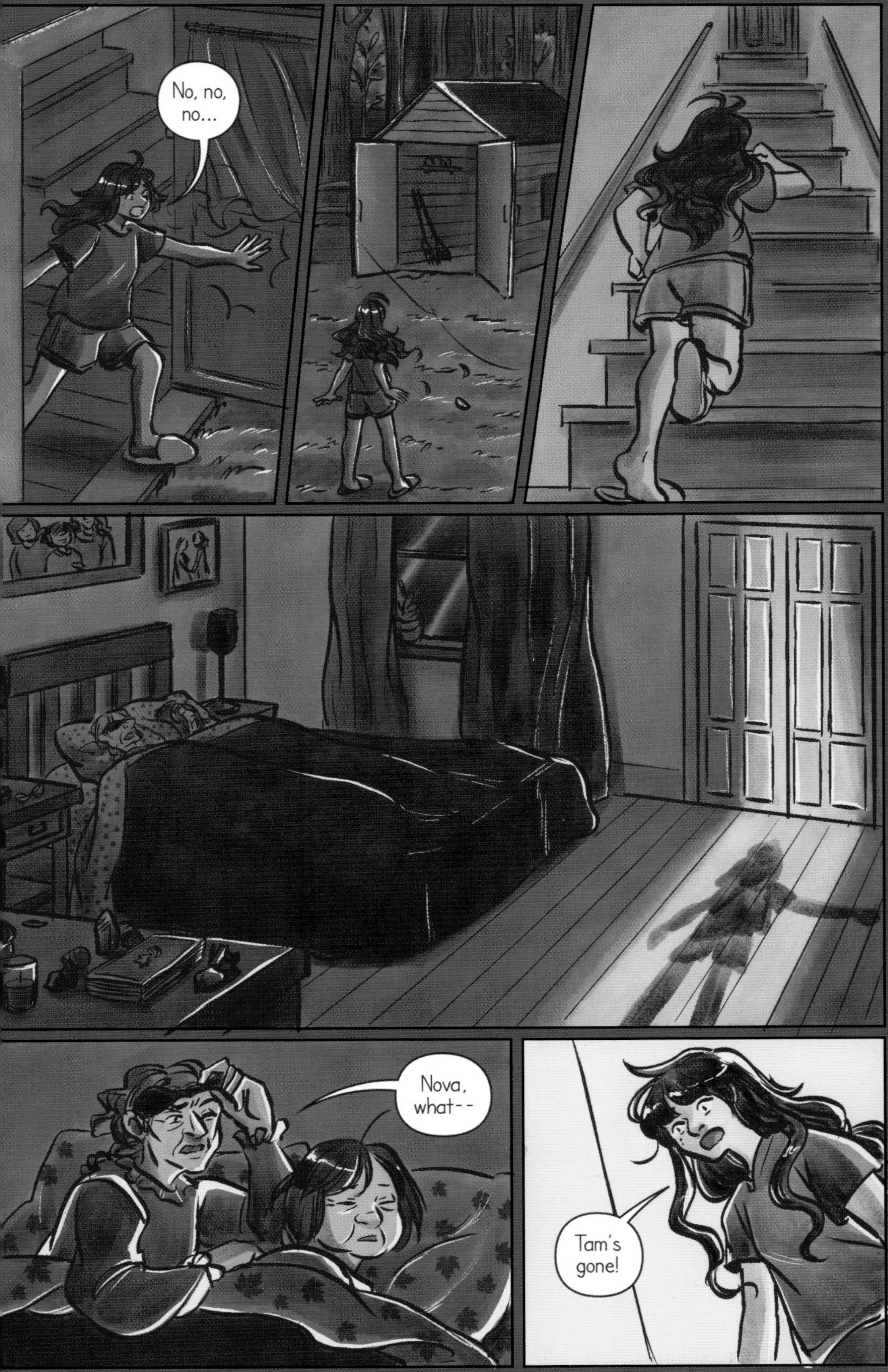

No, no, no...
Nova, what--
Tam's gone!

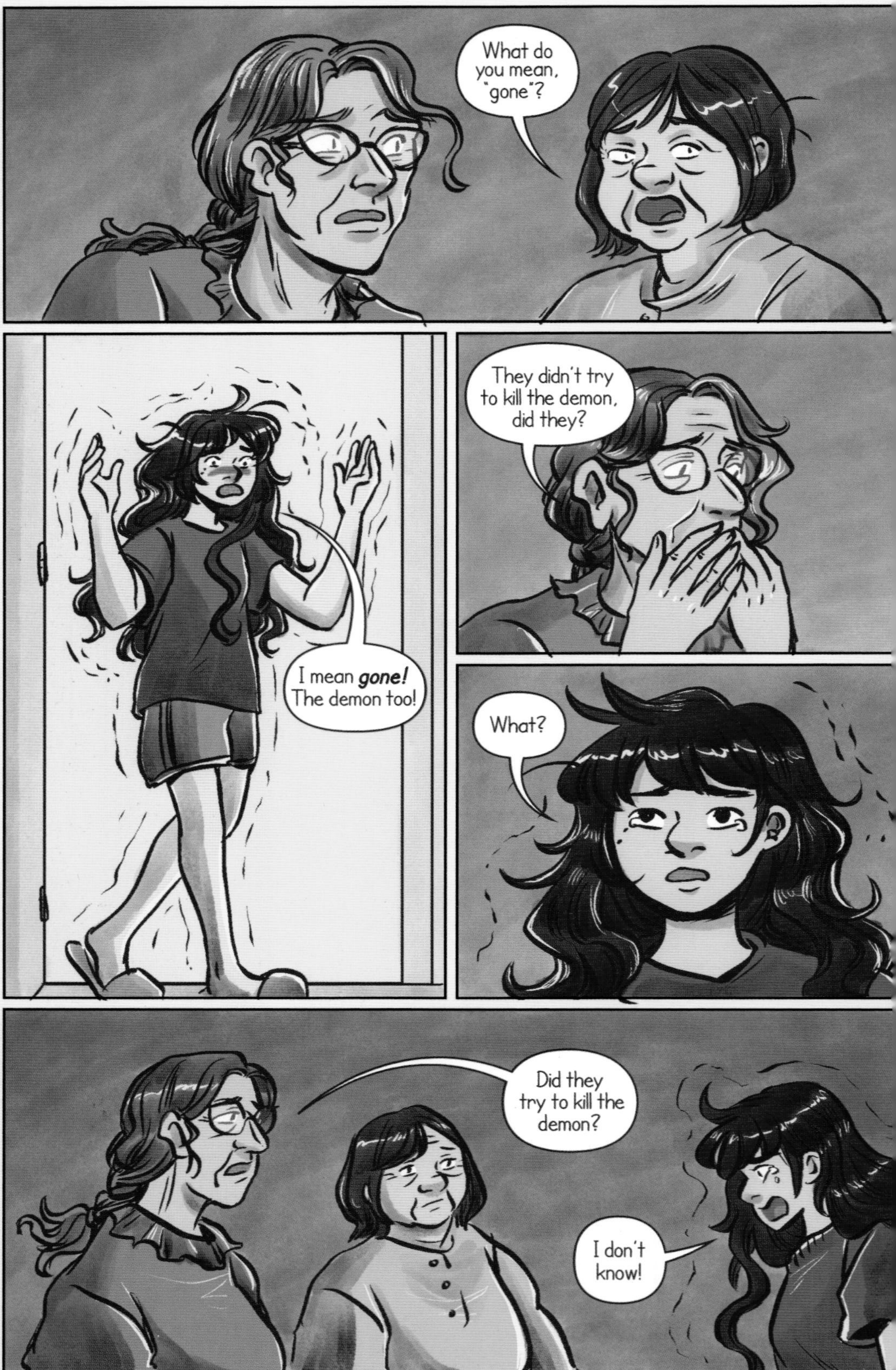
What do you mean, "gone"?
I mean **gone!** The demon too!
They didn't try to kill the demon, did they?
What?
Did they try to kill the demon?
I don't know!

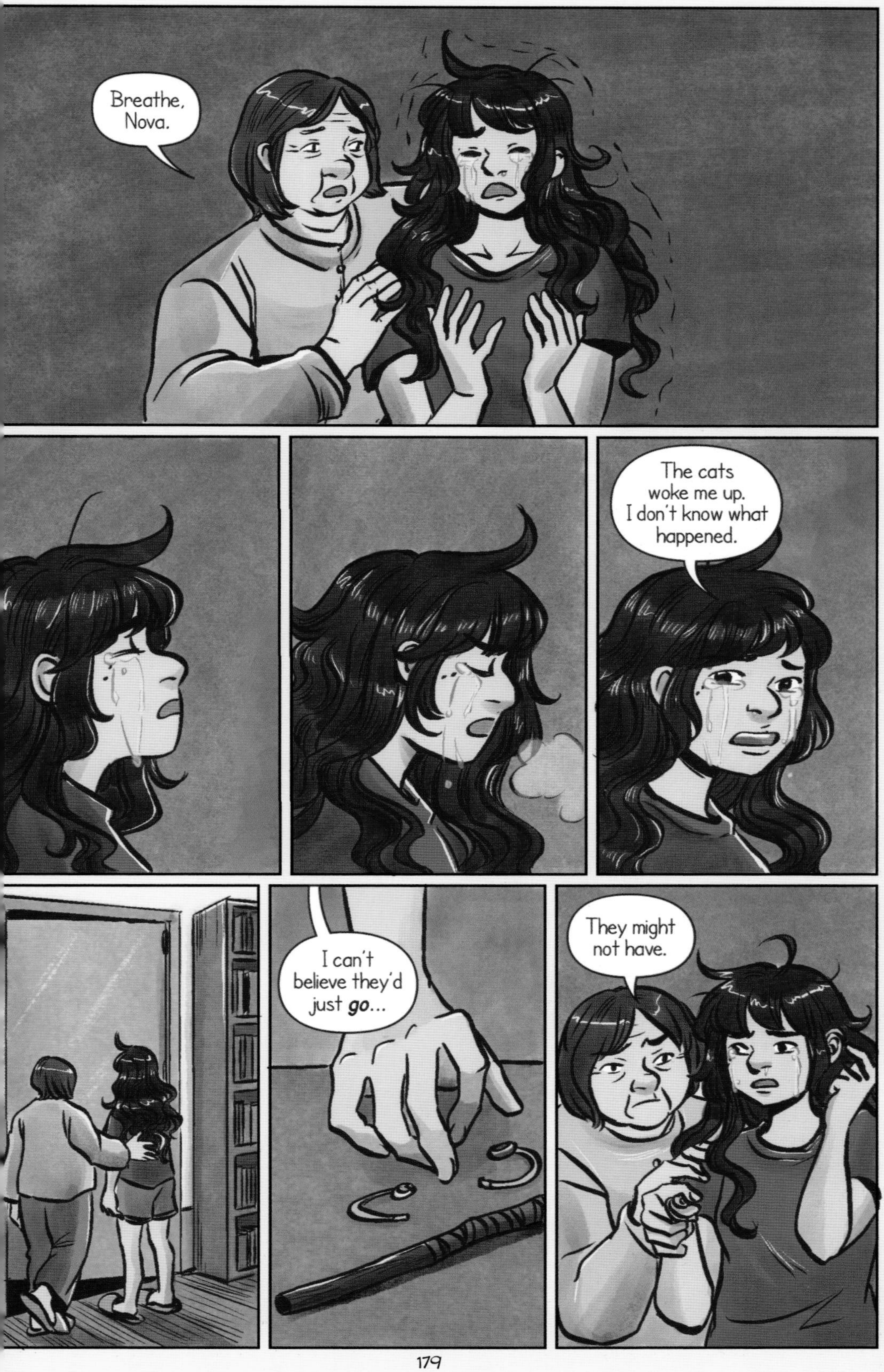
Breathe, Nova.
The cats woke me up. I don't know what happened.
I can't believe they'd just *go*...
They might not have.

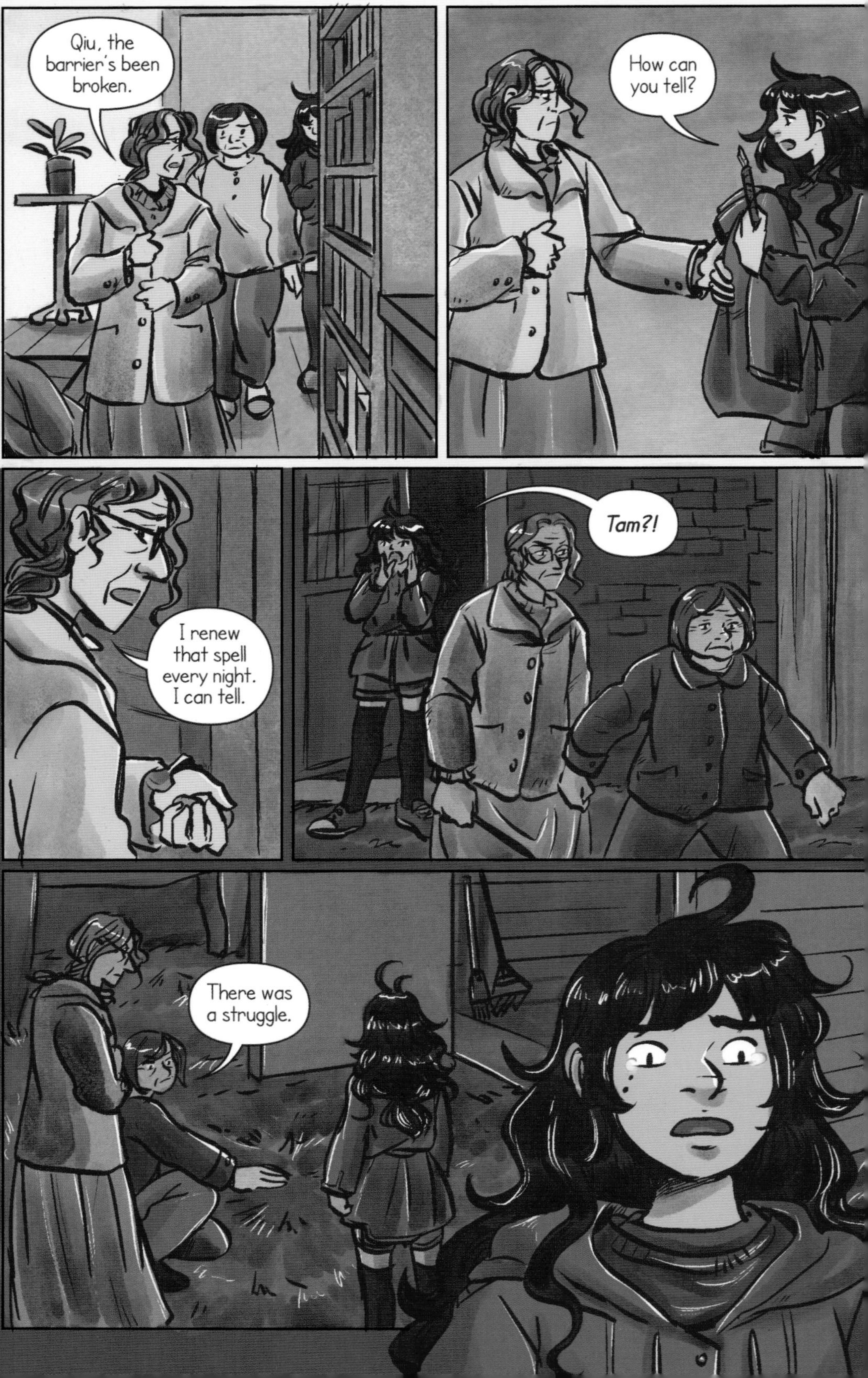
Qiu, the barrier's been broken.
How can you tell?
I renew that spell every night. I can tell.
Tam?!
There was a struggle.

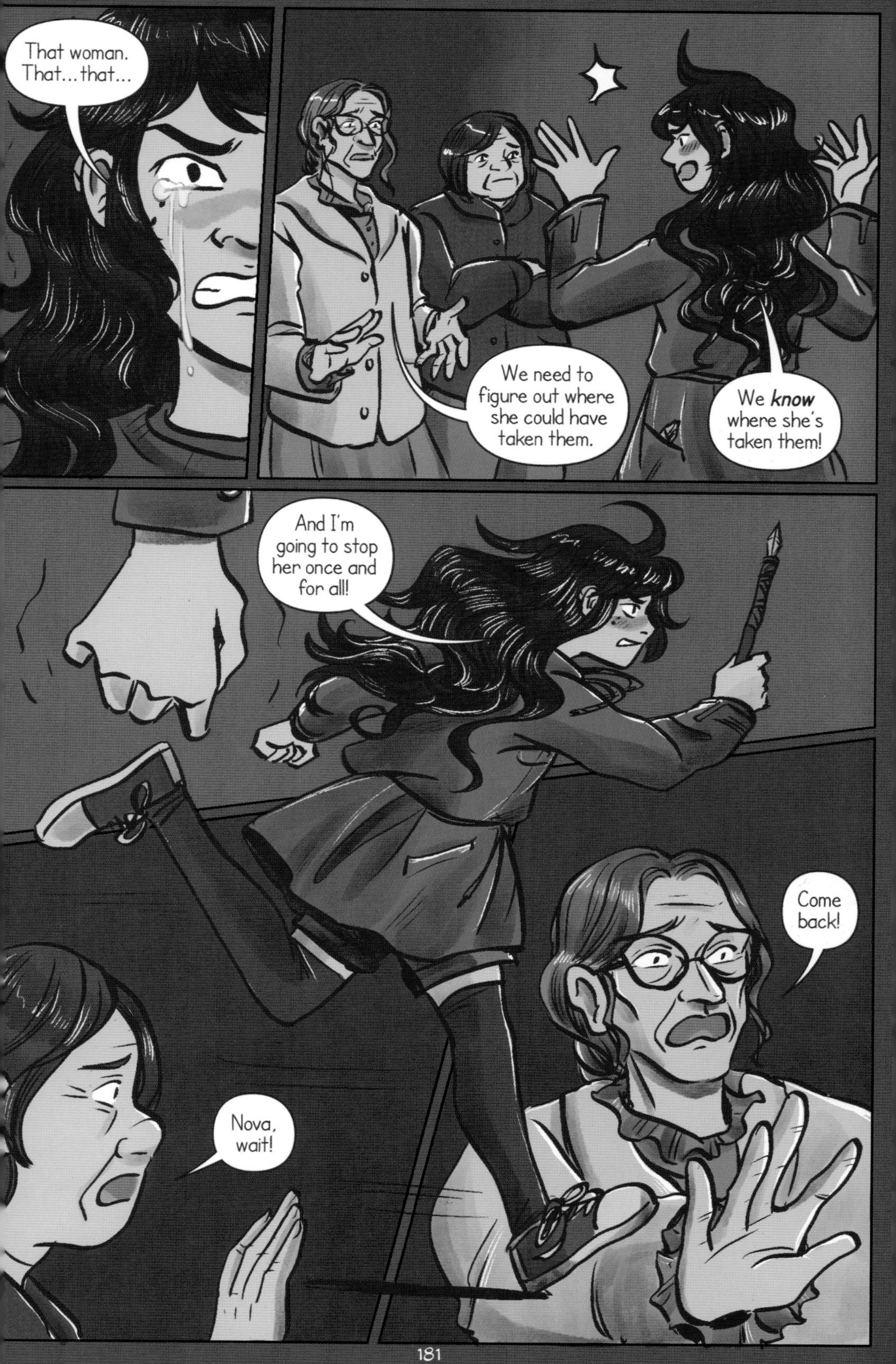

That woman. That... that...
We need to figure out where she could have taken them.
We **know** where she's taken them!
And I'm going to stop her once and for all!
Come back!
Nova, wait!

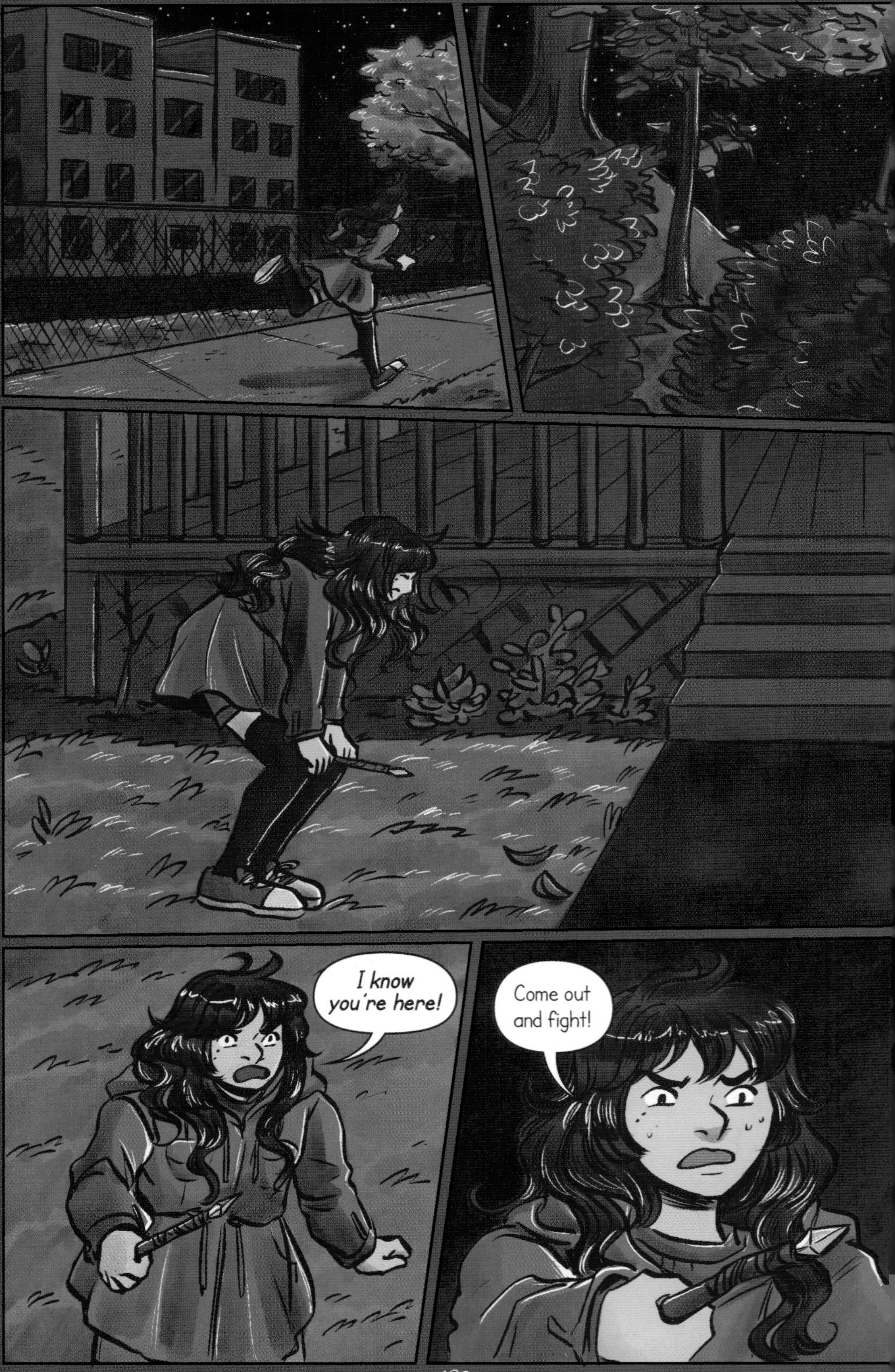
I know you're here!
Come out and fight!

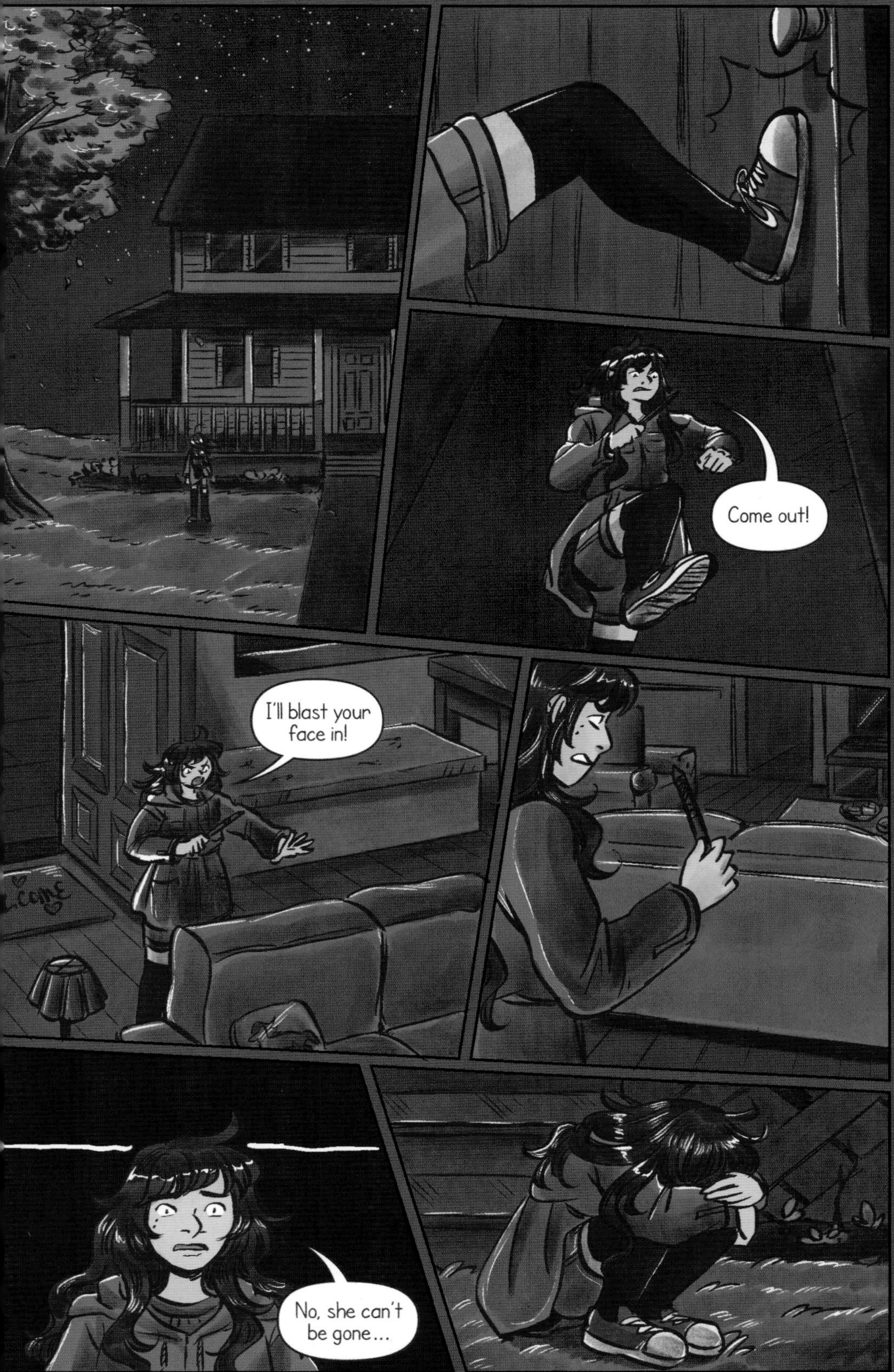
Come out!
I'll blast your face in!
No, she can't be gone...

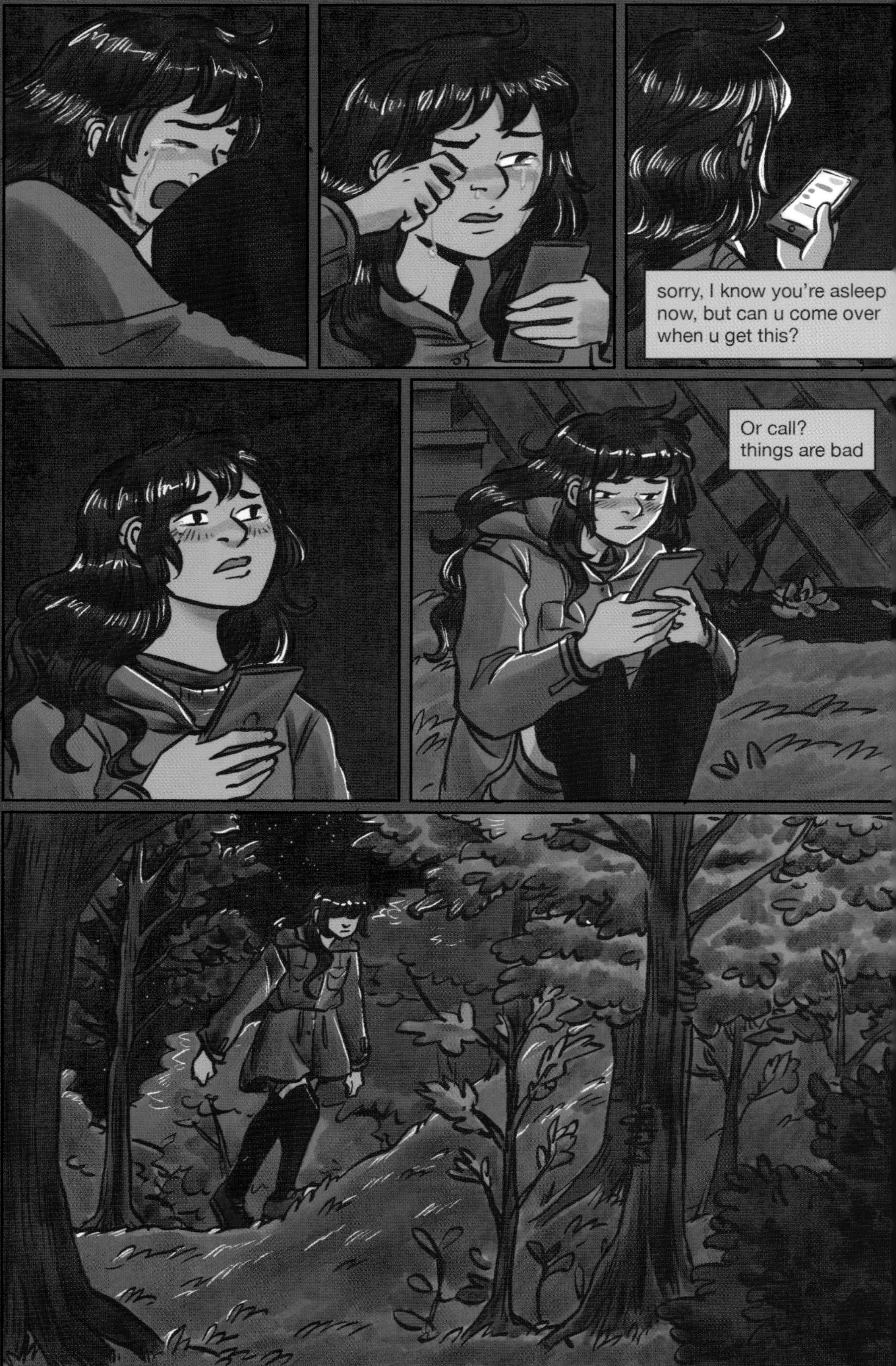
sorry, I know you're asleep now, but can u come over when u get this?
Or call? things are bad

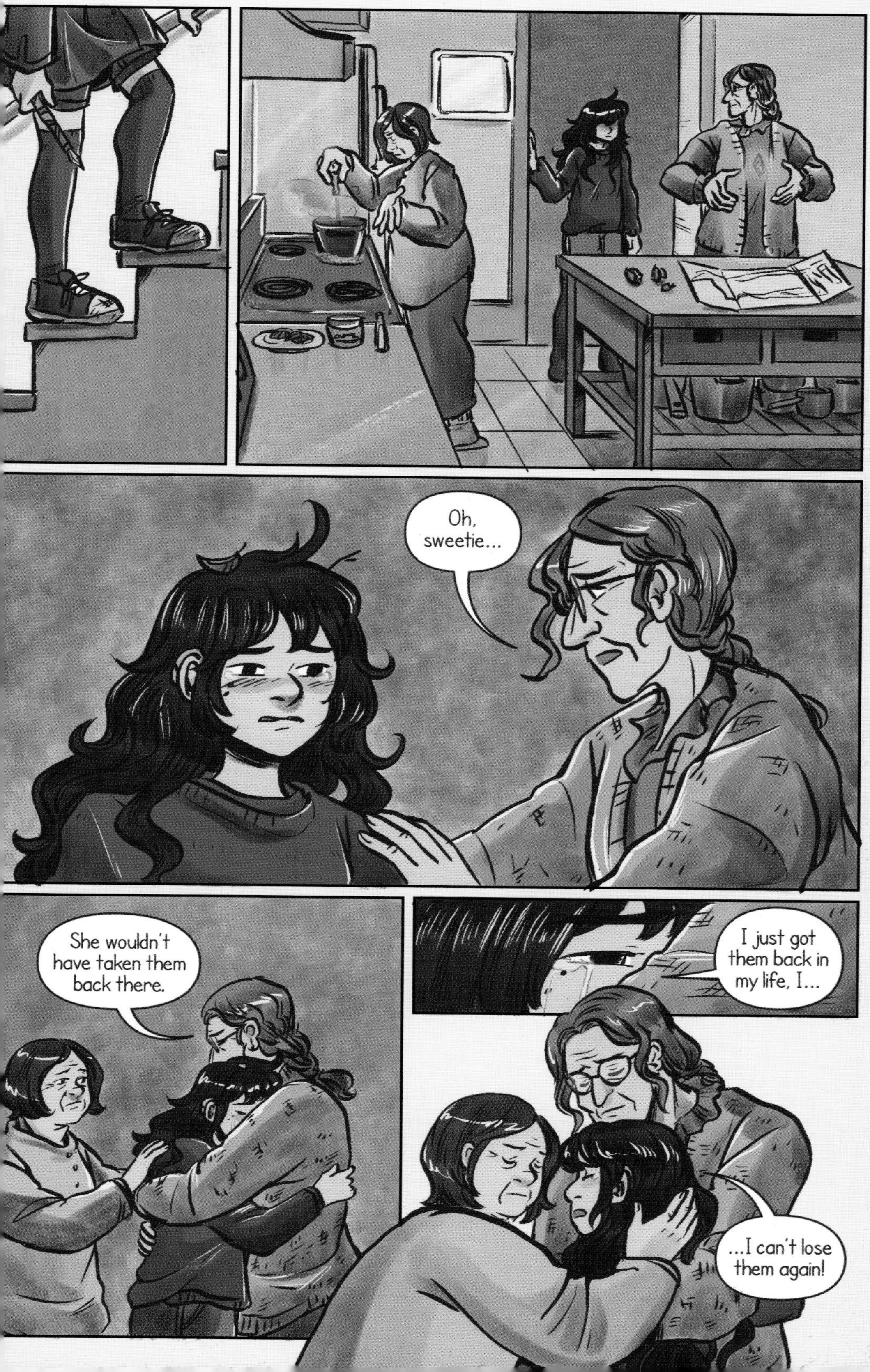
Oh, sweetie...
She wouldn't have taken them back there.
I just got them back in my life, I...
...I can't lose them again!

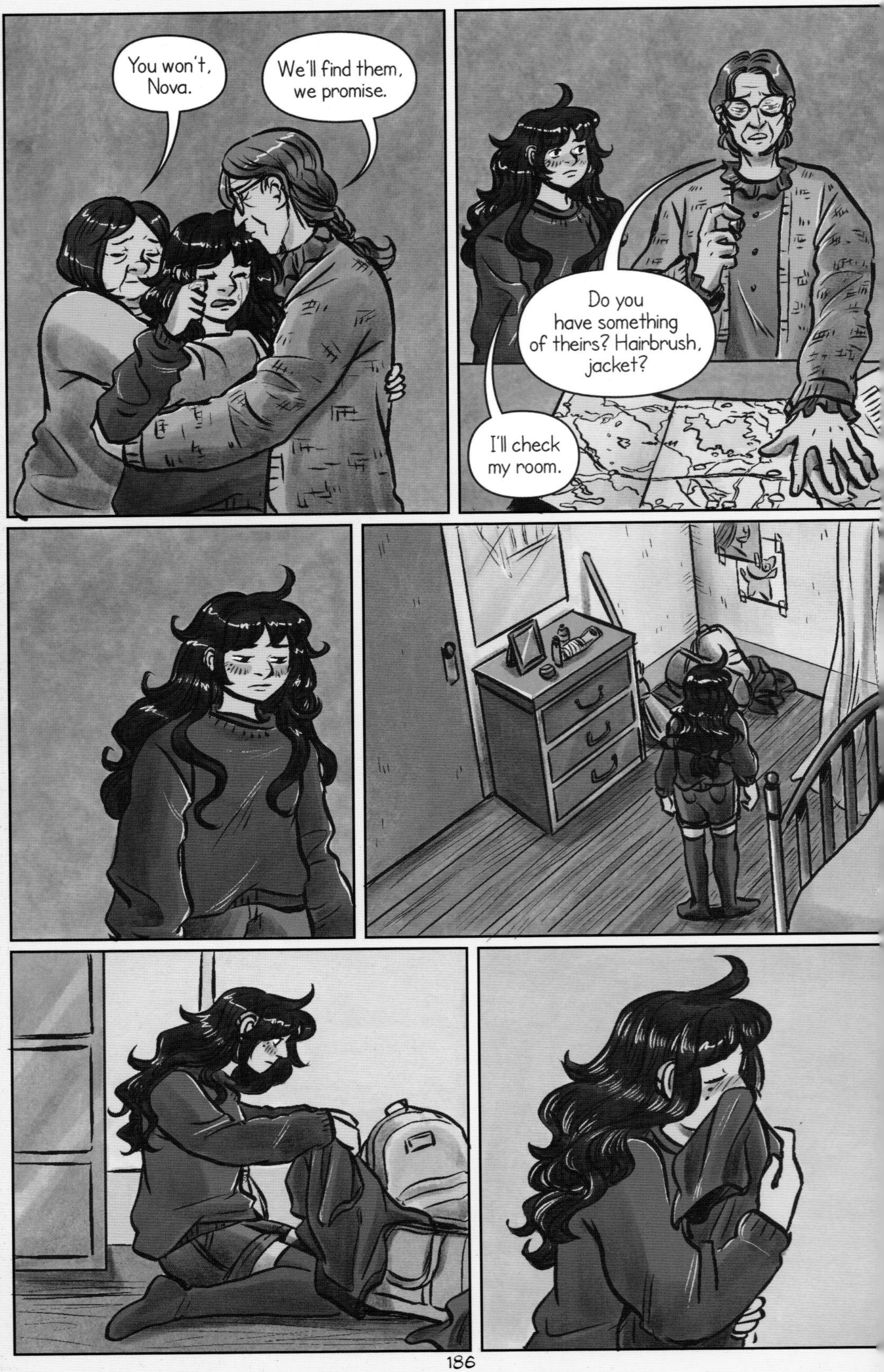
You won't, Nova.
We'll find them, we promise.
Do you have something of theirs? Hairbrush, jacket?
I'll check my room.

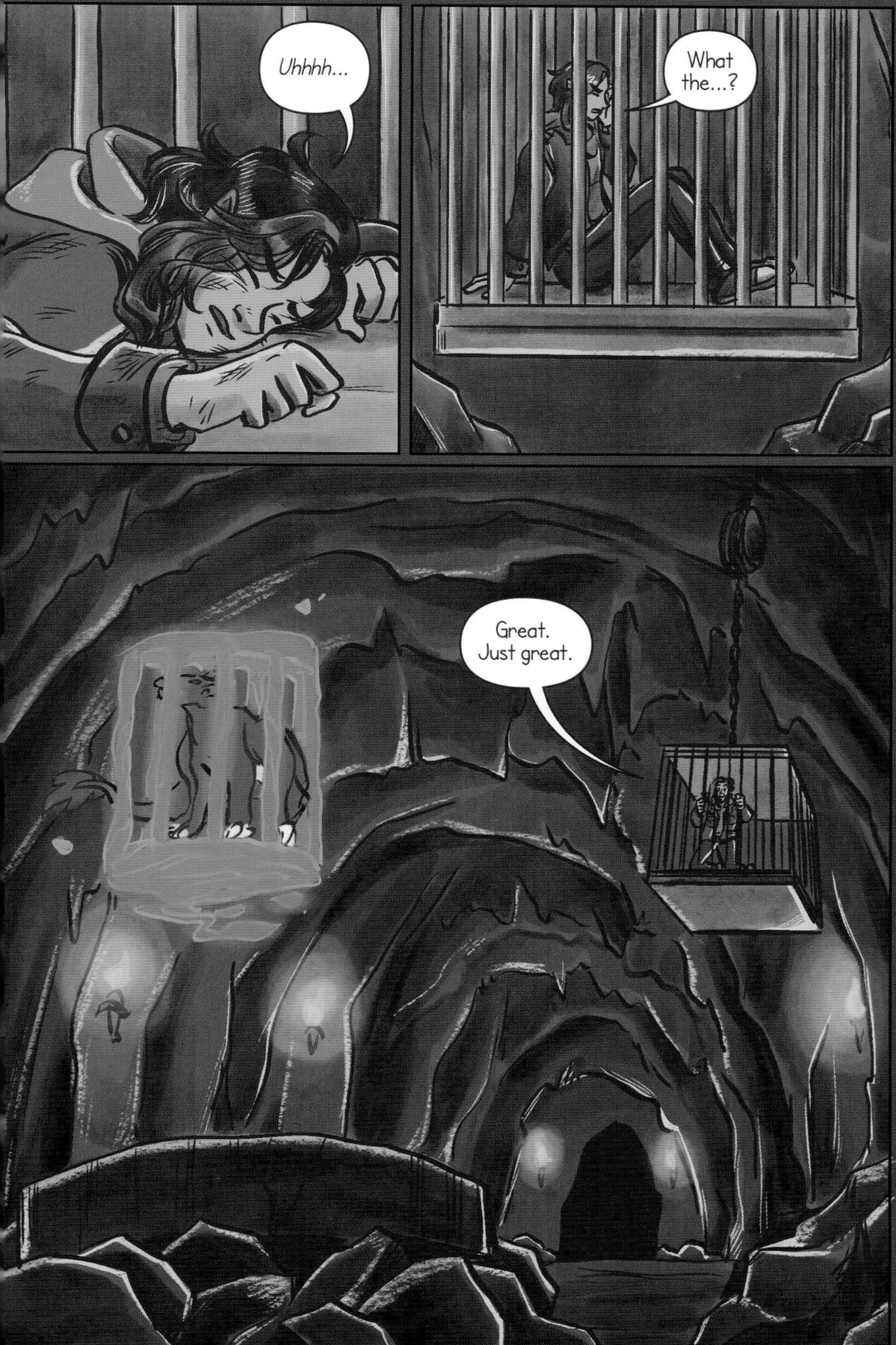
Uhhhh...
What the...?
Great. Just great.

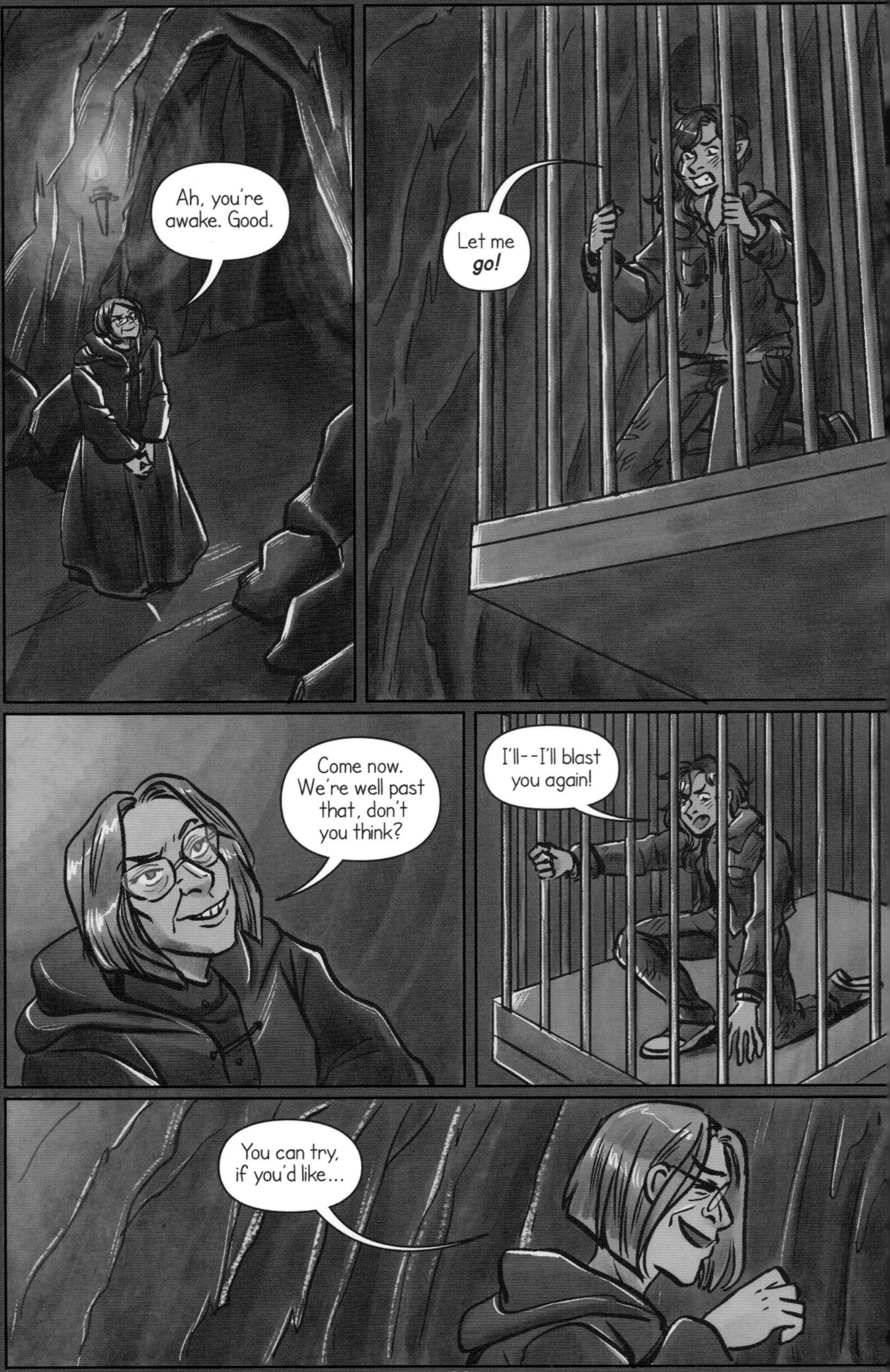
Ah, you're awake. Good.
Let me **go!**
Come now. We're well past that, don't you think?
I'll--I'll blast you again!
You can try, if you'd like...

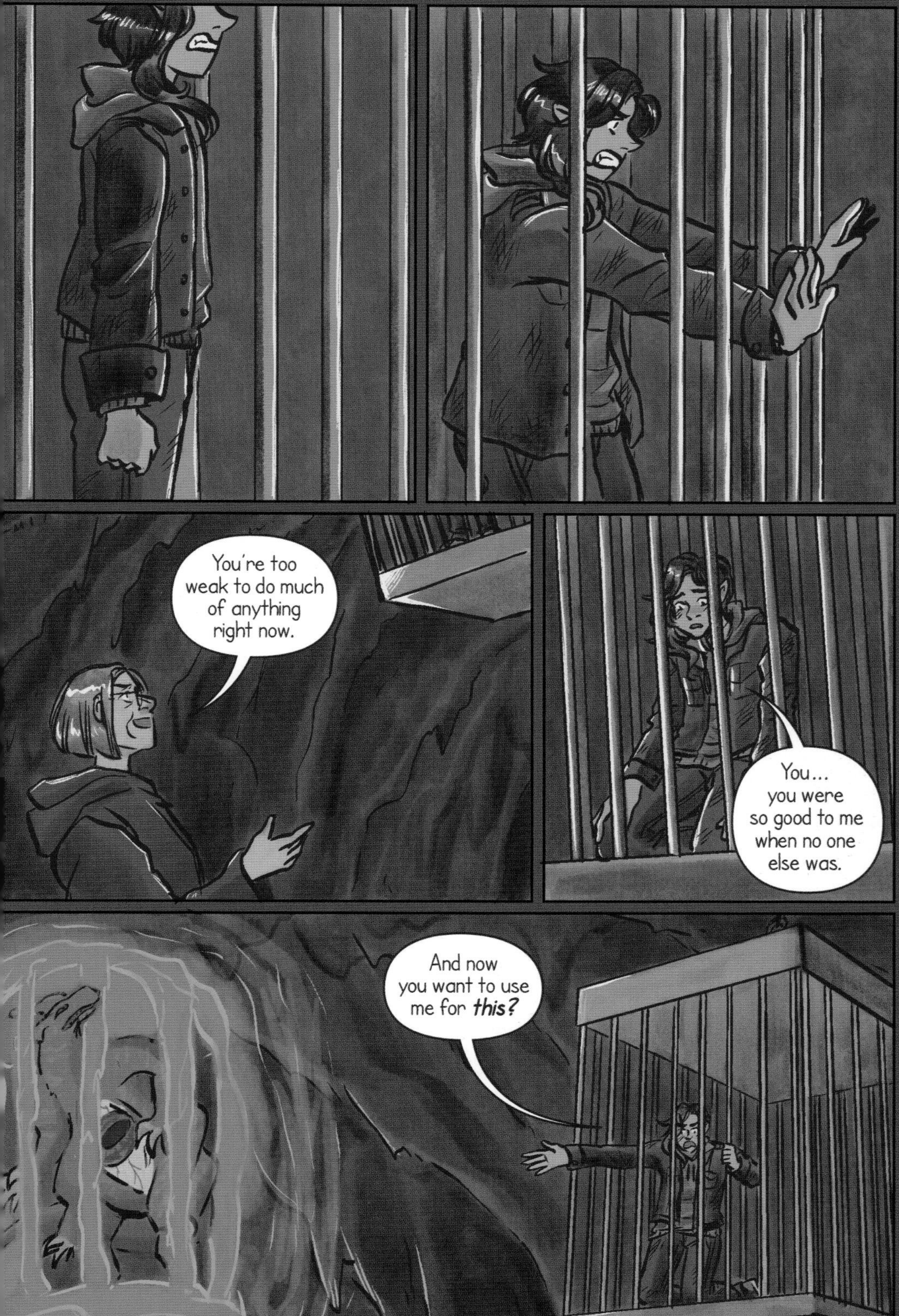
You're too weak to do much of anything right now.
You... you were so good to me when no one else was.
And now you want to use me for *this?*

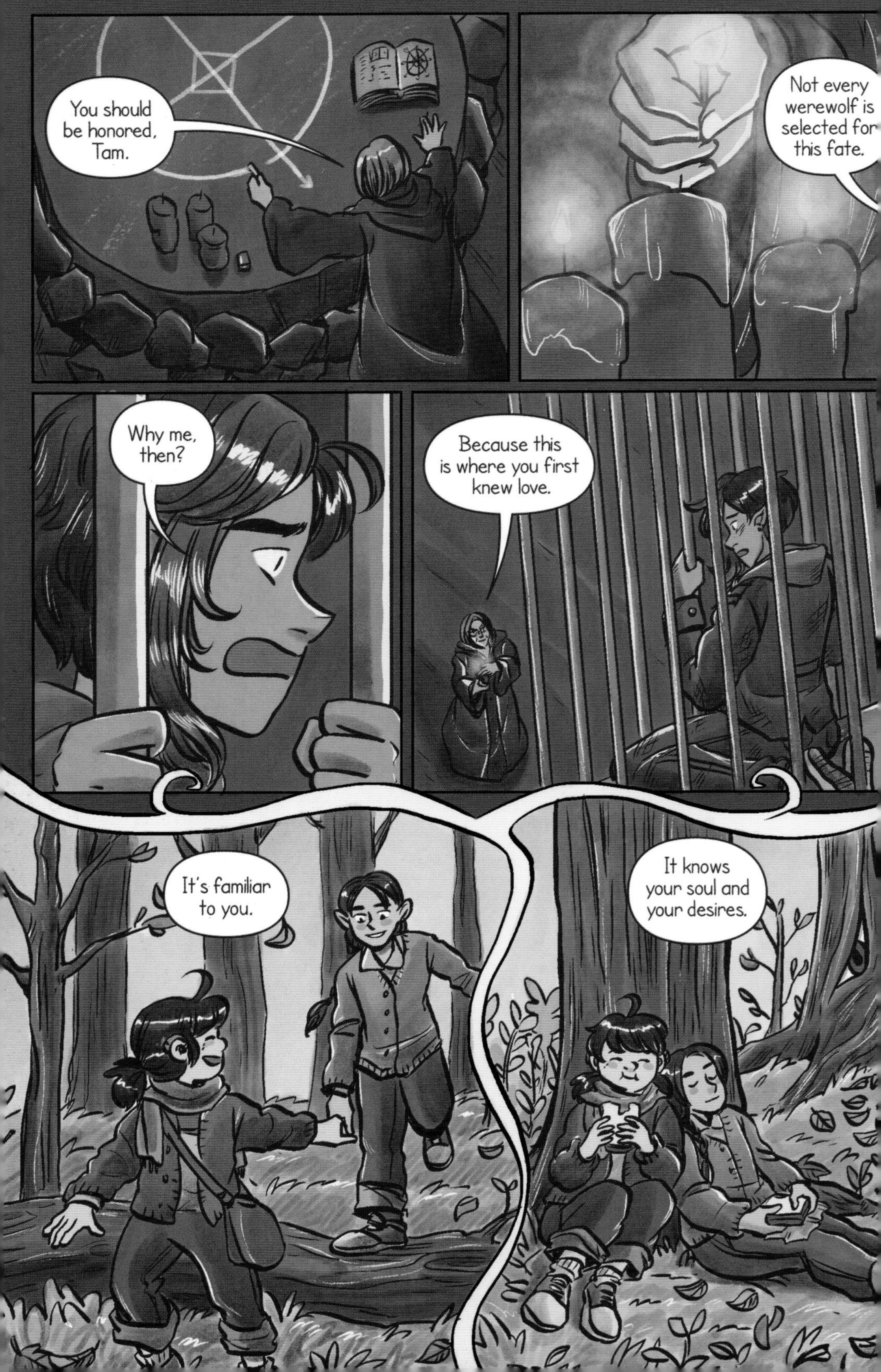
You should be honored, Tam.
Not every werewolf is selected for this fate.
Why me, then?
Because this is where you first knew love.
It's familiar to you.
It knows your soul and your desires.

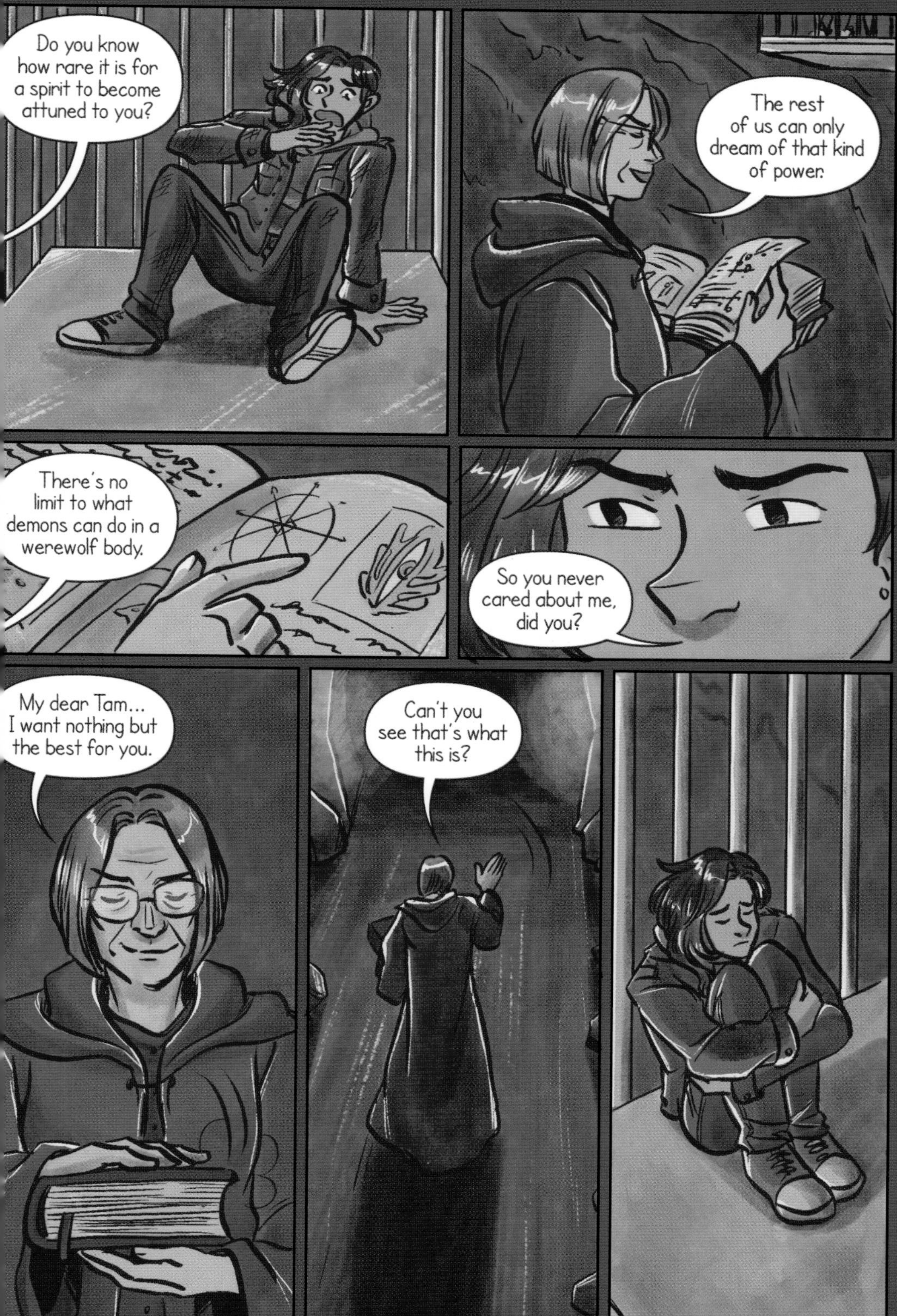
Do you know how rare it is for a spirit to become attuned to you?
The rest of us can only dream of that kind of power.
There's no limit to what demons can do in a werewolf body.
So you never cared about me, did you?
My dear Tam... I want nothing but the best for you.
Can't you see that's what this is?

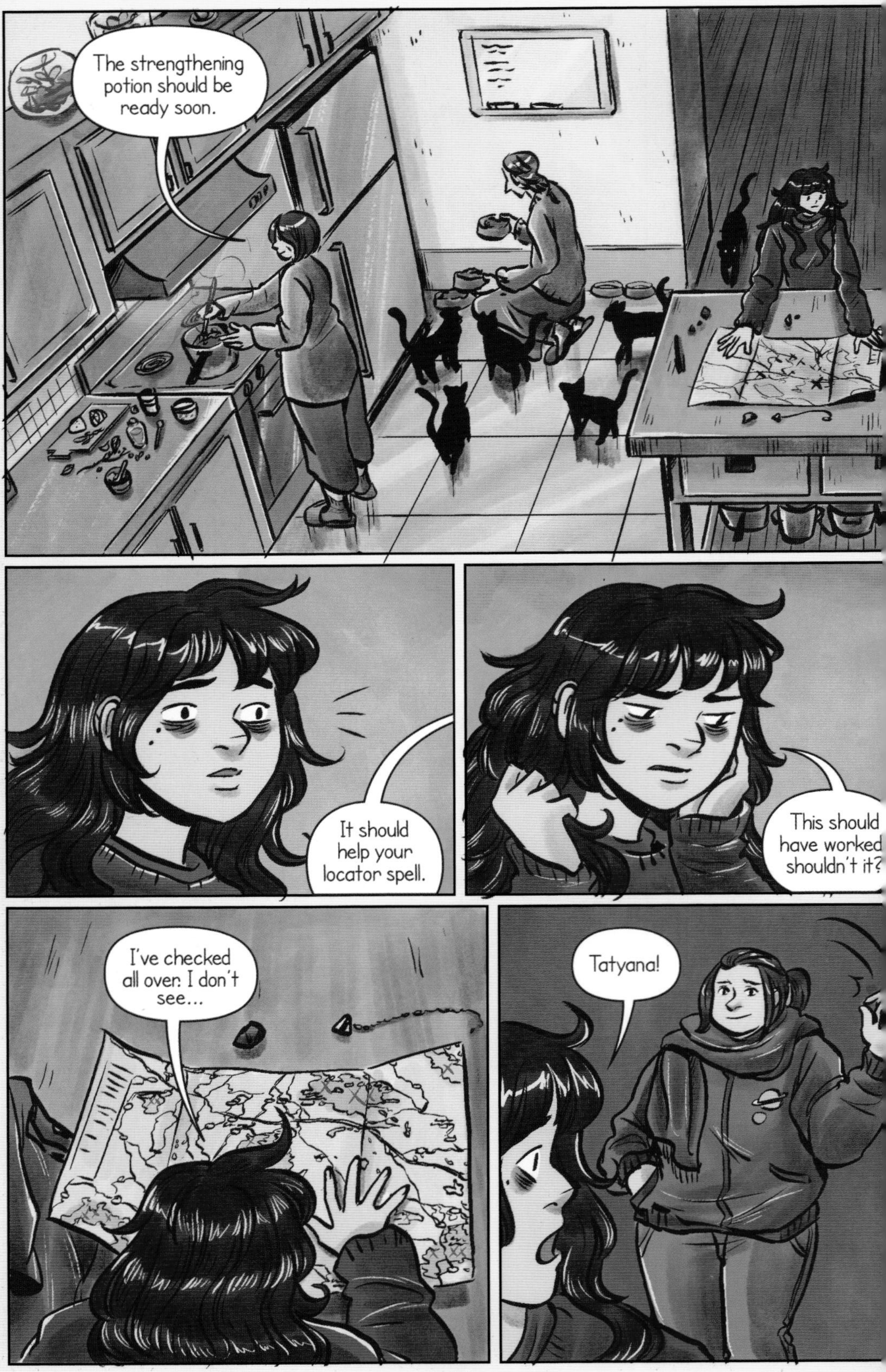
The strengthening potion should be ready soon.
It should help your locator spell.
This should have worked shouldn't it?
I've checked all over. I don't see...
Tatyana!

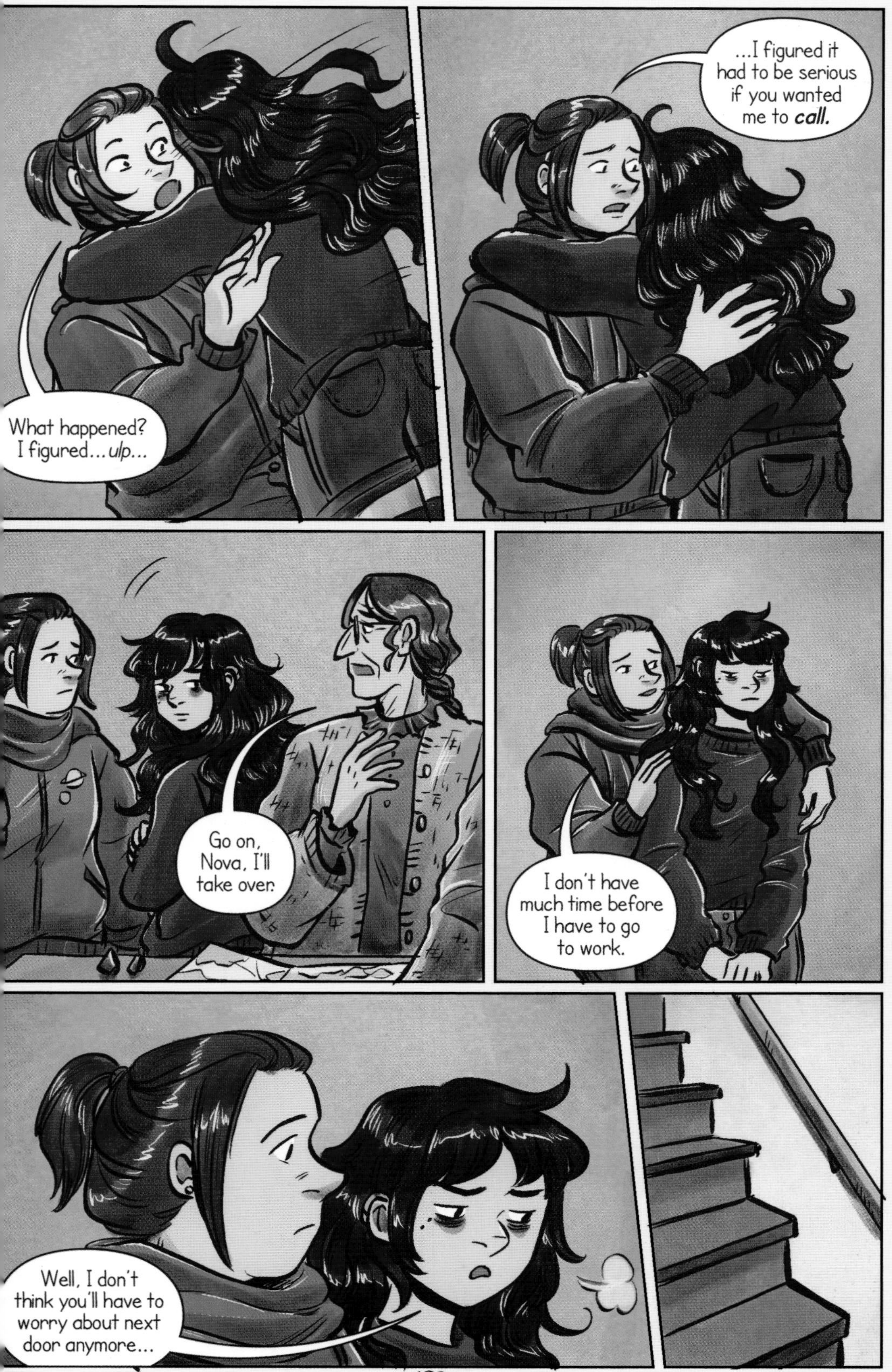
What happened? I figured... *ulp...*
...I figured it had to be serious if you wanted me to ***call.***
Go on, Nova, I'll take over.
I don't have much time before I have to go to work.
Well, I don't think you'll have to worry about next door anymore...

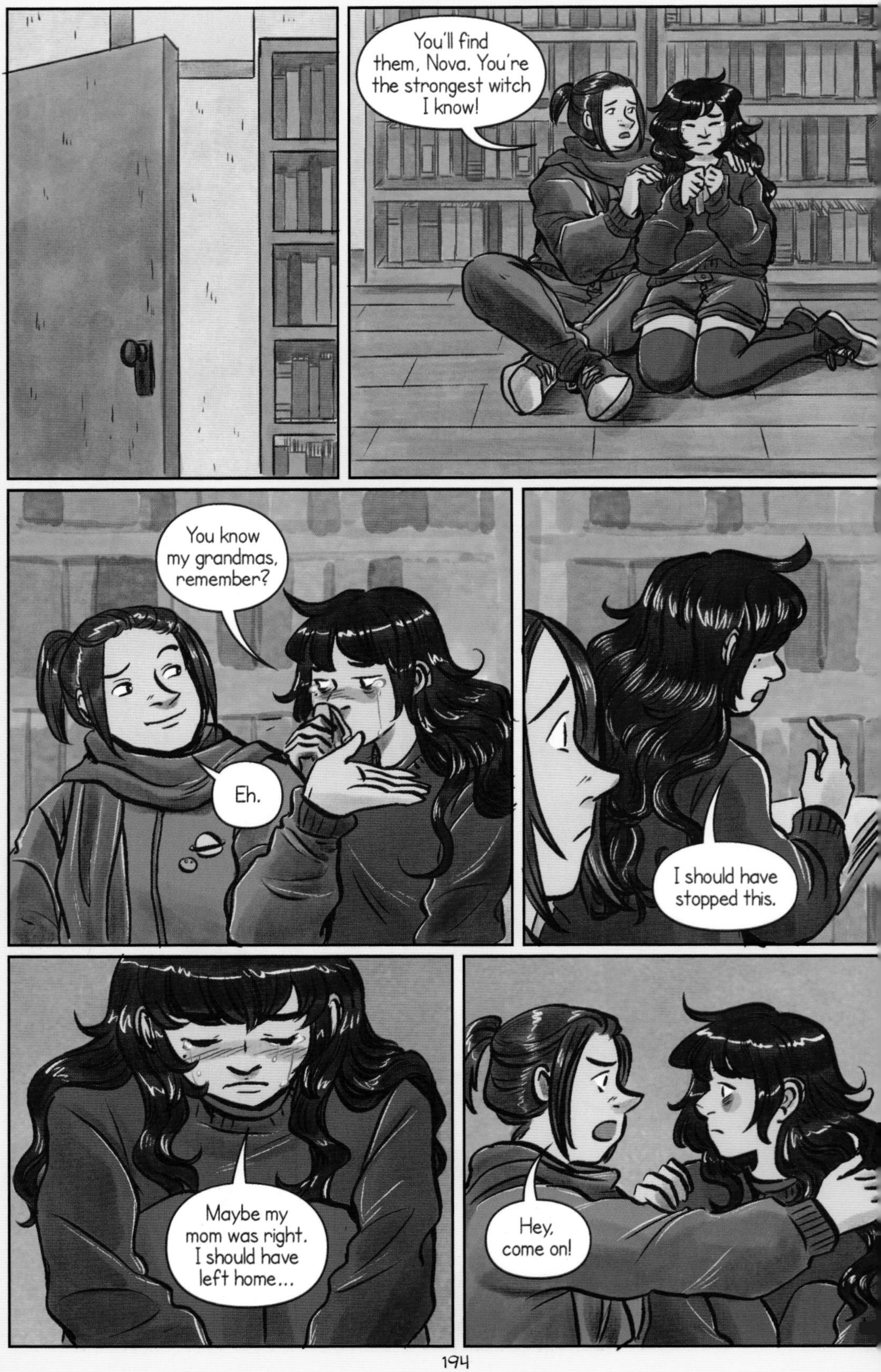
You'll find them, Nova. You're the strongest witch I know!
You know my grandmas, remember?
Eh.
I should have stopped this.
Maybe my mom was right. I should have left home...
Hey, come on!

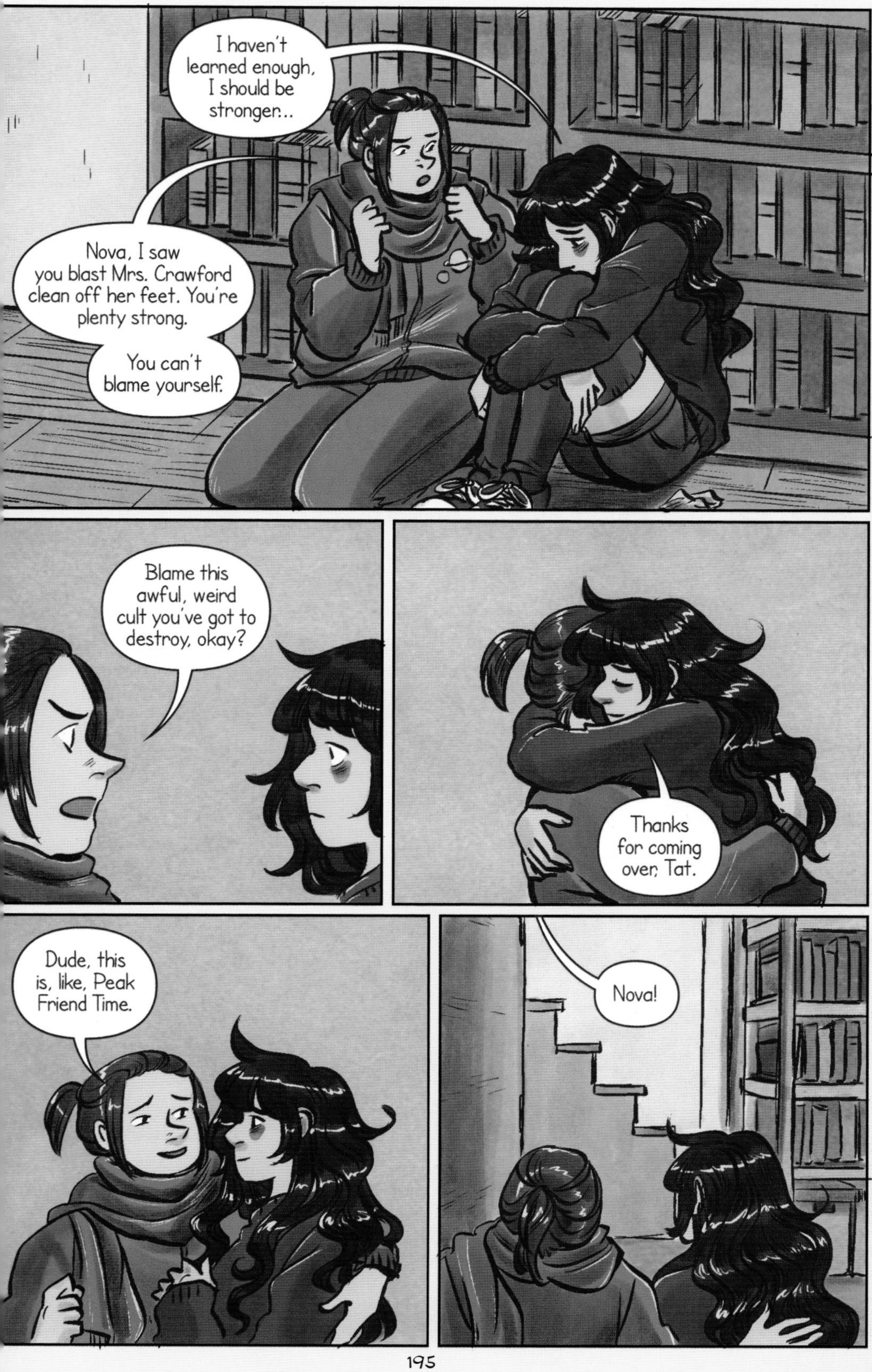
I haven't learned enough, I should be stronger...
Nova, I saw you blast Mrs. Crawford clean off her feet. You're plenty strong.
You can't blame yourself.
Blame this awful, weird cult you've got to destroy, okay?
Thanks for coming over, Tat.
Dude, this is, like, Peak Friend Time.
Nova!

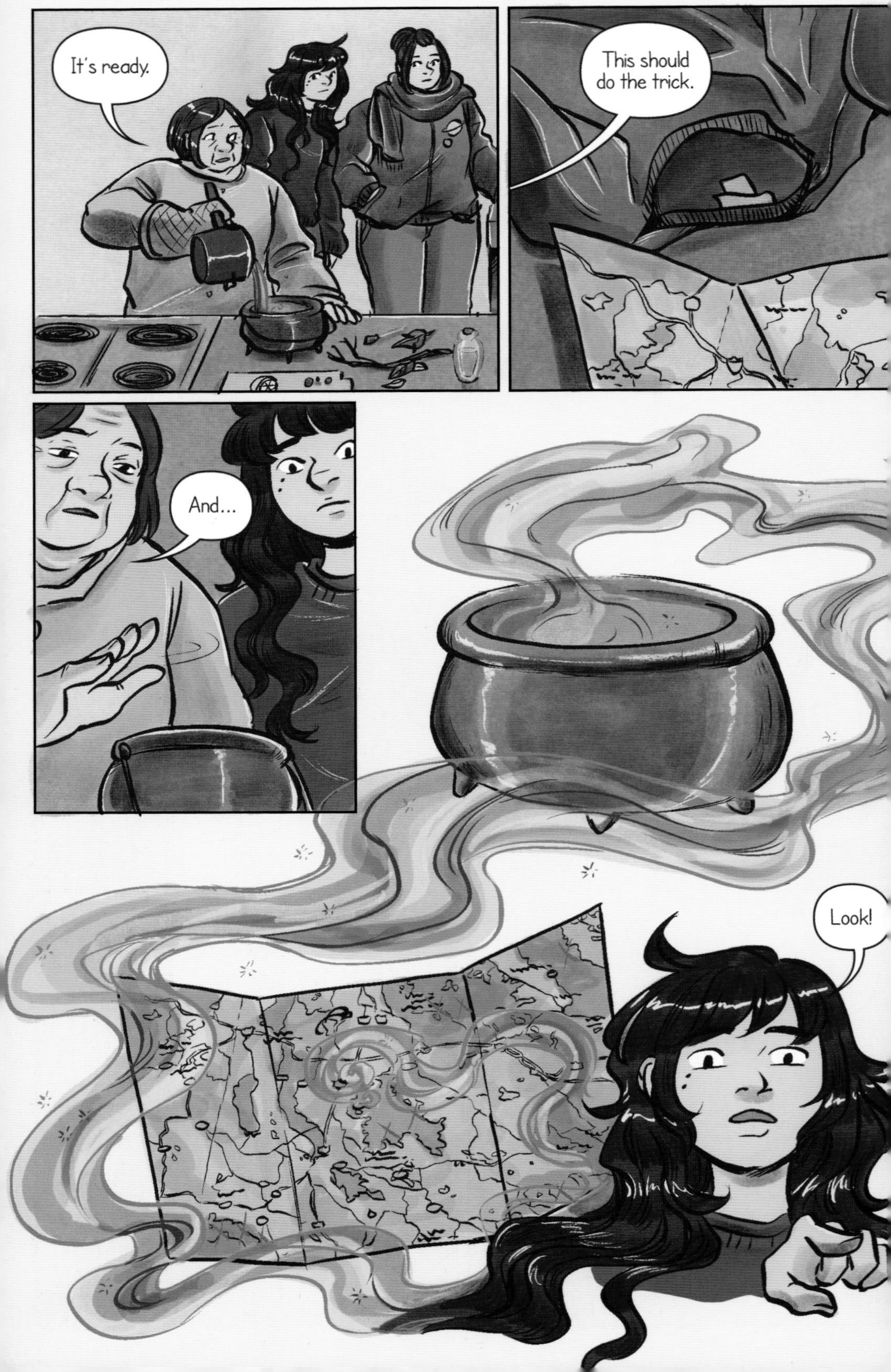
It's ready.
This should do the trick.
And...
Look!

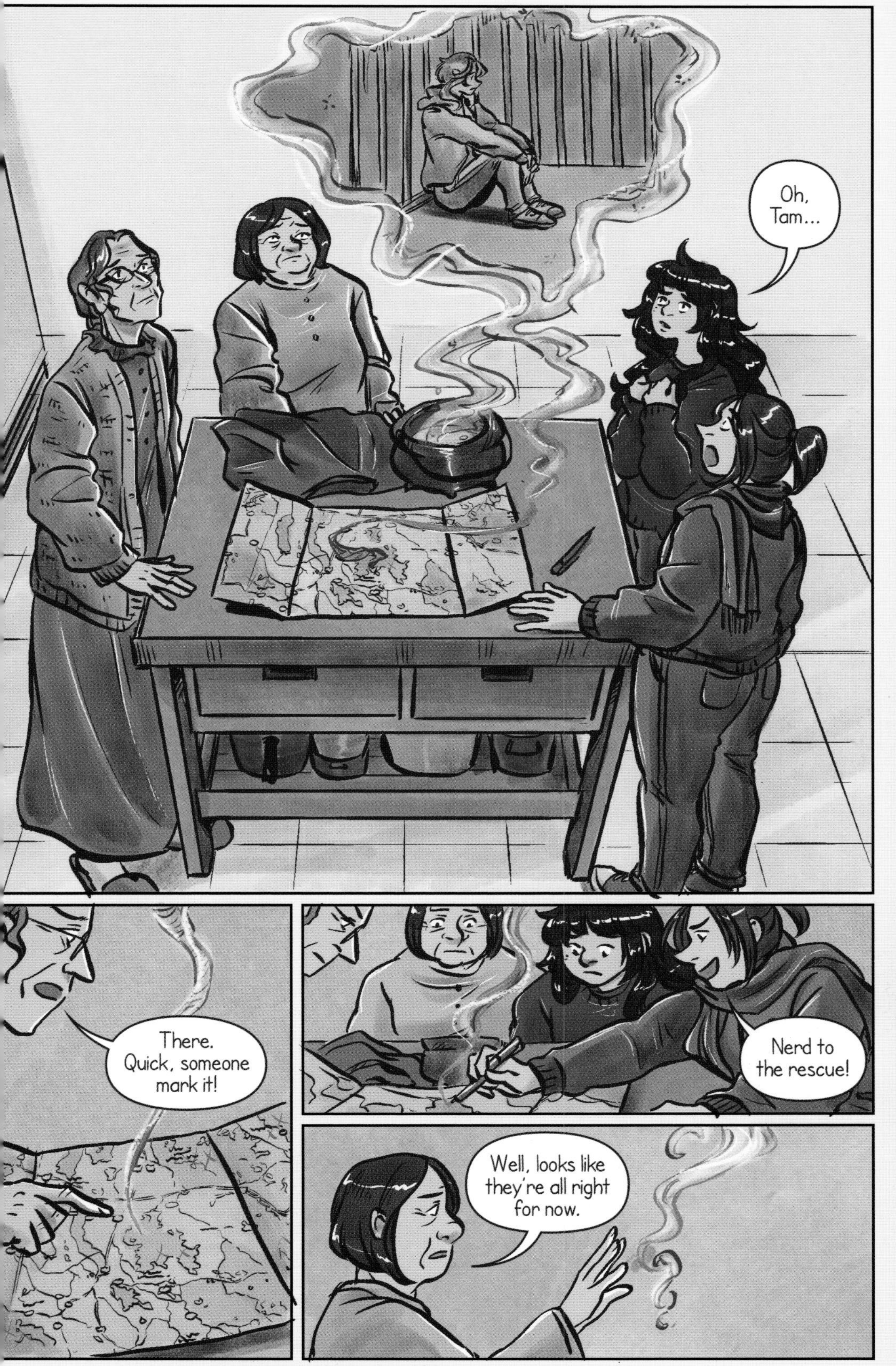
Oh, Tam...
There. Quick, someone mark it!
Nerd to the rescue!
Well, looks like they're all right for now.

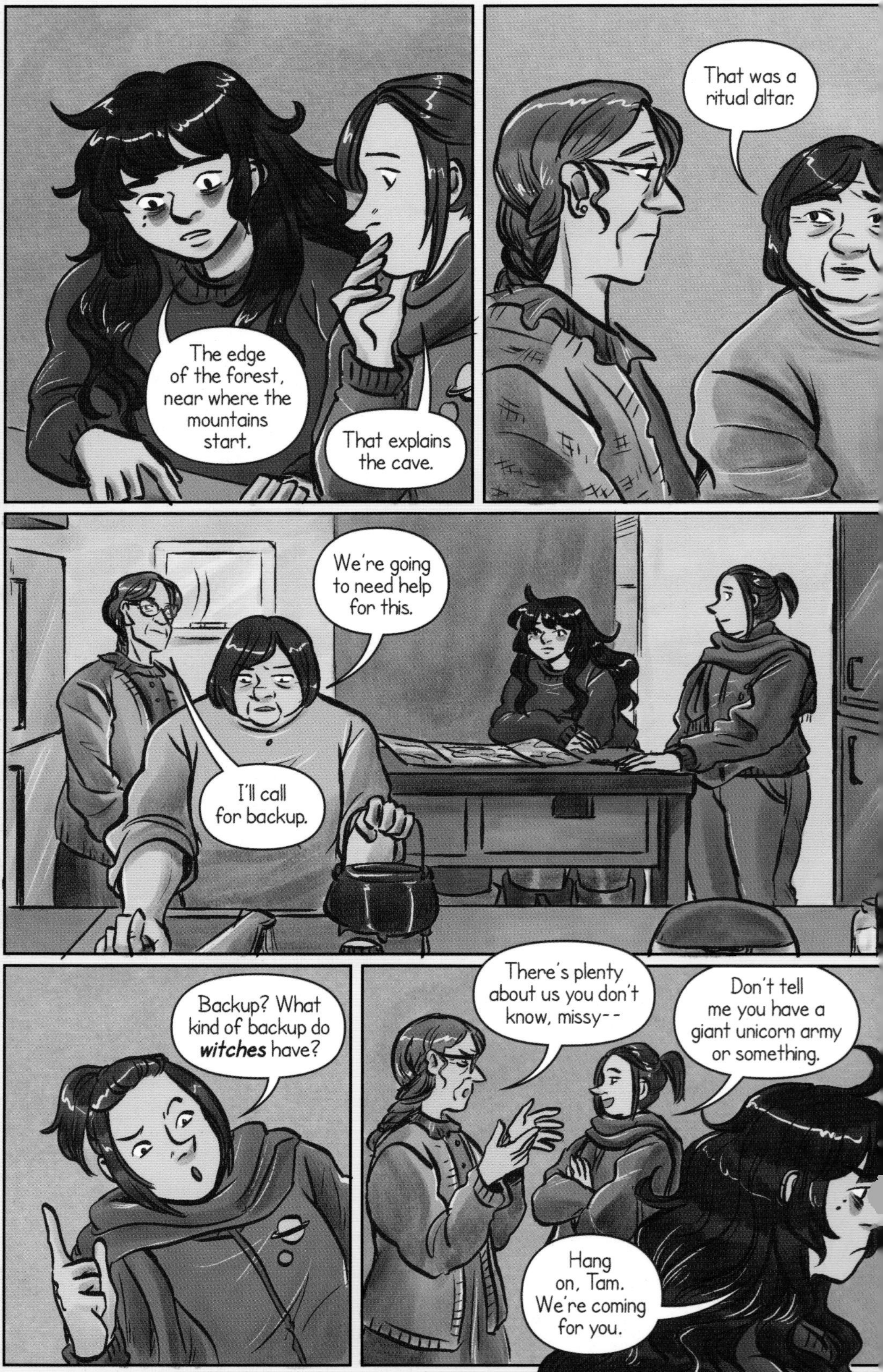
The edge of the forest, near where the mountains start.
That explains the cave.
That was a ritual altar.
We're going to need help for this.
I'll call for backup.
Backup? What kind of backup do ***witches*** have?
There's plenty about us you don't know, missy--
Don't tell me you have a giant unicorn army or something.
Hang on, Tam. We're coming for you.

Chapter 8

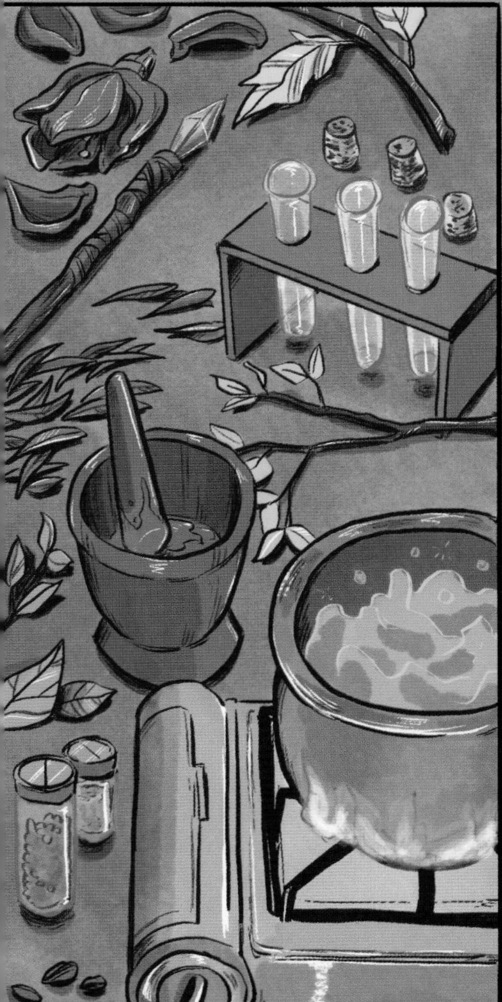

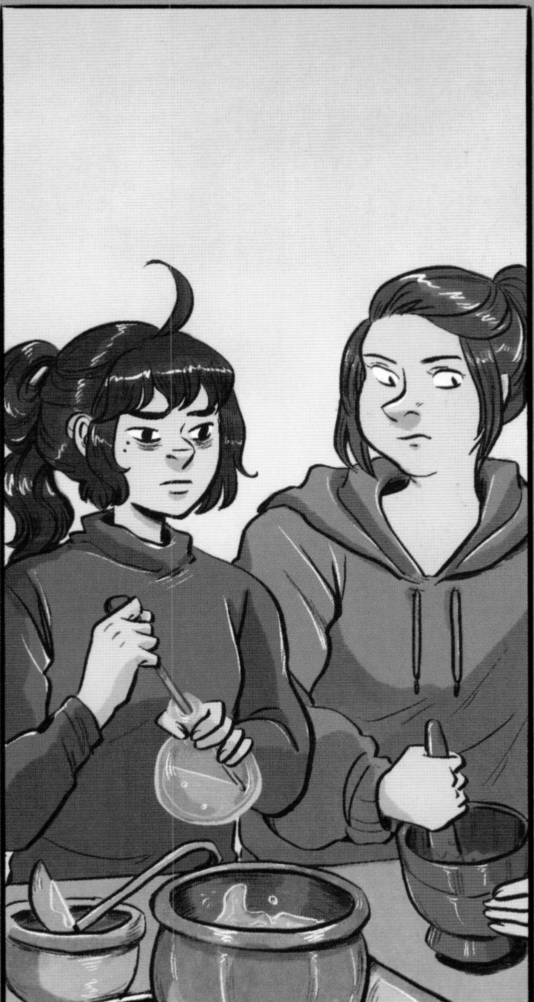

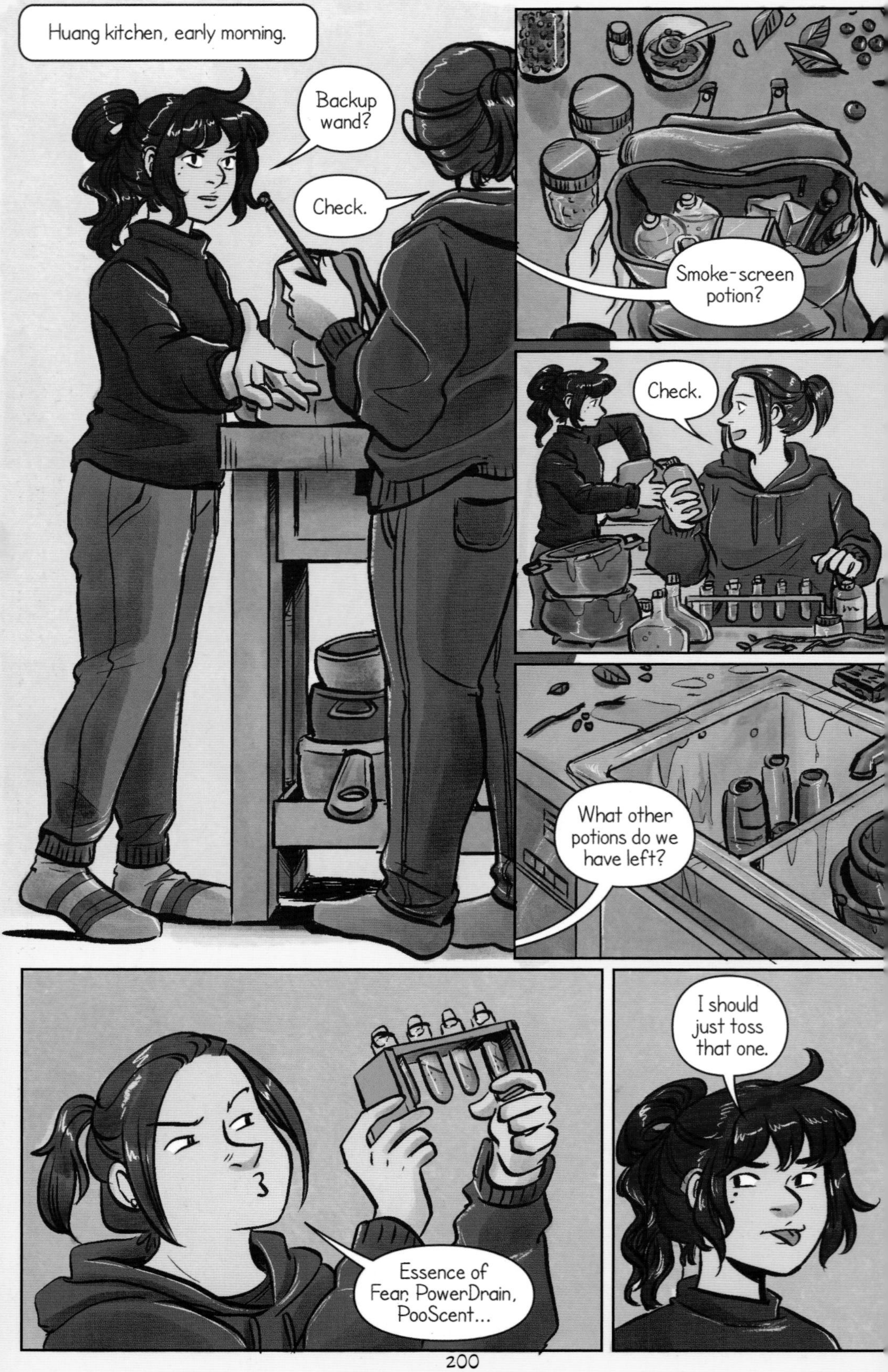
Huang kitchen, early morning.
Backup wand?
Check.
Smoke-screen potion?
Check.
What other potions do we have left?
Essence of Fear, PowerDrain, PooScent...
I should just toss that one.

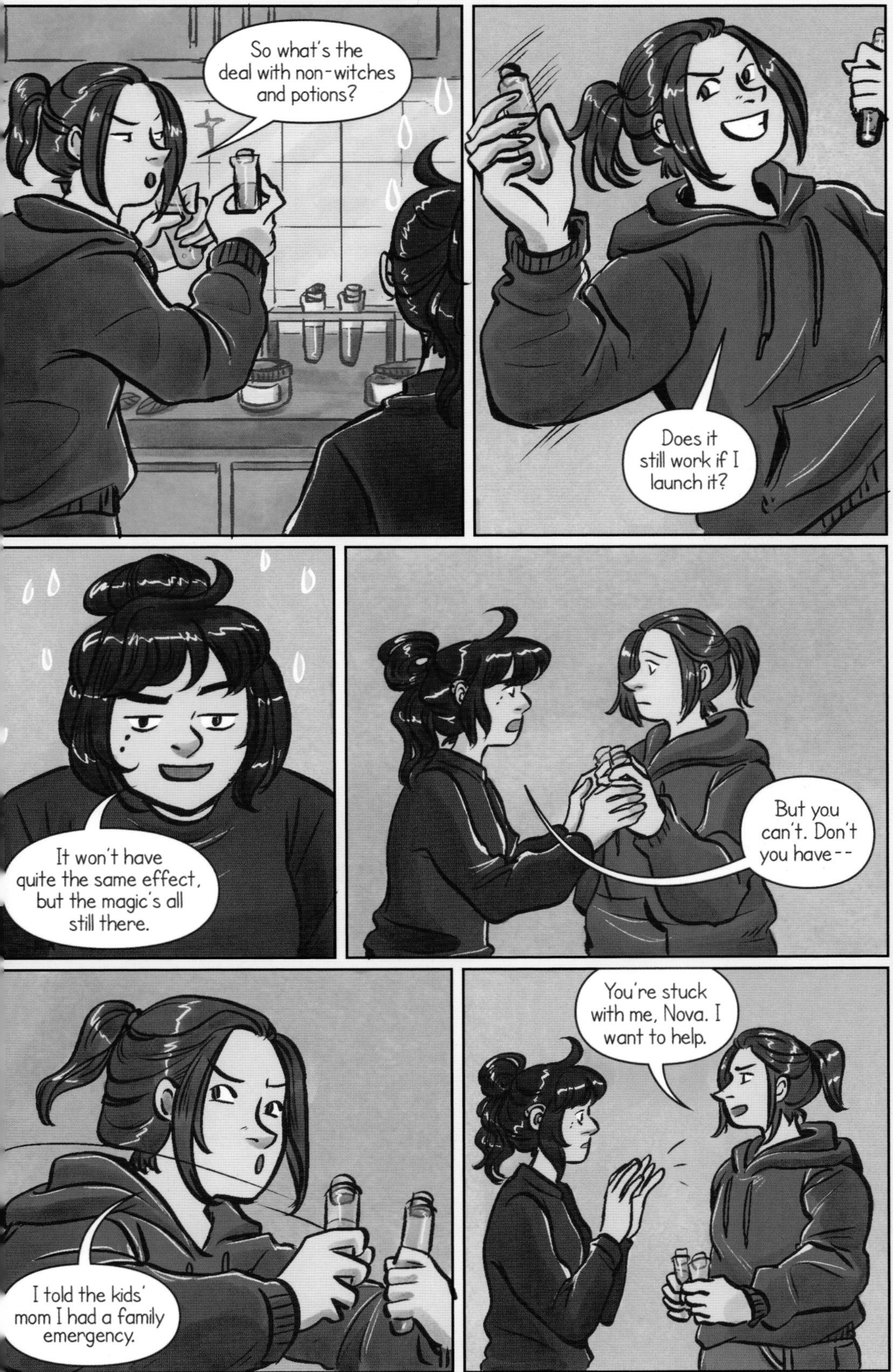
So what's the deal with non-witches and potions?
Does it still work if I launch it?
It won't have quite the same effect, but the magic's all still there.
But you can't. Don't you have--
I told the kids' mom I had a family emergency.
You're stuck with me, Nova. I want to help.

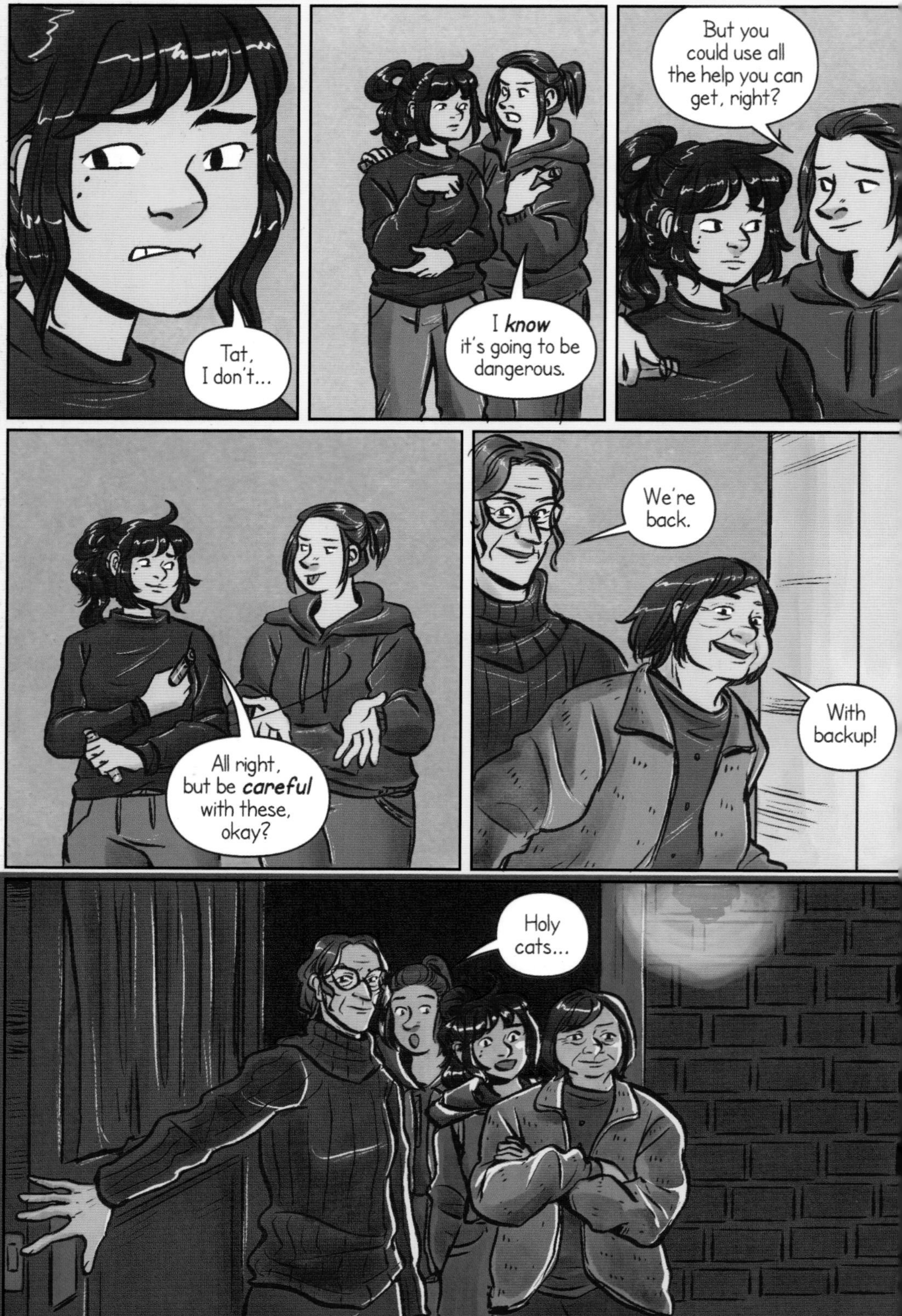
Tat,
I don't...
I **know**
it's going to be
dangerous.
But you
could use all
the help you can
get, right?
All right,
but be ***careful***
with these,
okay?
We're
back.
With
backup!
Holy
cats...

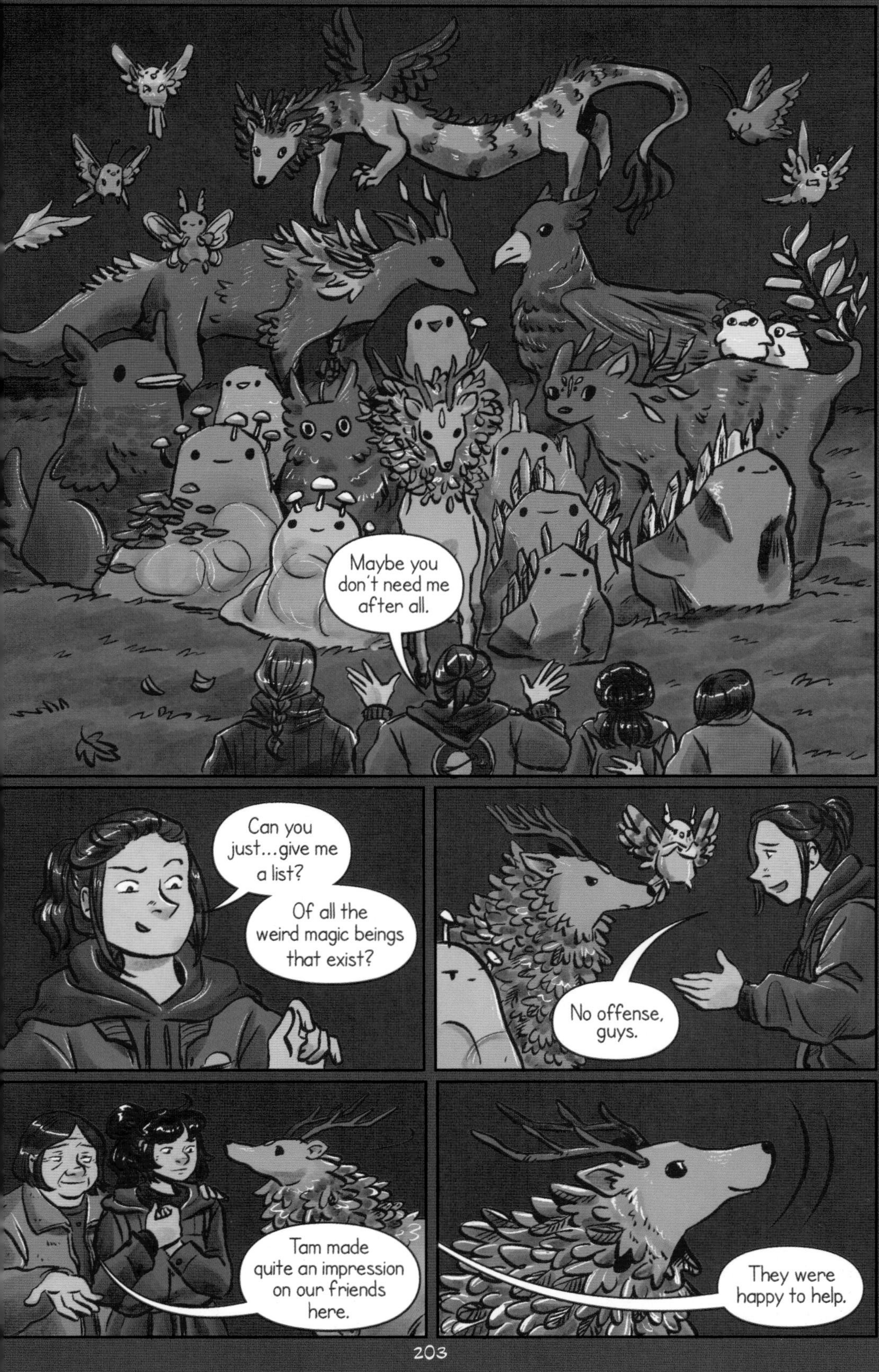
Maybe you don't need me after all.
Can you just...give me a list?
Of all the weird magic beings that exist?
No offense, guys.
Tam made quite an impression on our friends here.
They were happy to help.

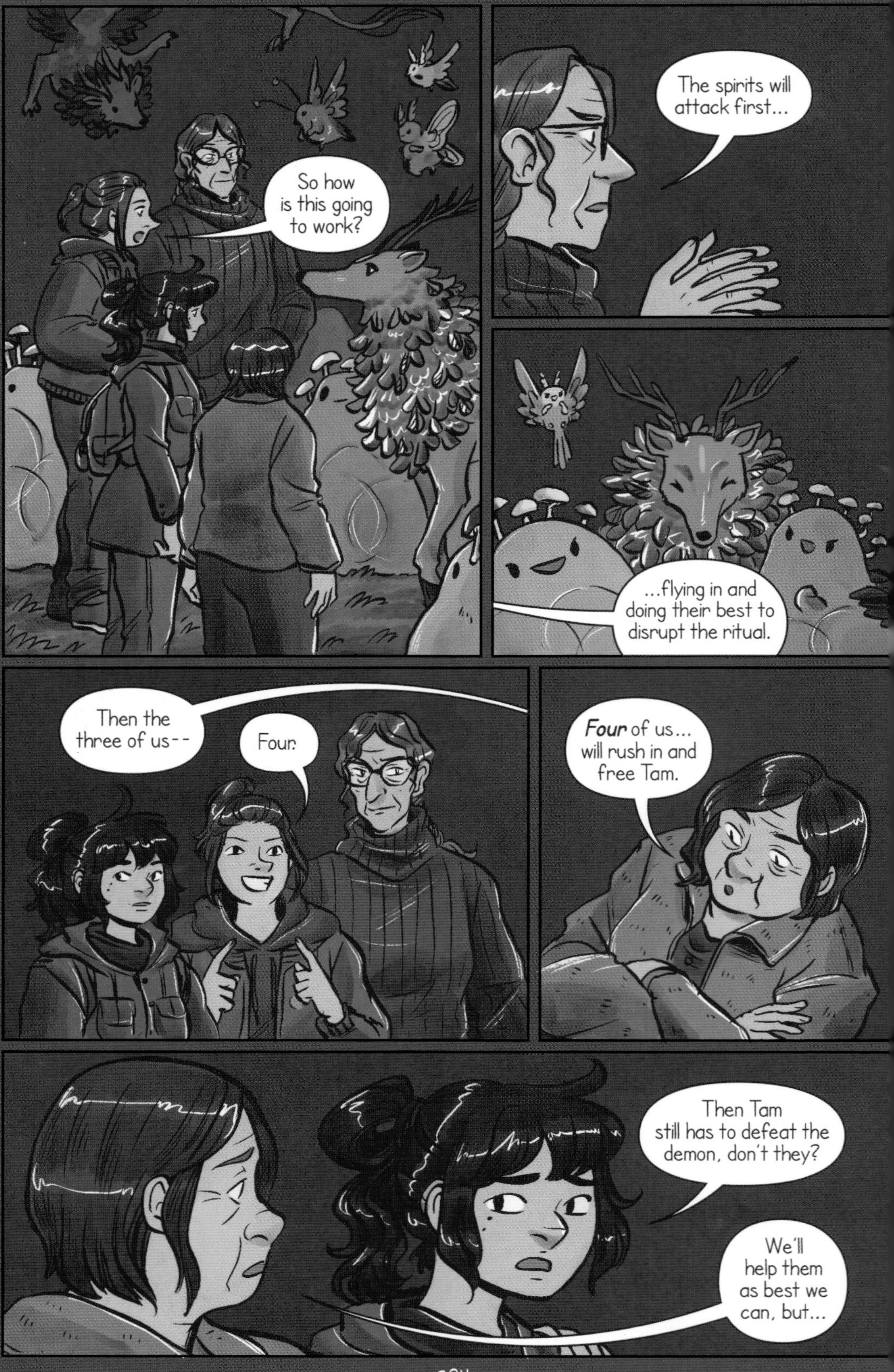
So how is this going to work?
The spirits will attack first...
...flying in and doing their best to disrupt the ritual.
Then the three of us--
Four.
Four of us... will rush in and free Tam.
Then Tam still has to defeat the demon, don't they?
We'll help them as best we can, but...

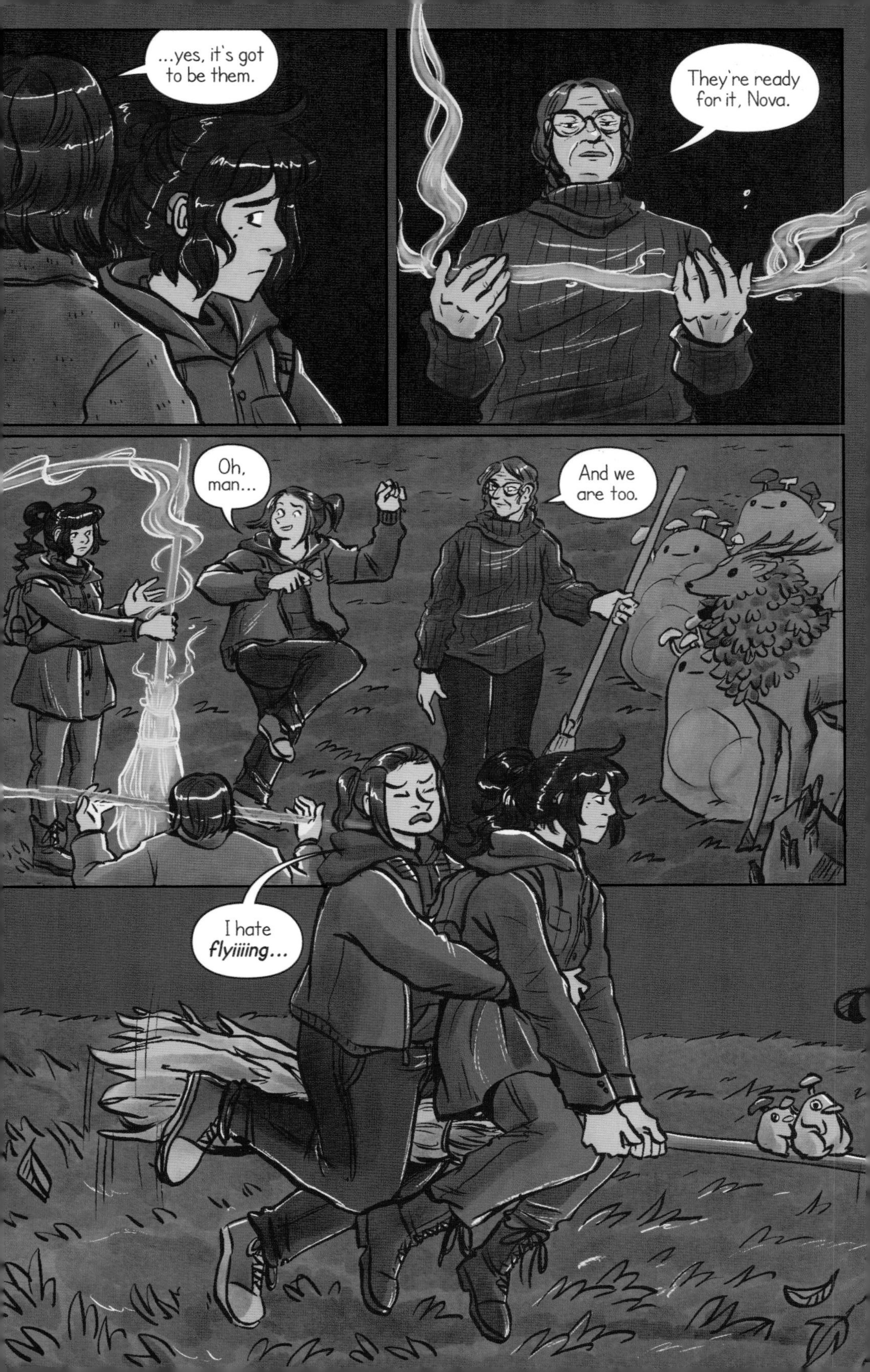
...yes, it's got to be them.
They're ready for it, Nova.
Oh, man...
And we are too.
I hate *flyiiiing...*

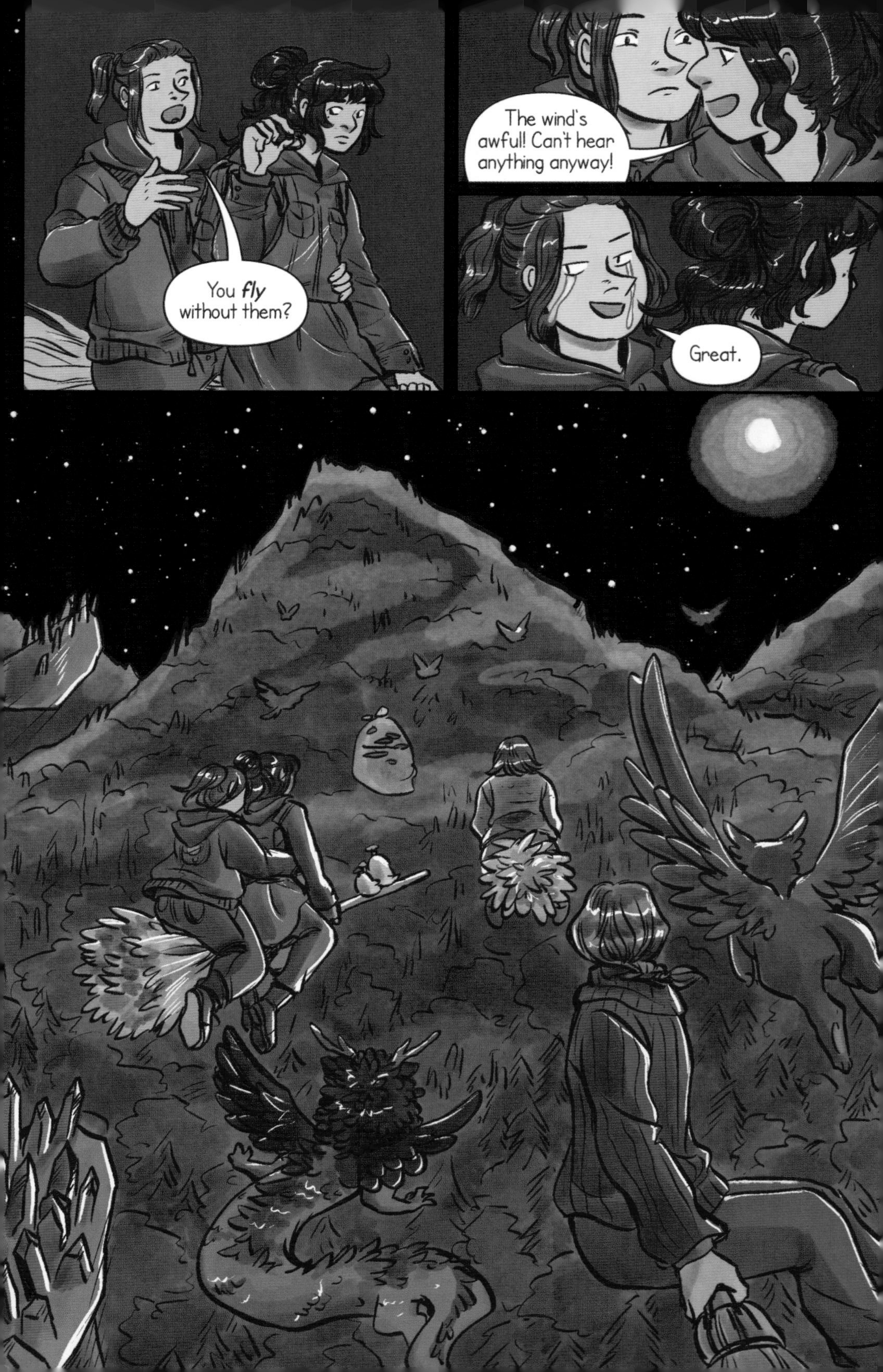
You *fly* without them?
The wind's awful! Can't hear anything anyway!
Great.

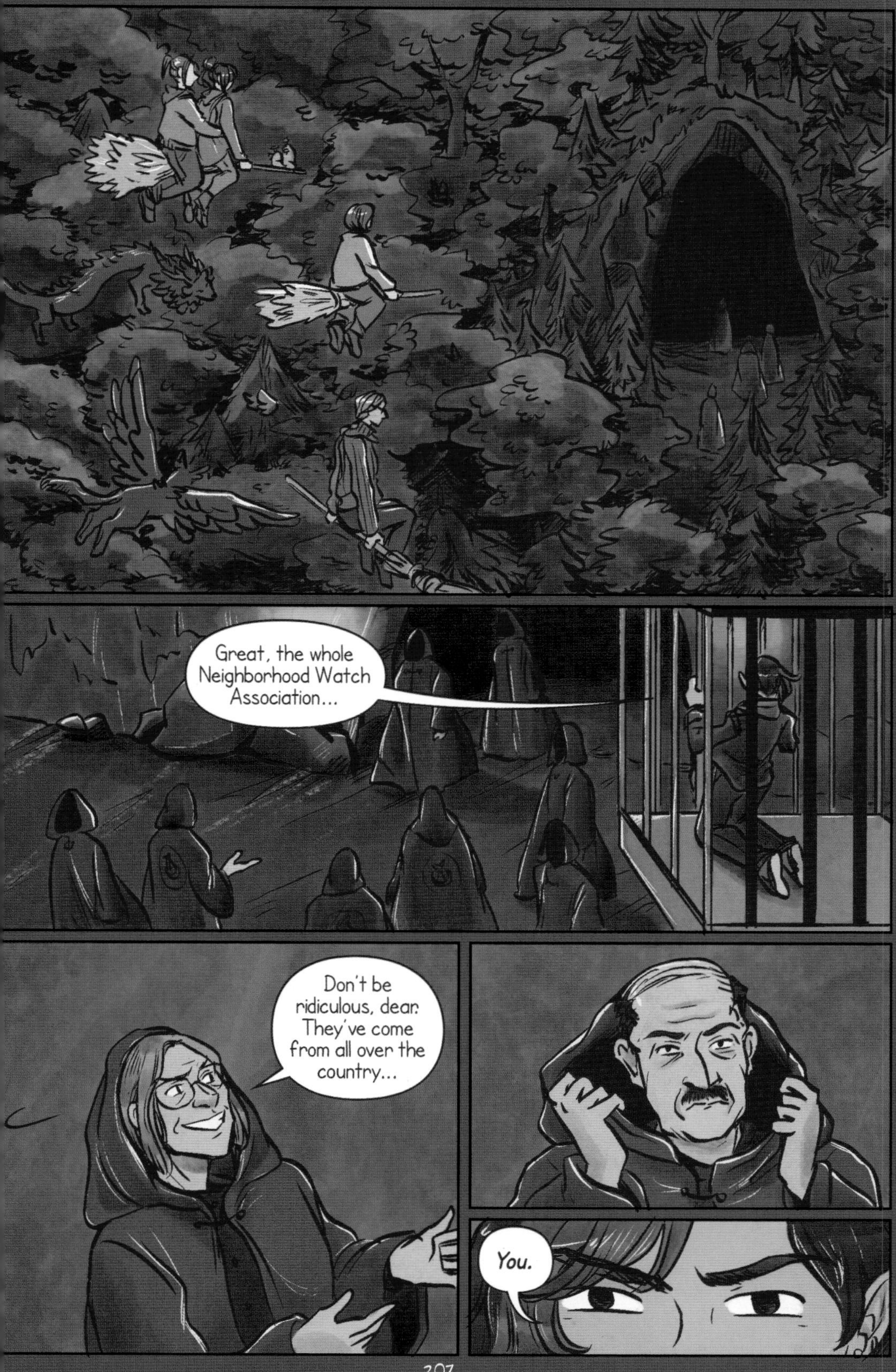
Great, the whole Neighborhood Watch Association...
Don't be ridiculous, dear. They've come from all over the country...
You.

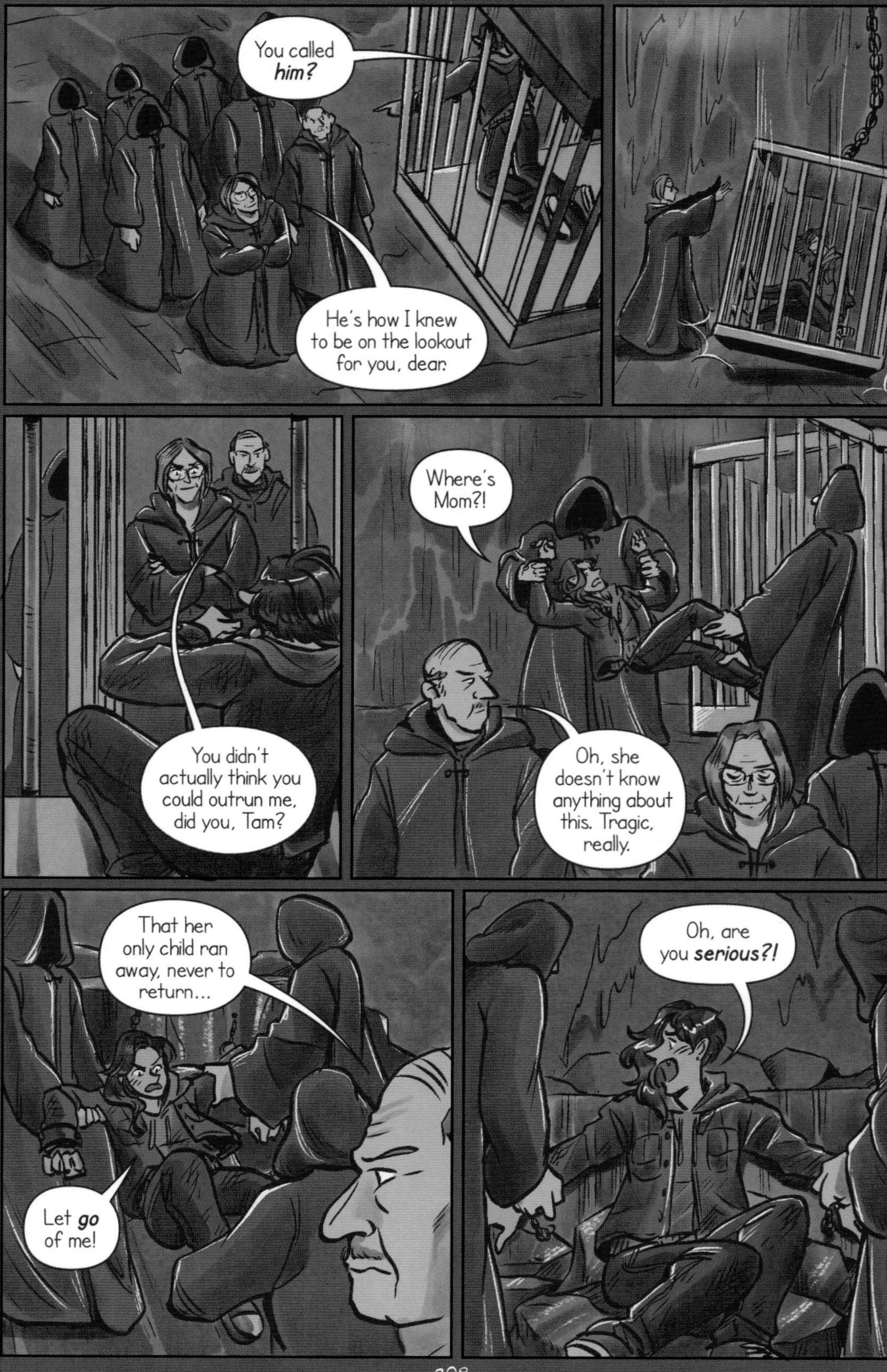
You called *him?*
He's how I knew to be on the lookout for you, dear.
You didn't actually think you could outrun me, did you, Tam?
Where's Mom?!
Oh, she doesn't know anything about this. Tragic, really.
That her only child ran away, never to return...
Let *go* of me!
Oh, are you *serious?!*

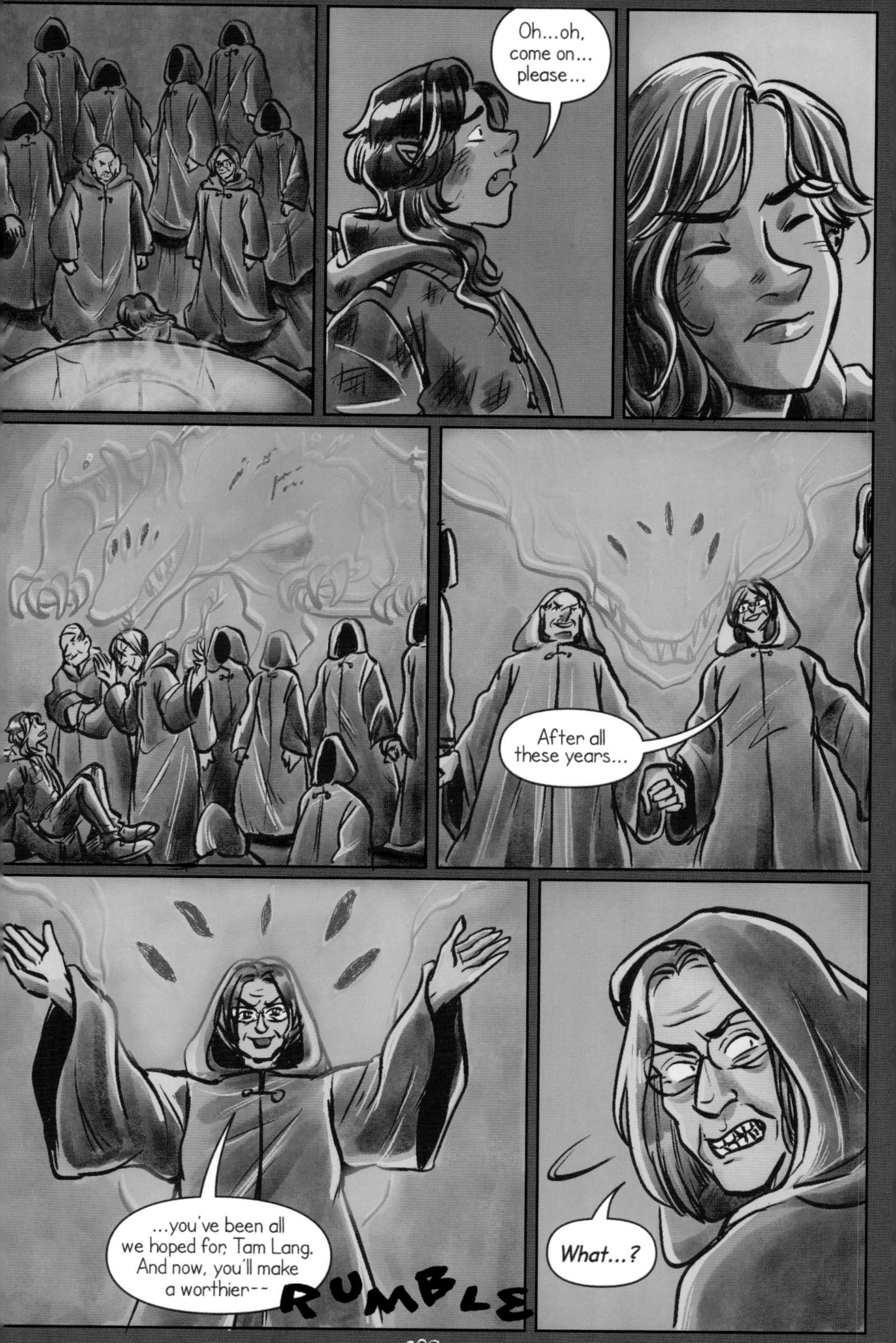
Oh...oh, come on... please...
After all these years...
...you've been all we hoped for, Tam Lang. And now, you'll make a worthier--
RUMBLE
What...?

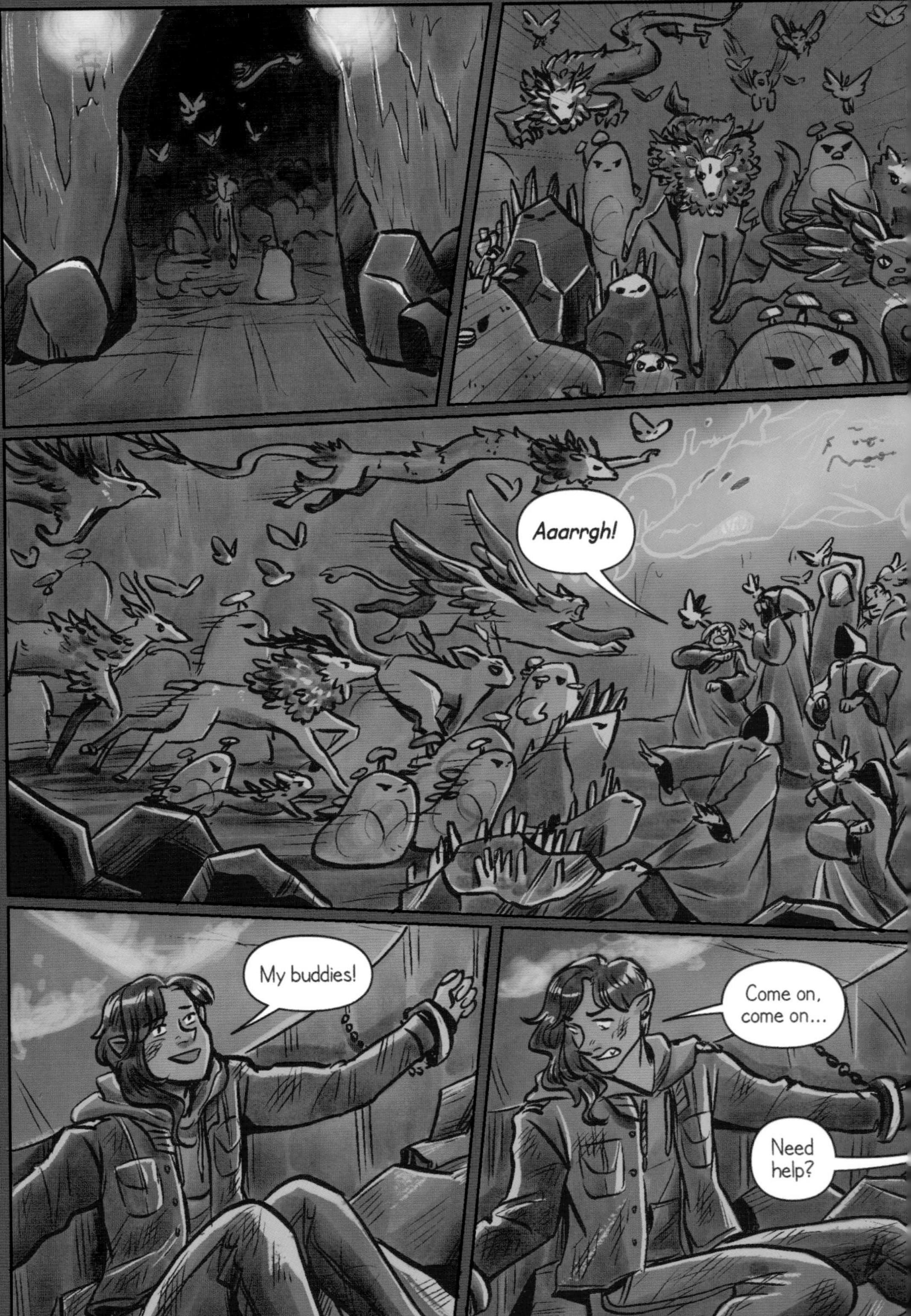
Aaarrgh!
My buddies!
Come on, come on...
Need help?

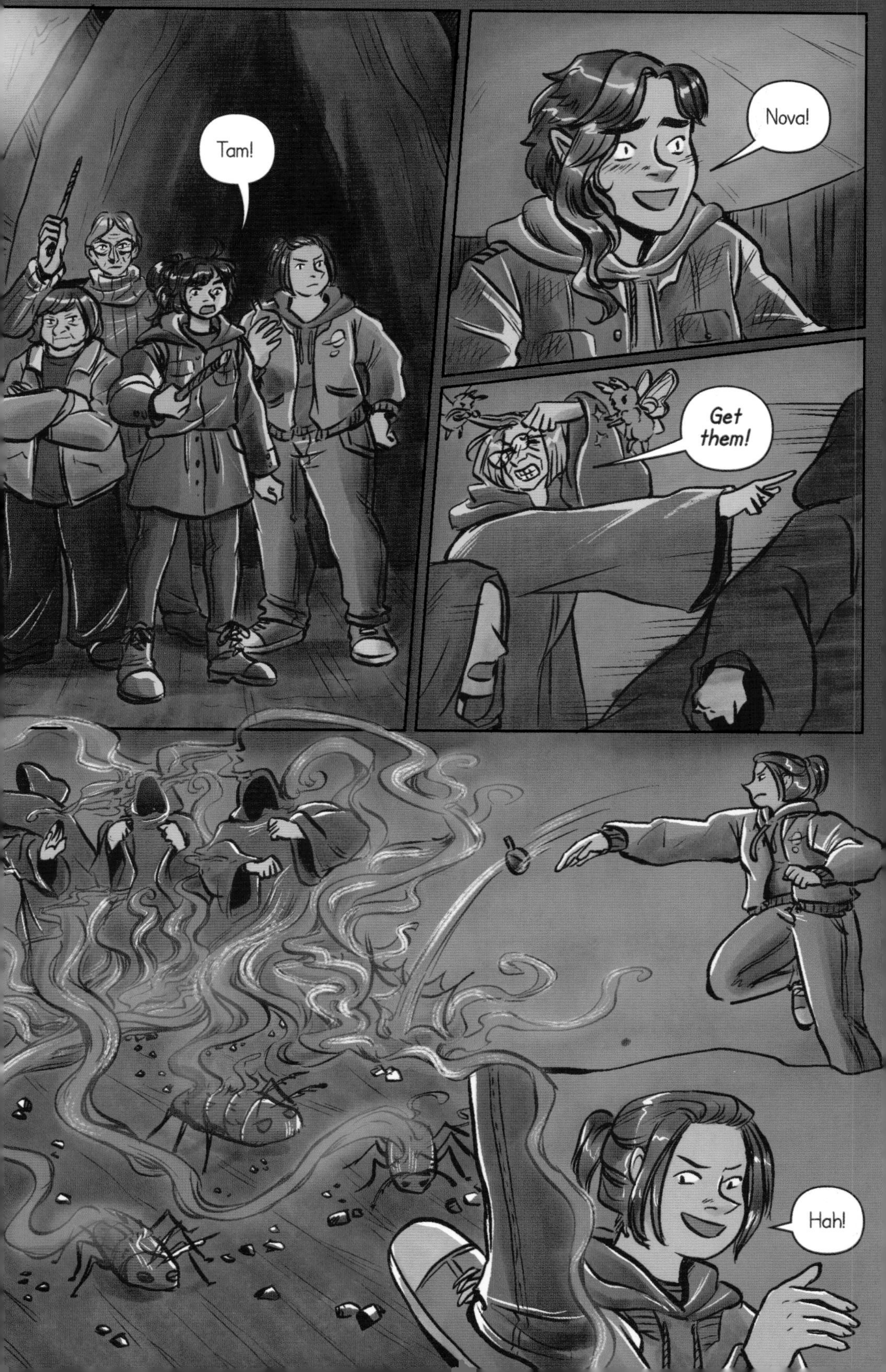
Tam!
Nova!
Get them!
Hah!

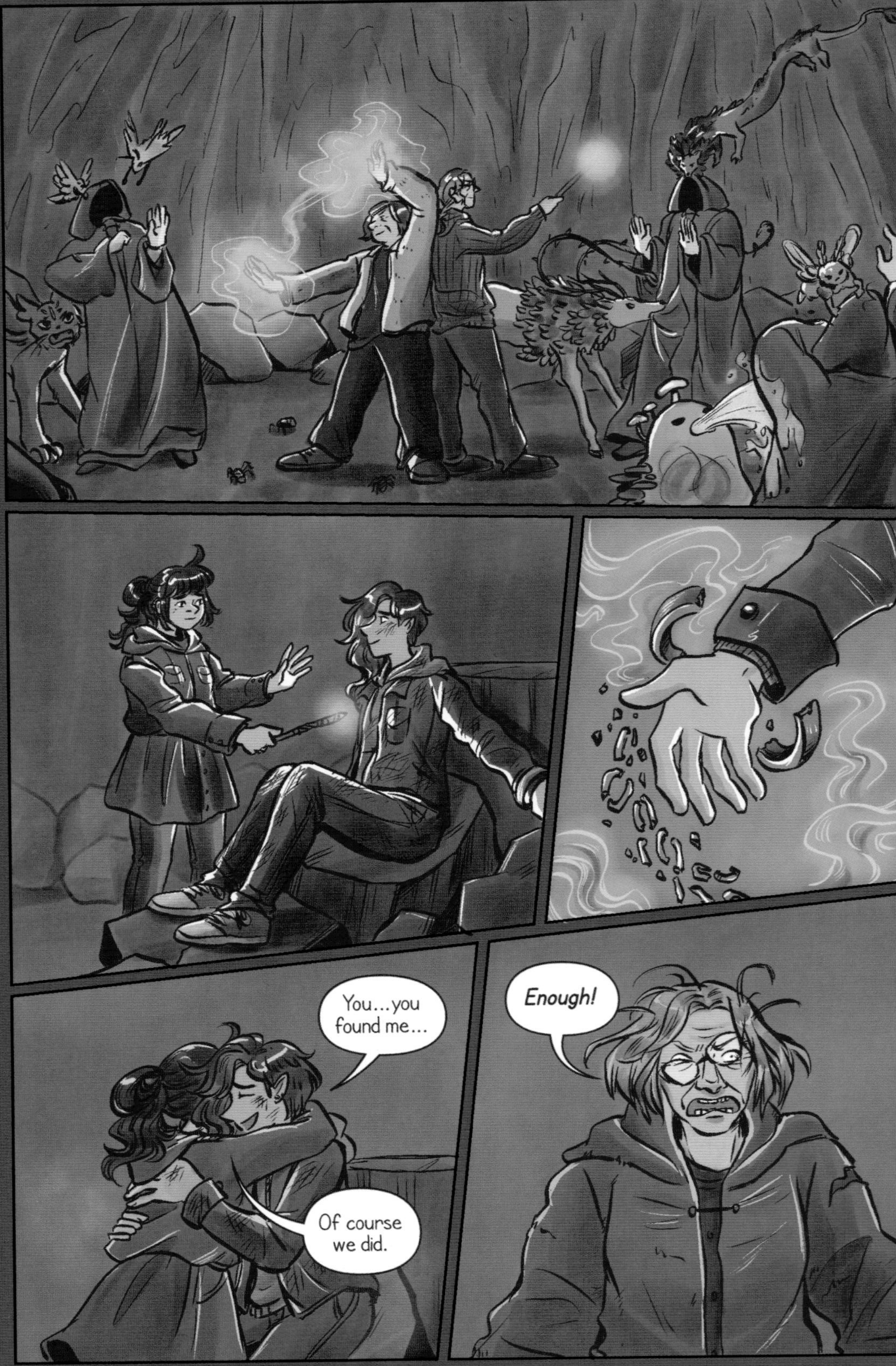
You...you found me...
Of course we did.
Enough!

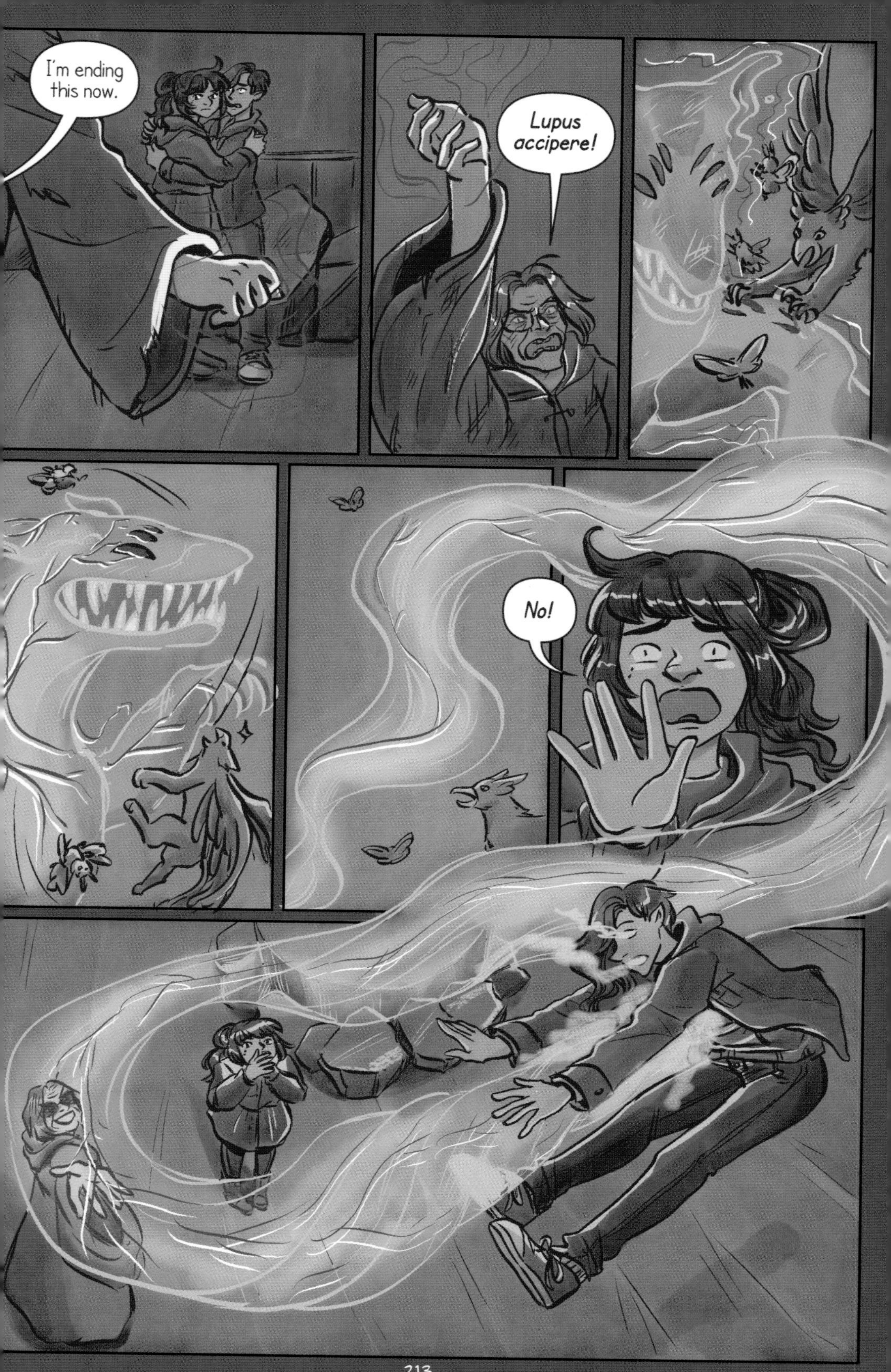
I'm ending this now.
Lupus accipere!
No!

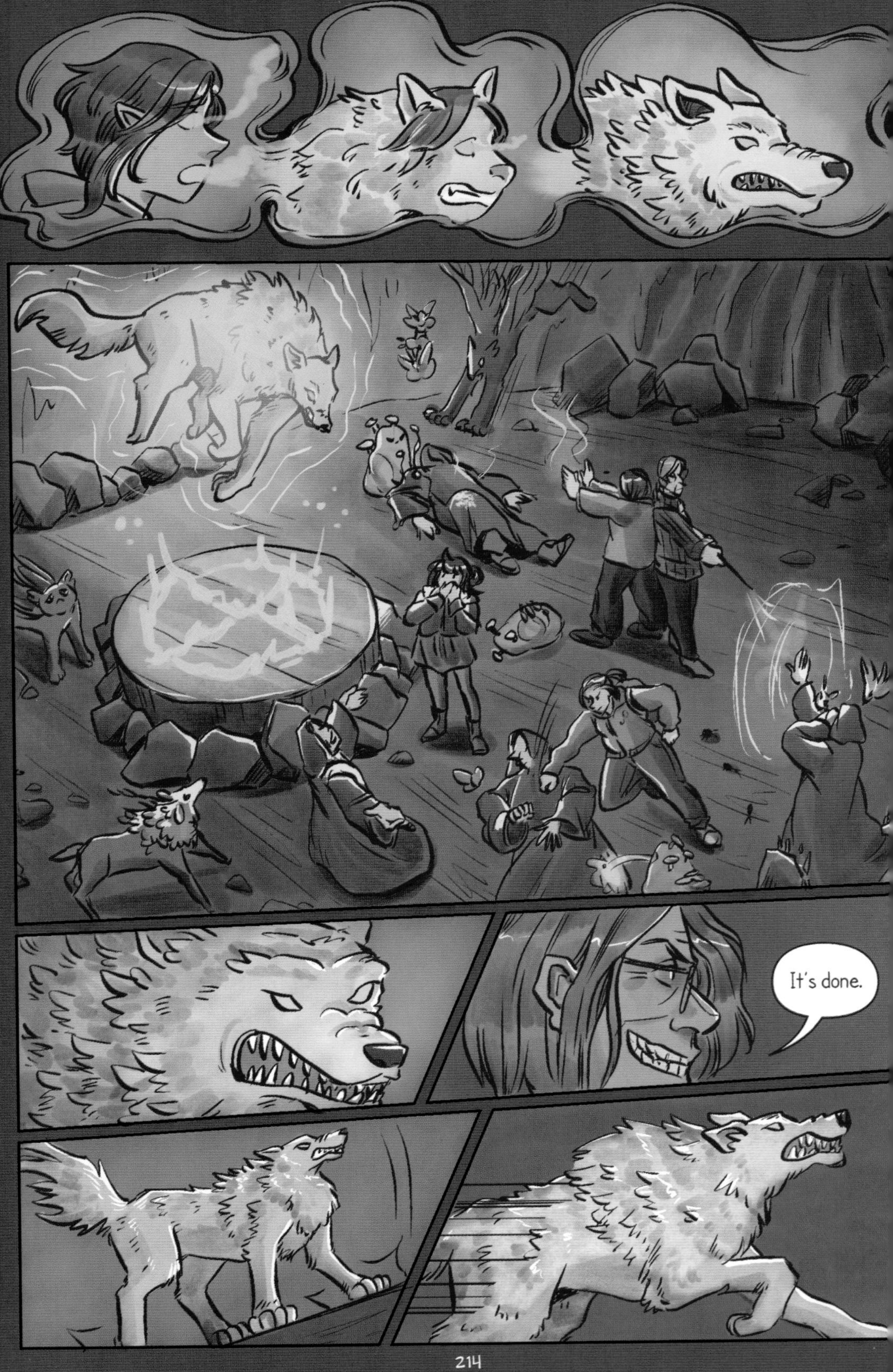
It's done.

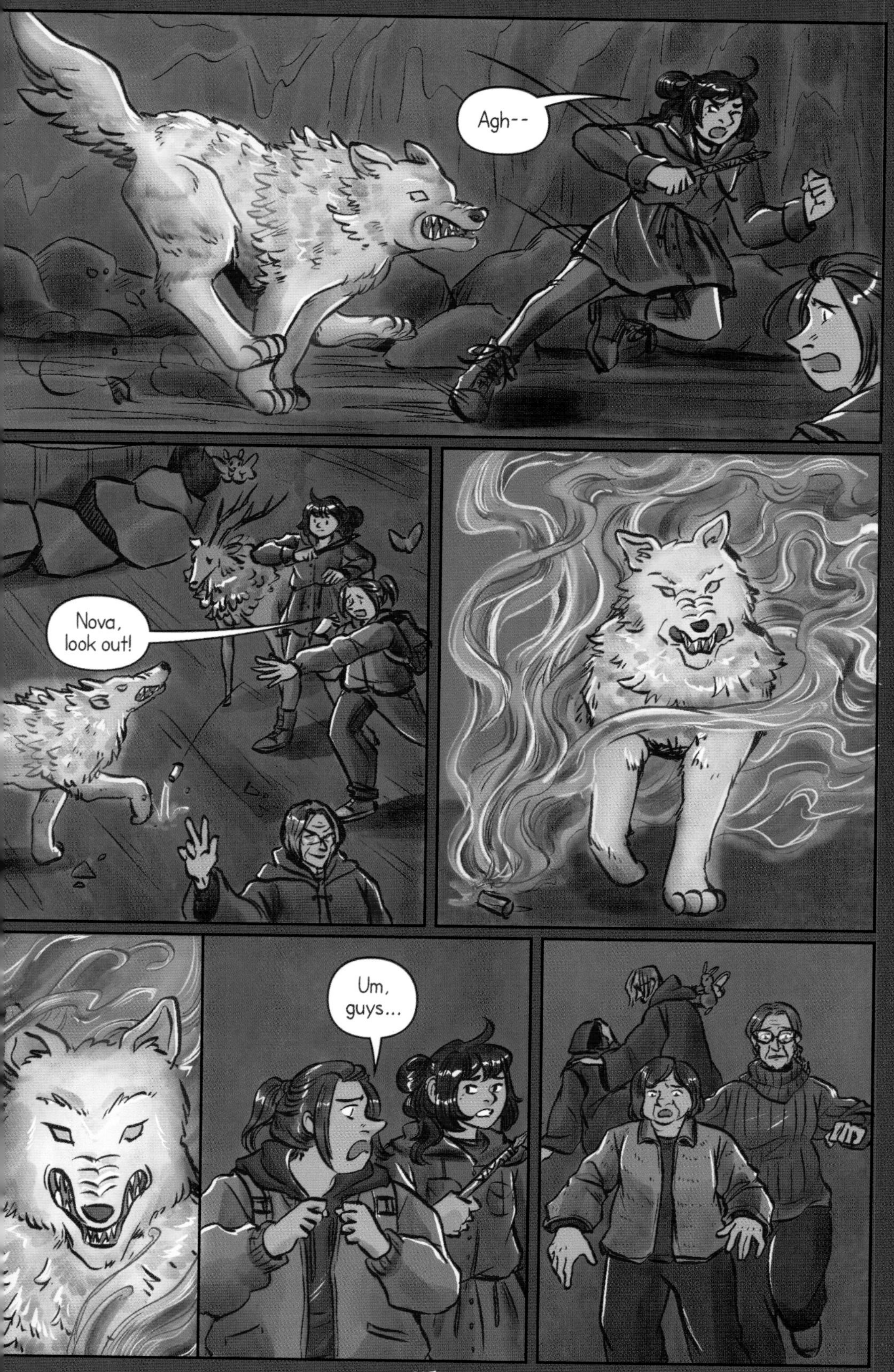
Agh--
Nova, look out!
Um, guys...

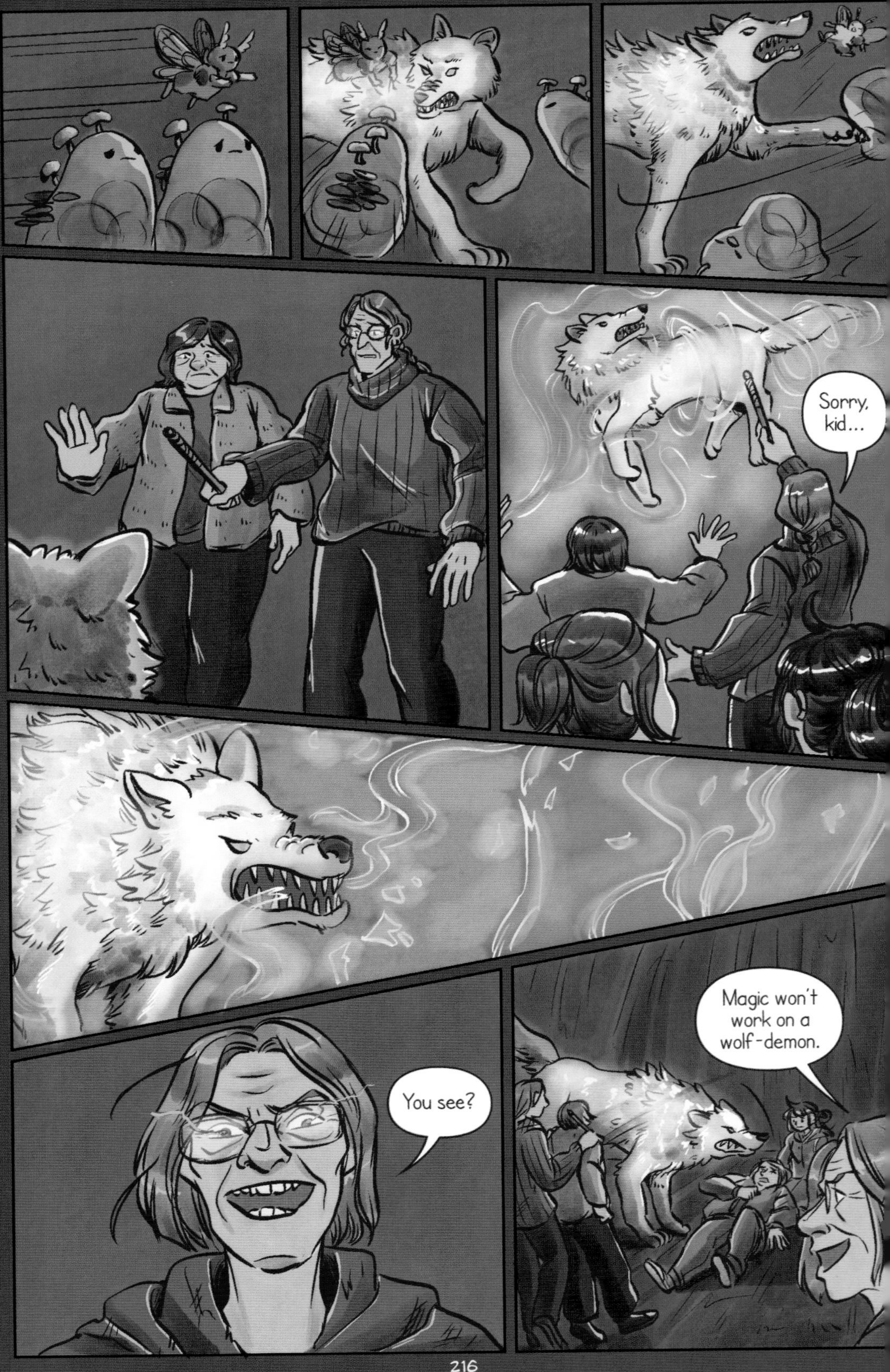
Sorry, kid...
You see?
Magic won't work on a wolf-demon.

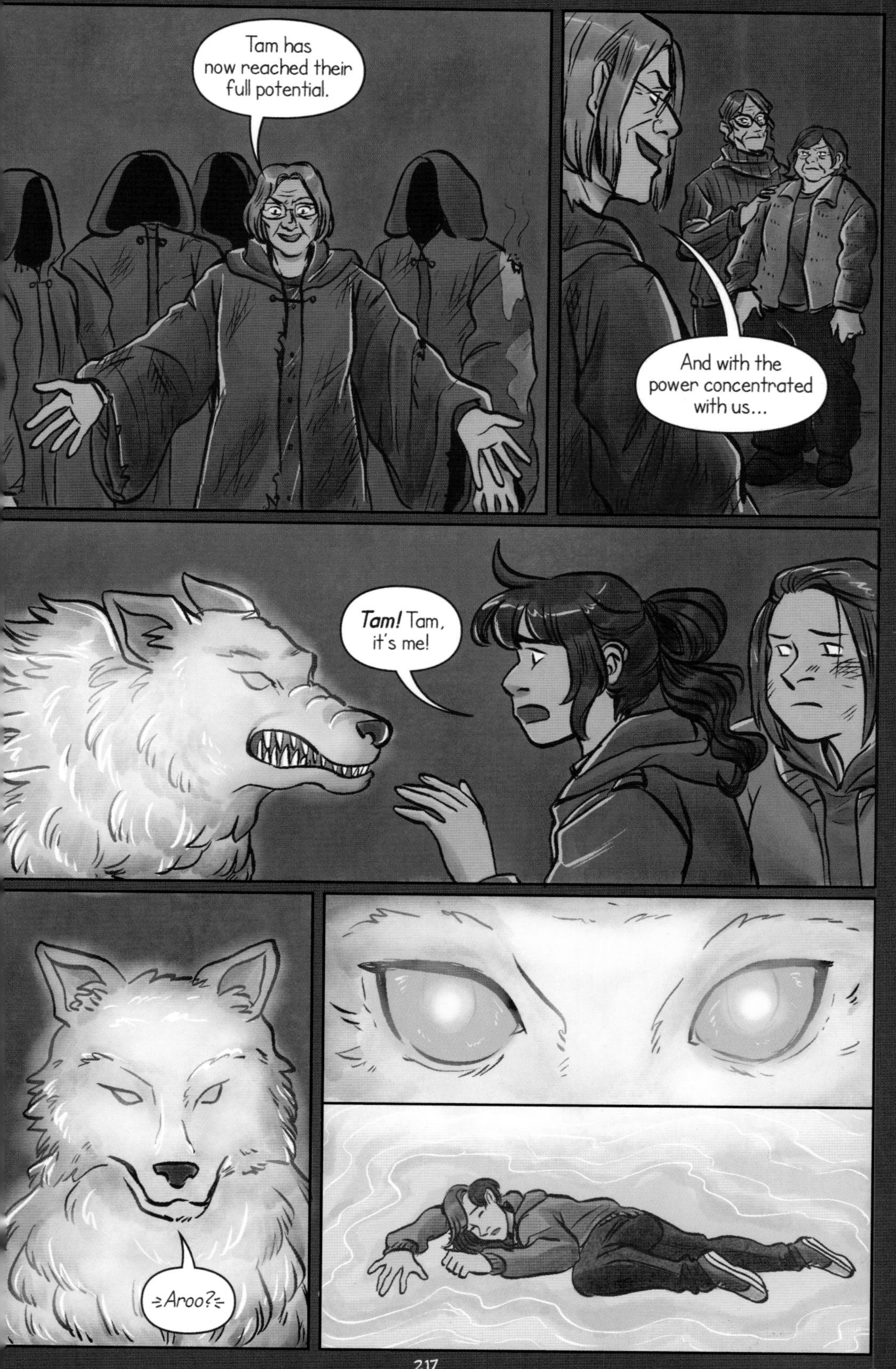
Tam has now reached their full potential.
And with the power concentrated with us...
Tam! Tam, it's me!
Aroo?

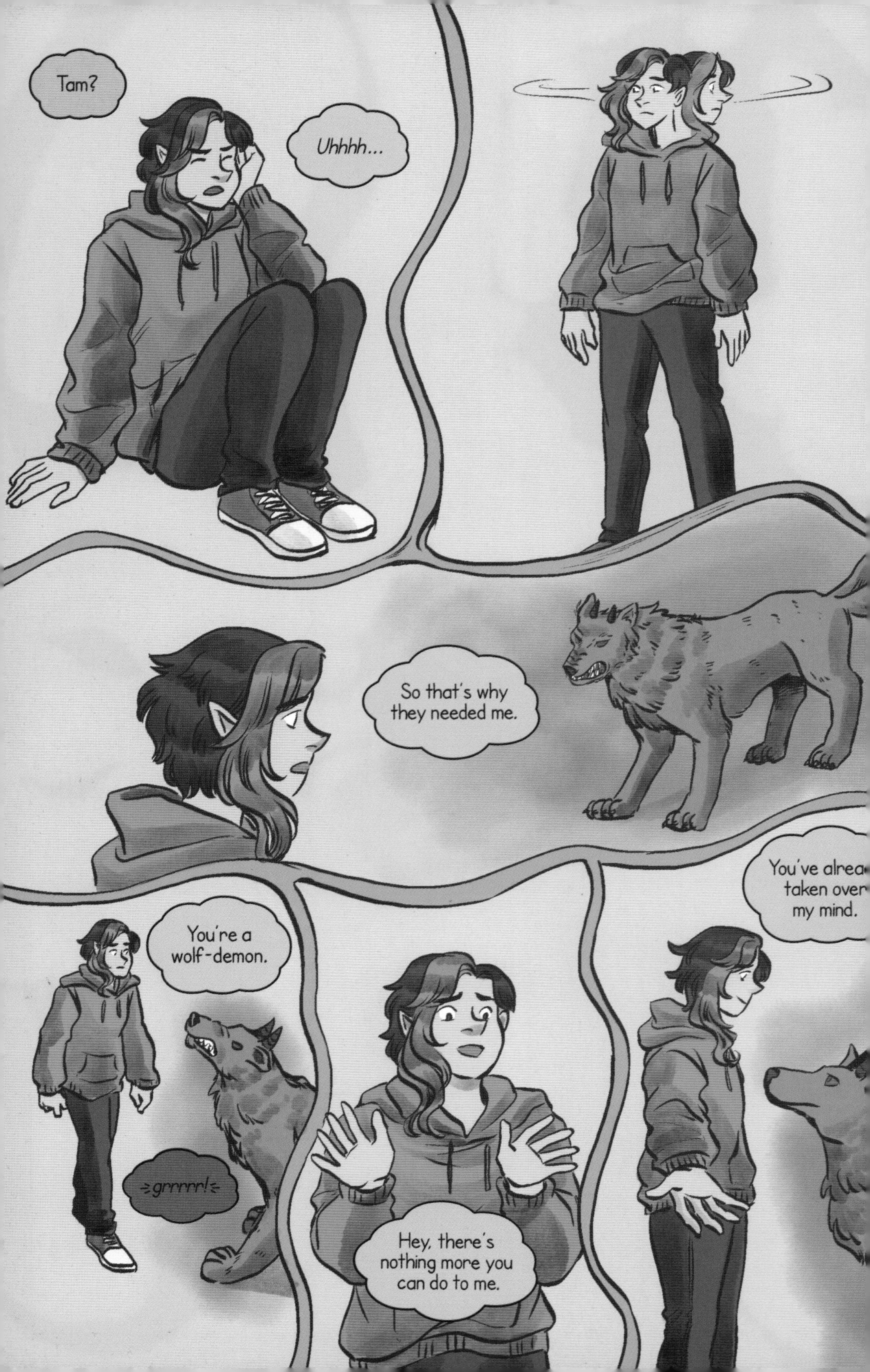
Tam?
Uhhhh...
So that's why they needed me.
You're a wolf-demon.
grrrrr!
Hey, there's nothing more you can do to me.
You've alrea taken over my mind.

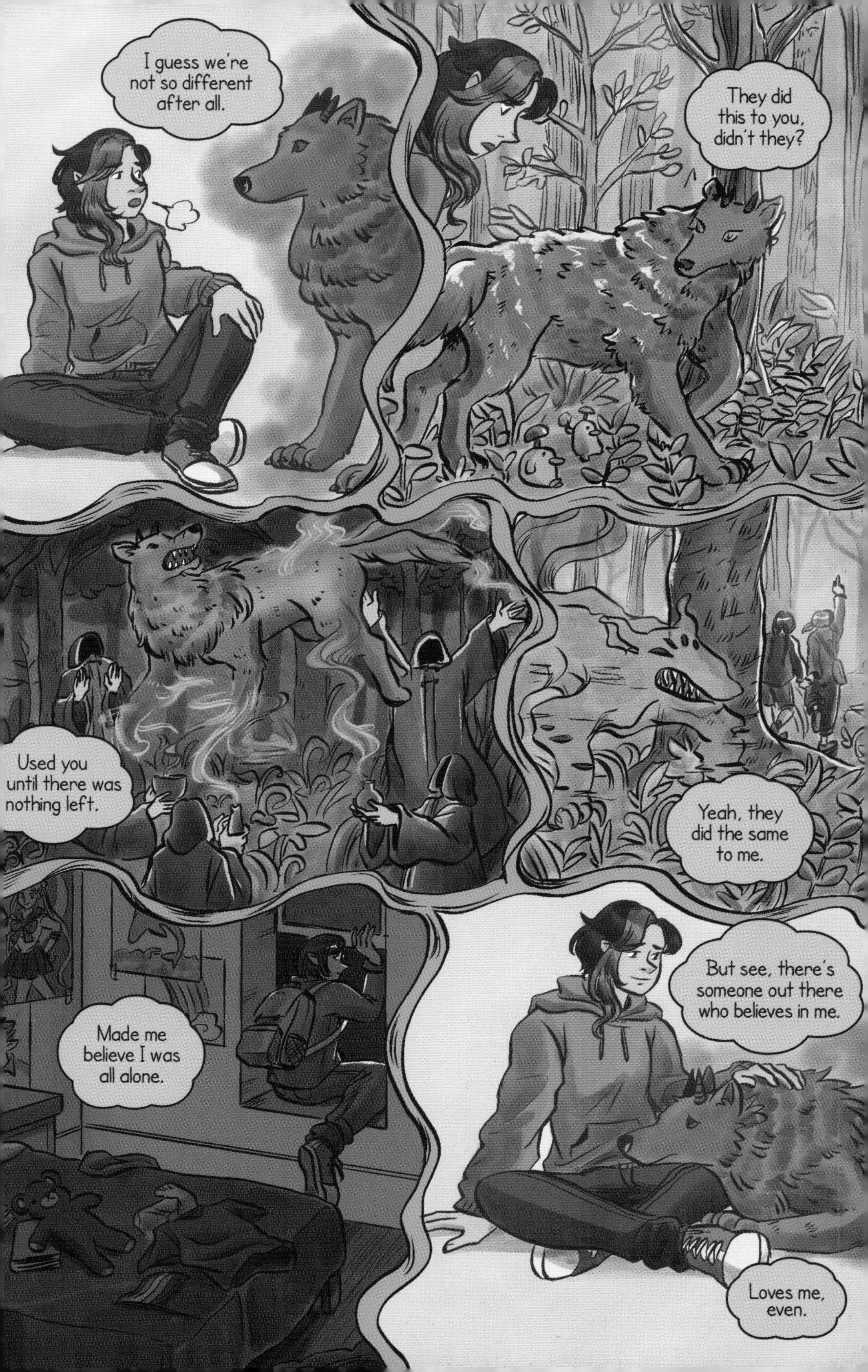
I guess we're not so different after all.
They did this to you, didn't they?
Used you until there was nothing left.
Yeah, they did the same to me.
Made me believe I was all alone.
But see, there's someone out there who believes in me.
Loves me, even.

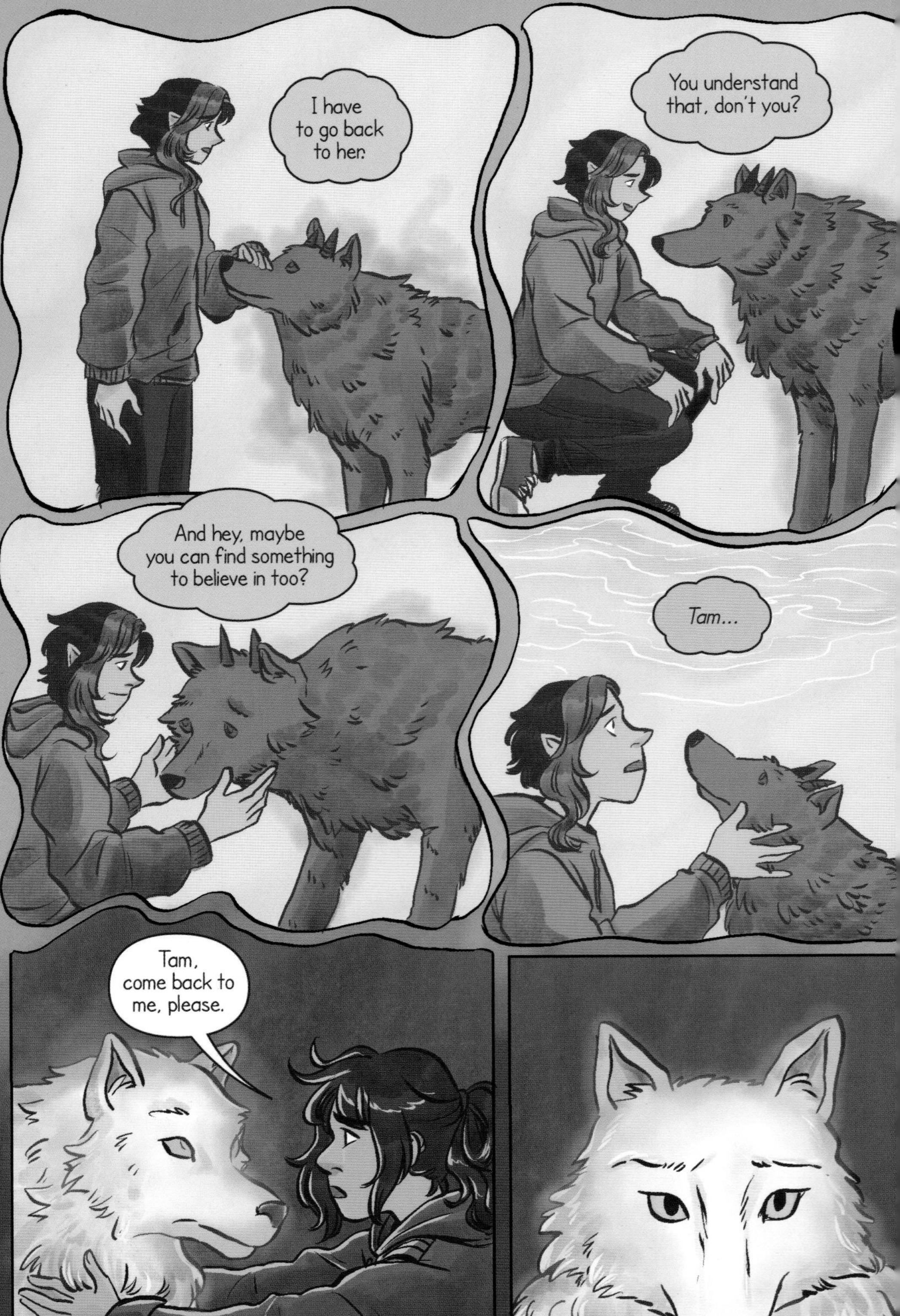
I have to go back to her.
You understand that, don't you?
And hey, maybe you can find something to believe in too?
Tam...
Tam, come back to me, please.

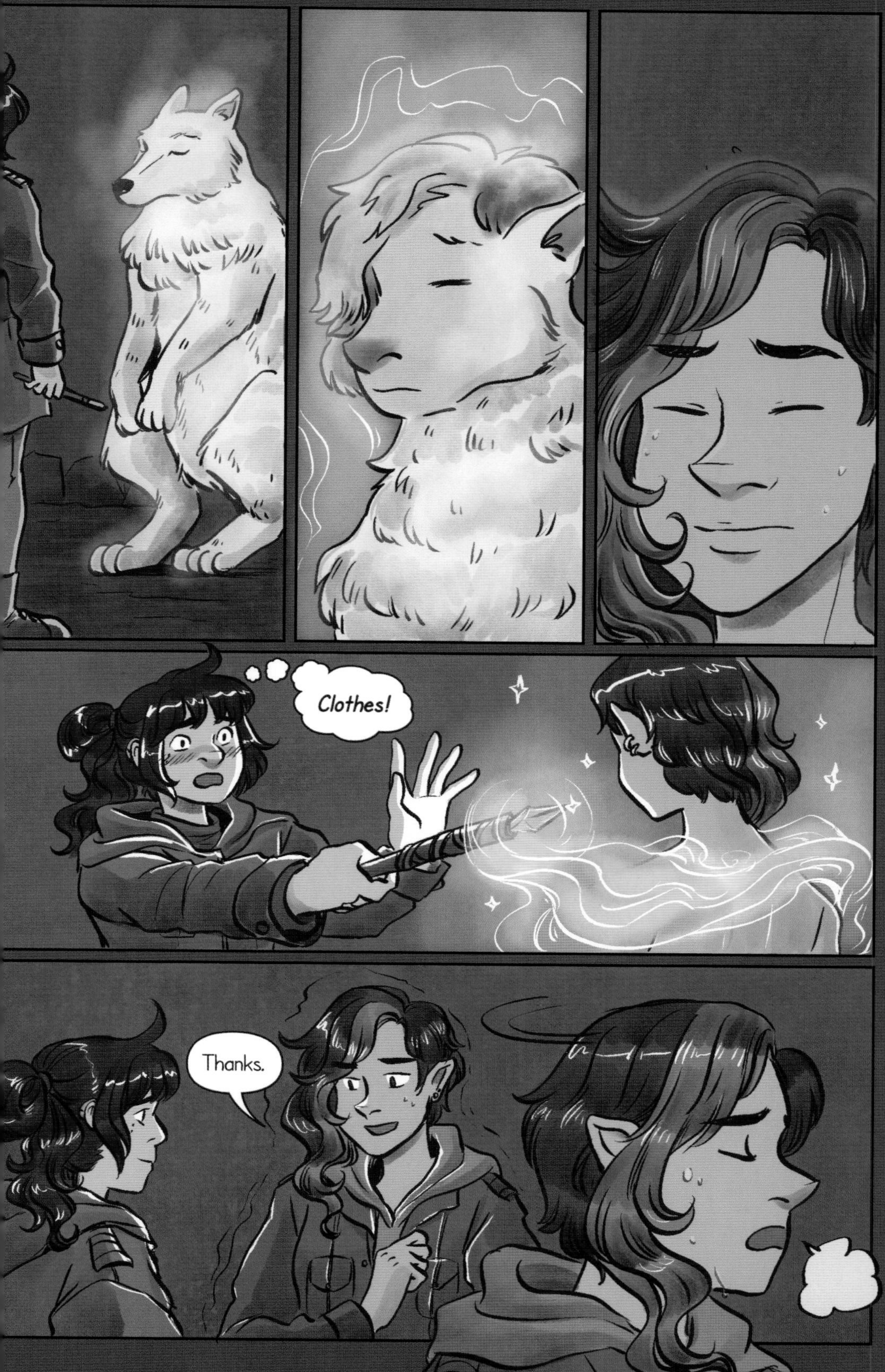
Clothes!
Thanks.

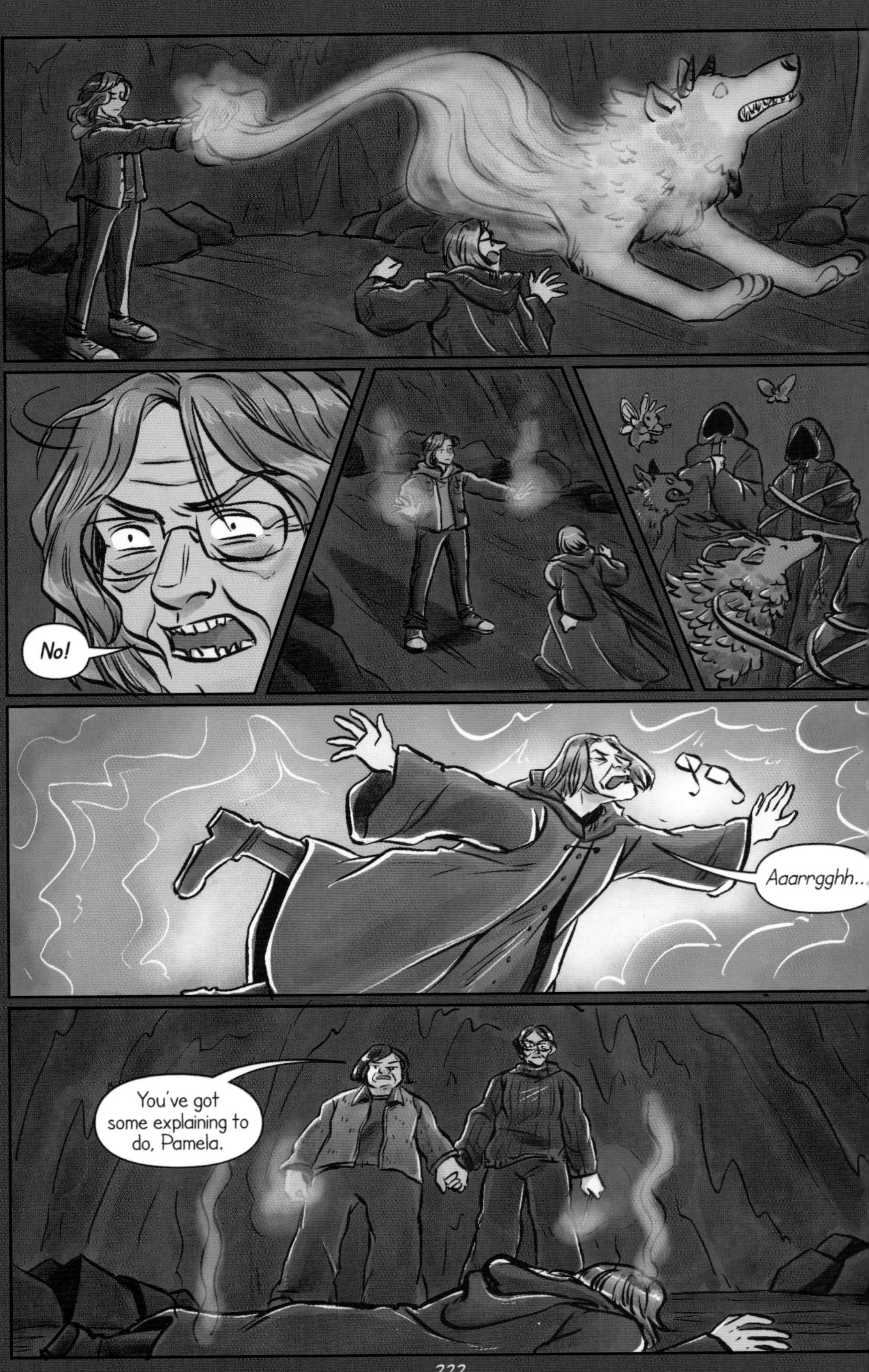
No!
Aaarrgghh...
You've got some explaining to do, Pamela.

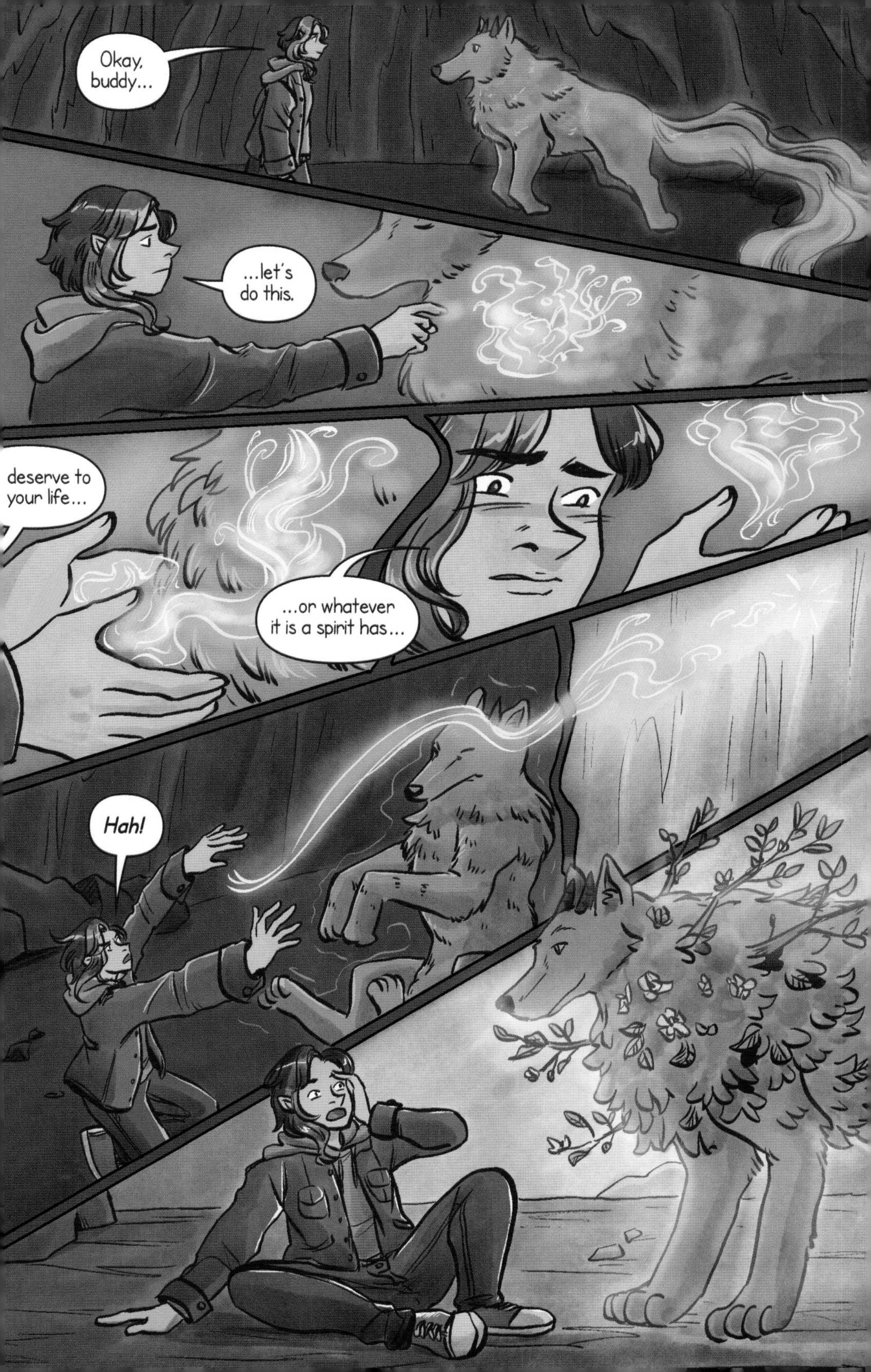
Okay, buddy...
...let's do this.
deserve to your life...
...or whatever it is a spirit has...
Hah!

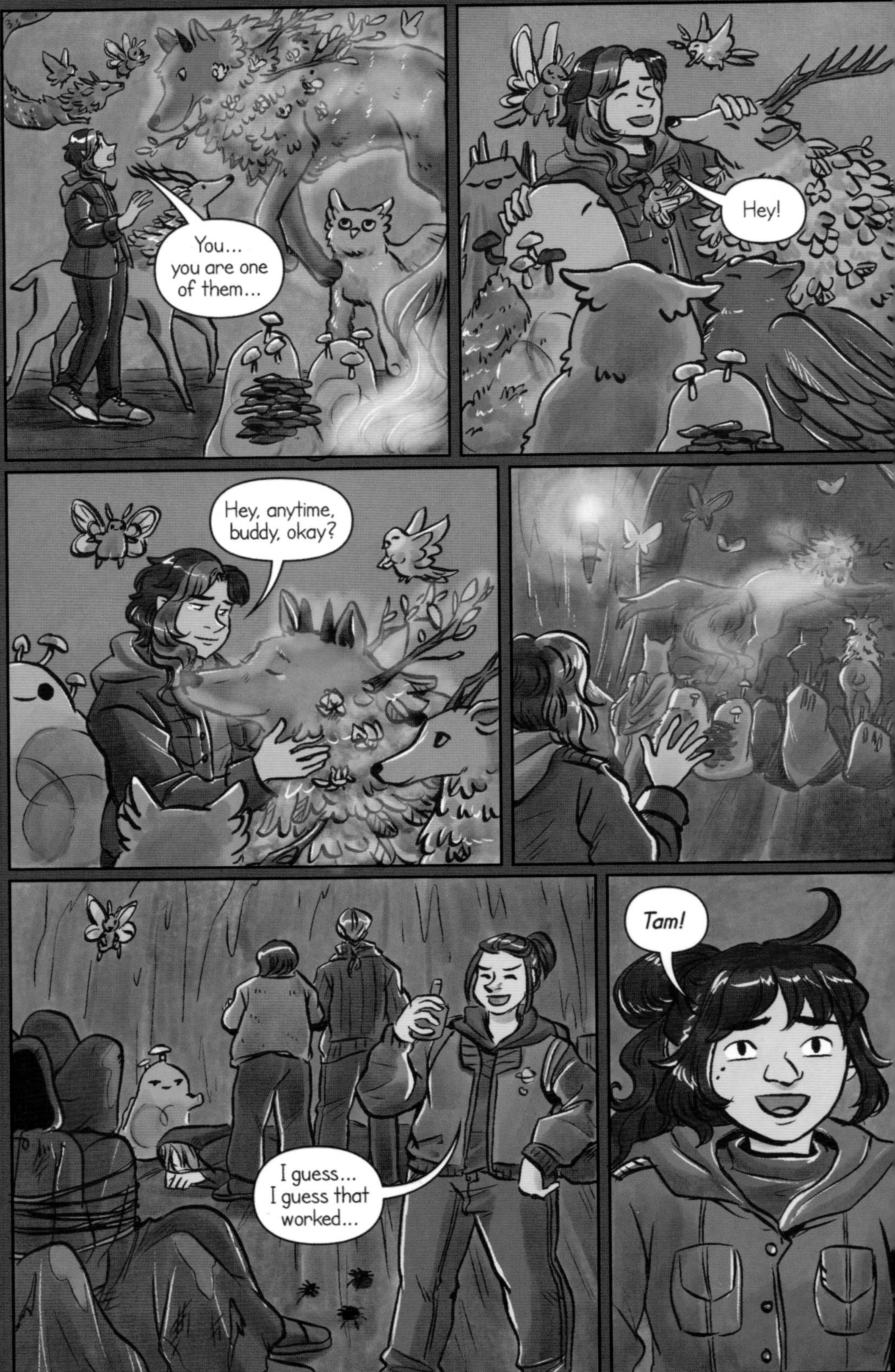
You...
you are one
of them...
Hey!
Hey, anytime,
buddy, okay?
I guess...
I guess that
worked...
Tam!

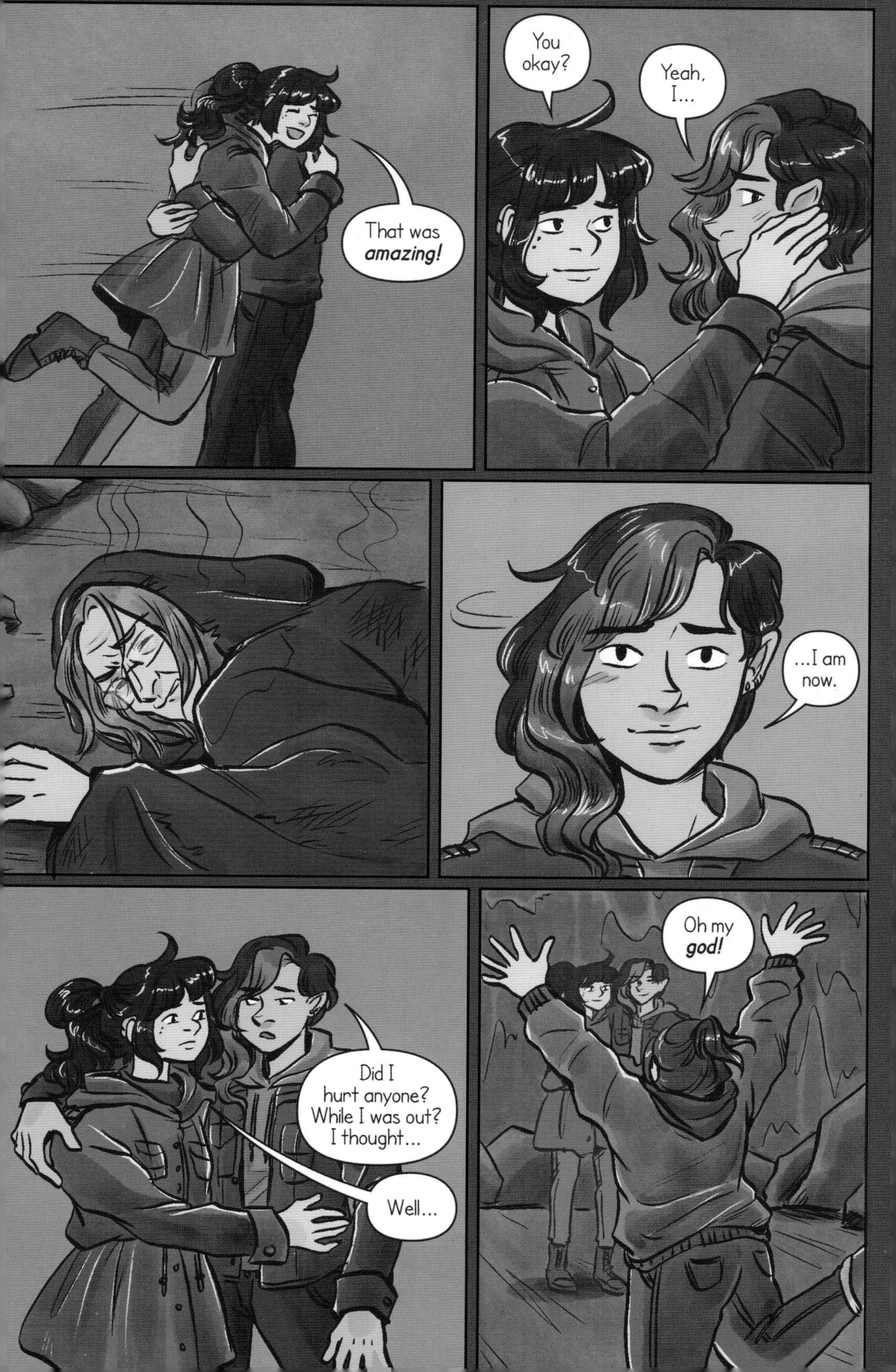
That was *amazing!*
You okay?
Yeah, I...
...I am now.
Did I hurt anyone? While I was out? I thought...
Well...
Oh my *god!*

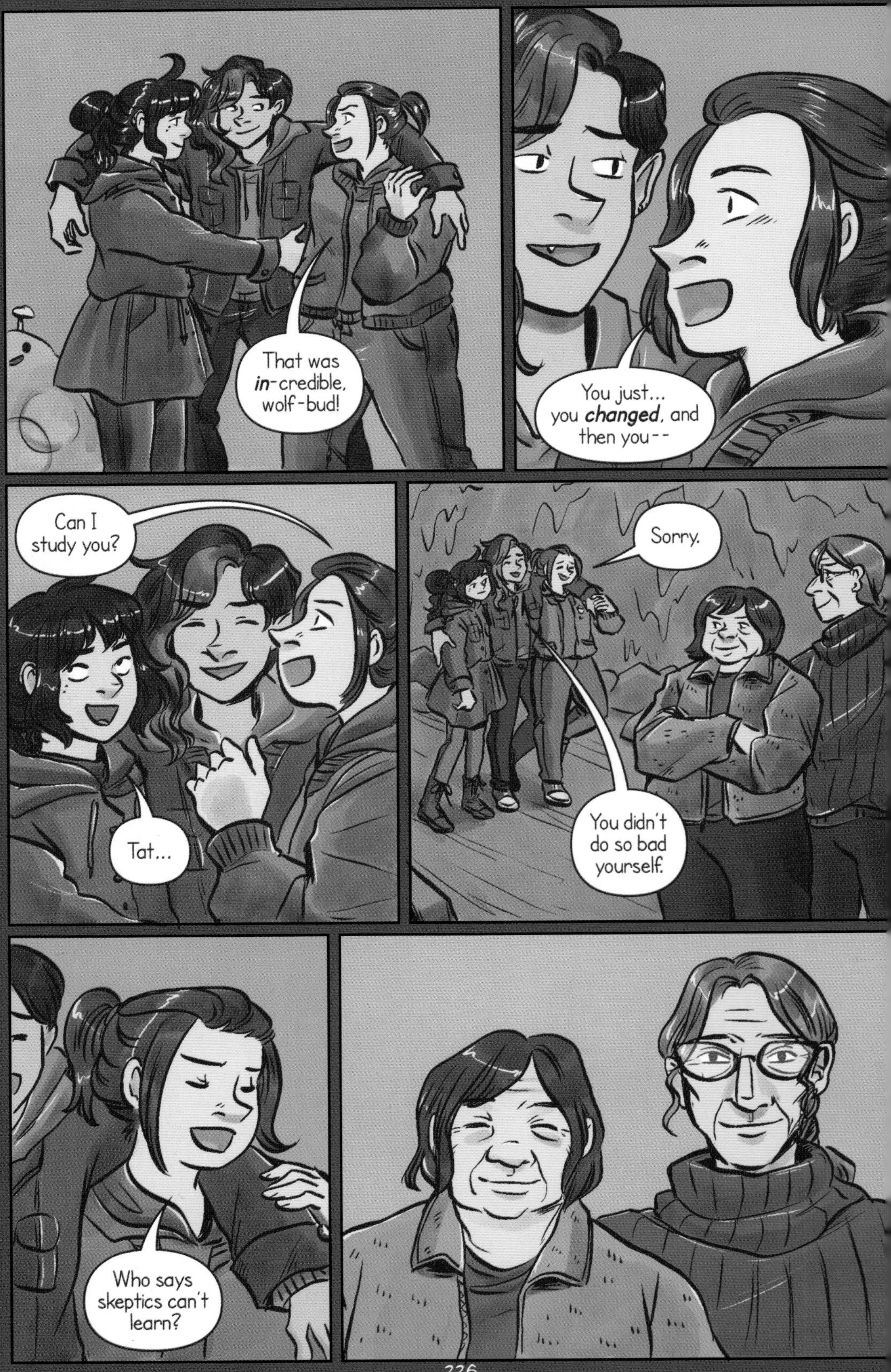
That was *in*-credible, wolf-bud!
You just... you ***changed***, and then you--
Can I study you?
Tat...
Sorry.
You didn't do so bad yourself.
Who says skeptics can't learn?

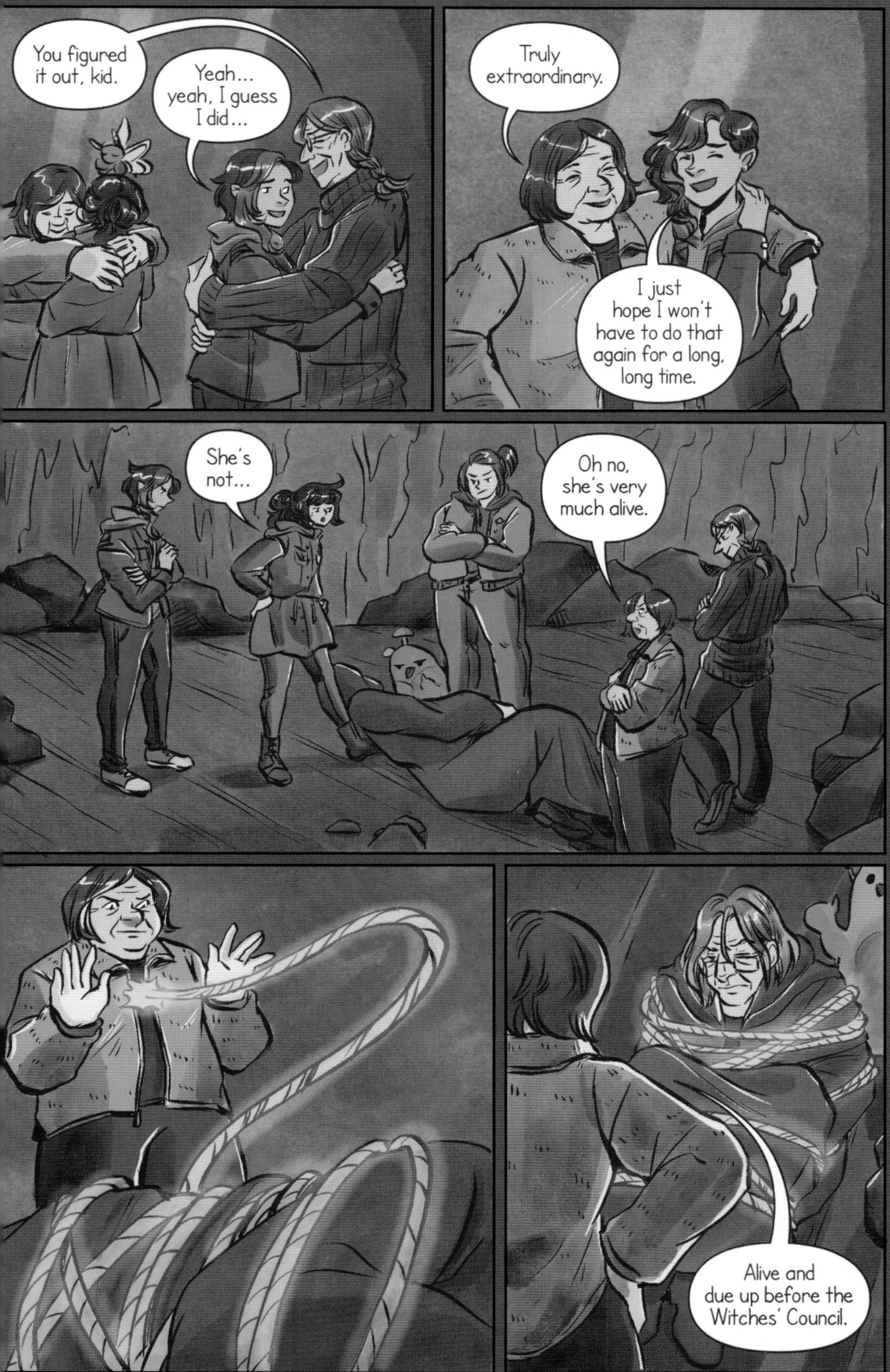
You figured it out, kid.
Yeah... yeah, I guess I did...
Truly extraordinary.
I just hope I won't have to do that again for a long, long time.
She's not...
Oh no, she's very much alive.
Alive and due up before the Witches' Council.

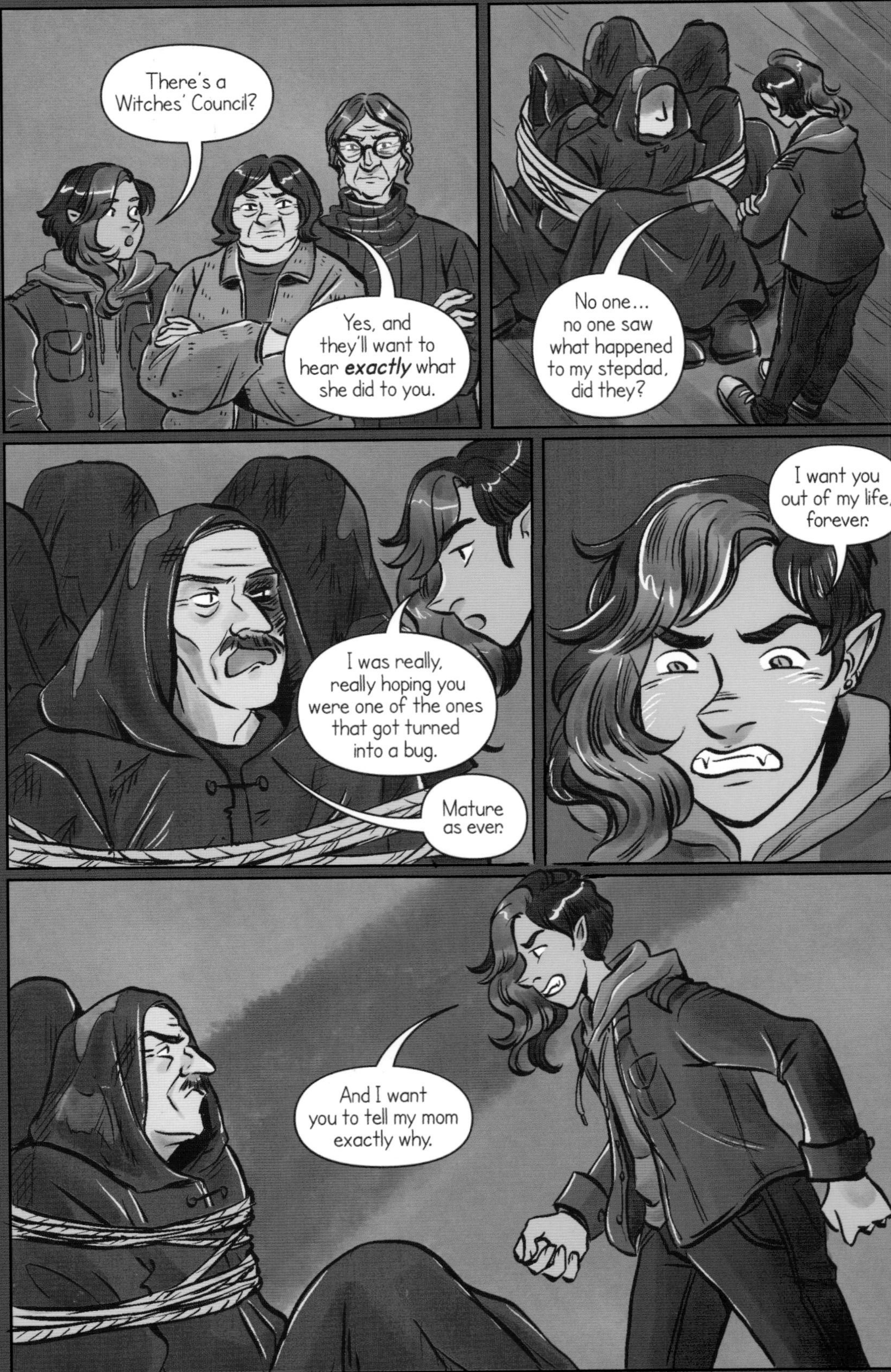
There's a Witches' Council?
Yes, and they'll want to hear *exactly* what she did to you.
No one... no one saw what happened to my stepdad, did they?
I was really, really hoping you were one of the ones that got turned into a bug.
Mature as ever.
I want you out of my life, forever.
And I want you to tell my mom exactly why.

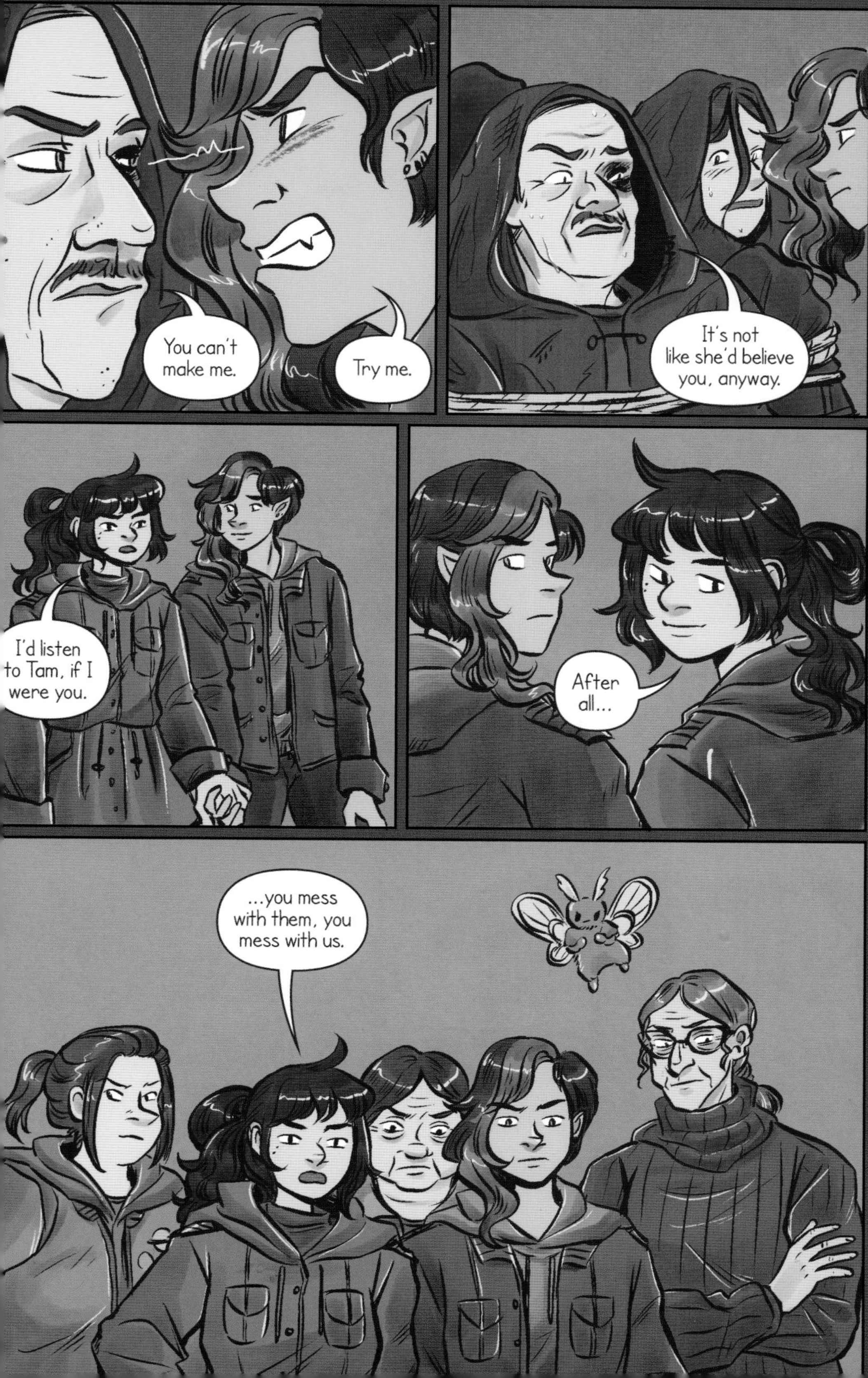
You can't make me.
Try me.
It's not like she'd believe you, anyway.
I'd listen to Tam, if I were you.
After all...
...you mess with them, you mess with us.

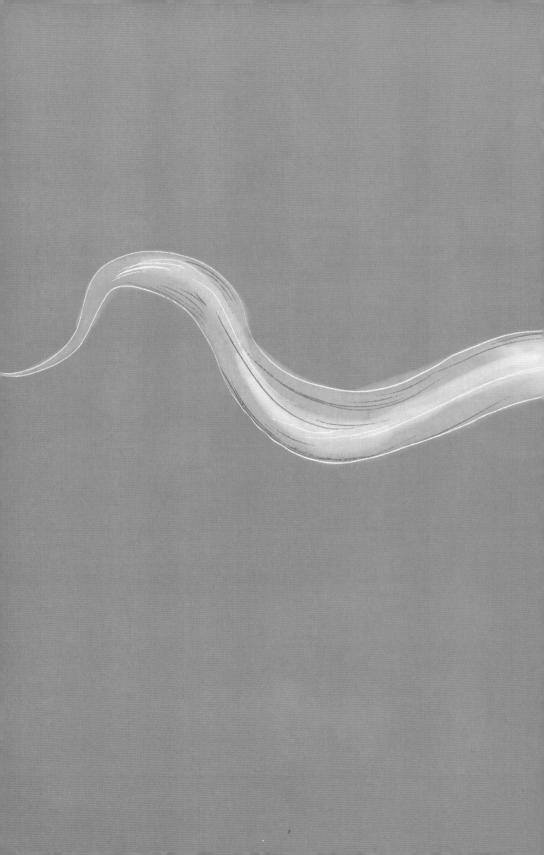

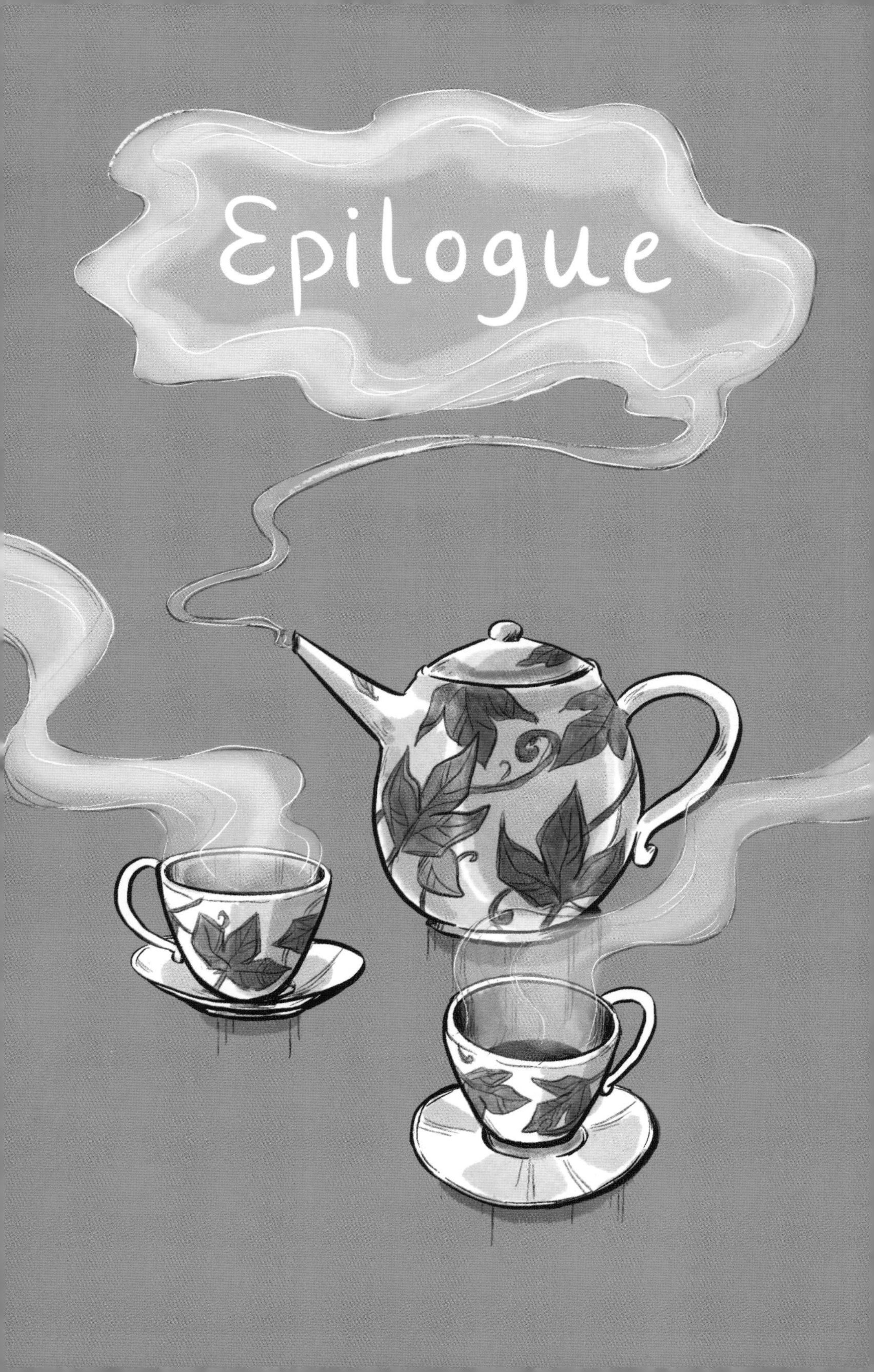
Epilogue

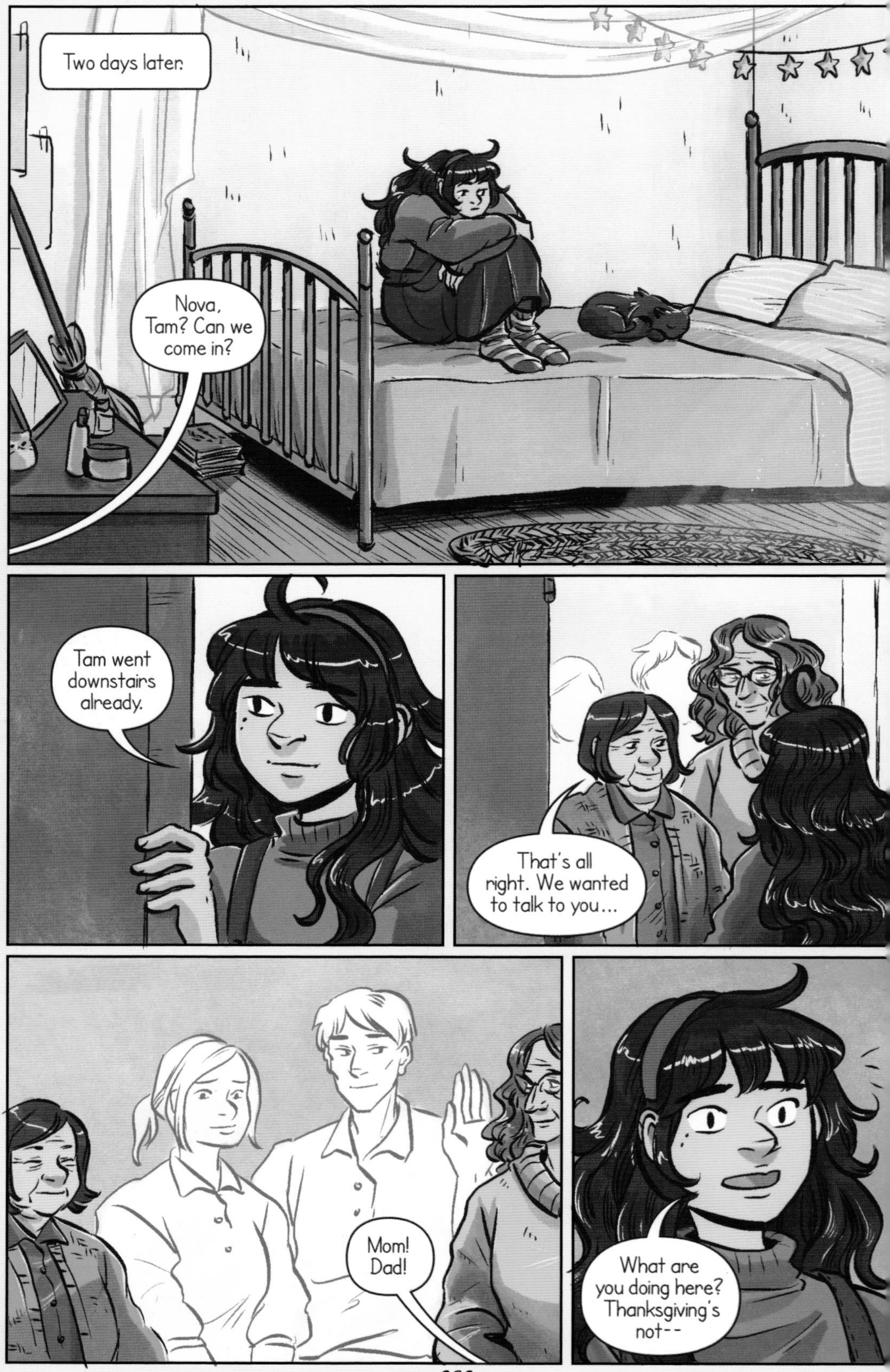

Two days later.
Nova, Tam? Can we come in?
Tam went downstairs already.
That's all right. We wanted to talk to you...
Mom! Dad!
What are you doing here? Thanksgiving's not--

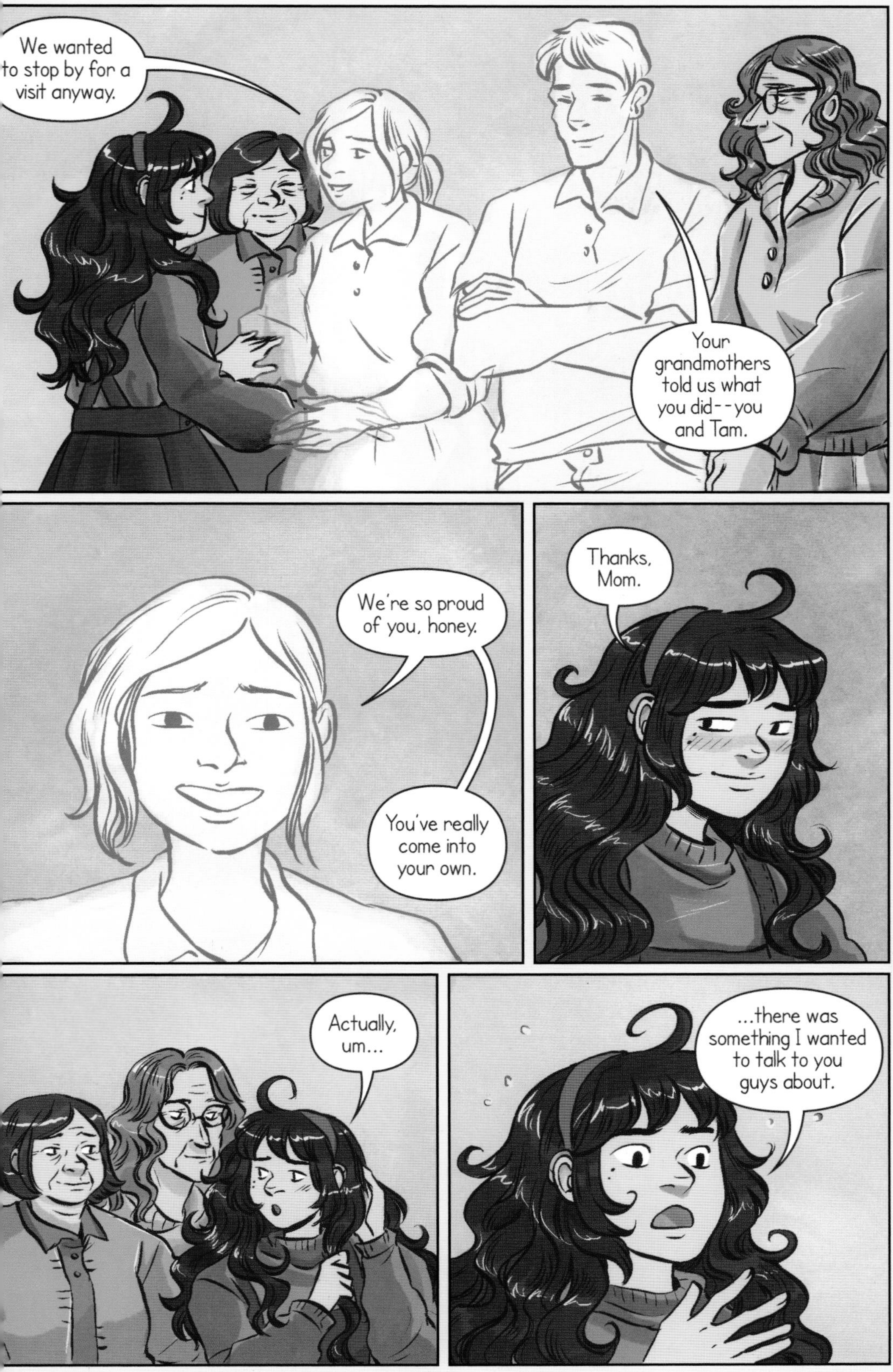
We wanted to stop by for a visit anyway.
Your grandmothers told us what you did--you and Tam.
We're so proud of you, honey.
You've really come into your own.
Thanks, Mom.
Actually, um...
...there was something I wanted to talk to you guys about.

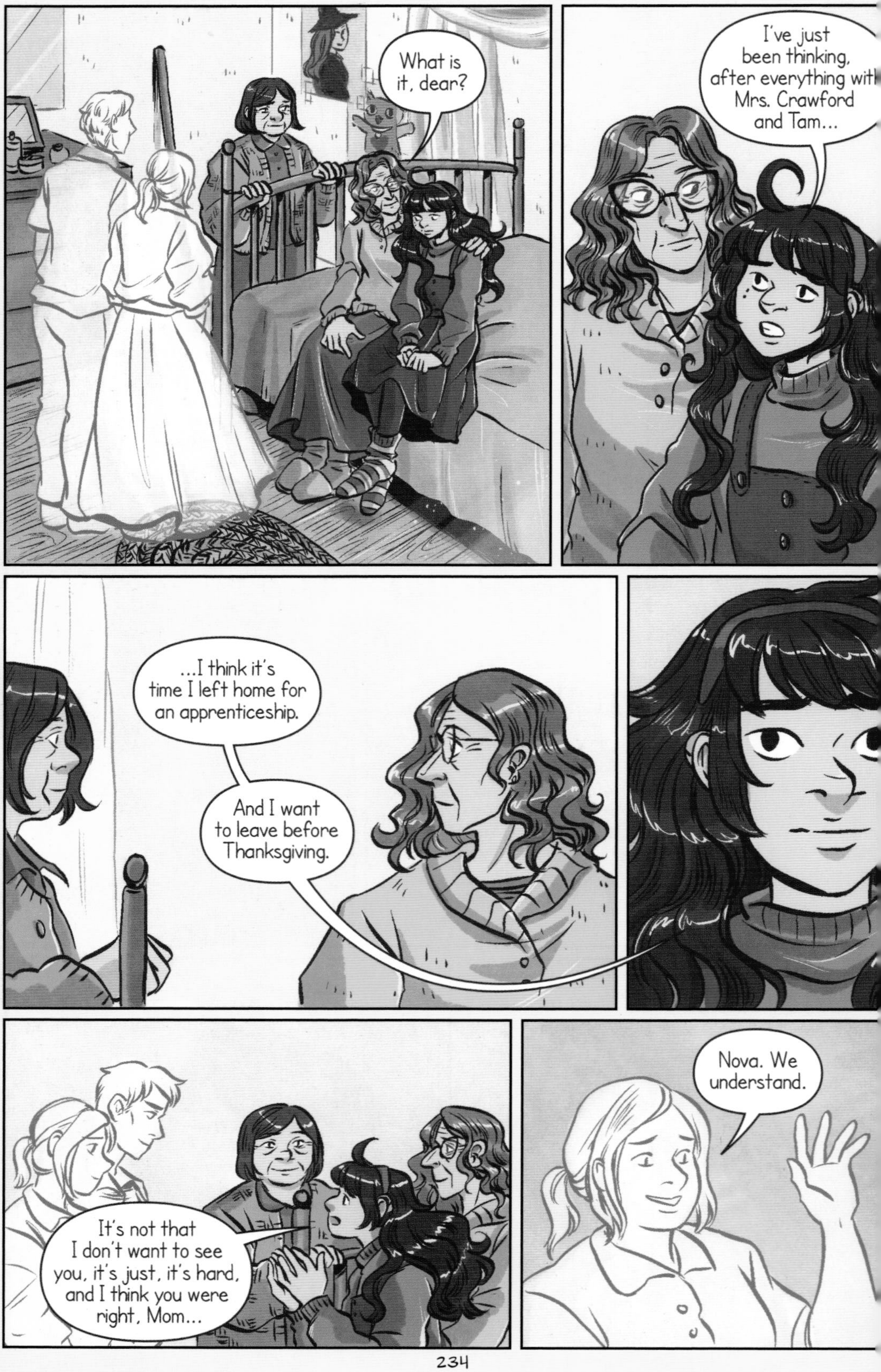
What is it, dear?
I've just been thinking, after everything with Mrs. Crawford and Tam...
...I think it's time I left home for an apprenticeship.
And I want to leave before Thanksgiving.
It's not that I don't want to see you, it's just, it's hard, and I think you were right, Mom...
Nova. We understand.

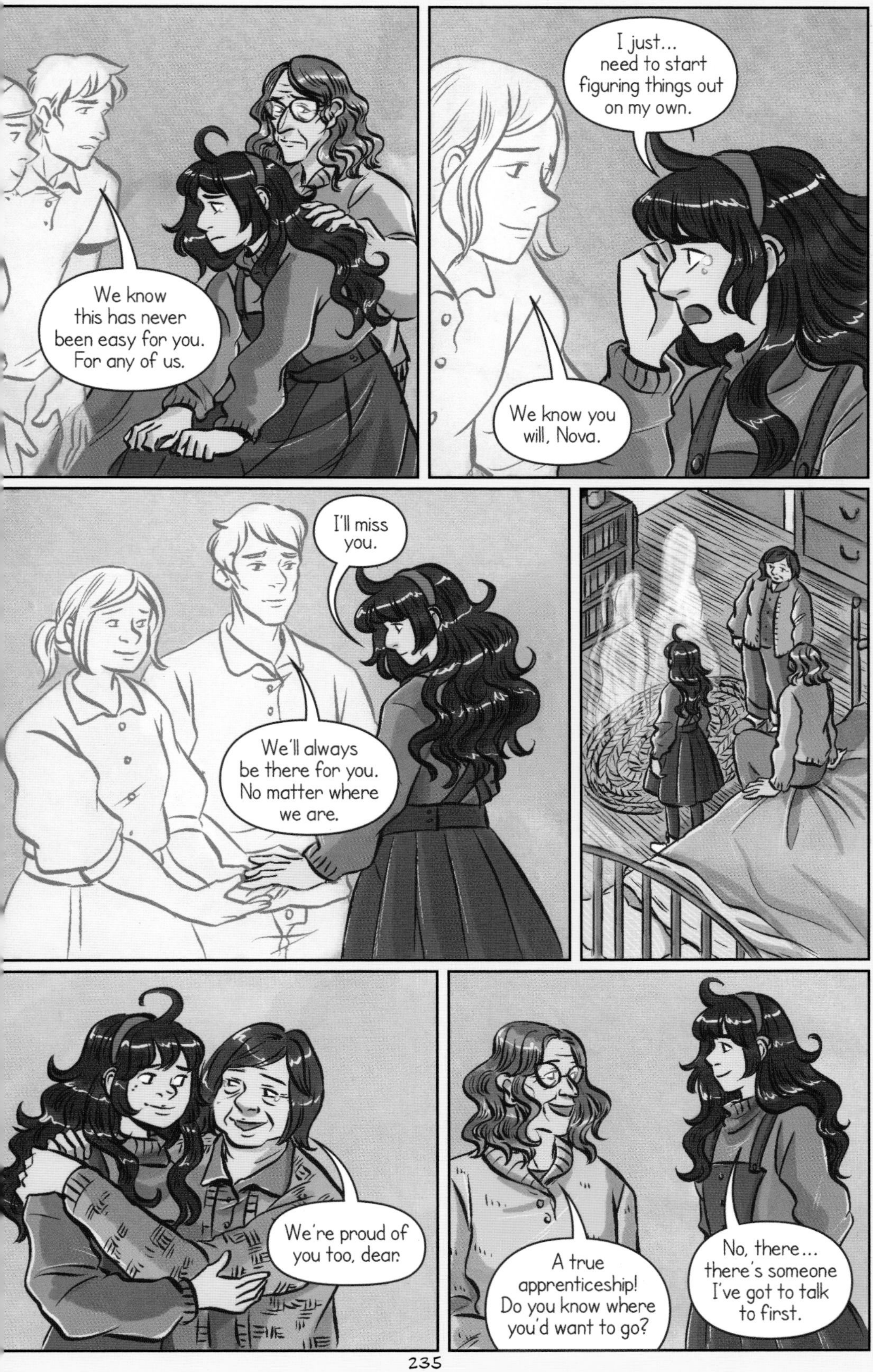
We know
this has never
been easy for you.
For any of us.
I just...
need to start
figuring things out
on my own.
We know you
will, Nova.
I'll miss
you.
We'll always
be there for you.
No matter where
we are.
We're proud of
you too, dear.
A true
apprenticeship!
Do you know where
you'd want to go?
No, there...
there's someone
I've got to talk
to first.

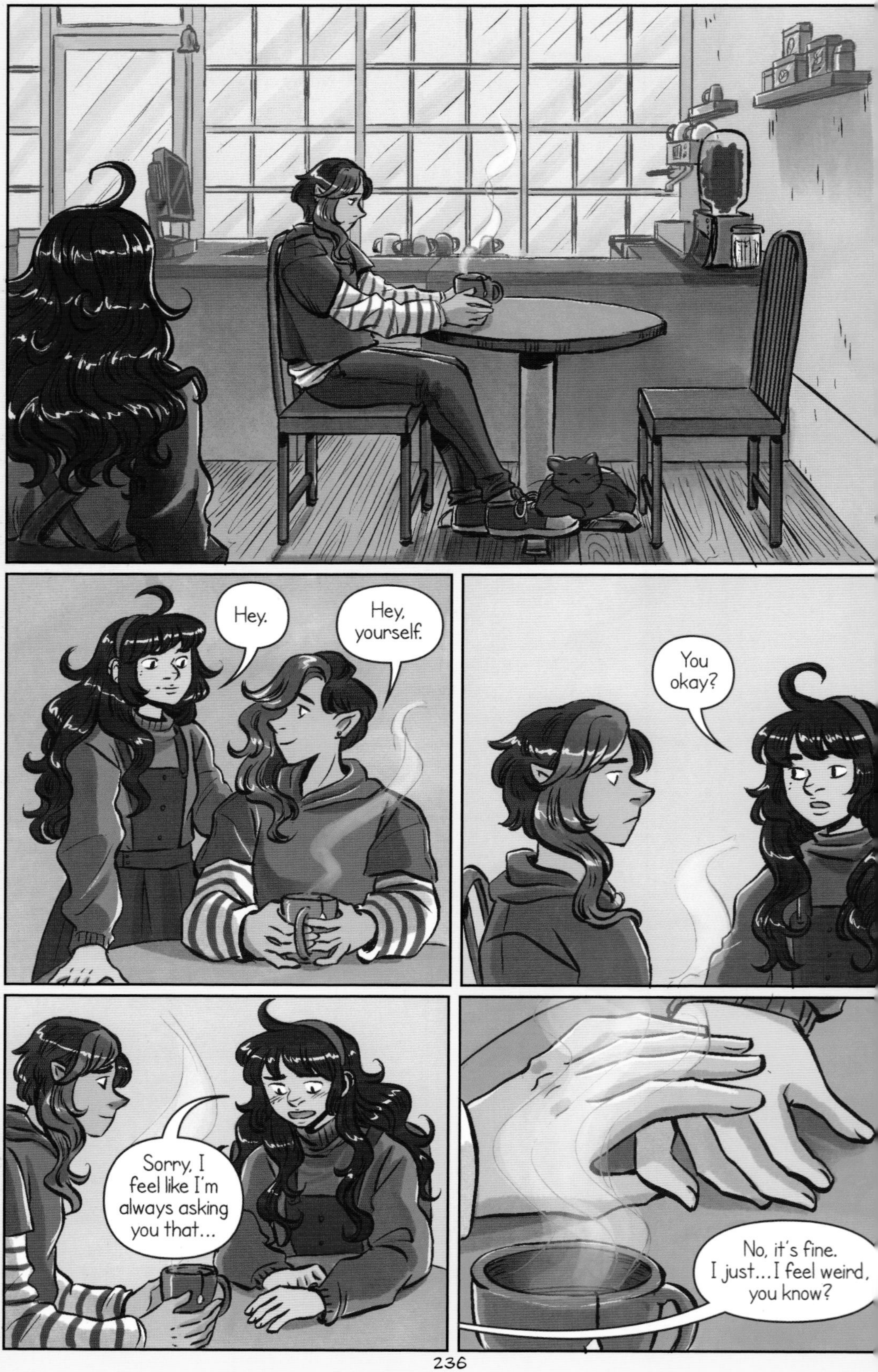
Hey.
Hey, yourself.
You okay?
Sorry, I feel like I'm always asking you that...
No, it's fine. I just... I feel weird, you know?

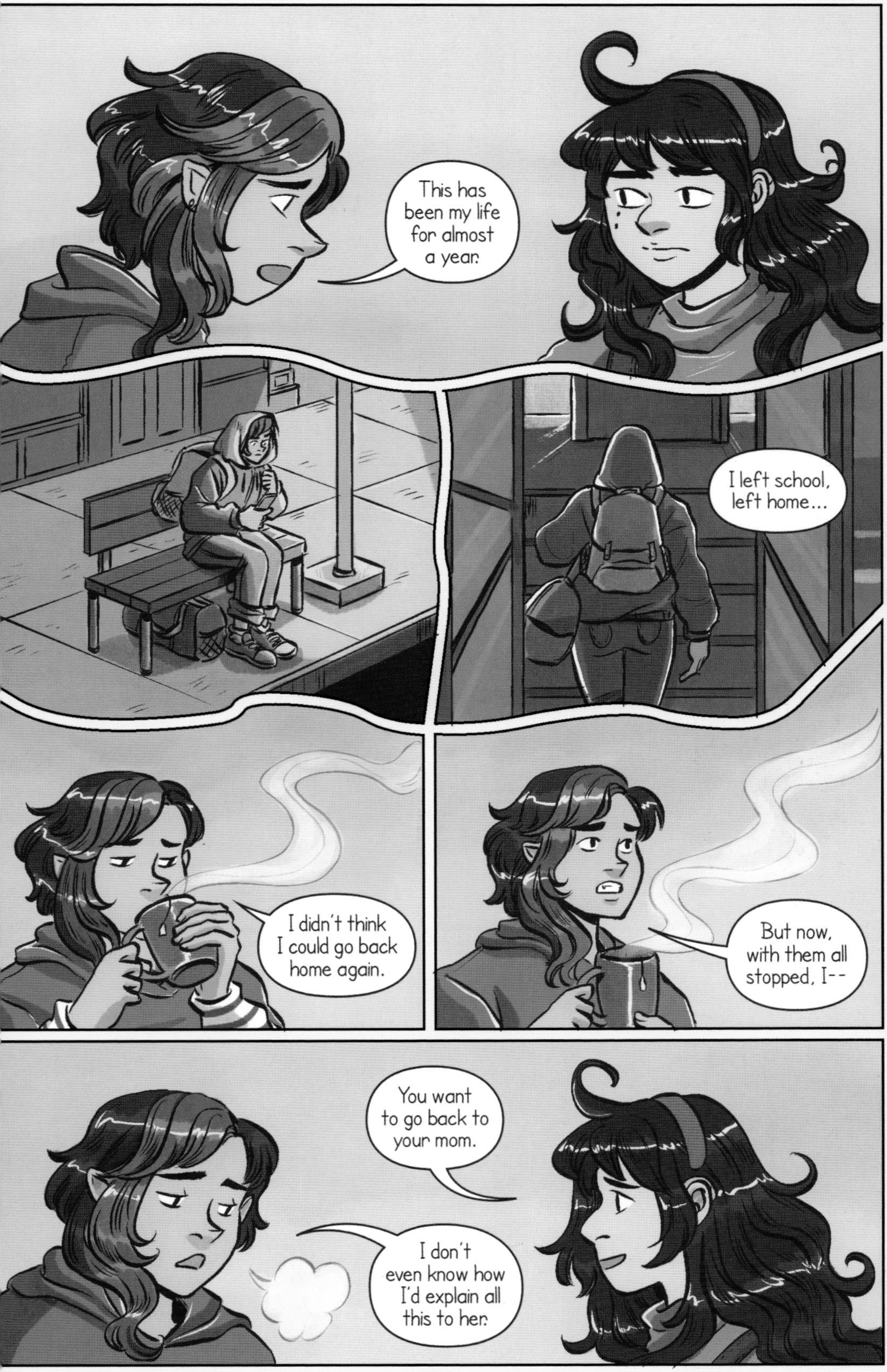
This has been my life for almost a year.
I left school, left home...
I didn't think I could go back home again.
But now, with them all stopped, I--
You want to go back to your mom.
I don't even know how I'd explain all this to her.

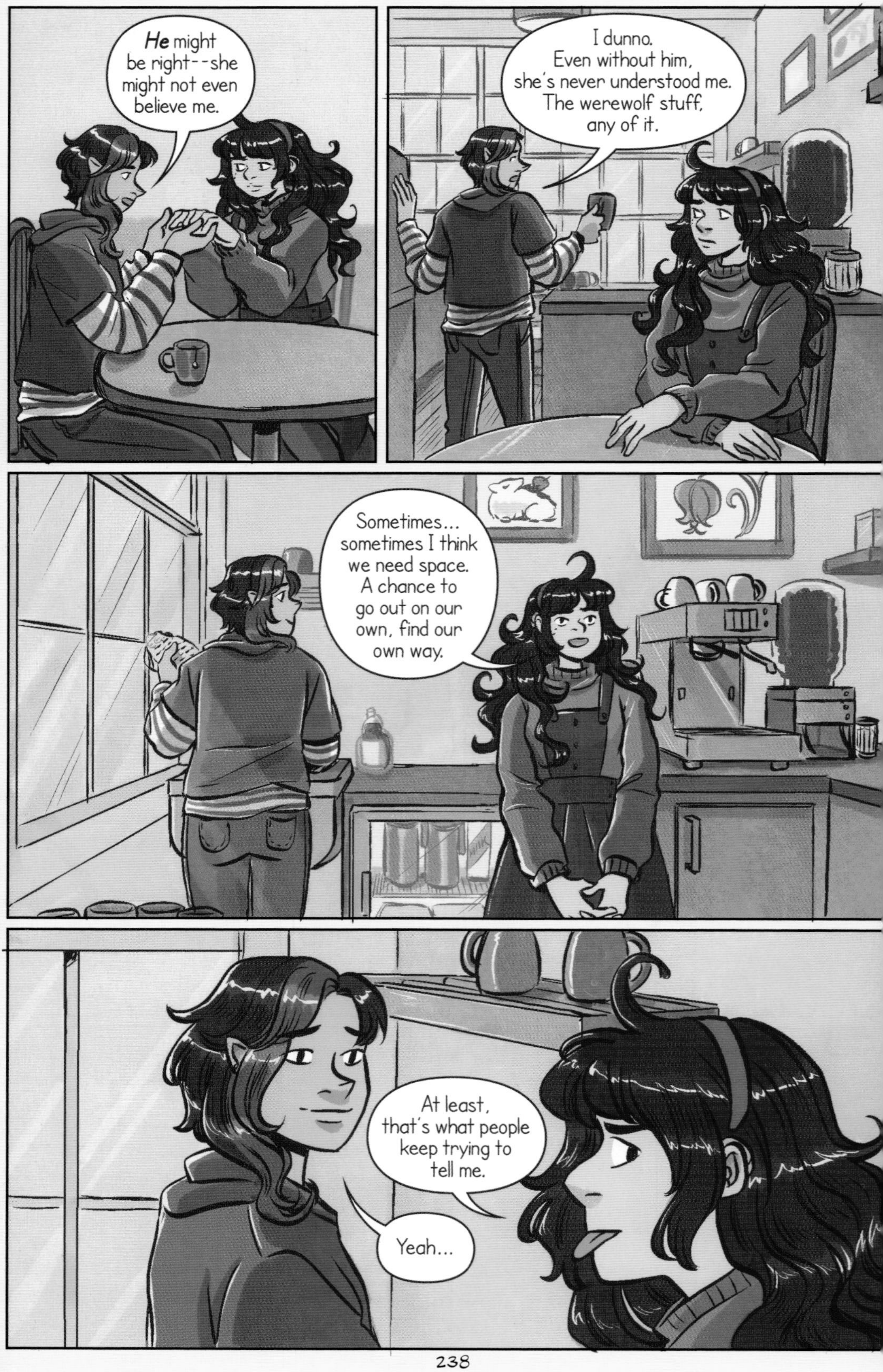
He might be right--she might not even believe me.
I dunno. Even without him, she's never understood me. The werewolf stuff, any of it.
Sometimes... sometimes I think we need space. A chance to go out on our own, find our own way.
At least, that's what people keep trying to tell me.
Yeah...

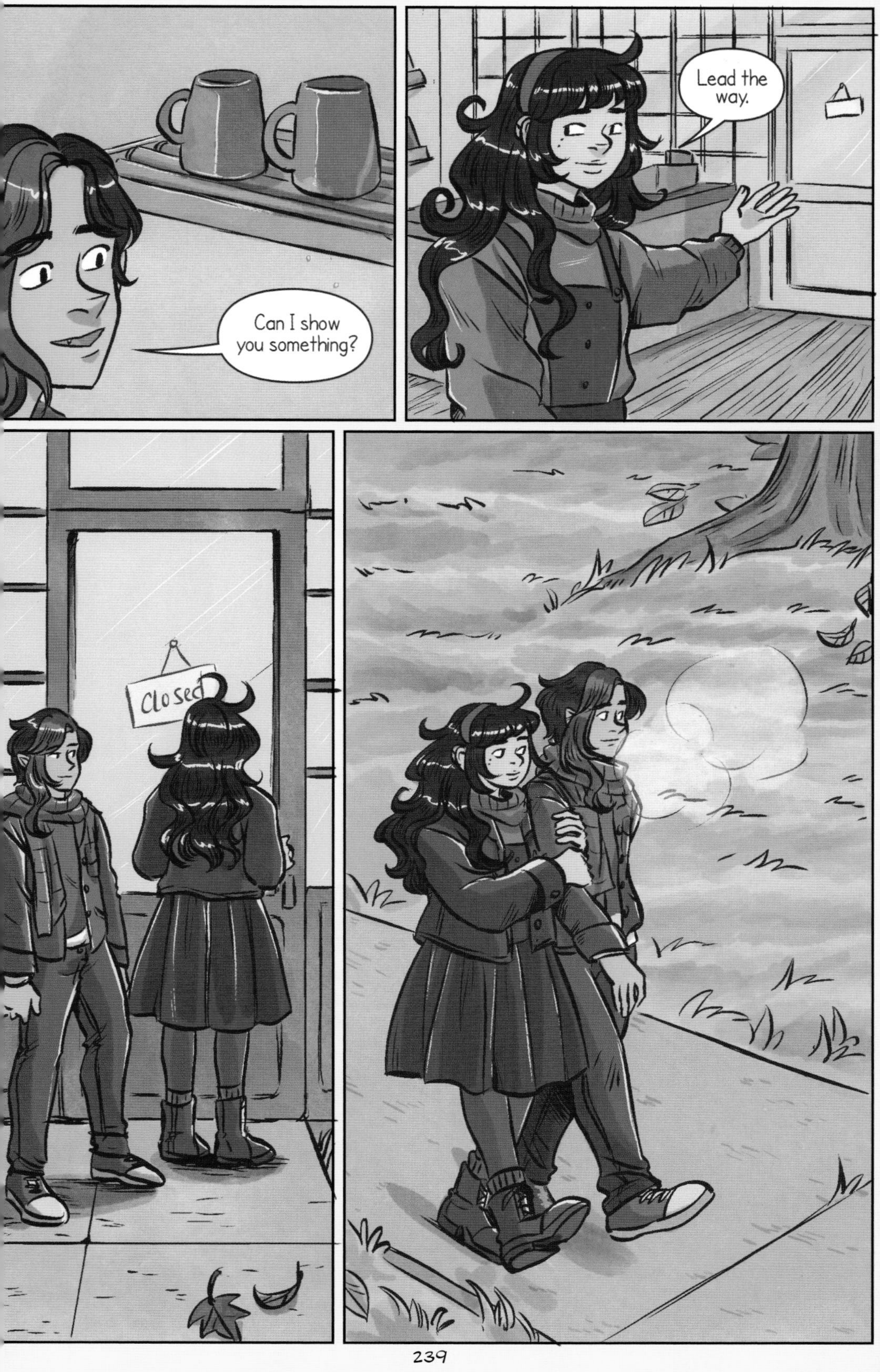
Can I show you something?
Lead the way.
Closed

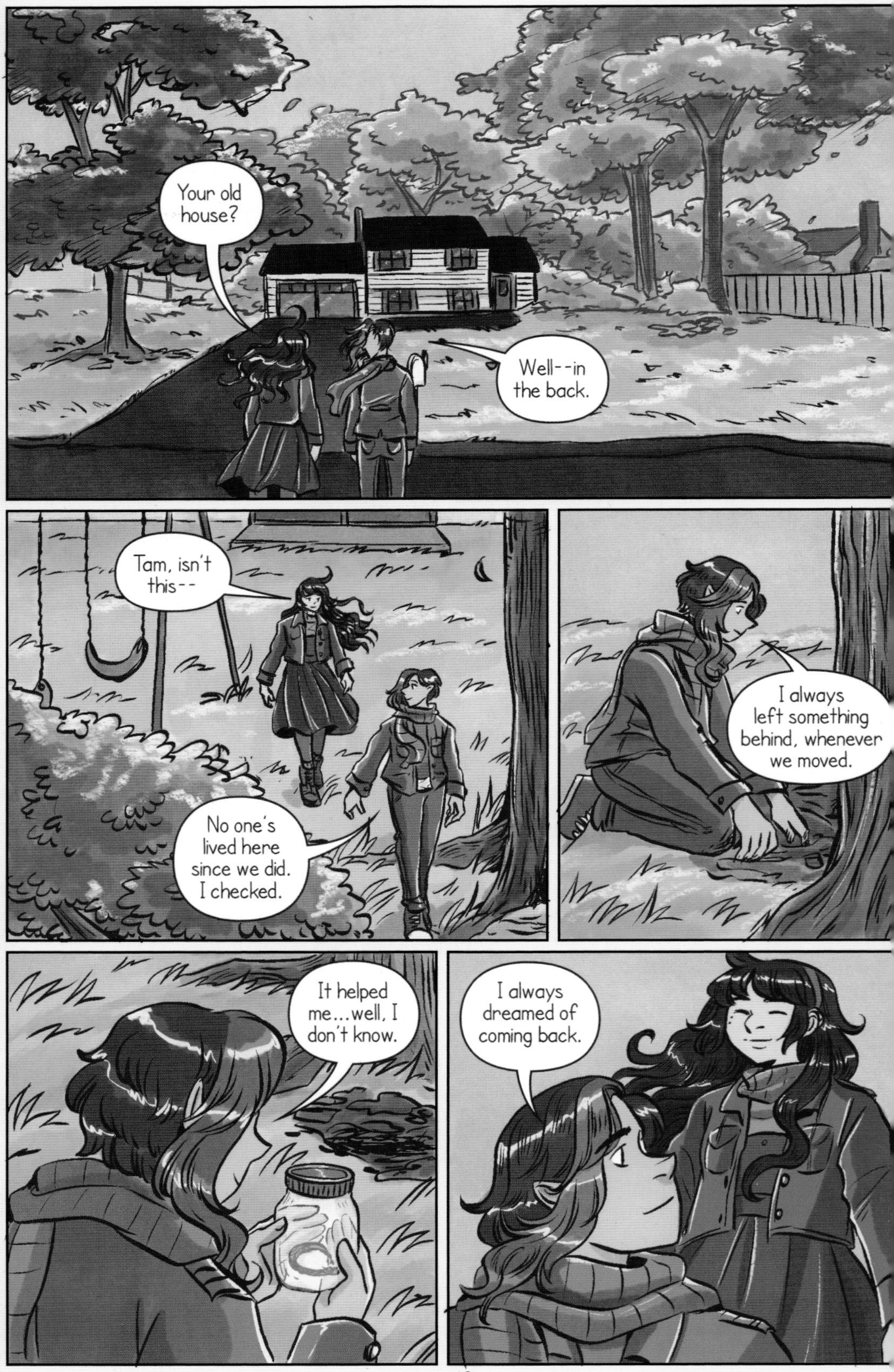
Your old house?
Well--in the back.
Tam, isn't this--
No one's lived here since we did. I checked.
I always left something behind, whenever we moved.
It helped me...well, I don't know.
I always dreamed of coming back.

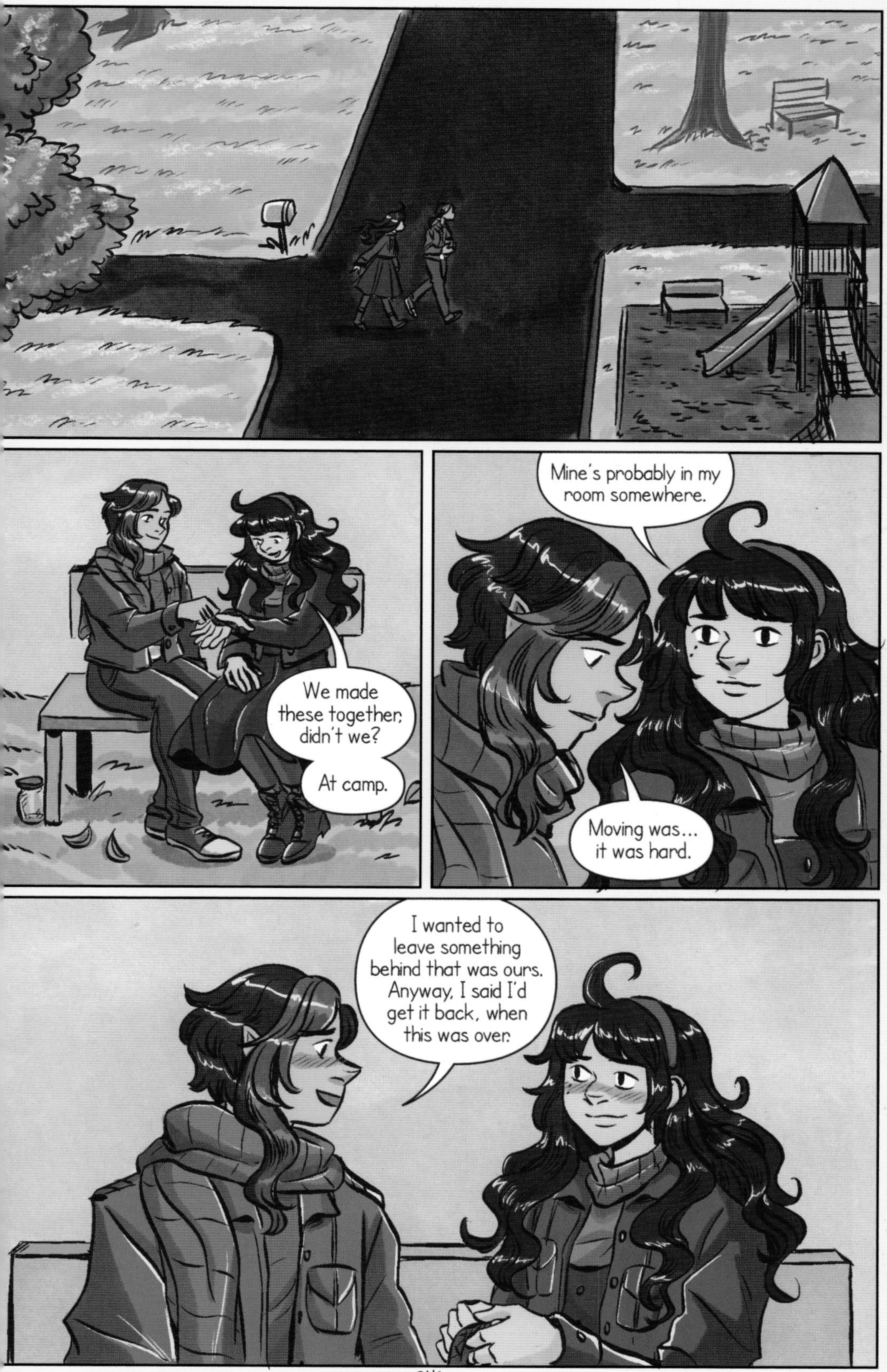

We made these together, didn't we?
At camp.
Mine's probably in my room somewhere.
Moving was... it was hard.
I wanted to leave something behind that was ours. Anyway, I said I'd get it back, when this was over.

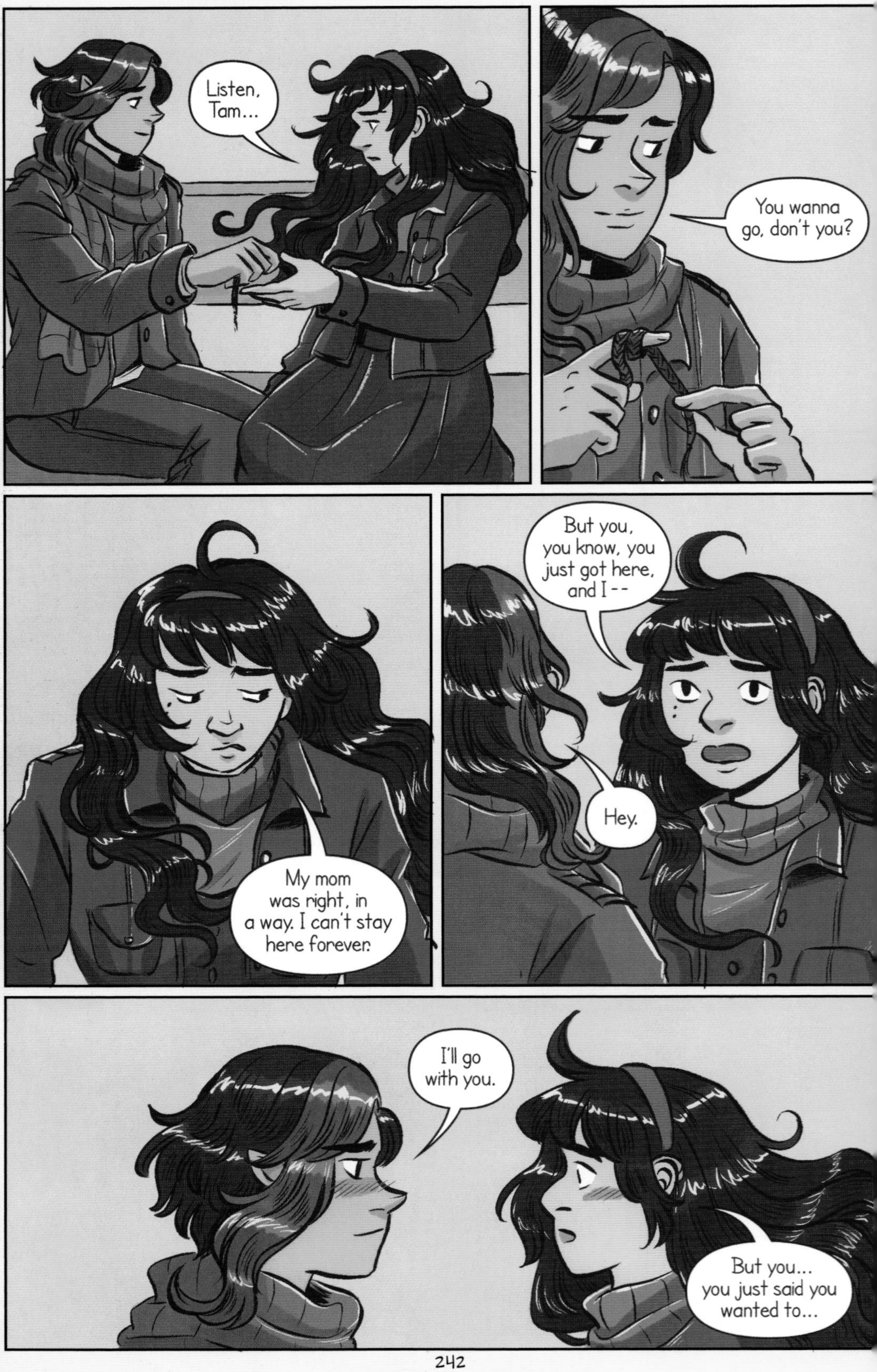
Listen, Tam...
You wanna go, don't you?
My mom was right, in a way. I can't stay here forever.
But you, you know, you just got here, and I --
Hey.
I'll go with you.
But you... you just said you wanted to...

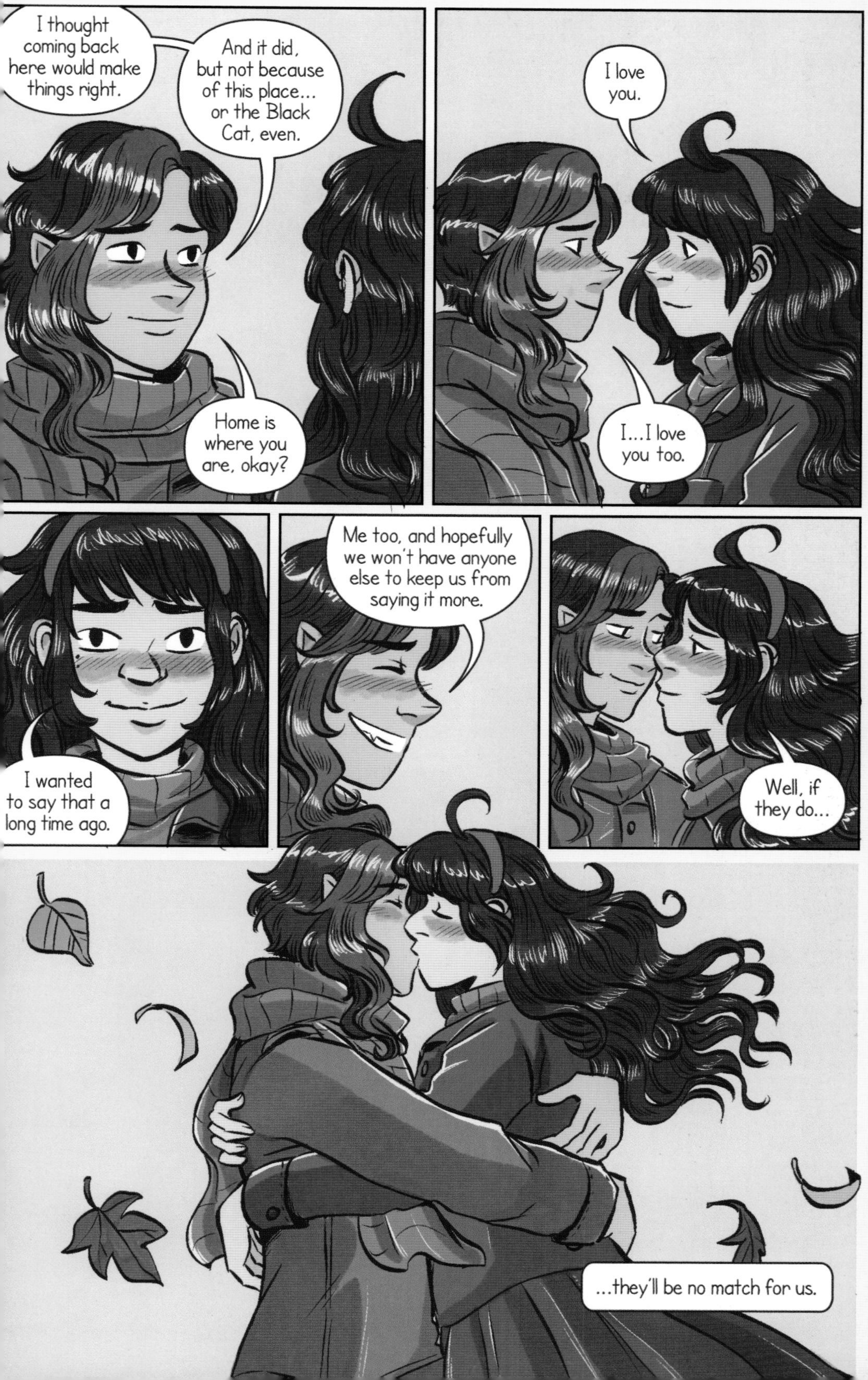
I thought coming back here would make things right.
And it did, but not because of this place... or the Black Cat, even.
Home is where you are, okay?
I love you.
I...I love you too.
I wanted to say that a long time ago.
Me too, and hopefully we won't have anyone else to keep us from saying it more.
Well, if they do...
...they'll be no match for us.

Additional Materials

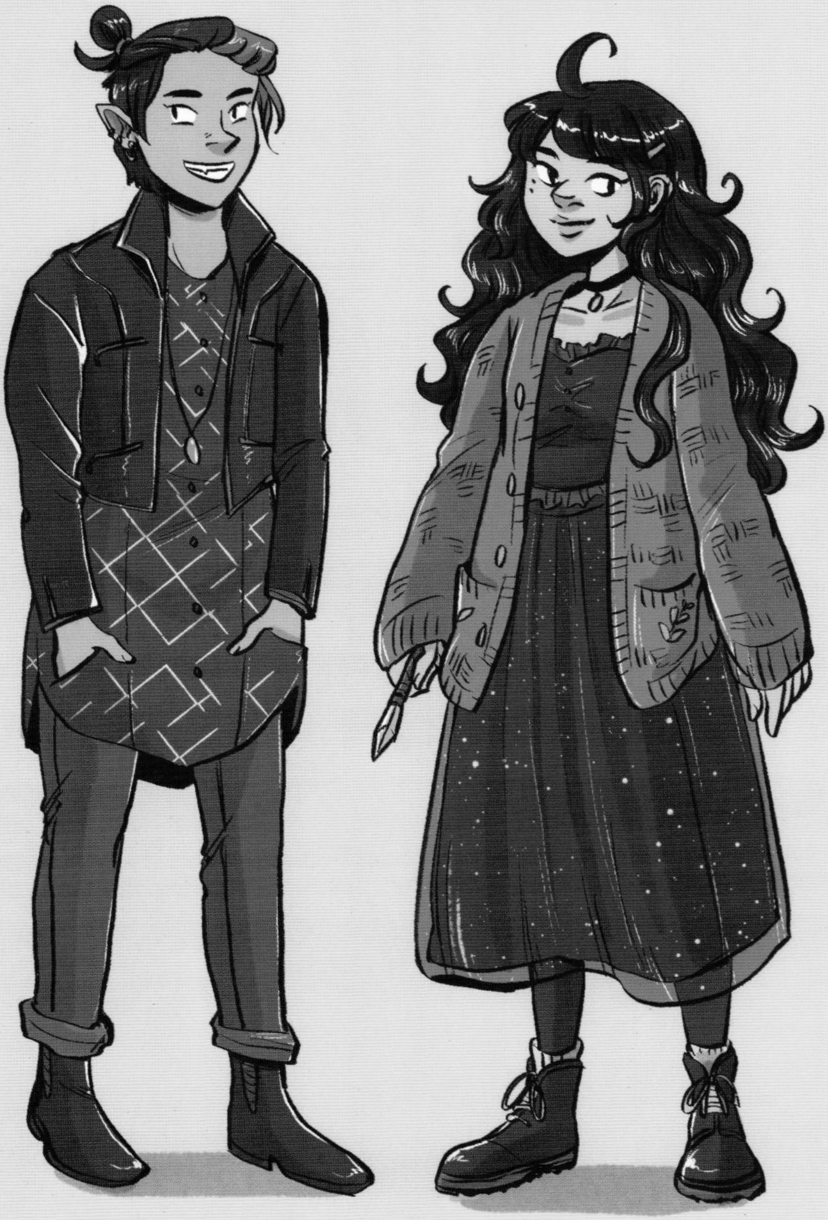

Concept Art

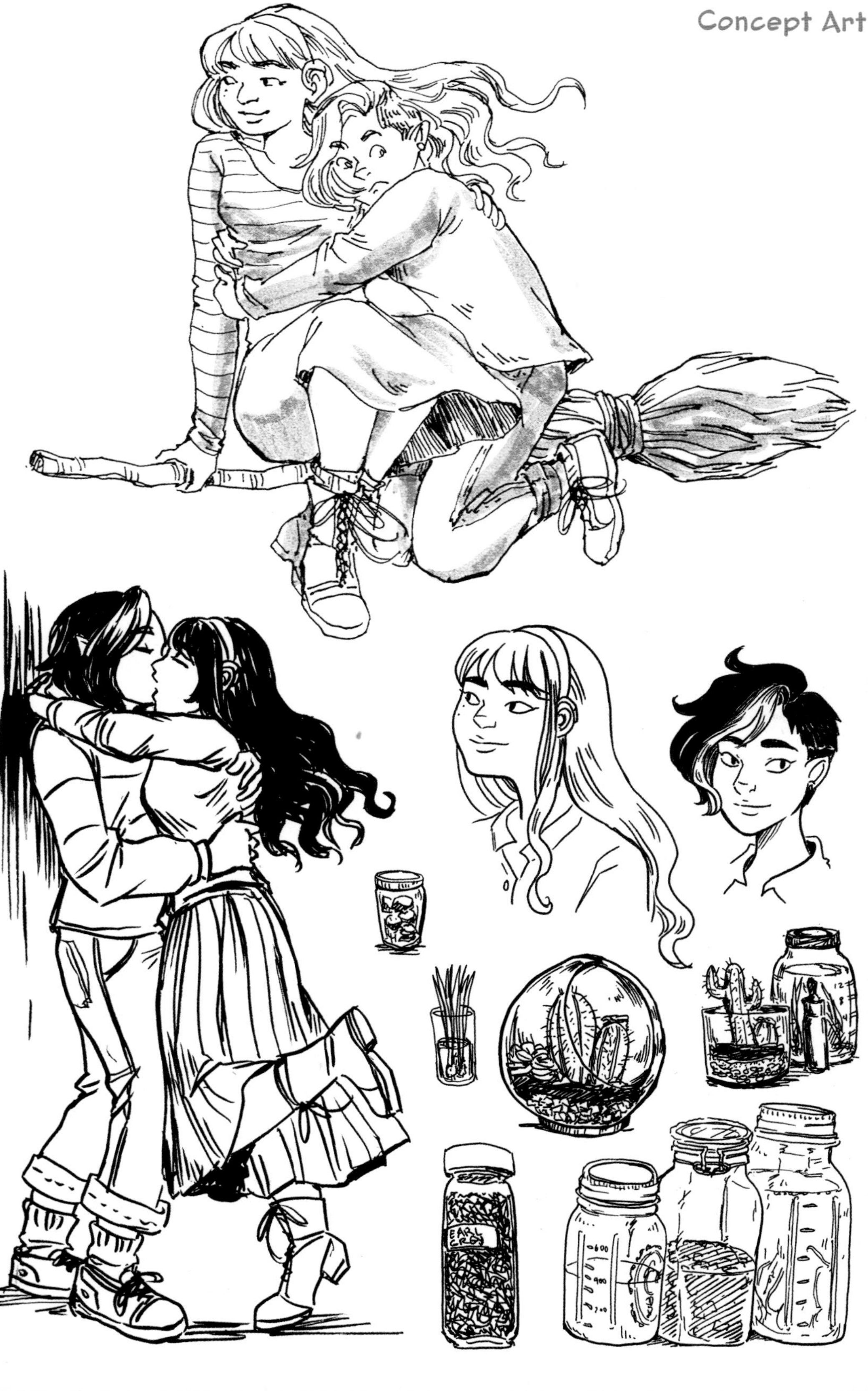
EARL

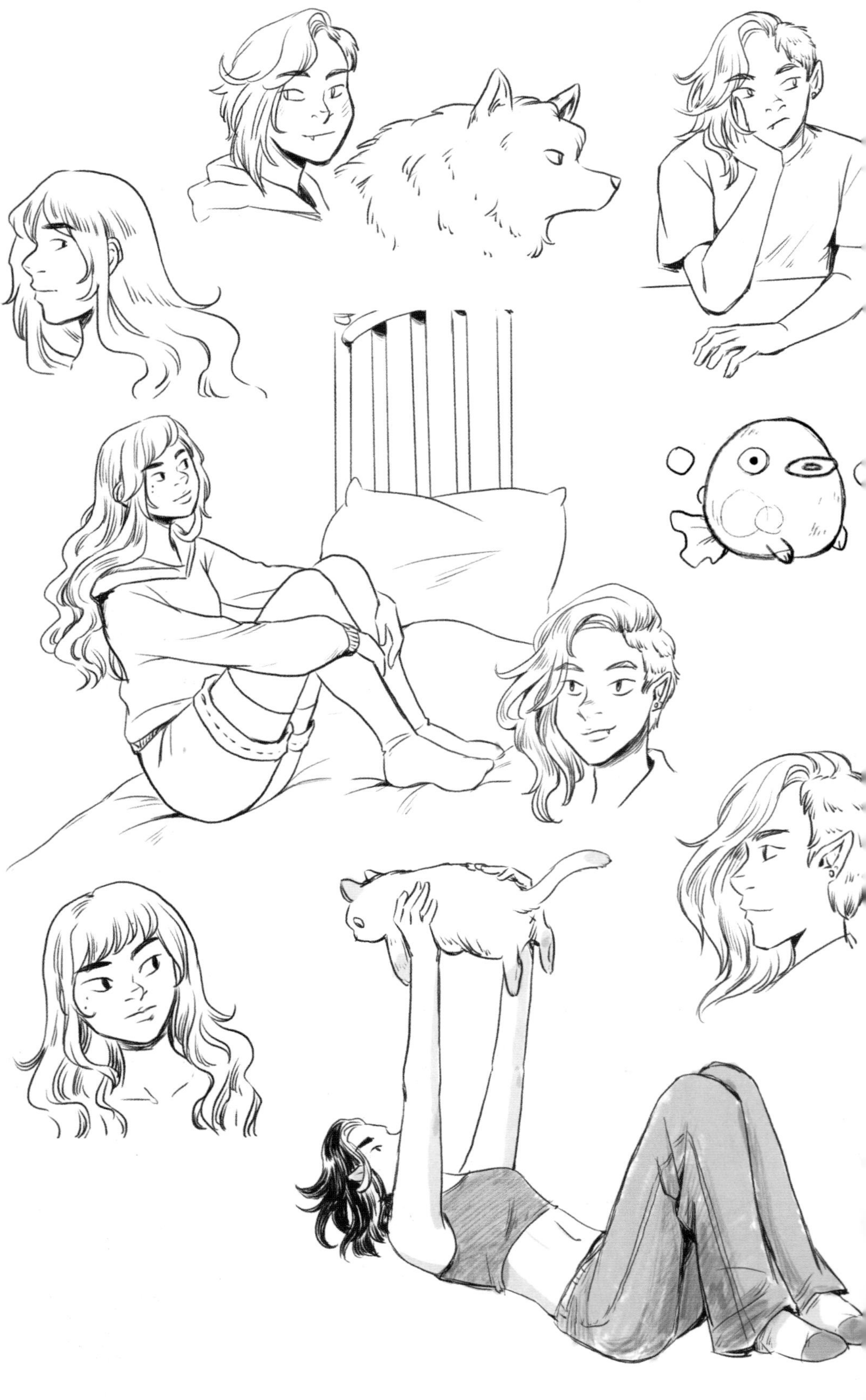

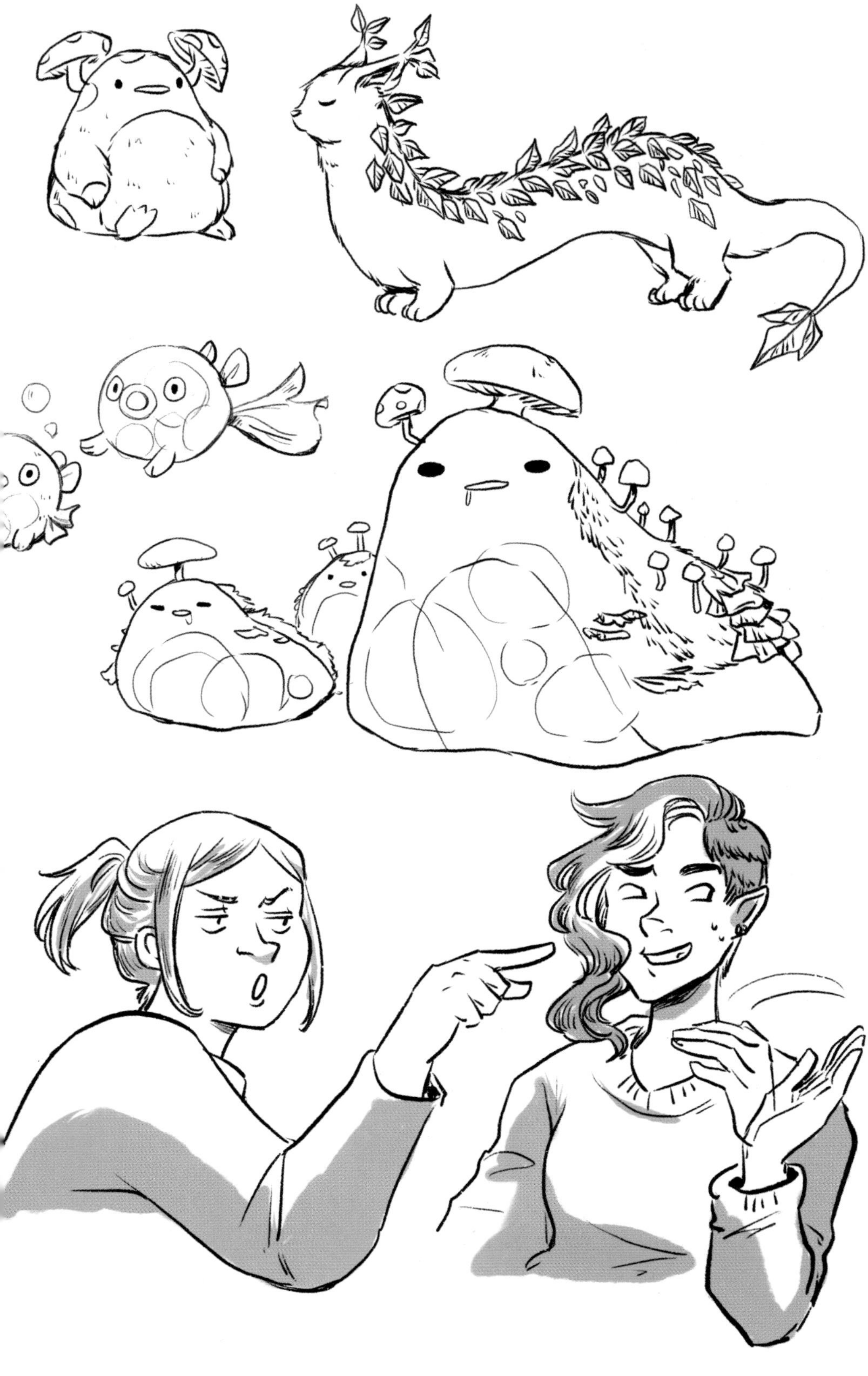

Script Breakdown

Page Twenty-One

Panel One
Nova runs around to the front, and we see a parked car on the street in front of the Black Cat. Most of its occupants are still in the car, and we see the shadow of a bird head in the backseat window. The front passenger's door has opened, with Nova's aunt Dawn stepping out. She's dressed nicely for the holidays, with pressed black pants, a red blouse, and fancyish trench coat over it, and she's holding a steaming dish in her hands.

> Dawn: Nova, darling!

Panel Two
Nova kisses her aunt on the cheek while taking the dish out of her hands.

> Nova: Let me help you with that, Auntie.
> Dawn: Careful, it's hot—

Panel Three
View from Dawn's perspective of Tam, who is standing in the sidewalk awkwardly—also without a jacket, hugging themselves against the cold. Nova squeezes her eyes shut in embarrassment from having forgotten introductions (she's still holding the dish, otherwise she would have smacked her hand to her forehead).

> Dawn: And who's this?
> Nova: Oh! Sorry.

Panel Four
Nova smiles and makes introductions.
> Nova: Tam, this is my Aunt Dawn, Uncle Joe…

Panel Five
We see Nova's Uncle Joe, dressed in a button-down shirt, sport coat and khakis, who's come around from the front of the car to stand next to Aunt Dawn. He gives a little wave to Nova and Tam. On the right-hand side of the panel, we can see that the back door of the car has opened.

Panel Six
OUR FIRST VIEW OF TERRY SHIN. He is also dressed fancy, wearing a black sport coat, button-down shirt, and green polka dot ascot. He has one hand jammed into his pocket and the other hand is waving at Tam.

> Nova [overlaid]:…and my cousin Terry.

Original script for chapter 3, page 21.

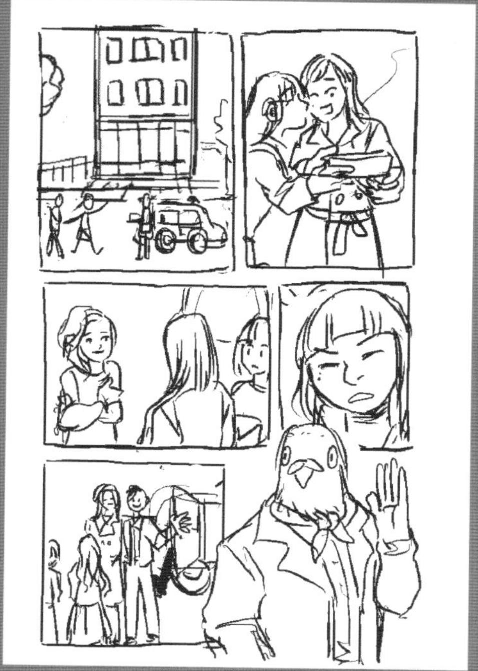

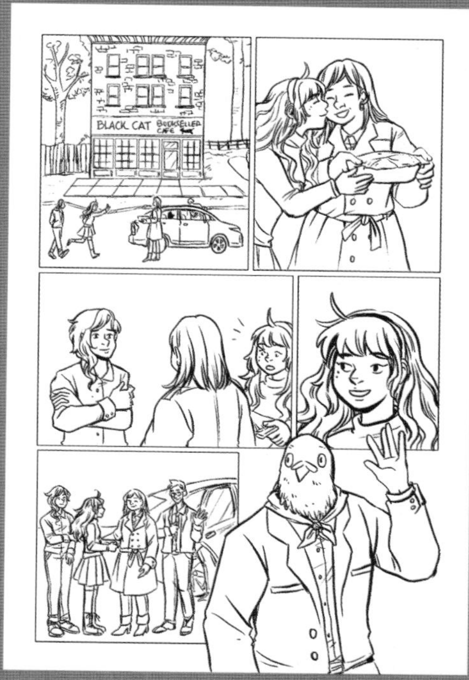

BLACK CAT BOOKSELLER CAFE

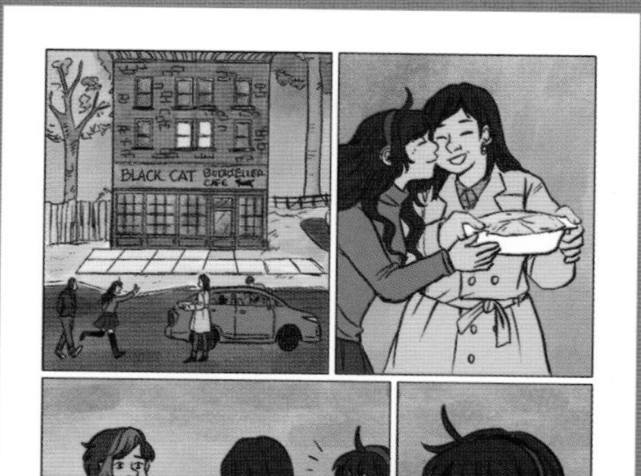

BLACK CAT BOOKSELLER CAFE

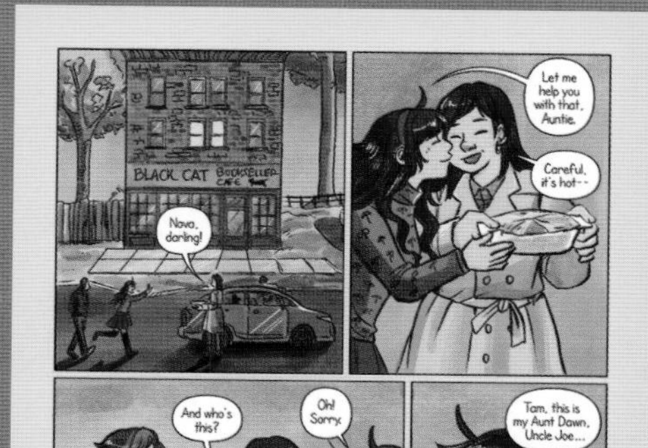

BLACK CAT BOOKSELLER CAFE
Nova, darling!
Let me help you with that, Auntie.
Careful, it's hot--
And who's this?
Oh! Sorry.
Tam, this is my Aunt Dawn, Uncle Joe...
...and my cousin Terry.

Thumbnail, inks, flat colors, and final art for chapter 3, page 21.

Page Twenty-two

Panel One
Tam is gobsmacked, to say the least, but they try to cover it up as best they can and they hold out a hand to Terry.

Tam: Uh…hi.
Terry: Cooo.

Panel Two
Aunt Dawn also holds out her hand for Tam to shake.

Tam: It's nice to meet you.
Dawn: It's nice to meet you too.

Panel Three
Dawn turns to Nova, eyebrows raised. She raises a hand and wiggles her fingers in a fairly obvious code for "does your S.O. know about the family business??".

Dawn: I assume, Nova, that…
Nova [off-panel]: Oh, Tam's a werewolf. They know all about magic.

Panel Four
Dawn's expression changes to one of surprised pleasure.

Dawn: Oh! Then you'll fit right in, Tam.

Panel Five
Dawn and Joe start to walk up the driveway, around the house to the backyard. Behind them, Terry claps his hand on Tam's shoulder in what's meant to be a very bro-y, bonding kind of way, and pecks Tam gently on the top of their head. Tam is still completely baffled by Terry.

Terry: [peck]*
text box: [I like you, fellow animal friend]

Panel Six
Tam trails behind Terry to walk with Nova, still carrying the dish. They lean in to speak very softly in Nova's ear.

Tam: So, um…

Original script for chapter 3, page 22.

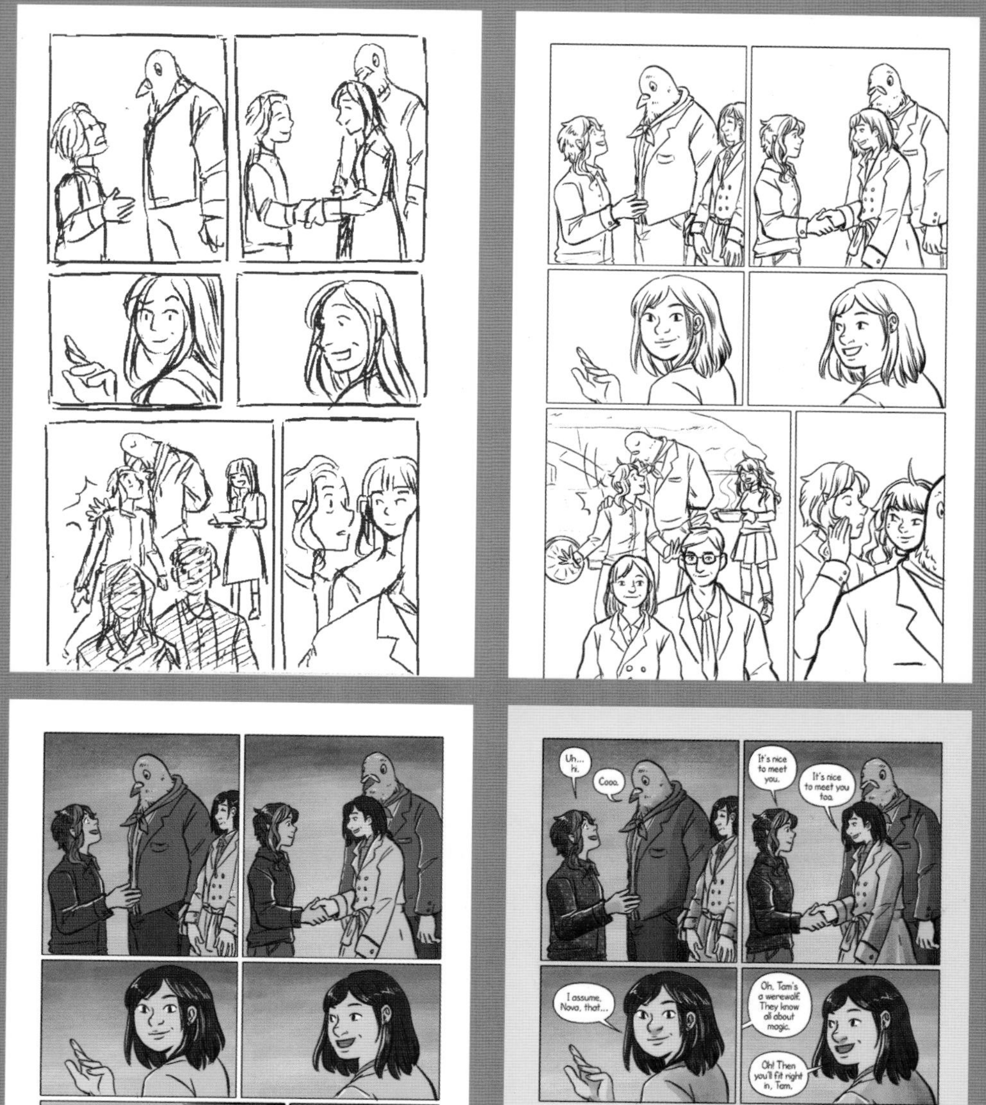
Uh... hi.
Cooo.
It's nice to meet you.
It's nice to meet you too.
I assume, Nova, that...
Oh, Tam's a werewolf. They know all about magic.
Oh! Then you'll fit right in, Tam.
peck
*I like you, fellow animal friend.
So, um...

Thumbnail, inks, flat colors, and final art for chapter 3, page 22.

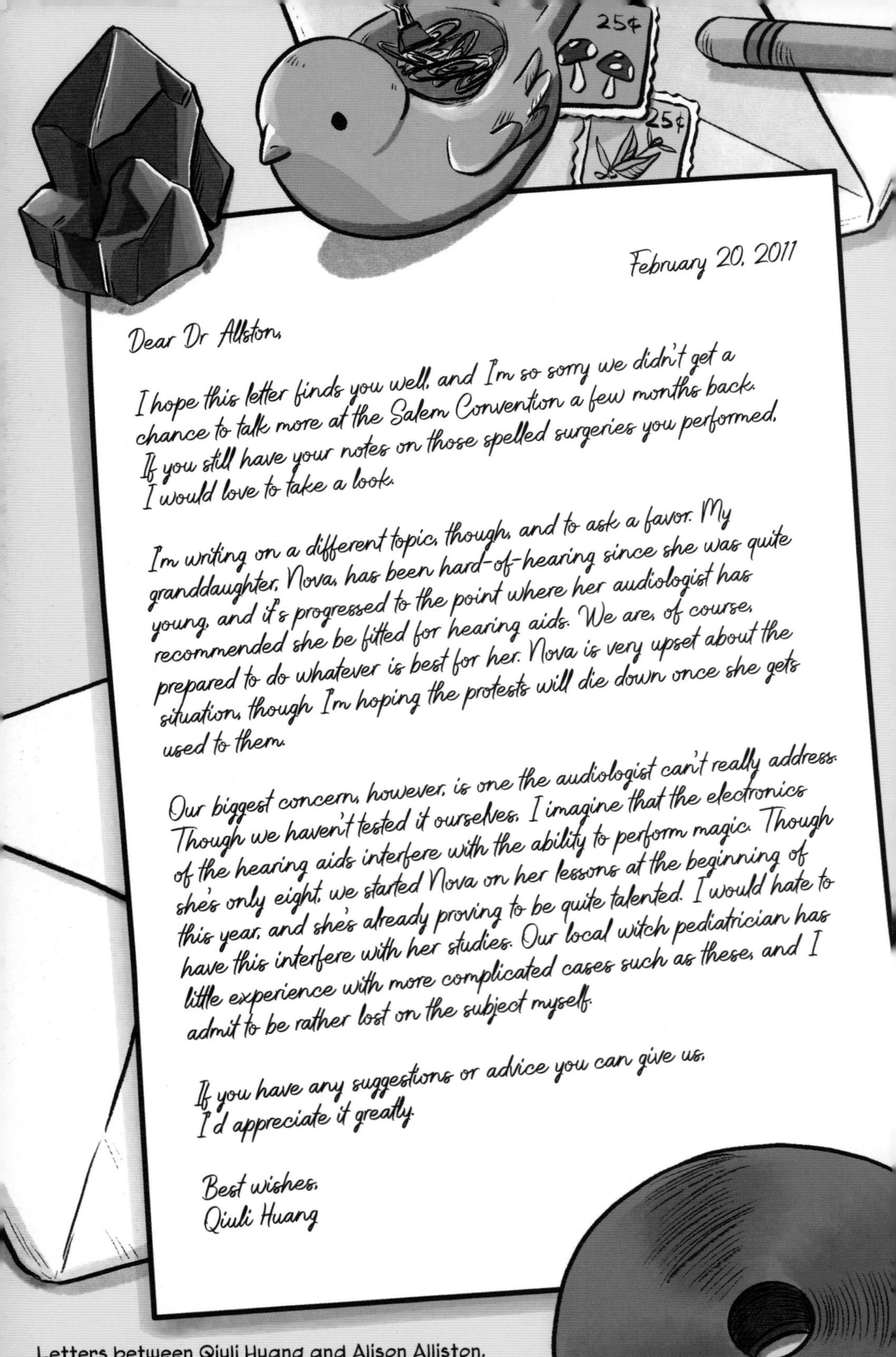

February 20, 2011

Dear Dr Allston,

I hope this letter finds you well, and I'm so sorry we didn't get a chance to talk more at the Salem Convention a few months back. If you still have your notes on those spelled surgeries you performed, I would love to take a look.

I'm writing on a different topic, though, and to ask a favor. My granddaughter, Nova, has been hard-of-hearing since she was quite young, and it's progressed to the point where her audiologist has recommended she be fitted for hearing aids. We are, of course, prepared to do whatever is best for her. Nova is very upset about the situation, though I'm hoping the protests will die down once she gets used to them.

Our biggest concern, however, is one the audiologist can't really address. Though we haven't tested it ourselves, I imagine that the electronics of the hearing aids interfere with the ability to perform magic. Though she's only eight, we started Nova on her lessons at the beginning of this year, and she's already proving to be quite talented. I would hate to have this interfere with her studies. Our local witch pediatrician has little experience with more complicated cases such as these, and I admit to be rather lost on the subject myself.

If you have any suggestions or advice you can give us, I'd appreciate it greatly.

Best wishes,
Qiuli Huang

Letters between Qiuli Huang and Alison Alliston.
Originally exclusive for Mooncakes patrons.

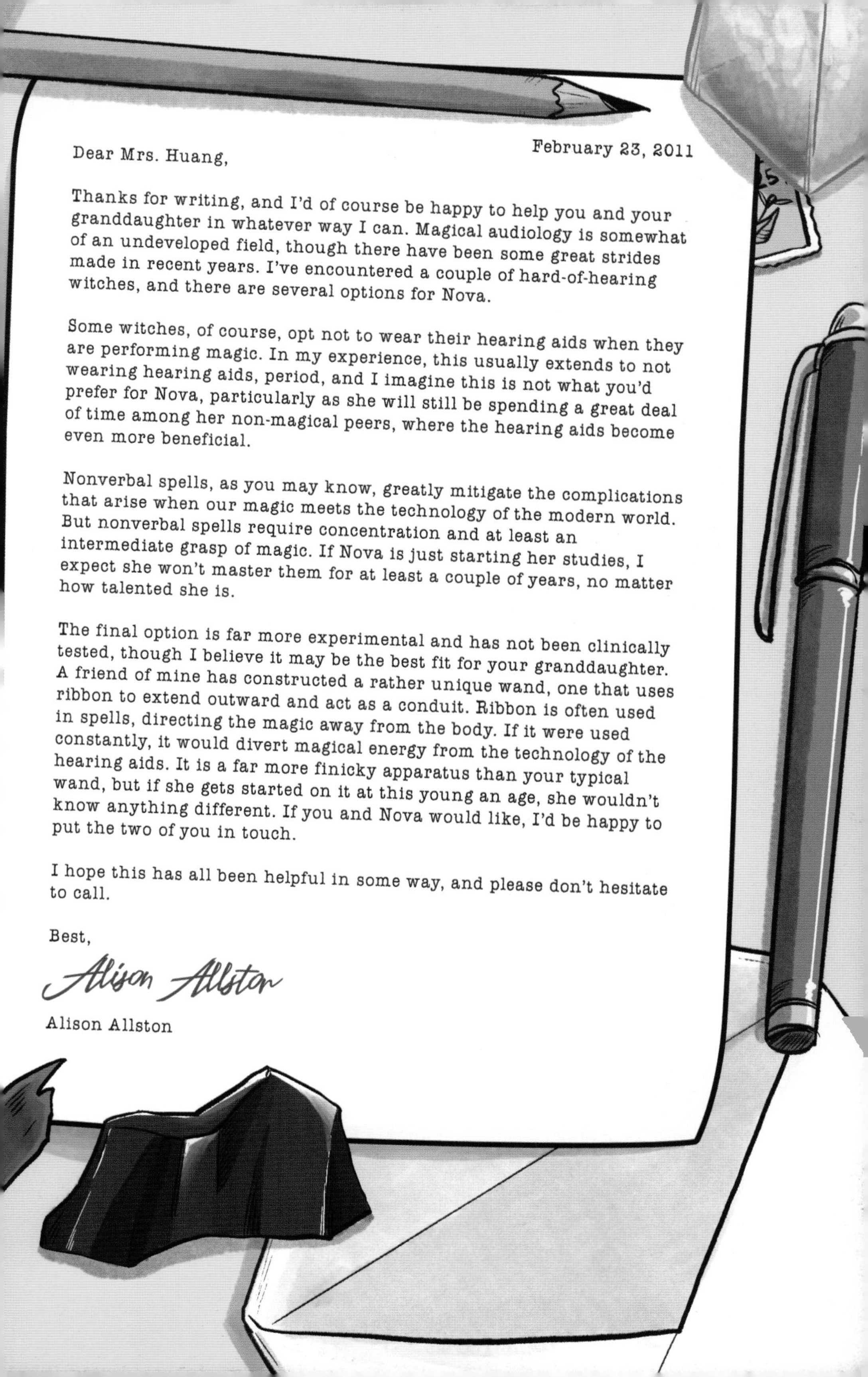

February 23, 2011

Dear Mrs. Huang,

Thanks for writing, and I'd of course be happy to help you and your granddaughter in whatever way I can. Magical audiology is somewhat of an undeveloped field, though there have been some great strides made in recent years. I've encountered a couple of hard-of-hearing witches, and there are several options for Nova.

Some witches, of course, opt not to wear their hearing aids when they are performing magic. In my experience, this usually extends to not wearing hearing aids, period, and I imagine this is not what you'd prefer for Nova, particularly as she will still be spending a great deal of time among her non-magical peers, where the hearing aids become even more beneficial.

Nonverbal spells, as you may know, greatly mitigate the complications that arise when our magic meets the technology of the modern world. But nonverbal spells require concentration and at least an intermediate grasp of magic. If Nova is just starting her studies, I expect she won't master them for at least a couple of years, no matter how talented she is.

The final option is far more experimental and has not been clinically tested, though I believe it may be the best fit for your granddaughter. A friend of mine has constructed a rather unique wand, one that uses ribbon to extend outward and act as a conduit. Ribbon is often used in spells, directing the magic away from the body. If it were used constantly, it would divert magical energy from the technology of the hearing aids. It is a far more finicky apparatus than your typical wand, but if she gets started on it at this young an age, she wouldn't know anything different. If you and Nova would like, I'd be happy to put the two of you in touch.

I hope this has all been helpful in some way, and please don't hesitate to call.

Best,

Alison Allston

Alison Allston

Thanks first and foremost to TEAM MOONCAKES!

To Hazel Newlevant, for their insightful and heroic editing—this book would not be what it is without you. To Joamette Gil, letterer extraordinaire. To Andrea Colvin and everyone else at Lion Forge for all the work they put in to making this book a reality, and to Katie O'Neill, Charlie Jane Anders, and Tillie Walden for the lovely blurbs.

From Wendy

Thank you, thank you, thank you to Suz, who sat down with me one summer's day and made an extremely vague idea about a witch and a werewolf a big, beautiful reality.

Thank you to Linda Camacho, SUPERSTAR AGENT, who encouraged and championed my work. You're the best. Thank you Sona Charaipotra, for pushing me to talk to Linda-- I needed that firm auntie hand! Thank you, the Day Job Team: my boss, Susan; manager Le and coworkers Eunice, Trevor, Maria, Sophia, Alex, Sam, Liz, Dan, and Lucas for their kindness, patience, and neverending support as I drew and colored this book.

To the friends who answered frantic messages with love, soothed my anxiety, kvetched with me, pushed me to grow as a creator, and wrote/drew alongside me in coffee shops on and off the Internet: Shivana Sookdeo, Chris Kindred, Olivia Stephens, Shannon Wrigh Ethan Aldridge, Steenz Stewart, Bianca Xunise, Joamette Gil, Sam Maggs, Toril Orlesky, Katie O'Neill, Autumn Crossman-Serb, Mey Rude, Karuna Riazi, and Jade Feng Lee.

To Julie Leung, Tiff Liao, Rhoda Belleza, Sarah Guan, Amanda Shih-Goel, and the rest of the Publishing Aunties for all the hotpot, ice cream, and excellent company.

To my mom, dad, and sister.

Thank you, especially, weird lizard-loving, Hutt-hugging fiance Richard, for waving various cute stuffed animals in my face when I'm having a bad day, doing all the chores get neglectful of, and feeding the cat in the mornings. For making me part of your family.

From Suzanne

A thousand thanks and more to Wendy Xu for creating with me, challenging me, and growing with me. I couldn't ask for a better collaborator and friend. We did it!!

Thank you to my friends for supporting me and laughing with me every step of the way: Emma Candon, Kyra Davies, J.A. Micheline, Caitlin Casiello, Anna Goldbeck, Mara Kenyor Michi Trota, Caitlin Rosberg, Melanie Jones, Suzanne Davies, and especially Hillary Ford.

To everyone at The Perfect Cup for keeping me caffeinated and providing a great space to write. To Jennie Kassanoff and Abby Gross, who believed in my creative career long before I did myself; to Karen Green for fostering my love of comics; and to Kelly-Sue DeConnick and the Carol Corps for being my first comics community. To the Ladies (and Kevin) for making the day job worthwhile. Thanks to my hydration pals for everything under the sun, and to Ellen for the same.

To my family near and far, especially my parents and sister, for their love, support, and encouragement.

And thanks to my cat, who reminded me, rudely, every night, when it was time to stop working and time to start eating.

Wendy Xu is a Brooklyn-based illustrator and comics artist. Her work has been featured on Catapult, Barnes & Noble Sci-Fi/Fantasy Blog, and Tor.com, among other places.

She currently works as an assistant editor curating young adult and children's books. You can find her on twitter @angrygirlcomics or on instagram as @artofwendyxu.

Suzanne Walker is a Chicago-based writer and editor. She has short fiction in *Clarkesworld*, and nonfiction articles in *Uncanny Magazine*, *Women Write About Comics*, and *Barriers and Belonging: Personal Narratives of Disability*.

She has spoken at numerous conventions on topics from disability representation in sci-fi/fantasy to the importance of fair compensation for marginalized SF/F creators.

You can find her posting pictures of her cat and yelling about baseball on Twitter: @suzusaur.

Written by Suzanne Walker
Illustrated by Wendy Xu
Lettered by Joamette Gil
Jacket and backmatter designed by Rachel Dukes

Mooncakes, published 2019 by the Lion Forge LLC. Illustrations © 2019 Wendy Xu; Text © 2019
Suzanne Walker. ROAR™ LION FORGE™ and its associated distinctive designs are trademarks
of The Lion Forge, LLC. All rights reserved. No similarity between any of the names, characters,
persons, or institutions in this book with those of any living or dead person or institution is
intended, and any such similarity which may exist is purely coincidental. Printed in China.

ISBN: 978-1-5493-0304-3

Library of Congress Control Number: 2019938044

10 9 8 7 6 5 4 3 2